continued . . .

Praise for
FURIES OF CALDERON

"Epic fantasy in the best way, inspired by Tolkien."
—Simon R. Green, *New York Times* bestselling author

"Filled with plot twists and white-knuckled suspense, this is a ripping good yarn that delivers terrific magic and nonstop action."
—Deborah Chester, national bestselling author of *The King Betrayed*

"A fascinating world and magic system . . . the start of a promising series." —*Locus*

"A stay-up-all-night-till-you-finish-it book, *Furies of Calderon* is a marvelous read."
—Patricia Briggs, author of *Raven's Shadow*

"With strong, likable characters and a graceful storytelling style, this series debut should appeal to fans of epic fantasy."
—*Library Journal*

"Absorbing fantasy . . . Butcher does a thorough job of world-building, to say nothing of developing his action scenes with an abundance of convincing detail. This page-turner bodes well for future volumes." —*Publishers Weekly*

"A real page-turner, with the classic plot of a kingdom threatened by both an outside invader and internal treachery enlivened by an abundance of original details and sheer storytelling gusto . . . A promising series-launcher."
—*Booklist*

Ace Books by Jim Butcher

ACADEM'S FURY

BOOK TWO OF THE CODEX ALERA

JIM BUTCHER

ACE BOOKS, NEW YORK

THE BERKLEY PUBLISHING GROUP
Published by the Penguin Group
Penguin Group (USA) Inc.
375 Hudson Street, New York, New York 10014, USA
Penguin Group (Canada), 90 Eglinton Avenue East, Suite 700, Toronto, Ontario M4P 2Y3, Canada
(a division of Pearson Penguin Canada Inc.)
Penguin Books Ltd., 80 Strand, London WC2R 0RL, England
Penguin Group Ireland, 25 St. Stephen's Green, Dublin 2, Ireland (a division of Penguin Books Ltd.)
Penguin Group (Australia), 250 Camberwell Road, Camberwell, Victoria 3124, Australia
(a division of Pearson Australia Group Pty. Ltd.)
Penguin Books India Pvt. Ltd., 11 Community Centre, Panchsheel Park, New Delhi—110 017, India
Penguin Group (NZ), Cnr. Airborne and Rosedale Roads, Albany, Auckland 1310, New Zealand
(a division of Pearson New Zealand Ltd.)
Penguin Books (South Africa) (Pty.) Ltd., 24 Sturdee Avenue, Rosebank, Johannesburg 2196, South Africa

Penguin Books Ltd., Registered Offices: 80 Strand, London WC2R 0RL, England

This is a work of fiction. Names, characters, places, and incidents either are the product of the author's imagination or are used fictitiously, and any resemblance to actual persons, living or dead, business establishments, events, or locales is entirely coincidental. The publisher does not have any control over and does not assume any responsibility for author or third-party websites or their content.

ACADEM'S FURY

An Ace Book / published by arrangement with the author

PRINTING HISTORY
Ace hardcover edition / July 2005
Ace mass-market edition / December 2006

Copyright © 2005 by Jim Butcher.
Cover art by Steve Stone.
Cover design by Rita Frangie.
Interior text design by Kristin del Rosario.

ISBN: 978-0-441-01340-1

ACE
Ace Books are published by The Berkley Publishing Group,
a division of Penguin Group (USA) Inc.,
375 Hudson Street, New York, New York 10014.
ACE and the "A" design are trademarks belonging to Penguin Group (USA) Inc.

PRINTED IN THE UNITED STATES OF AMERICA

16 15 14 13 12 11 10 9 8

*For all the old gang at AmberMUSH and on Too.
We all wasted way too much time together,
and I wouldn't have it any other way.*

ACKNOWLEDGMENTS

There are always lots of people to thank for helping out with any project as lengthy as a novel, but this time I want to thank the one person who always does the most for me, and who never expects anything in return.

Thank you, Shannon. For too many things for me to even remember, much less list.

I don't know how you put up with me, my angel, but I hope you don't stop.

◦◦◦◦◦ PROLOGUE

If the beginning of wisdom is in realizing that one knows nothing, then the beginning of understanding is in realizing that all things exist in accord with a single truth: Large things are made of smaller things.

Drops of ink are shaped into letters, letters form words, words form sentences, and sentences combine to express thought. So it is with the growth of plants that spring from seeds, as well as with walls built of many stones. So it is with mankind, as the customs and traditions of our progenitors blend together to form the foundation for our own cities, history, and way of life.

Be they dead stone, living flesh, or rolling sea; be they idle times or events of world-shattering proportion, market days, or desperate battles, to this law, all things hold:

Large things are made from small things.

Significance is cumulative—but not always obvious.

FROM THE WRITINGS OF GAIUS SECONDUS,
FIRST LORD OF ALERA

Wind howled over the rolling, sparsely wooded hills of the lands in the care of the Marat, the One-and-Many people. Hard, coarse flecks of snow fled before it, and though the One rode high in the sky, the overcast hid his face.

Kitai began to feel cold for the first time since spring. She turned to squint behind her, shielding her eyes from the sleet with one hand. She wore a brief cloth about her hips, a belt to hold her knife and hunting pouch, and nothing else. Wind threw her thick white hair around her face, its color blending with the driving snow.

"Hurry up!" she called.

There was a deep-chested snort, and a massive form paced into sight. Walker the gargant was an enormous beast, even of its kind, and its shoulders stood nearly the height of two men above the earth. His shaggy winter coat had already come in thick and black, and he paid no notice to the snow. His claws, each larger than an Aleran saber, dug into the frozen earth without difficulty or hurry.

Kitai's father, Doroga, sat upon the gargant's back, swaying casually upon the woven saddlecloth. He was dressed in a loincloth and a faded red Aleran tunic. Doroga's chest, arms, and shoulders were so laden with muscle that he had been obliged to tear the sleeves from the red tunic—but as it had been a gift, and discarding it would be impolite, he had braided a rope from the sleeves and bound it across his forehead, tying back his own pale hair. "We must hurry, since the valley is running from us. I see. Maybe we should have stayed downwind."

"You are not as amusing as you think you are," Kitai said, glowering at her father's teasing.

Doroga smiled, the expression emphasizing the lines in his broad, square features. He took hold of Walker's saddle rope and swung down to the ground with a grace that belied his sheer size. He slapped his hand against the gargant's front leg, and Walker settled down amicably, placidly chewing cud.

Kitai turned and walked forward, into the wind, and though he made no sound, she knew her father followed close behind her.

A few moments later, they reached the edge of a cliff that dropped abruptly into open space. The snow prevented her from seeing the whole of the valley below, but for the lulls between gusts, when she could see all the way to the bottom of the cliff below them.

"Look," she said.

Doroga stepped up beside her, absently slipping one vast arm around her shoulders. Kitai would never have let her father see her shiver, not at a mere autumn sleet, but she leaned against him, silently grateful for his warmth. She watched as her father peered down, waiting for a lull in the wind to let him see the place the Alerans called the Wax Forest.

Kitai closed her eyes, remembering the place. The dead

trees were coated in the *croach*, a thick, gelatinous substance layered over and over itself so that it looked like the One had coated it all in the wax of many candles. The *croach* had covered everything in the valley, including the ground and a sizeable portion of the valley walls. Here and there, birds and animals had been sealed into the *croach*, where, still alive, they lay unmoving until they softened and dissolved like meat boiled over a low fire. Pale things the size of wild dogs, translucent, spiderlike creatures with many legs once lay quietly in the *croach*, nearly invisible, while others prowled the forest floor, silent and swift and alien.

Kitai shivered at the memory, then forced herself to stillness again, biting her lip. She glanced up at her father, but he pretended not to have noticed, staring down.

The valley below had never in her people's memory taken on snow. The entire place had been warm to the touch, even in winter, as though the *croach* itself was some kind of massive beast, the heat of its body filling the air around it.

Now the Wax Forest stood covered in ice and rot. The old, dead trees were coated in something that looked like brown and sickly tar. The ground lay frozen, though here and there, other patches of rotten *croach* could be seen. Several of the trees had fallen. And in the center of the Forest, the hollow mound lay collapsed and dissolved into corruption, the stench strong enough to carry even to Kitai and her father.

Doroga was still for a moment before he said, "We should go down. Find out what happened."

"I have," Kitai said.

Her father frowned. "That was foolish to do alone."

"Of the three of us here, which has gone down and come back alive again the most often?"

Doroga grunted out a laugh, glancing down at her with warmth and affection in his dark eyes. "Maybe you are not mistaken." The smile faded, and the wind and sleet hid the valley again. "What did you find?"

"Dead keepers," she replied. "Dead *croach*. Not warm. Not moving. The keepers were empty husks. The *croach* breaks into ash at a touch." She licked her lips. "And something else."

"What?"

"Tracks," she said in a quiet voice. "Leading away from the far side. Leading west."

Doroga grunted. "What tracks?"

Kitai shook her head. "They were not fresh. Perhaps Marat or Aleran. I found more dead keepers along the way. As if they were marching and dying one by one."

"The creature," Doroga rumbled. "Moving toward the Alerans."

Kitai nodded, her expression troubled.

Doroga looked at her, and said, "What else?"

"His satchel. The pack the valleyboy lost in the Wax Forest during our race. I found it on the trail beside the last of the dead spiders, his scent still on it. Rain came. I lost the trail."

Doroga's expression darkened. "We will tell the master of the Calderon Valley. It may be nothing."

"Or it may not. I will go," Kitai said.

"No," Doroga said.

"But father—"

"No," he repeated, his voice harder.

"What if it is looking for him?"

Her father remained quiet for a time, before he said, "Your Aleran is clever. Swift. He is able to take care of himself."

Kitai scowled. "He is small. And foolish. And irritating."

"Brave. Selfless."

"Weak. And without even the sorcery of his people."

"He saved your life," Doroga said.

Kitai felt her scowl deepen. "Yes. He is irritating."

Doroga smiled. "Even lions begin life as cubs."

"I could break him in half," Kitai growled.

"For now, perhaps."

"I despise him."

"For now, perhaps."

"He had no right."

Doroga shook his head. "He had no more say in it than you."

Kitai folded her arms, and said, "I hate him."

"So you want someone to warn him. I see."

Kitai flushed, heat touching her cheeks and throat.

Her father pretended not to notice. "What is done is done," he rumbled. He turned to her and cupped her cheek in one vast hand. He tilted his head for a moment, studying her. "I like his eyes on you. Like emerald. Like new grass."

Kitai felt her eyes begin to tear. She closed them and kissed her father's hand. "I wanted a horse."

Doroga let out a rumbling laugh. "Your mother wanted a lion. She got a fox. She did not regret it."

"I want it to go away."

Doroga lowered his hand. He turned back toward Walker, keeping his arm around Kitai. "It won't. You should Watch."

"I do not wish to."

"It is the way of our people," Doroga said.

"I do not wish to."

"Stubborn whelp. You will remain here until some sense soaks into your skull."

"I am *not* a whelp, father."

"You act like one. You will remain with the *Sabot-ha*." They reached Walker, and he tossed her halfway up the saddle rope without effort.

Kitai clambered up to Walker's broad back. "But father—"

"No, Kitai." He climbed up behind her, and clucked to Walker. The gargant placidly rose and began back the way they had come. "You are forbidden to go. It is done."

Kitai rode silently behind her father, but sat looking back to the west, her troubled face to the wind.

Miles's old wound pained him as he trudged down the long spiral staircase into the depths of the earth below the First Lord's palace, but he ignored it. The steady, smoldering throb from his left knee was of little more concern to him than the aching of his tired feet or the stretching soreness of weary muscles in his shoulders and arms after a day of hard drilling. He ignored them, his face as plain and remote as the worn hilt of the sword at his belt.

None of the discomfort he felt disturbed him nearly as much as the prospect of the conversation he was about to have with the most powerful man in the world.

Miles reached the antechamber at the bottom of the stairs and regarded his distorted reflection in a polished shield that hung upon the wall. He straightened the hem of his red-and-blue surcoat, the colors of the Royal Guard, and raked his fingers through his mussed hair.

A boy sat on the bench beside the closed door. He was a lanky, gangling youth, a young man who had come to his growth recently, and the hems of his breeches and sleeves both rode up too far, exposing his wrists and ankles. A mop of dark hair fell over his face, and an open book sat upon his lap, one finger still pointed at a line of text though the boy was clearly asleep.

Miles paused, and murmured, "Academ."

He jerked in his sleep, and the book fell from his lap and to the floor. The boy sat up, blinking his eyes, and stammered, "Yes, sire, what, uh, yes sire. Sire?"

Miles put a hand on the boy's shoulder before he could rise. "Easy, easy. Finals coming up, eh?"

The boy flushed and ducked his head as he leaned down to recover the book, "Yes, Sir Miles. I haven't had much time for sleep."

"I remember," he said. "Is he still inside?"

The boy nodded again. "As far as I know, sir. Would you like me to announce you?"

"Please."

The boy rose, brushing at his wrinkled grey academ's tunic, and bowed. Then he knocked gently on the door and opened it.

"Sire?" the boy said. "Sir Miles to see you."

There was a long pause, then a gentle male voice responded, "Thank you, Academ. Send him in."

Miles walked into the First Lord's meditation chamber, and the boy shut the soundproof door behind him. Miles lowered himself to one knee and bowed his head, waiting for the First Lord to acknowledge him.

Gaius Sextus, First Lord of Alera, stood in the center of the tiled floor. He was a tall man with a stern face and tired eyes. Though his skills at watercrafting caused him to resemble a man only in his fifth decade of life, Miles knew that he was twice that age. His hair, once dark and lustrous, had become even more heavily sown with grey in the past year.

On the tiles beneath Gaius, colors swirled and changed, patterns forming and vanishing again, constantly shifting.

Miles recognized a portion of the southern coastline of Alera, near Parcia, which remained in place for a moment before resolving into a section of mountainous wilderness that could only have been in the far north, near the Shieldwall.

Gaius shook his head and passed his hand through the air before him, murmuring, "Enough." The colors faded away completely, the tiles reverting to their usual dull, stationary colors. Gaius turned and sank down into a chair against the wall with a slow exhalation. "You're up late tonight, Captain."

Miles rose. "I was in the Citadel and wanted to pay my respects, sire."

Gaius's greying brows rose. "You walked down five hundred stairs to pay your respects."

"I didn't count them, sire."

"And if I am not mistaken, you are to inspect the new Legion's command at dawn. You'll get little sleep."

"Indeed. Almost as little as you will, my lord."

"Ah," Gaius said. He reached out and took up a glass of wine from the bureau beside his chair. "Miles, you're a soldier, not a diplomat. Speak your mind."

Miles let out a slow breath and nodded. "Thank you. You aren't getting enough sleep, Sextus. You're going to look like something the gargant shat for the opening ceremonies of Wintersend. You need to get to bed."

The First Lord waved one hand. "Presently, perhaps."

"No, Sextus. You're not going to wave this off. You've been here every night for three weeks, and it shows. You need a warm bed, a soft woman, and rest."

"Unfortunately, I'm likely to have none of the three."

"Balls," Miles said. He folded his arms and planted his feet. "You're the First Lord of Alera. You can have anything you want."

Gaius's eyes flickered with a shadow of surprise and anger. "My bed is unlikely to be warm so long as Caria is in it, Miles. You know how things stand between us."

"What did you expect? You married a bloody child, Sextus. She expected to live out an epic romance, and she found herself with a dried-up old spider of a politician instead."

Gaius's mouth tightened, the anger in his eyes growing more plain. The stone floor of the chamber rippled, the tremor making the table beside the chair rattle. "How dare you speak so to me, Captain?"

"You ordered me to, my lord. But before you dismiss me, consider. If I wasn't in the right, would it have angered you as much as it did? If you weren't so tired, would you have revealed your anger so obviously?"

The floor quieted, and Gaius's regard grew more weary, less angered. Miles felt a stab of disappointment. Once upon a time, the First Lord would not have surrendered to fatigue so easily.

Gaius took another sip of wine, and said, "What would you have me do, Miles? Tell me that."

"Bed," Miles said. "A woman. Sleep. Festival begins in four days."

"Caria isn't leaving her door open to me."

"Then take a concubine," Miles said. "Blight it, Sextus, you need to relax and the Realm needs an heir."

The First Lord grimaced. "No. I may have ill-used Caria, but I'll not shame her by taking another lover."

"Then lace her wine with aphrodin and split her like a bloody plow, man."

"I didn't realize you were such a romantic, Miles."

The soldier snorted. "You're so tense that the air crackles when you move. Fires jump up to twice their size when you walk through the room. Every fury in the capital feels it, and the last thing you want is for the High Lords arriving for Wintersend to know you're worried."

Gaius frowned. He stared down at his wine for a moment, before he said, "The dreams have come again, Miles."

Worry struck Miles like a physical blow, but he kept it from his face as best he could. "Dreams. You're not a child to fear a dream, Sextus."

"These are more than mere nightmares. Doom is coming to Wintersend."

Miles forced a note of scorn into his voice. "You're a fortune-teller now, sire, foreseeing death?"

"Not necessarily death," Gaius said. "I use the old word. Doom. Fate. Wyrd. Destiny rushes toward us with Wintersend, and I cannot see what is beyond it."

"There is no destiny," Miles stated. "The dreams came two years ago, and no disaster destroyed the Realm."

"Because of one obstinate apprentice shepherd and the courage of those holders. It was a near thing. But if destiny doesn't suit you, call it a desperate hour," Gaius said. "History is replete with them. Moments where the fate of thousands hangs at balance, easily tipped one way or the next by the hands and wills of those involved. It's coming. This Wintersend will lay down the course of the Realm, and I'll be blighted if I can see how. But it's coming, Miles. It's coming."

"Then we'll deal with it," Miles said. "But one thing at a time."

"Exactly," Gaius said. He rose from the chair and strode back onto the mosaic tiles, beckoning Miles to come with him. "Let me show you."

Miles frowned and watched as the First Lord passed his hand over the tiles again. Miles sensed the whisper of subtle power flowing through the tiles, furies from every corner of the Realm responding to the First Lord's will. From upon the tiles, he got the full effect of the furycrafted map, colors rising up around him until it seemed that he stood like a giant over the ghostly image of the Citadel of Alera Imperia, capital of Alera itself. His balance wavered as the image blurred, speeding westward, to the rolling, rich valley of the Amaranth Vale, and past it, over the Blackhills and to the coast. The image intensified, resolving itself into an actual moving picture over the sea, where vast waves rolled under the lashing of a vicious storm.

"There," Gaius said. "The eighth hurricane this spring."

After a hushed moment, Miles said, "It's huge."

"Yes. And this isn't the worst of them. They keep making them bigger."

Miles looked up at the First Lord sharply. "Someone is crafting these storms?"

Gaius nodded. "The Canim ritualists, I believe. They've never exerted this much power across the seas before. Ambassador Varg denies it, of course."

"Lying dog," Miles spat. "Why don't you ask the High Lords on the coast for assistance? With enough windcrafters, they should be able to blunt the storms."

"They already are helping," Gaius said quietly. "Though

they don't know it. I've been breaking the storm's back and letting the High Lords protect their own territory once it was manageable."

"Then ask for further help," Miles said. "Surely Riva or Placida could lend windcrafters to the coastal cities."

Gaius gestured, and the map blurred again, settling in the far north of the Realm, along the solid, smooth stone of the Shieldwall. Miles frowned and leaned down, looking closer. Leagues away from the wall, he could see many figures moving, mostly veiled by clouds of finely powdered snow. He started making a count and quickly realized the extent of the numbers there. "The Icemen. But they've been quiet for years."

"No longer," Gaius said. "They are gathering their numbers. Antillus and Phrygia have already fought off two assaults along the Shieldwall, and matters are only growing worse. The spring thaw was delayed long enough to promise a sparse crop. That means the southerners will have the chance to gouge the Shield cities for food, and with matters as tense as they are already, it could well trigger further unpleasantness."

Miles's frown deepened. "But if more storms strike the southerners, it will ruin their crop."

"Precisely," Gaius said. "The northern cities would starve, and the southerners would be unprepared to face the Icemen that pour over the wall."

"Could the Canim and the Icemen be working together?" Miles asked.

"Great furies forbid," Gaius said. "We must hope that it is merely coincidence."

Miles ground his teeth. "And meanwhile, Aquitaine makes sure everyone hears that your incompetence is the cause of it all."

Gaius half smiled. "Aquitaine is a rather pleasant, if dangerous opponent. He is generally straightforward. I am more concerned with Rhodes, Kalare, and Forcia. They have stopped complaining to the Senate. It makes me suspicious."

The soldier nodded. He was quiet for a moment, the worry he'd felt before settling in and beginning to grow. "I hadn't realized."

"No one has. I doubt anyone else has enough information to understand the magnitude of the problem," Gaius said. He passed his hand over the mosaic tiles again, and the ghostly image of the map vanished. "And it must remain that way. The Realm is in a precarious position, Miles. A panicked re-action, a single false step could lead to division between the cities, and leave Alera open to destruction at the hands of the Canim or the Icemen."

"Or the Marat," Miles added, not bothering to hide the bitterness in his voice.

"On that front I am not unduly worried. The new Count of Calderon seems to be well advanced into forming friendly relations with several of their largest tribes."

Miles nodded his head, but said nothing more of the Marat. "You've much on your mind."

"All that and more," Gaius confirmed. "There are all the usual pressures of the Senate, the Dianic League, the Slaver's Alliance, and the Trade Consortium. Many see my reactivation of the Crown Legion as a sign of growing weakness, or possibly senility." He drew a breath. "Meanwhile the whole of the Realm worries that I may already have seen my last winter, yet have appointed no heir to succeed me—while High Lords like Aquitaine seem ready to swim to the throne through a river of blood, if necessary."

Miles considered the enormity of it for a moment in silence. "Balls."

"Mmm," Gaius said. "One thing at a time indeed." For a moment, he looked very old and very tired. Miles watched as the old man closed his eyes, composed his features, and squared his weary shoulders, steadying his voice to its usual brusque, businesslike cadence. "I have to keep an eye on that storm for a few more hours. I'll get what sleep I can then, Miles. But there is little time to spare for it."

The soldier bowed his head. "My words were rash, sire."

"But honest. I should not have grown angry with you for that. My apologies, Miles."

"It's nothing."

Gaius let out a pent-up breath and nodded. "Do something for me, Captain."

"Of course."

"Double the Citadel guard for the duration of Festival. I have no evidence to support it, but it is not beyond reason that someone might attempt dagger diplomacy during Wintersend. Especially since Fidelias left us." The First Lord's eyes grew more shadowed at this last, and Miles winced with sympathy. "He knows most of the passages in the Citadel and the Deeps."

Miles met Gaius Sextus's eyes and nodded. "I'll take care of it."

Gaius nodded and lowered his arm. Miles took it as a dismissal and walked toward the door. He paused there and looked back over his shoulder. "Rest. And think on what I said about an heir, Sextus. Please. A clear line of succession might lay many of these worries to rest."

Gaius nodded. "I am addressing it. I will say no more than that."

Miles bowed from the waist to Gaius, then turned and opened the door. A grating, buzzing sound drifted into the meditation chamber, and Miles observed, "Your page snores very loudly."

"Don't be too hard on him," Gaius said. "He was raised to be a shepherd."

xxx· CHAPTER 1

Tavi peeked around the corner of the boys' dormitories at the Academy's central courtyard, and said to the young man beside him, "You've got that look on your face again."

Ehren Patronus Vilius, a young man barely more than five feet tall, skinny, pale-skinned, and dark-eyed, fidgeted with the hems of his flapping grey academ's robes and overcoat. "What look?"

Tavi drew back from the corner, and tugged idly at his own student's uniform. It seemed that no matter how many times he got the garment adjusted, his body kept a pace ahead of the seamstress. The robes were too tight in the shoulders and chest, and the arms didn't come close to touching Tavi's wrists. "You know it, Ehren. The one you get when you're about to give someone advice."

"Actually it's the one I get when I'm about to give advice I'm sure will be ignored." Ehren peeked around the corner too, and said, "Tavi, they're all there. We might as well leave. There's only the one way to get to the dining hall. They're going to see us."

"Not all of them are there," Tavi insisted. "The twins aren't."

"No. Just Brencis *and* Renzo *and* Varien. Any one of whom could skin both of us together."

"We might be more of a handful than they think," Tavi said.

The smaller boy sighed. "Tavi, it's only a matter of time before they hurt someone. Maybe bad."

"They wouldn't dare," Tavi said.

"They're *Citizens*, Tavi. We aren't. It's as simple as that."

"That's not how it works."

"Do you ever actually listen to your history lessons?" Ehren countered. "Of course it's how it works. They'll say it was an accident, and they're terribly sorry. Assuming it even gets to a court, a magistrate will make them pay a fine to your relatives. Meanwhile, you'll be walking around missing your eyes or your feet."

Tavi set his jaw and started around the corner. "I'm not missing breakfast. I was up at the Citadel all night, he made me run up and down those crows-eaten stairs a dozen times, and if I have to skip another meal I'll go insane."

Ehren grabbed his arm. His lanyard, sporting one white bead, one blue, and one green bounced against his skinny chest. Three beads meant that the furymasters of the Academy thought Ehren barely had a grasp of furycrafting at all.

Of course, he had three beads more than Tavi.

Ehren met Tavi's gaze and spoke quietly. "If you go walking out there alone, you're insane already. Please wait a few minutes more."

Just then, the third morning bell sounded, three long strokes. Tavi grimaced at the bell tower. "Last bell. If we don't get moving, we won't have time to eat. If we time it right, we can walk past them when some others are coming out. They might not see us."

"I just don't understand where Max could be," Ehren said.

Tavi looked around again. "I don't know. I didn't leave for the palace until just before curfew, but his bed hadn't been slept in this morning."

"Out all night again," Ehren mourned. "I don't see how he expects to pass if he keeps this up. Even I won't be able to help him."

"You know Max," Tavi said. "He isn't big on planning." Tavi's belly cramped with hunger and made a gurgling noise. "That's it," he said. "We need to move. Are you coming with me or not?"

Ehren bit his lip and shook his head. "I'm not that hungry. I'll see you in class?"

Tavi felt a swell of disappointment, but he chucked Ehren on the arm. He could understand the smaller boy's reluctance. Ehren had grown up among his parents' quiet books and tables, where his keen memory and ability with mathematics far outweighed his lack of strong furycrafting. Before coming to the Academy, Ehren had never been faced with the kind of casual, petty cruelty that powerful young furycrafters could show their lessers.

Tavi, on the other hand, had been facing that particular problem for the whole of his life.

"I'll see you at class," he told Ehren.

The smaller boy fumbled at his lanyard with ink-stained fingers. "You're sure?"

"Don't worry. I'll be fine." With that, Tavi stepped around the corner and started walking across the courtyard toward the dining hall.

A few seconds later, Tavi heard running footsteps and Ehren puffed into place beside him, his expression nervous but resolved. "I should eat more," he said. "It could stunt my growth."

Tavi grinned at him, and the two walked together across the courtyard.

Spring sunlight, warmer than the mountain air around the capital of Alera, poured down over the Academy grounds. The courtyard was a richly planted garden with walkways of smooth white stone set in a number of meandering paths across it. The early blooms had accompanied the green grass up from the earth after winter's chill, and their colors, all reds and blues, decorated the courtyard. Students lounged at benches, talking, reading, and eating breakfast, all dressed in the uniform grey robes and tunics. Birds dipped and flashed through the sunshine, perching on the eaves of the buildings framing the courtyard before diving down to strike at insects emerging from their holes to gather in the crumbs dropped by careless academs.

It all looked peaceful, simple, and lovely beyond the scale of anything outside of the mighty capital of all Alera.

Tavi hated it.

Kalarus Brencis Minoris and his cronies had settled in their usual spot, at a fountain just outside the entrance to the dining hall. Just looking at the other boy seemed to make Tavi's morning grow darker. Brencis was a tall and handsome young man, regal of bearing and narrow of face. He wore his hair in long curls, considered fashionably decadent in the southern cities—particularly in his home of Kalare. His academ's robes were made of the finest of cloth, tailored personally to fit him, and embroidered with threads of pure gold. His lanyard shone with beads of semiprecious stones rather than cheap glass, and lay heavily on his chest with multiple representatives of all six colors—one for each area of furycrafting: red, blue, green, brown, white, and silver.

As Tavi and Ehren approached the fountain, the group of students from Parcia, golden brown skin shining in the morning sun, started passing between them and the bullies. Tavi hurried his steps. They only needed to avoid notice for a few more yards.

They didn't. Brencis rose from his seat at the fountain's edge, his lips curling into a wide and cheerful smile. "Well, well," he said. "The little scribe and his pet freak out for a walk. I'm not sure they'll let the freak into the dining hall if you don't put him on a leash, scribe."

Tavi didn't even glance toward Brencis, continuing on without slowing his steps. There was a chance that if he simply took no notice of the other boy, he might not bother to push.

Ehren, though, stopped and glowered at Brencis. The small boy licked his lips, and said, in a crisp tone, "He isn't a freak."

Brencis's smile widened as he came closer. "Of course he is, scribaby. The First Lord's pet monkey. It did a trick once, and now Gaius wants to show it off, like any other trained beast."

"Ehren," Tavi said. "Come on."

Ehren's dark eyes glistened abruptly, and his lower lip trembled. But the boy lifted his chin and didn't look away from Brencis. "H-he isn't a freak," Ehren insisted.

"Are you calling me a liar, scribe?" Brencis asked. His smile became vicious, and he flexed his fingers. "And I thought you had learned proper respect for your betters."

Tavi ground his teeth in frustration. It wasn't fair that idiots like Brencis should get to throw their weight around so casually, while decent folk like Ehren were constantly walked upon. Brencis obviously wasn't going to let them pass without incident.

Tavi glanced at Ehren and shook his head. The smaller boy would not have been here to begin with if he hadn't been following Tavi. That made Tavi responsible for what happened to him. He turned to face Brencis and said, "Brencis, please leave us alone. We just want to get some breakfast."

Brencis put his hand to his ear, his face reflecting feigned puzzlement. "Did you hear something? Varien, did you hear anything?"

Behind Brencis, the first of his two lackeys stood up and meandered over. Varien was a boy of medium height and heavy build. His robes were nowhere near so fine as Brencis's, though still superior to Tavi's. The extra fat gave Varien's face a petulant, spoiled look, and his baby-fine blond hair was too lank to curl properly, like Brencis's. His lanyard bore several beads of white and green that somehow clashed with his muddy hazel eyes. "I might have heard a rat squeaking."

"Could be," Brencis said gravely. "Now then, scribe. Would you prefer mud or water?"

Ehren swallowed and took a step back. "Wait. I'm not looking for trouble."

Brencis followed the small boy, his eyes narrowing, and grasped Ehren by his academ's robe. "Mud or water, you gutless piglet."

"Mud, my lord," urged Varien, eyes lit with an ugly sparkle. "Leave him up to his neck in it and let those clever wits of his broil in the sun for a while."

"Let me go!" Ehren said, his voice rising to a panicked pitch.

"Mud it is," said Brencis. He gestured to the ground with one hand, and the earth heaved and shivered. Nothing happened for a moment, then the ground began to stir, growing softer, a bubble rising up through the sudden mix of earth and fury-called water with a sodden "bloop."

Tavi looked around him for help, but there was none to be seen. None of the Maestros were passing through, and with the exception of Max, none of the other students were willing to defy Brencis when he was amusing himself at someone else's expense.

"Wait!" Ehren cried. "Please, these are the only shoes I have!"

"Well then," Brencis said. "It looks like your little freeholder family should have saved up for another generation before they sent someone here."

Tavi had to get Brencis's attention away from Ehren, and he could only think of one way to manage it. He bent over, dug up a handful of sodden earth into one scooped hand, and flung it at Brencis's head.

The young Kalaran let out a short sound of surprise as mud plastered his face. Brencis wiped at the mud and stared, shocked, at his soiled fingers. There was a sudden burst of stifled giggles from the students watching the exchange, but when Brencis stared around him, they all averted their gazes and hid smiles behind lifted hands. Brencis glowered at Tavi, his eyes flat with anger.

"Come on, Ehren," Tavi said. He pushed the smaller boy behind him, toward the dining hall. Ehren stumbled, then hurried that way. Tavi started to follow him without turning his back on Brencis.

"You," Brencis snarled. "How *dare* you?"

"Leave it, Brencis," Tavi said. "Ehren's never done you any harm."

"Tavi," Ehren hissed, warning in his tone.

Tavi sensed the presence behind him just as Ehren spoke, and ducked. He darted to one side, in time to avoid a pair of heavy-handed swipes from Brencis's second crony, Renzo.

Renzo was simply huge. Huge across, huge up and down, built on the same scale as barns and warehouses—big, roomy, and plain. He had dark hair and the scruffy beginnings of a full beard, and tiny eyes set in his square face. Renzo's academy tunic was made of unexceptional cloth, but its very size meant that it had to have cost twice what a normal outfit would have. Renzo had only heavy brown beads on his lanyard—lots and lots of them. He took another step toward Tavi and drove a huge fist forward.

Tavi hopped out of the way of that blow as well, and snapped, "Ehren, find Maestro Gallus!"

Ehren let out a startled cry, and Tavi looked over his shoulder to see Varien holding the little scribe, his arms around Ehren's shoulders, twisting painfully.

Distracted, Tavi was unable to avoid Renzo's next lunge, and the big, silent boy picked him up and threw him without ceremony into the fountain.

Tavi splashed into the water, and a shock of cold stole the breath from his lungs. He floundered for a minute, trying to tell up from down, and got himself more or less righted in the two-foot depth of water in the fountain. He sat up, spluttering.

Brencis stood over the fountain, mud dripping from one

ear and staining his beautiful clothing. His handsome face twisted into an expression of annoyance. He lifted one hand and flicked his wrist in a languid gesture.

The water around Tavi surged on its own accord. Steam, searing heat, washed up and away from the surface of the fountain's water, and Tavi let out a choked breath, lifting a hand to shield his eyes while the other supported him upright. The flood of heat passed as swiftly as it had come.

Tavi found himself completely unable to move. He looked around him and saw, as the steaming cloud cleared, that the fountain's water had transformed completely into solid, frozen ice. The cold of it began to chew into his skin a moment later, and he struggled to get a deep breath through the grip of the ice.

"H-how," he muttered, staring at Brencis. "How did you do that?"

"An application of furycrafting, freak," Brencis said. "Fire-crafting is all about arranging heat, after all. I just moved all the heat out of the water. It's an advanced application, of course. Not that I would expect you to understand how it works."

Tavi looked around the courtyard. Varien still held Ehren in a painful lock. The scribe was breathing in short, pained gasps. Many of the students who had been there a few moments before had left. Of the half dozen or so who remained, none were looking at the fountain, suddenly engrossed in their books, their breakfasts, or in the details of the roof of a building across the campus.

The cold's teeth became painful fangs. Tavi's arms and legs throbbed in pain, and it became harder to breathe. Fear raced through him, making his heart labor.

"Brencis," Tavi began. "Don't do this. The Maestros—"

"Won't care about *you*, freak." He regarded Tavi with a relaxed, calculating expression. "I am the eldest son of a High Lord of Alera. You're no one. You're nothing. Haven't you learned that by *now*?"

Tavi knew that the other boy was trying to hurt him, to anger him, and had chosen his words carefully. He knew that Brencis was deliberately manipulating him, but it seemed to make little difference. The words hurt. For most of his young life, Tavi had dreamed of leaving his aunt and uncle's steadholt, of coming to the Academy, to make something of himself despite his utter lack of ability in furycrafting.

Fate, it seemed, had delivered her most cruel stroke by granting his request.

The cold made it hard to speak, but Tavi did. "Brencis, we're both going to get demerits if the Maestros see this. Let me out. I'm sorry about the m-m-mud."

"You're sorry? As if that should matter to me?" Brencis said. "Renzo."

Renzo drew back his fist and hit Tavi in the mouth. Pain flashed through him, and he felt his lower lip split open and tasted coppery blood on his tongue. Anger joined his fear, and he stammered, "Crows take you, Brencis! Leave us alone!"

"He still has teeth, Renzo," Brencis noted.

Renzo said nothing, but hit Tavi again, and harder. Tavi tried to jerk his head away from the blow, but the ice held him fast, and he could no more avoid it than he could turn a cartwheel. The pain made his vision blur with tears he tried furiously to hold away.

"Let him go!" Ehren panted, but no one listened to him. The pain in Tavi's limbs continued to swell, and he felt his lips go numb. He tried to shout for help, but the sounds came out only feebly, and no help came.

"Well, freak," Brencis said. "You wanted me to leave you alone. I think I will. I'll stop by after lunch and see if there's anything else you have to say."

Tavi looked up and saw an opportunity approaching—but only if he could keep the bully's attention. He fixed his gaze on Brencis and snarled something under his breath.

Brencis tilted his head to one side, taking a step forward. "What was that?"

"I said," Tavi rasped, "that you're pathetic. You're a spoiled mama's boy who is too much a coward to face anyone strong enough to hurt you. You have to pick on people like Ehren and me because you're weak. You're nothing."

Brencis narrowed his eyes, leaning forward intently. "You know, freak. I don't have to leave you alone." He rested one hand on the ice, and it began to twitch and shift, letting out creaks and groans. Tavi felt a sharp twinge of pain in one shoulder, cutting through the frozen agony of the ice.

"If you like," Brencis said, "I can just stay right here with you."

Variens blurted, "Brencis!"

Tavi leaned forward and growled, "Go ahead, mama's boy. Go ahead and do it. What are you afraid of?"

Brencis's eyes flashed with anger, and the ice shifted more. "You've had this coming to you, paganus."

Tavi gritted his teeth over a pained scream.

"Good morning!" boomed a boisterous voice. A large, muscular young man in a *legionare*'s close-cropped haircut loomed up behind Brencis and casually seized him by the back of his coat and his long hair. Without preamble, the young man drove Brencis's head down into the ice, cracking his skull against the frozen surface near Tavi with a solid thump. Then the young man hauled Brencis back, and tossed him away from the fountain, sending the young lord sprawling bonelessly onto the green grass.

"Max!" Ehren shouted.

Renzo took a lumbering swing at the back of Max's neck, but the tall young man ducked under it and drove a stiff punch into the hulking Renzo's belly. Renzo's breath exploded from his chest, and he staggered. Max seized one of his arms and sent Renzo sprawling beside Brencis.

Max looked over at Varien and narrowed his eyes.

The young nobleman went pale, let go of Ehren, and backed away with his hands held before him. He and Renzo hauled the stunned Brencis onto his feet, and the three bullies retreated from the courtyard. Excited mutters and whispers from the academs in the courtyard rose as they left.

"Furies, Calderon," Max called to Tavi, loudly enough to be heard by anyone who wasn't deaf. "I am so clumsy in the morning. Look at how I went blundering right into those two." Without further delay, he moved over to the fountain and regarded Tavi's plight. Max nodded once, took a deep breath, and narrowed his eyes in concentration. Then he drew back his fist and slammed it down onto the ice near Tavi. A spiderweb of cracks exploded through it, and stinging chips struck against Tavi's numbed skin. Max pounded his fist down several more times, his fury-assisted strength more than equal to the task of pulverizing the ice imprisoning Tavi.

Within half a minute, Tavi felt himself come loose from his icy bonds, and Ehren and Max both hauled Tavi up from the ice and out onto the ground.

Tavi lay for a moment, gasping and gritting his teeth at the numbing cold still in his limbs, unable to speak.

"Crows," Max swore idly. He started rubbing briskly at Tavi's limbs. "He's near frostbitten."

Tavi felt his arms and legs twitch as fiery pins and needles started prickling against his skin. As soon as he could get his voice back, he gasped, "Max, forget this. Get me to breakfast."

"Breakfast?" Max said. "You're kidding, Calderon."

"I'm going to get a decent b-b-breakfast if it kills me."

"Oh. You're doing pretty well then," Max observed. He started helping Tavi up off the ground. "Thanks for keeping his attention off me until I could hit him, by the way. What happened?"

"B-Brencis," Tavi spat. "Again."

Ehren nodded earnestly. "He was going to bury me up to my neck again, but Tavi threw a bunch of mud at his face."

"Hah," Max said. "Wish I could have seen that."

Ehren bit his lip, then squinted up at the larger boy, and said, "If you hadn't been out all night, maybe you would have."

The large academ's face flushed. Antillar Maximus's features were not beautiful by anyone's standards, Tavi thought. But they were clean-cut, rugged, and strong. He had the wolfish grey eyes of the northern High Houses and combined a powerful build with a casual feline grace. Though usually he shaved scrupulously every day, he evidently hadn't had time to this morning, and shadowy stubble gave his features a roguish cast that went well with the dents in his twice-broken nose. Max's robes were plain and wrinkled, and had to struggle to contain his shoulders and chest. His lanyard, randomly arrayed with a hefty number of colored beads, had been carelessly knotted in several places where it had broken.

"I'm sorry," Max mumbled, as he helped Tavi stagger towards the dining hall. "It just kind of happened. There are some things that a man shouldn't miss."

"Antillar," murmured a female voice, a low and throaty purr drawling out consonants with an Attican accent. Tavi opened his eyes to see a ravishing young woman, her dark hair worn in a long braid that fell over her left shoulder. She was surpassingly lovely, and her dark eyes smoldered with a sensuality that had long since enraptured nearly every young man at the Academy. Her academ's robes did not manage to conceal the lush curves of her breasts, and the southern silks they were made from clung to her hips and hinted at the outlines of her thighs as she walked across the courtyard.

Max turned to face her and gave her a gallant little bow. "Good morning, Celine."

Celine smiled, the expression a lazy promise, and let Max take and kiss her hand. She let her hand rest on Max's and sighed. "Oh, Antillar. I know it amuses you to beat my fiancé unconscious, but you're so much . . . larger than he. It hardly seems fair."

"Life isn't fair," said a second female voice, and a second beauty, indistinguishable from Celine except that she wore her hair braided over the opposite shoulder, joined them. She slid one hand over Max's shoulder, on his other side, and added, "My sister can be such a romantic."

"Lady Celeste," Max murmured. "I'm just trying to teach him manners. It's for his own good."

Celeste gave Max an arch look, and said, "You are a vile brute of a man."

Max swept his arm back as he gave the young noble-women a gallant bow. "Celeste," he said. "Celine. I trust you slept well last night? You've almost missed breakfast."

Both of their mouths curved up into identical small smiles. "Beast," said Celine.

"Cad," her sister added.

"Ladies," Max bid them with another bow, and watched them walking away as he stood with Tavi and Ehren.

"You m-make me sick, Max," Tavi said.

Ehren glanced back over his shoulder at the twins, then to Max, his expression puzzled. Then he blinked, and said, "That's where you were all night? *Both* of them?"

"They *do* share the same quarters. Hardly would have been polite to only have one, and leave the other all lonely," Max said, his voice pious. "I was merely doing what any gentleman would."

Tavi glanced over his shoulder, his eyes drawn to the slow sway of the girls' hips as they walked away. "Sick, Max. You make me sick."

Max laughed. "You're welcome."

The three of them entered the dining hall in time to get the last of the food prepared by the kitchens that morning, but just as they found a place at one of the round tables, running foot-steps approached. A girl no older than Tavi, short, stocky, and plain, came to a halt at their table, her small scattering of green and blue beads flashing in a stray beam of sunlight against her grey robes. Her fine, mouse brown hair waved around her head where tiny strands had escaped their braid. "No time," she panted. "Put that down and come with me."

Tavi looked up from his plate, already laden with slices of ham and fresh bread, and scowled at the girl. "You would not believe what I had to go through to get this, Gaelle," he said. "I'm not moving an inch until my plate is empty."

Gaelle Patronus Sabinus looked around them furtively, then leaned down closer to their table to murmur, "Maestro Killian says that our combat final is to begin at once."

"*Now?*" stammered Ehren.

Max cast a longing glance down at his own heaping plate, and asked, "Before breakfast?"

Tavi sighed and pushed his chair back. "Blighted crows and bloody carrion." He stood up, wincing as his arms and legs throbbed. "All right, everyone. Let's go."

▭▭▭▭ CHAPTER 2

Tavi went first into the old grey stone study—a building of only a single story and perhaps twenty paces square residing in the western courtyard of the Academy, which was otherwise unused. No windows graced the study. Moss fought a silent war with ivy for possession of its walls and roof. It looked little different from the storage buildings but for a plaque upon its door that read in plain letters, MAESTRO KILLIAN—REMEDIAL FURYCRAFTING.

Several worn but well-padded old benches sat around a podium before a large slateboard. The others followed Tavi inside, Max last. The big Antillan shut the door behind them and glanced around the room.

"Everyone ready?" Max asked.

Tavi remained silent, but Ehren and Gaelle both answered that they were. Max put his hand flat against the door, closing his eyes for a moment.

"All right," he reported. "We're clear."

Tavi shoved the heel of his hand firmly against a particular spot on the slateboard, and a sudden crack appeared, straight as a plumb line. He set his shoulder to the slate, and with a grunt of effort pushed open the hidden doorway. Cool air rushed over him, and he peered down at a narrow stone stairway that wound down into the earth.

Gaelle passed him a lamp, and each of the others took one as well. Then Tavi set off down the stairs, the others close behind.

"Did I tell you? I found a way down to Riverside through the Deeps," Max mumbled.

Tavi snorted. The stone walls turned it into a hissing sound. "Down to the wine houses, eh?"

"It makes sneaking out to them simpler," Max said. "It's almost too much work to be bothered with, otherwise."

"Don't joke about such things, Max," Gaelle said, her voice somewhat hushed. "The Deeps run for miles, and great furies only know what you might run into down here. You should keep to the paths laid out for us."

Tavi reached the bottom of the stairway and turned left into a wide passage. He started counting off open doorways on his right. "It isn't all that bad. I've explored a little."

"Tavi," said Ehren, his tone exasperated. "That's the whole reason Master Killian loads you up with so much extra work. To keep you from getting into trouble."

Tavi smiled. "I'm careful."

They turned down another hall, the passage slanting sharply downward. Ehren said, "And if you make any mistakes? What if you fell into a fissure? Or into an old shaft filled with water? Or ran into a rogue fury?"

Tavi shrugged. "There's risk in everything."

Gaelle arched an eyebrow, and said, "Yet one so seldom hears of some fool drowning, starving, or falling to his death in a library or at the baker's."

Tavi gave her a sour look as they reached the bottom of the slope, where it intersected another hallway. Something flickered in the corner of his vision, and he turned to his right, staring intently down the hall.

"Tavi?" Max asked. "What is it?"

"I'm not sure," Tavi said. "I thought I saw a light down there."

Gaelle had already started down the hallway to the left, in the opposite direction, Ehren following her. "Come on," she said. "You know how much he hates to be kept waiting."

Max muttered, "He knows how much we hate to miss a meal, too."

Tavi flashed the larger young man a quick grin. The hallway led to a pair of rust-pitted iron doors. Tavi pushed them open, and the four academs moved into the classroom beyond.

The room was huge, far larger than the Academy's dining hall, its ceiling lost in shadow. A double row of grey stone pillars supported the roof, and furylamps mounted on the pillars lit the room in a harsh, green-white radiance. At the far end of the hall was a large square on the floor, composed of layers of reed matting. Beside it sat a hea\y bronze brazier, its coals glowing, giving the room its only warmth. To one side of one row of pillars was a long strip marked out on the floor for training in weaponplay. On the opposite side of the room was a cluster of ropes, wooden poles, beams, and various structures of varying heights—an obstacle course.

Maestro Killian sat on his knees beside the brazier. He was a wizened old man, his hair little more than a nimbus of fine white down drifting around his shining pate. Thin, small, and seemingly frail, his black scholar's robe was so old it had faded to a threadbare grey. Several pairs of woolen stockings covered his feet, and his cane rested on the ground beside him. As the group came closer, Killian lifted his face, his blind, filmy eyes turning toward them. "That was as soon as possible?" he asked, his voice annoyed and creaking. "In my day, Cursors-in-Training would have been lashed and laid down in a bed of salt for moving so slowly."

The four of them moved forward to the reed matting and sat down in a row, facing the old man. "Sorry, Maestro," Tavi said. "It was my fault. Brencis again."

Killian felt for his cane, picked it up, and rose to his feet. "No excuses. You're just going to have to find a way to avoid his attention."

"But, Maestro," Tavi protested. "I just wanted some breakfast."

Killian poked his cane at Tavi's chest, thumping him lightly. "Going hungry until lunch wouldn't have hurt you. It would at least have demonstrated self-discipline. Better yet, you might have demonstrated forethought and saved some of last night's dinner to eat in the morning."

Tavi grimaced, and said, "Yes, Maestro."

"Were you seen coming in?"

The four answered together. "No, Maestro."

"Well then," Killian said. "If you all don't mind too terribly, shall we begin the test? With you first, Tavi."

They stood to their feet. Killian doddered out onto the matting, and Tavi followed him. As he went, he felt the air tighten against his skin, grow somehow thicker as the old teacher called the wind furies that let him sense and observe movements. Killian turned toward Tavi, and nodded to him. Then the old man said, "Defend and counter."

With that, the little man whipped his cane at Tavi's head. Tavi barely ducked in time, only to see the old Maestro lift his stockinged foot and drive it down in a lashing kick aimed for Tavi's knee. The boy spun his body away from it, and used the momentum of the motion for a straight, driving kick, launched at Killian's belly.

The old Maestro dropped the cane, caught Tavi's foot at the ankle, and with a twist stole Tavi's balance and sent him flat down to the mat. Tavi hit hard enough to knock the wind from him, and he lay there gasping for a moment.

"No, no, no!" Killian scolded. "How many times do I need to tell you? You have to move your head as well as your legs, fool. You cannot expect an unaimed attack to succeed. You must turn your face to watch the target." He picked up his cane and rapped Tavi sharply on the head. "And your timing was less than perfect. Should you be on a mission one day and attacked, that kind of poor performance would mean your death."

Tavi rubbed at the spot on his head where Killian had reprimanded him, scowling. The old man had hardly needed to strike him that firmly. "Yes, Maestro."

"Go sit down, boy. Come, Antillar. Let's see if you can manage anything better."

Max went out onto the mat, and went through a similar sequence with Maestro Killian. He performed flawlessly, grey eyes flashing as he whipped his head around, keeping an eye on his target. Gaelle and Ehren went in their turns, and all of them responded better than Tavi had.

"Barely adequate," Killian snapped. "Ehren, fetch the staves."

The skinny boy got a pair of six-foot poles from a rack on the wall and brought them to the Maestro. Killian set his cane aside and accepted them. "Very well, Tavi. Let's see if you have managed to learn anything of the staff."

Tavi took the other staff from the Maestro, and the two saluted, staves lifted vertically before they both dropped into a fighting crouch.

"Defend," Killian snapped, and the old man spun his staff through a series of attacks, whirling, sweeping blows mixed with low, lightning thrusts aimed at Tavi's belly. He backed away from the Maestro, blocking the sweeping blows and slipping the thrusts aside. Tavi struck out with a counterattack, but he could feel an iron tension in his shoulders that slowed his thrust.

Killian promptly knocked aside Tavi's weapon, delivered a sharp thrust to the boy's fingers, and with a flick sent Tavi's staff spinning across the room to clatter against one of the stone pillars.

Killian thumped the end of his staff onto the mat, his expression one of frustrated disapproval. "How many times have I told you, boy? Your body must be relaxed until the instant you strike. Holding yourself too tightly slows your responses. Life and death are measured by the breadth of a hair in combat."

Tavi gripped his bruised hand into a fist, and grated out, "Yes, Maestro."

Killian jerked his head toward the fallen staff, and Tavi went to retrieve it.

The old man shook his head. "Gaelle. Attempt to show Tavi what I mean."

The others followed in turn, and they all did better than Tavi had. Even Ehren.

Killian passed the staves to Tavi and picked up his cane. "To the strip, children."

They followed him to the combat strip laid out on the floor. Killian walked to the center of the strip and thumped the floor with his cane. "And once more, Tavi. We might as well get it out of the way now."

Tavi sighed and walked to stand before Killian.

Killian lifted his cane into a guard position used for swords. "I am armed with a blade," he said. "Disarm me without leaving the strip."

The cane's tip darted at Tavi's throat. The boy lightly slapped the attack aside with one hand, retreating. The old man followed, cane sweeping at Tavi's head. Tavi ducked, rolled backward to avod a horizontal slash, and came to his feet to brush aside another thrust. He closed, inside the tip of the theoretical sword, hands moving to seize the old man's wrists.

The attack was too tentative. In the bare instant of delay, the Maestro avoided Tavi's attempt to grapple. The old man whipped the cane left and right, branding sudden pain into

Tavi's chest in an x-shape. He thrust the heel of one wrinkled hand into Tavi's chest, driving the boy a step back, then jabbed the tip of the cane firmly into Tavi's chest, sending him sprawling to the floor.

"What is wrong with you?" Killian snapped. "A sheep would have been more decisive than that. Once you decide to close range, you are committed. Attack with every ounce of speed and power you can muster. Or die. It's as simple as that."

Tavi nodded, not looking at the other students, and said, very quietly, "Yes, Maestro."

"The good news, Tavi," Killian said in an acid tone, "is that you won't need to worry about the entrails currently spilling over your knees. The fountain of blood spraying from your heart will kill you far more quickly."

Tavi climbed to his feet, wincing.

"The bad news," Killian continued, "is that I see no way that I can grade your performance as anything close to acceptable. You fail."

Tavi said nothing. He walked over to lean against the nearest pillar, rubbing at his chest.

The Maestro rapped his cane on the strip again. "Ehren. I hope to the great furies you have more resolve than he does."

The exam concluded after Gaelle had neatly kicked aside the Maestro's forearm, sending the cane tumbling away. Tavi watched the other three succeed where he had failed. He rubbed at his eyes and tried to ignore how sleepy he felt. His stomach rumbled almost painfully as he knelt beside the other students.

"Barely competent," Killian muttered, after Gaelle had finished. "You all need to spend more time in practice. It is one thing to perform well in a test on the training mat. It is quite another to do so in earnest. I expect you all to be ready for the infiltration test at the conclusion of Wintersend."

"Yes, Maestro," they replied, more or less in unison.

"Very well then," Killian said. "Off with you, puppies. You might become Cursors yet." He paused to glower at Tavi. "Most of you, at any rate. I spoke to the kitchen staff this morning. They're keeping some breakfast warm for you."

The students rose, but Killian laid his cane across one of Tavi's shoulders, and said, "Not you, boy. You and I are going to have words about your performance in the exam. The rest of you, go."

Ehren and Gaelle looked at Tavi and winced, then offered him apologetic smiles as they left.

Max clapped Tavi's shoulder with one big hand when he walked by, and said, quietly, "Don't let him get to you." Max and the others left the training hall, closing the huge iron doors behind them.

Killian walked back over to the brazier and sat down, holding his hands out toward its warmth. Tavi walked over and knelt down in front of him. Killian closed his eyes for a moment, his expression pained as he opened and closed his fingers, stretching out his hands. Tavi knew that the Maestro's arthritis had been troubling him.

"Was that all right?" Tavi asked.

The old man's expression softened into a faint smile. "You mimicked their weaknesses fairly well. Antillar remembered to look before he struck. Gaelle remembered to keep herself relaxed. Ehren committed without hesitation."

"That's wonderful. I guess."

Killian tilted his head. "You aren't happy that you appeared to your friends to be unskilled."

"I guess so. But . . ." Tavi frowned in thought. "It's hard to deceive them. I don't like it."

"Nor should you. But I think that isn't all."

"No," Tavi said. "It's because . . . well, they're the only ones who know that I'm undergoing Cursor training. The only ones I can talk to about most of the things I really care about. And I know they only mean to be kind. But I know what they aren't saying. How careful they are about trying to help me without letting me know that's what they're doing. Ehren thought he had to protect me from Brencis today. *Ehren.*"

Killian smiled again. "He's loyal."

Tavi scowled. "But he shouldn't have to do it. It isn't as if I'm not helpless enough already."

The Maestro frowned. "Meaning?"

"Meaning that I can learn all the unarmed combat I like and it won't help me against a strong furycrafter. Someone like Brencis. Even if I'm using a weapon."

"You do yourself an injustice."

Tavi said, "I don't see how."

"You are more capable than you know," Killian said. "You might not ever be the swordsman a powerful metalcrafter can become, or have the speed of a windcrafter or the strength of an earthcrafter. But furycrafting isn't everything. Few crafters develop the discipline to hone many skills. You have done so. You are now better able to deal with them than most folk who have only minor talents at furycrafting. You should take some measure of pride in it."

"If you say so." Tavi sighed. "But it doesn't feel true. It doesn't feel like I have very much to be proud about."

Killian laughed, the sound surprisingly warm. "Says the boy who stopped a Marat horde from invading Alera and earned the patronage of the First Lord himself. Your uncertainty has more to do with being seventeen than it does with any fury or lack thereof."

Tavi felt himself smile a little. "Do you want me to take the combat test now?"

Killian waved a hand. "Not necessary. I have something else in mind."

Tavi blinked. "You do?"

"Mmm. The civic legion is having trouble with crime. For the past several months, a thief has been stealing from various merchants and homes, some of which were warded by furycrafting. Thus far, the legion has been unable to apprehend the thief."

Tavi pursed his lips pensively. "I thought that they had the support of the city's furies. Shouldn't they be able to tell who circumvented the guard furies?"

"They do. They should. But they haven't."

"How is that possible?" Tavi asked.

"I cannot be certain," Killian said. "But I have a theory. What if the thief was managing the thefts without using any furycrafting? If no furies are brought into play, the city's furies could not be of any help."

"But if they aren't using any furies, how are they getting into warded buildings?"

"Precisely," Killian said. "And there is the substance of your test. Discover how this thief operates and see to it that he is apprehended."

Tavi felt his eyebrows shoot up. "Why me?"

"You have a unique perspective on this matter, Tavi. I believe you well suited to the task."

"To catching a thief the whole civic legion hasn't been able to find?"

Killian's smile widened. "This should be simple for the mighty hero of the Calderon Valley. Make sure it's done—and discreetly—before Wintersend is over."

"What?" Tavi said. "Maestro, with all of my courses, and serving in the Citadel at night, I don't know how you expect me to get this done."

"Without whining," Killian said. "You have real potential, young man. But if you are daunted by the difficulty of arranging your schedule, perhaps you would like to speak to His Majesty about returning home."

Tavi swallowed. "No," he said. "I'll do it."

The Maestro tottered back onto his feet. "Then I suggest you begin. You've no time to lose."

CHAPTER 3

Amara spread her arms and arched her back as she finally cleared the heavy cloud cover along the coast of the Sea of Ice, and emerged from the cold, blinding mist into the glorious warmth of the sunrise. For a few seconds, the edges of the clouds swirled as her wind fury Cirrus lifted her out of them, and she could see the fury's appearance in the motion of the clouds—the ghostly form of a lean, long-legged courser of a horse, swift and graceful and beautiful.

Clouds rose in peaks and valleys like vast mountains, an entire realm of slow grace and breathtaking beauty. The golden sunshine of spring turned them to flame, and in turn they shattered the light into bands of color that danced and spun around her.

Amara laughed for the sheer joy of it. No matter how often she flew, the beauty of the skies never ceased to fill her heart, and the sense of freedom and strength only grew more intense. Amara called to Cirrus, and the fury bore her straight up with such speed that the wind tightened her face to her cheekbones and a portion of cloud the size of the Citadel in Alera proper was drawn into a column in her wake. Amara angled her arms so that the wind of her passage spun her in dizzying circles, until her head spun, and the air began to grow thin and cold.

Cirrus's presence allowed her to breathe without difficulty, for a time at least, but the blue of the sky above her began to darken, and a few moments later she began to see the stars. The cold intensified, and Cirrus itself began to tire as the fury struggled to draw in enough air to keep her aloft.

Her heart pounding with excitement, she signaled Cirrus to cease.

She felt her ascent slow, and for a single delicious second she was suspended between the stars and the earth. And then, she twisted her body like a diver and fell. Her heart hammered with electric apprehension, and she closed her legs together and her arms in tightly to her sides, her face toward the ground below. Within seconds, she was rushing down more swiftly even than she had risen, and her eyes blurred with tears in the wind, until Cirrus slid a portion of its being over them to protect her.

As the air thickened, she willed Cirrus back into propelling her, and her speed doubled and redoubled, a faint nimbus of light forming around her. The rolling green hills of the Calderon Valley came into sight, already defying the winter with new growth. The Valley grew larger with deceptive deliberation.

Amara poured on the speed, focusing every ounce of her will to strengthen her furycrafting, and she picked out the causeway that ran the length of the Valley to the fortified steading at its east end. Then the outpost of Garrison itself came into sight.

Amara howled her excitement and stretched her power to its limits. There was a sudden and deafening thunder. She gasped and spread her arms and legs to slow her fall, only a thousand feet from the Valley's floor. Cirrus rushed to place himself in front of her, helping to slow her even more, then she and Cirrus pulled out of the dive, redirecting her momentum to send her flashing along the causeway in a howling cyclone of wind. Exhausted and panting from the effort of producing that much speed, Amara shot toward the gates of Garrison, swifter than an arrow from the bow. She drew the winds about her as she approached the gates, and the guard standing watch over them waved her in without rising from his stool.

Amara grinned, and altered her course to bring her down on the battlements over the gate. The winds around her sent dust and debris whirling up in a billowing cloud all around the guard—a grizzled centurion named Giraldi. The stocky old soldier had been peeling away the wrinkled skin of a winterstores apple with his dagger, and he flipped a corner of his scarlet and azure cloak over it until the dust settled. Then he resumed his peeling.

"Countess," he said casually. "Nice to see you again."

"Giraldi," she said. She loosened the straps of the sealed courier's pack she carried on her back and slid it off. "Most soldiers rise and salute when nobility visits."

"Most soldiers don't have an ass as grey as mine," he replied cheerfully.

Nor do most bear the scarlet stripe of the Order of the Lion, the mark of the First Lord's personal award for valor on their uniform trousers, Amara thought, and fought not to smile. "What are you doing standing a watch? I thought I brought the papers for your promotion last month."

"You did," Giraldi confirmed. He ate a wrinkled stripe of apple skin. "Turned it down."

"Your commission?"

"Crows, girl," he swore with a certain merry disregard for the delicacy tradition demanded be accorded her sex. "I made fun of officers my whole career. What kind of fool do you think I am to want to *be* one?"

She couldn't help it any longer, and laughed. "Could you send someone to let the Count know I'm here with dispatches?"

Giraldi snorted. "I reckon you already told him yourself. There ain't so many people that make great pounding bursts of thunder rattle every dish in the valley when they arrive. Everyone who ain't deaf knows you're here already."

"Then I thank you for your courtesy, centurion," she teased, slinging the pack over one shoulder and heading for the stairs. Her flying leathers creaked as she did.

"Disgraceful," Giraldi complained. "Pretty girl like you running around dressed like that. Men's clothes. And too tight to be decent. Get a dress."

"This is more practical," Amara called over her shoulder.

"I noticed how practical you look whenever you come to see Bernard" Giraldi drawled.

Despite herself, Amara felt her cheeks flush, though between the wind and cold of her passage, she doubted it would show. She descended into the camp's western courtyard. When Bernard had taken over command of Garrison from its previous Count, Gram, he had ordered it to be cleansed of the signs of the battle now two years past. Despite that, Amara always thought that she could still see stains of blood that had been overlooked. She knew that the spilled blood had all been cleaned.

What remained were the stains it had left in her thoughts, and in her heart.

The thought sobered her somewhat, without really marring

her sense of happiness in the morning. Life here, on the eastern frontier of Alera, she reminded herself, could be harsh and difficult. Thousands of Alerans had met their deaths on the floor of this valley, and tens of thousands of Marat. It was a place that had been steeped in hardship, danger, treachery, and violence for nearly a century.

But that had begun to change, in large part due to the efforts and courage of the man who oversaw it for the Crown, and whom she had braved the dangerous high winds to see.

Bernard emerged from the commander's quarters at the center of the camp, smiling. Though the cut of his clothing was a bit more stylish, and the fabrics more fine, he still wore the sober greens and browns of the free Steadholder he had been, rather than the brighter colors proclaiming his bloodlines and allegiance. He was tall, his dark hair salted with early grey, and like his beard cropped close in Legion fashion. He paused to hold the door open for a serving maid carrying an armload of laundry, then approached Amara with long, confident strides. Bernard was built like a bear, Amara thought, and moved like a hunting cat, and he was certainly as handsome as any man she had seen. But she liked his eyes best. His grey-green eyes were like Bernard himself—clear, open and honest, and they missed little.

"Count," she murmured, as he came close, and offered her hand.

"Countess," he responded. There was a quiet smoldering in his eyes that made Amara's heart race a bit more quickly as he took her hand in gentle fingers and bowed over it. She thought she could feel his deep voice in her belly when he rumbled, "Welcome to Garrison, lady Cursor. Did you have a nice trip?"

"Finally, now that the weather is clearing," she said, and left her hand on his arm as they walked to his offices.

"How are things at the capital?"

"More amusing than usual," she said. "The Slavers Consortium and the Dianic League are all but dueling in the streets, and the Senators can barely show their faces out of doors without being assaulted by one party or another. The southern cities are doing everything they can to run up the prices of this year's crops, screaming about the greed and graft of the Wall lords, while the Wall cities are demanding an increase in levies from the miserly south."

Bernard grunted. "His Majesty?"

"In fine form," Amara said. She made it a point to inhale through her nose as she walked. Bernard smelled of pine needles, leather, and woodsmoke, and she loved the scent of him. "But he's made fewer appearances this year than in the past. There are rumors that his health is finally failing."

"When aren't there?"

"Exactly. Your nephew is doing well at the Academy, by all reports."

"Really? Has he finally . . ."

Amara shook her head. "No. And they've called in a dozen different craftmasters to examine him and work with him. Nothing."

Bernard sighed.

"But otherwise, he's performing excellently. His instructors are uniformly impressed with his mind."

"Good," Bernard said. "I'm proud of him. I always taught him not to let his problem stand in his way. That intelligence and skill would carry him farther than furycrafting. But all the same, I had hoped . . ." He sighed, tipping a respectful nod to a pair of passing *legionares callidus*, walking from the mess hall with their officially nonexistent wives. "So, what word from the First Lord?"

"The usual dispatches, and invitations for you and the Valley's Steadholders to Festival."

He arched a brow. "He sent one to my sister as well?"

"Particularly to your sister," Amara said. She frowned as they went inside the command residence and up the stairs to Bernard's private offices. "There are several things you need to know, Bernard. His Majesty asked me to brief you both on the situation surrounding her attendance. In private."

Bernard nodded and opened the door. "I thought as much. She's already packed for the trip. I'll send word, and she should be here by this evening."

Amara entered, looking back over her shoulder, her head cocked. "By this evening, is it?"

"Mmm. Perhaps not until tomorrow morning." He shut the door behind him. And casually slid the bolt shut, leaning back against it. "You know, Giraldi's right, Amara. A woman shouldn't dress in tight leathers like that."

She blinked innocently at him. "Oh? Why not?"

"It makes a man think things."

She moved slowly. At his heart, Bernard was a hunter, and a man of great patience when need be. Amara had found that it was a distinct pleasure to test that patience.

And even more of a pleasure to make it unravel.

She started unbinding her honey brown hair from its braid. "What sorts of things, Your Excellency?"

"That you should be in a dress," he said, voice edged with the slightest low tone of a beast's growl. His eyes all but glowed as he watched her let her hair down.

She undid the plaits in her hair with deliberate precision and began to comb them out with her fingers. She'd worn her hair much shorter in the past, but she'd been growing it out since she found out how much Bernard liked it worn long. "But if I was in a dress," she said, "the wind would tear it to shreds. And when I came down to see you, milord, Giraldi and his men would all get to stare at what the shreds didn't cover." She blinked her eyes again and let her hair fall in mussed waves down around her face and over her shoulders. She watched his eyes narrow in pleasure at the sight. "I can hardly run around like that in front of a crowd of *legionares*. As I told the good centurion. It's merely practical."

He leaned away from the door and approached, a slow step at a time. He leaned close to her, and took the courier's pack from her. His fingertips dragged lightly over her shoulder as he did, and she almost felt that she could feel them through her jacket. Bernard was an earthcrafter of formidable power, and such people always carried a certain sense of purely instinctive, mindless physical desire around them like a tactile perfume. She had felt it when she first met the man, and even more so since.

And when he made the effort, it could cause her own patience to vanish first. It wasn't fair, but she had to admit that she could hardly complain about the results.

He set the pack of dispatches aside and kept stepping forward, and bodily pressed her hips against his desk and forced her to lean back a little from him. "No, it isn't," he said in a quiet voice, and she felt a slow, animal thrill course through her at his presence. He lifted a hand and touched her cheek with his fingertips. Then gently slid his hand down over her shoulder and flank to her hip. The touch of his fingers lingered and made her feel a little breathless with sudden need. He rested his hand on her hip, and said, "If they were practical, I could slide them out of my way at once. It would save time." He leaned down and brushed his lips against her cheek, nuzzling his nose and mouth in her hair. "Mmmm. Having you at once. That would be practical."

Amara tried to draw things out, but she hadn't seen him in weeks, and almost against her will she felt the sinuous pleasure of her body yielding and molding to his, one leg bending to slide her calf along the outside of his own. Then he bent his mouth to hers and kissed her, and the slow heat and sensual delight of the taste of his mouth did away with any thought whatsoever.

"You're cheating," she whispered a moment later, panting as she slipped her hands beneath his tunic to feel the heavy, hot muscles on his back.

"Can't help it," he growled. He parted the front of her jacket, and she arched her back, the air cool on her thin linen undershirt. "I want you. It's been too long."

"Don't stop," she whispered, though it was edged with a low moan. "Too long."

Boots thumped up the stairs outside Bernard's office.

One at a time.

Loudly.

Bernard let out an irritated groan, his eyes closed.

"Ahem," coughed Giraldi's voice from outside. "Achoo. My but what a cold I have. Yes, sir, a cold. I'll need to see a healer about that."

Bernard straightened, and Amara had to force her fingers to move away from him. She stood up and her balance wavered. So she sat down on the edge of Bernard's desk, her face flushed, and tried to get all the clasps on the jacket fastened closed again.

Bernard tucked his tunic more or less back through his belt, but his eyes smoldered with quiet anger. He went to the door, and Amara was struck by how *large* the man was as he unlocked it and stood in it, facing the centurion outside.

"Sorry, Bernard," Giraldi said. "But . . ." He lowered his voice to a bare whisper, and Amara couldn't hear the rest.

"Crows," Bernard spat in a sudden, vicious curse.

Amara jerked her head up at the tone in his voce.

"How long?" the Count asked.

"Less than an hour. General call to arms?" Giraldi asked.

Bernard clenched his jaw. "No. Get your century to the wall, dress uniform."

Giraldi frowned, head cocked to one side.

"We aren't preparing to fight. We're turning out an honor guard. Understand?"

"Perfectly, Your Excellency," Giraldi answered, his often-broken nose making the words thick. "You want our finest century on the wall in full battle gear so that we can beat some Marat around if they've got a mind to tussle, and if they don't, you want your most beautiful and charming centurion doing the greeting to make them feel all welcome."

"Good man."

Giraldi's smile faded, and he lowered his voice, his expression frank but unafraid. "You think there's a fight brewing?"

Bernard clapped the old soldier on the shoulder. "No. But I want you personally to tell Knight Captain Gregor and the other centurions it might be a good idea to run a weapons and arms inspection in their barracks for a while, in case I'm wrong."

"Yes, Your Excellency," Giraldi said. He struck his fist to his heart in a crisp Legion salute, nodded at Amara, and marched out.

Bernard turned to a large, sturdy wooden armoire and opened it. He drew out a worn old arming jacket and jerked it on with practiced motions.

"What's happening?" Amara asked.

He passed her a short, stout blade in a belted scabbard. "Could be trouble."

The *gladius* was the side arm of a *legionare*, and the most common weapon in the Realm. Amara was well familiar with it, and buckled it on without needing to watch her fingers. "What do you mean?"

"There's a Marat war party on the plain," Bernard said. "They're coming this way."

Amara felt a slow, quiet tension enter her shoulders. "How many?"

Bernard shrugged into the mail tunic and buckled and belted it into place. "Two hundred, maybe more," he answered.

"But isn't that far too small to be a hostile force?" she asked.

"Probably."

She frowned. "Surely you don't think Doroga would attack us at all, much less with so few."

Bernard shrugged, swung a heavy war axe from the cabinet, and slung its strap over his shoulder. "It might not be Doroga. If someone else has supplanted him the way he did Atsurak, an attack is a possibility, and I'm not taking any chances with the lives of my men and holders. We prepare for the worst. Pass me my bow."

Amara turned to the fireplace and took down a bow from its rack above it, a carved half-moon of dark wood as thick as her ankles. She passed it to him, and the big man drew a wide-mouthed war quiver packed with arrows from the armoire. Then he used one leg to brace the bow, and without any obvious effort he bent recurved staves that would have required two men with tools to handle safely, and strung the weapon with a heavy cord.

"Thank you."

She lifted her eyebrows at the bent bow. "Do you think that is necessary?"

"No. But if something bad happens, I want you to get word to Riva immediately."

She frowned. She would hate to leave Bernard's side in the face of danger, but her duty as a messenger of the First Lord was clear. "Of course."

"Shall I find you some mail?" he asked.

She shook her head. "I'm already tired from the trip in. If I need to fly, I don't want to carry any more weight than I must."

He nodded and stalked out of the office, and she kept pace with him. Together they headed through the eastern courtyard, to the looming, enormous expanse of the wall facing the spreading plains of the lands of the Marat. The wall was better than thirty feet high and thick, all black basalt that seemed to have been formed of a single, titanic block of stone. Crenellation spread seamlessly along the battlements. A gate high and wide enough to admit the largest gargants was formed of a single sheet of some dark steel she had never seen before, called from the depths of the earth by the First Lord himself, after the battle two years ago.

They mounted the steps up to the battlements, where Giraldi's eighty grizzled veterans, the men who had survived the Second Battle of Calderon, were assembling in good order. The bloodred stripe of the Order of the Lion was conspicuous on the piping of their trousers, and though they were dressed in their formal finery, each of the men wore his working weapons and armor of simple, battle-tested steel.

Far out on the plain, moving shapes approached the fortress, little more than dark, indistinct blotches.

Amara leaned into the space between two of the stone merlons and lifted her hands. She called to Cirrus, and the fury whirled between her hands, forming the air into a sheet of bent light that enlarged the image of the distant travelers.

"It's Doroga," she reported to Bernard. "If I'm not mistaken, that's Hashat with him."

"Hashat?" Bernard asked, frowning. "He needs her to patrol their eastern marshes and keep Wolf in line. It's dangerous for them to travel together in such a small company."

Amara frowned, studying them. "Bernard, Hashat is walking. Her horse is limping. There are more Horse on foot. They've got stretchers, too. Riderless horses and gargants. Wounded animals."

Bernard frowned, then nodded sharply. "You were right, centurion," he said. "It's a war party."

Giraldi nodded. "Just not here to fight us. Could be that they've got someone chasing them."

"No. Their pace is too slow," Bernard said. "If someone was after them, they'd have caught them by now. Stand down and get the healers into position."

"Yes, sir." The centurion signaled his men to sheathe their weapons, then started bawling out orders, sending men to fetch out bathing tubs to be filled with water, and summoning Garrison's watercrafters in order to care for the wounded.

It took more than an hour for Doroga's wounded band to reach the fortress, and by that time the cooks had the air filled with the smell of roasting meat and fresh bread, setting up trestles laden with food, stacking a small mountain of hay for the gargants, and filling the food and water troughs near the stables. Giraldi's *legionares* cleared out a wide area in one of the warehouses, laying out rows of sleeping pads with blankets for the wounded.

Bernard opened the gates and went out to meet the Marat party. Amara stayed at his side. They walked up to within twenty feet or so of the vast, battle-scarred black gargant Doroga rode, and the pungent, earthy smell of the beast was thick in her nose.

The Marat himself was an enormous man, tall and heavily built even for one of his race, slabs of thick muscle sliding under his skin. His coarse white hair was worn back in a fighting braid, and there was a cut on his chest that had closed itself with thick clots of blood. His features were brutish, but dark eyes glittering with intelligence watched Bernard from beneath his heavy brows. He wore the tunic the holders of Calderon had given him after the battle, though he'd torn it open down the front and removed the sleeves to make room for his arms. The cool wind did not seem to make him uncomfortable.

"Doroga," Bernard called.

Doroga nodded back. "Bernard." He hooked a thumb over his back. "Wounded."

"We're ready to help. Bring them in."

Doroga's wide mouth turned up into a smile that showed heavy, blocky teeth. He nodded his head at Bernard in thanks then untied a large pouch with a cross-shoulder sling on it from a strap on the gargant's saddle-mat. Then he took hold of a braided leather rope, and swung down from the beast's back. He closed on Bernard and traded grips with him, Marat fashion, hands clasping one another's forearms. "I'm obliged. Some of the wounds are beyond our skill. Thought maybe your people would be willing to help."

"And honored." Bernard signaled Giraldi to take over seeing to the injured among the Marat, while grooms came forth to examine wounded horses and gargants, as well as a pair of bloodied wolves. "You're looking well," Bernard said.

"How is your nephew?" Doroga rumbled.

"Off learning," Bernard said. "Kitai?"

"Off learning," said Doroga, eyeing Amara. "Ah, the girl who flies. You need to eat more, girl."

Amara laughed. "I try, but the First Lord keeps me busy running messages."

"Too much running does that," Doroga agreed. "Get a man. Have some babies. That always works."

A sickly little fluttering stab of pain went through Amara's belly, but she did her best to keep a smile on her face. "I'll think about it."

"Huh," Doroga snorted. "Bernard, maybe you got something broken in your pants?"

Bernard's face flushed scarlet. "Uh. No."

Doroga saw the Count's embarrassment and burst out into grunting, guffawing laughter. "You Alerans. Everything mates," Doroga said. "Everything likes to. But only your people try to pretend they do neither."

Amara enjoyed Bernard's blush, though the pain Doroga's words had elicited prevented her from blushing herself. Bernard would probably think she was just too worldly to be so easily embarrassed. "Doroga," she said, to rescue him from the subject, "how did you get that wound? What happened to your people?"

The Marat headman's smile faded, and he looked back out at the plains, his countenance grim. "I got it being foolish," he said. "The rest should first be for your ears only. We should go inside."

Bernard frowned and nodded at Doroga, then beckoned him. They walked together into Garrison and back to Bernard's office.

"Would you like some food?" Bernard asked.

"After my people have eaten," Doroga said. "Their *chala* too. Their beasts."

"I understand. Sit, if you like."

Doroga shook his head and paced quietly around the office, opening the armoire, peering at the bricks of the fireplace, and picking up several books off the modest-sized shelf to peer at their pages.

"Your people," he said. "So different than ours."

"In some ways," Bernard agreed. "Similar in many others."

"Yes." Doroga flipped through the pages of *The Chronicles of Gaius*, pausing to examine a woodcut illustration on one of them. "My people do not know much of what yours know, Bernard. We do not have these . . . what is the word?"

"Books."

"Books," Doroga said. "Or the drawing-speech your people use in them. But we are an old people, and not without our own knowledge." He gestured at his wound. "The ground powder of shadowwort and sandgrass took the pain, clotted the blood, and closed this wound. You would have needed stitches or your sorcery."

"I do not question your people's experience or knowledge, Doroga," Bernard said. "You are different. That does not make you less."

Doroga smiled. "Not all Alerans think as you."

"True."

"We have our wisdom," he said. "Passed on from one to another since the first dawn. We sing to our children, and they to theirs, and so we remember what has been." He went to the fireplace and stirred the embers with a poker. Orange light played lurid shadows over the shape of his muscles and made his expression feral. "I have been a great fool. Our wisdom warned me, but I was too foolish to see the danger for what it was."

"What do you mean?" asked Amara.

He drew a deep breath. "The Wax Forest. You have heard of it, Bernard?"

"Yes," he said. "I went there a time or two. Never down into it."

"Wise," Doroga said. "It was a deadly place."

"Was?"

The Marat nodded. "No longer. The creatures who lived there have departed it."

Bernard blinked. "Departed. To where?"

Doroga shook his head. "I am not certain. Yet. But our wisdom tells us of them, and warns of what they will do."

"You mean your people have seen such things before?"

Doroga nodded. "Far in the past, our people did not live where we live today. We came here from another place."

"Across the sea?" Amara asked.

Doroga shrugged. "Across the sea. Across the sky. We were elsewhere, then we were here. Our people have lived in many lands. We go to a new place. We bond with what lives there. We learn. We grow. We sing the songs of wisdom to our children."

Amara frowned. "You mean . . . is that why there are different tribes among your people?"

He blinked at her as her Academy teachers might have done at slow-witted students, and nodded. "By *chala*. By totem. Our wisdom tells us that long ago, in another place, we met a creature. That this creature stole the hearts and minds of our people. That it and its brood grew from dozens to millions. It overwhelmed us. Destroyed our lands and homes. It stole our children, and our females gave birth to its spawn."

Bernard sat down in a chair by the fire, frowning.

"It is a demon that can take many forms," the Marat continued. "It tastes of blood and may take the shape of the creature it tasted. It gives birth to its own brood of creatures. It transforms its enemies into . . . things. Things of its own creation, that fight for the creature. It keeps taking. Killing. Spawning. Until nothing is left to fight it."

Bernard narrowed his eyes, intent on Doroga. Amara took a few steps to stand behind his chair, her hand on his shoulder.

"This is not a campfire tale, Aleran," Doroga said quietly. "It is not a mistake. This creature is real." The big Marat swallowed, his expression ashen. "It can take many shapes and forms, and our wisdom warns us not to rely solely upon its appearance to warn us of its presence. That was my mistake. I did not see the creature for what it was until it was too late."

"The Wax Forest," Bernard said.

Doroga nodded. "When your nephew and Kitai returned from the Trial, something followed them."

"You mean wax spiders?" Bernard asked.

Doroga shook his head. "Something larger. Something more."

"Wait," Amara said. "Are you talking about many creatures or one creature?"

"Yes," Doroga said. "That is what makes it an Abomination before The One."

Amara almost scowled in frustration. The Marat simply did not use language the same way as Alerans did, even when speaking Aleran. "I don't think I've ever heard of anything like that here, Doroga."

Doroga shrugged. "No. That is why I have come. To warn you." He took a step closer to them, crouching down, and whispered, "The Abomination is here. The wisdom tells us the name of its minions. The *vordu-ha*." He shuddered, as if saying the words sickened him. "And it tells us the name of the creature itself. It is the vord."

There was heavy silence for a moment. Then Bernard asked, "How do you know?"

Doroga nodded toward the courtyard. "I gave battle to a vord nest yesterday at dawn with two thousand warriors."

"Where are they now?" Amara asked.

The Marat's expression stayed steady and on the fire. "Here."

Amara felt her mouth open in shock. "But you only had two hundred with . . ."

Doroga's features remained feral, stony, as her words trailed off into silence. "We paid in blood to destroy the vord in that nest. But the wisdom tells us that when the vord abandon a nest, they divide into three groups to build new nests. To spread their kind. We tracked and destroyed one such group. But there are two more. I believe one of them is here, in your valley, hiding on the slopes of the mountain called Garados."

Bernard frowned. "And where is the other?"

In answer, Doroga reached into his sling pouch and drew out a battered old leather backpack. He tossed it into Bernard's lap.

Amara felt Bernard's entire body go rigidly tense as he stared down at the pack.

"Great furies," Bernard whispered. "Tavi."

✗✗✗✗ CHAPTER 5

Whirls of dust from the collapse filled the inside of Isana-holt's stables, and made the sunshine slipping here and there through the roof into soft, golden rods of light. Isana stared at the enormous crossbeam in the steadholt's stables. It had broken and fallen without any warning whatsoever a moment after she had entered the barn to distribute feed to the animals. If she had been facing the wrong way, or if she had been any slower, she would be lying dead under it with the crushed and bloodied bodies of a pair of luckless hens instead of shaking with startled terror.

Her first thought was of her holders. Had any of them been in the barn, or the loft? Furies forbid, had any of the children been playing there? Isana reached out for her fury, and with Rill's help created a crafting that slid through the air of the barn—but the barn was empty.

Which was probably the point, she thought, suddenly struck with a possible explanation for the accident. She stood up, shaking still, and went to the fallen beam, examining it.

One end of the beam was broken, snapped off with ragged spikes and splinters of wood standing out from it. The other end was far smoother, almost as clean as if it had been trimmed with a mill-saw. But no blade had done it. The wood was crumbling and dusty, as if it had been attacked by an army of termites. A furycrafting, Isana thought. A deliberate furycrafting.

Not an accident. Not an accident at all.

Someone had tried to kill her.

Isana suddenly became more intensely aware of the fact that she was alone in the stables. Most of the holders were out in the fields by now—they had only a few more days to plow and sow, and the herders had their hands full with keeping track of mating cycles, assisting in the delivery of the new lambs, calves, kids, and a pair of gargant digs. Even the kitchens, the nearest building to the stables, were empty at the moment, while the steadholt women working there took time for a meal of their own in the central hall.

In short, it was unlikely that anyone heard the beam fall— and even more unlikely that they could hear her should she call for them. For a moment, Isana wished desperately that her brother still lived at the steadholt. But Bernard didn't. She would have to look out for herself.

She took a deep, steadying breath and stole a couple of steps to a wall where a pitchfork hung by a hook set into a beam. She took the tool down, straining to be silent, willing Rill's presence to continue sweeping through the barn. The furycrafting was hardly precise—and even if there was a murderer lurking nearby, if he was a man of enough detachment, he might not have enough of a sense of emotion for Rill to detect. But it was better than nothing.

Woodcrafters could, when they needed to, exert the power of their furies to hide their presence from other's eyes, if enough vegetable matter was nearby to use as material. At the behest of a woodcrafter, trees would shift their shadows, grass would twist and bend to conceal, and all manner of subtle illusions of light and shadow could hide them from even skilled, wary eyes. And the barn was almost ankle deep in the rushes laid to help keep it warm during the winter.

Isana remained in place for several silent moments, waiting for any sign of another's presence. Patience could only help her—it would not be long before the steadholt began to fill with holders returning from the fields for their midday meal. Her attacker, if he was here, would already have come for her if he thought her vulnerable. The worst thing she could do would be to lose her head and run headlong into a less subtle attack.

Outside, the beat of running hooves approached the steadholt, and someone rode a horse in through the gates. The animal chafed and stamped for a moment, then a young man's voice called, "Hello, the steadholt! Holder Isana?"

Isana held her breath for a moment, then let it out slowly, relaxing a little. Someone had come. She lowered the pitchfork and took a step toward the door she had entered.

There was a small, thumping sound behind her, and a

rounded pebble bounced once and then fell into the straw. Rill suddenly warned her of a wave of panic coming from immediately behind her.

Isana turned, raising the pitchfork by instinct, and only barely saw the vague outline of someone in the half-shadowed barn. There was a flash of steel, a hot sensation on one of her hips, and she felt the tines of the pitchfork bite hard into living flesh. She choked out a scream of terror and challenge and drove the pitchfork hard forward, throwing the weight of her entire body behind it. She drove the attacker back against the heavy door of one of the horse stalls, and she felt in exquisite detail the sudden burst of pain, surprise, and naked fear that came from her attacker.

The tines bit hard into the wooden door, and her attacker's crafting of concealment wavered and vanished.

He wasn't young enough to be called a youth, but not yet old enough to be considered a man, either. He seemed to be at that most dangerous of ages, where strength, skill, and confidence met naïveté and idealism; when young men skilled at the crafts of violence could be manipulated into employing those skills with brutal efficiency—and without questions.

The assassin stared at her for a moment, eyes wide, his face already pale. His sword arm twitched, and he lost his grip on the weapon, an odd blade slightly curved rather than the more typical *gladius*. He pushed at the tines of the pitchfork, but his fingers had no strength in them. One of the steel tines had severed a blood vessel in his belly, she judged, some part of her mind operating with clinical detachment. It was the only thing that could have incapacitated him so quickly. Otherwise, he would have been able to strike her again with the sword, even though wounded.

But the rest of her felt like wailing in sheer anguish. Isana's link to Rill was too open and too strong to set aside easily. All of what her attacker felt flowed into her thoughts and perceptions with a simple, agonizing clarity. She felt him, the screaming pain of his injuries, the sense of panic and despair as he realized what had happened, and that he had no way to avoid his fate.

She felt him as his fear and pain faded to a sense of dim, puzzled surprise, quiet regret, and a vast and heavy weariness.

Panicked, she withdrew her senses from the young man, her thoughts screaming at Rill to break the connection with the young killer. She all but sobbed with relief as the sensations of his emotion faded from her own, and she looked him in the face.

The young man looked up at her for a moment. He had eyes the color of walnuts and a small scar over his left eyebrow.

His body sagged, the weight pulling the tines of the pitchfork free of the door. Then his head lolled forward and a little to one side. His eyes went still. Isana shivered and watched him die. When he had, she pulled on the pitchfork. It wouldn't come out, and she had to brace one foot against the young man's chest to get enough leverage to withdraw the pitchfork. When it finally came free, lazy streams of blood coursed down from the holes in the corpse's belly. The corpse fell to its side, and its glazed eyes stared up at Isana.

She had killed the young man. She had killed him. He was no older than Tavi.

It was too much. She fell to her knees, and her belly lost control of its contents. She found herself staring down at the floor of the stables, shuddering, while waves of disgust and loathing and fear washed over her.

Footsteps entered the stables, but they meant nothing to her. Isana lowered herself to her side once her stomach had ceased its rebellion. She lay there with her eyes closed, while holders entered the stables, sure of only one thing: If she hadn't killed the man, he would certainly have killed her.

Someone with the resources to hire a professional killer wanted her dead.

She closed her eyes, too weary to do more, and was content to ignore the others around her and let oblivion ease her anguish and terror.

"How long has she been down?" rumbled a deep, male voice. Her brother, Isana thought. Bernard.

The next voice was old and quavered slightly. Isana recognized old beldame Bitte's quiet confidence. "Since just before midday."

"She looks pale," said another male voice, this one higher, less resonant. "Are you sure she's all right?"

Bernard answered, "As sure as I can be, Aric. There are no wounds on her." He let out a slow breath. "It looks like she might have collapsed, pushing her crafting too hard. I've seen her work herself into the ground before."

"It might also be a reaction to the struggle," Amara said. "Shock."

Bernard grunted agreement. "Green *legionares* do that after their first battle, sometimes. Great furies know it's a terrible thing to kill a man." Isana felt her brother's broad, warm hand on her hair. He smelled like sweating horses, leather, and road dust, and his voice was quietly anguished. "Poor 'Sana. Is there anything more we can do for her?"

Isana took a deep breath and made an effort to speak, though it came out as hardly more than a whisper. "Begin with washing your hands, little brother. They smell."

Bernard let out a glad cry, and she was immediately half-crushed in one of his bear hugs.

"I may need my spine unbroken, Bernard," she rasped, but she felt herself smiling as she did.

He laid her back down on the bed immediately, carefully restraining his strength. "Sorry, Isana."

She laid her hand on his arm and smiled up at him. "Honestly. It's all right."

"Well," said Bitte, her tone crisp. She was a tiny old woman, white-haired and hunched but with more wits than most, and she had been an institution in the Valley for years before the First Battle of Calderon had ever taken place, much less the more recent events. She stood up and made shooing motions. "Out, everyone, out. You all need to eat, and I daresay Isana could use a few moments of privacy."

Isana smiled gratefully at Bitte, then told Bernard, "I'll come down in a few moments."

"Are you sure you should—" he began.

She lifted a hand and said, more steadily, "I'll be fine. I'm starving."

"All right," Bernard relented, and retreated before Bitte like an indulgent bull from a herding dog. "But let's eat in the study," he said. "We have some things to discuss."

Isana frowned. "Of course, then. I'll be right there."

They left, and Isana took a few moments to pull her thoughts together while she freshened up. Her stomach twisted in revulsion as she saw the blood on her skirts and tunic, and she got out of the clothes as quickly as she possibly could, throwing them into the room's fire. It was wasteful, but she knew she couldn't have put them on again. Not after seeing the darkness close in on the young man's eyes.

She tore her thoughts away from that moment and stripped her underclothing off as well, changing into clean garments. She took her long, dark hair down from its braid, idly noting still more strands of grey. There was a small dressing mirror upon a chest of drawers, and she regarded herself in it thoughtfully as she brushed out her hair. More grey, but to look at her one would not know her age, of course. She was slim (far too much so, by fashionable standards), and her features were still those of a girl only a bit more than twenty years of age—less than half of the years she had actually lived. If she lived to be Bitte's age, she might look as old as a woman in her midthirties but for the grey hairs, which she refused to dye into darkness. Perhaps that was because between her too-thin body, and the apparent youth gifted to watercrafters, the grey hairs were the only things that marked her as a woman rather than a girl. They were a dubious badge of honor for what she had suffered and lost in her years, but they were all she had.

She left her hair down, rather than braiding it again, and frowned at herself in the mirror. Taking dinner in the study instead of the hall? It must mean that Bernard—or more likely

Amara—was concerned about what might be overheard. Which meant that she had come with some kind of word from the Crown.

Isana's stomach twisted again, this time in anxiety. The killer in the barn had arrived with quite improbable timing. What were the odds that such a thing would happen only hours before the Crown's messenger arrived in the Valley? It seemed that the two could hardly be unrelated.

Which begged the question—who had sent the killer after her? The enemies of the Crown?

Or Gaius himself.

The thought was not as ridiculous as others might think, given what she knew. Isana had met Gaius and felt his presence. She knew that he was a man of steel and stone, with the will to rule, to deceive and, when necessary, to kill to protect his position and his people. He would not hesitate to order her slain should she become a threat to him. And for all that he knew, she might be one.

She shivered, and pushed her worries down, forcing herself to wrap her fears with thoughts of confidence and strength. She'd been keeping secrets for twenty years, and she knew how to play the game as well as any in the Realm. As much as she liked Amara, and as much as she liked seeing that she made Isana's brother happy, Amara was a Cursor and loyal to the Crown.

She could not be trusted.

The stone halls of the steadholt would be cold as the evening blanketed the Valley, so she drew a heavy shawl of dark red about her shoulders to add to the deep blue dress, donned her slippers, and moved quietly through the hallways to Bernardholt—no, to *Isanaholt's* study. To *her* study.

The room was not a large one, and this deep in the stone walls of the steadholt there were no windows. Two tables filled up most of the space, and a slateboard and shelves filled the walls. In the winter, when there was more time than could be filled with work, the children of the steadholt learned their basic arithmetic, studied records of furycrafting for guidance in the use of their own furies, and learned to do at least a little reading. Now, Bernard, Amara, and Aric, the Valley's youngest Steadholder, occupied one table, which was laid out with the evening meal.

Isana slipped in quietly and shut the door behind her. "Good evening. I'm sorry I wasn't on hand to greet you properly, Your Excellencies, Steadholder."

"Nonsense," Aric said, rising and smiling at her. "Good evening, Isana."

Bernard rose as well, and they waited for Isana to sit down before they did themselves.

They ate in quiet conversation for a while, chatting about little of consequence, until the meal was finished. "You've hardly spoken at all, Aric," Isana said, as they pushed plates aside and sat sipping at cups of hot tea. "How did you and yours weather the winter?"

Aric frowned. "I'm afraid that's why I'm here. I . . ." He flushed a little. "Well. To be honest, I'm having a problem, and I wanted to consult with you before I bothered Count Bernard with it."

Bernard frowned. "For fury's sake, Aric. I'm still the same man I was two years ago, title or no. You shouldn't worry about bothering me when it's hold business."

"No, sir," Aric said. "I won't, Your Excellency, sir."

"Good."

The young man promptly turned to Isana, and said, "There have been some problems, and I'm concerned that I may need the Count's help."

Amara covered her mouth with her hand until she could camouflage the smile behind a cup as she drank. Bernard settled back with a tolerant smile, but Isana felt something else from him—a sudden stab of anxiety.

Aric poured a bit more wine into his cup and settled back from the table. He was a spare man, all arms and legs, and still too young to have the heavier, more muscular build of maturity. For all of that, he was considered to be uncommonly intelligent, and in the past two years had worked hard enough on the two steadholts under his authority to separate himself entirely from what was now generally considered to be an unfortunate blood relation with his late father, Kord.

"Something's been hunting on the eastern steadholt," he said in a serious tone. "We were missing nearly a third of the cattle we had to turn out to wild forage over the winter, and we assumed that they'd been taken by thanadents or even a herdbane. But we've lost two more cows from our enclosed pastures since we've brought them in."

Isana frowned. "You mean they've been killed?"

"I mean they've been lost," Aric said. "At night, they were in the pasture. In the morning they weren't. No tracks. No blood. No corpses. Just gone."

Isana felt her eyebrows lift. "That's . . . odd. Cattle thieves?"

"I thought so," Aric said. "I took two of my woodcrafters, and we went into the hills to track down whoever it was. We searched for their camp, and we found it." Aric took a large swallow of wine. "It looked like there might have been as many as twenty men there, but they were gone. The fires were out, but there was a spit of burnt meat sitting over one of them. There were clothes, weapons, bedrolls and tools lying out as if they'd all gotten up and walked away without taking anything with them."

Bernard's frown deepened, and Aric turned earnestly to face him.

"It was . . . *wrong*, sir. It was frightening. I don't know how else to describe it to you, but it made the hair on our necks stand up. And dark was coming on, so I took my men and headed back for the steadholt as quickly as we could." His face grew a little more pale. "One of them, Grimard— you remember him, sir, the man with the scar over his nose?"

"Yes. Attican *legionare*, I think, retired out here with his cousin. I saw him cut down a pair of Wolf warriors at Second Garrison."

"That's him," Aric said. "He didn't make it back to the steadholt."

"Why?" Isana asked. "What happened?"

Aric shook his head. "We were strung out in a line, with me in the middle. He wasn't five yards away. One minute he was there, but when I turned around to look a moment later, he was gone. Just . . . gone, sir. No sound. No tracks. No sign of him." Aric looked down. "I got scared, and I ran. I shouldn't have done that."

"Crows, boy," Bernard said, still frowning. "Of *course* you should have done that. That would have scared the hairs right off my head."

Aric looked up at him and down again, shame still on his features. "I don't know what to tell Grimard's wife. We're hoping he's still alive, sir, but . . ." Aric shook his head. "But I don't think he is. We aren't dealing with bandits, or Marat. I don't have a reason why. It's just . . ."

"Instinct," Bernard rumbled. "Never discount it, lad. When did this happen?"

"Last night. I've ordered the children kept in the steadholt walls, and that no one should leave in groups of less than four. I left first thing this morning to speak with Isana."

Bernard exhaled slowly and glanced at Amara. The Cursor nodded, stood up, and went to the door. Isana heard her whisper something while she touched the wood of the door, and her ears pained her briefly, then popped.

"We should be able to speak freely now," Amara said.

"Speak freely about what?" Aric asked.

"About something I learned from Doroga this morning," Bernard said. "He says that there is some manner of creature he called a vord. That it was dwelling in the Wax Forest, and that something happened that caused it to leave its home." Isana frowned, listening as Bernard told the rest of what Doroga had confided to him regarding the creature.

"I don't know, sir," Aric said, his voice dubious. "I've never heard of anything like this. A blood-drinking shapeshifter? We would have heard of such a thing, wouldn't we?"

"According to Doroga, by the time you hear about it, it might already be too late," Bernard said. "If he's correct about the location of the nest on Garados, it could explain the losses at your steadholt, Aric."

"Are you sure he isn't telling you stories?" Aric asked.

"I saw our healers patch up better than two hundred Marat and at least as many of their beasts, Aric. That wasn't done as a practical joke. If Doroga says he lost nearly two thousand warriors, I believe him." He went on to relay the rest of what Doroga had told him.

Isana folded her arms and shivered. "What about the third nest?"

Bernard and Amara traded another one of those looks, and she hardly needed any of her furycrafting gifts to know that her brother lied when he said, "Doroga has trackers on its trail. As soon as we find it, we'll hit it. But I want to focus on the nest we know about first."

"Two thousand men," Aric muttered. "What will you do to assault this nest? There aren't that many in the whole valley, Bernard."

"The Marat didn't have any Knights with them. We do. I think we should at least be able to contain these vord until reinforcements can arrive from Riva."

"If help arrives from Riva," Isana said.

Bernard looked at her sharply. "What do you mean?"

"You saw how Aric reacted when you told him your source of information, and he's actually met Doroga. Don't let it shock you if High Lord Riva discounts a barbarian's word altogether."

Amara chewed on her lip, eyes narrowed, "She could be right. Riva hates the Marat for a variety of reasons."

"But Alerans are dying, Amara," Bernard said.

"Your argument is reasonable," Amara said. "Riva might not be. He's already strapped for funds after rebuilding Garrison and assisting with repairs in the steadholts. He's going to find himself with empty pockets if he is forced to mobilize his Legions. He'll want to avoid that unless it's absolutely necessary, and he'll almost certainly drag his feet rather than waste money on the ghost stories of some furyless barbarian. It's even possible that he has already left to attend Wintersend ceremonies in the capital."

"It's also possible he hasn't."

Amara held up her hand in a pacifying gesture. "I'm only saying that it's going to be difficult to secure assistance based on the observations of a Marat hordemaster. Riva holds Doroga in contempt."

"I'd rather do something than nothing. And in any case, I've already sent the messenger. It's done. There isn't any time to waste."

"Why not?" Aric asked.

"According to Doroga, this nest will reproduce and divide into three more within a week's time. If we don't catch this one now, the vord may be able to spread more rapidly than we can find and destroy them. That being the case, if Riva doesn't respond at once, we may have to fend for ourselves."

Aric nodded, though he didn't look happy. "What can I do to help?"

"Return to your steadholt," Amara said. "Start filling containers with drinking water, preparing tubs for the healers, bandages, the like. We'll use Aricholt as our base of operations while we locate the nest."

"Very well," Aric said, rising from the table. "In that case, I wish to return immediately."

"It could be dangerous for you, after dark," Amara warned.

"I'll swing wide around the mountain," Aric said. "My place is with my holders."

Bernard stared at him for a moment, then nodded. "Be careful, Steadholder."

They murmured their good-byes, and Aric left the study.

After the door had shut, Amara turned to Isana and offered her an envelope.

"What's this?" Isana asked.

"An invitation to Wintersend, from the Crown."

Isana lifted her eyebrows. "But that's in a few days."

"I am given to understand that His Majesty has already set several Knights Aeris aside to fly you in."

Isana shook her head. "I'm afraid that isn't possible," she said. "Especially not before this vord situation is settled. Healers will be needed."

Amara frowned at her. "This isn't precisely a request, Steadholder Isana. You are needed in the capital. You've become quite the bone of contention."

Isana blinked. "I have?"

"Indeed. By elevating you to a position of equality with the male members of the gentry, Gaius has tacitly declared a sort of equality of status between men and women. As a result, many folk have taken it as permission to establish a number of equities formerly denied women. And others have taken shameless advantage of the opportunity. Various cities have begun to tax the sale of female slaves as heavily as males. The Slaver's Consortium is furious and demands legislation to reestablish the previous status quo, and the Dianic League has rallied against them."

"I don't see what that has to do with me attending Festival in the capital."

"The balance of power has begun to shift in the Senate. Gaius needs the support of the Dianic League if he is to prevent it from flying out of control. So he needs you there, at Festival, highly visible to everyone in the Realm, to show how strongly you support him."

"No," Isana said flatly. "I have more vital duties here."

"More vital than protecting the stability of the Realm?" Amara asked in a mild tone. "My. You must be very busy."

Isana rose sharply to her feet, her eyes narrowed, and snarled, "I don't need a child like you to tell me my duty."

Bernard rose, staring at Isana in shock. "'Sana, please."

"No, Bernard," Isana said. "I am not Gaius's pet dog to sit up and hop through hoops when he snaps his fingers."

"Of course not," Amara said. "But you *are* the only person who might give him the advantage he needs to prevent the Realm from falling into a civil war. Which is *why* someone ordered you killed in the first place—or hadn't that occurred to you?"

Bernard put a warm hand on Isana's shoulder to steady her, but Amara's words struck her like a cup of icy cold water. "Civil war? Has it come to that?"

Amara pushed her hair back tiredly. "It grows more likely each day. The Slaver's Consortium is supported by several of the southern cities, and the northern and Shieldwall cities favor the Dianic League. It is imperative that Gaius maintains control over the Senate's majority, and the Dianic League is the lever he needs. My orders were to give you this information, then accompany you and your brother to the capital."

Isana sat down again slowly. "But that has now changed."

Amara nodded. "If Doroga is right about the vord, they could be a deadly threat. They must be dealt with without delay, so Bernard and I will stay here and do so, and join you as soon as we are able."

"And," Bernard rumbled, "we think we know where the third group of vord is going."

Isana arched an eyebrow.

Bernard reached into a sack he'd brought with him and drew out an old, battered leather pack. "Doroga's scouts found this along a trail leading directly toward the capital."

Isana blinked at the pack. "Isn't that Fade's old pack?"

"Yes," Bernard said. "But Fade gave it to Tavi before he entered the Wax Forest. Tavi lost it during the battle there. His scent is all over it."

"Blood and crows," Isana swore. "Are you telling me that this creature is *following* him?"

"It appears so," said Amara. "The Knights Aeris will arrive in the morning. Isana, you need to get to the capital and gain an audience with Gaius as soon as possible. Tell him about the vord, and make him believe you. He needs to find their nest and stop them."

"Why can't you send a courier to him instead?"

"Too risky," Bernard answered. "If the courier is delayed, or if Gaius is preoccupied with preparations, we'd be better off having the extra help here."

Amara nodded. "He *will* see you, Holder Isana. You may be the only one who will be able to cut through protocol and get to him immediately."

"All right. I'll do it. I'll talk to him." Isana said. "But not until I am sure Tavi is safe."

Amara grimaced but nodded. "Thank you. It was never my intention to send you into that snake pit alone. There will be a lot of people interested in you. Some of them can be quite deceptive and dangerous. I can provide you with an escort— a man I trust, named Nedus. He'll meet you at the Citadel and should be able to help you."

Isana nodded quietly and rose. "Thank you, Amara. I'll manage." She took a step toward the door and wavered, nearly falling.

Bernard caught her before she could. "Whoa. Are you all right?"

Isana closed her eyes and shook her head. "I just need to rest. It will be an early morning." She opened her eyes and frowned up at her brother. "You *will* be careful?"

"I'll be careful," he promised. "If you promise that you will."

She smiled faintly at him. "Done."

"Don't worry, 'Sana," he rumbled. "We'll make sure everyone is kept safe. Especially Tavi."

Isana nodded, and started for the door again, steadier. "We will."

Presuming, of course, that they weren't already too late.

Between the time he saw Steadholder Isana found by her people and the time the sun set, Fidelias had run more than a hundred miles and left the Calderon Valley behind him. The furycrafted stones of the causeway lent their strength to his own earth fury, and through it to Fidelias. Though he was a man of nearly threescore years, the long run had cost him comparatively little effort. He slowed down when the hostel came into sight and walked the last several hundred yards, panting, his legs and arms burning lightly with exertion. Grey clouds rolled across the flaming twilight, and it began to rain.

Fidelias flipped his cloak's hood over his head. His hair had grown even thinner in the past few years, and if he didn't cover it, the cold rain would be both unpleasant and unhealthy. No self-respecting spy would allow himself to catch cold. He imagined the deadly consequences had he sneezed or coughed while inside the barn with Isana and her would-be assassin.

He didn't mind the thought of dying on a mission, but he'd stake himself out for the crows if he would ever allow it to happen because of a petty mistake.

The hostel was typical of its kind in the northern half of the Realm—a ten-foot wall surrounding a hall, a stables, a pair of barracks houses and a modest-sized smithy. He bypassed the hall, where travelers would be buying hot meals. His stomach rumbled. The music, dancing, and drinking wouldn't start until later in the evening, and until they did, he would not risk being recognized by bored diners with nothing better to do than observe and converse with their fellow travelers.

He slipped up the stairs of the second barracks house, opened the door to the room farthest from the entrance, and bolted it behind him. He eyed the bed for a moment, and his muscles and joints ached, but duty came before comfort. He sighed, built the fire laid in the fireplace to life, tossed aside his cloak, and poured water from a pitcher into a broad bowl.

Then he withdrew a small flask from his pouch, opened it, and poured a few splashes of water from the deep wellsprings beneath the Citadel in Aquitaine into the bowl.

The water in the bowl stirred almost immediately, rippling, and a long blob of liquid extruded from the surface of the contents in the bowl, wavering slowly into the miniature form of a woman in evening robes, striking rather than beautiful, apparently in her late twenties. "Fidelias," the woman's form said. Her voice sounded faint, soft, very far away. "You're late."

"My lady Invidia," Fidelias replied to the image, inclining his head. "I'm afraid the opposition wasn't overly considerate of our time constraints."

She smiled. "An agent had been dispatched. Did you learn anything of him?"

"Nothing stone solid. But he was carrying a Kalaran gutting knife, and he knew what he was doing," Fidelias said.

"A Kalaran bloodcrow," said the image. "Then the rumors are true. Kalarus has his own breed of Cursor."

"Apparently."

She laughed. "Only a man of great integrity could resist saying, 'I told you so.'"

"Thank you, my lady."

"What happened?"

"It was a near thing," Fidelias said. "When his first plan failed he panicked and went after her with that gutting blade."

"The Steadholder was slain?"

"No. She sensed him just before he struck, and killed him with a pitchfork."

The image's eyebrows shot up in surprise. "Impressive."

"She's a formidable woman, my lady, watercrafting aside. If I may ask, my lady, what were the results of the League's summit?"

The woman's image tilted her head, regarding him thoughtfully. Then said, "They have elected to support and promote Steadholder Isana's status."

Fidelias nodded. "I see."

"Do you?" the image asked. "Do you really see what this could mean? How it could affect the course of our history?"

Fidelias pursed his lips. "I suppose in the long term, it could mean an eventual state of legal and political parity between genders. I try not to think in terms of history, my lady. Only in practical cause and effect."

"Meaning?"

"Meaning that the most immediate effect will be economic, and therefore political. The establishment of a woman as a full Citizen in her own right will have immediate effects on the slave trade. If it becomes as costly to sell and purchase female slaves as male, it will have an enormous detrimental effect on the economy of the southern cities. Which is why, presumably, Kalarus dispatched an agent to remove Isana of Calderon."

"High Lord Kalarus is a debauched pig," Invidia said, her tone matter-of-fact. "I'm sure he went into some sort of seizure when he heard the news about Steadholder Isana."

Fidelias narrowed his eyes. "Ah. The First Lord knew precisely how High Lord Kalarus would react."

Her mouth curled up in an ironic smile. "Indeed. Gaius rather neatly divided his enemies by introducing this issue. My husband's alliance in the north, and Kalarus's in the south—and if the Steadholder appears in support of him, he may sweep the support of the Dianic League from my husband, as well."

"Would they not follow your lead, my lady?"

Invidia's image waved a hand. "You flatter me, but I do not control the League so completely. No one could. My husband simply understands the advantage that the support of the League gives him, and they see what they gain in return. Our relationship is one of mutual benefit."

"I assume your associates and allies are aware of the situation."

"Very," Invidia replied. "The woman's fate will be a demonstration of my husband's competence." She shook her head wearily. "The outcome of this situation is absolutely critical, Fidelias. Our success will solidify my husband's alliances while weakening the faith of Kalarus's followers. Failure could fatally cripple our plans for the future."

"In my judgment, the time seems premature for a confrontation with Kalarus."

She nodded. "I certainly would not have chosen this time and place, but by granting Citizenship to this woman, Gaius has forced Kalarus's hand." She waved her hand in a dismissive gesture. "But confrontation with Kalarus's faction was inevitable."

Fidelias nodded. "What are my orders, my lady?"

"You're to come to the capital at once for Wintersend."

Fidelias stared at the image for a moment. Then said, "You're joking."

"No," she said. "Isana will be presented formally to the Realm and the Senate at the conclusion of Wintersend, in public support of Gaius. We must stop it from happening."

Fidelias stared at the image for a moment, frustration welling up in his chest too sharply to keep it wholly from his voice. "I am a wanted man. If I am recognized in the capital, where many know my face, I will be captured, interrogated, and killed. To say nothing of the fact that the woman herself will know me on sight."

The image stared at him. "And?"

He kept his voice bland. "And it may somewhat hamper my ability to move around the city."

"Fidelias," the image chided, "you are one of the most dangerous men I know. And you are certainly the most resourceful." The image gave him a very direct, almost hungry look. "It's what makes you so attractive. You'll manage. It is my husband's command as well as my own."

Fidelias ground his teeth, but inclined his head. "Yes, my lady. I'll . . . think of something."

"Excellent," the image responded. "Isana's support for Gaius could cost my husband the support of the Dianic League. You must prevent it at any cost. Our future—and yours—hinges upon it."

The watery image slid smoothly back down into the bowl and vanished. Fidelias grimaced at it for a moment, then cursed and threw it across the room. The ceramic bowl shattered against the stones of the hearth.

Fidelias mopped his hands over his face. Impossible. What the Lord and Lady Aquitaine were asking was impossible. It would be the death of him.

Fidelias grimaced. There would be little point in trying to rest this night, and even the desire to eat had vanished with the tension that had filled him in the wake of his conversation with Lady Invidia.

He changed into dry clothing, seized his cloak and his belongings, and headed back out into the night.

CHAPTER 8

Tavi's legs burned from where he crouched on a rooftop over-looking the Domus Malleus, a building formerly a large smithy that had been rebuilt into one of the most popular din-ing houses in the trade quarter of the city of Alera. Twilight was laying siege to the day, and shadows had begun to fill the streets. Shops and merchants were closing their windows and doors for the night and rolling their goods away until the mar-ket opened again the next morning. The scent of fresh bread and roasting meat filled the air.

Tavi's leg twitched, threatening to begin cramping. Still-ness and patience were necessities for any hunter, and his uncle had taught Tavi all that he knew about tracking and hunting. Tavi had trailed the enormous sheep his uncle raised through rocky mountain trails, hunted down stray horses and calves, stalked the trails and learned the habits of the wildcats and thanadents that would prey upon his uncle's flocks.

As a final lesson, Bernard had taught him to stalk wild deer, creatures so quiet, alert, and swift that only the most skilled and persistent hunters would have any chance of tak-ing one. This thief was not a mountain buck; but Tavi rea-soned that someone so wily, so impossible to catch by even experienced civic *legionares* would have many of the same habits. The thief would be supremely wary, cautious, and swift. The only way to catch that kind of quarry was to deter-mine what he needed, and where he would go to get it.

So Tavi had spent the afternoon speaking to officers of the civic legion, learning where the thief had struck and what he had taken. The perpetrator had eclectic tastes. A jeweler had lost a valuable silver cloak-pin and several ebony combs—though more valuable trinkets stored in the same location had not been touched. A clothier had been taken for three valuable cloaks. A cobbler had lost a set of garim-hide boots. But most distinctively, a number of dining houses, grocers, and bakeries had suffered from frequent nocturnal robberies.

Whoever the thief was, he wasn't after money. In fact, from the wildly varying list of items taken, it was almost as though he was stealing his prizes purely on impulse, for enjoyment. But the reoccurring burglaries of kitchens and larders indicated a single common fact that he shared with the mountain bucks of Tavi's wild home.

The thief was hungry.

Once Tavi knew that, the rest was much less difficult. He had simply waited for the dining houses to begin preparing their evening meals, then followed his nose to the most delicious-smelling building he could find. He found a spot where he could watch the kitchen entrance, and settled down to wait for the deer to forage.

Tavi neither heard nor saw the thief coming, but the hairs on the back of his neck rose and an odd, tingling ripple washed down his spine. He froze, hardly daring to breathe, and a moment later he saw a slow, silent shape covered in a dark cloak slip over the peak of the Domus Malleus's roof and descend to leap lightly to the ground beside the kitchen door.

Tavi descended to the street and darted across the street to the alley behind the restaurant. He stalked deeper into the alley and concealed himself in a patch of thick shadows, waiting for his quarry to reappear.

The thief emerged from the kitchen a pair of heartbeats later, sliding something beneath his cloak.

Tavi held his breath as the thief ghosted down the alley toward him and passed within a long step of Tavi's hiding place. Tavi waited until the thief went by, then lunged out of the shadows, seized the thief's cloak and hauled hard.

The thief reacted with the speed of a wary cat. He spun as Tavi pulled on his cloak, and threw a clay pot of scalding soup at Tavi's head. Tavi darted to one side and out of the way, and the thief hurled a plate laden with the remains of a roast at him, striking him hard on the chest. He staggered and fell back, sent off-balance. The thief spun and sprinted away down the walkway.

Tavi regained his balance and set off in pursuit. The thief was light on his feet, and Tavi could barely keep up. They ran in silence down darkened streets and walkways, in and out of the colored, warm spheres of the furylights. The thief hauled a barrel to its side as he passed a cooper's shop, and Tavi had to jump it. He gained ground, and threw himself at the thief's back. He missed, but got the man on a leg, and wrenched, throwing him off-balance and to the ground.

There was a silent, mad struggle only a few seconds long. Tavi tried to pin one of the thief's arms behind him, but his opponent was too quick and writhed until he could throw an elbow at Tavi's head. Tavi ducked it, but the thief spun and struck him in the chin with the edge of one hand. Stars flashed in Tavi's eyes, and he lost his hold on the thief, who rose and vanished into the dark before Tavi could regain his feet.

He set off in pursuit, but it was in vain. The thief had made good his escape.

Tavi snarled a curse and stormed back out of the darkened alley, heading for the Domus Malleus. At least, he thought, he'd get himself a decent meal for all of his trouble.

He turned back out onto the street, scowling, and slammed directly into a large pedestrian.

"Tavi?" Max said, surprise in his tone. "What are you doing here?"

Tavi blinked at his roommate. "What are *you* doing here?"

"I'm being attacked by scowling academs from Calderon," Max said, a smile on the edges of his words. He shrugged his dark cloak to settle more solidly around him and brushed off his tunic.

The evening's mists were gathering thick and cold. Tavi felt himself start to shiver as the cold found its way to his sweating skin. He shook his head. "Sorry. I suppose I'm not at my most alert. But seriously, what are you doing down here?"

Max grinned. "There's a young widow a couple of streets down. She gets lonely on misty nights."

"This time of year, every night is misty," Tavi said.

Max beamed. "I noticed that, too."

"There's a reason people hate you."

"Jealousy is common among lesser men," Max agreed magnanimously. "My turn. What are you doing down here? Wouldn't do for Gaius's golden boy to get caught sneaking out past curfew."

"Meeting someone," Tavi replied.

"Sure you are," Max agreed amiably. "Who?"

"You aren't the only one who sneaks out of the Academy after dark."

Max burst out into a rolling laugh.

Tavi scowled at him. "What's so funny?"

"Obviously you aren't seeing a girl."

"How do you know?" Tavi demanded.

"Because even a virgin like you would try to look better than you do. Clean clothes, combed hair, freshly bathed, all that sort of thing. You look like you've been rolling around in the street."

Tavi flushed in embarrassment. "Shut up, Max. Go see your widow."

Instead, Max leaned against the wall of the dining house and folded his arms. "I could have rapped you on the head instead of letting you bump into me. And you'd never have known it happened," Max said. "It's not like you. You okay?"

"I'm just too busy," Tavi said. "I did calculations homework all day, after the test this morning—"

Max winced. "I'm sorry about how that went, Tavi. Killian might be able to furycraft his way around being blind, but he bloody sure doesn't see your strengths."

Tavi shrugged. "I expected it to go that way. And I've got to attend Gaius tonight."

"Again?" Max said.

"Yeah."

"So why aren't you back at the dorm getting some shut-eye?"

Tavi began to wave his hand vaguely, but then narrowed his eyes and smiled. "Ah-hah. Why aren't you running off to your eager widow, Max?"

"It's early. She'll keep," Max said, frowning.

"She'll keep until you complete your test for Killian?" Tavi asked.

Max's shoulders stiffened. "What are you talking about?"

"Your own test," Tavi said. "Killian gave you one of your own. He sent you to find out what I was doing."

Max couldn't hide an expression of surprise. Then he rolled his eyes. "Killian probably told you to keep yours secret, whatever it is."

"Of course. And no, I'm not telling you about it."

"Crows, Calderon. When you get this clever it makes me want to put a nice dent in your face."

"Jealousy is common among lesser men," Tavi said, with a small smile. Max mimed a punch, and Tavi ducked his head a little. "How long have you been shadowing me?"

"A couple of hours. Lost you when you moved off the roof."

"If Killian knew you'd shown yourself to me, he'd fail you on the spot."

Max rolled one shoulder in a shrug. "It's just a test. I've been dealing with tests of one kind or another since I could walk."

"High Lord Antillus wouldn't be pleased if you failed."

"I'm sure to lose sleep now," Max drawled.

Tavi half smiled. "Is there really a widow?"

Max grinned. "Even if there wasn't, I'm pretty sure I could find one. Or make one, if it came to that."

Tavi snorted. "What are your plans for the night, then?"

Max pursed his lips. "I could follow you around some more, but it doesn't seem fair." He drew an X over his belly. "Soothword. I'll leave you alone instead of making you spend an hour of your sleep shaking me."

Tavi nodded and gave his friend a grateful smile. Max had sworn himself to truth, an old northern custom. He would never so much as consider breaking a promise given under his soothword. "Thank you," Tavi said.

"But I *will* find out what you're up to," Max said. "Not so much for Killian, as it is because someone needs to show you that you aren't nearly as clever as you think you are."

"Better get to bed then, Max. That's only going to happen in your dreams."

Max's teeth flashed in the dimness as Tavi accepted the challenge. He struck his chest lightly with a fist, the salute of a *legionare*, then vanished into the misty night.

Once Max was gone, Tavi rubbed at his aching chest where the hurled plate had struck him. From the feel of it, there was going to be a bruise. A big one. But at least he'd get a decent meal for his pains. He stepped up onto the threshold of Domus Malleus.

The enormous chimes upon the top of the Citadel began to toll out the hour, each stroke sending out a low, vibrating pressure that could shake water within a bowl, accompanied by a shower of high, shivering tones, beautiful and somehow sad.

The chimes sounded nine times, and Tavi spat an oath. There would be no time to stop for a meal. If he set out at his best pace, it would take him nearly another hour to wind his way up through Alera's streets to the First Lord's Citadel, and subsequently descend into the depths beneath the stronghold. He would arrive smudged and stained from his skulking, covered in sweat and most of an hour late to his duties to the First Lord.

And he had a history examination in the morning.

And he still hadn't caught Killian's thief.

Tavi shook his head and started jogging back up through the capital. He'd only gone a couple of hundred yards when the skies rumbled, and drops of slow, heavy rain came down in sheets.

"Some hero of the Realm you are," Tavi muttered to himself, and set off to attend the First Lord.

Panting, dirty, and late, he paused at the door to the First Lord's chamber. He tried to straighten his cloak and tunic, then regarded them helplessly. Nothing short of a legion of cleaning experts could make him presentable. He chewed on his lip, shoved his dark mop of wet hair back from his face, and went inside.

Gaius stood upon the whirling colors of the mosaic tiles again. He stooped, as though with great weariness or pain. His face was ashen, and the stubble of his beard no longer seemed to contain any hairs but those gone white. But it was his eyes that were the worst. They were sunken, dark pits, the whites shot with blood around eyes whose colors had become faded and dull. Fell, sickly fires burned within them—not the determination, pride, and strength to which Tavi had become accustomed, but something more brittle, more frightening.

Gaius scowled down at him, and snapped, "You're late."

Tavi bowed his head deeply and left it that way. "Yes, sire. I have no excuse, and offer my apologies."

Gaius was silent for a moment, before he began to cough.

He waved an irritated hand at the tiles, dispersing the shapes and colors rising from them, and sat down at the little bureau against one wall until the coughing had passed. The First Lord sat with his eyes closed, his breath too shallow and too fast. "Go to the cupboard, boy. My spicewine."

Tavi rose immediately and went to the cupboard near the bench in the antechamber. Tavi poured and offered him the glass, and Gaius drank it with a grimace. He studied Tavi with a sour expression. "Why were you late?"

"Finals," Tavi replied. "They've taken up more of my time."

"Ah," Gaius said. "I seem to remember several such incidents during my own education. But it's no excuse for failing in your duties, boy."

"No, sire."

Gaius coughed again, wincing, and held out his glass for Tavi to refill.

"Sire? Are you well?"

The bitter, brittle flare of anger returned to Gaius's eyes. "Quite."

Tavi licked his lips nervously. "Well, sire, you seem to be . . . somewhat peaked."

The First Lord's expression grew ugly. "What would you know of it? I think the First Lord knows better than a bastard apprentice shepherd whether he is or is not well."

Gaius's words hit Tavi harder than a fist. He dropped back a step, looking away. "Your pardon, sire. I did not intend to offend you."

"Of course you didn't mean to," Gaius said. He set his wineglass down so hard that the stem snapped. "No one ever means to offend someone with power. But your words make your lack of respect for my judgment, my office, my *self* abundantly clear."

"No, sire, I don't mean that—"

Gaius's voice crackled with anger, and the ground itself quivered in reaction. "Be *silent*, boy. I will *not* tolerate further interruptions with good grace. You know *nothing* of what I have had to do. How *much* I have had to sacrifice to protect this Realm. This Realm whose High Lords now circle me like a pack of jackals. Like crows. Without gratitude. Without mercy. Without respect."

Tavi said nothing, but the First Lord's words rambled in pitch and tone so badly that he began to have trouble understanding Gaius's speech. He had never heard the First Lord speak with such a lack of composure.

"Here," Gaius said. He seized Tavi's collar with a sudden and terrifying strength and dragged the boy after him into the seeing chamber, out onto the whirling mosaic of tiles whose lights and colors pulsed and danced, creating a cloud of light and shadow that formed into a depiction of the lands of the Realm. At the center of the mosaic, Gaius slashed his other hand at the air, and the colors of the map blurred, resolving abruptly into the image of a terrible storm lashing some luckless coastal village.

"You see?" Gaius growled.

Tavi's fear faded a bit in the face of his fascination. The image of the town grew clearer, as though they were moving closer to it. He saw holders running inland, but the seas reached out for them with arms of black water. The waters rushed over the village, the holders, and all of them vanished.

"Crows," Tavi whispered. Tavi's belly quivered and twisted, and he was glad he hadn't eaten. He could barely whisper. "Can't you help them?"

Gaius screamed. His voice rolled out like the furious roar of some beast. The furylamps blazed to brilliant light, and the air in the chamber rolled and twisted in a small cyclone. The stone heart of the mountain shook and trembled before the First Lord's rage, bucking so hard that Tavi was thrown to the floor.

"What do you *think* I've been *doing*, boy!" Gaius howled. "Day! Night! AND IT ISN'T ENOUGH!" He whirled and snarled something in a savage tone, and the chair and table on one side of the room did more than burst into flame—there was a howling sound, a flash of light and heat, and the charred embers of the wooden furnishing flew throughout the room, rattling from the walls, leaving a fine haze of ash in the air. "ALL GONE! ALL! I HAVE NOTHING LEFT TO SACRIFICE, AND IT ISN'T ENOUGH!"

The First Lord's voice broke then, and he staggered to one knee. Wind, flame, and stone subsided again, and he was suddenly just an old man once more—his appearance that of someone aged too fast and too hard in a harsh world. His eyes were even more deeply sunken, and he trembled, and Gaius clutched at his chest with both hands, coughing.

"My lord," Tavi breathed, and went to the old man. "Sire, please. Let me find someone to help you."

The coughing wound down, though Tavi thought it was more a result of a weakening of Gaius's lungs than an improvement in his condition. The old man stared at the image of the coastal village with hazy eyes, and said, "I can't. I've tried to protect them. To help them. Tried so hard. Lost so much. And failed."

Tavi found tears in his eyes. "Sire."

"Failed," Gaius whispered. "Failed."

His eyes rolled back. His breaths came quick and shallow, rasping. His lips looked rough, chapped, dry.

"Sire?" Tavi breathed. "Sire?"

There was a long silence in which Tavi tried to rouse the First Lord, calling him by both title and name.

But Gaius did not respond.

CHAPTER 9

In that moment, Tavi understood a single, terrifying fact; the fate of the First Lord, and therefore of all Alera, was utterly in his hands.

What he did in the next moments, he knew, would have repercussions that would echo throughout the Realm. His immediate impulse was to run screaming for help, but he stopped himself and as Maestro Killian had taught them, he forced himself to slow down and set his emotion aside to work through the problem with cold logic.

He could not simply call for the guards. They would come, of course, and physicians would care for the First Lord, but then it would all be out in the open. If it became widely known that the First Lord's health had failed, it could prove disastrous in dozens of ways.

Tavi was not privy to the private counsels of the First Lord, but neither was he dull of ear or mind. He knew, from bits of conversation overheard while on his duties, more or less what was going on in the Realm. Gaius was in a tenuous position before several of the more ambitious High Lords. He was an old man without an heir, and should they begin regarding him as a *failing* old man with no heir, it could trigger uprisings, anything from the official processes of the Senate and Council of Lords to a full-fledged military struggle. That was precisely why Gaius had re-formed the Crown Legion, after all, to increase the security of his reign and reduce the chances of a civil war.

But it also meant that anyone determined to take power from Gaius would almost certainly be forced to fight. The very idea of the Legions and Lords of Alera making war on one another would have been incomprehensible to Tavi before the events of the Second Battle of Calderon. But Tavi had seen the results of furies wielded against Aleran citizens and soldiers, and those images still haunted his nightmares.

Tavi shuddered. Crows and furies, not that. Not again.

Tavi checked the old man. His heart was still beating, though not in steady rhythm. His breathing was shallow, but sure. Tavi could do nothing more for him, which meant that he had to have someone's help. But whom could he trust with this? Who would Gaius have trusted?

"Sir Miles, fool," he heard himself say. "Miles is captain of the Crown Legion. The First Lord trusts him, or Gaius wouldn't have given him command of five thousand armed men inside his own walls."

Tavi had no choice but to leave the fallen man's side to send for the grizzled captain. He rolled his cloak beneath Gaius's head, then tore a cushion from the First Lord's chair to elevate the old man's legs. Then he turned and sprinted up the stairs to the second guardroom.

But as he approached, he heard raised voices. Tavi stopped, heart pounding. Did someone already know what had happened? He slipped forward cautiously, until he could see the backs of the guards at the second duty station. The *legionares* were all standing, and all had hands on their weaponry. Even as Tavi watched, he heard boots hitting the floor in unison, and the men who had been taking their turns in sleep came out of the bunk room in hastily donned armor.

"I am very sorry, sir," said Bartos, the senior *legionare* at the station. "But His Majesty is unavailable while in his private chambers."

The voice that spoke next was not human. It was too vastly deep, too resonant, and the words twisted and oddly stretched, as if they'd been torn and rent by the fanged mouth where they'd been born.

One of the Canim had come down the stairs, and towered over the *legionares* in the guardroom.

Tavi had seen one of the Realm's deadliest enemies only once in two years, and that had been from a distance. He had heard the tales of them, of course, but they had not adequately impressed upon him the effect of the creatures' presence. Not adequately at all.

The Cane stood at its full height, and the ten-foot ceiling barely allowed it. Covered with fur the color of the darkest depths of night, the creature stood upon two legs, with the

mass of two or three big *legionares*. Its shoulders looked too
narrow for its height, and its arms were longer than human
proportions. Its long, blunt fingers were tipped with dark
claws. The Cane had a head that reminded Tavi unpleasantly
of the direwolves that had accompanied the Wolf Clan of the
Marat, though broader, its muzzle shorter. Massive muscles
framed the Cane's jawline, and Tavi knew that its sharp,
gleaming white-yellow teeth could snap through a man's arm
or leg without particular effort. The Cane's eyes were amber
yellow set against dark scarlet, and it gave the creature the
look of something that saw everything through a veil of
blood.

Tavi studied the creature more closely. This Cane was
dressed in clothing similar to Aleran in fashion, though made
with far greater lengths of cloth. It wore colors of grey and
black exclusively, and over that the odd Canim-style circular
cloak that draped over the back and half of the Cane's chest.
Where fur showed through, thin spots and white streaks
marked dozens of battle scars. One triangular ear, notched and
torn to ragged edges with old wounds, sported a gleaming
golden ring hung with a skull carved from some stone or gem
the color of blood. A similar ring glittered amidst the dark fur
covering its left hand, and at its side the Cane wore one of the
huge, scything war swords of its kind.

Tavi bit his lip, recognizing the Cane from its clothing, de-
meanor, and appearance. Ambassador Varg, the local packmaster of the Canim embassy and the spokesman for its
people to the Alerans.

"Perhaps you did not hear me, *legionare*," the Cane literally growled. More teeth showed. "I require counsel with your
First Lord. You will conduct me to him at once."

"With respect, Lord Ambassador," Bartos replied, his teeth
clenched over the words, "His Majesty has not apprised me of
your coming, and my standing orders are to see to it that he is
not disturbed during his meditations."

Varg snarled. Every *legionare* in the room leaned slightly
away from the Cane—and they were some of the best the
Realm had to offer. Tavi swallowed. If veteran fighting men
who had actually faced the Canim in battle were afraid of Ambassador Varg, it would be with good reason.

Anger and scorn rang in Varg's snarling words. "Obviously, Gaius could not know of my coming when it is an unexpected visit. The matter is of import to both your folk and mine." Varg took a deep breath, lips lifting away from an arsenal of fangs. One clawed hand fell to the hilt of its blade. "The commander at the first station was most polite. It would be polite for you to also stand out of my way."

Bartos's gaze flickered around the room as though searching for options. "It simply is not possible," the *legionare* said.

"Little man," said Varg, its voice dropping to a barely audible rumble. "Do not test my resolve."

Bartos did not respond at once, and Tavi knew, knew it by sheer instinct, that it was a mistake. His hesitation was a declaration of weakness, and to do such a thing before any aggressive predator was to invite it to attack. If that happened, the situation could only become worse, not better.

Tavi had to act. His heart thudded in fear, but he forced his face into a cold mask, and strode briskly into the guardroom. "*Legionare* Bartos," he said in a ringing tone. "The First Lord requires the presence of Sir Miles, immediately."

The room fell into a startled silence. Bartos turned his head and blinked at Tavi, his face covered in surprise. Tavi had never spoken in that tone of voice to the *legionares*. He'd have to apologize to Bartos later.

"Well, *legionare*?" Tavi demanded. "What is the delay? Send a man for Miles at once."

"Uh," Bartos said. "Well, the Ambassador here desires to meet with the First Lord as quickly as possible."

"Very well," Tavi said. "I will so inform him when I return with Sir Miles."

Varg let out a basso snarl that vibrated against Tavi's chest. "Unacceptable. You will lead me down to Gaius's chambers and announce me to him."

Tavi stared at Varg for a long and silent moment. Then slowly arched an eyebrow. "And you are?"

It was a calculated insult, given the Ambassador's notoriety in the Citadel, and Varg had to know it. Its amber eyes burned with fury, but it snarled, "Ambassador Varg of the Canim."

"Oh," Tavi said. "I'm afraid I did not see your name on the list of appointments for this evening."

"Um," Bartos said.

Tavi rolled his eyes and glared at Bartos. "The First Lord wants Miles *now, legionare*."

"Oh," Bartos said. "Of course. Nils."

One of the men edged his way around the furious Cane and set off up the stairs at a slow jog. He'd have a hard time of it in full armor, Tavi knew. Miles wouldn't get there anytime soon. "Have the captain report to the First Lord the moment he arrives," Tavi said, and turned to leave.

Varg snarled, and Tavi whirled in time to see it sweep out one arm and toss Bartos aside like a rag doll. The Cane moved with unearthly speed, and with a single bound landed beside Tavi and seized him in one clawed and long-fingered hand. Varg thrust its mouth down at Tavi's face, and the boy's vision filled with a view of wicked fangs. The Cane's breath was hot, damp, and smelled vaguely of old meat. The Cane itself smelled strange, an acrid but subtle scent like nothing Tavi had known before. "Take me to him now, boy, before I tear out your throat. I grow weary of—"

Tavi drew the dagger at his belt from beneath his cloak with liquid speed, and laid the tip of the blade hard against Ambassador Varg's throat.

The Cane stopped talking for a startled second, and its bloody eyes narrowed to golden slits. "I could tear you apart."

Tavi kept his voice in the same hard, commanding, coldly polite tone "Indeed. After which you will shortly bleed to death, Lord Ambassador." Tavi glared back hard into Varg's eyes. He was terrified, but knew that he did not dare allow it to show through. "You would ill serve your own lord by dying in such an ignominious fashion. Slain by a human cub."

"Take me to Gaius," Varg said. "Now."

"It is Gaius who rules here," Tavi said. "Not you, Ambassador."

"It is not Gaius whose claws rest near your heart, human cub." Tavi felt the Cane's claws press harder against his flesh.

Tavi showed his teeth in a mirthless grin. He pressed the dagger a bit more heavily into the thick fur beneath Varg's muzzle. "I, like His Majesty's *legionares*, obey his commands regardless of how inconvenient it may be to you. You will release me, Lord Ambassador. I will take your request to His Majesty at the earliest opportunity, and I will bring you his reply personally the instant he releases me to do so. Or, if you prefer, I can open your throat, you can tear me to bits, and we will both die for no reason. The choice is yours."

"Do you think I am afraid to die?" the Cane asked. Varg's dark nostrils flared, and it continued to study Tavi's face, teeth exposed.

Tavi stared back, praying that his hands didn't start shaking, and kept the pressure on the tip of his knife. "I think your death here, like this, will not serve your people."

A snarl bubbled in Varg's words. "What do you know of my people?"

"That they have bad breath, sir, if you are any indication."

Varg's claws twitched.

Tavi wanted to scream at himself for being a fool, but he kept his mask on, his dagger firm.

Varg's head jerked up, and it let out a barking sound. It released Tavi. The boy fell a step back, and lowered the knife, his heart pounding.

"You smell of fear, boy," Varg said. "And you are a runt, even of your kind. And a fool. But at least you know of duty." The Cane tilted its head to one side, baring a portion of its throat. The gesture looked exceedingly odd, but it reminded Tavi of a respectful nod of the head, somehow.

He dipped his head slightly in his own nod, never letting his gaze waver, and put the dagger away.

The Cane swept its eyes across the *legionares*, contempt in its expression. "You will all regret this. Soon."

And with that, Varg settled its cloak about it and stalked back out of the room to the winding staircase up. It made that same barking sound again, but the Cane did not look back.

Tavi's legs shook hard. He half stumbled to a trestle-bench, and sank down onto it.

"What the crows was that all about?" Bartos stammered a second later. "Tavi, what do you think you were playing at?"

Tavi waved his hand, trying not to let it tremble. "Bartos, sir, I'm sorry. I shouldn't have spoken to you like that. I offer you my apologies, but I felt it was necessary to appear to be your superior."

The *legionare* traded looks with some of his companions, then asked, "Why?"

"You hesitated. He would have attacked you."

Bartos frowned. "How do you know?"

Tavi fumbled for words. "I learned a lot on my steadholt. One of the things I learned was how to deal with predators. You can't show them any hesitation or fear, or they'll go for you."

"And you think I was showing him fear?" Bartos demanded. "Is that it? That I was acting like a coward?"

Tavi shook his head, and avoided looking at the *legionare*. "I think the Cane was reading you that way, is all. Body language, stance and bearing, and eye contact, it's all important to them. Not just words."

Bartos's face turned red, but one of the other *legionares* said, "The boy is right, Bar. You always try to slow down when you feel a stupid fight coming on. Try to find a way around it. Maybe today that was just the wrong thing."

The *legionare* glared at the speaker for a moment, then sighed. He went to the ale keg, drew a pair of mugs, and set one of them down in front of Tavi. The boy nodded to him gratefully, and drank the bitter brew, hoping it would help him calm down. "What did he mean?" Tavi asked. "When he said that we would regret this?"

"Seems pretty plain," Bartos said. "I'd be careful walking down dark passages alone for a while, lad."

"I should go back to the First Lord," Tavi said. "He seemed concerned. Could you please ask Sir Miles to hurry?"

"Sure, kid," Bartos said. Then he let out a low laugh. "Crows and furies, but you've got a set of balls on you. Pulling that knife."

"Bad breath," said one of the other *legionares*, and the room burst into general laughter.

Tavi smiled, got his hair rumpled by half a dozen soldiers, and made his exit as quickly as he could, to hurry down the stairs to the First Lord's side.

He hadn't made it all the way when he heard slow, hard, thudding boots on the stairs above him. He slowed down and Sir Miles appeared above him, leaping down stairs half a dozen at a step. Tavi swallowed. The pace had to be hideously painful to Miles's wounded leg, but the man was a strong met-alcrafter, and the ability to ignore pain was a discipline of furycrafting the strongest among them often developed.

Tavi started hurrying down as well, and he managed to arrive at the bottom of the stairs just behind Miles, who stopped in shock and stared at the still form of Gaius on the floor. He went to his side, felt the First Lord's throat, then peeled back an eyelid to peer at his eyes. Gaius never stirred.

"Bloody crows," Miles said. "What happened?"

"He collapsed," Tavi panted. "He said that he'd tried as hard as he could and that it wasn't enough. He showed me where a town by the ocean was torn apart by storms. He was . . . I'd never seen him like that, Sir Miles. Screaming. Like he wasn't . . ."

"Wasn't in control of himself," Miles said quietly.

"Yes, sir. And he was coughing. And drinking spicewine." Miles winced. "It isn't spicewine."

"What?"

"It's a health tonic he uses. A drug that dulls pain and makes you feel as if you aren't tired. He was pushing himself past his limits, and he knew it."

"Will he be all right?"

Miles looked up at him and shook his head. "I don't know. He might be fine after he gets some rest. Or he might not live the night. Even if he does, he might not wake up."

"Crows," Tavi said. A pain shot through his stomach. "Crows, I didn't do the right thing. I should have sent for a healer at once."

Miles's eyebrows shot up. "What? No, boy, you did exactly the right thing." The grizzled soldier raked his fingers back through his hair. "No one can know what has happened here, Tavi."

"But—"

"I mean *no one*," Miles said. "Do you understand?"

"Yes, sir."

"Killian," Miles muttered. "And . . . crows take it, I don't know if there's anyone else who can help."

"Help, sir?"

"We'll need a healer. Killian doesn't watercraft, but he has some skill as a physician, and he can be trusted. But I've got to have the Legion ready for review at Wintersend. It would cause too many questions if I did not. And Killian can't care for Gaius alone."

"I'll help," Tavi said.

Miles gave him a brief smile. "I had already assumed you would be willing. But you can't suddenly vanish from the Academy during the week of your finals. The absence of the First Lord's favorite page will not go unremarked."

"Then we'll need more help," Tavi said.

Miles frowned. "I know. But I don't know any others I can absolutely trust."

"None?" Tavi asked.

"They died twenty years ago," Miles said, his voice bitter.

"What about the Cursors?" Tavi said. "Surely they can be trusted."

"Like Fidelias?" Miles spat. "The only one of them I might take a chance on is Countess Amara, and she isn't here."

Tavi stared at the unconscious First Lord. "Do you trust me?"

Miles arched a brow sharply.

"Tell me what you need. Maybe I know someone who could help us."

Miles exhaled slowly. "No. Tavi, you're smart, and Gaius trusts you, but you're too young to know how dangerous this is."

"How dangerous will it be if we *have* no one to help, sir? Do we let him lie there and hope for the best? Is that less dangerous than taking a chance on my judgment?"

Miles opened his mouth, then closed it, clenching his teeth. "Crows. You're right. I hate it, but you are."

"So what do you need?"

"A nurse. Someone who can do all the day-to-day feeding and caring for him. And a double, if we can get one."

"Double?"

Miles clarified. "An imposter. Someone who can appear at events Gaius would attend. To be seen walking around. To eat the First Lord's breakfasts and otherwise make sure everyone thinks things are business as usual."

"So you need a strong watercrafter. Someone who can alter his appearance."

"Yes. And not many men have that much skill at water. Even if they have the talent. It's just . . . not masculine."

Tavi sat down on his heels, facing Miles. "I know two people who can help."

Miles's eyebrows went up.

"The first one is a slave. His name is Fade. He works in the kitchens and the gardens at the Academy," Tavi said. "I've known him since I was born. He doesn't seem very bright, but he hardly ever talks, and he's good at not being noticed. Gaius brought him here with me when I came."

Miles pursed his lips. "Really? Fine, I'll have him transferred to me to help with last-minute work. No one will notice something like that before Wintersend. The other?"

"Antillar Maximus," Tavi said. "He's got almost as many water beads on his lanyard as anyone at the Academy, and he's lost a bunch of them."

"High Lord Antillus's bastard?" Miles asked.

Tavi nodded. "Yes, sir."

"Do you really believe you can trust him, Tavi?"

Tavi took a deep breath. "With my life, sir."

Miles let out a rough laugh. "Yes. That's precisely what we're speaking about. Is he skilled enough to alter his form?"

Tavi grimaced. "You're asking exactly the wrong person about furycrafting, sir. But he hardly ever practices his crafting and still scores the highest in his classes. You might also consider letting me contact—"

"No," Miles said. "Too many people will know already. No more, Tavi."

"Are you sure?"

"I'm sure. You are to tell no one anything, Tavi. You are to make sure no one gets close enough to realize what has happened. You are to take any measures necessary to do so." He turned his face up to Tavi, and Miles's flat eyes chilled him to the core. "And I am going to do exactly the same thing. Do you understand me?"

Tavi shivered and looked down. Miles hadn't laid his hand on his sword for emphasis. He hadn't needed to. "I understand, sir."

"Are you sure you want your friends to be involved in this?"

"No," Tavi said, quietly. "But the Realm needs them."

"Aye, boy. It does." Miles sighed. "Though who knows? With luck, maybe it will work without trouble."

"Yes, sir."

"Now. I'll stay here. You fetch Killian and the others." He knelt by the First Lord again. "The Realm itself may be depending on us, boy. Keep everyone away from him. Tell no one."

"I'll keep everyone away from him," Tavi repeated dutifully. "And I'll tell no one."

"Stop worrying," Bernard said. "So long as you speak to Gaius right away, we should be fine."

"Are you sure?" Isana asked. "That it won't come to fighting?"

"As sure as anyone can be," Bernard assured his sister from the door to her bedroom. Morning sunlight slanted across the floor in golden stripes through the narrow windows. "I'm not eager to see more good people get hurt. All I want to do is make sure these vord stay where they are until the Legions arrive."

Isana finished binding her dark, silver-threaded hair into a tight braid, and regarded her reflection in the dressing mirror. Though she wore her finest dress, she knew perfectly well that the clothing would be laughably crude and lacking in style in Alera Imperia, the capital. Her reflection looked lean, uncertain, and worried, she thought. "Are you sure they won't attack you first?"

"Doroga seems confident that we have a little time before they'd be ready to do that," Bernard said. "He's sent for more of his own tribesmen, but they're in the southern ranges, and it may be two or three weeks before they arrive."

"And what if the First Lord does not order the Legions to help?"

"He will," Amara stated, her voice confident as she entered the room. "Your escorts are here, Isana."

"Thank you. Does that look all right?"

Amara adjusted the fore of Isana's sleeve and brushed off a bit of lint. "It's lovely. Gaius has a great deal of respect for Doroga, and for your brother. He'll take their warning seriously."

"I'll go to him at once," Isana replied. Though she by no means relished the notion of speaking to Gaius. That old man's eyes saw too much for her comfort. "But I know that there are many protocols involved in gaining an audience. He is the First Lord. I'm only a Steadholder. Are you sure I'll be able to reach him?"

"If you aren't, speak to Tavi," Amara said. "No one could deny you the right to visit your own nephew, and Tavi often serves as His Majesty's page. He knows the First Lord's staff and guards. He'll be able to help you."

Isana looked aside at Amara and nodded. "I see," she said. "Two years. Will I recognize him?"

Amara smiled. "You may need to stand a few stairs above him to get the same perspective. He's put on height and muscle."

"Boys grow," Isana said.

Amara regarded her for a moment, then said, "Sometimes the Academy can change people for the worse. But not Tavi. He's the same person. A good person, Isana. I think you have every right to be proud of him."

Isana felt a flash of gratitude toward Amara. Though she had never shared any such words or emotions before, Isana could feel the woman's sincerity as easily as she could see her smile. Cursor or not, Isana could tell that the words were precisely what they seemed to be—honest praise and reassurance. "Thank you, Countess."

Amara inclined her head in a gesture that matched the sense of respect Isana felt from the younger woman. "Bernard?" Amara said. "Would you mind if I had a few words with the Steadholder?"

"Not at all," Bernard said amiably.

Isana stifled a laugh that threatened to bubble from her mouth.

After a moment, Amara arched an eyebrow, and said, "Privately?"

Bernard blinked and stood up at once. "Oh. Right, of course." He looked back and forth between them suspiciously. "Um. I'll be out at the barn. We should be on the move in an hour. I've got to make sure Frederic—excuse me, Sir Frederic hasn't wandered off and forgotten his head."

"Thank you," Isana said.

Bernard winked at her, touched Amara's hand, and left the room.

Amara shut the door and laid her fingers against it. She

closed her eyes for a moment, and then Isana again felt that odd tightness to the room. There was a brief pain in her ears.

"There," Amara said. "I apologize. But I must be sure we are not overheard."

Isana felt her eyebrows rise. "Do you expect spies in my household now?"

"No. No, Steadholder. But I needed to speak with you about something personal."

Isana rose and tilted her head slightly to one side. "Please explain."

Amara nodded. The shadows under her eyes were deeper than they had been before. Isana frowned, studying the young woman. Amara was only a few years out of the Academy herself, though Isana was sure the Cursor had led a more difficult life than most. Amara had aged more quickly than a young woman should, and Isana felt a surge of compassion for her. In all that had happened, she sometimes forgot how very young the Countess was.

"Steadholder," Amara said, "I don't know how to ask this, but simply to ask it." She hesitated.

"Go on," Isana said.

Amara folded her arms and didn't look up. "What have I done to wrong you, Isana?"

The sense of raw pain and despair that rose from the girl closed around Isana like a cloud of glowing embers. She turned away and walked to the far side of the room. It required a significant effort to control her expression, and to keep her thoughts calm. "What do you mean?"

Amara shrugged with one shoulder, and Isana's sense of the young woman became tinged with embarrassment. "I mean that you don't like me. You've never treated me badly. Or said anything. But I also know that I am not welcome in your home."

Isana took a deep breath. "I don't know what you mean, Amara. Of course you're welcome here."

Amara shook her head. "Thank you for trying to convince me. But I've visited you several times over the past two years. And you've never once turned your back on me. You've never sat at the same table as me, or taken a meal with me—you serve everyone else instead. You never meet my eyes when you speak to me. And until today, you've never been alone in a room with me."

Isana felt her own brow furrow at the young woman's words. She began to answer, then remained silent. Was the Cursor right? She raked back through the memories of the past two years. "Furies." She sighed. "Have I really done that?"

Amara nodded. "I thought that . . . that I must have done something to warrant it. I was hoping that a little time would smooth things over, but it hasn't."

Isana gave her a fleeting smile. "Two years isn't much time when it comes to healing some hurts. It can take longer. A lifetime."

"I never meant to hurt you, Isana. Please believe me. Bernard adores you, and I would never intentionally do you wrong. If I have said or done anything, please tell me."

Isana folded her hands in her lap, frowning down at the floor. "You've never done anything of the sort. It was never you."

Frustration colored Amara's voice. "Then why?"

Isana pressed her lips together hard. "You're a loyal person, Amara. You work for Gaius. You are sworn to him."

"Why should that offend you?"

"It doesn't. But Gaius does."

Amara's lips firmed into a line. "What has he shown you other than generosity and gratitude?"

A stab of hot, bitter hatred shot through Isana, and her words crackled with it. "I was nearly killed today because of his gratitude and generosity. I'm only a country girl, Amara, but I'm not an idiot. Gaius is using me as a weapon to divide his enemies. Bernard's appointment to Count Calderon over the heads of the noble Houses of Riva is a direct reminder to them that Gaius, not Rivus, rules Alera. We are simply tools."

"That isn't fair, Isana," Amara said, but her voice was subdued.

"Fair?" Isana demanded. "Has he been fair? The status and recognition he gave us two years ago was not a reward. He created a small army of enemies for my brother and me, then whisked Tavi off to the Academy under his patronage— where I am certain my nephew has found others who strongly dislike and persecute him."

"Tavi is receiving the finest education in Alera," Amara stated. "Surely you don't begrudge him that. He's healthy and well. What harm has that done to him?"

"I'm sure he is healthy. And well. And learning. It's a marvelously polite way to hold Tavi hostage," Isana replied. The words tasted bitter in her mouth. "Gaius knows how much Tavi wanted to go to the Academy. He knows that it would destroy him to be sent away. Gaius manipulated us. He left us with no alternative but to throw in our lot with him as strongly as possible if we were to survive."

"No," Amara said. "No, I won't believe that of him."

"Of course you won't. You're loyal to him."

"Not mindlessly," Amara said. "Not without reason. I've seen him. I know him. He's a decent man, and you're interpreting his actions in the worst possible light."

"I have reason," Isana said. Some part of her felt shocked at the venom and ice in her voice. "I have reason."

Amara's expression and bearing flickered with concern. Her voice remained gentle. "You hate him."

"*Hate* is too mild a word."

Amara blinked several times, bewildered. "Why?"

"Because Gaius killed my . . . younger sister."

Amara shook her head. "No. He isn't that way. He is a strong Lord, but he is no murderer."

"He didn't do it directly," Isana said. "But the fault lies on him."

Amara fretted her lower lip. "You hold him responsible for what happened to her."

"He *is* responsible. Without him, Tavi might still have a mother. A father."

"I don't understand. What happened to them?"

Isana shrugged one shoulder. "My family was a poor one, and my sister did not wed by her twentieth birthday. She was sent to the Crown Legion camp for a term of domestic service. She met a soldier, fell in love, and bore him a child. Tavi."

Amara nodded slowly. "How did they die?"

"Politics," Isana said. "Gaius ordered the Crown Legion moved to the Calderon Valley. He was making a statement to Riva during a period of turmoil, and patronizing the Senate by placing a Legion in a position to deter a Marat horde from invading while simultaneously giving Lord Rivus a warning that his Legion was at hand."

Amara made a quiet, hissing sound. "The First Battle of Calderon."

"Yes," Isana said quietly. "Tavi's parents were there. Neither survived."

"But Isana," Amara said, "the First Lord did not mandate their deaths. He placed a Legion in harm's way. That's *why* they *exist*. The loss was tragic, but you can't blame Gaius for not foreseeing the Marat horde that even surprised his own commanders in the field."

"They were there on his orders. It was his fault."

Amara squared her shoulders and set her jaw. "Great furies, Steadholder. His own *son* was killed there."

"I know that," Isana spat. More words struggled to flow from her mouth, but she shook her head and stopped them. It was a struggle, so intense was the tide of hatred in her heart. "That isn't all that I blame him for." She closed her eyes. "There are other reasons."

"And they are?" Amara asked.

"My own."

The Cursor was silent for a long moment, then nodded. "Then . . . I suppose we must agree to disagree on this matter, Steadholder."

"I knew that before this conversation began, Amara," Isana said. The sudden tide of rage was failing, draining away, leaving her tired and unhappy in its wake.

"I know him as a disciplined, capable lord. And as an honorable and forthright man. He has sacrificed much for the sake of the Realm—even his own son. I am proud to serve him as best I may."

"And I will never forgive him," Isana said. "Never."

Amara nodded stiffly, and Isana could feel her distress beneath the polite expression she held on her face. "I'm sorry, Steadholder. After what you went through yesterday . . . I'm sorry. I shouldn't have pushed you."

Isana shook her head. "It's all right, Countess. It's good to have this in the open."

"I suppose," Amara said. She touched the door, and the

tense pressure in the very air of the room vanished. "I'll make sure your litter is ready and that your escorts have eaten."

"Wait," Isana said.

Amara paused, her hand on the door.

"You make Bernard very happy," Isana said in a quiet voice. "Happier than I've seen him in years. I don't want to come between you, Amara. We needn't agree about the First Lord for you to stay with him."

Amara nodded and gave her a silent smile, then left the room.

Isana stared at her mirror for a moment, then rose. She went to the chest at the foot of her bed and opened it. She took out piles of bedding, her extra pair of shoes, a spare pillow, and a small wooden box containing bits of silver jewelry she'd acquired over the years. Then she pushed hard on one end of the bottom of the chest, willing Rill to draw the water from the boards there, which shrank and came loose. She removed the dried slats, revealing a small and hidden space beneath them.

She picked up a small silk jewel-pouch. She untied and opened it, and upended the pouch into her palm.

An elegant ring of gleaming silver upon a slender silver chain fell into her palm. It was heavy and cool. The ring was set with a single gem that somehow changed from a brilliant blue diamond to a bloodred ruby down its seamless center. Two carved silver eagles, one slightly larger than the other, soared toward one another to form the setting, holding the gem aloft on their wings.

That old pain and loss filled her as she stared down at the ring. But she did not ask Rill to stop her tears.

She draped the chain over her head, and tucked it away into her dress. She stared at herself in the mirror for a moment, willing the redness from her eyes. She had no more time to waste looking back.

Isana lifted her chin, composed her expression, and left to go to the assistance of the family she loved with all of her heart and the man she hated with all of her soul.

Amara was waiting when the Knights Aeris sent by the Crown swept down from the dark grey clouds overhead. Spring this far north of the capital could be unpleasantly cold and damp, but the rain promised by occasional rumbles of thunder had not yet arrived. Amara recognized the man leading the contingent and briefly considered trying to provoke the water-laden clouds into emptying themselves a bit earlier. Onto his bloated head.

Sir Horatio flew in front of the enclosed litter, his ornamented armor doing its best to gleam on the cloudy day, his red velvet cloak spread behind him. A Knight in a travel harness flew at each corner of the litter, supporting its weight, and four more flew in a loose escort around it. The contingent descended more swiftly than was necessary, and their furies stirred up a miniature cyclone of wild wind that threw Amara's hair around her head and sent a herd of sheep in a nearby pen crowding to its far side for shelter. The holders rushing around preparing supplies and sundries for Bernard's cohort had to shield their eyes against flying straw and dust.

"Idiot," Amara said, sighing, willing Cirrus between herself and the flying debris. Horatio touched down lightly. As a subtribune and Knight of the Crown Legion, he was permitted the gold-and-silver filigree on his armor and the glittering gems on both his helmet and the hilt of his sword, but the gold embroidery on his velvet cloak was a bit much. Horatio had made a fortune winning the Wind Trials, the yearly race of aircrafters during Wintersend, and he liked everyone to know it.

Of course, he was less eager for them to know that he had lost the lion's share of his riches the first year Amara had entered the event. He would never let her forget that, though she supposed she might not feel inclined to be particularly polite to a person who had cost her that much money, either. She waited until the Knights had settled in the steadholt's court-yard, then approached.

"Good day, sir!" boomed Horatio in a brassy baritone. "Oh, wait. Not sir, at all. That's you, Countess Amara. Forgive me, but from there you looked like a young man."

A few years before, the insult to her physique would have stung her sorely. But that was before she'd become a Cursor. And before Bernard. "That's perfectly all right, Sir Horatio. We all expect men of your age to begin experiencing certain deficiencies." She bowed to him with courtly grace, and did not miss a low round of chuckles from the other Knights.

Horatio returned her bow with a brittle smile and glared at the men behind him. All eight Knights found other places to direct their gazes and assumed professionally bored expressions. "Of course. I assume our passenger is ready to leave?"

"Shortly," Amara said. "I'm sure the kitchen will have something hot for your men to eat while you wait."

"That isn't necessary, Countess," Horatio said. "Please inform Holder Isana that we await her arrival so that we may depart."

"You await *Steadholder* Isana's convenience," she said, deliberately letting her voice carry through the courtyard. "And as you are a guest at her steadholt, subtribune, I expect you to behave with the courtesy expected of a Knight and soldier of the Crown Legion to a Citizen of the Realm."

Horatio's eyes narrowed, hot with anger, but he gave her the smallest of bows in acknowledgment.

"Furthermore," she continued, "I strongly advise you to let your men rest and eat while they have the opportunity. If the weather worsens, they will need their strength."

"I do not take orders from you regarding the disposition of my command, Countess," Horatio snapped.

"Goodness," said a woman's voice from within the litter. "Perhaps we should hand you each a bone, and you can simply bludgeon one another to death. I can't think of a faster way to end this unseemly display. Rolf, please?"

One of the Knights immediately stepped to the side of the litter, opened the door, and offered a polite hand to assist as a tiny woman emerged into the grey light. She might have been almost five feet tall, but even at that height, she looked frail and delicate, as light-boned as a Parcian swallow. She had skin the color of dark honey, and fine, shining hair darker than wet coal. Her gown was made of rich silk, though in subtle shades of brown and grey, and its neckline plunged far more deeply than would be considered proper to any woman of any station whatsoever. Her features were hauntingly lovely, with dark eyes almost too large for her face, and twin ropes of the sunset-colored pearls from the seas near her home province wound through her hair and were matched by a second pair of strands around her throat.

The pearls of the necklace were priceless and lovely—but they did not conceal the fact that they were mounted to an elegant slave's collar.

"Amara," the woman said, her mouth parting in a wide smile. "Only a few years out of the civilized south, and you've turned savage." She extended her hands. "You've probably forgotten all about me."

Amara felt a laugh ripple from her mouth as she replied. "Serai," she said, stepping forward to take her hands. As always, standing before Serai's exquisite beauty made her feel tall and awkward, and, as always, she did not at all mind. "What are you doing here?"

Serai's eyes sparkled with silent laughter, and she swayed a little on her feet. "Oh, darling, I am simply perishing of fatigue. I thought I would be fine, but I've been so frail of late." She leaned on Amara's arm, and turned a gaze on Horatio that would have melted the heart of an Amaranth merchant. "Subtribune, I apologize for my weakness. But would it be all right with you if I sat down for a bit and perhaps had some refreshment before we depart?"

Horatio looked frustrated for a moment, glowered at Amara, then said, "Of course, Lady Serai."

Serai smiled wanly at him. "I thank you, milord. I hate to see you and your men suffer on my account. Will you not join me at the table?"

Horatio rolled his eyes and sighed. "I suppose a gentleman could do little else."

"Of course not," Serai said, patting his arm with a tiny hand, then lightly tracing the pearls at her throat. "The obligations of station enslave us all at times." She turned to

Amara, and said, "Is there somewhere I could freshen up, darling?"

"Of course," Amara said. "This way, Lady Serai."

"Bless you," Serai said. "Subtribune, I will join you and your men in the dining hall presently." She walked out, a hand still on Amara's arm, and gave a winsome smile to the Knights Aeris as she passed them. The men returned smiles and speculative looks as the slave passed.

"You're an evil woman," Amara murmured, once they were out of earshot. "Horatio will never forgive you for manipulating him like that in public."

"Horatio only has his continued command because of talented subordinates," Serai responded, laughter dancing in her words. A wicked glint touched her eyes. "In Rolf's case, *very* talented."

Amara felt her cheeks redden. "*Serai.*"

"Well, darling, what do you expect? One can hardly be a courtesan without indulging in certain improprieties." She touched her lips with her tongue. "In Rolf's case, quite a bit of indulgence. Suffice to say that Horatio is no threat to me, and how well he knows it." Serai's smile faded. "I almost wish Horatio would try something. It would be a pleasant diversion."

"What do you mean?"

Serai glanced up at her, her eyes opaque, and said, "Not outdoors, darling."

Amara frowned, then fell silent and led Serai into the steadholt, and to the guest quarters above the main hall. She gave Serai a few moments inside, then slipped in behind her, and asked Cirrus to seal off the room from potential listeners. Once the air had tightened around them, Serai sank down onto a stool and said, "It's good to see you again, Amara."

"And you," Amara answered. She knelt on the floor beside Serai, so that their eyes were on a level. "What are you doing here? I expected the Cursor Legate to send Mira or Cassandra."

"Mira was murdered near Kalare three days ago," Serai responded. She folded her hands, but not before Amara saw how the courtesan's fingers shook. "Cassandra has been missing from Parcia for several days. She is presumed dead or compromised."

Amara felt as though someone had punched her in the belly. "Great furies," she breathed. "What has happened?"

"War," Serai responded. "A quiet war fought in alleyways and service corridors. We Cursors are being hunted and killed."

"But who?" Amara breathed,

Serai moved a shoulder in a slow shrug. "Who? Our best guess is Kalare," she said.

"But how did he know where to hit us?"

"Treachery, of course. Our people have been killed in their beds, their baths. Whoever these people are, someone who knows us is telling them where to strike."

"Fidelias," Amara said. The word tasted bitter.

"Potentially," Serai said. "But we must assume that there may be someone else within the Cursors—and that means that we cannot trust anyone, Cursor or otherwise."

"Great furies," Amara breathed. "What about the First Lord?"

"Communications have been severely disrupted throughout the southern cities. Our channels to the First Lord have gone silent."

"*What?*"

"I know," Serai said. The tiny woman shivered. "My initial orders from the Cursor Legate were to dispatch an agent to your command to escort Steadholder Isana to Festival. But once this began happening it became clear that attempting to make contact with other Cursors would be dangerous. I had to speak to someone I trusted. So I came here."

Amara took Serai's hands in her own and squeezed tightly. "Thank you."

Serai answered with a wan smile. "We must assume that word has not reached the First Lord about the situation."

"You intend to use Isana to approach him in person," Amara said.

"Precisely. I can't think of a safer way to go about it."

"It might not be so safe," Amara said. "An assassin attempted to kill Steadholder Isana yesterday morning. He was using a Kalaran knife."

Serai's eyes widened. "Great furies."

Amara nodded with a grimace. "And she's lived her entire life in the provinces. She can't enter the capital unguided.

You'll need to show her around the political circles." She exhaled. "And you must be very careful, Serai. They'll try to remove her before the presentation ceremony."

Serai chewed on her lip. "I'm no coward, Amara, but I'm not a bodyguard, either. There's no way I can protect her from trained assassins. If that is the situation, I need you to come with us."

Amara shook her head. "I can't. Matters have developed locally." She explained what Doroga had told them about the vord. "We can't afford to let them spread and multiply. The local garrison will need every crafter they can get to make sure these creatures do not escape again."

Serai arched an eyebrow. "Darling, are you sure about this? I mean, I know you've had some contact with these barbarians, but don't you think that they might be exaggerating the truth?"

"No," Amara said quietly. "In my experience, they don't know how to exaggerate. Doroga arrived here yesterday with fewer than two hundred survivors from a force of two thousand."

"Oh come now," Serai said. "That must be an outright lie. Even a Legion's morale would break well before that."

"The Marat are not *legionares*," Amara said. "They aren't like us. But consider this—they fight, men and women and children together, beside their family and friends. They will not desert them, even if it means dying beside them. They consider the vord to be the same sort of threat—not just to their territory, but to their families and lives."

"Even so," Serai said. "You aren't a battlecrafter, Amara. You're a Cursor. Let those whose duties call them to a soldier's work do their part. But you must serve your calling. Come with me to the capital."

"No," Amara said. She paced to the window and stared out of it for a moment. Bernard and Frederic were lifting a pair of vast hogsheads of preserved foodstuffs onto racks on either side of a gargant's pack harness. The bull yawned, scarcely noticing what must have been half a ton of burden the two earthcrafters had casually lifted into place. "The garrison here lost most of its Knights Aeris at Second Calderon, and it has been difficult to replace them. Bernard may need me to help him by carrying messages or flying reconnaissance."

Serai let out a small gasp.

Amara turned, frowning, to find the tiny courtesan staring at her with her mouth open.

"Amara," Serai accused. "You're his lover."

"What?" Amara said. "That isn't what—"

"Don't bother trying to deny it," Serai said. "You were *looking* at him out there, weren't you?"

"What does that have to do with anything?" Amara asked.

"I saw your eyes," Serai said. "When you called him Bernard. He was out there doing something manly, wasn't he?"

Amara felt her face heat up again. "How did you—"

"I know these things, darling," she said airily. "It's what I do." The little woman crossed the room to stare out the window at the courtyard, and arched an eyebrow. "Which is he?"

"Green tunic," Amara supplied, stepping back from the window. "Loading the gargant. Dark hair, beard, a little grey in them."

"My," said Serai. "But hardly old. Went silver early, I'd say. That's always attractive in a man. It means he has both power enough to have responsibilities and conscience enough to worry over them. And—" She paused and blinked. "He's rather strong, isn't he?"

"He is," Amara said. "And his archery is amazing."

Serai gave her an oblique look. "I know it's petty and typical, but there *is* an undeniable, primal attraction in a man of strength. Wouldn't you agree?"

Amara's face burned. "Well. Yes. It suits him." She took a breath. "And he can be so gentle."

Serai gave her a dismayed look. "Oh, my. It's worse than I feared. You're not his lover. You're in *love*."

"I'm not," Amara said. "I mean. I see him fairly often. I've been Gaius's courier to the region since Second Calderon and . . ." Her voice trailed off. "I don't know. I don't think I've ever been in love."

Serai turned her back to the window. Over her shoulder, Amara could see Bernard giving directions to a pair of men hitching up heavy work horses to a wagon of supplies, then checking the beast's hooves. "Do you see him often enough?" Serai asked.

"I . . . I wouldn't mind being near him more."

"Mmmhmm," she said. "What do you like best about him?"

"His hands," Amara said at once. The answer came out before she'd had time to think it through. She felt herself blush again. "They're strong. The skin a little rough. But warm and gentle."

"Ah," said Serai.

"Or his mouth," Amara blurted. "I mean, his eyes are a lovely color, but his mouth is . . . I mean, he can . . ."

"He knows how to kiss," Serai said.

Amara stammered to a silence and simply nodded.

"Well," Serai said, "at this point, I think it's safe to say that you know what love feels like."

Amara bit her lip. "You really think that?"

The courtesan smiled, something wistful in it. "Of course, darling."

Amara watched the courtyard as a pair of boys, no more than six or seven years of age, leapt from hiding places in the wagon to Bernard's back. The big man roared in feigned outrage, and went spinning around for a few moments as though trying to reach them, until the boys lost their grips and fell to the ground, lurching dizzily and laughing. Bernard grinned at them, ruffled their hair, and sent them on the way with a wave of his hand. Amara found herself smiling.

Serai's voice became lower and very gentle. "You must leave him, of course."

Amara felt her spine stiffen. She stared past the other woman, out the window.

"You are a Cursor," Serai said, "One with the trust of the First Lord himself. And you have sworn your life to his service."

"I know that," Amara said. "But—"

Serai shook her head. "Amara, you can't do that to him if you truly love him. Bernard is a peer of the Realm, now. He has duties, responsibilities. One of them will be to take a wife. A wife whose first loyalty will be to him."

Amara stared at Bernard and the two children. Her vision suddenly blurred with hot tears.

"He has duties," Serai said, her voice compassionate, but resolute. "And among them is the duty to sire children so that the furycraft in his blood will strengthen the Realm."

"And I was blighted," Amara whispered. She pressed her

hand against her lower belly, and could almost feel the nearly invisible scars from the pockmarks the disease had left. She tasted bitter bile on her tongue. "I can't give him children."

Serai shook her head and turned to stare out the window down at the courtyard. Frederic herded a second pair of enormous gargants into the yard and began hitching up their cargo harnesses with Bernard, while other holders came and went in a constant stream, placing sacks and boxes on the ground to be loaded on the beasts once they were ready. Then Serai stood on tiptoe, and gently drew down the shade.

"I'm sorry, darling."

"I never thought it through," Amara said. More tears fell. "I mean. I was just so happy, and I never . . ."

"Love is a fire, Amara. Draw it too close and be burned." Serai stepped over to Amara and touched her cheek with the back of her hand. "You know what you must do."

"Yes."

"Then best to make it quick. Clean." Serai sighed. "I know what I'm talking about. I'm so sorry, darling."

Amara closed her eyes and leaned her head miserably against Serai's touch. She couldn't stop the tears. She didn't try.

"So much is happening, and all at once," Serai said after a moment. "It can't be a coincidence. Can it?"

Amara shook her head. "I don't think it can."

"Furies," Serai breathed. Her expressive eyes looked haunted.

"Serai," Amara said quietly, "I believe there is a real threat to the Realm here. I'm going to stay."

Serai blinked up at her. "Darling, of course you're going to stay. I don't need a bodyguard who is pining over a man like this—you're useless to me."

Amara choked on a small roll of laughter that came up through her at Serai's words, and she folded her arms around the courtesan in a tight hug. "Will you be all right?"

"Of course, darling," Serai said. But though her voice was warm, amused, Amara felt the little courtesan trembling. Serai probably felt Amara's shivering in return.

Amara drew back, her hands on Serai's shoulders, and met her gaze. "Duty. The vord may be inside the capital. More killers are probably looking for the Steadholder even now.

Cursors are being murdered. And if the Crown doesn't send reinforcements to the local garrison, more holders and *legionares* are going to die. Likely me with them."

Serai's eyes closed for a moment, and she bobbed her head in a brief nod. "I know. But . . . Amara, I'm afraid . . . afraid I am not suited for this kind of situation. I work in grand halls and bedchambers with wine and perfume. Not in dark alleyways with cloaks and knives. I don't like knives. I don't even *own* a knife. And my cloaks are far too expensive to risk bloodying."

Amara gently squeezed her shoulders, smiling. "Well. Perhaps it will not come to that."

Serai gave Amara a shaky smile. "I should hope not. It would be most awkward." She shook her head and smoothed the anxiety from her expression. "Look at you, Amara. So tall and strong now. Nothing like the farm girl I saw flying over the sea."

"It seems so long ago," Amara said.

Serai nodded, and touched a stray hair back from her cheek. Her expression became businesslike. "Shall we?"

Amara lifted her hand and the pressure of Cirrus's warding vanished. "Isana should be ready to leave shortly. Be cautious and swift, Serai. We are running out of time."

It took Tavi three hours to find Max, who was indeed at a young widow's house. He spent another hour finding a way into the house, and half an hour more to get his friend conscious, dressed, and staggering back up through the furylit streets of the capital to the Citadel. By the time the lights of the Academy loomed up above them, it was the most silent hour of the night, in the hollow, cold time just before dawn began to color the sky.

They entered through one of a sprinkling of unseen entrances provided for the use of the Cursors-in-Training at the Academy. Tavi dragged his friend down to the baths straightaway, and without ceremony shoved him into a large pool of cold water.

Max, of course, had the phenomenal recuperative abilities of anyone with his raw furycrafting power, but he had developed a correspondingly formidable array of carousing talents by way of compensation. It wasn't the first time Tavi had administered an emergency sobering after one of Max's nights on the town. The shock of the water had the large young man screaming and thrashing in a heartbeat, but when he lurched to the stairs up out of the water, Tavi met him, turned Max around, and pushed him back into the pool.

After a dozen more plunges into the freezing pool, Max pressed his hands against the sides of his head with a moan. "Great furies, Calderon, I'm awake. Would you let me out of the blighted, crows-begotten ice water?"

"Not until you open your eyes," Tavi said firmly.

"Fine, fine," Max growled. He turned a bloodshot glare upon Tavi. "Happy now?"

"Joyous," Tavi replied.

Max grunted, lumbered from the icy pool, and fumbled his clothes off, then shambled into the warm, sun gold furylit waters of one of the heated baths. As always, Tavi's eyes were drawn to the crosshatched network of scars on his friend's back—the marks of a whip or a ninecat that could only have been formed before Max came into his furycrafting power. Tavi winced in sympathy. No matter how many times he saw his friend's scars, they remained something startling and hideous.

He glanced around the baths. The room was enormous, with several different bathing pools trickling falls of water filling up a vast room with white marble walls, floor, pillars, and ceiling. Batches of plants, even trees, softened the severe, cold marble surroundings, and lounges were laid out in a dozen different areas, where bathers might idle in one another's company while awaiting their turn at a pool. Soft fury-lamps of blue, green, and gold painted each pool, giving an indication of its temperature. The sound of falling water bounded back and forth from the indifferent stone, filling the air with sound enough to mask voices more than a few steps away. It was one of the only places in the capital where one could be reasonably certain of a private conversation.

The baths were yet empty—the slaves who attended bathers would not arrive for more than an hour. Tavi and Max were alone.

Tavi stripped, though much more self-consciously than his friend. Back at the steadholt, bathing was a matter of privacy and practicality. It had been an adjustment to engage in the more metropolitan practice of bathing followed in most of the cities, and Tavi had never managed to lose entirely the twinge of discomfort he felt when disrobing.

"Oh for crying out loud, bumpkin," Max said, without opening his eyes. "It's the men's baths. There's no one else here, and my eyes aren't even open." He gave Tavi another glare, though it was less intense than the first. "If you'd left me where you found me, you could have had the baths to yourself."

Tavi slid into the pool beside Max and pitched his voice low, barely audible over the obscuring sounds of water. "There's trouble, Max."

Max's glower vanished, and his reddened eyes glittered with sudden interest. "What kind of trouble?"

Tavi told him.

"Bloody crows!" Max roared. "Are you trying to get me *killed*?"

"Yes. To tell you the truth, I never had much use for you, Max." Tavi watched his friend blink at him for a second, then scowl.

"Hah-hah," said Max. "You're hilarious."

"You should know better than that," Tavi replied. "If there was anyone else I thought could do this, I wouldn't have gotten you involved."

"You wouldn't?" Max asked, his tone suddenly offended. "Why not?"

"Because you've known what's going on for ten seconds, and you're already complaining."

"I like complaining. It's every soldier's sacred *right*," Max growled.

Tavi felt a smile tug at his lips. "You're not a *legionare* anymore, Max. You're a Cursor. Or a Cursor-in-Training, anyway."

"I'm still offended," Max declared. After a moment, he added, "Tavi, you're my friend. If you need help, just expect me to be there whether you want me there or not."

Tavi chewed at his lip, regarding Max. "Really?"

"It'll be simpler that way," Max drawled. "So. I'm to double for Gaius, eh?"

"Can you?" Tavi asked.

Max stretched out in the hot water with a confident smile in answer. "No idea."

Tavi snorted, went to the waterfall, took up a scrubber, and began raking it over his skin, cleaning the sweat and toil of the day from him before taking up a soaped comb and raking it quickly through his hair. He rose to rinse in a cooler pool and emerged shivering to towel himself dry. Max emerged from the pools a few moments later, similarly scrubbed, and the pair of them changed into the clean clothes they'd last left with the bath attendants, leaving their soiled garments behind on their respective shelves.

"What do I do?" Max asked.

"Go to the Citadel, down the south gallery and to the west hall to the staircase down."

"Guard station there," Max noted.

"Yes. Stop at the first station, and ask for Sir Miles. He's expecting to hear from you. Killian will probably be there, too."

Max raised his eyebrows. "Miles wanted to bring in the Cursors? I'd have thought he wouldn't hold with too much of that."

"I don't think Miles knows that Killian is still on active duty," Tavi said. "Much less that he's the current Legate."

Max slapped an annoyed hand at his head, sprinkling water out of his close-cropped hair. "I am going to lose my mind, trying to keep track of who is allowed to know what."

"You're the one who agreed to Cursor training," Tavi said.

"Stop walking on my sacred right, Calderon."

Tavi grinned. "Just do what I do. Don't tell anyone anything."

Max nodded. "That's a solid plan."

"Let's move. I'm supposed to bring someone else down. I'll meet you there."

Max rose to leave, but paused. "Tavi," he said. "Just because I'm not complaining doesn't mean this won't be dangerous. Very dangerous."

"I know."

"Just wanted to make sure you did," Max said. "If you get in trouble . . . I mean, if you need my help. Don't let your pride keep you from asking for it. I mean, it's possible that some serious battlecrafting could start happening. If it does, I'll cover you."

"Thank you," Tavi said, without much emotion. "But if it comes to that, we've probably failed so badly that my own personal legion wouldn't help."

Max gave a rueful laugh of agreement, squared his shoulders, and stalked out of the baths without looking behind him. "Watch your back."

"You too."

Tavi waited a moment until Max had left the baths, then hurried out of them and toward the servants' quarters. By the time he'd arrived, a swath of light blue on the eastern horizon of the night sky had arrived to herald the coming dawn, and the staff of the Academy was beginning to stir. Tavi wound his way cautiously down service corridors and cramped staircases, careful to avoid being seen. He moved in silence through the darkened corridors, bearing no lamp of his own, relying upon infrequent, feeble hallway lights. Tavi stalked down a final cramped corridor, and to a half-sized door that opened into a crawl space in the walls—Fade's chamber.

Tavi listened intently for any approach, and once he was sure he was not being idly observed, he opened the door and slipped inside.

The slave's room was musty, cold, and dank. It was nothing more than an inefficiency of design, bounded on two walls with stone of the Academy and on the others with rough plaster. The ceiling was barely five feet high and contained nothing more than a battered old trunk with no lid and an occupied sleeping palette.

Tavi moved in silence to the palette, and reached down to shake its occupant.

He realized half a breath later that the form under the blankets was simply a bundle of bedding, piled into place as a distraction. Tavi turned, crouched, his hand moving to his dagger, but there was swift and silent motion in the darkness, and someone smoothly took the weapon from his belt, slammed Tavi hard with a shoulder, and sent him off-balance to the ground. His attacker followed closely, and in another breath, Tavi found himself pinned by a knee on his chest, and the cold edge of his own weapon was pressed to his throat.

"Light," said a quiet voice, and an ancient, dim furylamp on the wall shone scarlet.

The man crouched over Tavi was of unremarkable height and build. His hair fell in ragged strands to his shoulders and over most of his face, brown streaked through with much grey, and Tavi could barely see the gleam of dark eyes behind it. What Tavi could see of the man's visage was hideously marred with the brand the Legions used upon those judged guilty of cowardice. His forearms were as lean and sinewy as the ancient leather slave-braid on his throat, and they were covered in white scars. Some were the tiny, recognizable pockmarks of burns gained at a smith's forge, but others were straight and fine, like those Tavi had seen only upon the arms of old Giraldi back at Garrison and on Sir Miles.

"Fade," Tavi said, his chest tight with the panic caused by the swift attack. His heart pounded hard and fast. "Fade. It's me."

Fade lifted his chin for a moment, staring down at him, then his body eased, moving away from the young man. "Tavi," Fade said, his voice thick and heavy with recent sleep. "Hurt you?"

"I'm fine," Tavi assured him.

"Sneaking," Fade said, scowling. "Sneaking into my room."

Tavi sat up. "Yes. I'm sorry if I startled you."

Fade reversed his grip, taking the dagger by its blade, and offered the hilt across his wrist to Tavi. The young man reclaimed his knife and slipped it back into its sheath. "Sleeping," Fade said, and yawned, adding a soft, slurring hooting sound to the end of it.

"Fade," Tavi said. "I remember the battlements at Calderon. I know this is an act. I know you aren't a brain-addled idiot."

Fade gave Tavi a wide and witless smile. "Fade," he stated in a vacantly cheerful tone.

Tavi glared at him. "Don't," Tavi said. "Keep your secrets if you want. But don't insult me with the charade. I need your help."

Fade became completely still for a long moment. Then he tilted his head to one side and spoke, his voice now low and soft. "Why?"

Tavi shook his head. "Not here. Come with me. I'll explain."

Fade let out his breath in a long exhalation. "Gaius."

"Yes."

The slave closed his eyes for a moment. Then he went to the trunk, and removed a handful of objects and a spare blanket. He pushed hard on the bottom of the trunk and there was a hollow-sounding crack. He withdrew a scabbard from the trunk, and drew a short, straight blade, the *gladius* of a *legionare*. Fade examined the weapon in the dim light, then sheathed it again, donned a voluminous old robe of worn sackcloth, and slipped the weapon beneath it. "Ready."

Tavi led Fade out into the corridors of the Academy, made his way toward the nearest of the secluded routes that led down into the uppermost layers of the Deeps, and emerged near the Citadel. The entrance to the Deeps wasn't precisely a secret door, but it lay within the deep shadows of a particularly cramped and crooked hallway, and if one didn't know where to look, the low, narrow opening to the stairwell was all but invisible.

Tavi led Fade down a series of little-traveled hallways, thick with moisture and chill air. His route led them briefly into the shallowest levels of the Deeps, then crossed beneath the Citadel's walls. They came to the stairway leading down to the First Lord's meditation chamber, and descended, challenged by alert *legionares* at each station. Tavi's legs throbbed with a brutal ache on every beat of his heart, but he forced himself to ignore the complaints of his tired body and kept moving.

Fade, Tavi noticed, studied the ground without looking up. His hair fell around his face and blended with the rough fabric of his robe. His gait was that of an older man's—stiff with apparent arthritis, halting and cautious. Or at least it was passing through each guard station. Once out of sight on the curving stairs, he moved with feline silence.

At the bottom of the stairs, the door to the First Lord's chamber was firmly closed. Tavi drew his knife and struck the hilt against the dark steel door in a set, staccato rhythm. After a moment, it opened, and Miles stood glowering in the doorway. "Where the crows have you been, boy?" he demanded.

"Um. Getting the man I told you about, Sir Miles. This is Fade."

"Took you long enough," Miles growled. He swept a cool gaze over the slave. "In four hours, Gaius must appear in his box at the preliminaries for the Wind Trials. Antillar isn't having much luck with his mimicry, but Killian can't stop to help him learn until he is sure the First Lord is attended. You should have brought the slave first."

"Yes, sir," Tavi said. "Next time this happens I'll be sure to remember."

Miles's expression turned sour. "Get in then," he said. "Fade, is it? I've had some bedding and a cot brought down. You'll need to assemble it and help me get Gaius into it."

Fade froze, and Tavi saw his eyes bright with shock behind his hair. "Gaius?"

"It looks as though he was trying to do too much furycrafting," Tavi said. "He may have broken his health on it. He collapsed several hours ago."

"Alive?" Fade asked.

"So far," Tavi said.

"But not if we don't get him into a proper bed and have him taken care of," Miles growled. "Tavi, you've got some messages to carry. Business as usual. Make everyone believe it. All right?"

There went the possibility of actually getting any sleep, Tavi thought. And at the rate things were going, he might well end up missing the test altogether. He sighed.

Fade shuffled into the chamber and went over to the bedding Miles had mentioned. The cot was a simple framework, standard Legion issue, and it didn't take Fade long to assemble it.

Miles went to Gaius's bureau against one wall and picked up a small stack of envelopes. He returned and gave them to Tavi without comment. Tavi was about to ask him which should be delivered first when Miles's eyes narrowed, and a frown wrinkled his brow.

"You," he said. "Fade. Turn around here."

Tavi saw Fade lick his lips and rise, turning to face Miles with his head down.

The Captain strode over to Fade. "Show me your face."

Fade made a quiet sound of distress, bowing in a panicked fashion.

Miles reached out a hand and flicked the hair from one side of Fade's face. It revealed the hideous scars of the coward's brand, and Miles frowned severely at it.

"Sir Miles?" Tavi asked. "Are you all right?"

Miles raked his fingers through his short-cropped hair. "Tired," he said. "Maybe I'm seeing things. He looks familiar, somehow."

"Perhaps you've seen him working, Captain," Tavi said, careful to keep his tone neutral.

"That's probably it," Miles said. He took a deep breath and squared his shoulders. "There's still a new Legion to run. I'm off for morning drills."

"Business as usual," Tavi said.

"Precisely. Killian will handle things until I can return. Obey him without question. Do you understand?"

Miles turned and left without waiting for an answer.

Tavi sighed and crossed the tiles to help Fade finish assembling the cot and bedding. On the other side of the room, Gaius lay on his back, his skin grey and pale. Killian knelt over him, his tea brazier alight, and some noxious-smelling steam drifted up from the coals.

"Tavi," Fade said, his voice low. "I can't do this. I can't be near Miles. He'll recognize me."

"That would be bad?" Tavi whispered back.

"I'd have to fight him." The words were simple, gentle, unadorned with anything but a faint tone of sadness or regret. "I must leave."

"We need your help, Fade," Tavi said. "Gaius needs your help. You can't abandon him."

Fade shook his head, then asked, "What does Miles know about me?"

"Your name. That I trust you. That Gaius sent you here to the Academy with me."

"Blighted furies." Fade sighed. "Tavi, I want you to do something for me. Please."

"Name it," Tavi said at once.

"Tell Miles nothing more about me. Even if he asks. Lie, make excuses, whatever you need to do. We can't afford for him to fly into a rage now."

"What?" Tavi asked. "Why would he do that?"

"Because," Fade said, "he's my brother."

CHAPTER 13

Though she had been unconscious for much of the day, by the time Isana had packed and settled into the covered litter, she was exhausted.

She had never flown in a litter before, either open to the elements or closed, and the experience felt far too familiar to be so terrifying. It looked little different than any covered coach, at least from the inside, which made it all the more disconcerting to see, out the coach's windows, the occasional soaring bird of prey or feathery tendril of cloud tinted dark gold by the deepening evening. She stared out at the gathering night and the land far below for a time, her heart beating too quickly in her chest.

"It's been getting dark for so long," Isana murmured, only half-aware that she'd said it out loud.

Serai looked up from the embroidery in her lap and glanced out the window. The light colored the pearls on her collar in shades of rose and gold. "We're flying into the sunset, Steadholder, high and quickly at that. The sun will outpace us in time. I've always loved evenings, though. I rather enjoy spending more time in them."

Isana turned her attention to the woman, studying her profile. Serai's emotional presence was barely there—something feather-light and nebulous. When the slave spoke, there was very little of the depth of emotional inflection Isana was used to feeling from those around her. Isana could count the people who had successfully concealed their emotions from her on the fingers of one hand.

Isana lifted her fingers to the front of her dress, touching them thoughtfully to the hidden ring on its chain. Serai was obviously more formidable than she appeared. "Do you fly often?" Isana asked her.

"From time to time," Serai replied. "The journey may take until this time tomorrow, possibly longer. We'll not stop until

Rolf's men need to change places in the harness, Steadholder, and that may be long after dark. You should rest."

"Do I look ill?" Isana asked.

"Amara told me of your encounter this morning," Serai replied. Her expression never changed, and the flicker of her needle did not slow, but Isana felt a faint current of trepidation in the courtesan's bearing. "It would be enough to exhaust anyone. You're safe now."

Isana regarded Serai quietly for a moment, and asked, "Am I?"

"As safe here as in your own home," Serai assured her, a dry edge lurking beneath the lightly given words. "I'll watch, and wake you if anything happens."

Serai's voice, presence, and manner rang with the subtle tone of truth, something few honest folk could ever hide successfully, and Isana felt herself relax, at least for a moment. The woman meant to protect her—of that much, at least, she felt certain. And Serai was right. The shock and startled fear on the face of the young man Isana had killed still tainted her every thought. She leaned her head back and closed her eyes.

She didn't expect to be able to sleep, but when she opened her eyes again, there was pale light flowing into the litter from the opposite windows, and her neck and shoulders felt stiff and uncomfortable. She had to blink her eyes for several moments to clear the unexpected sleep from them.

"Ah," Serai said. "Good morning, Steadholder."

"Morning?" Isana said. She fought back a yawn and sat up. There was a rolled cloak behind her head and a heavy, soft blanket covering her. "Did I sleep?"

"Most deeply," Serai confirmed. "You wouldn't stir when we stopped last night, and Rolf was a dear and loaned you his cloak when we got moving again."

"I'm sorry," Isana said. "Surely you rested as well?"

"Not just yet," the courtesan said. "I've been here, as I said I would—but for a few necessary moments, and Rolf sat here with you until I returned."

"I'm sorry," Isana repeated, embarrassed. She offered the cloak to Serai. "Here, please. You should rest."

"And leave you without conversation?" Serai said. "What kind of traveling companion would I be if I did such a thing."

She gave Isana a small smile. "I've a touch of metalcrafting in my family's blood. I can go for a few days without."

"That doesn't mean it's good for you," Isana said.

"I must confess that as a rule, things which may not be good for me seem to hold an unwholesome attraction," she said. "And in any case, we should be arriving in the capital within the hour."

"But I thought you said it would take at least a full day."

Serai frowned, staring out the window. The blue-white light of dawn, pure and clear, made her skin glow, and her dark eyes seemed all the deeper. "It should have. Rolf said that we were fortunate to be flying with an unusually swift wind at our backs. I've never experienced such a thing before, between any of the cities, much less flying from the far provinces."

Isana collected her thoughts for a moment. This development changed things. She had less than an hour to prepare herself for the capital, and it might be the only chance she had to speak with Serai in relative privacy. There was little time to discover whatever she could from the woman through conversation—which meant that there was little point to subtlety.

Isana took a breath and addressed the courtesan. "Do you travel this way often?"

"Several times each season. My master finds all sorts of reasons to send me to visit other cities."

"Master. You mean Gaius," Isana said.

Serai's lips pursed thoughtfully. "I am a loyal subject of the Crown, of course," she said. "But my owner is the Lord Forcius Rufus. He is the cousin to the High Lord of Forcia, and holds estates at the northern end of the Vale."

"You live in the Amaranth Vale itself?" Isana asked.

"At the moment, yes," Serai replied. "I'll be missing the orchards in bloom, which is a pity. It makes the whole Vale smell like paradise. Have you seen it?"

Isana shook her head. "Is it as beautiful as everyone says?"

Serai nodded and sighed. "If not more so. As much as I love to travel, I find that I miss my home there. Still, I suppose that I am glad to travel and even more glad to return. Perhaps I am doubly fortunate."

"It sounds like a lovely place." Isana folded her hands in her lap. "And an even lovelier conversational diversion."

Serai looked back to Isana, smiling. "Does it?"

"You are one of the Cursors, then?"

"Darling, I'm merely a glorified pleasure slave, doing Gaius a favor on behalf of her master. And even if I was free, I don't think I'd have the temperament for the profession. All the heroism and duty and so on. Exhausting."

Isana arched an eyebrow. "I suppose a spy for the Crown would be largely useless if she walked around announcing the fact."

Serai smiled. "That seems a reasonable statement, darling."

Isana nodded, her crafting senses once more all but blind to Serai's presence. It was an acutely frustrating sensation. Her companion was one of the First Lord's followers—of that much she was certain. Why else would the Cursors have chosen her to accompany Isana? That meant that she couldn't afford to let down her guard. Serai's duty would be to protect Gaius's interests, and not Isana's.

But at the same time, Isana wasn't so foolish as to think that she did not need an escort in Alera Imperia, capital of all the Realm. She had never been to one of the great cities that formed the heart of Aleran society. She knew that Wintersend in the capital was a time rife with the plotting of various political and economic factions. She had heard tales of such groups indulging in blackmail, extortion, murder, and worse, and her life in the countryside had not prepared her to deal with such matters.

Isana was fully aware that by coming to the capital, she was certain to face deadly peril. Gaius's enemies would strike at her not because of anything she had done, but because of what she represented. Isana was a symbol of the support for the First Lord. Gaius's enemies had already tried to destroy that symbol once. They would certainly do so again.

A sickly, wrenching sensation rippled through Isana's stomach.

Because Tavi was a symbol, too.

Isana would need an escort to navigate the treacherous waters of the capital, and Serai was her only guide and most vital ally. If she was to succeed in protecting Tavi from whatever deadly plots were afoot, Isana needed to secure the courtesan's support and cooperation in any way that she could. Flashes of sincerity were not enough.

"Serai," Isana said. "Do you have family?"

The little courtesan's face and bearing became abruptly opaque. "No, darling."

Isana felt nothing from Rill, but her eyes widened with sudden intuition. "You mean, not anymore."

Serai arched a brow, her expression surprised, but lifted her chin without looking away. "Not anymore."

"What happened?" Isana asked gently.

Serai was silent for a time, then said, "Our steadholt was blighted one year. Blighted badly. The blight took the lives of my husband and my daughter. She'd been born only three weeks before. My brother and my parents died as well. And the other holders. Of them all, I survived, but there will be no more family for me."

Serai looked away and out the window. She moved one hand to rest low on her belly, and her sudden pang of raw anguish struck Isana like a wave of scalding water.

"I'm sorry," she said to the courtesan. She shook her head. "I would never have thought you a holder."

Serai smiled without looking back at Isana, her eyes clear. "I entered into bondage after I recovered. To pay for decent arrangements for them. It was there that I became a"—she left a slight but deliberate pause—"courtesan. Many are found, just as I was."

"I'm so sorry," Isana said. "To make you remember the pain."

"You needn't be, darling. It was long ago."

"You don't look it."

"My family had—has a touch of watercraft in it as well," Serai said, her voice brightening with cheer that Isana knew must be forced. "Nowhere near as strong as you, Steadholder, but I can manage the occasional wrinkle."

The litter lurched, and Isana felt her head spin a little. She looked desperately out the window, but saw only thick, white fog. One of her feet lifted slightly from the floor, and fear froze her breath in her throat.

"It's all right," Serai said, and put a hand on Isana's knee. "We're descending. We're almost there. We'll land in moments."

Isana covered Serai's hand with her own. The courtesan's fingers felt fever-warm. Isana's hand must have been like ice. "There's not much time."

"What do you mean?"

Isana forced her eyes from the dizzying view out the window and to the other woman's. "Serai," she said, her voice shaking, "if you could have them back, would you?"

Serai's eyes widened in shock that quickly became a cool, agate-hard anger. "What sort of question is that, darling?" she replied, her tone unchanged. "Of course I would."

Isana covered Serai's hand with both of hers, and leaned forward, staring directly into her eyes. "That's why I'm coming to Festival. My family is in danger. I don't care about Gaius. I don't care about what man sits on the throne. I don't care about politics or plots or power. I only care that the child I raised is in danger, my brother may die if I cannot send him aid. They are all that I have in the world."

Serai tilted her head to one side in a silent question.

Isana felt her voice waver as she spoke. "Help me."

Serai straightened slowly, comprehension dawning in her eyes.

Isana squeezed her hand. "*Help me.*"

Serai's presence became acutely pained, but her face and her eyes remained calm. "Help you. At the expense of my duty to my master?"

"If need be," Isana said. "I'll do anything necessary to help them. But I don't know if I can do it alone. Please, Serai. They are my family."

"I am sorry, Steadholder, that your kin are in danger. But the servants of the Crown are the only family I know. I will do my duty."

"How can you say that?" Isana asked. "How can you be that indifferent?"

"I am not indifferent," Serai said. "I know what is at stake— better than anyone. Were it up to me, I would ignore the greater concerns of the Realm to save the lives of your family."

Silvery truth resounded in that whisper, but so did resolution. Another agonized stab of fear for her kin wrenched at Isana's chest. She bowed her head and closed her eyes, trying to sort through the courtesan's complex but shrouded tangle of emotion. "I don't understand."

"If it was up to me, I would help you. But it is not up to me," Serai replied. Her voice was both compassionate and unyielding. "I have sworn myself to the service of the Realm. The world of Carna is a cold, cruel place, lady. It is filled with danger and enemies to our people. The Realm is what keeps them safe."

Sudden and bitter scorn filled her throat with flame. Isana let out a breath, not quite a derisive laugh. "The irony. That someone the Realm failed to keep safe would be willing to sacrifice other families in service to it."

Serai withdrew her hands from Isana's, cold, controlled anger now in her voice and presence. "Without the Realm to protect them, there will be no families."

"Without families," Isana spat, "there is nothing for the Realm to protect. How can you say that when you may have the power to help them?"

Serai's bearing and tone remained aloof and unreadable. "As a woman using her own power to dredge up the most painful moment of my life in an attempt to manipulate me to her will, Isana, I hardly think you are in a position to criticize."

Isana clenched her hands in frustration. "I only ask you to help me protect my family."

"At the expense of my loyalty," Serai said, voice steady. "It isn't because I don't want to help you, Steadholder. Or your kin. But there are many women in the Realm with families. And if I could save ten thousand of them by sacrificing yours, I would do so. It wouldn't be right. But it would be necessary. And it is my duty. I have taken an oath as a servant to the Realm, and I will not be foresworn."

Isana looked out the window. "Enough. I understand." After a moment, she added, "And you're right. I apologize to you, lady. I shouldn't have tried to use the pain of your loss against you."

"Perhaps," Serai said, her tone matter-of-fact. "Or perhaps not. I have buried a family, Steadholder. It hurts more than I could ever have imagined. I might not be particular, either, were I trying to protect them."

"I'm terrified. What if I can't do it alone?"

Serai suddenly smiled. "That won't be an issue, darling. Hear me." She leaned forward, eyes intent. "I will do my duty to my master. But I will die myself before I allow you or yours to be harmed. That is my oath to you."

Sincerity rang in the words, a clear and silver tone of truth that not even Serai's composure could wholly contain.

"You do not have to make such an oath," Isana said.

"No," Serai said. "I do not. But it would make no difference in any case. I could not live with myself if I allowed it to happen to another family. Nor would I wish to." She shook her head. "I know it isn't what you wanted to hear, but I can do nothing more. Please believe that I will do nothing less."

"I believe you," Isana said quietly. "Thank you."

Serai nodded, her expression serene, her presence once more quiet and contained.

"Ladies," called a voice from outside the litter. One of their escorting Knights appeared at the window, a young man with sharp features and dark, intense eyes. He was unshaven, and looked beaten with weariness. "The currents can be unpredictable as we descend. There are a pair of restraining belts you should use."

Serai looked up with a sudden smile. "Yes, Rolf. I seem to remember having this conversation before. Where is the subtribune?"

The Knight grinned and bowed his head. Then he leaned closer, and whispered, "Sleeping on the roof. He got tired in the night. All but fell out of the sky."

"How humiliating to the great racing champion should he arrive in such a condition. Didn't he tell you to wake him before you fly into the capital?" Serai asked.

"It's odd," Rolf said. "I can't remember. I'm just that tired." He flicked a contemptuous glance up at the roof of the litter, then said, "If you please, ladies, strap in. Just a moment more."

Serai showed Isana how to secure herself with a pair of heavy woven belts that laced together, and a moment later the litter began to jostle, sway, and shake. It was a terrible sensation, but Isana closed her eyes and held on to the belts with both hands. There was a sudden, bone-rattling thud, and Isana realized that they were safely on the ground.

Serai let out a happy sigh and folded her sewing into a small cloth bag. They unfastened the belts and emerged from the litter into blinding golden sunlight.

Isana stared around her at Alera Imperia, heart of all the Realm.

They stood upon a platform of white marble, larger than the whole walled enclosure of Isanaholt. The wind was almost violent, and Isana had to shield her eyes against it. All around her, other litters were descending, the largest of them borne by a dozen windcrafters. The Knights Aeris were clad in the brilliant livery of the High Lords of each city, and men and women dressed in fantastically rich clothing, sparkling with jewels and embroidered with gold and silver emerged from them, their hair and garments untouched by the whirling winds.

Several men in brown tunics rushed around the litters as they touched down, where they immediately began picking up the litters with furycrafted strength and carrying them to a broad staircase leading down from the platform, so that others could land. Other men in brown tunics arrived, bearing food and drink for the newly arrived Knights, many of whom, including Rolf and the other Knights who had borne Isana and Serai, were sitting on the platform in sheer exhaustion.

"Isana," Serai called through the heavy winds. She stood on tiptoe to speak to the bent ear of another man in a brown tunic, who nodded and accepted a few gleaming coins from the courtesan with a polite bow. Serai beckoned. "Isana, come with me. It's this way."

"But my bag," Isana called back.

Serai approached and leaned up to half shout, "It will be delivered to the house. We need to get off the platform before someone lands on—*Isana*."

Serai suddenly drove herself hard against Isana's side. Utterly surprised, Isana fell—and so saw a short, heavy dagger as it swept past where her head had been an instant before.

There was a cracking sound, loud even over the wind's constant roar. Heads whipped around toward them. The tumbling dagger's hilt had struck one side of the litter with such force that it shattered the lacquered wood, shooting it through with splits and cracks.

Serai looked around wildly and pointed at the back of another man in a brown tunic, disappearing down the stairs. "Rolf!"

The Knight looked up from where he sat, exhausted, startled for a second, then rose unsteadily to his feet.

"Crows and bloody furies!" thundered a furious voice from atop the litter. Horatio sat up atop it, slipped, and fell from the litter's roof to the ground, screaming oaths at the top of his lungs.

Rolf hurried to the top of the stairs, breathing hard after only a few steps, and stared down them for a moment. He looked back at Serai and shook his head, his expression frustrated.

"I'll have your rank for this!" Horatio bellowed, struggling to his feet. All around them, Citizens of the Realm were pointing at the sleep-muddled subtribune, smiling and laughing. Few, if any, had realized that someone had just attempted bloody murder.

Serai's face was pale, and Isana could both see and feel the terror in her. She rose to her feet, offering Isana her hand. "Are you all right?"

"Yes," Isana said. She stumbled and lost her balance in the gale winds, nearly knocking down a tall woman in a red dress and black cloak. "Excuse me, lady. Serai, who was that?"

"I don't know," Serai said. Her hands were shaking, her dark eyes wide. "I saw stains on his tunic. I didn't realize until the last moment that they were blood."

"What?"

"I'll explain it later. Stay close."

"What do we do?"

The courtesan's eyes narrowed, fear replaced by hard defiance. "We hurry, Steadholder," Serai said. "Keep your eyes open and come with me."

"Very well," snapped Maestro Gallus in his querulous tenor. "Time is up."

Tavi's head snapped up from the surface of the table, and he blinked blearily around the lecture chamber. Nearly two hundred other academs sat in crowded rows at low tables, seated on the floor and writing furiously on long sheets of paper.

"Time," Gallus called again, an edge of anger in his voice. "Stop writing. If you haven't finished your proofs by now, another breath's worth of scribbling won't help you. Papers to the left."

Tavi rubbed at his mouth, blotting the drool from his lip with the sleeve of his grey tunic. The last few inches of his page remained conspicuously blank. He waited for the stack of papers to reach him, added his to it, and passed it to Ehren. "How long was I out?" he muttered.

"The last two," Ehren replied, straightening the pile with a brisk motion of his skinny arms before passing it on.

"You think I passed?" Tavi asked. His mouth felt gummy, and he ached with weariness.

"I think you should have slept last night," Ehren said primly. "You idiot. Did you want to fail?"

"Wasn't my idea," Tavi mumbled. He and Ehren stood and began shuffling out of the stuffy lecture chamber along with all the other students. "Believe me. Do you think I passed?"

Ehren sighed, and rubbed at his eyes. "Probably. No one but me and maybe you would have gotten the last two anyway."

"Good," Tavi said. "I guess."

"Calculations study is important," Ehren said. "In the greater sense, it's essential to the survival of the Realm. There are all sorts of things that make it absolutely necessary."

Tavi let irony creep into his tone. "Maybe I'm just tired. But calculating the duration of a merchant ship's voyage or tracking the taxation payments of outlying provinces seems sort of trivial to me at the moment."

Ehren stared at him for a moment, his expression shocked, as if Tavi had just suggested that they should bake babies into pies for lunch. Then said, "You're joking. You *are* joking, aren't you Tavi?"

Tavi sighed.

Outside the classroom, students burst into conversation, complaints, laughter, and the occasional song, and filed down the nearest walkway toward the main courtyard in a living river of grey robes and weary minds. Tavi stretched out the moment he got into the open air. "It gets too hot in there after a long test," he told Ehren. "The air gets all squishy."

"It's called humidity, Tavi," Ehren said.

"I haven't slept in almost two days. It's squishy."

Gaelle was waiting at the archway to the courtyard, standing up on tiptoe in a useless effort to peer over the crowd until she spotted Tavi and Ehren. The plain girl's face lit up when she saw them, and she came rushing over, muttering a string of apologies as she swam against the grey tide. "Ehren, Tavi. How bad was it?"

Tavi made a sound halfway between a grunt and a groan.

Ehren rolled his eyes and told Gaelle, "About what I thought it would be. You should be fine." He frowned and looked around. "Where's Max?"

"I don't know," Gaelle said, her eyes looking around with concern. "I haven't seen him. Tavi, have you?"

Tavi hesitated for a moment. He didn't want to lie to his friends, but there was too much at stake. Not only did he have to lie, but he had to do it well.

"What?" he asked blearily, to cover the pause.

"Have you seen Max?" Gaelle repeated, her voice growing exasperated.

"Oh. Last night he said something about a young widow," Tavi said, waving a hand vaguely.

"The night before an *exam*?" Ehren sputtered. "That's just . . . it's so wrong that . . . I think maybe I should lie down for a moment."

"You should, too, Tavi," Gaelle said. "You look like you're about to fall asleep on your feet."

"He did during the test," Ehren confirmed.

"Tavi," Gaelle said. "Go to bed."

Tavi rubbed at an eye. "I wish I could. But I couldn't finish all the letter-running before the test started. One more, then I can get some sleep."

"Up all night, then taking a test, and he's still got you running letters?" Gaelle demanded. "That's cruel."

"What's cruel?" Ehren asked.

Tavi started to answer, then walked straight into another student's back. Tavi stumbled backward, jolted from the impact. The other student fell, shoved himself up with a curse, and rounded on Tavi.

It was Brencis. The arrogant young lord's dark hair was mussed and stringy after the long exam. The hulking Renzo hovered behind him and a little bit to one side, and Varien stood to Brencis's left, eyes glittering with anticipation and malice.

"The freak," Brencis said in a flat voice. "The little scribe. Oh, and their sow. I should leave you all neck deep in a cesspool."

Varien said, "I should be pleased to help you with that, my lord."

Tavi tensed himself. Brencis wouldn't forget how Max had humiliated him the previous morning. And since there was little he could do to take vengeance on Max, he would have to find another target for his outrage. Like Tavi.

Brencis leaned down close to Tavi and sneered. "Count yourself lucky, freak, that I have more important matters today."

He turned around and swept away without looking back. Varien blinked for a moment, then followed. Renzo did the same, though his placid expression never changed.

"Huh," Tavi said.

"Interesting," Gaelle mused.

"Well. I wasn't expecting *that*," Ehren said. "What do you suppose is wrong with Brencis?"

"Perhaps he's finally growing up," Gaelle said.

Tavi exchanged a skeptical look with Ehren.

Gaelle sighed. "Yes, well. It could happen, you know. Someday."

"While we're all holding our breath," Tavi said, "I'm going to get this last letter delivered and get some sleep."

"Good," Gaelle said. "Who are you taking it to?"

"Uh." Tavi rummaged in his pockets until he found the envelope and glanced at the name on it. "Oh, bloody crows," he swore with a sigh. "I'll catch up to you later." He waved at his friends as he broke into a weary jog and headed for Ambassador Varg's quarters.

It wasn't a long way up to the Citadel, but Tavi's tired legs ached, and it seemed to take forever to reach the Black Hall— a long corridor of dark, rough-quarried stone very different from the rest of the First Lord's marble stronghold. The entrance to the hall had an actual gate upon it, bars of dark steel as thick and hard as the portcullis to any stronghold. Outside the gate stood a pair of soldiers from the Royal Guard in red and blue—younger members, Tavi noted, in full arms and armor as usual. They stood facing the gate.

On the other side of the gate, a single candle cast just enough light to show Tavi a pair of Canim crouched on their haunches. Half-covered in their round capes, Tavi could see little of them beyond the sharper angles of their armor at the shoulders and elbows, the gleam of metal upon the hilts of their swords and on the tips of their spears. The shape of their heads was half-hidden in their hoods, but their wolfish muzzles showed, and their teeth, and the faint red-fire gleam of their inhuman eyes. Though they squatted on the floor, their stance was somehow every bit as rigid, alert, and prepared as the Aleran guards facing them.

Tavi approached the gate. The scent of the Canim embassy surrounded him as he did—musky, subtle, and thick, somehow reminding him of both the smithy at his old steadholt and the den of a direwolf.

"Guard," Tavi said. "I bear a letter for His Excellency, Ambassador Varg."

One of the Alerans glanced over his shoulder and waved him past. Tavi approached the gate. On the other side, a leather basket sat in its usual place on the rough floor, an arm's length away from the bars, and Tavi leaned through to drop the letter into the basket. In his mind, he had already completed his task and was looking forward, finally, to sleeping.

He barely saw the Cane nearest him move.

The inhuman guard slid forward with a sudden, sinuous grace, and a long arm flashed out to snare Tavi's wrist. His heart lurched with a sudden apprehension too vague and exhausted to be proper panic. He could have swept his arm in a circle toward the Cane's thumb, to break the grip and draw back, but doing so would surely have caused him to lash open his own arm on the Cane's claws. There was no chance he could have pulled away from the guard by main force.

All of that flashed through his mind in the space of a heartbeat. Behind him, he heard the sharp intake of breath from the two Aleran guards and the sound of steel hissing against leather as they drew swords.

Tavi left his arm where it was in the Cane's grip, and raised his free hand to the guards. "Wait," he said, voice quiet. Then he looked up—a great deal up—to fix the Cane guard with a flat stare. "What do you want, Guard?" Tavi demanded, his tone impatient, peremptory.

The Cane regarded him with unreadable, feral eyes and released his wrist in a slow, deliberate motion that trailed the tips of the Cane's claws harmlessly against Tavi's skin. "His Excellency," the Cane growled, "requests the messenger to deliver the letter directly to his hands."

"Stand away from him, dog," snarled the Aleran guard.

The Cane looked up and bared its yellow fangs in a silent snarl.

"It's all right, *legionare*," Tavi said quietly. "It's a perfectly reasonable request. It is the Ambassador's right to receive missives directly from the First Lord should he wish."

Both the Canim started letting out low, stuttering growls. The one who had seized Tavi's arm opened the gate. Tavi stared for a moment at how easily the enormous Cane opened the massive steel portal. Then he swallowed, took up the single candle, clutched the envelope, and entered the Black Hall.

The Cane guard paced Tavi, slightly behind him. Tavi paused and slowed his steps until he could see the Cane in the corner of one eye. The guard prowled, each step sinuous and relaxed, regarding Tavi with what seemed to be open curiosity as they walked to the end of the Black Hall. They passed several open, irregular doorways on the way, but the shadows filling them were too thick to allow Tavi to see what lay beyond.

At the end of the hall was the only door Tavi had seen, made of some thick, heavy wood of some dark color that shone with deep red and heavy purple highlights in the light of Tavi's candle.

Tavi's guard strode past him in those too-long stalking steps of a grown Cane, and drew its claws slowly down the dark wood. Whatever it was, the wood was hard. The Cane's heavy claws scraped loudly, but no indentation or mark appeared on the wood.

There was a snarl from the room beyond, a sound that sent a quick chill racing down Tavi's spine. The guard replied with a similar sound, though higher in pitch. There was a brief silence, then a chuckling growl, and Varg's voice rumbled, "Send him in."

The guard opened the door and stalked away without giving Tavi a second glance. The boy swallowed, took a deep breath, and strode into the room.

As he crossed the threshold, a draft struck his candle and snuffed it out.

Tavi stood in utter darkness. There were a pair of low growls this time, one coming from either side of him, and Tavi became acutely aware of how entirely vulnerable he was, and how strongly the chamber smelled of musk and meat—the scent of predators.

It took his eyes a long moment to adjust, but he began to make out details of deep, scarlet light and black shadow. There was a bed of barely glowing coals in a shallow depression in the center of the floor, and some kind of heavy pads made from material he could not identify lay around the coals. The room was shaped like an overturned bowl, the walls curling up to a ceiling that was not much higher than Tavi could have reached with his hands. Several feet back in the shadows, there were what Tavi took to be two more guards, but upon second glance he recognized them as arming dummies—though taller and broader than the stands that typically bore the armor of off-duty *legionares*. One of the dummies bore the odd outline of a suit of Canish armor, but the other stood empty.

Against the back wall of the room, Tavi heard the trickle of water, and could barely see the shimmer of the dim red light against a pool, its surface broken by small and regular ripples.

On instinct, Tavi turned and faced almost directly behind him.

"Ambassador," he said in a respectful tone. "I've a message for you, sir."

Another low growl rippled through the room, oddly twisted by the shape of the walls, or by the composition of the stone, bouncing about as though from several sources at once. There was a gleam of red eyes two feet above Tavi's own, then Varg slid forward out of the darkness into the bloody light.

"Good," said the Cane, still dressed in cloak and armor. "The controlled use of instinct. Too often your kind are either ruled by them or pay them no mind."

Tavi had no idea how to respond to that, other than to offer Varg the envelope. "Thank you, Your Excellency."

Varg took the envelope and opened it with a single, negligent swipe of a claw that cut the paper with barely a whisper of sound. It flicked the missive inside open and scanned over it, growling again. "So. I am to be ignored."

Tavi regarded it with a blank expression. "I only carry the messages, sir."

"Do you?" said Varg. "Let it be on your own heads, then."

"You see, my lord," hissed a higher-pitched growling voice from the doorway. "They have no respect for you or for our people. We should be rid of this place and return to the Blood Lands."

Tavi and Varg both turned to face the doorway, where a Cane Tavi didn't recognize crouched. It wore no armor, but was draped in long robes of deep scarlet. Its pawlike hands were far thinner and more spidery than Varg's, and its reddish fur looked thin and unhealthy. The muzzle, too, was narrow and pointed, and its tongue lolled out to one side, flickering nervously.

"Sarl," Varg growled. "I did not send for you."

The second Cane drew its hood back from its head and tilted it to one side in an exaggerated gesture that Tavi suddenly understood. The Cane was baring its throat to Varg—a gesture of deference or respect, evidently.

"Apologies, mighty lord," Sarl said. "But I came to report to you that word has come, and that the change of guard would arrive in two days' time."

Tavi pursed his lips. He had never heard a Cane speak Aleran, except for Varg. He could not imagine that Sarl had addressed its superior in language Tavi could understand by mere chance.

"Very good, Sarl," Varg growled. "Out."

"As you wish, lord," Sarl replied, baring its throat again, bunching low. The Cane backed away, scraping, and hurried back into the corridor.

"My secretary," Varg said. Tavi could only guess, but he thought the Ambassador's growling tone was somewhere between pensive and amused. "He attends to matters he thinks beneath my notice."

"I am familiar with the concept," Tavi answered.

Varg's teeth showed as its muzzle lolled open. "Yes. You would be. That is all, cub."

Tavi began to bow, but then a thought struck him. The gesture might not be the same from the Cane's point of view. What was a motion of respect to Alerans might be something very different in a society whose members might fight to tear out one another's throats with their teeth, like wolves. A wolf who crouched and ducked its chin in closer to its body was preparing to fight. Certainly, Varg was aware of the difference in gestures, as it obviously didn't seem to regard bows as a challenge to combat, but it still seemed, to Tavi, to be impolite to make the gesture the Ambassador's instincts surely twinged at whenever it saw.

Instead, Tavi tilted his head a bit to one side, mimicking the gesture Varg himself had made earlier, and said, "Then I take my leave, Excellency."

He started to walk past Varg, but the Cane suddenly put out a heavy paw-hand and blocked Tavi's way.

Tavi swallowed and glanced up at the Cane. He met the Ambassador's eyes for a moment.

Varg regarded him, fangs gleaming, and said, "Light your candle at my fire before you go. Your night eyes are weak. I'll not have you stumbling in my corridor and bawling like a puppy."

Tavi exhaled slowly and tilted his head again. "Yes, sir."

Varg shifted its shoulders, an odd motion, and prowled back to the pool.

Tavi went to the coals and lit his candle against them, this time shielding the flame with his hand. He watched as the Cane crouched, as easy on all fours as upright, and drank directly from the pool. But he dared not simply stare, as fascinating as it might be. Tavi turned and hurried out.

Just before he crossed the threshold again, Varg growled, "Aleran."

Tavi paused.

"I have rats."

Tavi blinked. "Sir?"

"Rats," Varg growled. It turned its head to look over one armored shoulder. Tavi could see little more than the gleam of fangs and red eyes. "I hear them at night. There are rats in my walls."

Tavi frowned. "Oh."

"Out," said Varg.

Tavi hurried back into the hallway and started retreating back toward the Citadel proper. He walked slowly, mulling over the Ambassador's words. Clearly, it wasn't simply speaking about a rat problem. The rodents could be a nuisance, of course, but surely one the Cane could deal with. Even more puzzling was the reference to walls. The walls of the Canim enclosure in the Black Hall were made of stone. Rats were industrious tunnelers and gnawers, but they could not bore through solid rock.

Varg struck Tavi as the sort of being who did not spend his words idly. Tavi had already sized up the Ambassador as the kind of warrior who would fight with simple, deadly efficiency. It seemed reasonable to assume that given any choice in the matter, Varg would waste no more effort on words than on bloodshed.

Tavi's eyes fell to the flame on his candle. Then to the walls. He took a pair of quick steps to stand beside the wall nearest him and lowered his hand.

In the still air of the hallway, his candle flickered and leaned, very slightly.

His heart started pounding faster, and Tavi followed the direction of the flame, moving slowly down the wall. In only a moment, he found the source of the small draft—a tiny opening in the wall, one he had not seen before. He placed the heel of his hand against it and pushed.

A section of the stone wall slid open soundlessly, previously unseen seams splitting into visibility. Tavi held up the candle. Just beyond the hidden passageway, stairs led down into the stone.

The Canim had a passageway into the Deeps.

Tavi was still too far from the entrance to the Black Hall to see its guards clearly, and he could only hope that they could not see him clearly, either. Shielding the light of the candle in his hand once more, he slipped onto the stairs and went down them as silently as he possibly could.

Voices from ahead made him stop, listening.

The first speaker was Canim—Sarl, Tavi was sure of it. He recognized the cringing tone to its snarling voice. "And I tell you that all is in readiness. There is nothing to fear."

"Talk is cheap, Cane," said a human voice, so quiet that Tavi could hardly hear it. "Show me."

"That was not a part of our agreement," the Cane said. There was a shivering, flapping sound, like a dog shaking its chops. "You must believe my words."

"Suppose I don't?" asked the other.

"It is too late to change your mind now," said Sarl, a nasty slur to the words. "Let us not discuss what cannot—" The Cane's words cut off suddenly.

"What is it?" asked the second voice.

"A scent," Sarl said, a hungry little whine coloring his tone. "Someone near."

Tavi's heart raced, and he fled up the stairs as quietly as his weary legs could manage. Once in the hall, he all but sprinted down it, back toward the Citadel. As he approached, the Canim guards rose, growling, eyes intent upon him.

"His Excellency dismissed me," Tavi panted.

The guards traded a look, then one of them opened the gate. No sooner had Tavi fled out it and heard it shut behind him than the shadows stirred, and Sarl appeared in the Black Hall, hurrying along in a hunched shuffle. Its pointed ears went flat to its skull when he spied Tavi, and the Cane crouched a little, lips lifting away from the fangs on one side of its muzzle.

Tavi stared back at the Cane. He needed no intuition to understand the flash of raw, hungry hatred he saw in the Canim secretary's eyes.

Sarl spun and shuffled back into the shadows, motions purposeful. Tavi fled, fear making his legs tremble, to put as much distance as possible between himself and the residents of the Black Hall.

CHAPTER 15

Amara nudged her horse up to walk beside Bernard's in the morning sunlight, and murmured, "Something's wrong."

Bernard frowned and glanced at her. They were riding at the head of the column of *legionares* from Garrison. Two dozen local holders, veterans of the Legions themselves, rode armed and armored as auxiliary cavalry troops, and two dozen more bore the great hunting bows common to the holders of the region and marched in file behind the *legionares*. Behind them rumbled a pair of heavy gargant-drawn carts, followed by Doroga on his massive black gargant, and the column's rear guard, most of the Knights Bernard had under his command, mounted and grim.

Bernard himself had donned his helmet in addition to his mail, and carried his strung bow across his saddle in one hand, an arrow already on the string. "You noticed it, then."

Amara swallowed and nodded. "There are no deer."

Bernard nodded, a barely perceptible gesture. His lips scarcely moved when he spoke. "This time of year, the column should be scaring them out every few hundred yards."

"What does it mean?"

Bernard's shoulders shifted in a slight shrug. "Ordinarily, I'd think it meant that another body of troops had already driven them out, and that they may be preparing a surprise attack."

"And now?" Amara asked.

His lips lifted up away from his canines. "I think these creatures may already have driven them out, and that they may be preparing a surprise attack."

Amara licked her lips, glancing at the rolling woodlands around them. "What do we do?"

"Relax. Trust our scouts," Bernard said. "Keep an eye out. There might be a number of other explanations for some missing deer."

"Such as?"

"Aric's holders may have slaughtered all they could shoot quickly in preparation for our arrival, to help feed the troops, for one. I've had to put down a number of herdbane who remained in the valley after the battle. One of those could have killed the local does during birthing over the winter. They do that sometimes."

"What if that hasn't happened?" Amara asked.

"Then be ready to take to the air," Bernard said.

"I've been ready to do that since before we left the steadholt," she replied, her voice wry. "I'm not much one for feeling hunted."

Bernard smiled, and shared the warmth of it with her, meeting her eyes. "I'll not be hunted in my own home, dear Countess. And I'll not suffer my guests to be hunted, either." He gestured back toward the column with a tilt of his head. "Patience. Faith. Alera's Legions have seen her through a thousand years in a world where enemies of all sorts have tried to destroy her. They will see us through this, too."

Amara sighed. "I'm sorry, Bernard. But I've seen too many threats to Alera that a Legion could do precisely nothing about. How much farther to Aricholt?"

"We'll be there before midday," Bernard told her.

"You'll want to see the camp Aric told us about, I take it?"

"Naturally," Bernard said. "Before nightfall."

"Why not let your Knights Aeris handle it?"

"Because in my experience, wind rider, Knights Aeris miss a very great deal of what happens underneath branch and bough since they're soaring several dozen yards above them." He smiled again. "Besides, what fun would that be?"

Amara raised her eyebrows. "You're enjoying this," she accused.

Bernard's eyes returned to their casual, careful scan of the woods around them, and he shrugged. "It was a long winter. And I haven't been out in the field for more than a few hours at a time since I became Count Calderon. I hadn't realized how much I missed it."

"Madman," Amara said.

"Oh come now," Bernard said. "You have to admit, it's exciting. A mysterious, dangerous new creature. A possible threat to the Realm. The chance to challenge it, defeat it."

"Dear furies." Amara sighed. "You're worse than a boy."

Bernard laughed, and there was both joy and something unpleasant in it. The corded muscles in his neck tightened and relaxed with the horse's movements, and his broad hands held the great bow steady. Amara was again struck by the sheer size of the man, and well remembered the deadly skill and power in him. There was something wolfish in his manner, something that suggested that his quiet smile was only a mask. That something far more grim, and far more ready to taste blood, lay just beneath.

"Amara," he rumbled. "Something threatens my home. After what happened before, I know what is at stake. And I wouldn't want anyone else to be in charge of dealing with that threat." His hazel green eyes reflected bark and newly sprouted leaves in equal measure, dangerous and bright. "I am a hunter. I will hunt this creature down and hold it. And when the First Lord sends help enough, I will destroy it."

The words were calm, matter-of-fact, barely laced with that lurking ferocity, and Amara found herself feeling irrationally comforted by it. Her shoulders loosened a little, and the trembling that had been threatening her hands receded.

"Besides," Bernard drawled, "it's a lovely morning for a ride in the country with a pretty girl. Why not enjoy it?"

Amara rolled her eyes and began to smile, but Serai's words echoed quietly in her heart.

Of course you'll have to leave him.

She drew in a breath, forced her expression into a neutral mask, and said, "I think it's better for all of us if I remove any potential distraction, Your Excellency. Your mind should be upon your duty."

Bernard blinked and looked at her with open surprise on his face. "Amara?"

"If you will excuse me, Count," she said in a polite voice, and nudged her horse out of line, letting him nibble at new grass while she waited for the column to pass her. She felt Bernard's eyes on her for a moment, but she did not acknowledge him.

She waited until the carts had passed, then nudged her horse to pace alongside Doroga's giant gargant. The horse refused to move within twenty feet of the beast, despite Amara's best efforts.

"Doroga," she called up to the Marat chieftain.

"I am," he called back. He watched her struggle with the nervous horse, his expression amused. "You wish something?"

"To speak to you," she said. "I was hoping—" She broke off as a low branch slapped her in the face, a stinging annoyance. "Hoping to ask you some questions."

Doroga rumbled out a rolling laugh. "Your head will get knocked off. Your chieftain Gaius will come take it from my hide." He shifted an arm and tossed a rope of braided leather over the side of the saddle-mat to dangle five feet from the earth. "Come up."

Amara dipped her head to him and passed the reins of her horse off to a nearby holder. She dismounted and jogged over to pace Doroga's gargant. She seized the saddle rope and hauled herself carefully up to its back, where Doroga clamped a big fist down on her forearm and hauled her to a more stable perch.

"So," Doroga rumbled, turning back to face forward. "I see that Bernard ate the wrong soup."

Amara blinked at him. "What?"

Doroga smiled. "When I was young and had just taken my wife as mate, I woke up the next morning, went to my fire, and ate the soup there. I declared it the best soup that any woman ever made for a man. To everyone in the camp."

Amara lifted her eyebrows. "Your wife hadn't made it?"

"She had not," Doroga confirmed. "Hashat did. And after our wedding night, I spent the next seven days sleeping on the ground outside her tent to apologize."

Amara laughed. "I can't imagine you doing that."

"I was very young," Doroga said. "And I very much wanted her to be happy with me again." He glanced over his shoulder. "Just as Bernard wants you to be happy with him."

Amara shook her head. "It isn't anything like that."

"Yes. Because Bernard does not know he ate the wrong soup."

She sighed. "No. Because we aren't married."

Doroga snorted. "You are mates."

"No, not like that."

"You have mated," he said, patient as if he spoke to a small child. "Which makes you mates."

Amara's cheeks flamed. "We . . . did. We have. But we aren't."

Doroga looked back at her, his expression scrunched into a skeptical frown. "You people make everything too complicated. Tell him he ate the wrong soup and have done."

"It's nothing Bernard has done."

"You ate the soup?" Doroga asked.

"No," Amara said, exasperated. "There was no soup. Doroga, Bernard and I . . . we can't be together."

"Oh," Doroga said. He shook his head in a mystified gesture and briefly put his hand over his eyes, mimicking a blindfold. "I see."

"I have obligations to Gaius," Amara said. "So does he."

"This Gaius," Doroga said. "To me he seemed smart."

"Yes."

"Then he should know that no chieftain can command the heart." Doroga nodded. "He gets in the way of that, he will learn that love will be love, and he can do nothing but kill everyone or stand aside. You should learn that, too."

"Learn what?" Amara said.

Doroga thumped a finger against his skull. "Head got nothing to do with the heart. Your heart wants what it wants. Head got to learn that it can only kill the heart or else get out of the way."

"You're saying it would kill my heart to turn away from Bernard?" Amara asked.

"Your heart. His, too." Doroga rolled a shoulder in a shrug. "You get to choose."

"Broken hearts heal in time," Amara said.

Something washed over Doroga's features, making them look heavier, more sad. He lifted a hand to one of his braids, where he had braided his pale hair together with plaits of fine reddish tresses Amara had assumed were dyed. "Sometimes they do. Sometimes they don't." He turned to face her, and said, "Amara, you got something not everyone finds. Those who lose it would gladly die to have it again. Do not cast it away lightly."

Amara rode in silence, swaying in the rhythm of the gargant's long, slow steps.

It was difficult to consider Doroga's words. No one had

ever spoken to her of love in that way before. She had believed in it, of course. Her own mother and father had been very much in love, or so it had seemed to her as a small child. But since she had been taken in by the Cursors, love had been something that existed as a means to an end. Or as the lead player in a sad story about loss and duty. The only love a Cursor could allow herself to feel was for lord and Realm. Amara had known this since before she completed her training. What's more, she had believed it.

But in the past two years, things had changed. She had changed. Bernard had become, not so much important to her as he was natural to her whole being. He was as much a part of her thoughts as breath, food, and sleep. At once present and not present, conspicuous with his absence and filling her with a sense of completion when he was there.

For a man so strong, he was gentle. When his hands, his arms, his mouth were on her, he moved as if afraid she might shatter if held too tightly. Their nights together had been and remained a blaze of passion, for he was a wickedly patient lover who took delight in her responses to him. But more than that, in the quiet hours after he would hold her, both of them weary, content, sleepy. She would lie in his arms and feel no worry, or sadness, or anxiety. She only felt beautiful. And desired. And safe.

Safe. She had to make a sharp effort to keep tears from her eyes. She knew well how little safety truly existed in the world. She knew how much danger threatened the Realm; how a single mistake had the potential to bring it down. She could not allow emotions to cloud her judgment.

No matter how much she might want them to.

She was a Cursor. Sworn vassal of the Crown, a servant of the Realm of Alera, entrusted with its direst secrets, guarding against its most insidious foes. Her duty called for many sacrifices so that others could be safe and free. She had long ago given up the notion of a life of safety. Her duty called her to give up such luxuries as love as well.

Didn't it?

"I will consider your words," she told Doroga quietly.

"Good," he responded.

"But now is not the time for such things," Amara said. Already, her emotions were distracting her. She needed to know more about the dangers they currently faced, and for the moment Doroga was their sole source of information. "We have a more immediate problem."

"We do," Doroga agreed. "The ancient enemy. The Abomination before The One."

Amara looked from the Marat chieftain up to the sun and back, frowning. "Before the One. You mean, before the sun?"

Doroga looked at her blankly.

"The sun," Amara explained, adding a gesture. "That is what you mean by the One, yes?"

"No," Doroga said, laughter in his tone. "The sun is not The One. You do not understand."

"Then tell me," Amara said, exasperated.

"Why?" Doroga asked. The question was a simple one, but there was a weight behind the word that made Amara hesitate and think before answering.

"Because I want to understand you," she said. "I want to know more about you and your people. What makes you what you are. What we share and what we do not."

Doroga pursed his lips. Then he nodded once, to himself, and turned around completely, facing Amara, and crossing his legs. He folded his hands in his lap, then after a moment, began to speak to her in a tone that reminded her of several of her better teachers at the Academy.

"The One is all things. He is the sun, yes. And the sunlight on the trees. And the earth, and the sky. He is the rain in the spring, the ice of winter. He is the fire, the stars at night. He is the thunder and the clouds, the wind and the sea. He is the stag, the wolf, the fox, the gargant." Doroga put a broad hand on his chest. "He is me." Then he reached out and touched Amara's forehead with a finger. "And he is you."

"But I've seen your folk refer to The One, and indicated the sun by gesture."

Doroga waved a hand. "Are you Gaius?"

"Of course not," Amara said.

"But you are his sworn servant, yes? His messenger? His hand? And at times you command in his name?"

"Yes," Amara said.

"So it is with The One," Doroga replied. "From the sun

comes all life, just as from The One. The sun is not The One. But it is how we give him our respect."

Amara shook her head. "I've never heard that of your people."

Doroga nodded. "Few Alerans have. The One is all that is, all that was, all that will be. The worlds, the heavens—all a part of The One. Each of us, a part of The One. Each of us with a purpose and a responsibility."

"What purpose?" she asked.

Doroga smiled. "The gargant to dig. The wolf to hunt. The stag to run. The eagle to fly. We are all made to be for a purpose, Aleran."

Amara arched an eyebrow. "And what is yours?"

"Like all my people," Doroga said. "To learn." He leaned a hand down to rest on the steadily pacing gargant's back, almost unconsciously. "Each of us feels a call to other pieces of The One. We grow nearer to them. Begin to feel what they feel, and know what they know. Walker thinks all of this rusty metal your folk wear stinks, Aleran. But he smells winter apples in the wagons and thinks he should get a barrel. He is glad the spring is coming quickly, because he is tired of hay. He wants to dig down to find the roots of some young trees for his lunch, but he knows that it is important to me that we keep walking. So he walks."

Amara blinked slowly. "You know this about your gargant?"

"We are both a part of The One, and both stronger and wiser for it," Doroga said. He smiled. "And Walker is not mine. We are companions."

The gargant let out a rumbling call and shook its tusks, making the saddle-mat lurch back and forth. Doroga burst out into rumbling laughter.

"What did he say?" Amara asked, somewhat awed.

"Not so much say," Doroga said. "But . . . he makes me know how he feels. Walker thinks we are companions only until he gets too hungry. And then I can either give him more food or stand clear of those apples."

Amara found herself smiling. "And the other tribes. They are . . ."

"Bonded," Doroga provided.

"Bonded with their own totems?"

"Horse with horse, Wolf with wolf, Herdbane with herd-bane, yes," he confirmed. "And many others. It is how our people learn. Not just the wisdom of the mind." He put a fist on his chest. "But the wisdom of the heart. They are equally important. Each of them part of The One."

Amara shook her head. The beliefs of the barbarians were a great deal more complex than she would have believed possible. And if Doroga was telling the literal truth about the Marat bond with their beasts, it meant that they might be a great deal stronger than the Alerans had previously believed.

Hashat, for example, the chieftain of the Horse Clan, wore the cloak pins of three Royal Guardsman on her saber belt. Amara had assumed they had been looted from the field after the first day of First Calderon, but now she was not so sure. If the Marat woman, then a young warrior, had challenged the Princeps's personal guardsman on horseback, her bond with her animal may have given her a decisive advantage, even over Aleran metalcrafting. At Second Calderon, Doroga's gargant had smashed through walls built to withstand the pressures of battle of all kinds, from the great mauls of earthcrafter-borne strength to furycrafted blasts of fire and gale winds.

"Doroga," she said, "why have your people not made war on Alera more often?"

Doroga shrugged. "No reason to do it," he said. "We fight one another often. It is a test The One has given us, to see where the greatest strengths lie. And we have differences of thought and mind, just as your own folk do. But we do not fight until one side is dead. Once the strength is shown, the fight is over."

"But you killed Atsurak at the battle two years ago," Amara said.

Doroga's expression darkened with what looked like sadness. "Atsurak had become too savage. Too steeped in blood. He had betrayed his own purpose before The One. He had stopped learning and began to forget who and what he was. His father died at the Field of Fools—what my tribe call First Calderon—and he grew to manhood lusting for vengeance. He led many others with him in his madness. And he and his followers killed an entire tribe of my people." Doroga tugged at the braid again and shook his head. "As he grew, I had hoped he would learn to forget his hate. He did not. For a time, I feared I would hate him for what he did to me. But now it is over and done. I am not proud of what I did to At-surak. But I could do nothing else and still serve The One."

"He killed your mate," Amara said quietly.

Doroga closed his eyes and nodded. "She hated spending winters with my tribe, in our southlands, in the dunes by the sea. Too much sleeping, she said. That year, she stayed with her own folk."

Amara shook her head. "I do not want to disrespect your beliefs. But I must ask you something."

Doroga nodded.

"Why do you fight to destroy the ancient enemy if we are all a part of The One? Aren't they as much a part of it as your people? Or mine?"

Doroga was silent for a long moment. Then he said, "The One created us all to be free. To learn. To find common cause with others and to grow stronger and wiser. But the ancient enemy perverts that union of strengths. With the enemy, there is no choice, no freedom. They take. They force a joining of all things, until nothing else remains."

Amara shivered. "You mean, joined with them the way you are with your totems?"

Doroga's face twisted in revulsion—and, Amara saw with a sense of unease, the first fear she had ever seen on the Marat's face. "Deeper. Sharper. To join the enemy is to cease to be. A living death. I will speak no more of it."

"Very well," Amara said. "Thank you."

Doroga nodded and turned around to face forward.

She untied the saddle rope and dropped it over the gargant's flank, preparing to climb down it, when a call went down the column to halt. She looked up to see Bernard sitting his nervous horse with one hand lifted.

One of the scouts appeared on the road, his horse running at top speed toward the column. As the rider closed on Bernard and slowed, Bernard gave the man a curt gesture, and the two of them cantered side by side down the length of the column, until they were not far from Doroga's gargant.

"All right," Bernard said, gesturing from the scout to Amara and Doroga. "Let's hear it."

"Aricholt, sir," the man said, panting. "I was just there."

Amara saw Bernard's jaw clench. "What has happened?"

"It's empty, sir," the scout replied. "Just . . . empty. No one is there. There are no fires. No livestock."

"A battle?" Amara asked.

The scout shook his head. "No, lady. Nothing broken, and no blood. It's as if they all just walked away."

Bernard frowned at that and looked up at Amara. It didn't show on his face, but she could see the worry behind his eyes. It matched the worry and the fear she was feeling herself. Missing? An entire steadholt? There were more than a hundred men, women, and children who called Aricholt their home.

"It is too late to save them," Doroga rumbled. "This is how it begins."

CHAPTER 16

"I don't understand this," Isana said. "He's an academ. He's at the Academy. It isn't all that enormous. What do you mean that you can't find my nephew?"

The runner Serai had hired grimaced. He was a boy too young to labor on the docks but too old to be free of the need to work, and his sandy hair was limp with sweat from running back and forth between the Citadel and the private manor in the Citizens' Quarter.

"Pardon, my lady Citizen," the boy panted. "I did as you asked and inquired after him in every place in the Academy visitors are allowed."

"Are you sure you checked his quarters in the dormitories?"

"Yes, my lady," the boy said, apology in his tone. "There was no answer. I slipped your note under his door. He may be in examinations."

"Since *dawn*?" Isana demanded. "That's ridiculous."

Serai murmured from nearby, "Antonin's suggestion has merit, Steadholder. Final examination week is extremely demanding."

Isana settled down lightly onto the raised wall of flagstones surrounding the garden's central fountain, her back straight her eyes closed. "I see."

Birds chirped in the background, bright and cheerful in the warm afternoon that almost had the feel of spring to it. The manor to which Serai had brought Isana was a small one, by the standards of the capital, but its designer had crafted the home with an elegance that made the larger, richer homes surrounding it seem gaudy by comparison.

Isana opened her eyes. Though still marked by the chill of winter night, the garden had begun to awaken to the spring. Buds had already formed on the early-blooming plants and upon all three of the carefully pruned trees. Like the house, the garden was modest and beautiful. Surrounded upon all sides by the three-story manor, hanging and climbing vines hid the silvery marble of the building almost completely, so that the garden seemed more like a glade in a heavy forest than part of a metropolitan household. The bees had not yet awakened from their winter slumber, nor had most of the birds returned from their yearly journey, but it would not be long before the garden would be full of motion, bustling with the business of life.

Spring had always been her favorite time of year, and her own happiness had been infectious. Isana always felt her family's emotions quite clearly, regardless of the season, but in the spring they were the most happy.

That thought led her to Bernard. Her brother was walking into danger, and leading holders she had known for most of her life as he did. He would arrive at Aricholt today—and perhaps he already had. His men might be facing the danger the vord represented as early as the next morning.

And Isana could do nothing but sit in a garden, listening to the rustling waters of an elegant marble fountain.

She rose and paced the length of the garden and back, while Serai paid Antonin with five shining copper rams. The boy pocketed the coin in a flash, bowed to Isana and Serai, and retreated quietly from the garden. Serai watched him go, then settled down at the fountain again with her sewing. "You're going to wear a path in the grass, darling."

"This is taking too long," Isana said quietly. "We have to do something."

"We are," Serai said, her tone placid. "Our host, Sir Nedus, has dispatched word to the proper channels to request an audience."

"That was hours ago," Isana said. "It seems simple enough. How long can it take to give an answer?"

"The Wintersend ceremonies are extensive, Steadholder. There are thousands of Citizens visiting the capital, and there are quite literally hundreds of them also seeking an audience for one reason or another. It is quite prestigious to be granted an audience with Gaius during the festivities."

"This is different," Isana snapped. "He sent for me. And you are his envoy." Serai's eyes snapped up in a warning glance, and she cast a significant look at the house around them. Isana felt a flash of foolish embarrassment. "It is different," she repeated.

"Yes, it is," Serai said. "Unfortunately, the First Counselor's staff is not privy to the details of why. We must approach him through the usual channels."

"But we might not get through to him," Isana said. "We should present our request in person."

"Isana, only this morning a professional assassin attempted to take your life. If you leave this house, your chances of reaching the Citadel without further attempts are dubious, at best."

"I am prepared to take that risk," Isana replied.

"I am not," Serai said placidly. "In any case, it simply isn't how one approaches the First Lord of Alera, Steadholder. Were we to do as you suggest, it is most likely that we would be ignored."

"Then I will be insistent," Isana answered.

Serai's fingers moved with steady, calm speed. "In which case we would be arrested and held for trial until the end of the Festival. We must have patience."

Isana pressed her lips together and regarded Serai levelly for a moment. Then she forced herself to walk back to the fountain. "You're sure this is the fastest way?"

"It is not the fastest way," Serai said. "It is the only way."

"How much longer must we wait?"

"Nedus has friends and allies in the Citadel. We should have some kind of answer soon." She set the sewing down and smiled at Isana. "Would you care for a bit of wine?"

"No, thank you," Isana said.

Serai glided to a small table nestled in a nook of the garden, where glasses and a crystal decanter of wine rested. She poured rose-colored wine into a glass and sipped very slowly.

Isana watched her, and it was only with an effort that she could sense the woman's apprehension. Serai carried her wine over to the fountain and settled beside Isana.

"May I ask you something?" Isana said

"Of course."

"At the landing port. How did you know that man was an assassin?"

"The blood on his tunic," Serai said.

"I don't understand."

The tiny courtesan moved her free hand, to touch her side lightly, just under her arm. "Bloodstains, here." She glanced up at Isana. "Probably the result of a knife thrust to the heart, between the ribs and up through the lungs. It's one of the surest ways to kill a man quietly."

Isana stared at Serai for a moment, then said, "Oh."

The courtesan continued, her tone quiet and conversational. "If it isn't done perfectly, there can be quite a bit of excess blood. The assassin must have needed a second thrust to finish the dockworker whose tunic he stole. There was a long stain down the length of the fabric, and that was what made me take a second look at him. We were quite fortunate."

"A man died so that someone could try to murder me," Isana said. "In what way is that fortunate?"

Serai rolled her shoulder in a shrug. "His death was no doing of yours, darling. We were fortunate in that our assassin was both inexperienced and hurried."

"What do you mean?"

"He went to considerable lengths to acquire a tunic in order to disguise himself. With time to plan, he would never have jeopardized his mission with an unnecessary killing, nor approached with his disguise marred with a suspicious stain. It sharply limited his ability to be part of the background, and an older, more experienced operative would not have attempted it. We were also fortunate in that he was wounded."

"How can you know that?"

"The assassin was right-handed. He threw the knife at you with his left."

Isana frowned, then said, "The bloodstain was on the right side of the tunic."

"Precisely. The assassin approached the dockworker from behind and struck with the blade in his right hand. We know that the kill was not a clean one. We know that the dockworker was probably an earthcrafter. It is reasonable to assume that he struck back at his attacker with furycrafted strength—likely a glancing blow back with his right arm or elbow, striking the assassin's arm in the process.

Isana stared down at Serai. The practical, quiet tone of the courtesan's voice in discussing calculated violence and murder was chilling. A current of fear coursed through Isana, and she sat down at the fountain again. Men of terrible skill and intent were determined to end her life, and her only protection was a frail-looking slip of a woman in a low-cut silk gown.

Serai sipped again at her wine. "Had he been able to get any closer before being seen, or had he been throwing with his preferred arm, you would be dead, Steadholder."

"Great furies preserve us," Isana whispered. "My nephew. Do you think that he is in danger?"

"There's nothing to suggest that he is—and within the Citadel he's as safe as anywhere in the Realm." Serai touched Isana's hand with hers. "Patience. Once we contact Gaius, he will protect your family. He has every reason to do so."

Bitter, old sadness washed through Isana, and the ring on the chain about her throat suddenly felt very heavy. "I'm sure he has the best of intentions."

Serai's back straightened slightly, and Isana sensed a sudden wash of comprehension and suspicion from the courtesan. "Isana," Serai said quietly, dark eyes intent, "you know Gaius. Don't you?"

Isana felt a flutter of panic in her belly, but she held it from her voice, expression, and posture as she rose and paced away. "Only by reputation."

Serai rose to follow her, but before she could speak the courtyard was filled with the sound of the house bells ringing. Voices called out from the street outside, and only a moment later, an elderly but robust-looking man in fine robes limped quickly into the garden.

"Sir Nedus," Serai said, performing a graceful curtsey.

"Ladies," Nedus replied. Tall and slim, Nedus had been a Knight Captain for thirty years before retiring, and his every precise and efficient movement still reflected it. He bowed slightly to each of them, and grimaced, an expressive gesture given his bushy silver eyebrows. "Did you drink all my wine again, Serai?"

"I may have left a splash in the bottle," she said, walking to the little table. "Please, my lord, sit down."

"Steadholder?" Nedus asked.

"Of course," Isana replied.

Nedus nodded his thanks and thumped down on the stone

bench around the fountain, rubbing at his hip with one hand. "I hope you don't think me rude."

"Not at all," she assured him. "Are you in pain?"

"Nothing that doesn't happen every time I spend hours on my feet dealing with fools," Nedus said. "I must have walked for hours." Serai passed Nedus a glass of wine, and the old Knight downed it in a long swallow. "Furies bless you, Serai. Be a dear child and—"

Serai drew the bottle from behind her back, smiling, and refilled Nedus's glass.

"Wonderful woman," Nedus said. "If you could cook, I'd buy your contract."

"You couldn't afford me, darling," Serai said, smiling, and touched his cheek in a fond gesture.

Isana refrained from voicing a curse aloud and settled for asking, "What happened, sir?"

"Bureaucracy," Nedus spat. "The First Counselor's office was packed to the roof. If someone had set the building on fire, half the fools of the Realm would have burned to ash together and left us the richer for it."

"That many?" Serai asked.

"Worse than I've ever seen," Nedus confirmed. "The office wanted every request in writing, and they weren't supplying paper and ink to manage it with. The Academy refused to give any away during examinations, every shop in the Citadel was sold dry of them, and errand boys were gouging applicants for a bloody fortune to run and get them in the Merchants' Quarter, bless their avaricious hearts."

"How much did it cost you?" Serai asked.

"Not a copper ram," Nedus replied. "Something strange was up. The First Counselor's demands were just an excuse."

"How do you know?" Isana asked.

"Because I bribed a scribe in the office with a dozen golden eagles to find out," Nedus replied.

Isana blinked at Nedus. Twelve golden coins could buy supplies for a steadholt for a year or more. It was a small fortune.

Nedus finished the second glass of wine and set it aside. "Word came down that no further audiences with the First Lord were to be granted," he replied. "But that he'd commanded the First Counselor not to reveal the fact. The fool

was stuck with figuring out how to prevent anyone from seeing the First Lord without giving them an excuse as to why.
And from the looks of the folk in the office, he didn't expect
to last the day without someone setting his hair on fire."

Serai frowned and exchanged a long glance with Isana.

"What does it mean?" Isana asked quietly.

"That we cannot reach him that way," Serai said. "Beyond
that, I am not sure. Nedus, did you learn anything at all about
why the First Lord would do such a thing?"

Nedus shook his head. "Rumor was strong among the
Counselor's staff that the First Lord's health had finally broken, but no one knew anything solid." He took the bottle from
Serai's hand and drained the rest of it in a single pull. "I tried
to find Sir Miles and speak to him, but he was nowhere to be
found."

"Sir Miles?" Isana asked.

"Captain of the Royal Guard and the Crown Legion,"
Serai supplied.

"He was a water boy for Gaius's Knights, back in my day,"
Nedus added. "He and his brother Araris. Miles was a hopeless squire, but he grew up pretty good. He remembers me.
Might have helped out, but I couldn't find him. I'm sorry,
child. I failed you."

Serai murmured, "Of course you didn't, darling. Gaius is
making himself scarce, and his captain is nowhere to be
found. Clearly something is afoot."

"Not all that scarce," Nedus said. "He presided over the
qualifying runs of the Wind Trials this morning, as always."

"Perhaps," Serai said, her brow furrowed in thought. She
glanced back at Isana, and said, "We must now consider more
dangerous means of reaching him." She opened a small purse
affixed to her belt, withdrew a folded piece of paper, and offered it to Isana.

"What is this?" she asked.

"An invitation," Serai replied. "Lady Kalare is hosting a
garden party this evening."

Nedus's bushy eyebrows shot up. "Crows, woman. How
did you manage to get an invitation?"

"I wrote it," the courtesan replied serenely. "Lady Kalare's
hand is quite simple to reproduce."

Nedus barked out a laugh, but said, "Dangerous. Very dangerous."

"I don't want to go to a party," Isana said. "I want to reach the First Lord."

"Without being able to schedule an audience or reach your nephew, we must attempt something less direct. Each of the High Lords has an audience with the First Lord every year, as do the Senator Primus, the Regus of the Trade Consortium, and the head of the Dianic League. Most, if not all of them, will be at the fete."

Isana frowned. "You want to talk one of them into letting us accompany them on their audience?"

"It isn't uncommon," Serai said. "You would not be privileged to speak to the First Lord under normal circumstances, but then once we are actually in Gaius's presence, we should be able to resolve matters in short order."

"Very. Dangerous," Nedus said.

"Why?" Isana asked.

"Gaius's enemies will be there, Steadholder."

Isana inhaled slowly. "I see. You think someone might take the opportunity to kill me."

"It's possible," Serai confirmed. "Lord and Lady Kalare will be in attendance. Kalare is at odds with both Gaius and the Dianic League, and is probably the man behind the attempts upon your life. And you are already, I believe, acquainted with the political leanings of Lord and Lady Aquitaine."

Isana felt her hand clench into a fist. "Indeed. They will be there as well?"

"Almost certainly," Serai said. "Gaius's most loyal High Lords rule the Shield cities in the north. It is a rare year that more than one can attend, and this winter has been a particularly hard one on the northern High Lords."

"You mean that Gaius's supporters may not be there to protect me."

"In all probability," Serai said.

"Is there any chance at all of successfully reaching Gaius if we go to this party?"

"Slim," Serai said, her tone frank. "But it definitely exists. And your favor with the Dianic League should not be forgotten, either. They have long waited for a woman to attain

Citizenship outside the structure of marriage or the Legions. It is in their interest to preserve and support you."

Nedus growled, "Is the League going to walk the street next to her and make sure your assassin doesn't take her on the way there?"

Isana felt her fingers shaking. She pressed them against her forehead, and said, "You're sure we can't reach Gaius by any other means?"

"Not quickly," Serai said. "Until Wintersend is over, our options are severely limited."

Isana forced herself to ignore her fear, her worry. She had no desire to die, but she could not allow anything to stop her message, regardless of the danger. Wintersend would not conclude for days. Tavi could be in danger even now, and her brother would surely face it before another day had passed. She did not have time to wait. They did not have days.

"Very well," Isana said. "It would appear that we must go to a party."

It was late afternoon by the time Fidelias returned from gathering information from his contacts in the rougher parts of Alera Imperia. He emerged from the labyrinthine passages in the Deeps into the wine cellar of Aquitaine's manor, and it was a relief to arrive in an area where prying eyes were most unlikely to single him out for attention. He moved directly up the servant's staircase to the top floor of the mansion, where the lavish master suite of High Lord and Lady Aquitaine lay sprawled in luxurious splendor.

Fidelias entered the sitting room of the suite, walked across to the cabinet where a selection of spirits was kept, and helped himself to the contents of an ancient bottle of blue glass. He poured the clear liquid within into a broad, shallow glass, and took it over to a thickly padded chair before broad windows.

He sat down and closed his eyes, sipping slowly at the liquid that felt ice-cold to his lips.

A door opened behind him. Light footsteps moved into the room. "Icewine," murmured Lady Aquitaine. "You never struck me as the type."

"I arranged signals with my contacts a long time ago—in this case, ordering a drink. Back then I was fool enough to drink five or six firewines in a night."

"I see," Lady Aquitaine said, and sat down in the chair facing his own. Her personal presence was magnetic. She had the kind of beauty that most women would not know to envy— not that of transient youth, though her skill at watercrafting certainly allowed her to appear as young as she would wish. But instead, Invidia Aquitaine's beauty was something that could only be emphasized by the passing of years. It was founded on a rock-solid strength that carried through the lines of her cheekbones and jaw, and continued in the dark granite of her eyes. Lady Invidia's entire bearing and mien was one of elegant power, and as she sat down in her scarlet silk dress and faced Fidelias, he sensed that strength and felt the coolly restrained edge of anger that touched her voice as lightly as autumn's first frost. "And what did you learn?"

Fidelias took another slow sip of the cold drink, refusing to be rushed. "Isana is here. She is in the company of Serai."

Lady Aquitaine frowned. "The courtesan?"

"The Cursor," Fidelias said. "Or so I suspect her to be."

"One of Gaius's secret hands?"

Fidelias nodded. "Highly probable, though like the Cursor Legate, their identities are never openly revealed. She is staying with Isana in the home of Sir Nedus, on Garden Lane."

Lady Aquitaine arched an eyebrow. "Not in the Citadel?"

"No, my lady. And thus far I have not been able to discover why."

"Interesting," she murmured. "What else?"

"I'm certain that the assassin at the windport was one of Kalare's men."

"How can you be so sure?"

"He wasn't a local cutter," Fidelias answered. "My informants in the city would have known something—not necessarily who had done it, but *something*. They knew nothing. So it had to have come from out of town. Between that and the information gained from the assassin at Isanaholt, I'm convinced of it."

"I take it you have learned nothing that could be proven in court," Invidia said.

"I hadn't realized you were preparing a suit."

She gave him a smile as slim and fine as a dagger's edge.

"Kalare is still trying to remove Isana," Fidelias said. "I suspect that his operatives are using the Deeps to facilitate their movements."

Invidia frowned. "The caverns beneath the city?"

"Yes. Every source I spoke with reported men going missing in the Deeps. I presume that the bloodcrows are removing witnesses before they have a chance to spread word about them."

Invidia nodded. "Which would indicate multiple members of Kalarus's band."

"It would."

"But that hardly seems to make sense," Invidia said. "The attempt on Isana's life today was hurried—even sloppy. Why strike with one injured and wounded agent if others were available?"

Fidelias raised his eyebrows, impressed. "And I didn't even need to coach you to ask the right question."

"I'm not my husband, dear spy," she said, her mouth curving into a smile. "Well?"

He exhaled slowly. "You aren't going to like the answer, lady. But I do not know. There are other factors at work. These disappearances—I can't account for them. And . . ."

She leaned forward a little, arching an eyebrow. "And?"

"I can't be certain," Fidelias said. He took another drink of the burning cold liquid. "But I believe that there has been a disruption among the Cursors."

"What makes you think so?"

He shook his head. "Obviously, I couldn't speak to anyone directly connected to them. But those I spoke to should have known something about their recent movements, activities. But there was nothing. Not to mention that Serai is becoming very publicly involved in what is going on at great risk of revealing her allegiance."

"I don't understand," Invidia said.

"I'm not sure I do, either," Fidelias said. "There's a taste to the air." He fixed his gaze on Invidia's. "I think someone has declared war on the Cursors themselves."

Invidia arched an eyebrow. "That . . . would strike a crippling blow to Gaius."

"Yes."

"But who would have the knowledge to do such a thing?"

"Me," he said.

"That *had* crossed my mind," Invidia said. "Have you done it, then?"

Fidelias shook his head, glad that he had no need to veil his emotions in order to confound Invidia's ability at watercrafting. "No. I left the Cursors because I believe the Realm needs a strong leader—and that Gaius can no longer perform his duty as the First Lord. I bear no grudges or malice against the Cursors who serve him in good faith."

"Like the girl? What was her name?"

"Amara," Fidelias said.

"No grudge, my spy? No malice?"

"She's a fool," he said. "She's young. I have been both in my time."

"Mmmm," Invidia said. "How carefully you veil yourself from me when you speak of her."

Fidelias swirled the last bit of icewine around in his cup. "Did I?"

"Yes."

He shook his head and finished the drink. "I will learn whatever else I may. And I will move on Isana tonight."

"There are entirely too many mysteries here for my comfort," Lady Aquitaine said. "But keep in mind, my spy, that my primary concern is the Steadholder. I will not have the Realm know that Kalarus had her removed. I will be the one to weave her fate."

Fidelias nodded. "I have watchers around Sir Nedus's manor. When she steps outside, I'll know it, and be there."

"But why is she not in the Citadel?" Lady Aquitaine murmured. "Surely Gaius knows how vital she is to his continued authority."

"Surely, Your Grace."

"And with Serai." Invidia smiled faintly and shook her head. "I would never have guessed her to be Gaius's tool. I've spoken with her many times. I've never sensed any such thing about her."

"She's quite deadly at the arts of deception, my lady, and a valuable tool of the Crown. She has been sending messengers to the Citadel all during the day on behalf of the Steadholder."

Invidia frowned. "To Gaius?"

"To the boy at the Academy."

Invidia sniffed. "Family. Sentiment, I suppose."

"Word has it that he is one of Gaius's personal pages. Perhaps it is an attempt to reach the First Lord through him."

Lady Aquitaine pursed her lips. "If the palace guard is on heightened alert, and if, as you believe, the Cursors themselves are in disarray, then the channels of communication to Gaius may be entirely severed." A faint line appeared between her brows, then she smiled. "He's frightened. On the defensive."

Fidelias set his empty glass aside and nodded, rising. "It's possible."

"Excellent," she said, and rose with him. "Well. I have another dreary little gathering to prepare for, Fidelias—and at Kalarus's manor, no less. Perhaps I might glean some more information. I will leave you to see to the Steadholder."

Fidelias bowed to Lady Aquitaine and stepped back to withdraw.

"Fidelias," she said, just before he reached the door.

He paused, and looked over his shoulder.

"The Steadholder represents a significant political threat to our plans. You will deal with her tonight," she said. "Failure is unacceptable."

The last words held a frosted edge of steel.

"I understand, my lady," he told her, and paced back toward the shadowed entrance to the Deeps.

CHAPTER 18

Tavi slept like the dead and woke when someone gave his shoulder a brisk shake. He stirred slowly, his muscles tight with the discomfort of hours of motionless sleep, and wiped drool from his mouth.

"What?" he mumbled. The dormitory room he shared with Max was only dimly lit. From the quantity of light, it had to have been near dusk. He'd been asleep for hours.

"I said," replied a stern, rich voice, "that you should arise at once."

Tavi blinked and looked up at who had woken him.

Gaius fixed him with a stern glare. "I have no time to waste on apprentice shepherds who sleep too soundly to serve the First Lord of the Realm."

"Sire," Tavi blurted, and sat up. He shoved his hair from his eyes and tried to blink the sleep from them as well. "Forgive me."

"I expected better of you," Gaius said, his expression severe. "Behavior more like . . . like Antillus's bastard, for example. Fine figure of a young man, he is. An excellent reputation for loyalty. Honor. Duty. And handsome to boot."

Tavi rolled his eyes and slugged "Gaius" lightly in the stomach with one fist.

"Ooof," the false Gaius said, his voice sliding back into Max's usual pitch and cadence. The First Lord's features slid and changed, melting back into Max's own broken-nosed, rough good looks. The older boy's mouth was set in a wide grin. "Pretty good, eh? I had you going for a moment."

Tavi rubbed at the back of his neck, trying to work out a tight muscle. "Only for a moment."

"Ah," Max said. "But you *know* where he truly is, as well as his condition. No one else does—or that is the idea, anyway." He stretched out his legs and regarded his toes. "Besides, I've already attended the opening ceremonies to the

Wind Trials and half a dozen smaller functions. All I have to do is look grumpy and keep my verbal exchanges to one or two syllables, and everyone goes leaping out of their way to keep from angering me." Max bobbed his eyebrows. "It is good to be the First Lord."

"Quiet," Tavi warned his friend, glancing around. "These quarters aren't safe for such discussion."

"They aren't exactly the first place spies are going to be looking, either," Max said, with a careless flip of one booted foot. "You got some rest?"

"So it would seem," Tavi said, wincing.

"Time to get back to work then," Max said. "Change your clothes and come with me."

Tavi rose at once. "What are we doing?"

"I'm continuing my brilliant performance," Max said. "After we two pages attend the First Lord in his chambers, at any rate. You are advising me."

"Advising you?"

"Yes. You were the one who had the big thesis paper on furycrafting theory first year, and I'll be speaking to the . . . Board of someone or other."

"The Board of Speakers of the Crafting Society?" Tavi asked.

Max nodded. "Those guys. They're meeting with the First Lord to get approval for more studies of, uh . . ." Max squinted up his eyes. "Arthritic Beer, I keep thinking, but those aren't the right words."

Tavi blinked. "Anthropomorphic Theorem?"

Max nodded again, in exactly the same unconcerned way. "That's it. I've got to learn all about it by the time we walk up to the palace, and you're to teach it to me."

Tavi glared at his roommate and started ripping off his old clothes, changing into fresh ones. He hadn't even bothered to undress before he collapsed on his bed, after fleeing the Black Hall that morning. He started to awaken more thoroughly before he finished re-dressing and raked his comb through his hair. "I'm hurrying."

"Oh," Max said. He bent over and picked up an envelope on the floor. "Someone slid this under the door."

Tavi took the envelope and recognized the handwriting at once. "My aunt Isana."

Outside, the evening bells began to ring, signaling the coming of twilight.

"Crows," Max swore. He rose and started for the door. "Come on. I've got to be there in a quarter hour."

Tavi folded the envelope and thrust it into his belt pouch. "All right, all right." They left the room and started across the campus toward one of the hidden entries to the Deeps. "What do you need to know?"

"Well," Max said after a few steps. "Um. All of it."

Tavi stared at the larger boy in dismay. "Max, that class is required. Essentials of Furycrafting. You took that class."

"Well, yes."

"In fact, we had it *together*."

Max nodded, frowning.

"And you were *there* most of the time," Tavi said.

"Certainly," Max said. "It was in the afternoon. I have no objection to education as long as it doesn't interfere with my sleep."

"Did you *listen*?" Tavi asked.

"Um," Max said. "Keep in mind that Rivus Mara sat in the row in front of us. You remember her. The one with the red hair and the big . . ." He coughed. "Eyes. We spent some of those lectures seeing who could earthcraft the other the most."

Which explained both why Max had shown up nearly every day, and why he headed straight off for parts unknown after class, Tavi thought sourly. "How many is some?"

"All of them," Max said. "Except that day I was hungover."

"*What?* How did you manage to write a passing paper?"

"Well. You remember Igenia? That blonde from Placida? She was good enough to—"

"Oh, shut up, Max," Tavi growled. "That was a three-month course. How in the crows am I supposed to give you all of that in the next fifteen minutes?"

"Cheerfully and without complaint," Max replied, grinning. "Like a true and resourceful member of the Realm and servant of the Crown."

Tavi sighed as they made sure they weren't being observed, then slipped into an unlocked toolshed and down through the hidden trapdoor in its floor to the stairs that led into the Deeps. Max lit a furylamp and handed it to Tavi, then took one for himself.

"You ready to listen?" Tavi asked him.

"Sure, sure."

"Anthropomorphic Theorem," Tavi said. "Okay, you know that furies are the beings that inhabit the elements."

"Yes, Tavi," Max said drily. "Thanks to my extensive education, I did know that one."

Tavi ignored the remark. "There's been debate among furycrafters since the dawn of Aleran history as to the nature of those beings. That's what the various theories try to describe. There are a number of different ideas about how much of the furies are truly intrinsic to their nature, and how much is something that we cause them to become."

"Eh?" Max said.

Tavi shrugged. "We command furies with our thoughts." He went ahead using the inclusive plural. *We*. Though he was arguably the only Aleran alive who could have said *you* instead. "That's what Imposed Anthropomorphic Theory states. Maybe part of our thoughts also shape how our furies appear to us. Maybe a wind fury on its own doesn't look like anything much at all. But when a crafter meets it and uses it, maybe that crafter, somewhere in his head, believes that it should look like a horse, or an eagle, or whatever. So when that fury manifests in a visible form, that's what it looks like."

"Oh, oh, right," Max said. "We might give them form without realizing, right?"

"Right," Tavi said. "And that's the predominant view in the cities and among most Citizens. But other scholars support the Natural Anthropomorphic Theory. They insist that since the furies are each associated with some specific portion of their element—a mountain, a stream, a forest, whatever— that each has its own unique identity, talents, and personality."

"Which is why a lot of folks in the country name their furies?" Max guessed.

"Right. And why the city folk tend to sneer at the idea, because they regard it as *paganus* superstition. But everyone in the Calderon Valley named their furies. They all looked different. Were good at different things. They're also apparently a lot stronger than most city furies. Certainly the Alerans living in the most primitive areas of the Realm tend to command much more powerful furies than in other areas."

"Then why would anyone think that the Imposed Theory was correct?"

Tavi shrugged. "They claim that because the crafter is imagining a separate creature with a form and personality and range of abilities, even if he won't admit to himself that he is, that he is capable of doing more because so much less of it relies totally upon his own thought."

"So the crafter with a named fury can do more because he's too stupid to know he can't?" Max asked.

"That's the view of those in favor of Imposed Anthropomorphic Theory."

"That's stupid," Max said.

"Maybe," Tavi said. "But they may be right, too."

"Well. How do the Natural theorists explain why so many people have furies without a specific identity?"

Tavi nodded at the question. It was a good one. Max might not have had an ounce of self-discipline, but there wasn't a thing wrong with his wits. "Natural theorists say that the furies of increasingly domesticated lands tend to break down. They lose their specific identities as they get passed down from generation to generation and as the natural landscape becomes more and more settled and tamed. They're still present, but instead of being there in their natural form, the furies have been broken down into countless tiny bits that a crafter calls together when he wants to get something done. They aren't as strong, but they don't have the quirks and foibles, either, so they're more reliable."

Max grunted. "Might make some sense," he said. "My old man had some things to say when I named one of my furies." Max's voice took on a hard, bitter edge that Tavi could only barely hear. "Insisted that it was childish nonsense. That he had to break me of the habit before it ruined me. It was harder to do things, his way, but he wouldn't hear of anything else."

Tavi saw the pain in his friend's eyes and thought of all the scars on his back. Maybe Max had his reasons not to pay attention in that particular class that had nothing to do with his carousing. Tavi had thought himself alone in his painful sense of isolation when listening to the basic theory and history of furycrafting. But perhaps it dredged up as many painful memories for Max as it had for him.

"So"—Max sighed after a moment—"which is it?"

"No clue," Tavi said. "No one knows for sure."

"Yeah, yeah," Max said impatiently. "But which one does Gaius think it is? The Board of Speakers is going to be having some kind of debate."

"They do that every year," Tavi said. "I was there last year. Gaius doesn't take sides. They all get together to try to convince him with whatever they think they've learned, and he always listens and nods and doesn't make anyone angry and doesn't take sides. I think that the Board of Speakers really just wants the excuse to drink the First Lord's best wine and to try to one-up their opponents and rivals in front of him."

Max grimaced. "Crows. I'm glad I'm not the First Lord. This stuff would drive me insane in about a day and a half." He shook his head. "What do I do if someone tries to pin me down for an answer?"

"Evade," Tavi suggested, enjoying the heartlessly vague answer.

"What if they start talking about some kind of theory I have no clue about?"

"Just do what you do when the Maestros ask you a question during lecture and you don't know the answer."

Max blinked. "Belch?"

Tavi sighed. "No. No, Max. Divert the attention. Stall for time. Only try not to use any kind of bodily function to accomplish it."

Max sighed. "Diplomacy is more complicated than I thought it would be."

"It's just a dinner party," Tavi said. "You'll do fine."

"I always do," Max said, but his voice lacked some of its usual arrogance.

"How is he?" Tavi said.

"He hasn't moved," Max replied. "Hasn't woken up. But Killian says his heartbeat is stronger."

"That's good," Tavi said. He chewed at his lip. "What happens if . . ."

"If he doesn't wake up," Max said grimly.

"Yeah."

Max inhaled slowly. "Legions fight for the crown. A lot of people die."

Tavi shook his head. "But there is law and precedent for the death of a lord without an heir. The Council of Lords and the Senate would put forward candidates and determine the most fit to take the lordship. Wouldn't they?"

"Officially, sure. But whatever they decided, it wouldn't stick. The High Lords who want the throne might play nice for a little while, but sooner or later one of them would lose the political game and take it to a military venue."

"Civil war."

"Yeah," Max said. He grimaced. "And while we waited for it all, the southern cities would just love to cut the Shield cities loose. And without that support . . ." Max shook his head. "I served two tours on the Shieldwall. We hold it against the Icemen, but we aren't as invincible as everyone down in the rest of the Realm seems to believe. I've seen more than one near breach of the Shieldwall with my own eyes. Without Crown support, it would fall within three years. Four, at the most."

They walked in silence through the tunnels for a few moments. Tavi tended to forget that Max's knowledge of the military disposition of the various High Lords and their Legions was a match for his own knowledge of Aleran society, politics, and history, or for Gaelle's knowledge of the trade crafts and the movement of money, or for Ehren's knowledge of calculations and statistics. Each of them had their strengths, in accordance with their inclinations. It was one reason why they had been chosen to train for the Cursors.

"Max," Tavi said quietly, "you can do this. I'll be there. I'll help if you get into trouble."

His friend inhaled deeply and looked down at him. His mouth quirked in a half smile. "It's just that a lot depends on this act, Tavi. If I get this wrong, a lot of people could die." He sighed. "I almost wish I'd been paying attention in class."

Tavi arched one eyebrow.

Max winked. "I said almost."

All in all, things could have gone worse.

"Gaius" received the Board of Speakers in his own private reception chambers—which were as large as one of the Academy's lecture halls. Between the Board of Speakers, their wives, assistants, and *their* wives, there were fifty or sixty people in attendance, plus a dozen members of the Royal Guard. Max played his role well, circulating among the guests and chatting pleasantly while Tavi watched and listened from an unobtrusive seat in a curtained alcove. Max faltered once, when one particularly intent young Speaker brought up some obscure technical point of furycrafting, but Tavi promptly interceded, hurrying to pass the false First Lord a folded piece of paper with a scribbled missive. Max opened the paper, looked at it, then smoothly excused himself from the conversation to draw Tavi aside and issue apparent instructions.

"Thanks," Max said. "What the hell does inverted proportional propensity mean, anyway?"

"No idea, really," Tavi said, nodding as though in acknowledgment to a command.

"At least now I don't feel quite so stupid. How am I doing?"

"Stop looking down Lady Erasmus's bodice," Tavi said.

Max arched an eyebrow and sniffed. "I didn't."

"Yes, you did. Stop it."

Max sighed. "Tavi, I'm a young man. Some things just aren't in my control."

"Get them there," Tavi said, and inclined his head deeply, taking two steps back, then withdrawing to the alcove.

Beyond that, things had gone fairly well, until the midnight bell rang, signaling the guests that it was time to depart. Guests, serving staff, then guards cleared out of the reception chamber, leaving a pleasant quiet and stillness behind them.

Max exhaled noisily, picked a bottle of wine from one of the tables, and promptly flopped into a chair. He took a long pull from the bottle, then winced and stretched his back a little.

Tavi emerged from the curtained alcove. "What are you doing?"

"Stretching," Max growled. The tone sounded decidedly odd coming from the First Lord's mouth. "Gaius is about my size but his shoulders are narrower. After a while it starts to hurt like hell." He guzzled some more wine. "Crows, but I want a good long soak."

"At least get back into your own clothes and such before you start acting like that. Someone could see."

Max made a rude noise with his lips and tongue. "These are the First Lord's private chambers, Tavi. No one is going to come wandering into them uninvited."

No sooner had the words left Max's mouth than Tavi heard footsteps and the soft click of a doorknob turning from an unobtrusive doorway on the far side of the room. He reacted without thinking, and ducked back into the curtained alcove, peeking through a small gap.

The door opened, and the First Lady walked calmly into the room.

Gaius Caria, the First Lord's wife, was a woman not ten years older than Tavi and Max. It was widely known that her marriage to Gaius had been a political matching rather than one of romance, and Gaius had used it to drive a wedge between the High Lords of Forcia and Kalare, shattering a political alliance that had threatened even the power of the crown.

Caria herself was a young woman of impeccable breeding, formidable skill at furycraft, and stark, elegant beauty. Her long, straight, fine hair hung in a heavy braid worn over one shoulder, a strand of gleaming firepearls woven through the black tresses. Her gown was of the finest silks, the pure, ivory cream of her dress accented with royal blue and scarlet, the colors of the House of Gaius. Jewels gleamed upon her left hand, both wrists, her throat, and her ears, sapphires and blood-colored rubies that matched the colors in the dress. Her skin was very pale, her eyes dark, and her mouth was set in a hard, dangerous line.

"My lord husband," she said, and gave the false Gaius a little curtsey. There was restrained fury vibrating from every fiber of her.

Tavi's heart stuck in his throat. Stupid, stupid. Of course the First Lord's wife would be admitted to his presence. Their private chambers were linked by a number of hallways and doors, which had been the practice of the House of Gaius for centuries.

And crows take it all, in all that had happened he had never stopped to consider that Max might have to deceive Gaius's own wife. They were about to be discovered. Tavi hovered on the brink of emerging, telling the First Lady everything, before she discovered it on her own.

But he hesitated. His instincts screamed warnings at him, and though he had no reason at all to do so, he found himself feeling almost certain that exposing the charade to the First Lady would be a disastrous idea.

So he waited behind the curtains and did not move. He barely breathed.

Max managed to rise to a more believable seated position on the chair before the First Lady had entered the room. His expression became reserved and sober and he rose with a polite little bow that duplicated Gaius's own dignity perfectly. "My lady wife," he replied.

Her eyes flicked from his face down to the bottle and back. "Have I displeased you in some way, my lord?"

"Gaius" frowned, then pursed his lips thoughtfully. "And why should you think that?"

"I awaited your summons to the reception, my lord. As we discussed weeks ago. It never came."

Max raised both eyebrows, though it was an expression with more weariness than genuine surprise in it. "Ah. That's right. I'd forgotten."

"You forgot," Caria said. Her voice rang with scorn. "You forgot."

"I'm the First Lord of Alera, my lady," Max told her. "Not an appointments calendar."

She smiled and inclined her head, though the expression was a bitter one. "Of course, my lord. I'm sure that everyone will understand why you have insulted your own wife in front of the whole of the Realm."

Tavi winced. Not once had anyone asked about the First Lady's absence. Indeed, if the First Lord had apparently forbidden her to appear at his side at such a comparatively unimportant function, word of it would rapidly spread.

"It was not my intention to humiliate you, Caria," Max said, and rose from his chair to walk over to her.

"You never do anything without a reason," she spat back. "If that was not your intention, then why did you do this to me?"

Max tilted his head to one side and regarded her appraisingly. "Perhaps I wanted to keep the sight of you to myself.

That gown is lovely. The jewels exquisite. Though neither as much so as the woman wearing them."

Caria stood there for a moment in perfect silence, her lips parted in total surprise. "I . . . thank you, my lord."

Max smiled down at her, stepped close. He lifted a hand and put a forefinger under the tip of her chin. "Perhaps I wanted you to be here when I could have your attention to myself."

"My . . . my lord," she stammered. "I do not understand."

"If an enormous, boring crowd was standing around us right now," Max said, his eyes on hers, "I would hardly be able to do something like this."

Then he leaned down and kissed the First Lady of Alera, the wife of the most powerful man in the world, squarely, heatedly, upon the lips.

Tavi just stared at Max. That idiot.

The kiss went on for an utterly untoward amount of time, while Max's hand slid to the back of Caria's head, holding her there in the kiss in an utterly proprietary fashion. When he withdrew his mouth from the First Lady's, her cheeks were flushed pink, and she was breathing very quickly.

Max met her eyes, and said, "I apologize. It was an honest mistake, my lady. Truly. I'll find some way to make it up to you." As he said it, his eyes trailed down the front of her silken gown and then back to Caria's, heavy and warm.

Caria licked her lips and seemed to fumble for words for a few moments. Then she said, "Very well, my lord."

"My page should arrive at any moment," he said. His thumb caressed her cheek. "I've some business to attend. With luck, I'll have some of the night left when it is finished." He arched a brow in a silent question.

Caria's cheeks colored even more. "If duty permits, my lord. That should please me."

Max smiled. "I had hoped you would say that." He lowered his hand, then bowed slightly to her. "My lady."

"My lord," she replied, with another curtsey, before withdrawing through the door by which she'd entered.

Tavi waited for several long breaths before he came out of the alcove, staring at Max. His friend half staggered to the nearest chair, sat down in it, lifted the wine bottle to his mouth in a shaking hand, and drank the rest of it in a single, long pull.

"You're insane," Tavi said quietly.

"I couldn't *think* what else to do," Max said, and as he spoke the tenor of his voice changed, sliding back toward his own speaking voice. "Bloody crows, Tavi. Did she believe it?"

Tavi frowned, glancing at the door. "You know. I think she might have. She was totally off-balance."

"She'd better have been," Max growled. He closed his eyes and frowned, and the shape of his face began to change, slowly enough to make it difficult to say precisely what dimensions were shifting. "I hit her with enough earthcraft to inspire a gelded gargant bull to mate."

Tavi shook his head weakly. "Crows, Max. His *wife*."

Max shook his head, and in a few seconds more looked like himself again. "What else could I have done?" he demanded. "If I'd argued with her, she would have started bringing up past conversations and subjects that I would have no idea how to respond to. It would have given me away within five minutes. My only choice was to seize the initiative."

"Is that what you seized?" Tavi asked, his voice dry.

Max shuddered and stalked over to the alcove, tearing off the First Lord's clothing as he went to don his own once more. "I had to. I had to make sure she wasn't doing too much thinking, or she would have noticed something." He stuck his head through the neck of his own tunic. "And by the furies, Tavi, if there's anything I can do like a high lord, it's kiss a pretty girl."

"I guess that's true," Tavi said. "But . . . you'd think she'd know her own husband's kiss."

Max snorted. "Yeah, sure."

Tavi frowned and arched an inquisitive brow at Max.

Max shrugged. "It's obvious, isn't it? They're all but strangers."

"Really? How do you know?"

"Men of power, men like Gaius, have two different kinds of women in their life. Their political mates, and the ones they actually want."

"Why do you say that?" Tavi asked.

Max's expression became remote and bleak. "Experience." He shook his head and raked his fingers through his hair. "Believe me. If there's one thing a political wife doesn't know, it's what her husband's desire feels like. It's entirely possible that Gaius hasn't kissed her since the wedding."

"Really?"

"Yes. And of course, there's no one in the Realm who would risk crossing Gaius by becoming lovers with her. In that kind of situation, it's going to cause the poor woman considerable, ah, frustration. So I exploited it."

Tavi shook his head. "That's . . . that's so wrong, somehow. I mean, I can understand the political pressures when it comes to marriages among the lords, but . . . I guess I always thought there would be *some* kind of love."

"Nobles don't marry for love, Tavi. That's a luxury of holders and freemen." His mouth twisted in bitterness. "Anyway. I didn't know what else to do. And it worked."

Tavi nodded at his friend. "It looks that way."

Max finished dressing and licked his lips. "Um. Tavi. We don't really need to mention this to anyone, do we?" He glanced up at him uncertainly. "Please?"

"Mention what?" Tavi said, with a guileless smile.

Max let out a sigh of relief and smiled. "You're all right, Calderon."

"For all you know, I'll just blackmail you with it later."

"Nah. You don't have it in you." They headed for the door that led to a small stair down to the nearest portion of the Deeps. "Oh, hey," Max said. "What did your aunt's letter say?"

Tavi snapped his fingers and scowled. "Knew I was forgetting something." He reached into his pouch and withdrew his aunt Isana's letter. He opened it and read it in the light of the lamp at the top of the stairs.

Tavi stared at the words, and felt his hands start shaking.

Max noticed, and his voice became alarmed. "What is it?"

"I have to go," Tavi said, his voice choked almost to a whisper. He swallowed. "Something's wrong. I have to go see her. Right now."

CHAPTER 19

Amara reached Aricholt by midday. The column halted half a mile from the steadholt's walls, on a rise overlooking the hollow that held the steadholt's wall and buildings cupped in a green bowl of earth. Bernard overrode the objections of both his Knight Captain and First Spear, and stalked down into the deserted steadholt to search for any potential threat. Moments later, he returned, frowning, and the column had proceeded to march through Aricholt's gate.

The place had changed, and for the better, since Amara had first seen it. Years ago, under the rule of Kord, a slaver and murderer, the place had been little more than a collection of run-down buildings around a single stone storm shelter that had to hold the residents of the steadholt and their beasts as well. Since that time, Aric had attracted new holders to move to the potentially rich and certainly beautiful area. One of his new holders had found a small vein of silver on Aric's land, and not only had the revenue from the find paid off his father's enormous debts, but left him with money enough to last a lifetime.

But Aric hadn't hoarded the money away. He had spent it on his holders and his home. A new wall, as thick and solid as Isanaholt's, now shielded the steadholt's buildings, all of them also made of solid stone, including a large barn for the animals—even the four gargants Aric purchased for the heavy labor his steadholt needed to prosper. Over the past years, the steadholt had changed from a ragged, weed-choked cluster of shacks and hovels housing miserable no-accounts and pitiable slaves into a prosperous and beautiful home to more than a hundred people.

Which made it all the more eerie to look down upon it now. There was no bustle of activity within the walls or in the nearest fields outside. No smoke rose from the chimneys. No animals milled in the pens or in the pasture nearest the steadholt.

No children ran or played. No birds sang. In the distance to the west of the settlement, the enormous, bleak bulk of the mountain called Garados loomed in gloomy menace.

There was only a silence, as still and as deep as an underground sea.

Almost every door in the building hung open, swinging back and forth in the wind. The gates to the cattle pen stood open as well, as did the doors to the stone barn.

"Captain," Bernard said quietly.

Captain Janus, a grizzled veteran of the Legions and a Knight Terra of formidable skill, nudged his horse from the head of the column of Knights that had accompanied them to Aricholt. Janus, the senior officer of the Knights under Bernard's command as Count Calderon, was a man of under average height, but he had a neck as thick as Amara's waist, and his corded thews would have been tremendously powerful, even without furycrafting to enhance them. He was dressed in the matte black plated mail of the Legions, and his rough features sported a long, ugly scar that crossed one cheek to pull up his mouth at one corner in a perpetual, malicious smirk.

"Sir," Janus said. His voice was a surprisingly light tenor, marked with the gentle clarity of a refined, educated accent.

"Report, please."

Janus nodded. "Yes, milord. My Knights Aeris swept this entire bowl and found no one present, holders or otherwise. I put them on station in a loose diamond at a mile from the steadholt, to serve as sentinels in the event that anyone else attempts to approach. I have instructed them to observe extreme levels of caution."

"Thank you. Giraldi?"

"My lord," said the First Spear, stepping forward from the ranks of the infantry to slam his fist sharply against his breast-plate in salute.

"Establish a watch on the walls and work with Captain Janus to make this place defensible. I want twenty men working in teams of four to search every room in every building in this steadholt and make sure that they are empty. After that, round up whatever stores of food you can find here and get them inventoried."

"Understood, milord." Giraldi nodded and saluted again, then spun around to draw his baton from his belt and began bawling orders to his men. Janus turned to his subordinate, his voice much quieter than Giraldi's, but he moved with the same quality of purpose and command.

Amara stood back, watching Bernard thoughtfully. When she met him, he had been a Steadholder—not even a full Citizen himself. But even then, he had the kind of presence that demanded obedience and loyalty. He had always been decisive, fair, and strong. But she had never seen him in this setting, in his new role as Count Calderon, commanding officers and soldiers of Alera's Legion with the quiet confidence of experience and knowledge. She had known that he served in the Legions, of course, since every male of Alera was required to do so for at least one tour lasting two to four years.

It surprised her. She had regarded Gaius's decision to appoint Bernard the new Count of Calderon as a political gambit, mostly intended to demonstrate the First Lord's authority. Perhaps Gaius, though, had seen Bernard's potential more clearly than she. He was obviously comfortable in his role, and worked with the intent focus of a man determined to discharge his duties to the best of his ability.

She could see the reactions of his men to it—Giraldi, a grizzled old salt of a *legionare*, respected Bernard immensely, as did all of the men of his century. Winning the respect of long-term, professional soldiers was never easy, but he had done it. And amazingly enough, he enjoyed the same quiet respect with Captain Janus, who clearly regarded Bernard as someone competent at his job and willing to work as hard and face exactly the same situations he asked of his men.

Most importantly, she thought, it was evident to everyone who knew him what Bernard was: a decent man.

Amara felt a warm current of fierce pride flow through her. In spare moments of thought, it still seemed an amazing stroke of luck to her that she had found a man of both kindness and strength who clearly desired her company.

You must leave him, of course.

Serai's gentle, inflexible words killed the rush of warmth, turning it into a sinking in the pit of her stomach. She could not refute them. Bernard's duties to the Realm were a clear

necessity. Alera required every strong furycrafter it could get
to survive in a hostile world, and its Citizens and nobility represented the prime of that strength. Custom demanded that
Citizens and nobility alike seek out spouses with as much
strength as possible. Duty and law required the nobility to
take spouses who could provide strongly gifted children.
Bernard's strength as a crafter was formidable, and with more
than one fury, to boot. He was a strong crafter and a good
man. He would be a fine husband. A strong father. He would
make some woman very, very happy when he wed her.

But that woman could not be Amara.

She shook her head, forcing that line of thinking from her
thoughts. She was here to stop the vord. She owed it to the men
of Bernard's column to focus all of her thought on her current
goals. Whatever happened, she would not allow her personal
worries to distract her from doing everything in her power to
protect the lives of the *legionares* under Bernard's command,
and to destroy what would be a most deadly threat to the
Realm.

She watched Bernard kneel on the ground, his palm flat to
the earth. He closed his eyes and murmured, "Brutus."

The ground near him quivered gently, then the earth rippled
and broke like the still surface of a pool at the passing of a
stone. From that ripple, an enormous hound, bigger than some
ponies and made entirely of stone and earth rose up from the
ground and pushed his broad stone head against Bernard's outstretched hand. Bernard smiled and thumped the hound lightly
on the ear. Then Brutus settled down and sat attentively, its
green eyes—real emeralds—focused on Bernard.

The Count murmured something else, and Brutus opened
his jaws in what looked like a bark. The sound that came from
the earth fury was akin to that of a large rockslide. The fury
immediately sank back into the earth, while Bernard stayed
there, hunkered down, his hand still on the earth.

Amara approached him quietly and paused several steps
away.

"Countess?" Bernard rumbled after a moment. He sounded
somewhat distracted.

"What are you doing?" she asked.

There was another low shudder in the earth, this one sharp

and brief. Amara felt it ripple out beneath her boots. "Trying to see if anyone is moving around out there. On a good day, I could spot something three or four miles out."

"Really? So far?"

"I've lived here long enough," Bernard said. "I know this valley. That's what makes it possible." He grunted, frowning for a moment. "That isn't right."

"What isn't?"

"There's something . . ." Bernard suddenly lurched to his feet, his face gone white, and bellowed, "Captain! Frederic!"

In seconds, booted feet pounded on the stones of the court-yard, and Frederic came sprinting toward them from outside the walls, where the column's gargants, with Doroga's, waited for the steadholt to be searched for hidden dangers before entering. Seconds later, Captain Janus leapt from the steadholt's wall directly to the courtyard, absorbing the shock of the fall with furycrafted strength, and jogged over without delay or excitement.

"Captain," Bernard said. "There's been a chamber crafted into the steadholt's foundation, then sealed off."

Janus's eyes widened. "A bolt-hole?"

"It must be," Bernard said. "The steadholt's furies are trying to keep it sealed, and it's too much stone for me to move alone as long as they're set against me."

Janus nodded once, stripping his gloves off. He knelt on the ground, pressed his hands to the stones of the courtyard, and closed his eyes.

"Frederic," Bernard said, his voice sharp, controlled, "when I nod, I want you to open a way to that chamber, large enough for a man to walk through. The Captain and I will hold off the steadholt furies for you."

Frederic swallowed. "That's a lot of rock, sir. I'm not sure I can."

"You're a Knight of the Realm now, Frederic," Bernard said, his voice crackling with authority. "Don't wonder about it. Do it."

Frederic swallowed and nodded, a sheen of sweat beading his upper lip.

Bernard turned to Amara. "Countess, I need you to be ready to move," he said.

Amara frowned. "To do what? I don't know what you mean by bolt-hole."

"It's something that's happened on steadholts under attack before," Bernard said. "Someone crafted an open chamber into the foundation of the steadholt, then closed the stone around it."

"Why would anyone do—" Amara frowned. "They sealed their children in," she breathed, suddenly understanding. "To protect them from whatever was attacking the steadholt."

Bernard nodded grimly. "And the chamber isn't large enough to hold very much air. The three of us will open a way to the chamber and hold it open, but we won't be able to do it for very long. Take some of the men down and pull out whoever you can as quickly as you can."

"Very well."

He touched her arm. "Amara," he said. "I can't tell how long they've been sealed in there. It could be an hour. It could be a day. But I can't feel anything moving around."

She got a sickly, twisting feeling in the pit of her stomach. "We might be too late."

Bernard grimaced and squeezed her arm. Then he went to Janus's side and knelt, placing his own hands on the ground near the Captain's.

"Centurion!" Amara called. "I need ten men to assist possible survivors of the steadholt!"

"Aye, milady," Giraldi answered. In short order, ten men stood ready near Amara—and ten more, weapons drawn, stood next to them. "Just in case they *aren't* holders, my lady," Giraldi growled under his breath. "Doesn't hurt to be careful."

She grimaced and nodded. "Very well. Do you really think they could be the enemy?"

Giraldi shook his head, and said, "Sealed up in rock, for furies know how long? I doubt it will matter even if it is the vord." He took a deep breath, and said, "No need for you to go down when they open it, Countess."

"Yes," Amara said. "There is."

Giraldi frowned but said nothing else.

Bernard and Janus spoke quietly to one another for a few moments. Then Bernard said, his voice strained, "Almost there. Get ready. We won't be able to hold it open long."

"We're ready," Amara said.

Bernard nodded, and said, "Now, Frederic."

The ground trembled again, then there was a grating, groaning sound. Directly before Frederic's feet, the stones of the courtyard suddenly quivered and sank downward, as if the ground beneath them had turned to soupy mud. Amara stepped over to the opening hole, and took in the rather unsettling sight of stone running like water, flowing down to form itself into a steeply sloping ramp leading down into the earth.

"There," Bernard grated. "Hurry."

"Sir," Frederic said. He spoke in an anguished groan. "I can't hold it open for long."

"Hold it as long as you can," Bernard growled, his own face red and beginning to sweat.

"Centurion," Amara snapped, and she started down the ramp. Giraldi bawled out orders, and the sound of heavy boots on stone followed hard on Amara's heels.

The ramp went down nearly twenty feet into the earth and ended at a low opening into a small, egg-shaped room. The air smelled stale, thick, and too wet. There were shapes in the dimness of the room—limp bundles of cloth. Amara went to the nearest and knelt—a child, scarcely old enough to walk.

"They're children," she snapped to Giraldi.

"Move it," Giraldi barked. "Move it, boys, you heard the Countess."

Legionares stomped into the chamber, seized the still forms in it at random, and hurried out again. Amara left the chamber last, and just as she did, the smooth stone floor suddenly bulged upward just as the ceiling swelled downward. Amara shot a look over her shoulder, and was uncomfortably reminded of the hungry maw of a direwolf as the bedrock flowed and moved like a living thing. The opening to the room contracted, and the walls on either side of the ramp suddenly got narrower. "Hurry!" she shouted to the men ahead of her.

"I can't!" Frederic groaned.

Legionares sprinted up the ramp, but the stone was collapsing inward again too quickly. Scarcely noticing the weight of the limp child she carried, Amara cried out to Cirrus, and her fury came howling down into the slot in the stone like a hurricane. Vicious, dangerous winds abruptly swept down the ramp beneath and behind them, and then rushed up toward the surface like a maddened gargant. The winds threw Amara into the back of the *legionare* in front of her before it caught the man and his charge up, and sent them both into the next man in line, until in all a half dozen *legionares* flew wildly up the ramp and out of the grasp of the closing stone.

The ground grated again, a harsh, hateful sound, and the stone closed seamlessly back into its original shape, catching the end of Amara's braid as it did. The braid snared her as strongly as any rope, and the winds propelling her swung her feet out and up into the air as her hair was seized by the rock. She thumped back down to the stone flat on her back, and got the wind knocked out of her in a rush of breathless, stunned pain.

"Watercrafter!" bellowed Giraldi. "Healers!"

Someone took the child gently from Amara's arms, and she became vaguely aware of the infantry's watercrafter and several grizzled soldiers with healer's bags draped over one shoulder rushing over to them.

"Easy, easy," Bernard said from somewhere nearby. He sounded winded. Amara felt his hand on her shoulder.

"Are they all right?" she gasped. "The children?"

"They're looking at them," Bernard said gently. His hands touched her head briefly, then ran around the back of her head, gently probing. "You hit your head?"

Amara shook her head. "No. My braid caught in the rock."

She heard him let out a slow breath of relief, then felt him feeling his way along the length of the braid. When he got to the end of it, he said, "It's only an inch or two. It's right at the tie."

"Fine," Amara said.

She heard the rasp of Bernard's dagger being drawn from his belt. He applied the honed edge of the knife to the end of her braid and cut it loose from the rock.

Amara sighed as the pressure on her scalp eased. "Help me sit up," she said.

Bernard gave her his hand and pulled her to sit on the courtyard. Amara tried to get her breath back, and began methodically to work the now-loose braid out before it started tangling in knots.

"Sir?" Janus said. "Looks like we got here in time."

Bernard closed his eyes. "Thank the great furies. Who do we have here?"

"Children," Janus reported. "None of them over the age of eight or nine, and two infants. Four boys, five girls—and a young lady. They're unconscious but breathing, and their pulses are strong."

"A young lady?" Amara asked. "The steadholt's caretaker?"

Bernard squinted up at the sun and nodded. "It would make sense." He got up and paced over to the recumbent forms of the children and of one young woman. Amara rose, paused while her balance swayed a little, then followed him over.

Bernard grimaced. "It's Heddy. Aric's wife."

Amara stared down at a frail-looking young woman with pale blond hair and fair skin, only lightly weathered by sun and wind. "Sealed them in," she murmured. "And set their furies to make sure they stayed that way. Why would they do such a thing?"

"To make it impossible for anyone to get to them but the people who put them there," Bernard rumbled.

"But why?"

Bernard shrugged. "Maybe the holders figured that if they weren't around to get their children out, they didn't want whoever was attacking them to have the chance."

"Even if they died?"

"There are worse things than death," Doroga said. His rumbling basso startled Amara into a twitch of reflexive tension. The huge Marat headman had moved up behind them more silently than an Amaranth grass lion. "Some of them much worse."

One of the babies started squeaking out a stuttering little cry of complaint, and a moment later the infant was joined by the exhausted sobs of another child. Amara glanced up to find the children all beginning to stir.

Giraldi's watercrafter, a veteran named Harger, rose from the child beside Heddy and knelt over the young woman. He put his fingertips lightly on Heddy's temples, his eyes closed for a moment. Then he glanced up at Bernard, and said, "Her body is extremely strained. I don't know that her mind is straight right now, either. It might be better to give her the chance to sleep."

Bernard frowned and glanced at Amara, an eyebrow lifted.

She grimaced. "We need to talk to her. Find out what happened."

"Maybe one of the children could tell us," Bernard said.

"Do you think they could have understood what was going on?"

Bernard glanced at them, his frown deepening, and shook his head. "Probably not. Not well enough to risk more lives on what a small child remembers."

Amara nodded her agreement.

"Wake her up, Harger," Bernard said gently. "Careful as you can."

The old watercrafter nodded, his misgivings clear in his eyes, but he turned back to Heddy, touched her temples again, and frowned in concentration.

Heddy awoke instantly and violently, screaming in a raw, tortured wail. Her pale blue eyes flew open—torturously wide—the panicked eyes of an animal certain that its hungry pursuer had moved in for the kill. She thrashed her arms and legs wildly, and a sharp and sudden breeze, strong but unfocused, swept through the courtyard. It spun wildly, throwing up dust, straw, and small stones. "No!" Heddy shrieked. "No, no, no!"

She went on screaming the same word, over and over, and it sounded like she was tearing her own throat raw as she did.

"Heddy!" Bernard rumbled, eyes half-squinted against the wind-driven debris. "Heddy! It's all right. You're safe!"

She went on screaming, struggling, kicking, and bit the hand of one *legionare* who knelt along with Harger and Bernard in an attempt to restrain her. She struggled with a strength born of a fear so severe that it was its own kind of madness.

"Crows take it!" Harger snarled. "We'll have to sedate her."

"Wait," Amara snapped. She knelt beside the struggling holder. "Heddy," she said in the softest voice she could to be heard over the screams. "Heddy, it's all right. Heddy, the children are all right. The Count is here with the guard from Garrison. They're safe. The children are safe."

Heddy's panicked eyes flicked over to Amara, and her eyes focused on someone for the first time since she'd awoken. Her screams slowed a little, and her expression was tortured, desperate. It raked at Amara to see a woman in so much pain. But she kept her voice gentle, repeating quiet reassurances to the terrified holder. When Heddy had quieted even more, Amara put her hand on the young woman's head, stroking her cobweb-fine hair back from her forehead, never stopping.

It took nearly half an hour, but Heddy's screams died out into cries, then into groans, and finally into a series of piteous whimpering sounds. Her eyes stayed locked on Amara's face, as if desperate to find some kind of reference point. With a final shudder, Heddy fell silent, and her eyes closed, tears welling.

Amara glanced up at Bernard and Harger. "I think she'll be all right. Perhaps you gentlemen should leave me here with her for a little while. Let me take care of her."

Harger nodded at once and rose. Bernard looked less certain, but he nodded to Amara as well and walked over to Captain Janus and Centurion Giraldi, speaking in low tones.

"Can you hear me, Heddy?" Amara asked quietly.

The girl nodded.

"Can you look at me, please?"

Heddy whimpered and started trembling.

"All right," Amara soothed. "It's all right. You don't have to. You can talk to me with your eyes closed."

Heddy's head twitched into a nod, and she kept on shaking with silent sobs. Tears bled down over her cheekbones to fall upon the courtyard's stones. "Anna," she said after a moment. She twitched her head up off the ground, looking toward the sounds of crying children. "Anna's crying."

"Shhh, be still," Amara said. "The children are fine. We're taking care of them."

Heddy sank down again, trembling from the effort it had taken to partially sit up. "All right."

"Heddy," Amara said, keeping her voice smooth and quiet. "I need to know what happened to you. Can you tell me?"

"B-bardos," Heddy said. "Our new smith. Large man. Red beard."

"I do not know him," Amara said.

"Good man. Aric's closest friend. He sent us down into that chamber. Said that he was going to make sure that we weren't . . ." Heddy's face twisted in a hideous grimace of agony. "Weren't taken. Like the others."

"Taken?" Amara said quietly. "What do you mean?"

The young woman's voice became agony grinding in her throat. "*Taken.* Changed. Them and *not* them. Not Aric. Not Aric." She curled into a tight ball. "Oh, my Aric. Help us, help us, help us."

A huge, gentle hand settled on her shoulder, and Amara glanced back up at Doroga's quiet frown.

"Let her be," he said.

"We've got to know what happened."

Doroga nodded. "I will tell you. Let her rest."

Amara frowned up at the big Marat. "How do you know?"

He rose and squinted around the steadholt. "Tracks outside," he said. "Leading away. Shoes, no-shoes, male and female. Cattle, sheep, horses, gargants." He gestured around the steadholt. "Vord came in here two, maybe three days ago. Took the first. Not everyone at once. First they take a few."

Amara shook her head, her hand still resting on the curled form of the weeping holder. "*Took.* What do you mean?"

"The vord," Doroga said. "They get inside you. Go in through the mouth, nose, ear. Burrow in. Then you die. But they have your body. Look like you. Can act like you."

Amara stared at Doroga, sickened. "What?"

"Don't know what they look like exactly," Doroga said. "The vord have many forms. Some like the Keepers of Silence. Like spiders. But they can be little. Mouthful." He shook his head. "The Takers are small, so they can get inside you."

"Like . . . some sort of worm? A parasite."

Doroga tilted his head, one pale war braid sliding over a massive shoulder. "Parasite. I do not know this word."

"It's a creature that attaches itself to another creature," Amara said. "Like a leech or a flea. They feed on a host creature to survive."

"Vord are not like this," Doroga said. "The host creature doesn't survive. Just look like they do."

"What do you mean?"

"Say a vord gets into my head. Doroga dies. The Doroga

that is in here." He thumped his head with his thumb. "What Doroga feels. That is gone. But *this* Doroga"—he slapped his chest lightly with one hand—"this remains. You don't know any better, because you only know the true Doroga"—he touched his head—"through the Doroga you can see and talk to." He touched his chest.

Amara shivered. "Then what happened here?"

"What happened among my people," Doroga said. "Takers came. Took just a few. Looked around, maybe deciding who to take next. Then taking them. Until more were taken than were themselves. Took more than seven hundred Wolf Clan like that, one pack at a time."

"Is that what you fought?" Amara asked. "Taken Marat?"

Doroga nodded, his eyes bleak. "First, them. Then we found the nest. Fought the Keepers of Silence. Like big spiders. And their warriors. Bigger. Faster. They killed many of my people, our *chala*." He inhaled slowly. "And then we took the vord queen at that nest. A creature who . . ." He shook his head, and Amara saw something she never thought she might in Doroga—the shadow of fear in his eyes. "The queen was the worst. From her, all the others are born. Keepers. Takers. Warriors. We had to keep going, or the queen would have escaped. Founded another nest. Started over."

Amara pursed her lips and nodded. "That's why you fought as you did. To the end."

Doroga nodded. "And why the queen near this place must be found and destroyed. Before she spawns young queens of her own."

"What do you think happened here?" Amara said.

"Takers came in," Doroga said. "That was what she meant when she said them and not them. This Aric she speaks of was one who was taken. This other man, who sealed her into the stone, must have been free. Maybe one of the last of your people still free."

"Then where is he now?" Amara asked.

"Taken. Or dead."

Amara shook her head. "This isn't . . . this is too incredible. I've never heard of such a thing. No one has ever known anything like this."

"We have," Doroga rumbled. "Long ago. So long ago that few tales remained. But we have seen them."

"But it can't be," Amara said quietly. "It can't be like that."

"Why not?"

"Aric couldn't have been taken. He was the one who came to warn Bernard. If he was one of these vord now, then they would know . . ."

Amara felt a slow, vicious spike of cold lodge in her belly.

Doroga's eyes narrowed to slits. Then he spun to one side and took up the enormous war club he had left leaning against a wall. "Calderon!" he bellowed, and outside the walls of the steadholt, his gargant answered with a ringing trumpet of alarm. "Calderon! To arms!"

Amara staggered to her feet looking around wildly for Bernard.

And that was when she heard *legionares* begin to scream.

CHAPTER 20

Amara snapped an order to the nearest healer to watch over Heddy, then called to Cirrus. Her fury gathered around her, winds swirling up a cloud of dust that outlined the vague form of a long-legged horse in the midst of the winds. Amara cried out and felt Cirrus sweep her clear of the ground and into the open sky above Aricholt.

She spun in a circle, eyes flickering over the ground beneath her and the skies about her, taking in what was happening.

In the steadholt below her, she saw *legionares* emerge sprinting from the enormous stone barn. The last man out let out a cry and abruptly fell, falling hard to the stony ground. Something had hold of his ankle and began hauling him back into the barn. The soldier shouted, and his fellow *legionares* immediately turned back to help him.

Amara held up her hands to the level of her eyes, palms facing each other, and willed Cirrus into the air before her face, concentrating the winds to bend light and draw her vision to within several yards of the stone barn.

The *legionare*'s sword slashed through a shining, black, hard-looking limb like nothing that Amara had ever seen, save perhaps the pinching claws of a lobster. The sword bit into the vord's claw—but just barely. The *legionare* struck again and again, and even then only managed to cripple the strength of the claw, rather than severing it completely.

The men dragged their wounded companion away from the barn, his boot flopping and twisting at a hideous angle.

The vord warrior followed them into the sunlight.

Amara stared down at the creature, her stomach suddenly cold. The vord warrior was the size of a pony, and had to have weighed four or five hundred pounds. It was covered in slick-looking, lacquer-gloss plates of some kind of dark hide. Four limbs thrust straight out to the sides from a humpbacked central body, rounded and hunched like the torso of a flea. Its head extended from that body on a short, segmented stalk of a neck. Twists and spines of chitin surrounded its head, and a pair of tiny eyes recessed within deep grooves glared out with scarlet malevolence. Massive, almost beetlelike mandibles extended from its chitinous face, and each mandible ended in the snapping claw that had crippled the *legionare*.

The vord rushed out of the doorway, hard on the heels of its prey, its gait alien, ungainly, and swift. Two of the *legionares* turned to face it, blades in hand, while the third dragged the wounded man away. The vord bounded forward in a sudden leap that brought it down on top of one of the *legionares*. The man dodged to one side, but not swiftly enough to prevent the vord from knocking him to the earth. It landed upon him and seized his waist between its mandibles. They ground down, and the man screamed in agony.

His partner charged the vord's back, screaming and hacking furiously with his short, vicious *gladius*. One of the blows landed upon a rounded protrusion upon the creature's back, and it sprayed forth some kind of greenly translucent, viscous liquid.

A string of clicking detonations emerged from the vord, and it released the first *legionare* to whirl on its new attacker and bounded into the air as before. The *legionare* darted to one side, and when the vord landed, he struck hard at its thick neck. The blow struck home, though the armored hide of the vord barely opened. But it had been enough to hurt it.

More liquid, nauseating greenish brown, spurted from the wound, and more explosive clicks crackled from the monster. It staggered to one side, unable to keep its balance despite its four legs. The *legionare* immediately seized his wounded companion, and began to drag the other man away from the wounded, unsteady vord. He moved as quickly as he could.

It wasn't enough.

Another half dozen of the creatures rushed out of the barn like angry hornets from a nest, and the buzzing click of the wounded vord became a terrifying, alien chorus. The vibrating roar increased, and the humped, round backs of the things abruptly parted into broad, blackened wings that let them leap into the air and come sailing at the fleeing *legionares*.

The vord tore them to shreds before Amara's horrified eyes.

It happened quickly—start to finish in only a handful of seconds, and there was nothing anyone could have done to save the doomed *legionares*.

More vord emerged from other buildings in the steadholt, and Amara saw three of them leaping forth from the steadholt's well. She heard Giraldi bellowing over the rumble of angry clicking, and a sudden flash of fire boomed into the air as one of Commander Janus's Knights Ignus unleashed furies of fire upon a charging vord.

Another scream, this one very near, snapped Amara's gaze upward, to see one of the Knights Aeris struggling against a pair of winged vord warriors. The man slashed a hand at the air, and a burst of gale-force wind sent one vord tumbling to the side, spinning end over end as it fell toward the earth. But the second vord flared its wings at the last second and it struck him belly first, legs wrapping him, jaw-claws gripping and tearing. The Knight screamed, and the pair of them plummeted toward the ground.

Below her, the veterans of Giraldi's century had immediately linked up to stand together, their backs to one of the steadholt's stone walls and the nearest building securing one flank. Eight or nine of the vord bounded forward, only to be met by a solid wall of heavy Legion tower-shields and blades in the first rank, while the two ranks behind plied their spears in murderous concert with the front row. Supporting one another, Giraldi's veterans stopped the vord charge cold, steel flashing, men screaming defiance. Blood and nauseating vord-fluid sprinkled on the courtyard's stones.

The other century was in trouble. Only half of them had managed to draw together in concentration, and pockets of a half dozen *legionares* or a handful of armed holders were scattered on the walls and within the courtyard. The vord had already left a dozen dismembered corpses draining blood onto the stones. Trapped and on their own, Amara knew that the other isolated groups of Alerans would die within minutes.

There was another scream almost directly below her, a child's wail, and Amara's gaze snapped down to see three of the vord wheeling in perfect unison toward the healers and the survivors below. There was no one close enough to help them.

With a howl of terror and rage, Amnara drew her sword

and flung herself into a dive that could have outraced a hungry falcon. She swept her dive to the horizontal at the last possible instant, and swept in front of the lead vord. She struck with her sword as she passed, and though she was not herself particularly strong, the sheer speed of her dive delivered her blow with the force of a charging bull. The shock of the impact went all the way up her arm to her shoulder, and her fingers exploded with a tingling sensation and went partially numb.

Amara swept past and immediately turned to go to the defense of the endangered children and healers. The lead vord had been staggered by Amara's blow, which had taken off one of its mandibles cleanly halfway up its length. Sludgy brown-and-green ichor spurted from the broken limb.

The vord shook its head wildly, regained its balance, and turned to charge at Amara while its two companions assaulted the healers.

The vord bounded up into the air, attempting to land upon Amara, but the Cursor had seen the tactic already. As the vord leapt, she flung out one arm and called to Cirrus. A sudden flood of howling wind met the vord in midair and drove it hard into the outer wall of the steadholt. Snarling, Amara flicked her hand again, and the winds drove the creature's back straight down to the stones. When it hit, there was a snapping, crunching sound. The vord writhed and managed to roll back to its four feet, but now luminous green fluid dribbled down its outer plates to the ground. Within seconds, the vord settled smoothly to the earth, like a sail going limp as it lost the wind.

A scream behind Amara made her turn to see one of the vord seize Harger by the leg with its jaw-claw, breaking bone with a shake of its misshapen head. Amara could clearly hear the sickly snap.

The other vord snapped its mandibles around the waist of another healer, shook him hard, whipping back and forth until the man's neck broke. Then it dropped him and charged the terrified children and Heddy.

Amara wanted to scream with frustration—but then she shot a glance at the vord she had killed, and another at the one which had died beside the barn, realization dawning upon her.

If she was correct, she had found a weakness she could attack.

Amara snarled to Cirrus again, and shot across the stones of the courtyard, closing in upon the second vord, eyes seeking her target. She found it, and as she shot by the vord she lashed out with her short blade to strike the bulbous protuberance at the base of the rounded shell.

The sword bit through the vord's hide, and a sudden spray of green ichor splattered the air and the courtyard stones. The vord chattered and clicked in that bizarre fashion she had heard before, then it lurched back and forth in confusion, giving the children a chance to scramble frantically away from the creature. Amara somersaulted in midair, reversing her direction, and shot past the second vord, which had released Harger's ankle and attempted to seize him by the waist.

Amara lashed out as she passed, her sword again striking true. Half-glowing green ichor flowed. Harger rolled from beneath the vord's wildly flexing mandibles, face white with the pain of his injury. The vord whirled to charge drunkenly at Amara, but she swept herself up into the air before it could reach her. The vord staggered the last several feet, as though unable to see that its target was no longer there, and floundered down to the courtyard stones.

Amara came down near the children. Heddy and the remaining healer were trying to get them up and moving. Amara dashed to Harger's side.

"No!" Harger growled at her. Blood flowed from his ankle. "My lady, get these children clear. Leave me."

"On your feet, healer," Amara spat, and bent to seize the man's right arm and drag it over her shoulder so that she could help support him as he rose. "Head for Giraldi's century!" she shouted to the other two adults.

A shadow fell across her.

Amara looked up and saw more vord descending from above, their stiff wings buzzing in a tidal wave of furious sound. At least a dozen of the creatures were descending straight toward her, so swiftly that there was no time to flee, even had she been alone. She watched the vord coming down in a long and endless moment of fear and realized that she was about to die.

And then there was an explosion, and fire blossomed in the

air, directly amidst the ranks of the descending formation of vord. They tumbled and fell, chattering clicks sharp and deafening even among the thrum of blurred wings. Two of them burst into flame outright and were blasted from the sky. They tumbled and fell to their deaths in a drunken spiral, trailing black smoke and clouds of flesh charred to fine ash.

More deadly bursts of flame killed more of the vord, but one of the creatures managed to land on the stones a few steps away from Amara and the wounded Harger. It turned to leap at her, and as Amara tried to dodge, Harger's weight suddenly dragged her down.

Then there was the deep thrum of the heavy bow of a master woodcrafter, and an arrow buried itself into the vord's recessed left eye, striking so deeply that only the brown-and-green fletching showed. The vord rattle-clicked in what looked like agony, convulsing, and a breath later, a second arrow struck home into the creature's other eye.

Captain Janus charged the blinded vord, a heavy, two-handed greatsword held lightly in his right hand alone. Janus bellowed, whipped the sword with superhuman power, and struck cleanly through the vord's armored neck, severing its head from the body. Stinking ichor spewed.

"Come on!" Bernard shouted, and Amara looked up to see him running to her, his bow in hand, green-and-brown arrows riding in the war quiver at his hip. He seized Harger, dragged the man to his own shoulder, and hauled him toward the doorway of the steadholt's great hall.

Amara rose to follow him, and looked up to see two of the Knights Ignus under Bernard's command standing in the open doorway. One of them focused on a flying vord, suddenly clenched his fist, and another booming blossom of fire roared to life, charring the creature to dead, blackened flesh.

Amara made sure all the children were accounted for, and stayed close to Bernard. Behind them, she heard Janus bellow an order, and looked over her shoulder to see the Knight Captain trotting backward after them, sword in hand and ready to defend their backs. Two more firecraftings roared above them as Amara ran into the great hall, and other explosions, farther away, added their own sullen roars to the deafening chaos of battle.

Amara dropped to her knees once they were safely inside,

her body suddenly too weak and tired to support her anymore. She lay there for a few moments, panting hard, until she heard Bernard approach her and kneel next to her. He touched her back with one broad hand.

"Amara," he rumbled, "are you hurt?"

She shook her head mutely, then managed to whisper, "Tired. Too much crafting today." Dizziness and nausea, brought on by her fatigue, made it unthinkably difficult even to consider rising. "What's happening?"

"Isn't good," Bernard said, his voice grim. "They caught us unprepared."

Another set of boots approached quickly, and Amara looked up to see Janus standing over them. "Your Excellency, my Knights have saved everyone they could who had been cut off from Felix's century, but he's lost half his men so far. Giraldi's formation is holding for now."

"The auxiliaries?" Bernard asked, his voice tense.

Janus shook his head.

The Count's face went pale. "*Doroga?*"

"The Marat and that gargant of his have joined with what is left of Felix's century, along with my fighting men. Their defenses are firming."

Bernard nodded. "The Knights?"

"Ten down," Janus said, in a bleak, quiet voice. "All of our Knights Aeris fell trying to slow that second wave that came in. And Harmonus is dead."

Amara's belly quivered nervously. A full third of Garrison's Knights were dead, and Harmonus had been the most powerful watercrafter in Garrison. The Knights and the Legions both relied heavily upon the abilities of their watercrafters to return the wounded to action, and Harmonus's death would come as a crushing blow to both the troops' tactical capabilities and to their morale.

"We're holding them for now," Janus continued. "Giraldi's veterans haven't lost a man, and the Marat's stinking gargant is crushing these things like bugs. But my firecrafters are getting tired. They can't keep this pace up for long."

Bernard nodded sharply. "We have to concentrate our forces. Signal Giraldi to meet up with Felix's century. Get them here. We won't find a better place to defend."

Janus nodded and snapped his fist to his heart in salute, then turned to stalk out into the screaming chaos of the fighting again.

But even as he did, Amara heard a single, high-pitched squealing sound, almost like the shriek of a hawk. Before the sound had died away, buzzing thunder rolled over the entire steadholt. Amara lifted her head to the doorway, and without a word Bernard took her arm and helped her to her feet, then walked beside her to the door.

As they did, the thunder began to recede, and Amara looked up to see the vord in flight, dozens of them rising into the air and sailing away toward Garados.

"They're running," Amara said softly.

Bernard shook his head, and said quietly, "They're withdrawing the sortie. Look at the courtyard."

Amara frowned at him and did. It was a scene from a nightmare. Blood had run through the cracks in the cobblestone courtyard, outlining each stone in scarlet and leaving small pools of bright red here and there in the sunshine. The air stank of blood and offal, and of the acrid, stinging aroma of burnt vord.

The torn and mangled corpses of Knights and *legionares* littered the ground. Wherever she looked, Amara saw the remains of a soldier who had been alive under the morning sunshine. Now the dead lay in a hopelessly confused tangle of lifeless flesh that would make it impossible to lay them to rest in anything but a single grave.

Of the vord, fewer than thirty had been killed. Most of those had been blown out of the air by the Knights Ignus, though Giraldi's men had accounted for two more, and four lay crushed and dead on the far side of the courtyard, at the clawed feet of the chieftain's gargant, Walker.

She counted twenty-six dead vord. At least twice as many had risen into the skies when the vord retreated. Surely others must lie dead outside the steadholt's walls, but there could not have been many of them.

Amara had seen blood and death before. But this had been so savage, so abrupt and deadly that she felt as if what she had seen had entered her mind before she had the chance to armor it against the horror. Her stomach twisted with revulsion, and it was all that she could do to control herself. She did not have enough will to stop the tears from blurring her vision and mercifully shrouding the horrific scene in a watery haze.

Bernard's hand tightened on her shoulder. "Amara, you need to lie down. I'll send a healer to you."

"No," she said quietly. "We have wounded. They must be seen to first."

"Of course," Bernard rumbled. "Frederic," he said. "Get some cots out and set up. We'll bring the wounded in here."

"Yes, sir," Frederic said, somewhere behind them.

The next thing Amara knew, she was lying on a cot, and Bernard was pulling a blanket over her. She was too tired to protest it. "Bernard," she said.

"Yes?"

"Take care of the wounded. Get the men some food. Then we need to meet and decide our next step."

"Next step?" he rumbled.

"Yes," she said. "The vord hurt us badly. Another attack could finish us. We need to consider falling back until we can get more help."

Bernard was silent for a few moments. Then he said, "The vord killed the gargants and the horses, Countess. In fact, I suspect that was the purpose of this attack—to kill the horses, our healers, and cripple whatever *legionares* they could."

"Why would they do that?" Amara asked.

"To leave us with plenty of wounded."

"To trap us here," Amara said.

Bernard nodded. "We could run. But we'd have to leave our wounded behind."

"Never," Amara said at once.

Bernard nodded. "Then best take your rest while you can get it, Countess. We aren't going anywhere."

"I feel ridiculous," Isana said. She stared at the long dressing mirror and frowned at the gown Serai had procured for her. "I *look* ridiculous."

The gown was of deep blue silk, but cut and trimmed after the style of the cities of the northern regions of the Realm, complete with a beaded bodice that laced tightly across Isana's chest and pressed even her lean frame into something resembling a feminine bosom. She'd been forced to remove the ring on its chain, and now carried it in a cloth purse tucked into an inside pocket of the gown.

Serai produced plain, if lovely silver jewelry—rings, a bracelet, and a necklace, adorned with stones of deep onyx. After a calculating look, she unbound Isana's hair from its braid and brushed it all out into dark, shining waves threaded with silver that fell to her waist. After that, Serai insisted upon applying cosmetics to Isana's face, though at least the woman had done so very lightly. When Isana looked into the mirror, she scarcely recognized the woman looking back out at her. She looked . . . not real, somehow, as though someone else was simply pretending to be Isana.

"You're lovely," Serai said.

"I'm not," Isana said. "This isn't . . . it isn't . . . me. I don't look like this."

"You do now, darling. You look stunning, and I insist upon being given full credit for the fact." Serai, this time dressed in a silken gown of deep amber, touched a comb to several spots in Isana's hair, making adjustments, a wickedly amused glint in her eye. "I'm told that Lord Rhodes likes a girlish figure and dark hair. His wife will go into a fit when she sees him staring at you."

Isana shook her head. "I am not at all interested in making anyone stare at me. Particularly at a party hosted by a man who dispatched assassins to kill me."

"There's no proof that Kalare is behind the attacks, darling. Yet." The courtesan turned from Isana to regard her own flawless appearance in the mirror, and smiled in pleasure at her own image. "We're stunning—and we need to be, if we're to make a good impression and accomplish our goals. It's vain, it's stupid, and it's shallow, but that makes it no less true."

Isana shook her head. "This is all so foolish. Lives are in danger, and our only hope of getting anyone to do anything about it is to bow our knee to fashion in order to curry favor at a garden party. There isn't time for this nonsense."

"We live within a society, Isana, that has been built by a thousand years of toil and effort and war. We are by necessity victims of its history and its institutions." Serai tilted her head to one side for a moment, thoughtfully regarding her reflection, then artfully plucked a few curling strands from the clasps that held most of her hair back, so that they dropped to frame her face. The courtesan smiled, and Isana felt her squeeze her hand, her own fingers warm. "And admit it. That gown is perfect on you."

Isana felt herself smiling despite her concerns and turned back and forth in front of the mirror. "I suppose there's no harm in wearing something nice."

"Precisely," Serai said. "Shall we go then? Our carriage should arrive in a few moments, and I want to have time to gloat over the look on Sir Nedus's face when he sees you."

"Serai," Isana protested gently. "You know I have no such interest, or any such intentions of getting that sort of attention."

"You should try it. It can be quite satisfying." She paused, glancing at Isana, and asked, "Is there a man you'd prefer to see you tonight?"

Isana rested the fingers of her hand lightly on the ring, hidden in its pouch. "Once there was."

"He is not a part of your life?" Serai asked.

"He died." Isana hadn't meant her voice to sound quite so flat and hard, but it had, and she could not say that she regretted it. "I don't discuss it."

"Of course," Serai said, her voice thoughtful. "Forgive me for intruding." Then she smiled as though the exchange had never happened and took Isana's arm to walk her to the front of Sir Nedus's manor.

Serai took a few steps ahead of Isana at the last moment, to the top of the staircase leading down into the house's main hall, the better to gain their host's attention and make a dramatic little flourish of presentation as Isana stepped self-consciously into view.

The white-haired old Knight's seamed face immediately broke into a wide smile. "Furies, lass. I would never have guessed you cleaned up so well."

"Nedus!" Serai chided, and shook a finger at him. "How dare you underestimate my cosmetic skills."

Isana found herself smiling again and came down the stairs with Serai. "She tells me that I have you to thank for the gown, Sir Nedus. I am grateful for your generosity, and look forward to repaying it as soon as I may."

The old Knight waved his hand. "It is nothing, Steadholder. Foolish old men are wont to spend their gold on pretty girls." He flicked a glance at Serai. "Or so I am told. Ladies, permit me to escort you to the carriage."

"And I suppose you'll have to do," Serai sniffed. She took Nedus's offered arm with graceful courtesy, and Isana followed them out the front door of the house. A white-and-silver carriage drawn by four grey horses waited there, a driver in grey livery holding the reins while another stepped down from the stand at the back of the carriage, folded down its mounting steps, and opened its door for the women.

"Very nice," Serai murmured to Nedus. She glanced at the Knight, and said, "I notice that you wear your sword tonight, sir."

Nedus looked baffled. "Furies. Do I?"

"Indeed. And I further notice that your clothing looks a rather great deal like the livery of the coachmen."

"Astonishing," Nedus said, smiling. "Some sort of fascinating coincidence, no doubt."

Serai stopped and frowned firmly up at the old man. "And the seat beside the driver is empty of an armsman. What are you playing at?"

"Why, whatever do you mean?"

Serai sighed. "Nedus, darling, this isn't what I asked for. You've done more than enough for the Realm in your day. You're retired. I have no intention of dragging you into something dangerous. Stay here."

"I'm afraid I'm not sure what you're getting at, Lady Serai," Nedus replied affably. "I'm merely walking you to the carriage."

"You are *not*," Serai said, scowling.

The old Knight glanced up at Isana and winked. "Well. Possibly not. But it occurs to me that if I did intend to ride arms upon that carriage, there would really be nothing you could do about it, lady. Once you get in, I could mount the carriage and you'd be none the wiser for the extra protection, regardless of what you might be willing to accept from me."

Serai's mouth firmed into a line. "You aren't going to let me talk you out of this, are you?"

Nedus smiled guilelessly.

Serai let out an exasperated breath and touched his arm. "At least promise me you'll be careful."

"There are old swordsmen and bold swordsmen," Nedus said, idly employing the old Legion maxim. "But very few old, bold swordsmen." He opened the carriage door, and said, "Ladies, please."

Serai and Isana settled into the richly appointed carriage. Nedus shut the door and a moment later the carriage got under way. Isana watched Serai's face, sensing the Cursor's anxiety despite the habitual detachment she maintained.

"You fear for him," Isana murmured.

Serai gave her a pained smile. "In his day, he was one of the most dangerous men alive. But that was long ago."

"He adores you," Isana murmured. "Like a daughter."

Serai's smile became a little sad. "I know." The tiny courtesan folded her hands in her lap and stared pointedly out the carriage's window, and the remainder of the short trip to the garden party passed in silence.

The town house of Lord Kalare was larger than the whole of Isanaholt, and rose seven stories into the air. Balconies and stairs wound all over the outside of the building, thickly planted with broad-leafed plants, flowers, and small trees, all laid out in beautiful, miniature gardens, complete with several beautifully lit fountains. The coachman could have driven through the house's front doors without ducking his head or being particularly careful about the position of the carriage's wheels. Wintersend streamers and bunting in the green and grey of the city of Kalare festooned every balcony railing, window, and pillar, and had been wound round twin rows of statuary that led up to the front doors.

Forged invitation held in a confident hand, Serai led Isana up the lit walk toward the house's doors. "His house says something about our host, I think," Serai said. "Rich. Large. Gaudy. Indulgent. I'd say more, but I suppose it would sound unkind."

"I take it you do not care for Lord Kalare?" Isana asked.

"Nor ever have," Serai replied cheerfully. "Quite aside from his recent activities, I have always found the man to be a spineless, venomous boor. I have often hoped that he would contract some wasting disease that would expose him to lethal levels of humiliation."

Isana found herself laughing. "Goodness. But you're coming to his party anyway?"

"Why shouldn't I?" Serai said. "He adores me."

"He does?"

"Of course, darling. Everyone does. I'll be welcome here."

"If he adores you so much, why weren't you invited in the first place?"

"Because *Lady* Kalare made the lists," Serai said. "She does not adore any attractive woman whom her husband does, as a general rule." The courtesan sniffed, "She's quite petty about it, really."

"Why do I get the impression that you love to cast that dislike back into her face?"

Serai waved a hand airily. "Nonsense, darling. Gloating is hardly ladylike." She approached the doorman waiting at the threshold and presented her invitation. The man gave it only a brief glance and returned Serai's smile with a bow and a polite murmur of welcome. Serai led Isana into an immense entry hallway lined with statuary. They passed down it, slippers whispering quietly on the stone floor. They passed through pools of light from colored furylamps hung here and there among the statues, and it was very quiet within the hall.

Doubtless, the dimness and quiet had been intentionally established, for when Isana reached the end of the hallway, it opened up onto the sprawling garden that made up the heart of the manor house. The garden was a fabulous one, including topiary cut into the shape of horses and gargants, a section of the thick, green-purple foliage of the exotic trees of the Feverthorn Jungle, and dozens of fountains. Furylamps in every color blazed with light, and spark imps leapt rhythmically from lamp to lamp in long jets of color and light, each imp precisely following the steps of an impossibly complex dance—one echoed by jets of water leaping gracefully from one fountain to the next in rhythmic counterpoint.

The color of light falling upon any part of the garden changed between one breath and the next, and it left Isana feeling dazzled. Music floated throughout the garden, pipes, strings, a slow drum, and a wooden flute full of merry dignity.

And the people. Isana had rarely seen so many people in one place, and every one of them wore clothing that could have paid the taxes on her steadholt for a month, at the very least. There were folk with the golden coloring of the sunny southern coast, folk with the thin, somewhat severe features of the mountains west of the capital, and folk with the darker skin of the sailing folk of the western coast. Jewels flashed from their nests within rich clothing, rings, and amulets, their colors clashing and striking chords with the light as it continually changed.

The delicious odor of baking pastries and roasting meat filled the air, as did the fresh scents of flowers and new-cut grass, and Isana's nose touched upon half a dozen exotic perfumes as the attendees passed back and forth before them. In one nook of the garden, a juggler entertained half a dozen children of various ages, and in another drums beat more swiftly and intently, while three slave women sinuously weaved through the complex and demanding motions of traditional Kalaran dance.

Isana could only stare at it all, her mouth falling open. "Furies," she breathed.

Serai patted her hand. "Remember. As rich and powerful as they are, they're only people. And this house and garden—they're bought with mere money," she murmured. "Kalare is making an effort to display his wealth, his prosperity. Doubtless he is attempting to outdo whatever gatherings Aquitaine or Rhodes is planning."

"I've never seen anything like this," Isana said.

Serai smiled and looked around. Isana saw something wistful in her eyes. "Yes. I suppose it is quite lovely." She kept smiling, but Isana felt the faintest taint of bitterness as she spoke. "But I've seen what goes on in places like this, Steadholder. I can't appreciate the facade anymore."

"Is it truly so horrible?" Isana asked quietly.

"It can be," Serai said. "But after all, this is where I do my work. Perhaps I'm jaded. Here, darling, let's stand to one side for a moment so that those coming in behind us don't walk on your gown."

Serai pulled Isana aside and spent a moment peering around the garden. A small line appeared between her brows.

"What is it?" Isana asked quietly.

"Attendance tonight is quite a bit more partisan than I expected," Serai murmured.

"How so?"

"A great many of the High Lords are conspicuous by their absence," Serai replied. "Antillus and Phrygia aren't here, naturally, nor have they sent representatives. Parcia and Attica have not come—but they've sent their senior Senators as proxies. That's going to anger Kalare. It's a calculated insult." The little courtesan's eyes swept around the garden. "Lord and Lady Riva are here, as is Lady—but not Lord—Placida. Lord and Lady Rhodes are over there by the hedges. And my, it would seem that the Aquitaines are here as well."

"Aquitaine?" Isana said, her voice flat.

Serai gave her a sharp glance. Except for her eyes, the courtesan's smile was a firm and impenetrable mask. "Darling, you must contain your emotions. Very nearly everyone here has at least as much skill at watercraft as you. And while some feelings are better when shared with others, rage really isn't one of them—particularly when very nearly everyone here is hideously skilled at firecraft as well."

Isana felt her lips press tightly together. "His ambitions killed some of my friends, my holders, my neighbors. But for good fortune, they would have killed my family as well."

Serai's eyes widened with apprehension. "*Darling,*" she said, voice emphatic. "You must *not.* There are doubtless a dozen windcrafters listening to everything that they can. You must not say such things in public, where they might be overheard. The consequences could be dangerous."

"It's only the truth," Isana said.

"No one can prove that," Serai replied. Her hand tightened on Isana's arm. "And you are here in your capacity as a Steadholder. That means that you are a Citizen. And it means that if you slander Aquitaine in public, he will be forced to challenge you in the *juris macto*.

Isana turned to blink at Serai, startled. "Duel? Me?"

"If you fought him, he'd kill you. And the only way out of the duel would be to retract your statement in public—which would be an excellent way to help make sure that he can never be effectively accused." The courtesan's eyes became cold and hard as stones. "You *will* control yourself, Steadholder, or for you own good I will knock you senseless and drag you back to Nedus's manor."

Isana could only stare at the tiny woman, her mouth open.

"There will be a time of reckoning for those who have sought to undermine the authority of the Crown," Serai continued, iron in her eyes. "But it must be done properly if it is ever to be done at all."

In the face of Serai's reasoned determination, Isana forced her bitter anger aside. She'd had a lifetime of practice, resisting the influence of the emotions she could sense from others, and it afforded her some small advantage in containing her own. "You're right. I don't know what got into me."

The courtesan nodded, and her eyes softened to match her smile. "Furies, look what you've done. You've made me threaten you with physical violence, darling, which no proper lady would ever do. I feel so brutish."

"I apologize," Isana said.

Serai patted her arm, and said, "Fortunately, I am the most gracious and tolerant woman in the Realm. I will forgive you." She sniffed. "Eventually."

"Who should we talk to in the meanwhile?" Isana asked.

Serai pursed her lips thoughtfully, and said, "Let us begin with Lady Placida. She is the annalist of the Dianic League, and her husband has made it a point to remain rather distant from Kalare or Aquitaine."

"He supports the Crown, then?" Isana asked.

Serai arched a brow. "Not precisely. But he pays his taxes without complaining, and he and his sons have served terms in the Shieldwall Legions of Antillus. He'll fight for his

Realm, but he's mostly concerned with managing his lands with as little interference as possible. So long as he has that, he is unconcerned with the identity of the next First Lord."

"I shall never understand politics. Why would he help us?"

"He likely wouldn't, on his own," Serai said. "But there's a chance his wife will. I suspect the Dianic League will be most interested in establishing relationships with you."

"You mean, they want me to owe them favors as rapidly as possible," Isana said in a dry voice.

"Your understanding of politics seems sound enough to me," Serai replied, her eyes sparkling, and she led Isana over to meet Lady Placida.

Lord Placida's wife was an exceptionally tall woman with a thin, severe face and heavy-lidded brown eyes that bespoke the exceptional intellect behind them. She wore the single, deep color of the ruling house of Placida, a rich, deep emerald green whose dye was derived from a plant found only in the high reaches of the mountains near Placida. She wore golden jewelry set with emeralds and amethyst, each piece beautiful in its elegant simplicity. She looked no older than a girl in her midtwenties, though her medium brown hair, like Isana's, was touched lightly with silver and grey. She wore it bound up in a simple net that fell to the base of her neck, and she smelled of rose oil.

"Serai," she murmured, and smiled at the courtesan as she approached. Her voice was surprisingly light and sweet. She came forward, hands held out, and Serai took them, smiling. "It's been too long since you've visited us."

Serai inclined her head in a bow of deference to Lady Placida's station. "Thank you, Your Grace. And how is your lord husband, if I may ask?"

Lady Placida rolled her eyes the tiniest bit, and drily murmured, "He was not feeling well enough to attend tonight's festivities. Something in the air, no doubt."

"No doubt," Serai replied, her voice grave. "If I may be so bold, would you convey my best wishes to him for a speedy recovery?"

"Gladly," the High Lady said. She turned her face to Isana and smiled politely. "And you, lady. Would you happen to be Isana of Calderon?"

Isana bowed her head in reply. "If you please, Your Grace, just Isana."

Lady Placida arched a brow and studied Isana with intent, alert eyes. "No, Steadholder. I'm afraid I must disagree. Indeed, of all the women in the Realm, it would seem that you might be the one who most deserves the honorific. You've done something no other woman in all the history of Alera has ever done. You've earned rank and title without resorting to marriage or murder."

Isana shook her head. "The First Lord deserves the credit, if anyone. I had little say in the matter."

Lady Placida smiled. "History seldom takes note of serendipity when it records events. And from what I have heard, I suspect an argument could be made that you very much did earn the title."

"Many women have earned titles, Your Grace. It doesn't seem to have been a factor in whether or not they actually received them."

Lady Placida laughed. "True enough. But perhaps that is beginning to change." She offered her hands. "It is a distinct pleasure to meet you, Steadholder."

Isana clasped the other woman's hands for a moment, smiling. "Likewise."

"Please tell me that Serai is not your guide here in the capital," the High Lady murmured.

Serai sighed. "Everyone thinks the worst of me."

"Tut, dear," Lady Placida said calmly, her eyes shining. "I don't *think* the worst of you. I happen to *know* it. And I shudder to think to what kinds of shocking experiences the good Steadholder is about to be exposed."

Serai thrust out her lower lip. "Few enough. I'm staying at Sir Nedus's manor. I've got to be on my best behavior."

Lady Placida nodded in understanding. "Isana, have any of the Dianic League's council spoken to you yet?"

"Not yet, Your Grace," Isana replied.

"Ah," said Lady Placida. "Well, I'll not bore you with a recruiting speech here at the party, but I should enjoy the chance to discuss matters with you before the conclusion of Wintersend. I think there are many things that you and the League might have to offer one another."

"I don't know what I could offer, Your Grace," Isana said.

"An example, for one," Lady Placida replied. "Word of your appointment has spread like wildfire, you know. There are thousands of women in the Realm who have been shown that there are doors that might now be open to them that were not before."

"Your Grace," Serai lied smoothly, "I am afraid that the Steadholder's time is by and large accounted for, as a guest of the First Lord's—but I happen to know the outrageously beautiful slave in charge of her calendar, and I should be glad to speak to her on your behalf to see if we can open up a time."

Lady Placida laughed. "My own time is somewhat limited, you know."

"I do not doubt it," Serai said. "But perhaps something might be arranged. What are your mornings like?"

"Filled with endless receptions for the most part, but for my lord husband's audience with the First Lord."

Serai arched a thoughtful brow. "There is usually quite a bit of walking involved during the audience. Perhaps you might permit the Steadholder to accompany you for conversation?"

"An excellent notion," Lady Placida said. "But two days too late, I am afraid. My lord husband was first on the list this year." Her words were light and pleasant, but Isana saw something shrewd and calculating in her eyes for a moment. "I'll have one of my staff contact you to find a time to take tea with the Steadholder—if that is all right with you, of course, Isana."

"Oh. Yes, of course," Isana said.

"Excellent," Lady Placida said, smiling. "Until we meet again, then." She turned away to take up a conversation with a pair of grey-bearded men, each wearing the deep purple sash of a Senator.

Isana's stomach clenched in frustration and worry. She glanced at Serai, and said, "There must be someone else."

Serai frowned at the High Lady's back for a moment, and murmured to Isana, "Of course, darling. If at first you don't succeed, pick the next most likely course of action." The courtesan looked around the garden. "Mmm. Lord and Lady Riva probably aren't going to be very interested in helping you, I'm afraid. They very much resent how the First Lord appointed your brother as the new Count Calderon without consulting them on the matter."

"Who does that leave?" Isana asked.

Serai shook her head. "We'll keep trying until we've heard no from everyone. But let me go speak to Lord Rhodes."

"Shouldn't I come with you?"

"No," Serai said, firmly. "Remember, I think he's going to rather enjoy the look of you. I'd like to spring that on him as a surprise. It may warm him to the idea of taking you with him. Just watch me and come over when I wave, darling."

"All right," Isana said.

Serai glided through the attendees, smiling and exchanging courtesies as she went. Isana watched her, and felt suddenly vulnerable without the Cursor's presence and guidance. Isana glanced around, looking for a place she could wait without jumping like a frightened cat every time someone walked behind her. There was a long stone bench beside a nearby fountain, and Isana settled lightly down on it, making sure that she could see Serai.

A moment later, a woman in a red gown settled on the other end of the bench and nodded pleasantly at Isana. She was tall, her hair dark though shot with silver. She had clear grey eyes and lovely, if remote features.

Isana nodded back with a smile, then frowned thoughtfully. The woman seemed familiar, and a moment later she recognized her from the attack at the windport. She was the woman Isana had stumbled into.

"My lady," Isana said, "I'm afraid I didn't get the chance to beg your pardon at the windport this morning."

The woman arched a brow, expression quizzical, then she suddenly smiled. "Oh, on the landing platform. There were no broken bones—hardly a need to apologize."

"All the same. I left without doing so."

The woman smiled. "Your first time at the capital's windport?"

"Yes," Isana said.

"It can be overwhelming," the woman said, nodding. "So many windcrafters and porters and litters. All that dust blowing around—and, of course, no one can see anything. It's madness during Wintersend. Don't feel bad, Steadholder."

Isana blinked at the woman, startled. "You recognize me?"

"A great many would," the woman said. "You are one of the more famous women in the Realm this year. I am sure the Dianic League will be falling all over itself to welcome you."

Isana forced herself to smile politely, keeping a tight rein on her emotions. "It's quite flattering. I've spoken to High Lady Placida already."

The woman in red laughed. "Aria is many things—but none of them are flattering. I hope she was pleasant to you."

"Very," Isana said. "I had not expected this kind of . . ." She hesitated, searching for a phrase that would not give the noblewoman offense.

"Courtesy?" the woman suggested. "Common politeness uncommon in a noblewoman?"

"I would not describe it using any of those terms, lady," Isana replied, but she couldn't keep the wry humor out of her voice.

The woman laughed. "And I suspect that is because you have a conscience, whereas a great many of the people here would only be moved to it by their political ambitions. Ambitions are incompatible with consciences, you know. The two strangle one another straightaway and leave an awful mess behind them."

Isana laughed. "And you, lady? Are you a woman of conscience or of ambition?"

The lady smiled. "That's a question rarely asked here at court."

"And why is that?"

"Because a woman of conscience would tell you that she is a person of conscience. A woman of ambition would tell you that she is a person of conscience—only much more convincingly."

Isana arched a brow, smiling. "I see. I shall have to be more circumspect in my questions, then."

"Don't," the lady said. "It's refreshing to encounter a new mind with new questions. Welcome to Alera Imperia, Steadholder."

Isana inclined her head to the lady, and murmured, with genuine gratitude, "Thank you."

"Of course. It's the least I can do."

Isana looked up to see Serai speaking to a hollow-cheeked man in gold and sable, the colors of the House of Rhodes. The courtesan was laughing at something the High Lord was saying as she glanced over at Isana.

The smile froze on Serai's face.

She turned back to Rhodes and said something else, then turned and immediately crossed the garden to Isana and the woman in the red gown.

"Steadholder," Serai said, smiling. She curtseyed deeply to the woman in red. "Lady Aquitaine."

Isana's glance snapped from Serai to the woman in red, the heated anger she had felt before struggling to burst free. "You." She choked on the sentence and had to take a breath and begin again. "You are Lady Aquitaine?"

The lady regarded Serai with a cool glance and murmured, voice dry, "Did I not mention my name? How careless of me." She nodded to Isana, and said, "I am Invidia, wife to Aquitainus Attis, High Lord Aquitaine. And I should very much like to discuss the future with you, Steadholder."

Isana rose to her feet and felt her chin lift as she glared down at Lady Aquitaine. "I don't see what point there would be to that discussion, Your Grace," she said.

"Why ever not?"

Isana felt Serai step next to her, and the courtesan's fingers tightened on Isana's wrist, urging restraint. "Because in every future I can imagine, you and I have nothing to do with one another."

Lady Aquitaine smiled, a cool, self-contained expression. "The future is a winding road. It is not possible to foresee all of its turns."

"Perhaps not," Isana replied. "But it *is* possible to choose one's traveling companions. And I will not walk with a tr—"

Serai's nails dug hard into Isana's arm, and the Steadholder barely kept herself from saying the word "traitor." She took a deep breath and steadied herself before resuming. "I will not walk with a traveling companion I have small reason to like—and even less to trust."

Lady Aquitaine looked quietly from Isana to Serai and back. "Yes. I can see that your taste in companions and mine differ significantly. But bear in mind, Steadholder, that the road can be a dangerous one. There are many hazards both overt and unseen. It is wise to walk with someone who is able to protect you from them."

"And even wiser to choose companions who will not turn upon you when the opportunity presents itself," Isana replied. She lowered her voice to barely above a whisper. "I saw your husband's dagger, Your Grace. I buried men and women and children who died because of it. I will *never* walk willingly with such as you."

Lady Aquitaine's eyes narrowed unreadably. Then she nodded once, and her gaze moved to Serai. "I take it, Serai, that you are the Steadholder's guide within the capital?"

"His Majesty made a request of my master, who loaned me out to do so," Serai replied, smiling. "And if I happen to take in the new season's fashion in the course of my duties, well, I shall simply have to bear it."

Lady Aquitaine smiled. "Well, it isn't like our Midsummer ball, but it will have to do."

"Nothing compares to Midsummer at Aquitaine," Serai said. "And your gown is quite gorgeous."

Lady Aquitaine smiled in what looked like genuine pleasure. "This old thing?" she asked artlessly, and waved a hand. The scarlet silk of her dress swept through a haze of colors, then settled on a shade of amber like Serai's own dress, but more deeply steeped in crimson.

Serai's lips parted, and she smiled. "Oh, my. Is it difficult to do that?"

"No more so than any faucet or oven," Lady Aquitaine replied. "It's a new line of silks my Master Weaver has been working on for years." Another gesture returned the silk to its original hue, though it deepened from scarlet to black by gentle degrees at the ends of the sleeves and the hem of the skirts. "My lord husband suggested it be used to reflect the mood of its wearer, but for goodness' sake, it isn't as though we don't have trouble enough dealing with men. If they suddenly actually became able to gauge our moods, I'm sure it would be an utter disaster. So I insisted on mere fashion."

Serai regarded the dress wistfully. "Expensive, I take it, the new silk?"

Lady Aquitaine shrugged a shoulder. "Yes, but not

grotesquely so. And I might be able to arrange something for you, darling, should you join us at Midsummer."

Serai's smiling mask returned. "That's very generous, Your Grace. And certainly tempting. But I fear I must consult with my master before making any decisions."

"Naturally. I know how highly you value your loyalty. And he who commands it." There was a sudden silence, and Lady Aquitaine's smile put a mild but definite emphasis on it. "Are you sure you wouldn't like to come? These gowns are going to be all the rage in the next season or two. I'd love to see you in one—and you are, after all, an invaluable consultant on such matters. It would be a true shame were you not to be recognized as a leader in the newest styles."

Isana felt the courtesan's fingers tighten on her arm again. "You are very generous, Your Grace," Serai replied. She hesitated so briefly that Isana barely heard the awkward pause. "I'm afraid I'm still all turned about from all the travel I've done. Let me sleep on it and consider the possibilities."

"Of course, dear. Meanwhile, do good service to your master and to the Steadholder, Serai. The capital can be a dangerous place to those new to it. It would be a great loss to the League should anything happen to her."

"I assure you, Your Grace, that Isana is in the care of more hands than are easily seen."

"Of that," Lady Aquitaine said, "I am certain." She rose smoothly and inclined her head to Isana and Serai. Her steady grey eyes remained on Isana's. "Ladies. I am sure we will speak again."

It was a dismissal. Isana narrowed her eyes and prepared to stand her ground, but Serai's silent tugs on her arm drew her away from Lady Aquitaine to another part of the garden.

"She knew," Isana said quietly. "She knew how I would react to her had she introduced herself."

"Obviously," Serai said, and her voice was shaking.

Isana felt a thrill of apprehension flow into her from the courtesan, and she blinked at the smaller woman. "Are you all right?"

Serai looked around them, then said, "Not here. We'll speak again later."

"Very well," Isana said. "Did you speak to Lord Rhodes?"

"Yes."

"Where is he?"

Serai shook her head. "He and the other High Lords have gone to the far garden to bear witness to Kalare's official duel with his son, Brencis, for Citizenship. His audience with the First Lord is on the morrow, but his party is already over-large." She licked her lips. "I think we should leave, Stead-holder, as soon as possible."

Isana felt herself tensing again. "Are we in danger?"

Serai looked across the garden at Lady Aquitaine, and Isana felt her start trembling more severely. "Yes. We are."

Isana felt Serai's fear creep into her own belly. "What should we do?"

"I . . . I don't know . . ." The little courtesan took a deep breath and closed her eyes for a moment. Then she opened them, and Isana could feel her forcing steel into her voice. "We should leave as soon as possible. I'll make you enough introductions to satisfy courtesy, then we will return to the House of Nedus."

Isana felt her throat tighten. "We've failed."

Serai lifted her chin and patted Isana's arm firmly. "We have not yet succeeded. There is a difference. We'll find a way."

The courtesan's confident manner had returned, but Isana thought she could feel the faintest trembling yet in her hand. And she saw Serai spare another glance in Lady Aquitaine's direction, her eyes moving too quickly to be anything but nervous.

Isana looked back and met Lady Aquitaine's cool grey eyes from across the garden.

The Steadholder shivered and turned away.

Within half an hour, Serai had introduced Isana to more than a dozen nobles and prominent Citizens of the capital, charmed and complimented every one of them, and had somehow managed to leave each conversation with pleasant brevity. The courtesan was, Isana realized, a master fencer in the arts of wit and conversation. One friendly old Senator had threatened to drag the conversation out for hours, but Serai had deftly slipped in a joke that caused him to boom into a belly laugh in the middle of a sip of wine, requiring immediate steps to save the tunic he wore. A young Attican Lord had spoken to Serai in beautifully polite—and lengthy—phrases that were entirely out of sorts with his predatory eyes, but the Cursor had stood upon tiptoe to whisper something into his ear that made a slow smile curl one side of his mouth, and he had taken his leave "until later."

There were half a dozen other such incidents, and the courtesan reacted to each with precision, poise, wit, and blinding rapidity of thought. Isana was quite certain that with Serai's help, she had just set some kind of speed record for making a good first impression upon the cream of Alera's society. She'd done her best to smile, say polite things, and avoid tripping over either the nobles at the party or the hem of her silk gown.

Serai asked a servant to tell her coachmen to pick them up in front of the house. She and Isana had just turned to leave the garden when a man in a granite grey tunic salted with beads of green semiprecious stones stepped into their path, smiling pleasantly. He was not as tall as Isana, nor was he built with any particularly significant amount of athleticism. He had a weak chin hidden under a neatly trimmed goatee, rings on every finger, and wore a steel circlet across his brow. "Ladies," he said, and bowed very slightly. "I must apologize to you both for being remiss in my duties as a host. I must have overlooked your names on the guest list, or I would have made the time to visit with you both."

"Your Grace," Serai murmured, and dropped into a deep curtsey. "It is good to see you again."

"And you, Serai. You are as lovely as ever." The man's eyes were narrow and suspicious—not so much from active thought, Isana thought, as from ingrained habit. "I am surprised that my lady wife extended her invitations to you, I must admit."

Serai smiled winsomely up at him. "I suppose happy accidents can happen. High Lord Kalare, may I present Steadholder Isana of the Calderon Valley."

Kalare's narrowed eyes flicked to Isana and ran over her. There was no sense of emotion from him. He looked at Isana as other men might a column of numbers. "Ah. Well, this is a pleasant surprise." He smiled. There was no more emotion to that than there had been to his gaze. "I've heard so many things about you," he said.

"And I you, Your Grace," Isana murmured.

"Have you now. Good things, I hope?"

"Many things," Isana said.

Kalare's false smile vanished.

"My lord," Serai said, stepping into the silence before it could become more uncomfortable. "I fear that my recent travel has left me at somewhat less than perfect health. We were just leaving, before I fell down asleep and made a fool of myself."

"A fool of yourself," Kalare murmured. He stared at Serai for a moment, then said, "I have been considering purchasing you from your current master, Serai."

She smiled at him, somehow making it artless and vulnerable with fatigue. "You flatter me, my lord."

Kalare's voice was flat. "I do not offer it as a compliment, slave."

Serai lowered her eyes and curtseyed again. "Of course not, Your Grace. Please forgive my presumption. But I do not think my master has set a price for me."

"There's always a price, slave. Always." His mouth twitched at one corner. "I do not like to be made the fool. And I do not forget my enemies."

"My lord?" Serai asked. She sounded bewildered.

Kalare let out a harsh bray of bitter laughter. "You do your master good service, I think, Serai. But you will exchange his collar for another's, sooner or later. You should give careful thought to whom you might next serve." His eyes flicked to Isana, and he murmured, "And you should give careful thought to the company you keep. The world is a dangerous place."

Serai never lifted her eyes. "I will do so, my lord."

Kalare looked up at Isana, and said, "It was a pleasure to meet you, Steadholder. Allow me to wish you a safe journey home."

Isana faced him without smiling. "Certainly, my lord. And believe me when I say that I wish your own road to be of a kind."

Kalare's eyes narrowed to slits, but before he could speak a servant in the grey and green of House Kalarus approached him, carrying an arming jacket and a wooden practice sword. "My lord," he murmured, bowing. "Your son stands ready to face you, with Lords Aquitaine, Rhodes, and Forcia to bear witness."

Kalare's eyes snapped to the servant. The man paled a little and bowed again.

Serai licked her lips, looking from the servant to Kalare, and said, "My lord, is Brencis ready to challenge for Citizenship already? The last I saw of him, he wasn't so tall as me."

Kalare, without so much as glancing at Serai, struck her a blow to the cheek with his open hand. Isana knew that had he used fury-born strength to do so, the blow could have killed Serai—but it was merely a heavy, contemptuous slap that rocked the courtesan to stumble to one side.

"Lying bitch. Do not presume to speak to me as if you were my peer," Kalare said. "You are in my house. Your master is not here to speak for you. Keep to your place, or I will have that gown whipped from your flesh. Do you understand?"

Serai recovered herself. Her cheek had already begun to flush red where the blow had landed, and her eyes looked a bit glassy, stunned.

A startled silence settled over the garden, and Isana felt the sudden pressure of every gaze at the party being directed toward them.

"Answer me, slave," Kalare said, his voice quiet, even. Then he stepped toward Serai and lifted his hand again.

Isana's body was flooded with sudden, cold fury. She stepped forward between them, and raised one arm vertically, to intercept Kalare's swinging hand.

Kalare bared his teeth. "Who do you think you are, woman?"

Isana faced him, that same chill anger transforming her quiet speaking voice into a steely sword. "I think I am a Citizen of the Realm, my lord. I think that striking another Citizen is an offense in the eyes of the law of the Realm. I think that I am here at the invitation of my patron, Gaius Sextus, First Lord of Alera." She locked eyes with Kalare and stepped forward again, facing him from a handbreadth. "And, my lord, I think that you are neither foolish nor arrogant enough to believe for a single moment that you could strike *me* in public without repercussions."

The only sound in the garden was the gentle splash of water in the fountains.

Kalare shifted his weight uncomfortably, and his narrowed eyes relaxed, becoming more sleepy than suspicious. "I suppose so," he said. "But do not think I will forget this."

"That makes two of us, Your Grace," Isana said.

Muscles tightened along Kalare's jaw, and he spoke through clenched teeth. "Get out of my house."

Isana tilted her head in the barest nod of acknowledgment. She stepped back from Kalare, touched Serai's arm, and left the garden with her.

Instead of heading for the front door, Serai glanced around the hallway, took Isana's hand, and decisively led her into a side passage.

"Where are we going?" Isana asked.

"To the kitchen doors at the rear of the house," Serai said.

"But you told Nedus and his men to meet us at the front."

"I told the servant that for the benefit of whoever might be eavesdropping, darling," Serai said. "The better to keep anyone from following us home. After all, it *is* Kalare's house, and his servants will certainly report your movements. Nedus will know to meet us in the back."

"I see," Isana said, and in a moment the courtesan led her through the busy kitchens and out the back door of the house, to a dark, quiet street where Nedus and the coach waited. They hurried into the carriage without a word, and Nedus shut the door behind them. The driver clucked to the horses at once, and the carriage lurched forward into hurried motion.

"Lady Aquitaine," Isana said quietly. "She was not what I expected."

"She's the sort to smile while she twists the knife, Steadholder. Don't be deceived. She is a dangerous woman."

"You think she might be behind the attacks."

Serai stared at the curtains over the coach's windows and shrugged, her expression remote. "She is certainly capable of it. And she knows things she shouldn't."

"That you are one of the Cursors," Isana said.

Serai drew in a slow breath and nodded. "Yes. It would seem that I have been compromised. She knows, and from the way Kalare spoke, I would judge that he does as well."

"But how?"

"Remember that someone has been killing Cursors left and right, darling. It's possible that the information was extracted from one of them."

Or, Isana thought, *that one of them is a traitor.*

"What does it mean for you?" she asked Serai quietly. "Exposure."

"Any enemy of the Crown might take satisfaction in removing me," she said, her voice calm, matter-of-fact. "It will only be a matter of time. Secrecy was my greatest defense— and Gaius's enemies will face few, if any, consequences for murdering a slave. If nothing else, Kalare will do it simply to spite the First Lord."

"But wouldn't Gaius protect you?"

"If he could," Serai said. She shook her head. "He's been slowly losing power among the High Lords, and he isn't getting any younger. He won't be First Lord forever, and once he isn't . . ." The courtesan shrugged.

Isana felt sick at her stomach. "That's what that talk about the gown was all about. Lady Aquitaine was offering you a position with her, wasn't she?"

"More than that. I should think she meant to offer me my freedom, a title, and most likely a position in whatever would pass for the Cursors under her husband's rule."

Isana was quiet for a moment. "That's quite an offer," she said.

Serai nodded, silent.

Isana folded her hands in her lap. "Why didn't you take it?"

"Her price was too high."

Isana frowned. "Price? What price?"

"Isn't it obvious, darling? She knew that I was your guardian. She offered me power in exchange for you. And made it known that the results might be unpleasant if I denied her."

Isana swallowed. "Do you think she wants me dead?"

"Perhaps," Serai said, nodding. "Or perhaps only within her control. Which might be worse, depending on the next several years. From what she said, it seems obvious that her husband is very nearly ready to move against the Crown."

They rode in silence for a moment, then Isana said, "Or it might not have been a threat."

Serai arched a brow. "How so?"

"Well," Isana said slowly, "if word of your true allegiance has gotten out, and you didn't know about it . . . could what she said have been a warning? To point it out to you?"

Serai's eyebrows lifted delicately. "Yes. Yes, I suppose it could have been, at that."

"But why would she warn you?"

Serai shook her head. "Difficult to say. Assuming it was a warning, and assuming that Kalare and Aquitaine are not working together to bring Gaius down, it would be most likely that she warned me in an effort to deny Kalare the chance to kill me. Or capture me to learn what secrets I keep."

"We're both in the same oven, then. Whoever is killing Cursors would not mind seeing the pair of us dead."

"Indeed," Serai said. She glanced at her hands. Isana did as well. They were trembling harder. Serai folded them and held them tight against her lap. "In any case, given how little we know about the current climate, it seemed best to me that we leave before something unpleasant happened." She paused, then said, "I'm sorry we didn't manage to gain the First Lord's ear."

"But we must," Isana said quietly.

"Yes. But remember, Steadholder, that my first duty is to protect you—not to try to manage affairs in the Calderon Valley."

"But there's no *time*."

"You can't gain the support of the First Lord from the grave, Steadholder," Serai said, her tone frank, serious. "You're of no use to your family dead. And just between you and me, if I die before I get a chance to wear a gown of those new silks from Aquitaine, I will never forgive you."

Isana tried to smile at her attempt at levity, but it was too strongly underscored by an emotional undertow of anxiety. "I suppose. But what is our next step?"

"Get back to the house all in a piece," Serai said. "And from there, I think a nice glass of wine might soothe my nerves. And a hot bath."

Isana regarded her evenly. "And after that?"

"After wine and a steaming bath? I should be surprised if I didn't sleep."

Isana pressed her lips into a line. "I don't need you to try to amuse me with clever evasions. I need to know how we're going to get to Gaius."

"Oh," Serai said. She pursed her lips thoughtfully. "Going out of Nedus's house is a risk, Steadholder. For both of us, now. What do you think our next move should be?"

"My nephew," Isana said firmly. "In the morning we'll go to the Academy and find him so that he can carry the message to the First Lord."

Serai frowned. "The streets aren't safe enough for you to—"

"Crows take the streets," Isana said, the barest trace of an angry snarl in her voice.

Serai sighed. "It's a risk."

"One we have to take," Isana said. "We don't have time for anything else."

Serai frowned and looked away.

"And besides," Isana said, "I'm worried about Tavi. The message must have reached him by now—it was left in his own room, after all. But he hasn't come to see me."

"Unless he has," Serai pointed out. "He might well be waiting at Nedus's manor for us to return."

"Either way, I want to find him and make sure he's all right."

Serai sighed, and said, "Of course you do." She lifted a hand to press her fingers lightly against her reddened cheek, her eyes closed. "I hope you'll excuse me, Steadholder. I'm . . . somewhat shaken. Not thinking as clearly as I should." She looked up at Isana, and said, simply, "I'm afraid."

Isana met her eyes and said, in her gentlest voice, "That's all right. There's nothing wrong with being afraid."

Serai waved her hands in a frustrated little gesture. "I'm not used to it. What if I start chewing my nails? Can you imagine how horrid that would be? A nightmare."

Isana almost laughed. The courtesan might be afraid, but for all that she was playing in an unfamiliar field against lethally violent opponents, a mouse among hungry cats, she had the kind of spirit that refused to be kept down. The feigned vapid mannerisms and dialogue was her way of laughing at her fears. "I suppose we could always tie mittens onto your hands," Isana murmured. "If it is all that important to the security of the Realm to preserve your nails."

Serai nodded gravely. "Absolutely, darling. By any means necessary."

A moment later the coach came to a halt, and Isana heard the footman coming around to open the door. Nedus muttered something to the driver. The door opened, and Serai stepped out onto the folding stair. "It's a shame, really—all the politics. I hate it when I am forced to leave a party early."

The assassins came without sound or warning.

Isana heard a sudden, harsh exhalation from the driver of the coach. Serai froze in place on the stair, and a frozen gale of sudden fear swept over Isana's senses. Nedus shouted, and she heard the steely rasp of a sword being drawn. There were shuffling footsteps, and the ring of steel on steel.

"Stay back!" Serai cried. Isana saw a dark figure, a man with a sword, step up close to the coach. His blade thrust at Serai. The courtesan batted the blade aside with her left hand, and the flesh of her forearm parted, sending blood sprinkling down. The courtesan's other hand flew to her hair, to what Isana had taken as the handle of a jeweled comb. Instead, Serai drew forth a slender, needle-sharp blade and thrust it into the assassin's eye. The man screamed and fell away.

Serai leaned out to catch the handle of the coach's door and began to close it.

There was a hissing sound, a thump of impact, and the bloodied, barbed steel head of an arrow burst from Serai's back. Blood flooded over the ripped silk of her amber gown.

"Oh," Serai said, her voice breathless, startled.

"Serai!" Isana screamed.

The courtesan toppled slowly forward and out of the coach.

Isana rushed out of the coach to go to the woman's aid. She seized Serai's arm and hauled on it, trying to draw the Cursor back into the coach. Isana slipped in Serai's blood and stumbled. A second arrow sped past her shoulder as she did, driving itself to the feathers in the heavy oak wall of the coach.

She heard another scream to her right, and saw Nedus standing with his back to the wall of the coach, facing a pair of armed assassins, hard-looking men in drab clothing. A third attacker lay bleeding on the cobblestones, and even as Isana looked, the old metalcrafter's sword whipped up into a high parry and dealt back a slash that split open the throat of his attacker.

But the blow had left the old Knight open, and the other assassin lunged forward, his short, heavy blade thrusting sharply into Nedus's vitals.

Nedus whirled on the third man, showing no sign of pain, and seized his sword-arm wrist in one hand. Instead of pushing the man away, though, Nedus simply clamped down an iron grip, and with grim determination, rammed his sword into the assassin's mouth.

Assassin and Knight both collapsed to the ground, their blood pouring out like water from a broken cup.

Terrified, Isana pulled at Serai, struggling to get the Cursor back into the coach, before—

Something bumped into her, and there was a nauseating flash of sensation in her belly. Isana looked down to see another heavy arrow. This one had struck her, in the curl of her waist above her hipbone. Isana stared at it in shock for a moment, and then looked to see six inches of bloodied shaft emerging from her lower back.

Pain came next. Horrible pain. Her vision went red for a second, and her heart beat like thunder. She blinked down at Serai and reached for her again, unsure of what to do but doggedly determined to draw the fallen woman from beneath the hidden archer's shafts.

Serai rolled limply to one side, her eyes open and staring. The arrow had taken her through the heart.

Isana heard footsteps coming toward her. She looked up, agony making her vision almost seem to throb, and saw a man emerge from the darkness with a bow in his hand.

She recognized him. Shorter than average, grizzled with age, balding, stocky, and confident. His features were regular, unremarkable, neither ugly nor appealing. She had seen him once before—on the walls during the horrible battle at Garrison. She had seen him slaughter men with arrows, throw Fade from the walls with a noose tight around his neck, and attempt to murder her nephew.

Fidelias, a former Cursor Callidus, now a traitor to the Crown.

The man's eyes flicked around him as he walked, careful, wary and alert. He drew another arrow from his quiver and slipped its nock over the bowstring. He regarded the corpses dispassionately. Then his unreadable, merciless eyes fell upon Isana.

Pain took her.

CHAPTER 23

"Slow down," Max complained. "Furies, Calderon, what's all the crows-eaten rush?"

Tavi glanced back over his shoulder as he paced swiftly down the street from the Citadel. Colorful Wintersend fury-lamps lit the way in soft hues of pink, yellow, and sky-blue, and despite the late hour the streets were busy. "I'm not sure. But I know something is very wrong."

Max sighed and broke into a lazy lope until he caught up with Tavi. "How do you know? What does that letter say?"

Tavi shook his head. "Oh, the usual. How are you doing, little things that happened at home, that she's staying at the manor of someone named Nedus on Garden Lane."

"Oh," Max said. "No wonder you panicked. That's one horrifying letter. It certainly merits sneaking out on Killian and possibly endangering the security of the Crown."

Tavi glared at Max. "She wrote in details that weren't right. She called my uncle Bernhardt. His name is Bernard. She told me my little sister was doing well with her reading lessons. I don't have a sister. Something is wrong—but she didn't want to put it down on paper."

Max frowned. "Are you sure the letter is genuine? I can think of a few people who wouldn't mind catching up with you in a dark alley somewhere late at night."

"It's her handwriting," Tavi said. "I'm sure of it."

Max walked beside him in silence for a while. "You know what? I think you should go see her and find out what's going on."

"You think?"

Max nodded gravely. "Yeah. Better take someone large and menacing with you, too, just to be careful."

"That's a good idea, too," Tavi said. The pair turned onto Garden Lane. "How do we know which one is Nedus's house?"

"I've been there before," Max said.

"Is there a young widow?" Tavi asked.

Max snorted. "No. But Sir Nedus was the finest swordsman of his whole generation. He trained a lot of the greats. Princeps Septimus, Araris Valerian, Captain Miles of the Crown Legion, Aldrick ex Gladius, Lartos and Martos of Parcia, and dozens of others."

"You studied with him?" Tavi asked.

Max nodded. "Yes, all through first year. Solid man. Still a fair sword arm, too, and he's got to be eighty years old. Best teacher I ever had, including my father."

"You studying with him now?"

"No," Max said.

"Why not?"

Max shrugged. "He said that there wasn't anything else he could teach me on the training floor. That I'd have to learn the rest on my own in the field." .

Tavi nodded, chewing on his lower lip thoughtfully. "Where does he stand with the Crown?"

"He's a hard-line loyalist to the House of Gaius and the office of the First Lord. But if you ask me, I'd say that he detests Gaius, personally."

"Why would he do that?"

Max shrugged, but he spoke with absolute confidence. "There's some history between them. I don't know any details. But he'd never involve himself with traitors to the Crown, either. He's solid." Max nodded at a nearby house that was large and lovely but dwarfed by its neighbors. "Here it is."

But when they went to the door, they were informed that Lord Nedus and his guests were no longer there. Tavi showed the porter at the door the letter from his aunt, and the man nodded and returned with a second envelope, which he offered to Tavi.

Tavi took it and read it as they walked back down the street. "She's . . . oh great furies, Max. She's at the garden party being given by Lord Kalare."

Max's eyebrows shot up. "Really? From what you said of her, she never seemed like a socialite."

"She isn't," Tavi said, frowning.

"I bet the Dianic League is going to swarm over her like a pack of Phrygian waterpike." Max took the letter and read it, frowning. "She says she's hoping to get the chance to tour the palace with one of the High Lords." Max squinted up his eyes, frowning. "But the only time the High Lords are actually in the palace during Wintersend is during their meetings with the First Lord."

"She's trying to get to Gaius," Tavi said quietly. "She can't just come out and say it for fear of interception. But that's why she's been trying to contact me. To get to Gaius."

"Well that isn't going to happen," Max said calmly.

"I know," Tavi said quietly. "That's the problem."

"What?"

"My aunt . . . well, I get the impression that she and Sir Nedus would agree when it comes to the First Lord. She never wanted to come within a mile of him."

"So why is she trying to get to him now?" Max asked.

Tavi shrugged. "But she wouldn't do it if she wasn't desperate to get to Gaius. The coded messages. She's staying in the house of a Crown loyalist, instead of in the Citadel—and going out to noble functions."

"At Kalare's house, no less. That's dangerous."

Tavi frowned, thinking. "Kalare and Aquitaine are the strongest High Lords, and rivals. They both hate Gaius, too. And my aunt is in Gaius's favor."

"Yes," Max said. "She isn't going to get a warm welcome there."

"Surely she knows that. Why would she *go* there?" He took a deep breath. "I can't put my finger on it, but this really bothers me. I . . . it's like it was at Second Calderon. My instincts are screaming at me that this is serious stuff."

Max studied Tavi for a long minute, then nodded slowly. "Could be you're right. It was like this for me on the Wall a couple of times. Bad nights. But your aunt isn't going to get to Gaius, Tavi. Not even to me. Killian wouldn't hear of it."

"She doesn't have to," Tavi said. "Come on."

"Where to?" Max asked cheerfully.

"Kalare's manor," Tavi said. "I'll speak to her. I can pass word on to the First Lord for her. We keep the security intact, Killian's happy, and if she's here with something serious, then . . ."

"Then what?" Max asked pointedly. "You planning on issuing some royal commands to fix it?" Max met Tavi's eyes. "To tell you the truth, I'm scared as hell, Tavi. Whatever I do when I'm in costume, it's Gaius who will have to deal with the consequences. And I am *not* the First Lord. I don't have the authority to order Legions into action, or dispatch aid or Crown support."

Tavi frowned. "Killian would say that the Legions and the bursar legate don't know that."

Max snorted. "I know it. That's enough."

Tavi shook his head. "Do you think Gaius would prefer us to stand around doing nothing while his subjects and lands were jeopardized?"

Max gave Tavi a sour look. "You did better than me in Rhetoric. I'm not going to get into this with you. And no matter what you say, I'm not going to start setting policies and issuing proclamations in Gaius's name. Disobeying Academy rules meant to protect students' families from embarrassment is one thing. Sending men into harm's way is another."

"Fine. We go talk to my aunt," Tavi said. "We find out what's wrong. If it's something serious, we take it to Killian and let him and Miles decide what to do. Okay?"

Max nodded. "Okay. Though the furies help you if Brencis spots you at his father's party."

Tavi let out an irritated groan. "I'd forgotten about him."

"Don't," Max said. "Tavi, I've been meaning to talk to you about him. I don't think Brencis is quite right. You know?"

Tavi frowned. "In the head?"

"Yes," Max said, "He's dangerous. It's why I've always made it a point to smash him up a bit whenever I had the excuse. Establishing that he should be afraid of me and stay clear. He's fundamentally a coward, but he isn't afraid of you. Which means he probably enjoys thinking about hurting you—and you're going to be walking around in his family's home."

"I'm not afraid of him, Max."

"I know," Max said. "You idiot."

Tavi sighed. "If it makes you feel better, we'll get in and out fast. The sooner we get back to the Citadel, the less murderous Killian is going to be, in any case."

Max nodded. "Good thinking. This way he'll only murder us a little."

CHAPTER 24

Tavi paused outside Lord Kalare's manor on Garden Lane and studied it for a long moment, frowning. If he had not spent so much time in the First Lord's palace in the Citadel, Kalare's manor would have impressed him. The place was ridiculously large, Tavi thought. The whole of Bernardholt—Isanaholt now, he reminded himself—could have fit inside the manor, and there still would have been enough room to provide a pasture for the sheep. The place was richly appointed, lit, gardened, landscaped, and decorated, and Tavi could not help but be uncomfortably reminded of the harlots down near the river, with painted faces, gaudy clothes, and false smiles that never reached jaded eyes.

He took a deep breath and started toward the house down its double lines of statuary. Four men in plain, common clothing walked by him. They had hard faces, wary eyes, and Tavi saw the hilt of a sword beneath the cloak of the third man. He kept an eye on them as he approached the manor, and saw a harried-looking servant come running to meet them at the street, drawing four saddled horses with him.

"You see that?" Max murmured.

Tavi nodded. "They don't look much like visiting dignitaries, do they?"

"They look like hired help," Max said.

"But there's a valet rushing to bring them horses," Tavi murmured. "Cutters?"

"Probably."

The men mounted up, and at a quiet word from one of them, they kicked their horses into an immediate run.

"And in a hurry," Max said.

"Probably running off to wish someone a happy Wintersend," Tavi said.

Max snorted quietly.

The doorman stepped forward to meet them, his chin uplifted. "Excuse me, young masters. This is a private gathering."

Tavi nodded, and said, "Of course, sir." Then he held up the dispatch pouch he normally carried documents in, a fine piece of blue-and-scarlet leather bearing the golden image of the royal eagle. "I'm bearing dispatches on behalf of His Majesty."

The doorman relaxed his arrogant posture a bit, and said, "Of course, sir. I shall be pleased to deliver them on your behalf."

Tavi smiled at him and shrugged. "I'm sorry," he said, "but my orders are to place my charge directly into the hands of its recipient." He gestured back at Max. "I think it must be something sensitive. Captain Miles even sent a guard with me."

The doorman frowned at both of them, then said, "Of course, young sir. If you will come with me, I will take you to the garden while your escort waits."

Max said, in a voice of flat, absolute certainty, "I stay with him. Orders."

The doorman licked his lips and nodded. "Ah. Yes. This way please, gentlemen."

He led them through more of the same lavish decadence to the gardens at the center of the manor. Tavi walked along behind the man, trying to look bored. Max's boots hit the floor with the steady, disciplined cadence of a marching *legionare*.

The doorman—or rather, majordomo, Tavi supposed—paused at the entrance to the garden and turned to Tavi. Shifting colored lights flickered and flashed behind the man, and the garden buzzed with conversation and music. The aroma of food, wine, and perfume drifted through Tavi's breath. "If you will tell me the name of your party, sir, I will invite them to come receive your letter."

"Certainly," Tavi said. "If you would invite Steadholder Isana here, I would be most grateful."

The majordomo hesitated, and Tavi saw something shift uncertainly in his eyes. "The Steadholder is no longer here, young sir," the man said. "She departed not a quarter hour ago."

Tavi frowned and exchanged a glance with Max. "Indeed? For what reason?"

"I'm sure I could not say, young sir," the man replied.

Max gave Tavi the slightest nod, then rumbled, "The second missive is for High Lady Placida. Bring her."

The majordomo eyed Max suspiciously and glanced at Tavi. Tavi gave the man a between-us-servants roll of his eyes, and said, "Please invite her, sir."

The man pursed his lips in thought and shrugged. "As you wish, young sir. A moment." He vanished into the garden.

"Lady Placida?" Tavi muttered to Max.

"I know her," Max replied. "She'll know what is going on."

"We'll need some privacy," Tavi said.

Max nodded, then frowned in concentration and waved a hand vaguely at the air. Tavi felt a sudden pressure on his ears, sharp at first, but it subsided. "Done," Max said.

"Thank you," Tavi said. In only a moment, a tall woman with severe, distant features approached, wearing simple, elegant jewelry and a rich gown of a deep, compelling green, the majordomo at her elbow. She paused, studying them, and Tavi felt the weight of her gaze as palpably as the touch of a gentle hand. She frowned at him, and then frowned more deeply upon seeing Max. She dismissed the majordomo with a word and a curt flick of her wrist, and approached them.

She stepped into the area Max had protected from eavesdropping via wind furies and arched her eyebrow. Then she walked forward to stand over Tavi and murmur, "This isn't a missive from the First Lord, is it?"

Tavi opened the pouch and passed her a folded piece of paper. There was nothing written on it, but Tavi went through the motions for the benefit of those watching. "No, Your Grace. I'm afraid not."

She accepted the paper and opened it, glancing at it as if to read. "Oh, how I love Wintersend in the capital. Good evening, Maximus."

"Good evening, my lady. Your gown is lovely."

One corner of her mouth quirked into a tiny smile. "It's nice to see you took my advice about offering compliments to ladies."

"I have found it to be a most effective tactic, my lady," Max replied.

Lady Placida arched an eyebrow, and said, "I've created a monster."

"Ladies sometimes scream," Max said loftily. "But other than that, I would hardly say that I was a monster."

Her eyes hardened. "Which is something of a miracle. I know your father is on the Wall, but I expected to see your stepmother here."

"She was forbidden," Max said. "Or that's what I hear on the grapevine."

"They don't write," Lady Placida said, more than asked. "I suppose they wouldn't, though." She folded up the letter, and offered Max a brief smile. "It's nice to see you, Maximus. But would you very much mind telling me why you've very publicly associated me with the First Lord in front of half of the Lords Council and members of the Senate?"

"Your Grace," Tavi said. "I came here to speak to my aunt Isana. I think she's in some kind of trouble, and I want to help her."

"So you are he," Lady Placida murmured, and narrowed her eyes in thought.

"Tavi of the Calderon Valley, Your Grace," Max said.

"Please, lady," Tavi said. "Can you tell us anything you know of her."

"I would take it as a favor, lady," Max added, and put a solid hand on Tavi's shoulder.

Lady Placida's eyebrows rose sharply at the gesture. Then she studied Tavi again, and more intently. "She was here, along with the Amaranth Courtesan, Serai. They spoke to several different people."

"Who?" Tavi asked.

"Myself, Lady Aquitaine, any number of nobles and dignitaries. And Lord Kalare."

"Kalare?" Tavi said, frowning.

A strident male voice boomed in the garden, and was followed by a polite round of cheering and applause.

"Well," Lady Placida said. "It would seem that Brencis has won his duel to claim Citizenship. What a surprise."

"Brencis couldn't duel his way through a herd of sheep," Max snorted. "I hate show duels."

"Lady, please," Tavi said. "Do you know why she left early?"

Lady Placida shook her head. "Not for certain. But they had a less than pleasant discussion with Lord Kalare immediately prior to their departure."

Tavi glanced aside in the passageway as he felt a sudden

attention on him. Two young men stood not ten feet from him, and Tavi recognized them both. They were dressed in their nicest clothes, but blond and watery-eyed Varien and the hulking Renzo could not be mistaken for anyone else.

Varien blinked at Tavi for a second, then at Max. Then he muttered something to Renzo, and the two of them hurried away into the garden. Tavi's heart pounded. There was about to be trouble.

"How unpleasant a discussion?" Max asked.

"He struck Serai, openly." Lady Placida's lips pressed into a firm line. "I've little use for a man who strikes a woman simply because he knows he can."

"I can think of one or two things," Max growled.

"Be careful, Maximus," Lady Placida said in instant warning. "Guard your words."

"*Crows*," Tavi spat.

Both of them stopped to stare at Tavi.

"You say they left in a rush, Your Grace?" he asked.

"Very much so," Lady Placida answered.

"Max," Tavi said, his heart pounding, "those cutters we saw on the way in. They're going after my aunt."

"Bloody crows," Max said. "Aria, please excuse us?"

Lady Placida nodded once, and said, "Be careful, Maximus. I owe you my son's life, and I would hate to miss the chance to repay the debt."

"You know me, Your Grace."

"Indeed," Lady Placida said. She inclined her head to Tavi, smiled again at Max, then turned back to the garden, dismissing them with the same flick of her hand she'd used for the majordomo.

"Come on," Tavi said, his voice tense, and started trotting back through the house. "We have to hurry. Can you get us there any faster?"

Max hesitated for a second, then said, "Not in quarters this close. If I tried to windcraft us both there, I'd fly us into a building for sure." His face flushed with color. "It, uh, isn't my strong suit."

"Crows," Tavi spat. "But you could take yourself?"

"Yes."

"Go. Warn them. I'll catch up whenever I can."

"Tavi, we don't know that those cutters were after her," Max pointed out.

"We don't know that they *weren't*. She's my family. If I'm wrong, and she's safe, you can make fun of me for a year."

Max nodded sharply as they emerged from the front door. "What does she look like?"

"Long hair, dark with some grey, very thin, looks early twenties in the face,"

Max paused. "Pretty?"

"Max," Tavi snarled.

"Right, right," Max said. "I'll see you there." The young man took a pair of long steps and flung himself into a leap, bounding straight up into the air as sudden wind rose in a roar to carry him into the night sky, his hand on his sword the whole way.

Tavi stared bitterly after Max for a second, his emotions in a wash of fear, worry, and the raw and seething jealousy he rarely let himself feel. Of all the people of the Realm, comparatively few of them commanded enough power with wind furies to take flight. More young people were killed in windcrafting accidents than any other form of furycrafting as they attempted to push the limits of their skills and emulate those who could take to the skies. Tavi was hardly alone in his jealousy. But the possible danger to Aunt Isana made it a particularly bitter realization of his lack of power.

Tavi didn't let the sudden surge of emotion keep him from breaking into a dead run toward Nedus's house. He could not possibly match Max's time back to it, but he couldn't do less than his utmost, either, Not when it was Aunt Isana. He had never been a slow runner, and the years he'd spent in the capital had given him inches of height and pounds of muscle, all of it lean and hardened by his constant duties to the First Lord. There might have been a dozen men in the city who could have matched his pace without furycrafting, but no more. The boy all but flew down the festively lit and decorated Garden Lane.

If the cutters were there, they would almost certainly be skilled swordsmen, most likely metalcrafters, who tended to outshine all but the deadliest and most talented of swordsmen with no metalcrafting of their own. From the hard-bitten look of them, they were experienced, and that meant that they would work together well. Were it only one such man, Tavi might be able to steal upon him or arrange to bluff his way close enough to attempt some sort of surprise attack. But with four men, that would not be an option—and simply assaulting them, even had he been armed with more than the knife at his hip, would have been suicide.

Max, Tavi knew from experience in the training hall, was the kind of swordsman that might become a fencer of song and legend—or who might be killed by foolish overconfidence before he had the chance. Max was an absolutely deadly blade, but the training hall was far different than the street, and fencing partners were not likely to behave in the same way as professional killers. Even Max's experience in the Legions might not have prepared him for the kind of nasty fighting that might be used on the streets of the capital. Max had more confidence than any three or four other people Tavi knew, except perhaps for the First Lord, but Tavi was frightened for his friend.

Even so, he was more frightened for his aunt. Isana had, Tavi knew, spent her entire life in steadholts, and she had little idea of how treacherous the capital could be. He could not imagine that she would be keeping company with a courtesan if she knew the woman's profession. Tavi also could not imagine his aunt coming to the capital without *some* kind of guardian or escort, especially if she was here at Gaius's invitation. Surely she would have had the company of her younger brother Bernard at the very least. For that matter, why in the world hadn't the First Lord assigned Amara or one of the Cursors to accompany her while she guested in the palace? Gaius would have no reason at all to bring her to the capital only to allow her to be harmed. She was too much a symbol of his authority.

All of which meant that communications had to have broken down somewhere. Isana was vulnerable, perhaps unguarded, perhaps under the guidance of someone who would lead her into danger. Once Tavi found her, he would get her to the safety of the palace immediately. Even if he could tell her nothing of what was happening with the First Lord, it was in Gaius's best interests to protect her, and Tavi was sure that he could talk Killian into putting her into guest chambers where the presence of the Royal Guard would cover her from mortal danger.

Assuming that she was all right.

Cold fear ran through him, and lent still more speed to his limbs as he ran, tireless and focused and terrified for the woman who had raised him as if he had been her own.

When Renzo stepped out from behind a parked, riderless coach, Tavi barely had time to register it before the hulking boy struck him with a sweep of one enormous arm. Tavi twisted and caught the blow on both of his own arms, but the larger boy's fury-assisted strength was vicious, and sent Tavi into a running stumble that fetched him up hard against the stone wall surrounding the environs of another enormous manor.

He managed to avoid slamming his head or breaking his shoulder in the impact, but beyond that, Tavi did little more than fall to the ground. He could taste blood in his mouth. Renzo stood over him in his brown tunic, pig eyes narrowed, both hands clenched into fists the size of hams.

Someone let out a tittering laugh, and Tavi turned his head to see Varien approaching him from the same hiding place. "Good one," Varien said. "Look at him. I think he's going to cry."

Tavi tested his arms and legs, then pushed his hands down to rise from the ground. As he did, his fear and worry and humiliation coalesced into something made of nothing but hard edges and serrated blades. His aunt was in danger. The Realm could be in danger. And these two arrogant idiots had chosen now, of all times, to interfere.

"Varien," Tavi said, quietly. "I don't have time for this."

"You won't have to wait long," Varien told him, his tone taunting. "I flew the two of us in front of you, but Brencis will be along shortly to talk to you about your rudeness in coming to his party uninvited."

Tavi straightened and faced Varien and Renzo. When he spoke, a stranger's voice came from his lips, the tone hard, cold, ringing with command. "Get out of my way. Both of you."

Varien's sneer wavered and his watery blue eyes blinked several times as he stared at Tavi. After an uncertain pause, he began to speak.

"Open your mouth again," Tavi said, in that same, cold voice, "and I will break your jaw. Stand aside."

Varien's face flickered with fear, then with sudden anger. "You can't speak to me li—"

Tavi snapped his boot up into Varien's belly and the blow struck home, hard. The taller boy doubled over with a gasp, clasping at his stomach. Without pausing, Tavi seized him by the hair, and with all the weight of his body forced the boy down to the stones of the street, so that their combined weight landed at an oblique angle to Varien's chin. There was a sickly cracking sound, and Varien let out a wailing shriek of agony.

Tavi bounced back to his feet as a surge of exultation and savage joy flooded through him. Renzo rolled forward and slammed his arm at Tavi in another broad, sweeping blow. Tavi stepped under it and came up with his fist moving in a short, vertical blow, his arm and elbow in a single line with his forward leg. Every ounce of power in Tavi's body thudded into the tip of Renzo's jaw. The larger boy's head snapped back and up, but he didn't drop. He wobbled on his feet, eyes blinking in startled confusion, and drew back his huge fist to swing again.

Tavi gritted his teeth, took a step to one side, and kicked straight down and into the side of the larger boy's knee. With its crackling pop, Renzo let out a bellow and fell, roaring and cursing and clutching both hands at his wounded knee.

Tavi rose to his feet and stared down at the boys who had tormented him as they writhed and screamed in pain. Their yelling had already begun to attract attention from the nearby manor and from passersby on the street. Someone had already raised a cry for the civic *legionares*, and Tavi knew that they would arrive momentarily.

Varien's screams had subsided to wracking, moaning sobs of pain. Renzo wasn't in much better shape, but he managed to clench his teeth over the sounds of agony, so that they came out like the cries of a wounded beast.

Tavi stared down at them.

He had seen horrible things during the Second Battle of Calderon. He had looked down as Doroga rode his enormous bull through a sea of burned and bleeding Marat corpses, while the wounded screamed their agony to the uncaring sky.

He had seen the battle-wise crows of Alera descending in clouds to feast upon the eyes and tongue of the dead and the dying, Marat and Aleran alike, with a gruesome lack of preference between corpse and casualty. Tavi had seen the walls of Garrison almost literally painted in blood. He had seen men and women die crushed, slashed, pierced, and strangled while they fought for their lives, and he had splashed through puddles of still-hot blood as he ran through the carnage.

For a time, nightmares had haunted him. They had become less frequent, but the details had not faded from his memory. Too often, he found himself looking back at them, staring in a kind of fascinated revulsion.

He had seen terrible things. He had faced them. He hated them, and they terrified him still, but he had faced the simple existence of such hideous destruction without letting it control his life.

But this was different.

Tavi had harmed no one during Second Calderon—but the pain Renzo and Varien now suffered had been dealt to them by his own hands, his own will, his own choice.

There was no dignity in what he had done to them. There was nothing in which to take pride. The abrupt joy that had sung through his body during the swift, brutal fighting faded and vanished. He had looked forward to this moment, in some ways—to a time when he could put his skills to use against those who had always made him feel so helpless and small. He had expected to feel satisfaction, triumph. But in its place, he felt only an emptiness that filled with a sudden and sickening nausea. He had never hurt anyone so badly before. He felt stained, somehow, as if he had lost something valuable that he hadn't known he had possessed.

He had hurt the other boys, and hurt them terribly. It was the only way he could have beaten them. Anything less than a disabling injury would have left them able to employ their furies against him, and there would have been nothing he could have done but suffered whatever they intended for him. So he had hurt them. Badly. In the space of a few seconds, he had visited back all the misery and pain they had inflicted on him over two years twice over.

It had been necessary.

But that did not mean that it was right.

"I'm sorry," Tavi said quietly, though the ice in his voice yet filled the words. "I'm sorry I had to do that." He began to say more, but then shook his head, turned away, to resume running toward Sir Nedus's manor. He could sort out charges and legal problems with the civic legion once he was sure his aunt was safe.

But before he had gone more than a few steps, the stones beneath his feet heaved and flung him hard into the nearest stone wall. He had no warning of it at all, and his head smacked solidly against the rock, a flash of phantom light blinding him. He felt himself fall, and tried to rise, but a rough hand gripped him and threw him with a terrible, casual ease. He sailed through the air and landed on stones, and by the time he finished tumbling the stars had begun to clear from his eyes.

He looked up in time to see that he was in a darkened, blind alleyway between an expensive little wine shop and a goldsmith's. Inexplicably, a fog had risen, and as he blinked it built up, covering his face. Tavi pushed himself up to his knees to see Kalarus Brencis Minoris standing over him, dressed in a magnificent doublet of grey and green, a circlet of iron set with a green stone on his brow, and formal jewelry glittering on his fingers and throat. Brencis's hair had been drawn back into the braid the long-haired southern cities employed in their fighting men, and he wore a sword and dagger upon his belt. His eyes were narrow and cruel, and burned with something feral and unpleasant that Tavi could not begin to give a name.

"So," Brencis said quietly, as the fog continued to rise. "You thought it would be amusing to mock me by sneaking into my father's party? Perhaps drinking his wine? Pilfering a few valuables?"

"I was delivering a missive from the First Lord," Tavi managed to say.

He might as well not have spoken. "And now you have attacked and injured my friends and boon companions. Though I suppose you will claim that the First Lord instructed you to do so, eh, coward?"

"Brencis," Tavi said through clenched teeth, "this isn't about you."

"The crows it isn't," Brencis snarled. By then, the mist had risen in a thick blanket around them, and Tavi could see little more than a pair of running paces through the fog. "I've endured your insolence for the last time." Brencis casually drew the sword at his side, then took his dagger into his left hand. "No more."

Tavi stared at that disquieting light dancing behind Brencis's eyes and forced himself back to his feet. "Don't do this, Brencis. Don't be a fool."

"I will *not* be spoken to that way by a furyless freak!" Brencis snarled, and lunged at Tavi, sword extending into a clean thrust for Tavi's belly.

Tavi drew his own knife, managed to catch the thrust on it, and slide it away so that the tip of Brencis's sword went cleanly past him. But it had been a lucky parry, and Tavi knew it. Once Brencis began slashing, there was no way his little blade could help, and Tavi sprang back from his attacker, desperately looking for a way out of the alley. There was none.

"Stupid *pagunus*," Brencis said, smiling. "I've always known you were a gutless, stinking little pig."

"The civic *legionares* are already on the way," Tavi responded. His voice shook.

"There's time enough," Brencis said. "No one will see through the fog." His eyes glittered with an ugly amusement. "What an odd coincidence that it came up just now."

He came in again, the bright steel of his blade darting toward Tavi's throat. Tavi ducked under it, but Brencis's boot swept up to meet his head. Tavi managed to take part of the kick on his shoulder, but Brencis's fury-assisted strength was at least a match for Renzo's, and Tavi staggered to one side. Only the wall of the goldsmith's kept him from falling, and the world spun rapidly around him as Brencis raised his sword for a powerful, down-sweeping death blow.

Tavi's instincts screamed at him, and he somehow managed to stagger back as the sword came down. He felt a hot flash of pain on his left arm. He swept his dagger in a cut at Brencis's sword hand, but the taller boy avoided it with contemptuous ease. Then Brencis lifted a hand and flicked his wrist, and a blast of sudden wind threw Tavi bodily to the ground. It drove him back down the alley to the wall at its end. He fought his way back to his feet, only to have the wind flatten his back to the wall, where ugly, misshapen hands emerged smoothly from the stone and caught his wrists and legs in a crushing grip.

Brencis paced calmly down the alley and stared at Tavi, his expression smug. He sheathed his dagger and casually slapped Tavi across the face, then on the other side with his backhand swing. The blows, even delivered with an open hand, hit him like heavy fists, and the entire world narrowed down into a tunnel filled by the lean, arrogant shape of Kalarus Brencis Minoris.

"I can't believe how stupid you are. Did you think you could insult and defy me over and over again? Did you think that you could possibly survive such a thing? You're nothing, Tavi. You're no one. Not a crafter. Not even a Citizen. Just a favored pet dog of a senile old man." Brencis pressed the tip of his sword against Tavi's cheek. Tavi felt another sting of pain, and felt blood trail down over his jawline. Brencis stared into Tavi's eyes. The young noble's eyes were . . . strange. His pupils were far too wide, and his face shone with a sheen of perspiration. His breath reeked of wine.

Tavi swallowed and struggled to focus his thoughts clearly. "Brencis," he said quietly. "You're drunk. Intoxicated. You've taken drugs. You aren't in control of yourself."

Brencis slapped him twice more, contemptuous little blows. "I beg to differ."

Tavi reeled with disorientation, his stomach turning and twisting within him. "Brencis, you have to stop and think. If you—"

This time Brencis drove his fist into Tavi's belly, and though the boy managed to tighten his abdomen and let out a harsh breath in time with the blow, lessening its impact, it landed with more power than Tavi had ever felt before. It drove the breath from him.

"You don't tell me what I must do!" Brencis shrieked, his face white with fury. "You do as I will it. You *die* as I will it." He licked his lips and tightened his grip on the sword in his hand. "You have no idea for how long I've been looking forward to this."

Somewhere in the mist behind Brencis, there was the rasp of steel as a sword was drawn from its scabbard.

"Funny," Max said, and Tavi's friend stepped forward from the mist, *legionare*'s blade in hand. "I was just thinking that very thing."

Brencis went rigid, and though he did not take the sword's tip from Tavi's cheek, he looked over his shoulder.

"Get away from him, Brencis," Max said.

Brencis's lip twisted up into a sneer. "The bastard. No, Antillar. You get away. Walk away now, or I'll kill your little paganus friend."

"You just said that you intend to kill him anyway," Max said. "How stupid do I look to you?"

"Back off!" Brencis screamed. "I'll kill him! Right now!"

"I'm sure you would," Max said, his expression empty. "But then I would kill you. You know it. I know it. Be smart, Brencis. Leave."

Tavi saw Brencis's body start to quiver, and he looked swiftly back and forth between Tavi and Max. His eyes, too wide, too bloodshot, burned with desperate, alien fire, then abruptly narrowed.

"Max!" Tavi shouted, struggling to warn his friend.

At the same instant, Brencis turned from Tavi, his hand extended, and fire filled the narrow alley in a sudden and deadly storm that came from nowhere and howled down upon Max.

For a second, Tavi could see nothing, but then a shadow resolved within the flame, a dark shape dropped into a crouch, one arm up as though to shield his eyes. The flame abruptly vanished, and left Max crouched on one knee, his left forearm up to shield his eyes, his blade still in hand. The tip of the sword glowed cherry red, and Max's clothing had been blackened and burned away in places, but he came to his feet again, apparently unharmed, and started walking toward Brencis. "You'll have to do better than that," Max said quietly.

Brencis turned his back on Tavi and faced Max with a snarl. He gestured, and cobblestones before his feet tore themselves free of the ground and flew at Max in a heavy, deadly cloud.

Max lifted his left hand and clenched it into a fist, his expression grim. One of the stone walls of the alley abruptly flowed like water, stretching out between Max and the oncoming stones. They slammed into the sheet of stone before

Max, shattering into gravel as they struck. A second later, the wall snapped back into its original position. Max lowered his arm and kept walking forward.

Brencis snarled again, and a larger patch of stones began to rip their way from the ground, but Max gestured sharply at an almost-depleted pile of firewood stacked neatly against one wall, and a dozen logs, each the size of Tavi's thigh, suddenly flexed and bounded toward Brencis.

Brencis released the stones he had begun to raise, and his sword blurred into a web of steel that intercepted each log and cleanly severed it, sending the pieces spinning harmlessly away. Max charged forward, sword in hand, and with a cry of frustrated anger and fear, Brencis advanced to meet him. Blades rang harshly in the alley, steel chiming, sparks flowering into drizzling clouds of fiery rain where blade met blade. The two clashed and flowed past one another, then turned to do it again and again, their movements as graceful and smooth as any pair of dancers.

Tavi saw startled shock on Max's face for a second, after their third pass. He was a skilled fencer, Tavi knew, but he had evidently underestimated Kalare Brencis. The other boy was his match, and another pair of passes resulted in more ringing steel and no blood.

And then Brencis, facing toward Tavi, gave Max an ugly smile, lifted a hand, and cast it at Tavi. Fire lanced from his fingertips and screamed toward the helpless boy.

"No!" Max cried. He turned with a flick of his hand, and a wave of raw wind rose up before Tavi, holding the flames at bay, shielding Tavi from the fire, though the air grew hot enough to sear his lungs.

"Max!" Tavi screamed.

Brencis drove his glittering sword into Max's back. Its tip emerged from Max's belly.

Max's face went white, his eyes wide in shock.

Brencis twisted the blade once, twice, and then whipped it clear.

Max exhaled slowly, and crumpled to his hands and knees. Sudden silence filled the alley.

"Yes," Brencis said, panting, his eyes bright. "Yes. Finally." He gestured sharply, and a vicious lash of wind landed across Max's back in a line so fine that it sliced through his shirt and opened a long, bloody furrow in his skin. "Bastard. So smug. So sure of yourself." Brencis flicked his wrist again and again, opening the horrible scars on Max's back into fresh agonies and blood.

Max let out a groan, each blow driving him farther down. But when he looked up at Tavi, there was defiant determination in his face as well as agony and fear. Tavi felt the bonds on his wrists and ankles suddenly begin to loosen, and his frustrated fear and rage surged to new heights as he understood Max's intention.

Brencis paid Tavi no attention at all, utterly focused upon continuing to lash at Max, snarling and cursing at him the entire while. Max let out a harsh groan and sagged almost completely to the ground, and Tavi was abruptly free of the stone.

He set his feet, flicked his knife's handle, caught the flat of its blade between his fingers, and with a practiced, instinctive motion, threw the knife at Brencis's throat. It spun end over end through the air, and Brencis didn't know it was coming until the last instant. He flinched from the knife, and its blade struck home hard, drawing blood from one of Brencis's cheeks and sinking entirely through the boy's ear. Brencis screamed in sudden pain.

Tavi knew he had only seconds, if that, before Brencis recovered and killed them both. He launched himself forward, leaping over Max and driving his shoulder into Brencis's chest. They both went down. Brencis reached for his dagger, but Tavi drove his thumb into the other boy's eye with vicious desperation, and Brencis screamed.

There was no time for thought, for technique, for complex tactics. The struggle was too ugly, elemental, brutal. Brencis got his free hand on Tavi's throat and started to squeeze, trying to crush Tavi's windpipe with fury-born strength, but Tavi countered by getting his teeth into Brencis's forearm and biting down until blood filled his mouth. Brencis screamed. Tavi started hitting the other boy, pounding his fists down like clumsy sledgehammers while Brencis tried uselessly to bring his sword to bear in the close quarters of their grapple.

Tavi screamed and did not relent, terror and fury lending him more strength. Brencis tried to crawl away, but Tavi seized him by his braid and started slamming the other boy's face down onto the stones. Again and again he drove Brencis's face into the cobblestones, his weight on the other boy's back, until the body underneath him suddenly went limp and loose.

And then a hammer slammed into the top of his head and threw him back and away from Brencis.

Tavi landed in a heap, hardly able to see. But he looked up, his head pounding with nauseating throbs, and saw a man emerge from the mist, dressed in green and grey. Tavi dimly recognized him as High Lord Kalare. The man stared contemptuously at Tavi, then walked over to Breneis. He prodded his son with the tip of his boot.

"Get up," said Kalare, his voice seething with bitter anger. Behind him, Tavi saw the pathetic, hunched forms of Varien and Renzo, leaning on one another to keep from falling.

Brencis stirred, then slowly lifted his head. He sat up, his face a mass of cuts, blood, and bruises. His bloodied mouth hung open, and Tavi could see broken teeth.

"You are pathetic," Kalare said. There was neither compassion nor concern for his son in his voice. "You had them. And you allowed this . . . freakish little nothing to overcome you."

Brencis tried to say something, but it came out as a mush of sounds and sobs that meant nothing.

"There is no excuse," Kalare said. "None." He looked up at the two boys at the back of the alley. "No one can ever know that you, my son, were bested by this paganus. Never. We cannot allow word of this humiliation to leave this alley."

Tavi's heart lurched. Max, though breathing, was not moving, and he lay in a welter of his own blood. Tavi tried to gain his feet, but it was all he could do to keep from throwing up, and he knew High Lord Kalare was about to kill them. He watched helplessly as Kalare raised one hand and the earth began to shake around him.

But then light flooded the alley, a searing, golden light that burned away the mist and fog as swiftly as though the sun itself had come to Alera Imperia. The light stabbed at Tavi's eyes, and he lifted his hand to shield them against it.

Placida Aria, High Lady of Placida, stood at the other end of the alley with half a century of the civic Legion behind her.

One slender arm was lifted, wrist parallel to the ground, and upon it perched the form of a hunting falcon made of pure, golden fire. That light fell onto the alley, illuminating everything there.

"Your Grace," Lady Placida said, her voice ringing with the clarity of a silver trumpet, calm and unmistakably strong. "What passes here?"

The tremors in the ground abruptly ceased. Kalare stared at Tavi for a moment with empty eyes, and then turned to face Lady Placida and the *legionares*. "An assault, Your Grace. Antillar Maximus has attacked and badly injured my son and his companions from the Academy."

Lady Placida narrowed her eyes. "Indeed?" She looked from Kalare to the boys on the ground, to Brencis, Renzo, and Varien. "And you observed this assault?"

"The last of it," Kalare said. "Swords were drawn. Antillar was trying to murder my son after badly beating these other boys. My son and his friends can all testify to the facts."

"N—no," Tavi stammered. "That isn't what happened."

"Boy," Kalare snapped, fury in his voice. "This is Citizens' business. Hold your tongue."

"No! You aren't—" The air suddenly tightened in Tavi's throat, choking him to silence. He looked up to see Kalare frowning faintly.

"Boy," Lady Placida said in a cold voice. "You will hold your tongue. The High Lord is quite correct. This is Citizens' business." She stared at Tavi for a second, and Tavi thought he saw some expression flicker in her face, one of apology. Her next words were quieter, less frozen. "You must be silent here. Do you understand?"

The pressure in his throat eased, and Tavi could breathe again. He stared at Lady Placida for a moment, then nodded.

Lady Placida nodded back at him, then turned to the man next to him. "Captain, with your permission, I will see to the immediate wounds of those involved, before you take the accused into custody."

The *legionare* beside her said, "Of course, lady, and we are grateful for your assistance."

"Thank you," she told him, and started down the alley toward Tavi and Max.

As she did, Kalare turned to face her, clearly standing in her way.

Placida was inches taller than Kalare. She looked down at him with a serene, unreadable expression. The fire falcon on her wrist, still very much present, fluttered its wings restlessly, sending campfire sparks drifting to the ground. "Yes, Your Grace?"

Kalare spoke very quietly. "You do not wish me as an enemy, woman."

"Given what I know of you, Your Grace, I don't see how you could be anything else."

"Leave," he told her, his voice ringing with command.

Lady Placida laughed at him. It was a sound both merry and scornful. "How odd that Antillar Maximus inflicted all of these injuries with his hands. He does, you know, have considerable strength available to him at furycrafting."

"He is the bastard son of a stinking barbarian. It is to be expected," Kalare replied.

"As would be injuries to his knuckles after such barbarity. But his hands are unwounded. And what injuries Antillar does have are all upon his back."

Kalare stared at her in silent fury.

"Strange that the hands of the other boy are a frightful mess, Your Grace. Split knuckles on either hand. It seems odd, does it not? It is almost enough to make one think that the boy from Calderon overcame not only your son, but his companions as well." She pursed her lips in mock thought. "Is not the boy from Calderon the one with no ability whatsoever at furycraft?"

Kalare's eyes blazed. "You arrogant bitch. I will—"

Lady Placida's grey eyes remained as calm and as hard as distant mountains. "You will *what*, Your Grace. Challenge me to the *juris macto*?"

"You would only hide behind your husband," Kalare sneered.

"On the contrary," Lady Placida replied. "I will meet you here and now if that is Your Grace's desire. I am hardly a stranger to duels. As you remember from my own duel for Citizenship."

Kalare's cheek started a steady twitch.

"Yes," Lady Placida noted. "You do remember." She glanced

at Brencis and his companions. "See to your son, Your Grace. This round is over. So if you would please stand aside and let me assist the wounded . . . ?" The question was a polite one, but her eyes never wavered from Kalare's.

"I will remember this," Kalare murmured, as he stepped aside. "I promise you that."

"You would hardly believe how little that matters to me," Lady Placida responded, and walked past him without another glance, the fire falcon trailing falling sparks behind them.

She came to Tavi and Max and placed the falcon on the ground beside her, her expression businesslike. Tavi watched as Kalare helped his son to his feet and led him and his companions away and out of sight.

Tavi exhaled slowly, and said, "They're gone, Your Grace."

Lady Placida nodded calmly. Her eyes went flat for a moment as they saw the reopened scars on Max's back. She found the sword thrust through his lower back and winced.

"Will he live?" Tavi asked quietly.

"I think so," she replied. "He managed to close the worst of it on his own. But he isn't out of danger. It's fortunate that I followed Kalare when he left." She moved a hand, laying it across the wound, then slipped her other hand beneath Max, covering the wound where the sword had emerged on that side. She closed her eyes for two or three silent moments, then carefully drew her hands back. The sword wound had been closed, heavy with pink skin and scar tissue.

Tavi blinked slowly at it, and said, "You didn't even use a bath."

Lady Placida smiled slightly. "I didn't have one handy." She glanced back at the *legionares*, and asked, "What really happened?"

Tavi told her about the fight itself, as quietly and succinctly as he could. "Your Grace," he said, "it's important that Max return to the Citadel with me. Please, he cannot be arrested tonight."

She shook her head. "I am afraid that is impossible, young man. Maximus has been accused of a crime by a High Lord and three Citizens. I am sure that any reasonable court will acquit him, but there is no avoiding the process of a trial."

"But he *can't*. Not right now."

"And why not?" Lady Placida asked.

Tavi stared at her in helpless frustration.

"You'll be quite safe, at least from legal accusation," Lady Placida said. "There's no chance at all that Kalare would let his son accuse *you* of half-killing him."

"That isn't what I'm worried about," Tavi said.

"Then what is?"

Tavi felt his face flush, and he looked away from Lady Placida.

She sighed. "I suggest you be grateful that you are both alive," Lady Placida said. "It's something of a miracle that you are."

"Tavi?" asked Max. His voice was weak, thready.

Tavi turned to his friend immediately. "I'm here. Are you all right?"

"Had worse," Max murmured.

"Maximus," Lady Placida said firmly. "You must be silent until we can get you to a proper bed. Even if it is in a cell. You're badly hurt."

Max shook his head a little. "Need to tell him, Your Grace. Please. Alone."

Lady Placida arched a brow at Max, but then nodded and rose. At her gesture, the fire falcon took wing toward her, vanishing into nothingness as it did. She walked calmly back to the *legionares* and began speaking with them.

"Tavi," Max said. "Went to Sir Nedus's."

"Yeah?" Tavi leaned closer, his heart pounding in time with his head.

"Attacked outside his house. Sir Nedus is dead. So are the coachmen. The courtesan. So are the cutters."

The bottom fell out of Tavi's stomach. "Aunt Isana?"

"Never saw her, Tavi. She's gone. There was a blood trail. Probably took her somewhere." He started to say something else, but then his eyes rolled back into his head and closed.

Tavi stared numbly at his friend as the *legionares* gathered around him and carried him away to imprisonment. Afterward, he went to Sir Nedus's manor, to find the civic legion already moving over the grisly scene there. The bodies had all been laid out in a line. None of them were his aunt.

She was gone. Probably taken. She might already be dead.

Max, the only person who could maintain the illusion of Gaius's strength, was in jail. Without his presence as Gaius's double, the Realm might already be destined for a civil war that would let its enemies destroy them entirely. And it was Tavi's decision that had led to it.

Tavi turned and began to walk slowly and painfully up the streets to the Citadel. He had to tell Killian what had happened.

Because there was nothing else that he could do for either his family, his friend, or his lord.

Amara woke to the sensation of something small brushing past her foot. She kicked her leg at whatever it was, and heard a faint scuttling sound on the floor. A mouse, or a rat. A steadholt was never free of them, regardless of how many cats or furies were employed to keep them at bay. She sat up blearily and rubbed at her face with her hands.

The great hall of the steadholt was full of wounded men. Someone had gotten the fires going at the twin hearths at either end of the hall, and guards stood by both doors. She rose and stretched, squinting around the hall until she located Bernard at one of the doors, speaking in low voices with Giraldi. She crossed the hall to him, skirting around several wounded on cots and sleeping palettes.

"Countess," Bernard said with a polite bow of his head. "You should be lying down."

"I'm fine," she replied. "How long was I out?"

"Two hours or so," Giraldi replied, touching a finger to the rim of his helmet in a vague gesture of respect. "Saw you in the courtyard. That wasn't bad work for a, uh . . ."

"A woman?" Amara asked archly.

Giraldi sniffed. "A civilian," he said loftily.

Bernard let out a low rumble of a laugh.

"The survivors?" Amara asked.

Bernard nodded toward the darker area in the middle of the hall where most of the cots and palettes lay. "Sleeping."

"The men?"

Bernard nodded toward the heavy tubs against one wall, upended now and drying. "The healers have the walking wounded back up to fighting shape, but without Harmonus we haven't been able to get the men who were intentionally crippled back up and moving. Too many bones to mend without more watercrafters. And some of the bad injuries . . ." Bernard shook his head.

"We lost more men?"

He nodded. "Four more died. There wasn't much we could do for them—and two of the three healers left were wounded as well. It cut down on what they could do to help the others. Too much work and not enough hands."

"Our Knights?"

"Resting," Bernard said, with another nod at the cots. "I want them recovered from this morning as soon as possible."

Giraldi snorted under his breath. "Tell the truth, Bernard. You just enjoy making the infantry stay on their feet and go without rest."

"True," Bernard said gravely. "But this time it was just a fortunate coincidence."

Amara felt herself smiling. "Centurion," she said, "I wonder if you would be willing to find me something to eat?"

"Of course, Your Excellency." Giraldi rapped his fist against the center of his breastplate and headed for the nearest hearth and the table of provisions there.

Bernard watched the centurion go. Amara folded her arms and leaned against the doorway, looking outside at the late-afternoon sunshine pouring down upon the grisly courtyard. The sight threatened to stir up a cyclone of fear and anger and guilt, and Amara had to close her eyes for a moment to remain in control of herself. "What are we going to do, Bernard?"

The big man frowned out at the courtyard, and after a moment, Amara opened her eyes and studied his features. Bernard looked weary, haunted, and when he spoke, his voice was heavy with guilt. "I'm not sure," he said at last. "We only got done securing the steadholt and caring for the wounded a few moments ago."

Amara looked past him, to the remains in the courtyard. The *legionares* had gathered up the fallen, and they lay against one of the steadholt's outer walls, covered in their capes. Crows flitted back and forth, some picking at the edges of the covered corpses, but most of them found plenty to interest them in the remains too scattered to be retrieved.

Amara put her hand on Bernard's arm. "They knew the risks," she said quietly.

"And they expected sound leadership," Bernard replied.

"No one could have foreseen this, Bernard. You can't blame yourself for what happened."

"I can," Bernard said quietly. "And so can Lord Riva and His Majesty. I should have been more cautious. Held off until reinforcements arrived."

"There was no time," Amara said. She squeezed his wrist. "Bernard, there *still* is no time, if Doroga is right. We have to decide on a course of action."

"Even if it is the wrong one?" Bernard asked. "Even if it means more men go to their deaths?"

Amara took a deep breath and responded quietly, her voice soft, her words empty of rancor. "Yes," she said quietly. "Even if it means every last one of them dies. Even if it means you die. Even if it means I die. We are here to protect the Realm. There are tens of thousands of holders who live between here and Riva. If these vord can spread as swiftly as Doroga indicated, the lives of those holders are in our hands. What we do in the next few hours could save them."

"Or kill them," Bernard added.

"Would you have us do nothing?" Amara asked. "It would be like cutting their throats ourselves."

Bernard looked at her for a moment, then closed his eyes. "You're right, of course," he rumbled. "We move on them. We fight."

Amara nodded. "Good."

"But I can't fight what I haven't found," he said. "We don't know where they are. These things laid a trap for us once. We'd be fools to go charging out blind to find them. I'd be throwing more lives away."

Amara frowned. "I agree."

Bernard nodded. "So that's the question. We want to find them and hit them. What should our next step be?"

"That part is simple," she said. "We gather whatever knowledge we can." Amara looked around the great hall. "Where is Doroga?"

"Outside," Bernard said. "He refused to leave Walker out there by himself."

Amara frowned. "He's the only person we have who has some experience with the vord. We can't afford to risk him like that."

Bernard half smiled. "I'm not sure he isn't safer than we are, out there. Walker seems unimpressed by the vord."

Amara nodded. "All right. Let's go talk to him."

Bernard nodded once and beckoned Giraldi. The centurion came back over to the doorway bearing a wide-mouthed tin cup in one hand. He took his position at the doorway again and offered the steaming cup to Amara. It proved to be full of the thick, meaty, pungent soup commonly known as "*legionare*'s blood." Amara nodded her thanks and took the cup with her as she and Bernard walked outside to speak to Doroga.

The Marat headman was in the same corner he'd defended during the attack. Blood and ichor had dried on his pale skin, and it lent him an even more savage mien than usual. Walker stood quietly, lifting his left front leg, while Doroga examined the pads of the beast's foot.

"Doroga," Amara said.

The Marat grunted a greeting without looking up.

"What are you doing?" Bernard asked.

"Feet," the Marat rumbled. "Always got to help him take care of his feet. Feet are important when you are as big as Walker." He looked up at them, squinting against the sunlight. "When do we go after them?"

Bernard's face flickered into a white-toothed grin. "Who says we're going after them?"

Doroga snorted.

"That depends," Amara told Doroga. "We need to know as much as we can about them before we decide. What more can you tell us about the vord?"

Doroga finished with that paw. He looked at Amara for a moment, then moved to Walker's rear foot. Doroga thumped on Walker's leg with the flat of one hand. The gargant lifted the leg obligingly, and Doroga began examining that foot. "They take everyone they can. They destroy everyone they can't. They spread fast. Kill them swiftly or die."

"We know that already," Amara said.

"Good," Doroga answered. "Let's go."

"There's more to talk about," Amara insisted.

Doroga looked blankly up at her.

"For instance," Amara said. "I found a weakness in them—those lumps on their backs. Striking into them seemed to release some kind of greenish fluid, as well as disorient and kill them."

Doroga nodded. "Saw that. Been thinking about it. I think they drown."

Amara arched an eyebrow. "Excuse me?"

"Drown," Doroga said. He frowned in thought, looking up, as though searching for a word. "They choke. Smother. Thrash around in a panic, then die. Like a fish out of water."

"They're fish?" Bernard asked, his tone skeptical.

"No," Doroga said. "But maybe they breathe something other than air, like fish. Got to have what they breathe or they die. That green stuff in the lumps on their backs."

Amara pursed her lips thoughtfully. "Why do you say that?"

"Because it smells the same as what is under the *croach*. Maybe they get it there."

"Tavi told me about the *croach*," Bernard mused. "That coating that gave the Wax Forest its name. They had the stuff spread out all over that valley."

Doroga gave a grunt and nodded. "It was also spread over the nest my people destroyed."

Amara frowned in thought. "Then perhaps this *croach* isn't simply something like . . . like beeswax," she said. "Not just something they use to build. Doroga, Tavi told me that these things, the wax spiders, defended the *croach* when it was ruptured. Is that true?"

Doroga nodded. "We call them the Keepers of Silence. And yes. Only the lightest of my people could walk on the *croach* without breaking it."

"That might make sense," Amara said. "If the *croach* contained what they needed to survive . . ." She shook her head. "How long was the Wax Forest in that valley?"

Bernard shrugged. "Had been there as long as anyone could remember when I came to Calderon."

Doroga nodded agreement. "My grandfather had been down into it when he was a boy."

"But these spiders, or Keepers—they never appeared anywhere else?" Amara asked.

"Never," Doroga said with certainty. "They were only in the valley."

Amara looked over at one of the dead vord. "Then they

couldn't leave it. These things have been swift and aggressive. Something must have kept them locked into place before. They had to stay where the *croach* was to survive."

"If that's true," Bernard said, "then why are they spreading now? They were stationary for years."

Doroga put Walker's foot back down and said, quietly, "Something changed."

"But what?" Amara asked.

"Something woke up," Doroga said. "Tavi and my wh—and Kitai awoke something that lived in the center of the *croach*. It pursued them when they fled. I threw a rock at it."

"The way Tavi told it," Bernard said, "the rock was the size of a pony."

Doroga shrugged. "I threw it at the creature that pursued them. It struck the creature. Wounded it. The creature fled. The Keepers went with it. Protected it."

"Had you seen it before?" Amara asked.

"Never," Doroga said.

"Can you describe it?"

Doroga mused in thought for a moment. Then he nodded toward one of the fallen vord. "Like these. But not like these. Longer. Thinner. Strange-looking. Like it was not finished becoming what it would be."

Bernard said, "Doroga, your people had run this race for many years. How could Tavi and Kitai have wakened this creature?"

Doroga said, without expression, "Maybe you have not noticed. Tavi does things big."

Bernard arched an eyebrow. "How so?"

"He saw how the Keepers see the heat of a body. Saw how they respond to damage on the *croach*. So he set it on fire."

Bernard blinked. "Tavi . . . set the Wax Forest on *fire*?"

"Left out that part, did he?" Doroga said.

"Yes he did," Bernard said.

"The creature bit Kitai. Poisoned her. Tavi was climbing out. But he went back down for her when he could have left her there. They had been sent to recover a mushroom that grew only there. Powerful remedy to poison and disease. They each had one. Tavi gave his to Kitai to save her from the poison. Even when he knew it would cost him the race. His life." Doroga shook his head. "He saved her. And that, Bernard, is why I killed Atsurak in the battle. Because the boy saved my Kitai. It was bravely done."

"Tavi did that?" Bernard said quietly.

"Left out that part, did he?" Doroga asked again.

"He . . . he has a way of coloring things when he describes them," Bernard said. "He didn't speak of his own role in things quite so dramatically."

"Doroga," Amara asked. "If Tavi gave up the race to save your daughter, how did he win the trial?"

Doroga shrugged. "Kitai gave him her mushroom to honor his courage. His sacrifice. It cost her something she wanted very much."

"Left out that part, did you?" Bernard said, smiling.

Amara frowned and closed her eyes for a moment, thinking. "I believe I know what is happening." She opened her eyes to find both men staring at her. "I think that Tavi and Kitai woke up the vord queen. My guess is that it had been sleeping, or dormant for some reason. That somehow, whatever they did allowed it to wake up."

Doroga nodded slowly. "Maybe. First queen wakes. Spawns two new, lesser queens. They split up and found new nests."

"Which means they would need to cover new areas with the *croach*," Amara said. "If they truly need it to survive."

"We can find them," Bernard said, voice tight with excitement. "Brutus knew the feel of the Wax Forest. He can find something similar here."

Doroga grunted. "So can Walker. His nose better than mine. We can find them and give battle."

"We don't have to do that," Amara said. "All we really need to do is destroy the *croach*. If our guess is right, that will smother them all, sooner or later."

"If you're right," Bernard said, "then they will fight like mad to protect it."

Amara nodded. "Then we need to know what we're likely to face there. These wax spiders. What kind of threat are they?"

"Poison bite," Doroga said. "About the size of a small wolf. Bad enough, but nothing like these things." He nudged the shattered, flattened shell of a crushed vord with his foot.

"Do you think an armored *legionare* would be able to handle one?" Amara asked.

Doroga nodded. "Metal skin would stop Keeper fangs. Without the bite, they aren't much."

"That leaves the warriors," Amara said. She glanced around the courtyard. "Which are slightly more formidable."

"Not if we have the initiative," Bernard said. "Giraldi's century stood them off pretty well, working together."

"Yes," Doroga said, nodding. "Impressive. You people must get bored stupid practicing for that kind of fight, close together."

Bernard grinned. "Yes. But it's worth it."

"I saw," Doroga said. "We should think about going in at night. Keepers were always slowest then. Maybe the other vord are the same way."

"Night attacks," Bernard said. "Dangerous business. A lot can go wrong."

"What about their queen?" Amara asked. "Doroga, did you fight the queen at the nest you destroyed?"

Doroga nodded. "Queen was holed up under a big tangle of fallen trees with two queen whelps. Too many warriors guarding her for us to go in. So Hashat fired the trees and we killed everything as it came out. Queen whelps went down easy. The queen came last, vord around her. Hard to get a good look at her. Smaller than the vord, but faster. She killed two of my men and their gargants. All smoke and fire, couldn't see anything. But Hashat rode into it, called to me where to strike. Walker stomped on the queen. Wasn't much left."

"Could he do it again?" Amara asked.

Doroga shrugged. "His feet look fine."

"Then maybe we have a plan. We can handle the spiders, the vord, the queen," Amara said. "We move in and use the *legionares* to shield our Knights Ignus. They put fire to the *croach*. Once that is done, we can fall back and let the vord drown."

Doroga shook his head. "You are forgetting something."

"What?"

"The taken," Doroga said. The Marat leaned back against the wall, as far into the shadows of the wall as he could get, and glanced apologetically up at the sky. "The taken. They belong to the vord now. We'll have to kill them."

"You've talked about your folk being taken several times," Amara said. "What do you mean by it, exactly?"

"Taken," Doroga said. He seemed at a loss for a moment, searching for words. "The body is there. But the person is not. You look into their eyes and see nothing. They are dead. But the vord have partaken of their strength."

"They're under the vord's control?" Amara asked.

"Hardly seems possible," Bernard said, frowning.

"Not at all," Amara said. "Have you ever seen what discipline collars can do to slaves, when taken to extremes? Enough of it will make anyone easy to control."

"This is more than that," Doroga said. "There is nothing left on the inside. Just the shell. And the shell is fast, strong. Feels no pain. Has no fear. Does not speak. Only the outside is the same."

Amara's stomach did a slow twist of sickened horror. "Then . . . the holders here. Everyone who is missing . . ."

Doroga nodded. "Not just the men. Females. The old. Any children taken. They will kill until they are killed." He closed his eyes for a moment. "That was what made our losses so heavy. Hard to fight things like that. Saw a lot of good warriors hesitate. Just for an instant. They died for it."

The three of them were silent for a moment. "Doroga," she said quietly, "why did you call them shapeshifters, earlier?"

"Because they change," Doroga said. "In the stories, my people have met the vord three times. Each time, they looked different. Different weapons. But they acted the same. Tried to take everyone."

"How is the taking accomplished?" Amara pressed. "Is it some kind of furycrafting?"

Doroga grunted and shook his head. "Not sure what it is," he said. "Some stories, the vord just look at you. Control you like some kind of stupid beast."

Walker made the ground shake with a basso rumble ending in a snort, and bumped Doroga with one thick-furred leg.

"Shut up, beast," Doroga said absently, recovering his balance and leaning against the gargant. "Other stories, they poison the water. Sometimes they send something to crawl inside you." He shrugged. "Haven't seen it happening. Just saw the results. Whole hunting tribes all gone together. Doubt they knew it was happening until it was over."

They were all silent for a long moment.

"I hate to say it," Bernard said quietly. "But what if the holders who were taken . . . what if the vord can use their furies?"

A slow sliver of apprehension pierced Amara's spine. "Doroga?" she asked.

The Marat shook his head. "Don't know. Furies are not my world."

"That could change everything," Bernard said. "Our Knights' furies are our decisive advantage. Some of those holders are strongly gifted. You have to be, this far from the rest of the Realm."

Amara nodded slowly. "Assuming the vord do have access to furycraft," she said. "Does it change anything about our duty?"

Bernard shook his head. "No."

"Then we have to plan for the worst," Amara said. "Hold our Knights in reserve to counter their furycraft, until we are sure one way or another. If they do have it, the Knights may be able to counter them, at least long enough for the Knights Ignus to burn off the *croach*. Can we do it?"

Bernard frowned for a moment, then nodded slowly. "If our reasoning is sound," he said. "What do you think, Doroga?"

Doroga grunted. "I think we got too many *ifs* and *maybes*. Don't like it."

"Neither do I," Amara said. "But it's what we have."

Bernard nodded. "Then we'll move out. We'll take the Knights and Giraldi's century. I'll leave Felix here to guard the wounded."

Amara nodded, and her stomach growled. She lifted the forgotten cup of soup and drank. It tasted too salty but was pleasant going down. "Very well. And we'll need to establish passwords, Bernard. If taken Alerans can't speak, it will let us sort out friend from foe if there is any confusion. We can't assume we're any more immune to it than the holders were."

"Good idea," Bernard said. He looked around the courtyard, his eyes bleak. "Great furies, but this doesn't sit well on my stomach. Everything ran from those things. Except for the crows and us here, there isn't an animal stirring for half a mile. No birds. Not even a crows-begotten rat."

Amara finished the soup, then looked sharply at Bernard. "What?"

"It's got me spooked," he said. "That's all."

"What do you mean, there aren't any rats?" she demanded, and she heard her voice shaking.

"I'm sorry," he said. "Just thinking out loud."

Terror made the fingers in her hand go numb, and the tin cup fell to the ground. The tactile memory of something small creeping over her feet as she woke flooded through her thoughts in bright scarlet realization and fear.

Sometimes they send something to crawl inside you.

"Oh no," Amara breathed, whirling toward the darkened great hall, where weary Knights, *legionares*, and holders lay wounded, resting, sleeping. "Oh no, no, no."

CHAPTER 26

Behind her, Amara heard Bernard let out a startled oath, and then two sets of heavy steps following her back to the great hall, where Giraldi stood a laconic watch. The old centurion frowned as Amara came running up.

"Your Excellency?" he asked, frowning. "Is something wrong?"

"Get everyone," Amara snapped. "And get them all outside. Now."

Giraldi blinked. "Ev—"

"Do it!" Amara snarled, and Giraldi automatically went rigid at the sound of unwavering authority in her tone and banged a fist to his breastplate. Then he spun about and started barking out a string of booming orders.

"Amara?" Bernard asked. "What is this?"

"I felt a rat or a mouse brush past my foot as I woke," Amara said. Her hands were clenched into impotent fists. "But you said that there aren't any left."

Bernard frowned. "Maybe you dreamed it?"

"Great furies," Amara breathed. "I hope so. Because if the vord are taking people by sending things to crawl into them as they sleep, we have a problem. Most of the Knights were sleeping near me, on the cots where the lights were dimmest."

Bernard sucked in a sudden breath. "Crows and bloody carrion," he swore quietly. "You mean that you think that there were . . . things . . . crawling around in the hall?"

"I think that this is part of their first attack," Amara said. "It's just happening more quietly."

Doroga grunted. "Makes sense why the vord withdrew early, now. Gave you wounded to care for. Knew you would take them inside. Then they send takers."

Inside the hall, Giraldi continued bellowing orders. Every furylamp in the place had been brought to its most brilliant, and the hall was bright enough to hurt Amara's eyes. She stepped to one side of the door as the *legionares* nearest it took up their weapons and shields and headed outside at a quick jog. Several men limped painfully. The wounded had to be carried out on their cots, one man lifting either end.

Amara fought down an urge to scream for more haste in exiting the building. Giraldi was already doing plenty of that. Amara hoped desperately that she had leapt to an incorrect conclusion and that the evacuation of the building was an unnecessary measure. But something in her guts told her that she hadn't been wrong. That the carefully laid trap had already been sprung.

Two men carried the first of the cots outside, and Amara frowned down at them, chewing on one lip. Several of the heavily armored Knights Terra went out next, still carrying pieces of their armor to the courtyard. A few of the men were milling around in knots of two and three, speaking quietly, their expressions uncertain. Giraldi started to bellow an order at them, then stopped himself with a visible effort and turned around to continue berating the young *legionares* of Felix's century.

Amara frowned and studied the idle men whom Giraldi had declined to order around. They were Knights, every one of them. Why weren't they leaving?

"Gentlemen," Amara called to them. "With the rest of us, please."

The Knights glanced up at her, and several of them thumped a fist to their breastplate in response. They all headed for the door, falling into line behind those bearing stretchers.

They'd just been waiting for an order, Amara thought. *Surely Captain Janus would have deduced that the evacuation order was intended for everyone.*

Another cot went by, and Amara almost didn't notice that the man carrying the foot of the cot was Captain Janus. The captain's mouth started an irregular tic on one corner, and he glanced around until his eyes met Amara's.

She stared at him in shock. The man's eyes were . . . wrong. Simply wrong. Janus was an excellent, conscientious officer, whose mind was continually occupied with how best to lead and protect his men, attend to his duty, and serve the Realm. Even when he had been eating or at weapons practice, whether relaxed or angry, there had always been a sense of reflection to his eyes, his expression, as his mind assessed, planned, and weighed advantages.

That reflection had vanished.

Time stopped. Janus's eyes were half-hooded, unblinking, his expression oddly slack. He met Amara's gaze and whatever it was that now looked at her, it was *not* Captain Janus.

Great furies, Amara thought. *He's been taken.*

Something alien and mad flickered through the taken man's eyes in response to Amara's realization. He shifted his grip on the cot, then tore it bodily from the hands of the man at the other end. The wounded man in the cot screamed as he tumbled from it to the stone floor.

Janus swept the heavy cot in a two-handed swing that clipped Amara's shoulder and spun her to the floor. Then he turned, and with another swing of the cot, shattered the skull of the cot-bearing man walking backward in line behind him. The man went down without making a sound. Janus hurled the heavy cot at the next man, and the missile hit hard, knocking down several more.

Janus turned back to the door and broke into a run, but as he went past Amara, she thrust out her foot and deftly caught it on the man's ankle, sending him into a sprawling trip that carried him out the door.

"Bernard!" Amara shouted, rising to her feet to follow him. "Giraldi! Janus has been taken!" She came outside to find Janus walking calmly in a straight line toward Harger. "Stop him!" she shouted. "Stop that man!"

A pair of *legionares* near Janus blinked at her, but then stepped into the man's path. One of the men held up a hand, and said, "Excuse me, sir. The Countess would like to—"

Janus reached for the *legionare*'s upraised hand and with a single motion of casual, savage strength he crushed it to pulp and splintered bone. The *legionare* screamed and staggered as Janus released him. The second *legionare* stared for an instant, then his hand flashed toward the hilt of his sword.

Janus swept a fist at the *legionare*'s head and struck with such force that Amara clearly heard the man's neck snap. He dropped to the ground in a boneless heap.

"He's heading for Harger!" Amara shouted. "Protect the healer! Get him out of here!" She drew her sword, called to

Cirrus to lend to her of his swiftness, and rushed at Janus from behind.

Just before she closed to within reach of her blade, Janus spun to face her and threw a crushing fist at her head. Amara saw it as a lazy, slow swing rather than the pile-driving blow that she knew had to have lashed at her as swiftly as a slive's tongue. She altered her balance, her own movements sluggish and dreamlike, and let the blow slip past her head without landing. Then she slashed downward with the short, heavy *gladius*, and the blade bit deep into the muscle of Janus's right thigh.

From the reaction the taken captain showed, she might have struck him with a handful of down feathers. Without pausing, another blow swept at her head.

Amara let her legs go out from under her, diving to Janus's right, and hoped that the wound in his thigh would slow him down as she dropped into a forward roll and came back to her feet several paces away.

Janus stared at her for a blank second, then turned and walked toward Harger again. The exhausted healer, himself in a cot, had not awakened in the commotion. His face looked sunken, his iron grey beard shot through with white. Two more *legionares* bore him away while half a dozen others set themselves in a line of shields facing Janus, weapons in hand.

Janus lashed out with one boot in a stomping kick that landed in the middle of a *legionare*'s shield. The blow hurled the man several yards backward, and he landed awkwardly on the stones. The *legionare* beside the stricken man laid open Janus's arm from shoulder to elbow with a hard slash, but the taken man ignored it, seized that *legionare*'s shield in both hands, and threw him with bone-crushing force into the next man in the line.

And then Bernard appeared, facing Janus, his hands empty. Amara's heart leapt into her throat in sudden fear for him. Bernard growled a curse under his breath and swept his fist at Janus with the incredible fury-born strength Brutus gave him. The blow hit Janus like a battering ram and he arched up and landed on his back on the cobblestones. Bernard pointed at the taken man and called, "Brutus!"

The cobblestones heaved, then the jaws of the earthen hound emerged from them and clamped down hard on Janus's leg before the taken man could rise.

Janus's eyes widened, and his head snapped around to examine the stone hound that had him locked into place. His head tilted to one side, a slow and oddly rubbery movement. Then he looked back at Bernard and pushed the heel of his hand toward the Count.

The earth heaved and bucked up into a ripple a full two feet high. The stone wave leapt at Bernard with impossible speed, striking him hard on one leg and sending the Count to the ground.

Amara's heart leapt into her throat.

The taken could furycraft.

She dashed forward and drove her sword down at Janus's throat. The man turned as she approached, and her thrusting blade shot cleanly through Janus's upraised palm. He twisted his arm to one side in a half circle, and the blade, caught in the flesh and the bones of his hand, twisted from her grasp.

Amara darted to one side as Janus tried to seize her with his other hand.

"Amara!" Doroga bellowed.

She whipped her head around to see the Marat headman cast his heavy cudgel into the air from behind a crowd of confused *legionares* who blocked his way. The heavy end of the club hit the ground, and Amara seized the long club's grip as it bounded toward her. She could not afford to waste the momentum the cudgel provided, for it was far too heavy for her to wield with deliberate focus. Instead, she held on to the handle with both white-knuckled hands, spun in a full circle with the heavy, deadly weapon, and brought it down squarely on Captain Janus's head.

She felt the crackling, brittle fragility of the taken man's skull breaking under the incredible force the cudgel delivered in the blow. She staggered, the weight of the cudgel pulling her off-balance. The impact all but crushed Janus's skull down into his chest, and after several seconds of twisting, spasmodic motion, he slowly went still.

Amara heard other screams and cries. A *legionare* lay in the doorway to the great hall, shrieking in a horrible, high voice, a sound of agony and terror that could not have been recognized as coming from a human mouth. His left arm was missing from its socket and his blood became a spreading pool beneath him until his cries dwindled to silence seconds later. Amara heard the ring of steel on steel, more shouts, and Giraldi's barking, confident voice of command.

She looked around the courtyard, panting. The action had lasted for only seconds, but she felt exhausted and weak. Harger, now surrounded by *legionares*, appeared to be unharmed. Amara hurried over to Bernard and knelt beside him. "Are you hurt?"

"Wind knocked out of me," Bernard replied, his voice soft. He sat up stiffly and rubbed groggily at his head. "See to the men."

Amara nodded once, and rose.

Doroga came over to them and frowned at Bernard. "You dying?"

Bernard winced, the heel of his hand against the back of his skull. "I almost wish I was."

Doroga snorted. He recovered his cudgel and studied the end of it, then showed it to Bernard. "Your head is better off than his."

One side of the cudgel's striking end was covered in scarlet and dark hairs that clung to the blood. Amara saw it, and it made her feel sickened. Janus. She'd known the man for two years. Liked him. Respected him. He had been unfailingly courteous and thoughtful, and she knew how much Bernard valued his experience and professionalism.

And she'd killed him. She'd crushed his skull.

Amara fought not to throw up.

Doroga regarded her steadily, and said, "He was taken. Nothing you could do."

"I know."

"He would have killed anyone he could have."

"I know that, too," Amara said. "It doesn't make it any easier."

Doroga shook his head. "You did not kill him. The vord did. Just like the men who died during the ambush."

Amara didn't answer him.

A moment later, Giraldi strode over and snapped one hand to his breastplate. "Countess. Count Bernard."

"What happened?" Bernard rumbled quietly. "I heard more fighting."

Giraldi nodded. "Three of the wounded men just . . . sat up and started killing people. They were all almost earthcrafter strong. We had to kill them—which took some doing." He took a deep breath, staring at Janus's corpse for a second. "And Sir Tyrus went mad, too. Started in on Sir Kerns. Killed him. He made a pretty fair run at Sir Jager, and cut his leg up pretty well. I had to kill Tyrus."

Bernard stared at Giraldi for a moment. "Crows."

Giraldi nodded grimly, looking around the crow-infested courtyard with distaste. "Yes."

Doroga looked back and forth between them, frowning. "What does that mean?"

"We had three firecrafters with our Knights," Bernard said quietly. "They're our most powerful offensive assets. And now two of them are dead, one wounded. How mobile is he, Giraldi?"

Giraldi shook his head. "Lucky he's alive. There wasn't a watercrafter to handle the injury. I've got my best medic on him with needle and thread now. But he isn't going to be able to travel."

"Crows," Bernard said quietly.

"What happened?" Giraldi asked.

Amara listened as Bernard explained what they knew of vord takers. "So we think some of them must have been waiting inside the great hall, until some of our people went to sleep."

Footsteps thumped over the cobblestones and the young Knight, Frederic, came running from the great hall, holding a tin cup in his hands. "Sir!" Frederic said.

"A moment, Fred," Bernard said, turning back to Giraldi. "How did Tyrus kill Kerns?"

"Gladius," Giraldi said. "Right in the back."

Amara frowned. "Not firecrafting?"

"Thank the furies, no," Giraldi said. "Firecrafting in there would have killed everyone."

"What about the others who were taken?" Amara pressed.

"Bare hands," Giraldi said.

Amara stared at the centurion, then traded a puzzled glance with Bernard. "But Janus used an earthcrafting out here. Why didn't the taken inside the hall use furycraft?"

Bernard shook his head, baffled. "You think there's a reason for it?"

"Sir," Frederic said. His palm was pressed flat over the cup, and his expression was impatient or strained.

"Not now, please," Amara told Frederic. "It doesn't get us anywhere if we assume there was no logical reason for it," she told Bernard. "Something happened out here that was different than what happened inside. We need to discover what that was."

Bernard grunted. "Giraldi, what else can you tell me about the taken in the great hall?"

Giraldi shrugged. "Not much, sir. It was fast, bloody. Swords and knives. One of the men used the haft of his spear and broke one of the taken's necks with it."

"Weaponplay," Amara said. "Centurion, was there any crafting involved?"

Giraldi frowned. "Nothing overt, my lady. I've some metalcrafting, but it's never been something I actually *do* anything to use, if you follow me. One of the men maybe used some earthcraft to throw a trestle at one of the taken to slow it down when it went for one of the children."

Amara frowned. "But drawing upon a fury for strength is an internalized use of furycraft—just like your enhanced skills of swordplay. Or Bernard's archery." She glanced up at Bernard. "But you actually manifested Brutus to pin Janus down. It was after you did that he . . ." She frowned. "He almost seemed surprised when it happened, as if he could feel it, somehow. And then he loosed his own furycrafting against you, Bernard."

Bernard frowned. "But what does that mean?"

"I don't think he could have called upon any furycrafting when he first came outside," Amara said. "If he could have, I think he'd have turned it on Harger at once."

Bernard nodded slowly. "You think he couldn't have used it until . . . what? Until someone showed him how? Until someone else initiated a crafting?"

Amara shook her head. "Perhaps. I don't know."

Giraldi growled. "Janus was after our last healer? Crows."

Bernard nodded. "Our healers. Our firecrafters. These vord, whatever they are, are not stupid. They lured us into a trap, and they're striking deliberately at our strongest crafters. They've predicted several of our moves. Which means that they know us. They know us a lot better than we know them."

Bernard grunted and hauled himself unsteadily to his feet. "That's bad news, people."

"Sir," Frederic said.

"Wait a moment," Bernard said, holding up a hand to Frederic. "Amara, you said you felt something brush your foot while you were sleeping?"

"Yes," she said.

Bernard nodded. "So. Let's assume that these takers are something very small—about the size of a mouse or a small rat. We all must sleep sooner or later. We're still vulnerable to them. We need to work out some kind of defense."

"Can't we just make sure the great hall is emptied of them?" Amara asked.

"Not for certain," Bernard said. "In the first place, we don't even know what they look like. And secondly, something mouse-sized is going to be able to find cracks in the stone, holes in the walls, places to get in and places to hide. The rats do."

"And I don't think camping outside is an option," Amara mused.

"Definitely not."

"We need to know more about these takers," Amara said. "If we could get a look at one, it might help us work out a plan."

Frederic let out an explosively frustrated sigh, stepped forward between them all, and slammed the open mouth of the cup down onto the cobblestones in a swift gesture. Amara blinked at him in surprise. The young Knight looked up at them, and said, "They look like this."

He jerked the cup up off the ground.

Amara stared at the taker. It was as long as her hand and very slender. Its flesh was a sickly, pale color, streaked with scarlet blood, and its body was covered in overlapping segments of translucent chitin. Dozens of legs protruded from either side of its body, and antennae fully as long as its body sprouted from either end of the creature. Its head was a barely discernible lump at one end of the body, and was armed with short, sharp-looking mandibles.

The taker flinched into a writhing ball when the light touched it, as if it could not stand its brightness. Its legs and chitinous plates scraped against the stones.

"Look," Amara murmured, pointing at the taker. "Its back."

There were two lumps there, as there had been on the warriors. Amara reached down to touch one, and with blinding speed the taker's body whirled and those heavy mandibles snapped down upon Amara's finger. The Cursor let out a hiss and flicked her wrist. The taker's grip was surprisingly strong, and it took her several tries to dislodge the creature and fling it away from her.

Bernard spun around and stomped down with one boot. The taker's body made a crackling sound as he crushed it.

"Crows," Giraldi breathed quietly.

Everyone turned to look at Frederic.

"I was moving one of the corpses," Frederic said quietly. "Tyrus. His head had been chopped off. That thing crawled out of . . ." Frederic swallowed and looked a little green. "It crawled out of the head's mouth, sir."

An odd and unpleasant burning sensation had begun to throb through Amara's finger scarce seconds after the taker had bitten down. Over the next several heartbeats, the burning numbness spread to her entire finger and hand, to the wrist. She tried to clench her fingers, and found them barely able to move. "Its bite," she said. "Some kind of poison."

Frederic nodded and held up his own weakly flapping hand. "Yes, ma'am. Bit me a few times when I caught it, but I don't feel sick or anything."

Amara nodded with a grimace. "It wouldn't make sense for a taker's venom to be lethal. We'll have to hope for the best. These things must have approached men who were sleeping. Crawled into their mouths." She started to feel queasy herself. "And then took control of them."

Giraldi frowned. "But you'd feel it crawling into your mouth. Those things are big enough to choke you."

"Not if it bit you," Amara responded. "Not if you'd gone numb, so you couldn't feel it on you. Especially if you were asleep to begin with."

"Great furies," Bernard breathed.

Amara continued to follow the line of logic. "They didn't pick random targets, either. Janus. Our Knights." She took a steadying breath. "And me."

Frederic said, "Steadhold—uh, that is, Count Bernard. We've taken a head count inside. We're missing four other men."

Bernard arched an eyebrow. "They aren't in the steadholt?"

"We haven't found them," Frederic said. "But the far door of the hall was open."

"They were taken," Amara murmured. "Must have been. They went out the door on that side so that they could leave the steadholt without us or Doroga seeing them go." She took a deep breath. "Bernard. The longer we wait around, the more likely it is that we will suffer additional losses. We need to wipe out that nest immediately."

"Agreed," Bernard said quietly. "But can we do it? Without the firecrafters to set it ablaze and assist us in any fighting, I'm not sure how effective we can be."

"Do we have a choice?" Amara asked quietly.

Bernard folded his arms across his chest, squinted up at the sun, and shook his head. "I don't suppose we do," he rumbled. "Every advantage. We must create what we need." Bernard nodded once, sharply. He turned to Giraldi, and said, "I want your century ready to march in ten minutes. Tell Felix about the takers, and make sure all the men know about them. Have him create a record of what we've learned so far and leave it where any relief troops will find it in case we . . . aren't able to tell anyone ourselves. They'll need to stand watch for one another against the takers, and sleep in shifts."

Giraldi banged his fist on his breastplate and stalked off, bellowing orders again.

Bernard turned to Amara. "Countess, I'm appointing you Knight Commander. We'll need to make the most of our Knights' strength. I want you to do it."

Amara licked her lips and nodded. "Very well."

"Frederic," Bernard said, "get every Knight Terra we have left and have them cover you while you go through some of the buildings. I want every furylamp outside of the steadholt's great hall ready to go with us when we march. Move."

Frederic nodded and dashed off.

"Furylamps?" Amara murmured.

Bernard traded a look with Doroga, and the big Marat smiled broadly.

"Furylamps," Bernard said. "We attack the vord nest at nightfall."

Chapter 27

Fidelias opened the door of the room and stepped aside, letting in a haze of smoke and incense, the sound of reed pipes, and the low murmur of human sound that drifted through the halls of the brothel like cheap perfume. The cloaked and hooded figure on the other side slipped into the room and drew back her hood. Invidia Aquitaine looked around the room, her expression remote, and while she felt around her for any intrusive furycraftings, Fidelias shut and locked the door.

Lady Invidia nodded to herself in satisfaction, and Fidelias felt her own furycraftings rise up to keep their conversation private. Her voice was low, tense. "What happened? The streets were a madhouse of rumors."

"Kalare's men followed them back to Sir Nedus's manor," Fidelias reported. "Three cutters and an archer. They attacked as Isana dismounted from the carriage."

Invidia looked at the very still form lying on the room's bed. "And?"

"Sir Nedus was killed, along with Serai and the coachmen. The Steadholder was shot."

Invidia's cold, hard gaze flicked to Fidelias. "The assassins?"

"Dead. Sir Nedus killed the cutters, but the archer was well hidden. It took me longer than I thought to find him and kill him."

"And the Steadholder was shot as a result." Invidia crossed the room to the bed, staring down at the pale, unconscious face of Isana of Calderon. "How badly is she wounded?"

"Barring infection, she'll live, even without crafting. She was very lucky. I've removed the arrow and cleaned and dressed the wound." He shrugged. "I can't imagine she'll be very comfortable when she wakes up, though."

Invidia nodded. "We'll have to get her into a bath as soon as possible. Kalare's people won't give up now. Better if she's not an invalid." She frowned. "And I suppose it might engender some feeling of gratitude."

Fidelias arched an eyebrow. "For something she could do herself, once awake?"

Invidia shrugged a shoulder. "For offering her something Gaius did not: safety. She was here at his bidding, I am certain. Whatever has happened, the simple fact that he did not provide her with sufficient protection will weigh heavily against him."

"Against Gaius does not necessarily mean toward you, Your Grace," Fidelias pointed out. "If she is like many holders, she will wish to have nothing to do with any ranking nobility—much less with the wife of the man who orchestrated the attack that nearly destroyed her home and family."

"That wasn't personal," Invidia said.

"For Isana it was," Fidelias said.

She waved a hand and sighed. "I know, I know. When I met her at Kalare's garden party, I thought for a moment that she was about to assault me. I tried to warn them that they were in danger and that Serai's identity might be known. I had thought that they listened. They left quite quickly."

"It might have been a moot point by then," Fidelias said. "In any case, we have to assume that Kalare will have his people looking for her when her body doesn't turn up."

Invidia nodded. "How secure is this location?"

"Not as much as I would like," Fidelias said. "I should have ample warning in the event I need to leave. That's as much as I can realistically expect without moving into the Deeps—or to your manor."

"Definitely not," Invidia said. "Kalare's bloodcrows haunt the Deeps, if your suspicion is correct—and it would be embarrassing for you to be discovered at my husband's manor. And I am sure that there are more than a few people looking for you. If the Cursors are not so rattled as you seem to think, they would make it a point to assume that if you were in town, you might well be in the manor."

Fidelias nodded. "I suggest, Your Grace, that you consider bringing Isana to your manor to stay, if not me."

"She does not care for me, dear spy."

Fidelias half smiled. "I promise you that she cares for me even less."

"I trust you to deal with that," Invidia replied. "I want you to care for her personally until she wakes. Do whatever you must—but make sure she understands her vulnerability before you contact me again." She paused for a moment. "The messages that she has been sending, the company she has kept. Isana has . . . the sense of a desperate woman about her. Find out why."

"She is unlikely to take me into her confidence," he said in a dry voice.

"If I am right, it might not matter," Invidia said. She drew the hood back over her face. "She is motivated by powerful emotions. I suspect that she believes her family is in danger. To protect them, she might willingly lend me her support."

"Perhaps," Fideiias agreed. "But I do not think that you will find her as forgiving as other players in the game, Your Grace. You and I understand the necessity of allying oneself today with the political opponent of yesterday. But for someone like her, you will always be the wife and helpmate of the man who attempted to destroy her home and kin. That is the way of folk in the country."

"She isn't in the country anymore, Fidelias. She needs to realize that. Impress it upon her if you can. Contact me when you judge her as willing as she is likely to be."

"Very well."

"She's critical to us, dear spy. If she is killed, the lords will understand that Kalare has won the round. If she appears to the Senate under Gaius's oversight, the First Lord will have controlled the situation. She must appear before the Senate, and in my lord husband's colors. Then we will have outmaneuvered Kalare and Gaius alike."

"I understand, Your Grace," Fidelias said. "But I don't know if this victory is possible."

"Now, now, Fidelias. Of course it is possible, if we work hard enough and intelligently enough." She crossed to the door and opened it slowly. "And don't take too long, my spy," she cautioned him. "Time is fleeting."

"When is it not?" he replied.

Invidia's teeth gleamed white as she smiled from within her hood. Then she slipped out of the room and closed the door behind her.

Fidelias locked the door and sank down into the room's only chair. He ached all the way to his bones, and he was more than a little tired, but he didn't dare let his guard down. Those interested in claiming the reward for him offered by the Crown would certainly be looking for him. But bounty hunters were a secondary concern. Kalare's bloodcrows would be more organized, more formidable, and much more capable trackers. The fact that they had, in fact, seemingly stretched their influence into the Deeps, traditionally the haunt of the Cursors and the criminal underworld of the capital, spoke volumes about how they must have prospered.

Not only did Fidelias have to worry about bounty hunters and rival assassins, but the Steadholder had already proven herself capable of decisive, deadly action. If he went to sleep with her yet wounded and senseless, when she woke she might well prove it again, and he did not care to be on the receiving end of further violence. He had been weary before. He could wait for her to waken.

Beyond that, he was not sure. What Invidia required of him might well be impossible. But she was not the kind to suffer failure lightly. It could be worth as much as his life if Isana of Calderon refused to cooperate.

Fidelias tried not to think about that. He had not survived a lifetime of service in the shadows by allowing his fears and doubts to rule his mind.

So he settled back in his chair, listened to the music and talk and cries of those enjoying the hospitality of the brothel, and waited for the Steadholder to waken, so that he could convince her to help topple the First Lord of Alera on behalf of Lord and Lady Aquitaine.

CHAPTER 28

Killian lifted a shaking hand to his face and leaned his forehead down against his palm. He was silent for a moment, but to Tavi that moment seemed days long. Maybe longer.

Tavi licked his lips and glanced at Fade, apparently asleep on the floor beside Gaius's cot. He wasn't sleeping. Tavi wasn't sure how he knew, but he felt certain that Fade was awake and listening carefully. The First Lord looked little different than when Tavi had last seen him. Gaius still seemed shrunken in upon himself, his face colorless and frail.

Sir Miles, who had been sitting at the replacement desk in one corner of the meditation chamber, methodically reading the messages sent to the First Lord, looked as though someone had kicked him in the stomach.

"I didn't mean for any of that to happen," Tavi said into the silence. "Neither did Max."

"I should hope not," Killian said in a mild voice.

"You . . ." Miles took a deep breath, clearly struggling to restrain his anger. Then he bared his teeth, and just as clearly lost the struggle. "You *idiots!*" he shouted. "You stupid, crows-begotten *fools*! How could you *do* something like this? What treacherous moron dashed the *brains* from your witless *skulls*?" He clenched his hands into fists and opened them again several times, as though strangling baby ducks. "Do you have any idea what you've *done*?"

Tavi felt his face heat up. "It was an accident."

Miles snarled and slashed his hand at the air. "It was an accident that the two of you left the Citadel when you knew you should stay close at hand? When you *knew* what was at stake?"

"It was my aunt," Tavi said. "I went to help her. I thought she was in trouble." Tavi felt his eyes blur with frustrated tears, and he scrubbed savagely at them with one sleeve. "And I was right."

"Your aunt," Miles growled, "is one person, Tavi. What you've done may have endangered the whole of Alera."

"I'm not related to the whole of Alera," Tavi shot back. "She's almost my only blood relation. My only family. Do you understand what that means? Do you have any family, Sir Miles?"

There was a heavy silence. Some of the anger faded from the captain's face.

"Not anymore," Miles said, his voice quiet.

Tavi's eyes went back to Fade, who lay in exactly the same position. Tavi thought he could feel a kind of quivering attention in him at Miles's mention of family.

Miles sighed. "But furies, boy. Your actions may have endangered us all. The Realm is only barely holding together. If word of Gaius's condition gets out, it could mean civil war. Attack from our enemies. Death and destruction for thousands."

Tavi physically flinched at the captain's words. "I know," he said. "I know."

"Gentlemen," Killian said, raising his head, "we all know what is at stake. Recriminations are useless to us for the time being. Our duty now is to assess the damage and take whatever steps we can to mitigate it." His blind eyes turned toward Tavi, and his voice took on a faint, but definite edge of frost. "After the crisis is past us, we will have time to consider appropriate consequences for the choices made."

Tavi swallowed. "Yes, sir."

"Damage," Miles spat. "That's a pretty way to phrase it. We don't have a First Lord to appear at the highest profile social functions of the entire Realm. When he doesn't show up, the High Lords are going to start asking questions. They're going to start spreading money around. Sooner or later, someone is going to realize that no one knows where Gaius is."

"At which point," Killian mused, "we can expect them to attempt some sort of action to test the First Lord's authority. Once that is done, with no response from Gaius, an attempt to seize the Crown will only be a question of time."

"Could we find another double?" Miles asked.

Killian shook his head. "It was little short of a miracle that Antillar was able to impersonate him at all. I know of no other crafter both capable and trustworthy enough. It may be best to make excuses for the First Lord for the remainder of Winters-end and focus on ways to respond to any probes from the High Lords."

"You think we can cow them?" Miles asked.

"I think that they will need time to become certain that they have an opportunity," Killian said. "Our response would be designed to extend that time in order to give the First Lord a chance to recuperate."

Miles grunted. "If the First Lord does not appear at Wintersend—or to the presentation of new Citizens to the Senate and Lords—his reputation may never recover."

"I'm not sure that we can reasonably hope to attain anything better," Killian replied.

"Um," Tavi said. "What about Max?"

Killian arched an eyebrow. "What about him?"

"If we still need him so badly, can't we get him out of holding?" Tavi shook his head. "I mean, we have the First Lord's signet dagger. We could issue an order."

"Impossible," Miles said flatly. "Antillar is accused of the deadly assault and attempted murder of a Citizen—and the son of a High Lord at that, not to mention two other young men who are already being groomed as Knights for Kalare's Legions. Antillar must be held by the civic legion until his trial. Not even Gaius can defy that law."

Tavi chewed on his lip. "Well. What if we . . . sort of got him out unofficially?"

Miles frowned. "A jailbreak." He scrunched up his nose in thought. "Killian?"

"Lord Antillus has never made Maximus's heritage a secret," Killian answered. "They'll hold him in the Grey Tower."

Miles winced. "Ah."

"What's the Grey Tower?" Tavi asked. "I haven't heard of it."

"It isn't a place one discusses in polite company," Killian replied, his voice tired. "The Tower is meant to be capable of containing any crafter in the Realm—even the First Lord, if necessary—so that not even the High Lords would be beyond the reach of the law. The Lords Council itself crafted the security measures around the Grey Tower."

"What kind of measures?" Tavi asked.

"The same as you might find around the palace, prominent

jewelers, or a lord's treasury—only a great deal more potent. It would take several High Lords working in concert to furycraft a way in or out. And the Grey Guard stand watch on the conventional thresholds."

"Who are they?" Tavi asked.

"Some of the finest metalcrafters and swordsmen in the Realm," Miles said. "To get in without furycrafting, we'd have to kill some damned decent men to get Antillar out. And doing so during Wintersend would set half the Realm on our trail. He'd be useless to us."

Tavi frowned. "Bribery?"

Miles shook his head. "The Grey Guard are handpicked specifically because they have enough integrity to resist bribery. Not only that, but the law states that the Crown will pay a bonus of double the amount of any attempted bribe if the guardsman turns in whoever tried it. In the past five hundred years, not one Grey Guardsman has taken a bribe, and only a handful of idiots have attempted to give them one."

"There must be some way in," Tavi said.

"Yes," Killian said. "One can go through furycrafted guardians and wards too powerful to simply overcome, or one can fight his way through the Grey Guard. There are no other ways in or out." He paused for a beat, and said, "That's rather the point in having a prison tower in the first place."

Tavi felt himself flush again. "I only mean that there must be some course of action we could take. He's only there because he saved my life. Brencis was going to murder me."

"That was noble of Maximus."

"Yes."

Killian's voice turned severe. "The unpleasant truth is that the Cursors have little need of nobility. We desire foresight, judgment, and intelligence."

"Then what you're saying," Tavi said, "is that Max should have left me to die."

Miles frowned, but said nothing, watching Killian.

"You both should have brought the information to me first. And you certainly should not have left the Citadel without consulting me."

"But we can't leave him there. Max didn't even—" Tavi began.

Killian shook his head and spoke over him. "Antillar has been taken out of play, Tavi. There is nothing we can do for him."

Tavi scowled down at the floor and folded his arms. "What about my aunt Isana? Are you going to tell me that there's nothing we can do for her, either?"

Killian frowned. "Is there a viable reason for us to divert our very limited current resources to assist her?"

"Yes," Tavi said. "You know as well as I do that the First Lord was using her to divide what he suspected was an alliance of several High Lords. That he appointed her a Steadholder without consulting Lord Rivus in the matter. She has become a symbol of his power. If he has invited her to Wintersend, and something happens to her, it will be one more blow to his power base." Tavi swallowed. "Assuming she isn't dead already."

Killian was quiet for a moment. Then he said, "Normally, you would have a point. But we are now in the unenviable position of choosing which of Gaius's assets to sacrifice."

"She is *not* an asset," Tavi said, and his voice rang with sudden strength and authority. Miles blinked at him, and even Killian tilted his head quizzically. "She is my aunt," Tavi continued. "My blood. She cared for me after my mother died, and I owe everything in my life to her. Furthermore, she is an Aleran Citizen here at the invitation and in support of the Crown. He owes it to her to provide protection in her hour of need."

Killian half smiled. "Even at the expense of the rest of the Realm?"

Tavi took a deep breath through his nose. Then he said, "Maestro. If the First Lord and we his retainers are no longer capable of protecting the people of the Realm from harm, then perhaps we should not be here at all."

Miles growled, "Tavi. That's treason."

Tavi lifted his chin and faced Miles. "It isn't treason, Sir Miles. It's the truth. It isn't a pretty truth, or a happy truth, or a comfortable truth. It simply is." He stared at Miles's eyes levelly. "I'm with the First Lord, Sir Miles. He is my patron, and I will support him regardless of what happens. But if we aren't living up to the obligations of the office of First Lord, then how can we pretend to be justified in holding its power?"

Silence reigned.

Killian sat perfectly still for a long moment. Then he said, quietly, "Tavi, you are morally correct. Ethically correct. But to best serve the First Lord we must make a difficult choice. No matter how horrible it seems." Killian let Tavi absorb the words for a moment, then turned his head vaguely toward Miles in search of support. "Captain?"

Miles had fallen silent, and now stood leaning against the wall, studying Tavi with his lips pursed. His thumb rapped a quiet rhythm on the hilt of his sword.

Tavi met the old soldier's eyes and did not look away.

Miles took a deep breath, and said, "Killian. The boy is right. Our duty in this hour is to perform as the First Lord would wish us to—not to safeguard his political interests. Gaius would never abandon Isana after asking her here. We therefore owe it both to the First Lord and to the Steadholder to protect her."

Killian's lips shook a little as he pressed them together. "Miles," he said, a gentle plea in his tone.

"It's what Gaius would want us to do," Miles said, unmoved. "Some things are important, Killian. Some things cannot be abandoned without destroying what we and our forebears have worked all our lives to build."

"We cannot base our decision on passion," Killian said, his voice suddenly raw. "Too much depends upon us."

Tavi lifted his head suddenly, staring at Killian as comprehension dawned. Then he said, "You were his friend. You were friends with Sir Nedus."

Killian answered quietly, his voice smooth, precise, and steady. "We served our Legion terms together. We entered the service of the Royal Guard together. He was my friend for sixty-four years." Killian's voice did not change as tears slid down from his sightless eyes. "I knew that she was coming to the capital, and that given our circumstances that she might not be secure in the palace. Nedus was protecting your aunt because I trusted him. I asked him to. He died because I put him in harm's way. And all of that changes nothing about our duty."

Tavi stared at him. "You knew my aunt was here? That she might be in danger?"

"Which is why I made sure Nedus knew to offer his hospitality," Killian said, his voice suddenly brittle and sharp. "She was supposed to stay in his manor until this situation settled. She would have been as safe there as anywhere. I cannot imagine what drove her to leave the manor—or why Nedus permitted it. He must have been trying to contact me, but . . ." He shook his head. "I didn't grasp what was happening. I didn't see."

"What if he had good reason to take the chance?" Tavi asked quietly. "Something he judged to be worth the risk?"

Killian shook his head and didn't answer.

"The boy is right," Miles said. "He was a Royal Guard in his own day and was never a fool. He was my *patriserus* of the blade. Rari's too. He knew better than anyone the risks in exposing the Steadholder. If he did so, he did it only because it was a necessity."

"Don't you think I know that?" Killian said quietly. "If I allow this to distract our focus, we may lose all of Alera. And if I ignore Nedus's sacrifice, it may mean that we are exposed to some unforeseen threat he was desperate to warn us about. I must choose. And I must not let my feelings, however strong, dictate that choice. Too much is at stake."

Tavi stared at Killian and suddenly perceived not the razor intellect and deadly calm of the Cursor Legate, but the deep and bitter grief of an old man struggling to hold himself together in the face of an overwhelming storm of anxiety, uncertainty, and loss. Killian was not a young man. The future of literally the entire Realm rested on his slender shoulders, and he had found them more brittle than strong beneath so heavy a burden. His fight to retain his control, to rely upon pure intellect to guide his choices, was his only defense against the storm of danger and duty that demanded that he act—and which instead held him pinned and motionless.

And Tavi suddenly understood what might tip that balance. He hated himself for thinking of the words. He hated himself for even considering saying them. He hated himself for drawing the breath that would carry them to the wounded, bleeding soul within the old man.

But it was the only way he could help Aunt Isana.

"Then the question is whether or not you trust Sir Nedus's

judgment. If you do, and if we leave the Steadholder to her fate," Tavi said quietly, "then he will have died for nothing."

Killian bent his head sharply, as though to stare at a dagger suddenly buried in his guts.

Tavi forced himself to watch the old man's pain. The pain he'd driven hard into Killian in his moment of weakness. The pain he knew would compel Killian to act. There was another silence, and Tavi felt suddenly sick with an anger directed nowhere but at himself.

He looked up to find Miles staring at him, something hard in the captain's eyes. But he never stirred and did not speak, letting his silence stand substitute for his support.

"I don't know how we can help her," Killian said at last, his voice a croak. "Not with only the three of us."

"Give me Ehren and Gaelle," Tavi said at once. "Free them of their final exercise. Let them investigate and see what they can find. They don't have to know anything about Gaius. Isana is my aunt, after all. Everyone knows that already. It would be natural for me to ask for their help in finding her. And . . . I might be able to ask Lady Placida as well. She's one of the leaders in the Dianic League. The League has a vested interest in keeping my aunt safe. They might be willing to expend some effort to locate her."

Killian's shaggy white brows knitted together. "You know that she may already be dead."

Tavi inhaled slowly. His tactics, the topic of the discussion, and the horrible images running through his head were terrifying. But he kept his breathing steady, and spoke of nightmarish scenarios in a calm, reasoned tone, as if discussing theoretical situations in a classroom. "Logically, it is likely that she is alive," he said. "If the cutters we saw wanted her dead, they would have found her body next to Sir Nedus's and Serai's. But she was taken from the scene. I think someone hopes to make use of her somehow, rather than removing her entirely."

"Such as?" the old Cursor asked.

"Asking for her support and allegiance, perhaps," Tavi said. "Hoping to gain the support of a very visible symbol if possible, rather than simply destroying it."

"In your estimation, will she do so?" Miles asked.

Tavi licked his lips, thinking through his answer as carefully as he possibly could. "She has little love for Gaius," he said. "But even less for those who arranged the Marat attack on the Calderon Valley. She'd rather gouge out her own eyes than stand with someone like that."

Killian exhaled slowly. "Very well, Tavi. Ask Ehren and Gaelle to help you, but do not tell them it is my desire that they do so, and reveal nothing further to them of the situation. Contact Lady Placida to request her help—though I wouldn't expect her to be terribly eager to assist you. By delivering a message from Gaius to her in public, you have tacitly claimed that Lord and Lady Placida are loyalists."

"Are they not loyal?" Tavi asked.

"They are not interested in choosing sides," Killian replied. "But you may have forced them to do it. In my judgment, they will not be appreciative of your actions. Walk carefully when you see them."

Miles grunted. "Maestro, I have some contacts in town. Retired Legion, mostly. There are two or three men who I could ask to look into Isana's disappearance. I'd like to contact them at once."

Killian nodded, and Miles pushed off the wall and headed for the door. He paused beside Tavi and glanced at the young man. "Tavi. What I said earlier . . ."

"Was completely justified, sir," Tavi said quietly.

Miles regarded the boy for a moment more, then the pain in Killian's features. "Maybe it wasn't enough."

The captain gave Tavi a stiff, formal nod and strode from the room, his boots thudding in a swift, angry cadence.

He left Tavi with Killian, Fade, and the unconscious Gaius.

They sat in silence for a moment. Gaius's breathing sounded steadier and deeper to Tavi, but it could have been his imagination. Fade stirred and sat up, blinking owlishly at Tavi.

"With the captain gone," Killian said, "I'll have to handle the First Lord's mail. I know you want to move immediately, Tavi, but I'll need you to read it to me before you go. It's on the desk."

"All right," Tavi said, rising and forcing himself not to give voice to an impatient sigh. He paced to the desk, sat on the chair, and took up a stack of about a dozen envelopes of various sizes, and one long, leather tube. He opened the first letter and scanned over it. "From Senator Parmus, informing the Crown of the status of the roads in—"

"Skip that one for now," Killian said quietly.

Tavi put that letter down and went to the next. "An invitation from Lady Riva to attend her yearly farewell gathering in—"

"Skip it."

He opened the next letter. "From Lord Phrygius, bidding the First Lord a merry Wintersend in his absence, which is due to military considerations."

"Details?" Killian asked. "Tactical intelligence?"

"Nothing specific, sir."

"Skip it."

Tavi went through several more routine letters such as those, until he came to the last one, in the leather scroll tube. He picked it up, and the case felt peculiar against his hand, sending a slow shiver up his spine. He frowned at the peculiar leather, then suddenly understood the source of his discomfort.

It was made from human skin.

Tavi swallowed and opened the tube. The cap made an ugly, quavering, scraping sound against the substance of the tube. Tavi gingerly drew out a sheet of leather parchment, trying not to touch the case any more than he absolutely had to do so.

The parchment, covered in large, heavy letters, was also made from thin-scraped human skin. Tavi swallowed uncomfortably, and read over the message.

"From Ambassador Varg," he read. "And in the Ambassador's own hand, it says."

Killian's heavy, white brows furrowed. "Oh?"

"It advises the First Lord that the Canim courier ship has arrived with the change of his honor guard and will depart the capital to sail down the Gaul in two days."

Killian thumped his forefinger against his chin. "Interesting."

"It is?" Tavi asked.

"Yes."

"Why?"

Killian rubbed at his chin. "Because it is absolutely not interesting. It is an entirely routine notification."

Tavi began to follow the Maestro's line of thought. "And if it is entirely routine," he said, "then why is it in the Ambassador's own hand?"

"Precisely," Killian said. "The Canim courier passes back and forth every two months or so. The Ambassador is permitted six guards at any one time, and four replacements are brought with every ship, so that no two guards spend more than four months on duty here. It is a common enough sight." He waved vaguely at his blind eyes. "Or so I am told."

Tavi frowned. Then he said, "Maestro, when I took that message to the Ambassador, he made it a point to tell me that he was having problems with rats. He . . . well indirectly pointed me at a hidden doorway, and I found an entry to the Deeps in the Black Hall."

Killian's frown darkened. "They found it, then."

"It was always there?" Tavi asked.

"Obviously," Killian said. "Gaius Tertius, I believe, made sure a way in was available to us, in the event that we needed to force entry. But I thought it undiscovered."

"Why would Varg take the time to tell us that he knew about it?" Tavi asked.

Killian mused for a moment and then said, "Honestly, I don't know. I can't think of any reason but for spite, to show us that he had not been deceived. But our knowledge of his knowledge could only have reduced any advantage he gained from knowing about the door—and it isn't like Varg to give away an advantage."

"I went down the passage a little," Tavi said. "I heard Varg's second, Sarl, speaking with an Aleran."

Killian's head tilted. "Indeed. What did they say?"

Tavi thought about it for a moment, then repeated the conversation.

"How nonspecific," Killian murmured.

"I know," Tavi said. "I'm sorry I didn't bring this to you at once, sir. I was scared when I left and I hadn't slept and . . ."

"Relax, Tavi. No one can go on forever without rest. Young men your age seem to need more than most." The old Cursor blew out a breath. "I suppose it's true for all of us. It bears thinking on, later, when there is less urgent business at hand," he said. "Is there any more mail?"

"No, sir. That's all."

"Very well. Then be about your assignment."

Tavi rose. "Yes, sir." He started for the door and paused. "Maestro?"

"Mmm?" Killian asked.

"Sir . . . do you know who the captain meant when he said that Nedus had also trained 'Rari'?"

Tavi saw Fade's attention snap toward him in the corner of his vision, but he didn't look at the slave.

"Araris Valerian," Killian replied. "His older brother."

"There was bad blood between them?" Tavi asked.

Killian's expression flickered with irritation, but his answer was in a patient voice. "They had a falling-out. They hadn't recovered from it when Araris was killed at First Calderon, with the Princeps."

"What kind of falling-out?" Tavi asked.

"The famous duel of Araris Valerian and Aldrick ex Gladius," Killian replied. "Originally, you see, Miles was to duel Aldrick over . . ." He waved a hand. "I forget. Some kind of disagreement over a woman. But on the way to the duel, Miles slipped and fell into the street into the path of a water wagon. It ran over his leg and shattered his knee so badly that not even watercrafters could make it entirely whole again. Araris, as Miles's second, fought the duel in his place."

"And that came between them?" Tavi asked. "Why?"

"Miles accused Araris of pushing him in front of the wagon," Killian said. "Said he did it out of a desire to protect him."

Tavi watched Fade in the corner of his eye, but the slave had gone completely still. "Is it true?"

"Had they faced one another, Aldrick would have killed Miles," Killian stated. There was no doubt whatsoever in his tone. "Miles was very young, then, not even fully grown, and Aldrick was—is—a terror with a blade."

"Did Araris really push Captain Miles?" Tavi asked.

"I doubt anyone will ever know the truth of it. But Miles was wounded too badly to accompany the Princeps and his Legion to the Battle of the Seven Hills. He was on the way to the Calderon Valley to rejoin the Princeps when the Marat attacked and began the First Battle of Calderon. Araris died beside the Princeps. Miles and his brother never saw one another again. Never had the chance to reconcile. I suggest you avoid the topic."

Tavi turned to look at Fade.

The slave averted his eyes, and Tavi could not read the man's marred features. "I see," he said quietly. "Thank you, Maestro."

Killian lifted a hand, cutting Tavi off. "Enough," the old man murmured. "Be about your duties."

"Yes, sir," Tavi said, and retreated from the meditation chamber to seek out Ehren and Gaelle.

CHAPTER 29

"Do you have any idea what time it is?" Ehren mumbled. "And we have a history examination at third bell." He turned his back, resettled himself onto his pillow, and mumbled, "Come back after the exam."

Tavi glanced across the cot at Gaelle, then the two of them reached down and hauled Ehren bodily up out of bed. The skinny boy let out a yelp as they dragged him toward the door of his dorm room. On the way, Tavi scooped up a pair of trousers, stockings, and boots, neatly laid out in preparation for the morning.

"Quiet," he said to Ehren. "Come on. We don't want the night watchman to come looking for us."

Ehren subsided and began to stagger along with them, keeping pace, until after several dozen paces he blinked, and murmured, "What's going on?"

"Tell you in a minute," Tavi said. He and Gaelle steered Ehren toward the overgrown area of the campus where Killian's supposed classroom was located. Tavi snagged the key to its door from beneath a nearby stone, unlocked it, and the three young people hurried inside.

Once there, Tavi made sure the shades were drawn tight closed, and murmured, "All right," to Gaelle, who coaxed the flame of a furylamp to dim life.

Ehren gave Gaelle a self-conscious glance, reached for his clothing, and started jerking it on with considerable haste, even though his nightshirt came to well below his knees. "We're going to get in trouble," he said. "Tavi, what are you doing?"

"I need your help," he said quietly.

"Can't it wait?" Ehren asked.

Tavi shook his head, and Gaelle suddenly frowned at him. "Tavi," she murmured. "What's wrong? You look awful."

At that, Ehren frowned and studied him as well. "Tavi? Are you all right?"

"I am," Tavi replied. He took a deep breath. "My aunt isn't. She came to the capital for the presentation at the conclusion of Wintersend. Her party was attacked. Her companion and her armsmen were murdered. She's been taken."

Gaelle drew in a quick breath. "Oh, furies, Tavi, that's horrible."

Ehren pushed his fingers idly through his tangled hair. "Crows."

"She's in danger," Tavi said quietly. "I have to find her. I need your help."

Ehren snorted. "Our help? Tavi, be reasonable. I'm sure the Civic Legion is looking for her already. And the Crown is going to turn the Realm upside down and shake it until she falls out. Gaius can't afford to let something happen to Steadholder Isana."

Gaelle frowned. "Ehren's right, Tavi. I mean, I'm your friend, and I want to do whatever I can to help you, but there are going to be much more capable people handling your aunt's disappearance."

"No," Tavi said quietly. "There aren't. At least, I don't think anyone with a real chance of success is going to look for her."

Ehren's expression became uncertain. "Tavi? What do you mean?"

Tavi took a deep breath. Then he said, "Look. I'm not supposed to tell you about this. But the Crown is, for the moment, extremely limited in what it can do to help."

"What does that mean?" Gaelle asked.

"I can't share specifics," Tavi said. "Suffice to say that the Crown isn't going to be turning anyone upside down looking for my aunt."

Gaelle blinked in slow surprise. "What about the Cursors? Surely they will be able to help?"

Tavi shook his head. "No. There . . ." He grimaced. "I can't tell you any more. I'm sorry. The only help my aunt is going to get is whatever I can bring to her myself."

Ehren frowned. "Tavi, don't you trust us?"

"It isn't that," Tavi said. "Because I do."

Gaelle stared at him, then mused aloud, "Which means you are under orders not to speak to us about it."

Ehren nodded thoughtfully. "And the only one who could give you an order like that is Maestro Killian."

"Or the First Lord," Gaelle murmured. "Which means . . ." Her face went a little pale.

Ehren swallowed. "Which means that something very serious is happening—something serious enough to divert the entire resources of the Cursors and the Crown elsewhere. And that whoever gave him the order is afraid of treachery from within the Citadel, because even we aren't getting the whole story."

Gaelle nodded slowly. "And as students newly introduced to matters of intelligence, we present less risk to security matters." She frowned at Tavi. "Has something happened to the First Lord?"

Tavi used every ounce of experience he'd gained growing up with a powerfully sensitive watercrafter watching over him to keep any kind of expression from his face or voice as he answered. "I can't tell you anything more than I have."

"But if we do this," Gaelle said, "we will be in danger."

"Probably," Tavi said quietly.

Ehren shivered. "I would have thought you'd ask Max first," he said. "Why isn't he here?"

"I'm not sure where he is," Tavi said. "But as soon as I see him, I'm going to ask him, too."

Ehren frowned and glanced down at the floor. "Tavi, we have examinations for two more days—and we still have to complete our final exercises for Killian. There's no way I can do that and an investigation, too."

"I know," Tavi said. "I'm asking for a lot—from both of you. Please believe me when I say that I wouldn't do it if I wasn't desperate. We've got to find my aunt—both for her own sake and to help the Crown."

"But . . ." Ehren sighed. "History."

"I think we can get the Academy to give us special consideration later," Tavi said. "But I can't promise you anything, Ehren. I'm sorry."

"My admittance to the Academy was conditional. If I fail any courses, they're going to send me back home," Ehren said.

Tavi shook his head. "You've been training as a Cursor, Ehren. The Crown won't let them send you away if you were pulled away from your studies by duty."

Gaelle arched her brows. "But *is* this duty, Tavi?"

"It is," Tavi said.

"How do we know that?' Gaelle asked.

"You'll just have to trust me." Tavi gazed at her steadily.

Gaelle and Ehren traded a long look, then Gaelle said, "Well, of course we'll help you, Tavi." She took a shaking breath. "You're our friend. And you are right about your aunt's importance to the Crown." She grimaced. "I wasn't exactly having a good time with my assignment for Killian in any case."

"Oh, dear." Ehren sighed. "Yes, of course we'll help."

"Thank you," Tavi told them. He smiled a little. "If you like, I'll even help you with your assignments for the Maestro. We'll make it our own little secret."

Ehren let out a wry laugh. "I can hardly imagine where *that* could lead," he said. He finished lacing his boots. "So, tell us whatever you can about the attack on your aunt."

Tavi told them about the visit to Lord Kalare's garden party and what they had learned there and after, omitting any mention of Max or Brencis and his cronies from the tale.

"It would appear," Ehren said, "that Kalare dispatched these cutters who killed your aunt's entourage."

"It seems a rather glaringly obvious conclusion," Gaelle replied. "It may have been a deliberately planted encounter for Tavi's benefit."

"It hardly matters," Tavi said. "The men who took her wouldn't bring her back to Kalare's property in any case. He'd be protecting himself from any association with the murders and kidnapping."

"True," Ehren said. He glanced at Gaelle. "The staff of Kalare's household may have seen something. And odds are very good the house's chef employed the services of caterers for some of the food. They might also have seen something without realizing it."

Gaelle nodded. "There were any number of people on the streets nearby. We could knock on doors, speak to people still there. There are bound to be rumors flying about, too. One never knows when they might be useful. Which do you prefer?"

"Streets," Ehren said.

Gaelle nodded. "Then I will approach Kalare's staff and the caterers."

"If she's been taken," Tavi said, "they might be preparing to leave with her. I'll take the riverfront and check in with the dockmaster and the causeway wardens to make sure they know to keep an eye out." He half smiled. "Listen to us. We sound almost like Cursors."

"Amazing," Gaelle said, mouth curving into a small smile.

The three young people looked around at one another, and Tavi could feel the quivering nervousness in his own belly reflected in his friends' eyes.

"Be careful," he said quietly. "Don't take any chances, and run at the first sign of trouble."

Ehren swallowed and nodded. Gaelle rested her hand briefly on his.

"All right," Tavi said. "Let's go. We should leave separately."

Gaelle nodded and doused the light of the furylamp. They waited until their eyes had adjusted to the low light, then she slipped out of the classroom. A few moments later, Ehren breathed, "Good luck, Tavi," and vanished into the late-night darkness himself.

Tavi crouched in the darkness with his eyes closed, and suddenly felt very small and very afraid. He had just asked his friends to help him. If they were harmed, it would be his fault. Max now languished in the Grey Tower, a prisoner because he had tried to help Tavi. That, too, was his fault. And no matter what he told himself, he felt responsible for what had happened to Aunt Isana as well. If he had not become involved in the matters leading up to the Second Battle of Calderon, the First Lord might never have seen an opportunity to use her by appointing her a Steadholder.

Of course, if he hadn't gotten involved, his aunt might well be dead, too, along with everyone else in the Calderon Valley. But even so, he couldn't keep the heavy, ugly pressure of guilt from weighing on him.

If only Max hadn't been taken, Tavi thought. If only Gaius could waken. Direct orders from the First Lord could galvanize the Civic Legion to furious action, dispatch the Crown Legion to help search, call in favors owed by Lords, High Lords, and Senators alike, and generally change the entire situation.

But Gaius was unable to take action. Max was locked

away behind the heaviest security in the Realm, furycraftings
that no one could overcome . . .

Unless there was someone who could.

Tavi jerked his head upright in sudden, astonished realization. There was indeed someone capable of circumventing the
kinds of security craftings that kept Max locked away in the
Grey Tower. Someone who had, without using craftings of his
own, managed to outmaneuver, circumvent, or render impotent the furycraftings that protected the businesses of jewelers, goldsmiths, and more humble bakeries and smithies alike.

And if those furycraftings had been so effortlessly overcome, then perhaps he might be able to enter the Grey Tower
as well. If someone could reach Max and withdraw him quietly from his prison, the guards might remain ignorant for
time enough to enable Max to return to the Citadel and resume the role of Gaius Sextus. And *then* there would indeed
be a First Lord able to have the city turned upside down in
order to recover Aunt Isana from her captors.

Which meant that Tavi's next move was obvious.

He had to find and catch the Black Cat.

This was no mere exercise, upon which hung nothing more
than his final grade. Tavi had to convince the thief to help him
enter the Grey Tower and liberate his friend Max. And soon.
Every moment that the stars wheeled overhead was a moment
in which whoever had his aunt might dispose of her.

Tavi narrowed his eyes in thought, then rose from the
floor, left the classroom, and locked the door behind him. He
returned the key to its resting place, and hurried with silent,
determined paces into the night.

CHAPTER 30

Tavi didn't know quite what it was that made him decide to head for Craft Lane at the base of the mountain crowned by the Citadel high above. It was far from the elegant celebrations and garden parties of the streets that rose above the rest of the city. No jeweler's shop or goldsmith would be found there. Craft Lane was inhabited by those who worked with their hands for a living—blacksmiths, farriers, carters, weavers, bakers, masons, butchers, vendors, carpenters, and cobblers. By the standards in the countryside, any one of the households there was extremely prosperous, and yet Craft Lane was still poor compared to the Citizens' Lanes above them, and the ascending ranks of the nobility that followed.

But what Craft Lane lacked in extravagance, it made up for in enthusiasm. For folk who toiled every day to earn their keep, the celebration at Wintersend was one of the most anticipated times of the year, and great effort went into the planning of celebrations. As a consequence, there was literally no hour of the day or night that some (if not all) of Craft Lane would be host to street gatherings where food, drink, music, dance, and games ran with a constant, merry roar.

Tavi had dressed in his darkest clothes and wore his old green cloak with its hood pulled forward to hide his face. Upon reaching Garden Lane, he studied it for a moment with a kind of half-amused dismay. The celebrations were running in full swing, with furylamps brightening night to near day. He could hear at least three different groups of musicians playing, and numerous areas along the crowded streets had been marked out on the cobblestones with chalk to reserve space for the dancers who whirled and reeled through their steps.

Tavi wandered down the Lane, looking up only occasionally. He focused his attention on what his ears and his nose told him of his surroundings, then at the intersection with Southlane he abruptly stopped.

The first thing he noticed about the background was the difference in music. Rather than instruments, there was a small vocal ensemble singing a complex air that rang down the street with merry energy. At the same time, the overwhelming scent of baking sweetbread flooded his senses and made his mouth water. He hadn't eaten in hours and hours, and he looked up to stare hungrily at the baker's shop, which by all rights should have been locked up and quiet, and was instead turning out sweetbread and pastries by the bushel.

Tavi glanced around him, ducked to one side of the road and between two of the shops, and found a box to stand on. He used it to reach up for the top of the windowsill, and with a carefully directed explosion of effort, he heaved himself up, grabbing at the eaves of the roof and hauling himself swiftly up to the rooftop. Once there, he was able to turn and spring lightly from that roof to the next, which offered a split level that rose another story into the air. Tavi scaled that as well, then started down Crafter Lane, springing lightly from one closely spaced rooftop to the next, his eyes and ears and nose open.

A sudden quivering excitement filled him for no reason whatsoever, and Tavi abruptly felt certain that his instincts had not led him astray. He found a pocket of deep shadows behind a chimney and slipped into it, crouching into cautious immobility.

He didn't have long to wait. There was a flicker of motion on the far side of Crafter Lane, and Tavi saw a cloaked and hooded figure gliding over the rooftops just as lightly and quietly as he had. He felt his lips tighten into a grin. He recognized the grey cloak, the flowing motion. Once again, he had found the Black Cat.

The figure eased up to the edge of the roof to stare down at the vocalists, then dropped into a relaxed crouch, hands reaching down to rest his fingers lightly on the rooftop. Beneath the cloak's hood, the Cat's head tilted to one side, and he went completely still, evidently fascinated by the singers. Tavi watched the Cat in turn, an odd and nagging sense of recognition stirring briefly. Then the Cat rose and ghosted down to the next rooftop, his covered face turned toward the bakery, with its tables piled high with fresh, steaming sweetbread while a red-cheeked matron did a brisk business selling the loaves. A quality of tension, of hunger, entered the Cat's movements, and he vanished over the far side of the building upon which he stood.

Tavi waited until the Cat was out of sight, then rose and leapt to the roof of the bakery. He found another dark spot to conceal his presence just as the dark-cloaked Cat emerged from between the two buildings across the street and walked calmly through the crowded street, feet shuffling in a rhythmic step or two as he passed the vocal ensemble. The Cat slowed his steps by a fraction and passed the table just as the matron behind the table turned to deposit small silver coins into a strongbox. The Cat's cloak twitched as he passed the table, and if Tavi hadn't been watching carefully he would never have seen the loaf vanish under the thief's cloak.

The Cat never missed a step, sliding into the space between the bakery and the cobbler's shop beside it and walking quietly and quickly down the alleyway.

Tavi rose and padded silently along the rooftop, reaching to his belt for the heavy coil of tough, flexible cord looped through it. He dropped the open loop at the end of the lariat clear of his fingertips, and opened the loop wider with the practiced, expert motions his hands had learned through years of dealing with the large, stubborn, aggressive rams of his uncle's mountain sheep. It was a long throw and from a difficult angle, but he crouched by the edge of the roof and flicked the lariat in a circle before sending it sharply down.

The loop in the lariat settled around the Cat's hooded head. The thief darted to one side, and managed to get two fingers under the loop before Tavi could snap the line tight. Tavi planted his feet and hauled hard on the line. The line hauled the Cat from his feet and sent him stumbling to one side.

Tavi whipped the cord twice around the bricks of the bakery's chimney, slapped it through a herder's loop in a familiar blur of motion, then slid down the roof to drop to the alley, landing in a crouch that bounced into a leap that carried him into the Black Cat's back. He hit hard, driving the Cat into the wall with a breath-stealing slam.

The Cat's foot smashed down hard on his toes, and if he hadn't been wearing heavy leather boots, it might have broken them. Tavi snarled, "Hold still," and hauled at the rope, trying to keep his opponent from finding his balance. There was a rasping sound and a knife whipped at the hand Tavi had on the rope. He jerked his fingers clear, and the knife bit hard into the tightened lariat. The cord was too tough to part at a single blow, but the Cat reached up with his free hand to steady the rope and finish the cut.

The lariat parted. Tavi slammed the Cat against the wall again, seized the wrist of the thief's knife hand and banged it hard against the bakery's stone wall. The knife tumbled free. Tavi drove the heel of his hand into the base of the Cat's neck, through the heavy cloak, a stunning blow. The Cat staggered. Tavi whirled and threw the thief facedown to the ground, landing on his back and twisting one slender arm up far behind him, holding the Cat in place.

"Hold *still*," Tavi snarled. "I'm not with the Civic Legion. I just want to *talk* to you."

The Black Cat abruptly stopped struggling, and something about the quality of that stillness made him think it was due to startled surprise. The Black Cat eased away the tension in the muscles that quivered against Tavi, and they softened abruptly.

Tavi blinked down at his captive and then tore the hood back from the Black Cat's head.

A mane of fine, silvery white curls fell free of the cloak, framing the pale, smooth curve of a young woman's cheek and full, wine-dark ups. Her eyes, slightly canted at their corners, were a brilliant shade of green identical to Tavi's own, and her expression was one of utter surprise. "Aleran?" she panted.

"Kitai," Tavi breathed. "*You're* the Black Cat?"

She turned her head as much as she could to look up at him, her wide eyes visible even in the dimness of the alley. Tavi stared down at her for a long moment, his stomach muscles suddenly fluttering with excited energy. He became acutely conscious of the lean, strong limbs of the young Marat woman beneath him, the too-warm fever heat of her skin, and the way that her own breathing had not slowed, though she had ceased to struggle against him. He slowly released her wrist, and she just as slowly withdrew her arm from between their bodies.

Tavi shivered and leaned a little closer, drawing in a breath through his nose. Strands of fine hair tickled his lips. Kitai smelled of many scents, faint perfumes likely stolen from expensive boutiques, the fresh warmth of still-warm sweetbread and, beneath that, of heather and clean winter wind. Even as he moved, she turned her head toward him as well, her temple brushing his chin, her breath warm on his throat. Her eyes slid almost closed.

"Well," she murmured after another moment. "You have me, Aleran. Either do something with me or let me up."

Tavi felt his face flare into a fiery blush, and he hurriedly pushed his arms down and lifted his weight from Kitai. The Marat girl looked up at him without moving for a moment, her mouth curled into a little smirk, before she rose with a thoughtless, feline grace to her own feet. She looked around for a moment and spotted her ill-gotten loaf of sweetbread on the ground, crushed during their struggle.

"Now look what you've done," she complained. "You've destroyed my dinner, Aleran." She frowned and stared at him for a moment, annoyance flickering in her eyes as she looked him up and down, then stood directly before him with her hands on her hips. Tavi blinked mildly at her expression and stared down at her. "You've grown," she accused him. "You're taller."

"It's been two years," Tavi said.

Kitai made a faint, disgusted sound. Beneath the cloak she wore a man's tunic of dark, expensive silk, hand-stitched with Forcian nightflowers, heavy, Legion-issue leather trousers, and fine leather shoes that would have cost a small fortune. The Marat girl had changed as well, and though she was obviously little taller than before, she had developed in other, extremely interesting ways, and Tavi had to force himself not to stare at the pale slice of smooth flesh revealed by the neckline of the tunic. Her cheek had a reddened patch of abraded flesh sharing space with a steadily darkening bruise, where Tavi had first slammed her into the wall. There was a similar mark upon her throat, though it was slender and precise, from where Tavi's lariat had caught her.

If she felt any pain, it didn't show. She regarded Tavi with intelligent, defiant eyes, and said, "Doroga said you would do this to me."

"Do what?" Tavi asked.

"Grow," she said. Her eyes raked him up and down, and she seemed to feel no compunction at all about staring at him. "Become stronger."

"Um," Tavi said. "I'm sorry?"

She glowered at him, and looked around until she spotted her knife. She reclaimed it, and Tavi saw that the blade was inlaid with gold and silver, the handle set with a design of amber and amethysts, and would probably have cost him a full year's worth of the modest monthly stipend Gaius permitted him. More jewelry glittered at her throat, on both wrists, and in one ear, and Tavi gloomily estimated that the value of the goods she had stolen would probably merit her execution should she be captured by the authorities.

"Kitai," he said. "What in the world are you doing here?"

"Starving," she snapped. She poked at the ruined loaf with the tip of her shoe. "Thanks to you, Aleran."

Tavi shook his head. "What were you doing before that?"

"*Not* starving," she said with a sniff.

"Crows, Kitai. Why did you come here?"

Her lips pressed together for a moment before she answered. "To stand Watch."

"Uh. What?"

"I am Watching," she snapped. "Don't you know anything?"

"I'm starting to think that I don't," Tavi said. "Watching what?"

Kitai rolled her eyes in a gesture that conveyed both annoyance and contempt. "You, fool." She narrowed her eyes. "But what were you doing on that roof? Why did you attack me?"

"I didn't know it was you," Tavi said. "I was trying to catch the thief called the Black Cat. I suppose I did."

Kitai's eyes narrowed. "The One sometimes blesses even idiots with good fortune, Aleran." She folded her arms. "You have found me. What do you want?"

Tavi chewed on his lip, thinking. It was dangerous for Kitai to be in Alera at *all*, much less in the capital. The Realm's experiences with other races upon Carna had invariably been tense, hostile, and violent. When the Marat had wiped out Princeps Gaius Septimus's Legion at the First Battle of Calderon, they had created an entire generation of widows and orphans and bereaved families. And since the Crown Legion had been recruited from Alera Imperia, there were thousands, tens of thousands of individuals in this city with a bitter grudge against the Marat.

Kitai, because of her athletic build, pale skin, and hair—
and *especially* because of her exotically slanted eyes—would
be recognized immediately as one of the barbarians from the
east. Given all that she had stolen (and the humiliation she
had inflicted upon the Civic Legion in the process), she would
never see the inside of a jail or a court of law. If seen, she
would probably be seized by an angry mob and stoned,
hanged, or burned on the spot, while the Civic Legion looked
the other way.

Tavi's neglected stomach gurgled a complaint, and he
sighed. "First thing," he said, "I'm going to get us both some
food. Will you wait here for me?"

Kitai arched an eyebrow. "You think I cannot steal food for
myself?"

"I'm not going to steal it," Tavi said. "Think of it as an
apology for ruining your sweetbread."

Kitai frowned at that for a moment, then nodded cautiously and said, "Very well."

He had just enough money to purchase a couple of heavy
wildfowl drumsticks, a loaf of sweetbread, and a flagon of
apple cider. He took them back into the dim alley, where Kitai
waited in patient stillness. Tavi passed her a drumstick and
broke the loaf in half, then let her choose one. Then he leaned
back against the wall, standing beside her, and got down to the
serious business of eating.

Evidently, Kitai was at least as ravenous as Tavi, and they
demolished meat and bread alike in moments. Tavi took a
long drink from the flask and offered the rest to Kitai.

The Marat girl drank and wiped her mouth with one
sleeve, then turned to Tavi, exotic eyes glittering. She dropped
the empty flask and studied him while she licked the crumbs
and grease from her fingers. Tavi found it fascinating, and
waited in silence for a moment.

Kitai gave him a slow smile. "Yes, Aleran?" she asked. "Is
there something you want?"

Tavi blinked and coughed, looking away before he started
blushing again. He reminded himself sternly of what was at
stake and that he did not dare allow himself to be distracted
when it could cost so many people their lives. The terrifying
weight of his responsibility drove away thoughts of Kitai's

fingers and mouth, replacing them with twisting anxiety. "Yes, actually," he said. "I need your help."

Kitai's playful little smile vanished, and she peered at him, her expression curious, even concerned. "With what?"

"Breaking into a building," he said. "I need to learn how you've managed to get around all the security precautions in the places you have raided."

Kitai frowned at him. "For what reason?"

"A man is locked inside a prison tower. I need to get him out of the Grey Tower without tripping any furycrafted alarms and without anyone seeing us. Oh, and we need to do it so that no one knows that he's missing for at least a quarter of an hour."

Kitai took that in stride. "Will it be dangerous?"

"Very," Tavi said. "If we're caught, they will imprison or kill us both."

Kitai nodded, her expression thoughtful. "Then we must not be caught."

"Or fail," Tavi said. "Kitai, this could be important. Not just for me, but for all of Alera."

"Why?" she asked.

Tavi furrowed his brow. "We don't have much time for explanations. How much do you know about Aleran politics?"

"I know that you people are all insane," Kitai said.

Despite himself, a low bark of laughter flew from his lips. "I can see how you'd think that," Tavi said. "Do you need a reason other than insanity, then?"

"I prefer it," Kitai said.

Tavi considered it for a moment, then said, "The man who is locked away is my friend. He was put there for defending me."

Kitai stared at him for a moment and nodded. "Reason enough," she said.

"You'll help me?"

"Yes, Aleran," she answered. She studied his features with thoughtful eyes. "I will help you."

He nodded seriously. "Thank you."

Her teeth shone white in the dim alley. "Do not thank me. Not until you see what we must do to enter this tower."

CHAPTER 31

Tavi stared across an enormous span of empty air at the Grey Tower, and his heart pounded with what some people might characterize as abject terror.

It was not difficult to find someone who would tell Tavi where to find the Grey Tower. He simply asked a civic *legionare* with a little too much good cheer showing in his reddened nose and nearly flammable breath, explaining that he was visiting from out of town and would like to see it. The *legionare* had been obliging and friendly, and given Tavi directions made only marginally unintelligible by all the mushy, slurred S sounds. After that, Tavi and Kitai slipped through the streets of the capital, taking care to avoid the more energetic celebrations like the ones on Crafter Lane.

Now, they stood atop an aqueduct that carried water from a wellspring in the mountains outside the capital to run through the great green bowl of fields and steadholts that surrounded the city. There the aqueduct diverted into a dozen offshoots that directed clean water to reservoirs around the city. From where they stood, Tavi could look down the almost imperceptible slope of the aqueduct, where it passed over entire neighborhoods, its stately arches holding up the stone trough, gurgling water a constant babble as he and Kitai paced steadily forward. Only a few hundred yards ahead, the aqueduct swept past the headquarters and barracks of the Civic Legion upon the one side and the Grey Tower upon the other.

Kitai glanced over her shoulder at him, her steps never slowing, walking with perfect confidence despite the evening breezes and the narrow, water-slicked stone footing of the aqueduct's rim. "Do you need me to slow down?"

"No," Tavi said irritably. He focused on their destination, trying not to think about how easy it would be to fall to a humiliating death. "Just keep going."

Kitai shrugged, a small, smug smile playing on her lips, and turned away from him again.

Tavi studied the Tower as they approached it. It was a surprisingly simple-looking building. It didn't look terribly towerlike, either. Tavi had imagined something suitably elegant and grim, maybe something bleak and straight and menacing, where the prisoners would be lucky to be able to throw themselves off the top of the tower to fall to humiliating deaths of their own. Instead, the building looked little different than the Legion barracks nearby. It was taller, and featured very narrow windows, and there were fewer doors in evidence. There was a wide lawn around the tower and a palisade around the lawn. Guards were in evidence at the gate in the fence, at the front doors to the building, and patrolling around the exterior of the fence.

"It looks . . . nice," Tavi murmured. "Really rather pleasant."

"There is no pleasant prison," Kitai replied. She abruptly stopped, and Tavi nearly bumped disastrously into her. He recovered his balance and glowered at her as another group of wandering singers passed on the street beneath the aqueduct they stood upon. Each member of the group held a candle as they walked, performing one of the traditional airs of the holiday.

Kitai watched the group closely as they passed.

"You like the music?"

"You all sing wrong," Kitai said, eyes curious and intent. "You don't do it properly."

"Why do you say that?"

She flipped a hand irritably. "Among my people, you sing the song on your lips. Sometimes many songs together. Everyone who sings weaves their song with the ones already there. At least three of them, or it is hardly worth the trouble. But you Alerans only sing one. And you all sing it the same way." She shook her head, her expression baffled. "All the practice you need to do that must bore your folk to death."

Tavi grinned. "But do you like the results?"

Kitai watched the group pass out of sight, and her voice was wistful. "You don't do it properly."

She started moving again, and Tavi followed her until they had drawn even with the Grey Tower. Tavi looked over the edge of the stone aqueduct. There was a good fifty-foot drop to the boot-packed, hardened earth of a Legion training field that butted up against the wall around the Tower. A fresh spring wind whipped down from the mountains, cold and swift, and Tavi had to lean back to keep from swaying off the edge and into a fall. He forced his eyes to remain on the roof of the tower, instead of looking down.

"That's got to be fifty feet," he told Kitai quietly. "Not even you could jump that."

"True," Kitai said. She cast her cloak back from her arms and opened a large, heavy pouch of Marat-worked leather. She drew out a coil of greyish, almost metallic-looking rope.

Tavi watched, frowning. "Is that more of that rope made from Iceman hair?"

"Yes," she replied. Her hand dipped into her pouch again, and came out with three simple metal hooks. She slid them together, small grooves and tabs locking the hooks' spines together, and linked them solidly with a piece of leather cord, so that the hooks reached out with steely fingers in a circle around the spine.

"That grappling hook isn't Marat-made," Tavi said.

"No. An Aleran thief had it. I watched him rob a house one night."

"And stole it from him?"

Kitai smiled, fingers flying as they knotted the cord to the hook. "The One teaches us that what one gives to others, one receives in return." She flashed him a sharp-toothed grin, and said, "Get down, Aleran."

Tavi dropped to one knee just as Kitai raised the hook and whirled it in a circle, letting out the line and gathering speed. It didn't take her long. Four circles, five, and she let out a hiss and flung the hook and the line across the distance to the roof. Metal clinked faintly on stone.

Kitai began drawing the cord in, very slowly and carefully. The rope suddenly tightened, and she continued to lean back, steadily increasing the pressure. "Here," she said. "In the pouch. There is a metal spike there, a hammer."

Tavi slipped his hand into the pouch and found them. The spike had an open ring set into the butt end, and Tavi grasped its use at once. He knelt with the spike and the hammer. He took off his cloak and folded it a few times, then drove the spike carefully into the stone of the aqueduct, the cloth muffling the sound of the hammerblows. Tavi drove it in at an angle opposite the pull of the rope, and when he was finished he glanced up to find Kitai looking down at the spike with approval.

She passed him the end of the Marat rope, and Tavi threaded it through the eye on the end of the spike. He took in the last few feet very slowly, with Kitai careful to keep the pressure against the grappling hook, until he was able to lean his full weight against it, holding it in place.

Kitai nodded sharply and her hands flew through another knot, one Tavi was not familiar with. She tied off the rope, using the knot to draw it tight and to tighten it even more before she released it, leaned back, and nodded to Tavi.

The boy released the rope slowly. It made a faint, strong thrumming sound, and stretched out between the aqueduct and the Tower, glistening like spider silk in the ambient radiance of the city's thousands upon thousands of furylamps. "So," he said. "We cross on the rope to avoid the earth and wood furies in the lawn. Right?"

"Yes," Kitai said.

"That's going to leave wind furies on watch around the roof," he said. "And it looks like there might be a gargoyle at either end. See, those lumps there?"

Kitai frowned. "What is this, gargoyle?"

"It's an earth fury," Tavi explained. "A statue that is able to perceive and to move. They're not very fast, but they are strong."

"They will try to harm us?"

"Probably," Tavi said quietly. "They'll respond to movement on the roof."

"Then we must not touch foot to the roof, yes?"

Tavi nodded. "It might work. But I don't see how else we're going to get inside but the door on the roof. There are guards at all the lower doors."

"Give me your cloak," Kitai said.

Tavi passed it over to her. "What are you doing?"

"Seeing to the wind furies," she said. She slipped her cloak off and thrust them both into the cold current of water running through the aqueduct, soaking them. Then she opened another pouch and drew out a heavy wooden canister, which proved to be full of salt. She started spreading it heavily over the damp cloaks.

Tavi watched that, frowning. "I know salt is painful to wind furies," he said. "But does that actually work?"

Kitai paused and gave him an even look. Then she glanced down at her clothing and jewelry and back up to Tavi.

He lifted his hands. "All right, all right. If you say so."

She rose a moment later and tossed him the cloak. Tavi caught it, and drew the wet, sodden mass on. Kitai did the same. "Are you ready, Aleran?"

"Ready for what?" Tavi asked. "I'm still not sure how we're going to get in without touching down on the roof."

Kitai nodded at the narrow windows on the topmost floor. "I will go in through there. Wait until I am all the way across before you start. The rope is not designed to hold two."

"Better let me go first," Tavi said. "I'm heavier. If it's going to collapse, it will be for me."

Kitai frowned at him, but nodded. She gestured to the rope, and said, "Go on. Leave me space to work when I get there."

Tavi nodded, then turned to look at the slender rope stretching across to the Grey Tower. He swallowed and felt his fingers trembling. But he forced himself to move, sliding over to the rope and taking it in his hands. He let himself drop down, head toward the Grey Tower, hands on the rope, his heels crossed in an X to hold up his legs. The wind blew, the rope quivered, and Tavi prayed that the grappling hook would not slip from its purchase. Then, as carefully and smoothly as he could, he started pulling himself over the gap to the Grey Tower. He glanced back once to see Kitai watching him, her eyes glittering with mischief, one hand covering her mouth without really hiding the amusement on it.

Tavi forced himself to concentrate on his task, upon the steady, sure motion of arms and legs and fingers and hands. He did not hurry, but moved with deliberate caution until he had crossed the gap. He was able to spot a window ledge, and dropped his feet carefully down to rest on it until he was sure it would hold his weight. Then he stepped more firmly onto the ledge and looked back at Kitai, one hand steadying himself on the rope.

The Marat girl did not lower herself to the rope as he had. Instead, she simply stepped out onto it as though it were as wide and steady as a crossbeam of heavy timber. Her arms akimbo, she moved with a kind of casual arrogance for the deadly drop beneath her, crossed the rope in a third the time it had taken Tavi, and hopped down, turning in midair and landed with her heels steady on the ledge beside him.

Tavi stared at her for a moment. She cocked an eyebrow at him. "Yes?"

He shook his head. "Where did you learn that?"

"Rope walking?" she asked.

"Yes. That was . . . impressive."

"It is a whelp's game. We all play it when we are young." She grinned. "I was better at it when I was younger. I could have run along it." She turned to the window and peered through the glass. "A hall. I see no one."

Tavi looked. "I don't either," he said. He drew his knife from his belt and tested the edges of the glass over the window. It was a single pane, crafted directly into the stone. "We'll have to break it," he told Kitai.

She nodded sharply, then drew a roll of some kind of thick cloth from another pouch. She rolled it out with a flick, then drew out a small bottle and opened it. There was a sharp stench as she poured some kind of thick, oily substance onto her palm and smeared it all over her window. She hurriedly scrubbed the substance from her skin with the cloth, then frowned, her lips moving.

"What are you doing?" Tavi asked.

"Counting," she replied. "You'll make me lose my place." She went on that way for another minute or so, then flattened the cloth against the window, where it adhered almost instantly. Kitai smoothed the cloth out as much as she could, waited a moment more, then drew her knife and brought the rounded hilt sharply down onto the glass in a short, precise blow.

The glass broke with a crunching snap. Kitai hit it again, in several different places, and drew the cloth out slowly. The window glass, Tavi saw, stuck to the cloth. Kitai then took the portion of the cloth she had wiped her hand upon and pressed it to the wall beside the window, where it clung as strongly as it had to the glass.

She glanced at Tavi as she broke off a few jagged pieces of glass the cloth had missed, dropped them, then bent nimbly and slid through the window and into the Grey Tower.

Tavi shook his head and made his way over to the next window, carefully holding the rope as he did it. He felt clumsy and slow in comparison to the Marat girl, which was vaguely annoying. But at the same time, he took a real sense of pleasure in seeing her ability and confidence. Like himself, she had no furycraft of her own, but it was clear to him that she did not think herself disadvantaged. And she had reason not to, having spent the last several months sneering at furycrafted security measures and defeating them with intelligence and skill.

Tavi filed away that trick with the adhesive and the cloth for future reference and slid inside to drop into a crouch beside Kitai.

They were in a hallway, one side lined with windows, the other with heavy wooden doors. Tavi crossed to the nearest door and tested the handle. "Locked," he reported in a whisper, and dipped a hand into his own belt pouch. He drew out a roll of leather containing several small tools.

"What are you doing?" Kitai whispered.

"Unlocking," he replied. He slipped the tools into the keyhole, closed his eyes, and felt his way through the lock's mechanism. A moment later, he locked his grip on the tools and twisted slightly, springing the lock open.

Tavi opened the door on a small and barren bedchamber. There was a bed, a chair, a chamber pot, and nothing else but smooth stone walls.

"A cell," he murmured, and closed the door again.

Kitai plucked the tools from his hand and stared at them, then at him. "How?" she asked.

"I've been learning this kind of thing," Tavi replied. "I can show you later. How did you steal all of that without learning how to open a lock?"

"I stole the keys," Kitai said. "Obviously."

"Obviously," Tavi muttered. "Come on."

They went down the hall, and Tavi checked every door. Each room was the same—drab, plain, and empty. "He must not be on this floor," Tavi murmured, as they reached the end of the hall. There was a door there, and Tavi opened it, to reveal a stairway curling down, lit by dim orange furylamps. Sound would bounce merrily around the stairs, and Tavi made a motion cautioning Kitai to silence, before slipping out the door and to the stairs. He hadn't gone down more than three or four when he heard the sound of song ringing through the tower below, another Wintersend round, though this one performed with the benefit of far more drink than practice.

Tavi grinned and moved a little more quickly. If the guards were that raucous below, it would be a far simpler matter to move around the tower.

They took the stairs to the next floor, and Tavi opened the door on the landing, only to find another row of holding rooms just as there had been on the top floor. They left that one to slip down one floor more, when Kitai suddenly seized Tavi's shoulder, the tight grip of her fingers a warning.

Then just below him was the sound of a heavy door bolt opening, and men's voices speaking to one another. Tavi froze. Their footsteps started down the stairs toward the singing.

Tavi waited until they were gone before stealing down the rest of the stairs, struggling to keep his excitement from making him sloppy. He handled the lock on the door to the stairway as easily as the others and opened it onto a very different area than on the floors above.

Though still furnished very plainly, the whole floor was given over to a single, large suite. There was an enormous bath, several bookshelves complete with simple couches and chairs upon which to sit while reading, a table for four where food might be served, and a large bed—all of which were behind a heavy grid of steel bars with a single door. The windows were likewise barred.

"Told you I'm fine," said a heavy, tired voice, from somewhere beneath a large lump under the bed's covers. "Just need to rest."

"Max," Tavi hissed.

Max, his short hair still damp and plastered to his head, sat bolt upright in bed, and his jaw dropped open. *"Tavi?* How the crows did you get in here? *What* the crows are you doing here?"

"Breaking you out," Tavi said. He crossed to the barred door, while Kitai left the stairway door open a crack and stood watch. He started on the lock.

"Don't bother," Max said. "It's on the table on the north wall."

Tavi looked around, spotted the key, and fetched it. "Not terribly secure of them."

"Anyone who winds up in this cell is being held by politics more than anything," Max said. "The bars are just for show." He grimaced. "Plus furycrafting doesn't work in here."

"Poor baby, no furycrafting," Tavi said, taking the key to the lock. "Come on. Get dressed and let's go."

"You're kidding, right?"

"No. We need you, Max."

"Tavi," Max said. "Don't be insane. I don't know how you got in here, but—"

"Aleran," Kitai hissed. "We have little time before dawn." She turned her head to Tavi, and her hood had fallen back from her face. "We must leave, with or without him."

"Who is that?" Max asked. He blinked. "She's a *Marat*."

"That's Kitai. Kitai, this is Max."

"She's *Marat*," Max breathed.

Kitai arched a pale brow, and asked Tavi, "Is he slow in the head?"

"There are days when I think so," Tavi replied. He entered the cell and went to Max's side. "Come on. Look, we can't let that idiot Brencis send the entire Realm into chaos. We get you out of here. We go down into the Deeps and come up near the palace and get you to Killian without anyone being the wiser. You get back to work and help my aunt."

"Fleeing custody is a Realm offense," Max said. "They could hang me for it. More to the point, they could hang *you* for helping me. And great bloody furies, Tavi, you're doing it with a *Marat* at your side."

"Don't mention Kitai to Killian and Miles. We'll fix the rest of it," Tavi said.

"How?"

"I don't know. Not yet. But we will, Max. A lot of people could get hurt if this situation goes out of control."

"Can't be done," Max said. "Tavi, you might have gotten in here, but the craftings to block the way out are twice as thick and strong. They'll sense anything I try to do, and—"

Tavi picked up a pair of loose linen trousers and flung them at Max's head. "Put these on. We got in here without using any furies at all. We'll go out the same way."

Max stared at Tavi for a second, skeptical. "How?"

Kitai made a disgusted sound. "Everyone here thinks nothing can happen without sorcery, Aleran. I say it again. You are all mad."

Tavi turned to Max and said, "Max, you saved my life once already tonight. But I need more of your help. And I swear to you that once my family is safe, I will do everything in my power to help make sure that you are not punished for it."

"Everything in your power, huh?" Max said.

"I know. It isn't much."

Max regarded Tavi evenly for a second, then swung his legs down to the side of the bed and put on the linen trousers. "It's enough for me." He let out a hiss of discomfort as he rose, unsteady on his feet. "Sorry. They healed the wounds, but I'm still pretty stiff."

Tavi stuffed the bed's pillows under the blankets in a vague Max-sized lump, then got a shoulder under his friend's arm for support. With luck, the guards would leave "Max" to sleep in peace for hours before they noticed that the prisoner was no longer in his cell. They left, and Tavi locked the cell behind them and replaced the key.

"Tavi," Max mumbled, as they went up the stairs again, Kitai pacing along behind them. "I've never had a friend who would do something like this for me. Thank you."

"Heh," Tavi said. "Don't thank me until you see how we're going to leave."

CHAPTER 32

"And then we left the same way we came in, Maestro, and now we're here. We were not seen entering the Deeps or moving here, except at the guard post on the stairs." Tavi faced Killian, working hard to keep his expression and especially the tone of his voice steady and calm.

Killian, sitting in the chair beside Gaius's bed, drummed his fingers on his cane, slowly. "Let me see if I understand you correctly," the old teacher said. "You went out and found the Grey Tower. Then you entered through the seventh-floor window, by means of a grappling hook and rope thrown from the top of the aqueduct, shielding yourself from air furies with a salted cloak, and from earth furies by not touching the ground. You then searched for Antillar floor by floor and found him, freed him, and extracted him, all without being seen."

"Yes, Maestro," Tavi said. He nudged Max with his hip.

"He didn't seem to leave much out," Max said. "Actually, the room they had me in was quite a bit nicer than any I've ever had to myself."

"Mmmm," Killian said, and his voice turned dry. "Gaius Secondus had a prison suite installed when he arrested the wife of Lord Rhodes, eight hundred years ago. She was charged with treason, but was never tried or convicted, despite interrogation sessions with the First Lord, three times a week for fifteen years."

Max barked a laugh. "That's a rather extreme way to go about keeping a mistress."

"It avoided a civil war," Killian replied. "For that matter, the records suggest that she actually was a traitor to the throne. Which makes the affair either more puzzling or more understandable. I'm not sure which."

Tavi exhaled slowly, relieved. Killian was pleased—and maybe more than pleased. The Maestro only turned raconteur of history when he was in a fine mood.

"Tavi," Killian said. "I'm curious as to what inspired you to attempt these methods."

Tavi glanced aside at Max. "Um. My final examination with you, sir. I had been doing some research."

"And this research was so conclusive that you bet the Realm on it?" he asked in a mild voice. "Do you understand the consequences if you had been captured or killed?"

"If I succeeded, all would be well. If I'd been arrested and Gaius didn't show up to support me, it would have exposed his condition. If I'd been killed, I wouldn't have to take my final history examination with Maestro Larus." He shrugged. "Two out of three positives aren't terrible odds, sir."

Killian let out a rather grim little laugh. "Not so long as you win." He shook his head. "I can't believe how reckless that was, Academ. But you pulled it off. You will probably find, in life, that successes and victories tend to overshadow the risks you took, while failure will amplify how idiotic they were."

"Yes, sir," Tavi said respectfully.

Killian's cane abruptly lashed out and struck Tavi in the thigh. His leg buckled, nerveless and limp for a second, and he fell heavily to the floor in a sudden flood of agony.

"If you ever," Killian said, his voice very quiet, "disobey another of my orders, I will kill you." The blind Maestro sat staring sightlessly down at Tavi. "Do you understand?"

Tavi let out a breathless gasp in the affirmative and clutched at his leg until the fire in it began to pass.

"We aren't playing games, boy," Killian went on. "So I want to make absolutely sure that you realize the consequences. Is there any part of that statement that you don't comprehend?"

"I understand, Maestro," Tavi said.

"Very well." The blind eyes turned toward Max. "Antillar, you are an idiot. But I am glad you have returned."

Max asked, warily, "Are you going to hit me, too?"

"Naturally not," Killian said. "You were injured tonight. Though I will hit you when the crisis is past if it makes you feel better."

"It doesn't," Max said.

Killian nodded. "Can you still perform the role?"

"Yes, sir," Max said, and Tavi thought his voice sounded a great deal more steady than his friend looked. "Give me a few hours to rest, and I'll be ready to go."

"Very good," Killian said. "Take the cot. We can't have you seen running back and forth to your room."

"Maestro?" Tavi asked. "Now that Max is here . . ."

Killian sighed. "Yes, Tavi. I will write up orders to begin a full-scale search for Steadholder Isana. Will that be satisfactory?"

"Perfectly, sir."

"Excellent. I have some more missives for you to deliver. After that, I want you to get some more rest. Report back to me after your history examination. Dismissed."

"Yes, sir," Tavi said. He took up the stack of letters and turned to walk toward the door, favoring his still-throbbing leg.

Just as he got there, Killian said, "Oh, Tavi?"

"Sir?"

"Who else entered the Grey Tower with you?"

Tavi suppressed a rush of surprise and adrenaline. "No one, sir. Why do you ask?"

Killian nodded. "You stated that 'we' exited the way 'we' came in. It implies that someone else was with you."

"Oh. Slip of the tongue, Maestro. I meant to say that I was alone."

"Yes," Killian murmured. "I'm sure you did."

Tavi said nothing to that, and the old Maestro stared at him with those unseeing eyes for a solid minute of silence.

Killian chuckled then, and lifted a hand, his voice mild and not at all amused. "As you wish. We can take this up again later." He flicked his hand in a curt dismissal.

Tavi hurried from the meditation chambers and set about delivering the letters. Before the morning's second bell tolled, he delivered his last letter, another missive to Ambassador Varg in the Black Hall.

Tavi approached the guard post and found the same pair who had been there the day before. There was something about their expressions and bearing that seemed odd, somehow, and Tavi stared around the entrance to the Canim embassy until it dawned on him what was out of place.

The Canim guards were not present. The Alerans stood as

always, facing the Canim embassy, but their Canim minors were gone. Tavi slipped in and nodded to them, dropping the letter through the bars and into the basket waiting there. Then he turned to the Alerans on duty and asked, "Where are the guards?"

"No idea," one of them said. "Haven't seen them all morning."

"That's odd," Tavi said.

"Tell me about it," the guard said. "This place is odd enough without adding anything else to it."

Tavi nodded to the men and hurried out of the palace, back to the Academy to return to the room he shared with Max.

On the way, he suddenly found himself trembling, and his breathing started coming swiftly, though he was only walking. His belly twisted around inside him.

Aunt Isana, taken and missing. And if he'd been faster, or more clever, or if he had slept a little more lightly to hear her messenger arrive, she almost certainly would not have been abducted. Assuming she *had* been abducted. Assuming she hadn't simply been taken elsewhere to be killed.

Tears blurred his vision, and his steps faltered for a second. His mind had run out of things to occupy it, he thought dully. As long as he'd been in motion, hunting Kitai, entering the Grey Tower, rescuing Max, and lying to Maestro Killian, he had been focused on the task at hand. Now, though, he had a temporary respite from those duties, and all the feelings he had forced down rose up into his thoughts, inevitable as the tides.

Tavi slammed open the door to his room, swung it shut, and leaned his back against it, eyes lifted to the ceiling. The tears wouldn't stop. He should have been able to control himself, but he couldn't. Perhaps he was simply too strained, too tired.

In the unlit room, Tavi heard movement, and then a moment later Kitai asked softly, "Aleran? Are you unwell?"

Tavi swept his sleeve over his eyes and looked at Kitai, who stood before him with a puzzled expression. "I . . . I'm worried."

"About what?"

He folded his arms over his stomach. "I can't tell you."

Kitai's pale eyebrows shot up. "Why not?"

"Security," he replied.

She looked at him blankly.

"Dangerous secrets," he clarified. "If Gaius's enemies learned them, it could get a lot of people hurt or killed."

"Ahhh," Kitai said. "But I am not Gaius's enemy. So it is all right to tell me."

"No, Kitai," Tavi began. "You don't get it. It . . ." He blinked for a second and thought it over. Kitai obviously was not a threat to Gaius. In fact, of everyone in Alera Imperia, she was probably the *only* person (other than Tavi himself) who he could be sure was not an enemy of the Crown. Obviously, Kitai would have no political leanings, no power or authority at stake, no conflicts of interest. She was a stranger to the Realm, and because of that, Kitai was immune to the influence of political and personal pressures.

And he wanted to talk to someone, very much. If only to get the twisting knot of serpents out of his belly.

"If I tell you," he said, "will you promise me never to speak of it with anyone but me?"

She frowned a little, her eyes intent on his face, then nodded. "Very well."

Tavi breathed out very slowly. Then he let himself slide down the length of the door to sit on the floor. Kitai settled cross-legged in front of him, her expression a mixture of interest, concern, and puzzlement.

Tavi told her all that had happened to him in recent days. She sat patiently through it, stopping him only to ask questions about words or people she didn't know.

"And now," Tavi finished, "Aunt Isana is in danger. It may already be too late to help her. And what's worse is that I'm almost certain that she wanted to reach the First Lord because there was some kind of trouble back in Calderon."

"You have friends there," Kitai said quietly. "And family."

Tavi nodded. "But I don't know what to do. That bothers me."

Kitai leaned her chin against the heel of one of her hands and studied him, frowning faintly. "Why?"

"Because I'm worried that there's something I'm missing," he said. "Something else I could be doing that would help. What if there's a way to solve this whole situation, and I'm just not smart enough to think of it?"

"What if a stone falls from the sky and kills you where you sit, Aleran?" Kitai said.

Tavi blinked. "What is that supposed to mean?"

"That not all things are in your control. That worrying about those things will not change them."

Tavi frowned and looked down. "Maybe," he said. "Maybe."

"Aleran?"

"Yes?"

Kitai chewed on her lower lip thoughtfully. "You say this creature, Varg, has been acting strangely?"

"Looks that way," Tavi said.

"Is it possible that he does so because he is involved in what is happening to your headman?"

Tavi frowned. "What do you mean?"

Kitai shrugged. "Only that of all the things you describe, Varg is the one with no stomach to match his hands."

Tavi blinked. "What?"

She grimaced. "It is a Horse Clan saying. It does not translate well. It means that Varg has no reason to act as he has. So the question you must ask is why does he do this?"

Tavi frowned, mind racing. "Because maybe he does have a reason to do all these things. Maybe we just can't see it from where we're standing."

"Then what might that reason be?" Kitai asked.

"I don't know," Tavi said. "Do you?"

"No," Kitai said, undisturbed. "Perhaps you should ask Varg."

"He isn't exactly the type to engage in friendly conversation," Tavi said.

"Then watch him. His actions will speak."

Tavi sighed. "I'll have to speak to Maestro Killian about it. I don't think he can spare me to follow Varg around. And in any case, it isn't important to me."

"Your aunt is," Kitai said.

Aunt Isana. Tavi suddenly ached from head to foot, and his anxiety threatened to overwhelm him once more. He felt so helpless. And he hated the feeling with a burning passion of a lifetime of experience. His throat seized up again, and he closed his eyes. "I just want her to be safe. I want to help her. That's all." He bowed his head.

Kitai moved quietly. She prowled over to sit down beside him, her back against the door. She shifted, pressed her side to his, and settled down, relaxing, saying nothing but providing the solid warmth of her presence in a silent statement of support.

"I lost my mother," Kitai said after a time. "I would not wish that pain on anyone, Aleran. I know that Isana has been a mother to you."

"Yes. She has."

"You once saved my father's life. I am still in your debt for that. I will help you if I am able."

Tavi leaned against her a little, unable to give a voice to the gratitude he felt. After a moment, he felt warm fingertips on his face and opened his eyes to stare into Kitai's from hardly a handbreadth away. He froze, not daring to move.

The Marat girl stroked her fingers over his cheek, the line of his jaw, and tucked errant, dark hairs into place behind his ears. "I have decided that I do not like it when you hurt," she said quietly, her eyes never leaving his. "You are weary, Aleran. You have enemies enough without tearing open your own wounds over things you could not have prevented. You should rest while you have a chance."

"I'm too tired to sleep," Tavi said.

Kitai stared at him for a moment, then sighed. "Mad. Every one of you."

Tavi tried to smile. "Even me?"

"Especially you, Aleran." She smiled back a little, luminous eyes bright and close.

Tavi felt himself relaxing a little, leaning more toward her, enjoying the simple warmth of her presence. "Kitai," he asked. "Why are you here?"

She was quiet for a moment, before she said, "I came here to warn you."

"Warn me?"

She nodded. "The creature from the Valley of Silence. The one we awoke during the Trial. Do you remember?"

Tavi shivered. "Yes."

"It survived," she said. "The *croach* died. The Keepers

died. But it left the Valley. It had your pack. It had your scent."

Tavi shivered.

"It came here," Kitai said quietly. "I lost its trail in a storm two days before I came here. But it had run straight for you the entire way. I have been looking for it for months, but it has not appeared."

Tavi thought about it for a moment. Then he said, "Well something like that could hardly have gone unnoticed in the capital," he said. "A giant, hideous bug would tend to stand out."

"Perhaps it also died," Kitai said. "Like the Keepers."

Tavi scratched at his chin. "But the Black Cat has been stealing for months," he said. "You've been here for months. If you'd only come to warn me, you could have done it and been gone. Which means there must be another reason you stayed."

Something flickered in her deep green eyes. "I told you. I am here to Watch." Something in her voice lent the word quiet emphasis. "To learn of you and your kind."

"Why?" Tavi asked.

"It is the way of our people," Kitai said. "After it is known that . . ." Her voice trailed off, and she looked away.

Tavi frowned. Something told him that she would not take well to him pressing the question, and he did not want to say anything to make her move away. Just for a moment, he wanted nothing more than to sit there with her, close, talking.

"What have you learned?" he asked her instead.

Her eyes came back to his, and when they met, Tavi shivered. "Many things," she said quietly. "That this is a place of learning where very few learn anything of value. That you, who have courage and intelligence, are held in contempt by most of your kind here because you have no sorcery."

"It isn't really sorcery," Tavi began.

Kitai, never changing expression, put her fingertips lightly over Tavi's lips, and continued as if he hadn't spoken. "I have seen you protect others, though they consider you to be weaker than they. I have seen a very few decent people, like the boy we took from the tower." She paused for a moment in consideration. "I have seen women trade pleasure for coin to feed their children, and others do the same so that they could ignore their children while making themselves foolish with wines and powders. I have seen men who labor as long as the sun is up go home to wives who hold them in contempt for never being there. I have seen men beat and use those whom they should protect, even their own children. I have seen your kind place others of their own in slavery. I have seen them fighting to be free of the same. I have seen men of the law betray it, men who hate the law be kind. I have seen gentle defenders, sadistic healers, creators of beauty scorned while craftsmen of destruction are worshiped."

Kitai shook her head slowly. "Your kind, Aleran, are the most vicious and gentle, most savage and noble, most treacherous and loyal, most terrifying and fascinating creatures I have ever seen." Her fingers brushed over his cheek again. "And you are unique among them."

Tavi was silent for a long moment. Then he said, "No wonder you think us mad."

"I think your kind could be great," she said quietly. "Something of true worth. Something The One would be proud to look down upon. It is within you to be so. But there is so much hunger for power. Treachery. False masks. And intentional mistakes."

Tavi frowned faintly. "Intentional mistakes?"

Kitai nodded. "When one says something, but it is not. The speaker is mistaken, but it is as though he intends to be incorrect."

Tavi thought about it for a second and then understood. "You mean lies."

Kitai blinked at him in faint confusion. "What lies? Where does it lie?"

"No, no," Tavi said. "It is a word. Lies. When you say what is not true, intentionally, to make another think it *is* true."

"Lies means to . . . recline. For sleep. Sometimes implies mating."

"It also means to speak what is not so," Tavi said.

Kitai blinked slowly. "Why would you use the same word for these things? That is ridiculous."

"We have a lot of words like that," Tavi said. "They can mean more than one thing."

"That is stupid," Kitai said. "It is difficult enough to communicate without making it more complicated with words that mean more than one thing."

"That's true," Tavi said quietly. "Call it a falsehood instead. I think any Aleran would understand that."

"You mean all Alerans do this?" Kitai asked. "Speak that which is not correct? Speak falsehood."

"Most of us."

Kitai let out a faintly disgusted little breath. "Tears of The One, *why*? Is the world not dangerous enough?"

"Your people do not tell li—uh, falsehoods?" Tavi asked.

"Why would we?"

"Well," Tavi said, "sometimes Alerans tell a falsehood to protect someone else's feelings."

Kitai shook her head. "Saying something is not so does not cause it to *be* not so," she said.

Tavi smiled faintly. "True. I suppose we hope that it won't happen like that."

Kitai's eyes narrowed. "So your people tell falsehoods even to themselves." She shook her head. "Madness." She traced light, warm fingers over the curve of his ear.

"Kitai," Tavi asked, very quietly. "Do you remember when we were coming up the rope in the Valley of Silence?"

She shivered, her eyes steady on his, and nodded.

"Something happened between us. Didn't it?" Tavi didn't realize he had lifted a hand to Kitai's face until he felt the warm, smooth skin of her cheek under his fingertips. "Your eyes changed. That means something to you."

She was silent for a long moment, and, to his astonishment, tears welled up in her eyes. Her mouth trembled, but she did not speak, settling instead for a slow, barely perceptible nod.

"What happened?" he asked gently.

She swallowed and shook her head.

Tavi felt a sudden intuition and followed it. "That's what you mean when you say that you came to Watch," he said. "If it had been a gargant, you'd be Watching gargants. If it had been a horse, you'd be Watching horses."

Tears fell from her green eyes, but her breathing stayed steady, and she did not look away.

Tavi ran his fingers lightly over her pale hair. It was almost impossibly fine and soft. "Your people's clans. Herdbane, Wolf, Horse, Gargant. They . . . join with them somehow."

"Yes, Aleran," she said quietly. "Our *chala*. Our totems."

"Then . . . that means that I am your *chala*."

She shuddered, hard, and a small sound escaped her throat. And then she sagged against him, her head falling against one side of his chest.

Tavi put his arm around her shoulders without thinking about it, and held her. He felt faintly surprised by the sensation. He'd never had a girl pressed up against him like this. She was warm, and soft, and the scent of her hair and skin was dizzying. He felt his heart and breath speed, his body reacting to her nearness. But beneath that was another level of sensation entirely. It felt profoundly and inexplicably *right*, to feel her against him, beneath his arm. His arm tightened a little and at the same time Kitai moved a little closer, leaned against him a little harder. She shook with silent tears.

Tavi began to speak, but something told him not to. So he waited instead, and held her.

"I wanted a horse, Aleran," she whispered, in a broken little voice. "I had everything planned. I would ride with my mother's sister Hashat. Wander over the horizon for no reason but to see what is there. I would race the winds and challenge the thunder of the summer storms with the sound of my Clanmates running over the plains."

Tavi waited. At some point, he had found her left hand with his, and their fingers clasped with another tiny shock of sensation that was simply and perfectly *right*.

"And then you came," she said quietly. "Challenged Skagara before my people at the *horto*. Braved the Valley of Silence. Defeated me in the Trial. Came back for me at risk to your own life when you could have left me to die. And you had such beautiful eyes." She lifted her tear-stained face, her eyes seeking out Tavi's once more. "I did not mean this to happen. I did not choose it."

Tavi met her gaze. The pulse in her throat beat in time with his own heart. They breathed in and out together. "And now," Tavi said quietly, "here you are. Trying to learn more about me. Everything is strange to you."

She nodded slowly. "This has never happened to one of my people," she whispered. "Never."

And then Tavi understood her pain, her heartache, her fear. "You have no Clanmates," he said softly. "No Clan among your people."

More tears fell from her eyes, and her voice was low, quiet, steady. "I am alone."

Tavi met her eyes steadily and could all but taste the anguish far beneath the calm surface of her words. The girl still trembled, and his thoughts and emotions were flying so fast and thick that he could not possibly have arrested any one of them long enough for consideration. But he knew that Kitai was brave, and beautiful, and intelligent, and that her presence was something fundamentally good. He realized that he hated to see her hurting.

Tavi leaned forward, cupping her face with one hand. Both of them trembled, and he hardly dared move for fear of shattering that shivering moment. For a little time, he did not know how long, there was nothing but the two of them, the drowning depths of her green eyes, the warmth of her skin pressed against his side, smooth under his fingertips, her own fever-hot fingers trailing over his face and throat, and through his hair.

Time passed. He didn't care how much. Her eyes made time into something unimportant, something that fit itself to their needs and not the other way around. The moment lasted until it was finished, and only then was time allowed to resume its course.

He looked into Kitai's eyes, their faces almost touching, and said, his voice low, steady, and certain, "You are *not* alone."

Amara stared down at the outlaw's cave through the magnifying field of denser air Cirrus created between her outstretched hands. "You were right," she murmured to Bernard. She beckoned him with her head, and held her hands out so that he could lean down and peer over her shoulder. "There, you see, spreading out from the cave mouth. Is that the *croach*?"

The ground for two hundred yards in every direction from the cave mouth was coated with some kind of thick, viscous-looking substance that glistened wetly in the light from the setting sun. It had engulfed the heavy brush in front of the cave entrance, turning it into a semitranslucent blob the size of a small house. The trees near the cave, evergreens mostly, had been similarly engulfed, with only their topmost branches free of the gummy coating. All in all, it gave the hillside around the cave a pustuled, diseased look, especially with the ancient mass of the mountain called Garados looming over it in the background.

"That's the stuff from the Wax Forest, all right," Bernard said quietly. "This cave has always been trouble. Outlaws would lie up there, because it was close enough to Garados that none of the locals would be willing to go near it."

"The mountain is dangerous?" Amara asked.

"Doesn't like people," Bernard said. "I've got Brutus softening our steps so that the old rock won't notice us. As long as we don't get any closer, the mountain shouldn't give us any trouble."

Amara nodded, and exclaimed, "There, do you see that? Movement."

Bernard peered through her upheld hands. "Wax spiders," he reported. He swallowed. "A lot of them. They're crawling all over the edges of the *croach*."

Doroga's heavy steps approached and paused close beside them. "Hngh," he grunted. "They are spreading the *croach*.

Like butter. Grows out by itself but I figure they are trying to make it grow faster."

"Why would they do that?" Amara murmured.

Doroga shrugged. "It is what they do. If they get their way, it will be everywhere."

Amara felt a cold little chill run down her spine.

"They won't," Bernard said. "There's no sign of any of our people, taken or otherwise. I don't see any of their warriors, either."

"They are there," Doroga said, his rumbling voice confident. "They get in there in the *croach*, you can't see them. Blend right in."

Bernard put his hand on Amara's shoulder and stood, inhaling slowly. "I'm of a mind to go ahead with our plan," he told her. "We'll wait for dark and hit them hard. Get close enough to make sure the vord are in there, and finish them. Countess?"

Amara released Cirrus and lowered her hands. "We can hardly stand about and wait for them to come after us," she said. She glanced back at Bernard. "But these are your lands, Count. I'll support your decision."

"What is there to decide?" Doroga asked. "This is simple. Kill them. Or die."

Bernard's teeth showed. "I prefer hunting to being hunted," he said. "Doroga, I'm going to go circle that cave a good ways out. See if I can find out if they've got any other surprises hidden in there waiting for us. Want to come along?"

"Why not?" Doroga said. "Walker is foraging. Better than standing around watching him root things up."

"Countess," Bernard said, "if you're willing, I'd like to see what you can spot from the air before we lose the light."

"Of course," she said.

"Three hours," Bernard said after a moment. "I'm telling Giraldi to be ready to hit them in three hours, just after full dark. If we don't find any surprises waiting, that's when we'll take the fight to them."

Amara inhaled and exhaled deeply, then rose with a forced calm and poise she did not feel, and called Cirrus to carry her up and into the air. She was still weary from an excess of windcrafting, but she had enough endurance for a short flight over the proposed battlefield. It would take her only a few moments.

And once it was done, the remaining hours before they moved would feel like an eternity.

Once Amara returned from her uneventful (and unenlightening) flight over the vord nest, she had settled down with her back to a tree to rest. When she woke, she was lying on her side, half-curled, her head pillowed on Bernard's cloak. She recognized the scent without needing to open her eyes, and she lay there for a moment, breathing slowly in and out. But around her, Giraldi's veterans were stirring, and weapons and armor made quiet sounds of metal clicking on metal and rasping against leather as they secured their arms and gear and prepared to fight. No one spoke, except for short, hushed phrases of affirmation as they checked one another's gear and tightened buckles.

Amara sat up slowly, then rose to her feet. She stretched, wincing. The mail hadn't been made to fit her, though it was tolerably close to functional, but her muscles weren't used to the weight of the armor, and they twitched and clenched painfully at odd moments and places as she put the strain on them again. She looked for the man closest to the vord nest and walked toward him.

"Countess," rumbled Bernard. There was a weak half-moon in the sky, occasionally veiled by clouds, and there was barely enough light for her to recognize his profile as he stared at the vord nest. His eyes glittered in the shadows over his face, steady and unblinking.

The vord nest, by night, looked eerie and beautiful. Green light flowed up from the *croach*, a faint, spectral color that created shapes and swirls of color while not managing to give much in the way of illumination. The green werelight pulsed slowly, as though in time to some vast heartbeat, making shadows shift and roil in slow waves around it.

"It's beautiful," Amara said quietly.

"Yes," he said. "Until you think about what it means. I want it gone."

"Absolutely," she said quietly. She stepped up beside him and stared at the nest for a while, until she shivered and turned to Bernard. "Thank you," she said, and held out his rolled cloak.

Bernard turned to her to accept it, and she heard the smile

in his voice. "Anytime." He slung the cloak around his shoulders and clasped it again, leaving his left arm clear for shooting. "Or maybe not anytime," he said then. His voice was thoughtful. "You've changed your mind. About us."

Amara suddenly went very still and was glad that the darkness hid her expression. She could keep her voice steady. She could tell that much of a lie. She couldn't have looked him in the face as she did it. "We both have duties to the Realm," she said quietly. "I was blighted when I was a child."

Bernard was silent for a very long time. Then he said, "I didn't know."

"Do you see why it must be?" she asked him.

More silence.

"I could never give you children, Bernard," she said. "That alone would be enough to force you to seek another wife, under the law. Or lose your Citizenship."

"I never sought it to begin with," Bernard said. "For you, I could do without it."

"Bernard," she said, frustration on the edges of her voice, "we have few enough decent men among the Citizenry. Especially among the nobles. The Realm needs you where you are."

"To the crows with the Realm," Bernard said. "I have lived as a freeman before. I can do it again."

Amara inhaled, and said, very gently, "I have oaths, too, Bernard. Ones that I still believe in. That I will not disavow. My loyalty is to the Crown, and I cannot and will not set aside my duties. Or take upon myself others that could conflict with them."

"You think I am in conflict with the Crown?" Bernard asked quietly.

"I think that you deserve someone who can be your wife," Amara said. "Who can be the mother of your children. Who will stand at your side no matter what happens." She swallowed. "I can't be those things to you. Not while my oaths are to Gaius."

They both stood there for a time. Then Bernard shook his head. "Countess, I intend to fight you about this. Tooth and nail. In fact, I intend to wed you before the year is out. But for the time being, both of us have more pressing business, and it's time we focused on it."

"But—"

"I want you to get with Giraldi and make sure every man

has his lamps," Bernard said. "And after that, get into position with Doroga."

"Bernard," Amara said.

"Countess," he interrupted, "these are my lands. These men are in my command. If you will not serve with them, then you have my leave to go. But if you stay, I expect to be obeyed. Clear?"

"Perfectly, Your Excellency," Amara replied. She wasn't sure if she was more annoyed or amused at his tone, but her emotions were far too turbulent to allow herself to react other than professionally. She inclined her head to Bernard and turned to walk back toward the *legionares* and to find Giraldi. She confirmed that each *legionare* carried two furylamps with him, and after that she found her way to the rear of the column, where the pungent scent of Walker, Doroga's gargant, provided almost as good a guide as the feeble light.

"Amara," Doroga said. He stood in the dark, leaning against Walker's flank.

"Are you ready?" Amara asked him.

"Mmm. Got him loaded up easy enough. You sure about this?"

"No," she said. "But then, what *is* sure in this life?"

Doroga smiled, his teeth a sudden white gleam. "Death," he said.

"That's encouraging," she said, her voice dry. "Thank you."

"Welcome," he said. "You afraid to die?"

"Aren't you?" she asked.

The Marat headman's head tilted thoughtfully. "Once I would have been. Now . . . I am not sure. What comes after, no one knows. But we believe that it is not the end. And wherever that path leads, there are those who went before me. They will keep me company." He folded his massive arms over his chest. "My mate, Kitai's mother. And after our battle last night, many of my people. Friends. Family. Sometimes, I think it will be nice to see them again." He looked up at the weak moon. "But Kitai is here. So I think I will stay for as long as I can. She might need her father, and it would be irresponsible to leave her alone."

"I think I will also try not to die," Amara told him. "Though . . . my family is waiting there, too."

"Then it is good you ride with me tonight," Doroga said. He turned, seized a heavy braided mounting cord, and swarmed easily up it onto Walker's back. He leaned over, tossing the line down to Amara and extending his hand to help her up, grinning. "No matter what happens, we have something to look forward to."

Amara let out a quiet chuckle and climbed up to settle behind Doroga on the woven saddle-mat stretched over Walker's broad back. The gargant shifted his weight from side to side, restless. Liquid sloshed in the wooden barrels attached to either side of the gargant's saddle.

Doroga nudged Walker forward, and the beast lumbered with slow, silent paces toward the area where the *legionares* were forming into their ranks. Amara watched as Giraldi prowled up and down their lines, baton in hand, giving each man an inspection in the wan moonlight. There was none of the centurion's usual bluster and sarcasm. His eyes were intent, his expression hard, and he pointed out flaws on two different *legionares* with a hard rap of the baton. The men themselves did not speak, jostle, or silently roll their eyes as the centurion passed. Every face was intent, focused on the task at hand. They were afraid, of course—only fools wouldn't be, and the veteran *legionares* were not fools. But they were professional soldiers, Aleran *legionares*, the product of a thousand years and more of tradition, and fear was one enemy to whom they would never surrender or lose.

Giraldi glanced up at her as the gargant lumbered quietly by and touched his baton to his chest in salute. Amara returned it with a nod, and the gargant went by to stop near Bernard and his remaining Knights—half a dozen each of earth and wood, none of them as gifted as Janus or Bernard, but each of them a solid soldier of several terms in the Legions. Shields had been abandoned entirely, the woodcrafters bearing thick bows while the earthcrafters bore heavy mauls and sledgehammers—except for the young Sir Frederic, who had opted to carry his spade into battle instead.

Bernard glanced up at Amara and Doroga. "Ready?"

Doroga nodded.

"Centurion?" Bernard asked the shadows behind him.

"Ready, my lord," came Giraldi's quiet reply.

"Move out," Bernard said, and rolled his hand through a short circle in the air that ended with him pointing at the nest.

The gargant's broad back swayed as the beast began walking forward, at no visible signal from Doroga. Amara heard a few soft creaks of worn leather boots and one rattle of what must have been a shield's rim against a band of steel armor, but beyond that the *legionares* and Knights moved in total silence. Glancing around, she could barely see the front rank of the *legionares* behind them, though they were no more than a dozen steps away. Shadows bent and blurred around them, the results of layers of subtle woodcraftings.

Amara's heart started pounding harder as they drew closer to the spectral green light of the *croach*. "Is this what your people did?" she asked Doroga in a whisper.

"More yelling," Doroga said.

"What if they come early?" she whispered.

"Won't," Doroga said. "Not until the Keepers warn them."

"But if they do—"

"We make them pay to kill us."

Amara's mouth felt dry. She tried to swallow, but her throat didn't feel as though it could move. So she fell silent and waited as they walked in tense, ready silence.

Bernard and his Knights reached the forward edge of the *croach*. He paused there, giving the *legionares* behind a chance to settle into their formation, then took a deep breath. He lifted his bow even as he knelt, a broad-bladed hunting arrow lying across the straining wood. He lined up the edge of the arrow with the surface of the *croach*, then released the arrow. The great bow thrummed. The arrow swept across the ground and, thirty or forty yards in, started cutting a long, fine incision in the surface of the *croach*. The waxy substance split, bursting like a boil, and luminous green fluid bubbled up out of the yards-long wound.

The vord nest erupted into violent motion, an alien wailing, whistling chorus rising into the night sky. Wax spiders, creatures as big as a medium-sized dog, burst up out of the *croach*. Their bodies were made of some kind of pale, partially translucent substance that blended in with the *croach*. Plates overlapped one another to armor their bodies while chitinous, many-jointed legs propelled them into leaps and jumps that covered twenty yards at a bound. The spiders emitted wailing shrieks and keening whistles, rushing for the long cut in the *croach*. Amara flinched in shock. She would never have *believed* that so many of them could have been so close, virtually under her nose, but invisible. There were dozens of them, moving over the *croach*, and as she watched the dozens became scores, then hundreds.

Bernard and his Knights Flora bent their bows and went to work. Arrows hissed unerringly into the wax spiders as they scuttled and leaped across the *croach*, these mounted with stiletto-shaped heads for piercing through armor. Launched from the heavy bows only a woodcrafter could bend, they proved deadly. Arrows flew home over and over again, ripping through the spiders, leaving them thrashing and dying, and they did not realize that they were being attacked at all for better than a minute.

Some of the nearer spiders spun to face the Aleran troops, eyes whirling with more luminous light and began bobbing up and down, letting out more whistling shrieks. Others picked up the call, and in seconds the whole horde of them had turned from the wounded croach and begun rushing at their attackers.

"Now!" Bernard roared. The bowmen fell back, still shooting, arrows striking wax spiders out of the air even as they flew toward the Alerans. Half of Giraldi's infantry advanced onto the surface of the *croach*, grounded their shields hard on the waxy substance, and stood fast as the wave of wax spiders rolled into their shieldwall.

The *legionares* worked together, their usual spears discarded in favor of their short, heavy blades that hacked down upon the spiders without mercy or hesitation. One man faltered as three spiders overwhelmed him. Venomous fangs sank into his neck, and he staggered, creating a dangerous breach in the line of shields. Giraldi bellowed orders, and fellow *legionares* in the ranks behind the first seized the wounded man and hauled him back, then stepped into his place in the line. The slaughter went on for perhaps half a minute, then there was a brief hesitation in the wax spiders' advance.

"Second rank!" bellowed Giraldi. As one, the *legionares* in the shieldwall pivoted, allowing the second rank of fresh soldiers to advance, ground their shields a pace beyond the first, and ply their blades with deadly effect. Endless seconds later, another break in pressure allowed the third rank to advance in their turn, then the fourth, each one allowing more rested *legionares* to advance against the tide of wax spiders.

Their heavy boots broke through the surface of the *croach* so that the viscous fluid within oozed and splashed around every step, and made for poor footing—but they had drilled, maneuvered, and fought in mud before, and Giraldi's veterans held their line and steadily advanced toward the cave, while Bernard's archers warded their flanks, arrows striking down the spiders that attempted to rush from the sides.

"Just about halfway there," Doroga rumbled. "They'll come soon. Then we—"

From the mouth of the cave there came another shriek, this one somehow deeper, more strident and commanding than the others. For a second there was silence, then motion. The spiders began bounding away from the Alerans, retreating, and as they did the vord warriors boiled forth from the cave's mouth.

They rushed the Aleran line, dark plates of armor rattling and snapping, vicious mandibles spread wide.

"Doroga!" Bernard bellowed. "Giraldi, fall back!"

The Marat headman barked something at Walker, and the gargant hauled himself around and began to lumber back the way they had come, following the channel crushed through the *croach*. As he did, Amara leaned over the barrels mounted on Walker's saddle and struck away the plates that covered large tap holes at their bases. Lamp oil mixed with the hardest liquor Giraldi's veterans could find flooded out in a steady stream as Walker retreated, leaving two wide streams that spread out through the channel of broken *croach*. Giraldi's veterans broke into a flat-out run, racing toward the edge of the *croach*, and the vord followed in eager pursuit.

As the first *legionares* came to the end of the *croach*, Giraldi snapped another order. The men whirled, snapping into their lines again, this time on either side of the channel, shieldwalls aligned to funnel the vord warriors between them. The vord, reckless and aggressive, flooded directly toward the Alerans, their course guided by the shieldwalls, which channeled them directly into Doroga, Walker, and the crushing strength of Bernard's Knights Terra.

Walker let out a fighting bellow, rising up onto his rear

legs to slash one vord from the air as it tried to take wing, and the gargant's crushing strength was more than a match for the vord's armor. It fell broken to the ground, while Amara clutched desperately on to Doroga's waist to keep from falling off the beast's back entirely.

The Knights Terra held the gargant's flanks, and ripples of earth, furycrafted by the Knights, lashed out at the vord as they closed, shattering the momentum of their charge and exposing them to well-timed blows from the savage hammers that crushed vord armor plates like eggshells.

And all of it was nothing but a prelude to the true attack.

"Giraldi!" Bernard cried.

"Fire!" the centurion bellowed. "Fire, fire, fire!"

Along the whole of the Legion shieldwall, furylamps blazed into full and blinding brilliance.

And as one, the *legionares* hurled the lamps down into the viscous liquid of the broken *croach* mixed with lamp oil and alcohol.

Flames spread with astonishing speed, the individual fires in nearly a hundred places rapidly meeting, melding, feeding one another. Within seconds, the fire blazed up and began to consume the entrapped vord warriors.

Now the *legionares* had to fight in earnest, as desperate vord tried to batter their way out of the trap. Men screamed. Black smoke and a hideous stench filled the air. Giraldi bellowed orders, hardly audible over the frenzied rattling and clicking of the armored vord.

And the lines held. The vord at the rear of the trap managed to reverse their direction, streaming back toward the cave.

"Countess!" Bernard cried.

Amara reached out for Cirrus and felt the sudden, eager presence of her wind fury. She took a deep breath, focused her concentration, and shouted, "Ready!"

"Down, down, down!" Giraldi barked.

Amara saw everything moving very, very slowly. All along the lines, *legionares* abruptly drew back a pace and dropped to one knee, then to their sides, their curving tower shields closing over them like coffin lids. Desperate vord staggered and thrashed their way to their deaths, while those who had managed to retreat drove directly for the cave.

Amara drew Cirrus into her thoughts and sent it, with every ounce of her will, to fly toward the fleeing vord.

A hurricane of violent wind swept down from the air at Amara's command. It caught up the blazing liquid and hurled it in a sudden, blinding storm of blossoming flame. Fire engulfed the air itself, fed wildly by the wind, and the heat burned away the *croach* wherever it touched, melting it like the wax it resembled. *Croach*-covered trees burst into individual infernos, and still the frantic fire, driven by Amara's wind, rolled forward.

It engulfed the last of the vord who had attacked fifty feet short of the mouth of the cave—and then kept right on going, fires spreading and whirling madly, burning away the *croach* wherever it touched it.

Amara's concentration and will faltered in a sudden, nauseating spasm of fatigue, and she slumped hard against Doroga's back. Without the gale winds to feed and push them, the fires began to die down into individual blazes. There was no sign whatsoever of any *croach* anywhere upon the surface—only blackened earth and burning trees.

They'd done it.

Amara closed her eyes in exhaustion. She didn't feel herself listing to one side until she actually began to fall, and Doroga had to turn and catch her with one heavily muscled arm before she pitched off Walker's back and to the ground.

Things were blurry for a few moments, then she heard Bernard giving orders. She forced herself to lift her head and look around until she spotted Bernard.

"Bernard," she called weakly. The Count looked up from where he knelt, supporting a wounded soldier while a healer removed a broken shard of vord mandible from the man's leg. "The queen," Amara called. "Did we kill the queen?"

"Can't say yet," he replied. "Not until we check the cave, but it's a death trap. Has a high ceiling, but it isn't deep. It wouldn't surprise me if the firestorm cooked everything inside."

"We should hurry," she said, while Doroga slowly turned Walker around to face away from the cave. "Finish it before it has the chance to recover. We have to kill the queen or it's all for nothing."

"Understood. But I've got men dying here, and no water-crafter. We see to them first."

"Hey," Doroga growled. "You two. The queen is not in the cave."

"What?" Amara lifted her head blearily. "What do you mean?"

Doroga nodded grimly toward the crest of the hill behind them, back toward Aricholt.

The taken holders were there in a silent group, a simple crowd of people of all ages and both sexes who stood there in the weak moonlight and stared down at the Aleran forces with empty eyes.

Beside them stood Felix's century, together with what looked like every single *legionare* they'd been compelled to leave behind at Aricholt.

And all of them had been taken.

At the head of the silent host, something crouched low, and Amara had no doubts whatsoever as to what she was looking at. It was man-sized, more or less, and little more than an oddly shaped shadow. If it hadn't been for the luminous glow of its eyes, Amara would have thought that the vord queen was only an illusion of bad light and heavy shadows.

But it was real. It took a slow, steady pace down the slope of the hill, moving weirdly, as if walking on four legs when it was meant for two, and at precisely the same instant the entire taken host stepped forward as well.

"Furies," Amara breathed, almost too tired to be terrified at what she saw. Even as they had sprung their trap on the vord, the vord had been circling behind them to strike at the weaker target. Back at Aricholt, even a few taken had proved to be deadly—and now they outnumbered the *legionares* still left to face them.

"Bernard," she said quietly. "How many wounded?"

"Two dozen," he said tiredly.

The taken poured down the hill, in no great hurry, led by the glowing-eyed shadow at their forefront. Something like hissing, moaning laughter echoed through the night, dancing among the popping sparks of the burning trees.

"There are too many of them," Amara said quietly. "Too many. Can we run?"

"Not with this many wounded," Bernard said. "And even if we could move them, we've got our backs pinned to

Garados. We'd have to retreat over his slopes, and no one could conceal that much movement from the mountain."

Amara nodded and drew in a deep breath. "Then we have to fight."

"Yes," Bernard said. "Giraldi?"

The centurion appeared. He had blood on his leg, and there was a savage dent in the overlapping plates guarding one shoulder, but he struck his fist to his breastplate sharply. "Yes, my lord."

"Get everyone moving," he said quietly. "We'll fall back to the cave. We can fight in shifts there. Maybe hold out for a while."

Giraldi looked at Bernard for a moment, and there was no expression on his face but for troubled eyes. Then he nodded, saluted again, turned, and started giving quiet orders.

Amara closed her eyes wearily. Some part of her wondered if it might not be better to just go to sleep and let events take their course. She was so very tired. She tried to find some reason to keep herself moving forward, to keep pushing away despair.

Duty, she thought. She had a duty to do her utmost to protect the nobles, *legionares*, and holders of the Realm. That duty did not permit simple surrender to death. But it felt hollow. More than anything, she wanted to be someplace warm and safe—but duty was a cold and barren shelter for a wounded spirit.

She looked up again and saw Bernard helping a wounded man rise and hobble along to the cave while leaning on the haft of his spear. He helped the man get started, encouraging him, and turned to the next man in need of help while he organized their retreat—however temporarily it might extend their lives.

He was reason enough.

Doroga abruptly started laughing.

"What is so amusing?" she asked him quietly.

"Good thing we talked before this," Doroga rumbled, eyes merry. "Otherwise, I might have forgotten that no matter what happens, we got something to look forward to." He was still laughing to himself under his breath as he turned Walker to bring up the rear of the Aleran column.

Amara turned her head as they rode and watched the vord queen and the taken slowly closing in behind them.

CHAPTER 34

Tavi frowned at Ehren, and whispered, "What do you mean, nothing?"

"I'm sorry," Ehren whispered back. "I did as much as I could in the time I had. During the attack, someone apparently killed the streetlamps. Several people heard fighting, two even saw the beginning of the attack, but someone put the lamps out and after that, nothing."

Tavi exhaled slowly and leaned his head back against the wall. The examination room was more than mildly stifling. The history examination's written portion had begun after the noon meal and concluded a mere four hours later—to be followed by individual oral examinations. Sunset light slipped orange fingers through the upper windows of the hall, and there wasn't one of the hundred-odd students present who wasn't wild to leave.

Maestro Larus, a slump-shouldered man with an impressive mane of silver hair and an immaculate white beard, nodded to the student standing before his chair and flicked his hand in curt dismissal. He took a moment to make a note on the uppermost of a stack of parchments, then glared at Tavi and Ehren.

"Gentlemen," he said, sonorous voice edged with annoyance. "I would hope that you would show enough courtesy to your fellow students to remain politely silent during their examination. Just as I hope they will do for you." He narrowed his eyes at Tavi, specifically. "In fact, if that is not the case, I would be obligated to speak to the gathering on the subject of academic courtesy—at some length. I trust it will not be necessary?"

There was a rustle of clothing as the class turned to face them. A hundred irritated, threatening glares focused on Tavi and Ehren, the silent promise of mayhem lurking behind them.

"No, Maestro," Tavi replied, trying to sound contrite.

"Sorry, Maestro," Ehren said. Either he was better at it than Tavi, or else he actually *did* feel contrite.

"Excellent," Larus replied. "Now then, let us see. Ah, Demetrius Ania, if you would approach the front. You are next. If you would, please account for me the economic advances of the rule of Gaius Tertius and their effect upon the development of the Amaranth Vale . . ."

The young woman started fumbling for an answer under Larus's steady, menacing gaze.

Tavi leaned back to Ehren, and whispered, "It doesn't make sense. Why would an attacking *archer* put the lights out? He couldn't see to shoot."

Ehren gave Tavi a look of protest, bobbing his eyes toward Larus.

Tavi scowled. "Just keep your voice down. He won't hear it over everyone's stomach growling."

Ehren sighed. "I don't know why someone would do that, Tavi."

Gaelle, standing on the far side of Ehren from Tavi, leaned over, and whispered, "I didn't find much more. None of the staff I talked to remembered these cutters you mentioned. But I looked in their refuse bin and found several sets of perfectly serviceable clothing, some bedding, some cups and other such articles, as if they'd thrown out everything in a room or two. Breakfast refuse was on top of them, so it must have happened late last night."

"Crows," Tavi muttered. He settled back against the wall, restless. The examination had gone on for entirely too long. Kitai had agreed to remain quietly in Tavi's room until night fell to cover her exit from the Academy grounds, but he had told her he would be back well before now. Every moment made it more likely that she would take it upon herself to leave.

"Tavi?" Ehren asked. "Didn't the Civic Legion find out anything?"

Tavi shook his head in frustration. "Not when I came in here two hundred years ago," he muttered. He glowered at the student fumbling to cover the simple question. "Crows, Tertius's policies arrested inflation, which made the domestication of silkbats feasible and began the entire silk industry. The crows-eaten apple orchards didn't have anything to do with it."

"Be nice, Tavi," Gaelle murmured. "She's from Riva, and I hear the people from up that way are none too bright."

Ehren frowned. "I never heard that. I mean, Tavi's from near Riva and . . ." He blinked, then rolled his eyes, and said, "Oh."

Tavi glared at Gaelle, who only smiled and listened as Ania finally mentioned something about silk farms in her rambling answer. Maestro Larus dismissed her with another flick of his hand and an acidic look, before he marked his paper again and turned it over to the last page.

"Well then," Larus murmured. "That leaves us with only one more student. Tavi Patronus Gaius, please come to the front." He shot Tavi a hard look, and said, "If you can spare the time from your conversation, that is."

Tavi felt his face flush but said nothing as he stepped away from his place by the wall and walked up to the front of the room and stood before Maestro Larus.

"Very well then," the Maestro drawled. "If it isn't too much trouble, I wonder if you might enlighten me about the so-called Romanic Arts and their supposed role in early Aleran history."

A low murmur ran through the hall. The question was a loaded one, and everyone knew it. Tavi had argued the point with Maestro Larus on four separate occasions over the past two years—and now the Maestro had brought it into an examination. Clearly, he intended to force Tavi to surrender the point they had argued before, or else fail his course. It was a deliberate bully's tactic, and Tavi found it incredibly petty and annoying in the face of the matters that had ruled his life over the past few days.

But he felt his jaw setting, and the calm and logical part of his mind noted with some alarm that the stubborn apprentice shepherd in him had no intention of surrendering.

"From which perspective, sir?"

Maestro Larus blinked his eyes very slowly. "Perspective? Why, from the perspective of history, of course."

Tavi's mouth set into a harder line. "Whose history, sir?

There have, as you know, been several schools of thought upon the Romanic Arts."

"I hadn't realized," Larus said mildly. "Why don't we begin with an explanation of precisely what the Romanic Arts were?"

Tavi nodded. "It is, in general, a reference to the collection of skills and methods embraced by the earliest Alerans of historical record."

"Reportedly embraced, I believe you mean," Larus said smoothly. "As no authentic records of their generation are known to survive."

"Reportedly embraced," Tavi said. "They included such areas of knowledge as military tactics, strategic doctrine, philosophy, political mechanics, and engineering without the use of furycraft."

"Yes," Larus said, his warm, mellow voice turning smug. "Furyless engineering. They also included such matters as the reading of the intestines of animals in order to predict the future, the worship of beings referred to as 'gods,' and such ridiculous claims as that their soldiers were paid with salt, not coin."

Low titters of laughter ran through the room.

"Sir, the ruins of the city of Appia in the southern reach of the Ameranth Vale, as well as the old stone highway that runs ten miles to the river, seem to indicate that their ability to build without the benefit of furycraft was both certain and considerable."

"Really?" asked Maestro Larus mildly. "According to whom?"

"Most recently," Tavi said, "Maestro Magnus, your predecessor, in his book, *Of Ancient Times.*"

"That's right. Poor Magnus. He really was quite the moving speaker, in his day. He remained so, right until he was dismissed by the Academy Board in order to prevent his insanity from influencing the youth of Alera." Larus paused, then said, with insulting patience, "He was never very stable."

"Perhaps not," Tavi said. "But his writings, his research, his observations, and conclusions are both lucid and difficult to controvert. The ruins of Appia feature architecture comparable both in quality and scale to modern construction techniques, but were clearly made from hand-quarried blocks of stone that were—"

Maestro Larus waved a hand in casual dismissal. "Yes, yes, you would have us all believe that men without any furycraft carved marble blocks with their bare hands, I suppose. And that next, again without fury-born strength, they proceeded to lift these massive blocks—some of which weighed as much as six or seven tons—with nothing but their backs and arms, as well!"

"Like Maestro Magnus—"

Larus made a rude, scoffing sound.

"—and others before him," Tavi continued, "I believe that the capabilities of men using tools and heavy equipment, combined with coordinated effort, have been vastly underestimated."

"You do sound a great deal like Magnus, toward the end," Larus replied. "If such methods were indeed as feasible as you claim, then why do workmen not still employ them?"

Tavi took a calming breath, and said, "Because the advent of furycrafting made such methods unnecessary, costly, and dangerous."

"Or perhaps such useless methods never existed at all."

"Not useless," Tavi said. "Only different. Modern construction techniques have not proven themselves substantially superior to the ruins of Appia."

"Oh for crying out loud, Calderon!" someone shouted from the center of the hall. "They couldn't have done it without furycrafting! They weren't as useless as you! And the nonfreaks in the room are hungry!"

Nervous laughter flitted around the room. Tavi felt a flash of sudden rage, but he didn't let it touch his face or look away from Maestro Larus.

"Academ," Larus said. "The position is an interesting—and romantic one, I suppose—from your point of view. But the fact of the matter is that the small, primitive, limited society of the earliest Alerans was clearly unable to support the kind of mass, collective effort that would have been required for such construction. They simply did not have the means to build it without furycrafting—which in turn makes it fairly obvious that Alerans have never been without furycraft, even if their more limited skill at it, in their day, mandated the use of assembled-parts construction, rather than modern methods that extrude all stone from the bedrock. It is the only reasonable view.

"It is *your* view, Maestro," Tavi replied. "There are many scholars and historians beyond Magnus who would disagree."

"Then they should be at the Academy sharing their views, shouldn't they?" Larus said, and his eyes had gone flat. "Well. I suppose allowances must be made for your . . . unique perspective."

Tavi's face burned again, anger and humiliation making it hard to keep his expression calm.

"While you are clearly misguided in your knowledge, Academ, I must admit that you have indeed read the material. I suppose that's more than many have done." Larus looked down to his sheaf and marked down Tavi's final grade—an absolutely minimum acceptable mark. He flicked his wrist at Tavi. "Enough."

Tavi gritted his teeth, but withdrew back to his place on the wall, while Maestro Larus looked over his sheets, then asked, "Have I overlooked anyone?" he asked. "If you haven't had the oral portion of the exam, you will receive a failing mark." He looked around the room, which had already begun to buzz with talk and movement. "Very well, then," he said. "Dismissed."

Before he got to "then" every student in the room was on their feet and crowding toward the door.

"Petty tyrant," Gaelle told Tavi on the way out. "Furies, but that man is an arrogant ass."

"He's an idiot," Tavi said. "He's never been to Appia, never studied it. Magnus might be insane, but that doesn't make him *wrong*."

"That wasn't what his question was about," Ehren said quietly. "Tavi, you can't just argue with a Maestro of the Academy like that. He wanted to put you in your place."

Tavi snarled under his breath and drove his fist savagely against his palm several times. Then he winced. The bruises on his knuckles throbbed, and the torn skin reopened in a couple of places.

"Furies, Tavi," Gaelle said, her voice worried. "How did you get those?"

"I don't want to talk about it," Tavi answered.

"Let's just get something to eat," Ehren said.

"You go ahead," Tavi replied. "I've got to report to Gaius immediately. He'll probably be mad the test ran over so long."

"Maybe they'll have found your aunt," Ehren suggested. "She might even be waiting for you."

"Sure," Tavi said. "See what else you can find out, all right? I'll talk to you as soon as I can."

He turned away and stalked back toward his rooms, ignoring looks of concern from both of his friends. He thought he heard one or two sniggers from students who watched him going by, but he could have been imagining them, and he didn't have the time or the inclination to take issue with them in any case. Only the very last light of day was in the sky, and he had to get Kitai out of the Academy before Killian started snooping around to find out who had been with Tavi. He didn't think that Killian would do anything dangerous, at least not once things were explained, but he would feel better once Kitai had gotten clear of the Citadel, at least.

He walked back to his rooms, stomach growling along the way, and hoped that she had remained in the room as he'd asked her to.

Tavi turned the corner that led to the room he shared with Max and stopped himself short. He frowned, staring ahead at the already-deep shadows down the row of doors to individual student quarters. This tier of student housing was flush up against the outer wall of the Citadel, and between the dark wall of stone and the doorways of the rooms the darkness was already complete.

Tavi could see nothing ahead of him, but his instincts warned him not to proceed. He licked his lips. He had not been carrying so much as his knife when he went to the test, as such things were not permitted in lecture halls, and he missed the comforting weight of the modest weapon.

He stepped quickly from the walkway to stand against the outer wall, where he, too, would be in shadow, not backlit from the feeble light falling through the more open areas behind him. He closed his eyes for a moment and tried to focus on his senses, to understand what had caused his instinctive alarm.

He heard steps, long and very soft, somewhere ahead of him in the darkness, retreating. And then a breath later, he caught the acrid, caged-animal scent of the Black Hall.

His heart leapt into his throat. One of the Canim was waiting in the darkness before his door. His first instinct was to flee, a simple reaction of terror, but he repressed it ruthlessly. Not only was Kitai nearby, possibly unaware of the danger, but to one of the Canim, such flight would have been an invitation to attack. In fact, even had he been carrying his knife and a dozen like it besides, it would have made little difference. A fight would be very nearly suicide. He had only one choice of action that seemed likely to protect him from a lurking Canim—bold confidence.

"You there!" Tavi spat into the shadows, his voice ringing with authority. "What business do you have here? Why have you wandered from the Black Hall?"

From the darkness, there was a low, rumbling, stuttering growl that Tavi interpreted as a Cane's chuckle. And then there was a snarl and the shockingly loud sound of splintering wood—a door breaking inward. A slice of candlelight fell through the shattered door into the darkness outside, and Tavi saw something huge and furred outlined in that lonely spill of light as it surged through the broken door and into Tavi's room.

There was a cry from inside the room, and Tavi's ears abruptly sang with the thrill of battle. He raced forward. There was a rasp of a blade being drawn, the sound of something being knocked over, then a bestial roar of surprise and anger and pain. Kitai's voice trilled out a battle cry, scornful laughter in it, until a rising, bubbling snarl drowned it out; and then Tavi was at the doorway.

Ambassador Varg filled the room with its bulk, its hulking form doubled down, its crouch so low that it might have looked painful if the Cane had not moved with such incredible, lithe agility as it darted at Kitai.

The Marat girl faced Varg, crouched on top of Max's dresser, her eyes glittering, her mouth set in a sneer. Her knife was in one hand, its blade wet with dark blood, and she grasped Tavi's blade in the other. As Varg reached for her, she whipped both knives at the extended claws, and one of the cuts swept drops of blood onto the ceiling.

Varg's bellowing snarl shook the room, and with casual strength the Ambassador kicked the dresser out from under Kitai. The girl let out a shocked sound and fell, landing on all fours like a cat. Quick though she was, she was not fast enough to avoid Varg's claws, and the Cane hauled her from the floor and shook her as a terrier might a rat. The knives clattered from her hands, and Varg whirled to face the door.

Tavi did not pause a beat on his way into the room. When Varg turned to him, he had already picked up the heavy clay water pitcher from its place on the table beside the door, and he threw it with all the strength of both hands and his entire upper body. The pitcher shattered on Varg's snout, driving its weight back onto its rear foot. The Cane's blood-colored eyes widened with actual surprise, pain, and anger, and the dark lips pulled back from yellow-white fangs in a snarl of outrage.

"Let her go!" Tavi snarled, already throwing the plate the pitcher usually rested upon, but Varg swept it out of the air with casual precision and leapt at Tavi in a blur of fur, fangs, and bloodred eyes.

The Cane hit him, and Tavi felt the sheer power as a shock of utter surprise. Varg bulled through him as if he had weighed no more than a few feathers, and the force of the impact sent Tavi flying up from the ground to land clumsily on his back and elbows ten feet away.

"Aleran!" Kitai gasped.

Varg growled, crouched over Tavi with his naked teeth gleaming white in the dark. "Follow or she dies."

Varg turned and bounded down the shadowed row of doors, then across the open courtyard beyond it, down a servant's path which, Tavi knew, led to a grate that could be pulled up to gain entrance to the Deeps.

Tavi stared after Varg for a second, then let out a snarling curse. He picked himself up and snatched up both knives. He seized the lit candle and slapped it into his little tin lantern, then burst out of the room, sprinting along on Ambassador Varg's trail.

It was madness, Tavi knew. He could not fight Varg and win. For that matter, he could not fight Varg and *survive*. But neither could he allow the Canim to take Kitai from him, nor abandon the Marat girl to her fate when she had trusted him to shelter her for the day.

He knew that Varg would outrun him easily, and that Tavi would only be able to catch up to him when he was allowed to do so, but he had no choice.

He had promised Kitai that she was not alone, and though it cost him his life, he would make good on it.

Amara stared out of the mouth of the cave and murmured, "What are they waiting for?"

Outside, the silent host of taken had descended the hill and advanced to the edge of the blackened earth that had been the *croach*. For a time, they had been visible in the light of the burning trees, but as those fires slowly died down, the trees crashing one by one to earth, darkness swallowed them until the silent forms of the taken were now no more than motionless outlines in the gloom. The moon sank from the sky, deepening the night's blackness dramatically.

Standing in the cave itself was like standing in a vast fireplace long overdue for cleaning. Soot covered every surface, where the wind-driven firestorm had roared into the cave, consuming whatever had been inside. All that was left when the Alerans entered had been ugly, blackened lumps and scorched bits of heat-warped vord armored hide. A sickly-sweet scent filled the cave, a noxious cloud of unseen fumes, and even though it had been hours since they entered, the smell had not faded or become unnoticeable.

"Waiting for sunrise, maybe," Doroga rumbled.

"Why?" Amara said, staring out at the silent enemy.

"So they can see," Doroga said. "Vord can see in the dark pretty good. So can Marat. Your people, not so good. So taken, they don't see so good."

"That might be it," Amara murmured. "But if that was the case, they should have assaulted us immediately, while they still had the light from the fires and the moon."

"They got to know we don't have much water," the Marat headman rumbled. "Or food. Maybe they think they can wait us out."

"No," Amara said, shaking her head. "They've behaved intelligently all along—very intelligently. They've been aware of their enemy, of our capabilities, of our weaknesses. They have to be aware that we are only a small part of a much larger nation. They have to know that a relief force will arrive within days at the most. They don't have time for a siege."

"Maybe they are sending more takers," Doroga said.

"They'd have moved by now," Amara said. "I've got you and Walker guarding the cave mouth. Everyone wounded or sleeping has a partner to watch for more takers. No one has seen any of them."

Doroga grunted, folded his arm, and leaned against Walker's shoulder, where the great gargant bull rested placidly on his belly, chewing cud from his earlier foraging. The beast filled up most of the cave's mouth and regarded the silent enemy outside without particular fear. Amara envied the gargant that. The strength of a mere Aleran was no match for the berserk power of a taken Aleran, but both were of little consequence to something the gargant's size, and Doroga seemed to share Walker's calm.

Bernard moved up from the rear of the cave, silent for all of his size. Though they had placed several furylamps on the ground outside the cave to illuminate any possible approach, lights within the cave were kept dim to hide them from observation. It took Amara a moment to sense the weariness and worry in him.

"How is he?" she asked quietly.

"Giraldi is a tough old bastard," Bernard replied. "He'll make it. If we get out of this." He stared out at the silent forms of the vord for a moment, and said, "Three more dead. If we'd had a watercrafter, they all would have made it. But the rest look like they'll pull through."

Amara nodded, and the three of them stared out at the silent foe.

"What are they waiting for?" Bernard sighed. "I don't mind if they keep doing it, but I wish I knew why."

Amara blinked, then said, "Of course."

Bernard said, "Hmmm?"

"They're afraid," Amara murmured.

"Afraid?" Bernard said. "Why would they be, now? They've got us by the throat. If they storm this cave, they can probably finish us. They've got to know how hurt we are."

"Bernard," she said. "Don't you see? They made it a point

to attack our Knights early on—first the watercrafters, then the firecrafters. They understood what kind of threat they represented and eliminated them."

"Yes," Bernard said. "So?"

"So we just wiped out the vord nest with fire," Amara said. "When they thought they had killed our firecrafters. We've done something that they didn't expect, and it's shaken them."

Bernard shot a glance out at the enemy and lowered his voice to a bare whisper. "But we don't have any firecrafters."

"They don't know that," Amara replied as quietly. "They probably expect us to come out to them and do it again. They're waiting because they think it's their smartest option."

"Waiting for what?" Bernard said.

Amara shook her head. "Better light? For us to be weaker or more tired? For our wounded to expire? I don't know enough about them to make a better guess."

Bernard frowned. "If they think we've got firecrafters here, then they must think it's suicide to come into the cave. We'd fry them here at the mouth, before they ever got close to combat range. They're waiting for us to come out to burn them down, out where they can use the advantage of numbers against us." He let out a quiet chuckle. "They think they're the ones in trouble."

"Then all we have to do is wait them out," Amara said. "Surely a relief force will be here soon."

Bernard shook his head. "We have to figure that they'll understand that, too. Sooner or later, when we don't come out to them, they're going to realize it's because we don't have what they think we have. And then they'll come in."

Amara swallowed. "How long will they wait, do you think?"

Bernard shook his head. "No way to tell. But they've been too bloody smart all along."

"Dawn," Doroga said, his voice lazy and confident.

Amara looked at Bernard, who nodded. "His guess is as solid as anyone's. Probably more so."

Amara stared out at the darkness for several moments. "Dawn," she said quietly. "Had the First Lord dispatched Knights Aeris to us, they would have been here already."

Bernard stood beside her and said nothing.

"How long until then, do you think?" Amara asked.

"Eight hours," Bernard said quietly.

"Not time enough for the wounded to recover without crafting."

"But time enough to rest," Bernard said. "Our Knights needed it. As do you, Countess."

Amara stared out into the darkness, and it was then that the vord queen stepped into the light of the furylamps.

The queen walked upon two legs, but something in its motion was subtly off, as though it were performing a trick rather than moving naturally. A worn old greatcloak covered all but a few portions of the queen. Its feet were long, the toes spreading out and grasping at the ground as it moved. Its face, where not covered by the cloak's deep hood, was strangely shaped—its features almost human, but carved from some kind of rigid green material incapable of changing expression. Its eyes emitted a soft green-white glow, round orbs of color with no detectable lids or pupils.

Its right hand was raised above its head. Its arm was too long, jointed strangely, but the hand that grasped a broad strip of white cloth was also nearly human.

Amara just stared stupidly for a moment.

The vord queen spoke, its voice a slow, wheezing wail of sound, painful to hear and difficult to understand. "Alerans," the creature said.

Amara shuddered in reaction to the creature's voice, the alien tones and inflections.

"Aleran leader. Come forth. White talk, of truce."

"Crows," Bernard breathed quietly. "Listen to that. Makes my blood cold."

Doroga regarded the queen with flat eyes, and Walker let out a rumbling sound of displeasure. "Do not trust the words of the queen," he said. "It is mistaken and knows it."

Amara frowned at Doroga. "Mistaken?"

"It's lying," Bernard clarified. He squinted at Doroga. "Are you sure?"

"They kill," the Marat said. "They take. They multiply. That is all that they do."

Bernard squinted out at the vord queen, now remaining perfectly, unnaturally still as it waited. "I'm going to talk to it," he said.

Doroga's frown deepened. He never took his eyes from the vord queen. "Unwise."

"If it's busy talking to me," Bernard said, "it isn't leading an attack on us. If I can buy us some time with talks, it might make a difference."

"Doroga," Amara said. "These queens are dangerous, are they not?"

"More so than a warrior," Doroga said. "Speed, power, intelligence, sorcery if you get too close."

Amara frowned. "What sorcery?"

Doroga stared at the vord through eyes that appeared to be lazily unconcerned. "They command the vord without need for speech. They can make phantoms appear, distract, and blind, create images with no substance. Trust nothing you see when a vord queen is near."

"Then you can't risk it, Bernard," Amara said.

"Why not?"

"Because Giraldi is wounded. If something happens to you, command falls to me, and I am no soldier. We need your leadership too badly for you to take chances." She shook her head. "I'll go."

"The crows you will," Bernard spat.

Amara lifted a hand. "It makes sense. I can speak for us. And frankly, between the two of us I suspect I have more experience in manipulating conversations and evaluating responses."

"If Doroga's right, and it is a trap—"

"Then I am the most likely to be able to escape," she pointed out.

"Doroga," Bernard growled, "tell her how stupid it is."

"She's right," Doroga said. "Fast enough to escape a trap."

Bernard stared hard at Doroga, and said, "Thank you."

Doroga smiled. "You Alerans pretty stupid about how you treat your females. Amara is not a child to be protected. She is a warrior."

"Thank you, Doroga," said Amara.

"A *stupid* warrior to go out there," Doroga said. "But a warrior. Besides. If she goes, you can stay here with your bow. Queen tries anything, shoot it."

"Enough," Amara said. She flicked her cloak back to clear her sword arm, loosened her weapon in its sheath, then strode forward out of the cave and into the steady light of the fury-lamps. She stopped about ten feet in front of the vord queen, enough to one side to give Bernard a clear line of fire to the creature. She regarded the vord queen in silence for a moment. The entire while, the creature did not move, its luminous eyes tracking her.

"You asked for a talk," Amara said. "So talk."

The vord queen's head rotated oddly within the hood, eyes coming to rest at a slant. "Your people are trapped. You have no escape. Surrender and spare yourselves pain."

"We will not surrender," Amara said. "Attack us at your own peril. Once battle is joined, we will show no mercy."

The vord queen's head tilted in the opposite direction. "You believe that your First Lord will dispatch forces to save you. That will not happen."

There was something about the vord's statement, a certainty about the way it spoke that shook Amara's confidence. She kept her face and voice steady, and replied, "You are mistaken."

"No. We are not." The vord queen shifted in place, and the cloak stirred and moved inhumanly. "Your First Lord lies near death. Your messengers are dead. Your nation will soon be divided by war. No help comes for you."

Amara stared at the vord queen for a moment, fear a sudden, steady sensation at the base of her spine. Again, the creature spoke with total certainty. If it was telling the truth, it meant that the vord were working in several places at once. That the vord queen Doroga worried about had, in fact, reached the capital.

More pieces fell into place, and Amara's sense of horror rose as they did. The Wintersend Festival was attended by most of the nobility of the Realm. Public victories during Wintersend were that much more valuable—and public defeats that much more disastrous. It was surely no coincidence that the Cursors had come under attack at this time. If Gaius truly was incapacitated, his intelligence forces reeling, it would be an almost laughably easy matter to engineer the revelation of his weakness, and after that it would be a short step indeed to open civil war.

Amara stared at the vord queen with a rising sense of despair. Oh yes, the vord had fought intelligently. They had taken the time to get to know their enemy. Amara could not make more than vague guesses as to the extent of what the vord were doing, but if they were truly working in concert with disruptive efforts within the capital . . .

Then they might very well *be* doomed.

Amara stared at the vord queen as the thoughts reeled through her mind.

"Intelligent," said the vord queen. "Intuitive. Rapid analysis of disparate facts. The logic of the hypothesis is sound. Surrender, Alcran. You will make an excellent addition to the Purpose."

Cold horror drove Amara back a pair of steps and sent her heart into frantic racing.

It had heard her thoughts.

"You have fought commendably," the vord queen said, and it seemed that with every word the vord's pronunciation became more clear. "But it is over. This world is now part of the Purpose. You will perish. I offer you the opportunity for a painless end. It is the most you can hope for. Yield."

"We do *not* yield," Amara snarled, shocked at how high and thready her voice sounded. "Our Realm is not yours. Not today." She lifted her chin, and said, "We choose to fight."

The vord queen's glowing eyes narrowed, pulsing from green-white to a deep shade of golden red, and it rasped, "So be it." It opened its hand and released the white cloth to fall to the ground. Then it turned and bounded with inhuman grace and speed into the darkness. Amara retreated quickly to the cave, her legs shaking almost too much to walk.

Bernard, bow in hand, kept watching the shadows beyond the furylamps, frowning. "What happened?"

"It . . ." Amara sank down to the ground abruptly and sat there shivering. "It . . . looked into my thoughts. Saw what was going on in my mind."

"What?" Bernard said.

"It saw . . ." She shook her head. "I never said a word about some of the things, and it talked about them anyway."

Bernard chewed on his lips. "Then . . . it saw that we didn't have a firecrafter with us."

"Told you," Doroga observed. "Stupid."

Amara blinked. "What?" She stared at him for a moment, then said, "Oh, no. No, I didn't even consider that possibility. Which I suppose is just as well." She rubbed her arms with her hands. "But it claimed that Gaius had been incapacitated. That our messengers had been killed. That no help was coming, so we might as well give up. Bernard, it claimed to be working together with others of its kind inside the Realm— perhaps even in the capital."

Bernard exhaled slowly. "Doroga," he said. "I wonder if you would go tell Giraldi what has passed? And ask him to pick a squad for duty. I want us ready to repel an attack at any time."

Doroga looked between Bernard and Amara skeptically, but then nodded and rose, thumped Walker on the shoulder, and headed deeper into the cave.

When he was gone, Amara slumped against Bernard and abruptly started sobbing. It felt humiliating, but she was unable to stop herself. Her body was shivering severely, and she could barely get a breath between her lips.

Bernard held her, drawing her into his arms, and she just shuddered against him for a while. "It . . . it was so alien. So certain, Bernard. We're going to die. We're going to die."

He held her, but said nothing, arms strong and warm around her.

She couldn't stop crying, or babbling. "If it was telling the truth, it could be over, Bernard. Over for everyone. The vord could spread everywhere."

"Easy," he told her. "Easy. Easy. We don't know anything yet."

"We do," Amara said. "We do. They're going to destroy us. We fought them as hard as we could, but they only grew stronger. Once they begin to spread out, nothing can stop them." She shuddered again, and felt like something was tearing apart inside her. "They'll kill us. They'll come for us and kill us."

"If it comes to that," Bernard said quietly, "I want you to leave. You can take flight and warn Riva, and the First Lord."

She lifted her head to stare at him through a blur of tears. "I don't want to leave you behind." She suddenly froze, panicked. She had tried so hard to push him away from her, for both their sakes. But the finer concerns of duty and loyalty had become grossly insignificant in the past hours and moments. Her voice dropped to a whisper as she met his eyes, and said, "I don't want to be without you."

He smiled, only with his eyes. "Really?"

She nodded, her breathing too shaky to risk speech.

"Then don't be," he said quietly. One thumb gently brushed tears from her cheek. "Marry me."

She stared at him, her eyes widening in shock. "What?"

"Right here," he said. "Right now."

"Are you mad?" she said. "We'll be lucky to live the night."

"If we don't," he said, "then at least we'll have some of the night together."

"But . . . but you have to . . . your vows of . . ."

He shook his head. "Countess. We'll be lucky to live the night, remember? I do not think the First Lord would begrudge a few hours of not-quite-approved marriage to his sworn vassals who have given their lives in service to the Realm."

She had to stifle a sudden burst of laughter that fought with the tears for space in her throat. "You madman. I should kill you for asking me at a time like this. You're heartless."

He captured her hand between his. Her own hand felt so slender and fragile between his. His fingers were callused, warm, strong, and always so gentle. "I am only heartless, Countess, because I have given mine to a beautiful young woman."

She suddenly couldn't look away from his eyes. "But . . . you don't want . . . don't want *me*. I . . . we've never spoken of it, but I know you want children again."

"I don't know everything that is going to happen tomorrow," he said. "But I know I want to see it happen with you, Amara."

"You madman," she said quietly. "Tonight?"

"Right now," he said. "I've checked the bylaws. Doroga qualifies as a visiting head of state. He can pronounce us wed."

"But we . . . we . . ." She gestured outside the cave.

"Are not needed to stand watch," he said quietly. "And we'll serve when it comes time. Did you have anything else planned before morning?"

"Well. No. No, I suppose not."

"Then will you, Amara? Marry me."

She bit her lower lip, her heart still surging, her hands now shaking for an entirely different reason. "I don't suppose it will matter, in the long run," she whispered.

"Maybe not," Bernard said. "I have no intention of lying down to die, Amara. But if this is to be my last night as a man, I would have it be as your man."

She lifted her hand to touch his cheek. Then said, "I never thought anyone would want me, Bernard. Much less someone like you. I would be proud to be your wife."

He smiled, mouth and eyes, the expression warm, his eyes bright, the gleam in them a sudden and potent defiance of the despair around them. Amara smiled back at him, and hoped he could see the reflection of that strength in her own eyes. And she kissed him, most gently, most slowly.

Neither of them had noticed Doroga's silent return, until the Marat headman snorted. "Well," he said. "Good enough for me. I pronounce you man and wife."

Amara twitched and looked up at Doroga, then at Bernard. "What?"

"You heard the man," Bernard said, stood up, and scooped Amara into his arms.

She began to speak, but he kissed her again. She was dimly aware of him walking, and of a small alcove that someone had crafted into the back of the cave, curtained off with Legion cloaks hung from a spear behind a wall of stacked shields. But most of all, she was aware of Bernard, of his warmth and strength, of the gentle power of his hands and his heart. He kissed her, undressed her, and she clung as tightly as she could to him, cold and eager to feel his warmth, to share the heat between them in the darkness.

And for a time, there was no deadly struggle. No waiting

enemy. No certain death awaiting them somewhere in the night. There was only their bodies and mouths and hands and whispered words. Though her life would soon be over, she at least had this time, this warmth, this comfort, this pleasure.

It was terrifying, and it was wonderful.

And it was enough.

CHAPTER 36

Isana awoke to pain and a sense of smothering confinement. Dull fire burned in her side. She struggled, pushing against something soft that held her close, and only after several seconds of flailing was she able to escape it. It took long seconds after that for her to come to her senses and realize that she was in a bed, upon a lumpy mattress, in a darkened room.

"Lights," murmured a male voice, and a pink-tinted fury-lamp on a battered card table against one wall came up to low, sullen life.

Isana began to sit up, but the pain flashed into a blaze of agony and she subsided, settling for twisting her neck until her eyes fell upon the form of the assassin sitting in a chair in front of the door. She stared at the middle-aged man for a silent moment, and he returned her look with veiled eyes that somehow made her feel off-balance. It took her a moment to realize that it was because she had no emotional sense of him whatsoever. Her skills as a watercrafter cursed her with the constant empathy that came with them—but from him she felt an utter void of emotions. It took her a moment to realize that he was concealing his emotions from her, and doing it better than even Tavi had ever managed.

Isana stared at the man, at his expression, his eyes, searching for some clue about his emotions, his intentions. But there was nothing. He might have been made from cold, featureless stone.

"Well," she spat. "Why don't you go ahead and finish the job?"

"Which job is that?" he responded. His voice was mild, and matched his unremarkable appearance admirably.

"You killed them," she said quietly. "The coachmen. Nedus. You killed Serai."

His eyes flickered with something, and there was a very

brief sense of regret from him. "No," he said quietly. "But I did kill the archer who shot Serai. And you, for that matter."

Isana looked down to find herself clothed only in the silk shift she'd worn beneath her gown. It was stained with blood where she had been wounded and had been sliced open along the side to make room for someone, presumably the assassin, to clean and bind her wounds. Isana closed her eyes, touching upon Rill to feel her way through her body to the injury. It could have been a great deal worse. The arrow had ruptured flesh and fat and injured muscles, but it hadn't broken through into her vitals. The man had done a competent job of removing the arrow, cleaning the wound, and stopping the bleeding.

Isana opened her eyes, and asked, "Why should I believe you?"

"Because it's the truth," he said. "By the time I found the archer it was too late to help Serai. I regret that."

"Do you," Isana said, her voice flat.

Fidelias arched an eyebrow. "Yes, actually. She was someone I respected, and her death served no purpose. I hit him just as he loosed at you, Steadholder."

"Which saved my life?" Isana asked. "I suppose now I should feel grateful to you for rescuing me from my would-be killer."

"I think you'd rather send me to join him," Fidelias said. "Especially given what happened in Calderon two years ago."

"You mean when you tried to murder my family, my holders, and my neighbors."

"I was doing a job," Fidelias said. "I did what I had to do to complete it. I took no joy in that."

Isana could sense the man's apparent sincerity, but it only made her anger sharper, more clear. "You got more joy of it than the folk of Aldoholt. More than Warner and his sons. More than all the men and women who died at Garrison."

"True enough," Fidelias agreed.

"Why?" Isana demanded. "Why did you do it?"

He folded his arms over his chest and mused for a moment. "Because I believe that Gaius's policies and decisions over the past decade or so are leading our Realm to disaster. If he remains as First Lord or dies without a strong heir, it will only be a matter of time before the strongest High Lords attempt to seize power. That kind of civil war would destroy us."

"Ah," Isana said. "To save the people of Alera, you must kill them."

He gave her a wintry smile. "You could put it that way. I support the High Lord I regard as the most likely to provide leadership for the Realm. I don't always agree with his plans and methods. But yet I deem them less damaging to the Realm in the long term."

"It must be nice to have so much wisdom and confidence."

Fidelias shrugged. "Each of us can only do as he sees best. Which brings us to you, Steadholder."

Isana lifted her chin, and waited.

"My employer would like you to pledge your public support to his house."

Isana let out a pained laugh. "You can't be serious."

"On the contrary," Fidelias said. "You should consider the advantages such an alliance would bring you."

"Never," Isana said. "I would never betray the Realm as you have."

Fidelias arched an eyebrow. "Exactly which part of the Realm is it you feel deserves such loyalty?" he asked. "Is it Gaius? The man who made you and your brother into symbols of his own power and made you targets of all of his enemies? The man who holds your nephew virtually hostage in the capital as a guarantee of your loyalty?"

She stared at him, and said nothing.

"I know you've come here to seek his help in something. And I know that you have had no luck in making contact with him—and that he has clearly made no effort at all to protect you from harm, despite the danger he placed you in by inviting you here. If not for the intervention of my employer, you would now be dead beside Nedus and Serai."

"That changes nothing," she said quietly.

"Doesn't it?" Fidelias said. "What has he done, Steadholder? What action has Gaius ever taken to command your loyalty and respect?"

She did not answer him.

After another silent moment, he said, "My employer would like you to meet with his second-in-command."

"Do I have a choice?" Isana spat.

"Of course," Fidelias said. "You are not a prisoner here, Steadholder. You are free to leave at any time you wish." He shrugged. "You need not meet with my employer, either. The room is paid for until sunrise, at which point you will need to either leave or make your own arrangements with the mistress of the house."

Isana stared at him for a moment, eyebrows lifted. "I . . . see."

"I assumed you would wish to care for your injury, so I've taken the liberty of having the house prepare a bath for you." He nodded toward a broad copper tub on the floor beside the fireplace. A heavy kettle bubbled on a hook over the fire. "Steadholder, you're free to do as you wish. But I would ask you to give serious consideration to the meeting. It might present you with some options you don't currently have."

Isana frowned at the tub, then at Fidelias.

"Do you need help getting to the tub, Steadholder?" he asked.

"Not from you, sir."

He smiled faintly, rose, and gave her a small bow of his head. "There is a change of clothes for you in the trunk beside the bed. I will be in the hall. You should be safe here, but if you become at all suspicious of an intruder, call me at once."

Isana arched a brow. "Be assured, sir," she said, "that if I feel myself in danger, you will certainly weigh heavily in my thoughts."

The faint smile warmed to something almost genuine for a moment. Then he bowed and left the room.

Isana grimaced down at her wounded flank and pushed herself heavily upright on the bed. She closed her eyes against a wave of pain and waited for it to recede. Then she rose, slowly and carefully, and walked deliberately across the room, one step at a time. She pushed the bolt on the door to, and only then did she make her way to the copper tub. The kettle on the fire was mercifully mounted on a swinging arm, and Isana swung it slowly out over the tub and poured from the kettle until the bathwater was comfortably warm. Then she slid the stained slip from her shoulder, loosened the bandages about her waist, and made her way painfully into the tub.

She felt Rill's presence at once, closing about her in a gentle cloud of concern and affection. Isana cleared the injury of bandages and directed Rill to her flank, carefully willing the fury through the process of repairing the injury. There was burning pain at first, then a tingling numbness as the fury went to work, and after several moments of concentration Isana sank back into the tub with a languid weariness. The pain was all but gone, though she still felt stiff and brittle. The water had been stained with blood, but the skin that now covered the wound was pink and new as a baby's. She added a little more hot water from the kettle and sank into the tub.

Nedus was dead.

Serai was dead.

They had died trying to protect her.

And she was now alone, far from any friends, any family, anyone she could trust.

No, not far from any family. Tavi was in the city, somewhere. But he was, it would seem, beyond her reach, as had been everyone else since she arrived. Even if her letters had found him, they would only have directed him to Nedus's house.

Oh furies. If he had been at Nedus's house, if he had come in response to her letter, if he had been there waiting when the assassins had taken position . . .

And Bernard. She had a horrible intuition that he was facing danger enough to kill him and his entire command, and yet she still had not reached the First Lord with word of the danger. For all the good she had done her brother and her nephew, she might as well have died in the barn when the first assassin had attacked her.

Isana closed her eyes and pressed the heels of her hands against them. The fear, the worry, the wrenching hopelessness of her futile efforts overwhelmed her, and she found herself curling up in the tub, arms around her knees as she wept.

When Isana lifted her head again, the water in the tub had become tepid. Her eyes felt heavy and sore from weeping.

Her purpose, she realized, had not changed since coming to the capital. She had to secure help for those she loved.

By whatever means necessary.

As soon as she was dressed, she unbolted the door and

opened it. Fidelias—assassin, traitor, murderer, and servant to a ruthless lord—waited politely in the hallway. He turned to her with an inquiring expression.

She faced him, chin lifted, and said, "Take me to the meeting. At once."

CHAPTER 37

Ambassador Varg fled through the tunnels of the Deeps, and Tavi followed.

For the first hundred steps, Tavi had been frantic with fear. Without weapons, position, *something* he could use to his advantage, Varg would tear him to pieces, and so actually catching up to the Cane would be suicide. And yet, Varg still carried Kitai. How could Tavi do anything else?

But then another thought occurred to him. Even carrying his prisoner, Varg could have outpaced Tavi on foot without more than moderate effort. Canim battlepacks could often outmarch even the Legions in the field, unless the Alerans countered their natural speed by using the roads to lend speed and endurance to their troops. And yet, while Varg fled at great speed, it never quite pulled away from Tavi. The young man actually slowed his steps for a time, but Varg's lead did not lengthen.

Suspicion came over him, and his brain started chewing furiously over the facts. As Tavi pelted along the tunnels, he used his knife to strike the stone walls at each intersection, drawing small bursts of sparks and leaving the stone of the tunnels clearly marked. He knew the tunnels near the Citadel well, but Varg swiftly descended through a gallery Tavi had never explored and began working his way deeper into the mountain, to the tunnels that connected to the city below, the walls growing slick with moisture the lower they went.

Tavi rounded a final corner, to find the tunnel opening up into a long and slender chamber. He slid to a halt, lantern in hand, only to feel a sudden impact on the lantern that tore it from his hands and extinguished the candle in it.

Tavi got his back to the nearest wall and gripped his knife tightly, while struggling to keep his labored breathing quiet enough to allow him to hear. There was a quiet, steady trickling of water, where runoff from above the mountain escaped cisterns and flowed into the subterranean channels beneath the mountain's skin. After a long moment, he made out a dim red glow, the same as from one of the barely visible Canim lamps in Varg's chambers. Over another moment or two, his eyes adjusted, until he could make out the silent, enormous form of Ambassador Varg, crouched a dozen yards in front of Tavi, one hand holding Kitai's back to its front by the waist, the other pressing black claws against her throat.

The Marat girl looked more angry than frightened, a fierce glitter in her green eyes, and her expression was proud and cold. But she did not struggle against the vastly more powerful Cane.

Varg stared at Tavi, its eyes hidden in the shadows of its muzzle and fur. Varg lifted black lips from his fangs.

"I'm here," Tavi said, very quietly. "What do you want me to see?"

Varg's tongue lolled over its fangs for a moment in what looked like a pleased grin. "Why do you think that, pup?"

"You don't need something this complicated to kill me. You could have done it already, without bothering to lead me somewhere first. So I figure you wanted to show me something. That's why you took Kitai."

"And if it is?" Varg growled.

"You wasted your time. You didn't have to do this to get me here."

"No?" Varg asked. "Sooth, pup, would you have followed me deep into these tunnels simply because I asked it of you?" The Cane's white teeth showed. "Would you have walked this far from any help with me, given any choice?"

"Good point," Tavi said. "But I'm here now. Release her."

A bone-rattling deep growl rolled up from Varg's chest.

"Release her, Ambassador," Tavi said, and kept his tone even and uninflected. "Please."

Varg stared for a moment more, then nodded and released Kitai with a little shove. She stumbled away from the Cane and to Tavi's side.

"You all right?" Tavi asked her.

She seized her knife from where he had thrust it through his belt and turned around to face the Cane with murder in her eyes.

"Wait," Tavi told her, and clasped his hand down over her shoulder. "Not yet."

Varg let out a coughing, snarling laugh. "Ferocious, your mate."

Tavi blinked, then said, "She is not my mate."

At the same time, Kitai said, "He is not my mate."

Tavi glanced at Kitai, cheeks flushing, while she favored him with an acidic look.

Varg barked another laugh. "Plenty of fight in both of you. I can respect that."

Tavi frowned. "I assume you are the one who broke my lantern."

Varg made a guttural, affirmative sound.

"Why?"

"The light," Varg said. "Too bright. They would see it."

Tavi frowned. "Who would?"

"We put our fangs away for now," Varg said, white teeth still gleaming. "Truce. And then I will show you."

Tavi nodded sharply and without any hesitation. He sheathed his knife, and said, "Kitai, please put it away for the moment."

Kitai glanced at him, wary, but slipped her knife back into its own sheath. Varg's stance changed to something more relaxed, and it let its lips fall over its teeth. "This way."

Varg stooped to pick up the Cane lamp, a small affair of glass that looked like a bottle full of liquid embers only moments from dying. As it did, Tavi took note of the fact that Varg now wore the armor he'd seen on the mounting dummy in the Black Hall, and wore its enormous sword on its belt. Varg set the bottle on the floor next to an irregular opening in the cavern wall, and growled, "No light past here. We crawl. Stay to the left-side wall. Look down and to your right."

Then he dropped to all fours and wriggled his long, lean frame through the opening and into whatever lay beyond.

Tavi and Kitai exchanged glances. "What is that creature?" she asked him.

"A Cane," Tavi said. "They live across the sea to the west of Alera."

"Friend or enemy?"

"Their nation is very much an enemy."

Kitai shook her head. "And this enemy lives in the heart of your headman's fortress. How stupid are you people?"

"His nation may be hostile," he murmured, "but I'm starting to wonder about Varg. Wait here. I'll feel better if someone is watching my back while I'm in there with him."

Kitai frowned at him, "Are you sure you should go?"

Varg's growl bubbled out of the opening in the wall.

"Um. Yes. I think I'm sure. Maybe," Tavi muttered. He dropped down into the opening, which led to a very low passage and started forward before he could think too much about what he was doing. Had he tried, he could have crawled forward with his knees on the floor and his back brushing the rough spots in the ceiling.

Within a few feet, the cave became completely black, and Tavi had to force himself to keep going, his left shoulder pressed against the wall on that side. Varg let out another, almost inaudible growl in front of him, and Tavi tried to hurry, until Varg's feral scent and the odor of iron filled his nose. They went on that way for a time, while Tavi counted his "steps" each time he moved and planted his right hand. The sound of falling water grew louder as they proceeded. At seventy-four steps, Tavi's eyes made out a faint shape in front of him—Varg's furry form. Ten steps beyond that, he saw pale, green-white light ahead of him.

And then the wall on his right fell away, and the low tunnel they were in became a dangerously narrow shelf at the back of a gallery of damp, living stone. The Cane rose to a low hunting crouch, glanced at Tavi, and jerked its muzzle at the cavern beneath them. Tavi drew himself up beside Varg, instinctively keeping every move silent.

The cavern was enormous. Water dripped steadily down from hundreds of stalactites above, some of them longer than the outer walls of the Citadel were tall. Their floor-level counterparts rose in irregular cones, many of them even longer than those above. A stream spilled out of a wall on the far side of the gallery, fell several feet into a churning pool, and rushed on down a short channel and beneath the back wall, continuing down toward the river Gaul. Tavi stared at the scene illuminated in green-white light, and his mouth dropped open in sickened horror.

Because every surface in the cavern was covered in the *croach*.

It had to be. It was exactly the same as he had seen in the Wax Forest two years before. It did not look as thick as the wax that had covered that alien bowl of a valley, but it gave off the same pulsing, white-green glow. Tavi saw half a dozen wax spiders gliding with sluggish grace over the *croach*, pausing here and there, their luminous eyes glowing in shades of green, soft orange, and pale blue.

Tavi stared down at them for a moment, too shocked to do anything more. Then his eyes picked out an area where the *croach* had grown up into a kind of enormous, lumpy blister that covered several of the largest stalagmites. The surface of the blister pulsed with swirling green lights and was translucent enough to reveal shadows moving within it.

Outside the blister were Canim. They crouched in the Cane four-legged guard stance along the base of it in a steady perimeter, no more than four or five feet apart, every one of them armed and armored, their heads mostly covered by the deep hoods of their dark red mantles. Not one of them moved. Not a twitch. From where he crouched, Tavi could not see them breathing, and it made them look like full-color statues rather than living beings. A wax spider made its slow way across the *croach* and climbed over a crouching Cane as if it was a simple feature of the landscape.

There was a sudden snarling bellow that rattled off the cavern walls, and from somewhere almost directly beneath them, several Canim appeared. Tavi watched as three of them hauled a bound and struggling Cane into the cave. The Cane was wounded, and its steps left bloody footprints on the cave floor. Its hands had been bound at the wrists, fingers interlaced, and several twists of rope bound its jaws shut. There was a mad gleam in its bloody eyes, but struggle as it might, the Cane could not shake the grip of its captors.

By contrast, the Canim dragging the prisoner were silent and calm, letting out no snarls, no growls, and wearing no expression whatsoever on their ferocious faces. They stepped onto the *croach*, dragging their prisoner, crushing the surface of the material as they went. Wax spiders moved with lazy grace to the damaged area and began repairing it, multiple legs stroking and smoothing the *croach* back into its original form.

Beside him, Varg's chest rumbled with another, quietly furious growl.

They dragged the prisoner forward to what proved to be an opening in the wall of the blister. They hauled the Cane inside. A second later, another shrill, smothered snarl erupted from within the blister.

Beside him, stone crunched as Varg's claws dug into it. The Cane's ears were laid flat back, and it bared its teeth in a vicious, silent snarl.

For a moment, nothing happened. And then four Canim emerged from the blister. They paced along the wall of the blister until they reached the end of the row of Canim, where they settled down into identical crouches and went still. The last Cane was the prisoner, now freed of its bonds. A pair of wax spiders appeared and began crawling lightly over the Cane, legs smoothing gelatinous *croach* into the Cane's wounds.

"Rarm," Ambassador Varg growled, in a voice barely audible over the sound of the cascading stream. "I will sing your blood song."

A moment later, more shadows stirred in the blister, and another Cane emerged from within it. Sarl still looked thin, furtive, and dangerous. His scarlet eyes flicked around the chamber, and when a wax spider brushed against him on the way to repairing the *croach* he had broken, Sarl let out a snarl and kicked the wax spider into the nearest stalagmite. It struck with a meaty-sounding splat and fell to the *croach*, legs quivering.

Without so much as hesitating, two more spiders diverted their course and began sealing the dying spider into the *croach*, where Tavi knew it would be dissolved over time into food for the creatures.

A second form emerged from the blister, this one smaller, no more than human-sized. It wore a deep grey cloak, and its hood covered its head altogether—but the way it moved was eerily inhuman, too graceful and poised.

"Where is the last?" the cloaked figure asked. Its voice was absolutely alien in tone and inflection, and revealed nothing about what might be concealed beneath the cloak.

"He will be found," Sarl growled.

"He must be," the figure said. "He could warn the Aleran leader of us."

"Varg is hated," Sarl said, "He was unable to so much as gain an audience with the Aleran leader. Even if he managed to speak to him, the Alerans would never believe him."

"Perhaps," the cloaked figure said. "Perhaps not. We must not chance discovery now."

Sarl gave its shoulders an odd shake and said nothing.

"No," the figure said. "I am not afraid of them. But there is little logic in allowing our chances of success to be endangered."

Sarl gave the cloaked figure a sullen look and eased a step away.

"Are your allies prepared?" the figure asked.

"Yes. Storms will strike the whole of the western coast this night. It will force him to his chamber to counter them. There is only one path to the chamber. He will not escape."

"Very well," the figure said. "Find your packmaster. If he cannot be found before the setting of the moon, we will strike without him."

"He is dangerous," Sarl objected. "As long as he lives we will not be safe."

"He is no threat to me," the figure said. "Only to you. We will strike at the setting of the moon. After which—"

The cloaked figure broke off and turned abruptly, staring up at the ledge and seemingly directly at Tavi.

Tavi froze, and his mouth went dry.

The moment passed in silence, then the cloaked figure turned to Sarl again. As it did, a pair of Cane rose from their stance beside the blister and moved to take position beside Sarl. "Take these. Hunt him down."

Sarl's teeth snapped in a sharp clash of bone on bone, and the Cane whirled to stalk out of the chamber.

The hooded figure stared up at the ledge for a moment more, then turned and glided back into the blister.

Varg pressed against Tavi and nodded toward the tunnel. Tavi turned and dropped to crawl back along it, to the chamber where Kitai waited with her knife and the Canim lamp. Tavi rose immediately, unnerved at the silent, dangerous presence of the Cane behind him, and stepped over to stand with Kitai, their backs to a wall, facing Varg.

"What did you see?" she whispered.

"Keepers of the Silence," he replied. "*Croach*. A great big nest, a lot like the one in the old Wax Forest."

Kitai inhaled sharply. "Then it *did* come here."

"Yes," Tavi said.

The Cane emerged from the tunnel and rose to its full height, stretching. Though it wasn't showing its teeth, Varg's ears were still laid flat back against its skull, and rage boiled off it in an invisible cloud.

Tavi looked at Varg and asked, "What happened to them?"

Varg shook its head. "They are bewitched, somehow."

"But who are they?"

"Members of my battlepack," Varg replied. "My guards."

Tavi frowned. "But you arc only allowed six. There were twenty there."

"Twenty-one," Varg corrected him. "Garl got a belly wound when the others came for us. I sent him to the blood lands ahead of us before those things could take him as they did Rarm."

"You knew they were coming for you?" Tavi asked.

Varg nodded. "Started to figure it out two days ago, when four of my guards were getting ready to leave. They mentioned rats in their quarters. Hadn't ever been any. But the month before, Morl and Halar said the same thing. Next day, when they left, they acted strange."

"Strange how?" Tavi asked.

The Ambassador shook its head. "Silent. Distant. More than usual." His eyes narrowed. "Their ears didn't look right."

Tavi frowned, and said, "Then . . . the departing guards, the ones you thought were going back to your lands, did not actually leave. They've been going down here into the Deeps instead."

Varg grunted. "And Sarl is behind it. With the cloaked one working witchery on my wolves."

"Why would he do that?" Tavi asked.

Varg growled. "Among my kind are several . . . castes, your word is. Warriors are the largest, the strongest caste. But also very strong are the Ilrarum. The blood prophets. Sorcerers.

Deceivers, treacherous. Sarl is one of the Ilrarum, though he pretends to be of lower caste, working for me in secret. As if I did not have a brain in my head. The blood prophets hate your kind. They are determined to destroy you by whatever means."

"Then Sarl's working together with the cloaked one," Tavi said.

"And coming to kill Gaius," Varg said. "He wants to cripple your leadership. Leave you vulnerable." Varg rested a hand on the hilt of its sword and showed its teeth in an easy grin. "I attempted to warn your First Lord. But some pup with more guts than brains stopped me with a knife."

"So you tried to point me at it," Tavi said. "And hoped I would figure it out for myself. That's why you sent the letter to Gaius like that, too. So that he would investigate the ship and see that the guards weren't actually leaving."

Varg let out a growl that somehow sounded affirmative. "Didn't work. So I brought you here."

Tavi tilted his head and studied Varg closely. "Why?"

"Why what?"

"Why expose this to us at all? You are an enemy of my people."

Varg looked at Tavi for a moment, then said, "Yes. And one day my people will come for you, pup. And when I rip the throat from your First Lord, it will be on the battlefield, when I have burned your lands, destroyed your homes, and slain your warriors—and you. There will be no secrets. No sorcery. No betrayal. One day I will tear the belly from the whole of your breed, Aleran. And you will see me coming all the while."

Tavi swallowed, suddenly very afraid.

Varg continued. "I have no stomach for Sarl's methods. He would sacrifice the lives of my pack for the sake of a treachery he thinks will give us your lands. He defies my authority. He makes pacts with unknown forces employing strange witcheries. He would rob our victory of honor, of passion." Varg held up the claws of its right hand and regarded them for a moment. "I won't have it."

"He wants you dead, too," Tavi pointed out.

Varg's teeth showed again. "But I found him out too late.

All but two of my battlepack had already been bewitched. They are now gone. They will hunt me. They may well kill me. But I will not let Sarl say that he bested me entirely. So the next step is yours, pup."

"Me?" Tavi asked.

Varg nodded and growled, "There is not much time before Sarl moves. And we both know that even if I spoke to Gaius, he would be slow to believe me." Varg pulled up the hood on his cloak and strode to a side passage leading off from the long gallery. "It will not be long before Sarl is on my trail. I will lead him away. You are the only one who can stop them now, pup."

Varg vanished into the darkness of the tunnels, leaving the dim scarlet lamp behind.

"Crows," Tavi said weakly. "Why does this keep happening to me?"

CHAPTER 38

Fidelias had to give Steadholder Isana credit: The woman had courage. Only hours ago, she had been wounded in an attack that had killed virtually everyone she knew within the capital. She had missed death by the width of a few fingers and by the fraction of a second it had taken Fidelias to steady his aim on the assassin-archer and release his own shaft. She was, as far as she was concerned, consorting with murderers and traitors to the Realm, even now.

And yet she walked with a quality of quiet dignity as they left the relative security of the room within the brothel. She had covered herself in a large cloak without complaint, though upon entering the raucous main hall of the house, her face had turned a decided shade of pink upon observing the activities there.

"This second-in-command," Isana asked as they walked outdoors. "Will he have the support of your employer?"

Fidelias mused over the woman's choice of words. She could as easily have said, "Lady Aquitaine" and "Lord Aquitaine," but she had not. She had understood that Fidelias had avoided mentioning their names where it might be overheard, and had respected that. It gave him hope that the woman might actually have enough flexibility of thought to work with them.

"Completely," he told her.

"I have conditions," she warned him.

Fidelias nodded. "You will need to take it up at the meeting, Steadholder," he replied. "I'm only a messenger and escort. But I think it likely that some sort of exchange can be negotiated."

Isana nodded within her hood. "Very well. How far must we walk?"

"Not much farther, Steadholder."

Isana let out an exasperated little breath. "I have a name. I'm getting tired of everyone calling me Steadholder."

"Think of it as a compliment," Fidelias advised her. The hairs on the back of his neck abruptly rose, and he forced himself not to turn and stare around like a spooked cat. Someone was following him. He had played the game long enough to know that. For the moment, at least, he did not need to know the details. He had shown his face too often the previous day, and one of any number of opportunists would love to turn him in to the Crown and collect his bounty prize. "No other woman in the Realm can lay claim to the same title."

"No other woman in the Realm knows my recipe for spice-bread, either," Isana said, "but no one says anything about that."

Fidelias turned to smile briefly at her. He used the moment to catch sight of their followers in the corner of his vision. Two of them, large rough types, doubtless river rats for one of the hundreds of riverboats now docked at the city for the festivities. He could see little more than that they were not dressed well, and one of them had a drunken hesitation to his step. "Do you mind if I ask you a question?"

"Yes," she said. "But ask."

"I cannot help but take note that you have no husband, Steadholder. Nor any children. That is . . . unusual, for a woman of our Realm, given the laws. I take it that you did spend your time in the camps when you came of age?"

"Yes," she said, her tone flat. "As the law requires."

"But no children," he said.

"No children," she replied.

"There was a man?" Fidelias asked.

"Yes. A soldier. We were together for a time."

"You bore him a child?"

"I began to. It ended prematurely. He left me shortly after. But the local commander sent me home." She glanced aside at him. "I have fulfilled my duties under the law, sir. Why do you ask?"

"It's something to pass the time," Fidelias said, trying for an amiable smile.

"Something to pass the time while you look for a place to deal with the two men following us, you mean," she said.

Fidelias blinked up at her, for the Steadholder was a hand taller than he and more, but this time his smile was genuine. "You've a remarkable eye for a civilian."

"It isn't my eyes," she said. "Those men are putting off greed and fear like a sheep does stink."

"You can feel them from here?" Fidelias felt himself grow even more impressed with the woman. "They must be fifty feet away. You have a real gift for watercrafting."

"Sometimes I think I would prefer not to have it," she said. "Or at least not quite this much of it." She pressed fingers against her temple. "I do not think I shall go out of my way to visit cities in the future. They're far too loud, even when most are asleep."

"I sympathize to some degree," Fidelias said, and turned their path down a side lane that wandered among several homes and was thick with shadow. "I've seen watercrafters who were unable to maintain their stability when their gifts were as strong as yours."

"Like Odiana," she said.

Fidelias felt disquieted at the mention of the mad water witch's name. He did not care for Odiana. She was too much of an unknown quantity for his liking. "Yes."

"She told me about when she first came into her furies," Isana said. "Frankly, I'm surprised she's as stable as she is."

"Interesting," Fidelias said, and found a nook between two buildings. "She's never spoken to me about it."

"Have you asked?" Isana said.

"Why would I?"

"Because human beings care about one another, sir." She shrugged. "But then, why would you?"

Fidelias felt a faint twist of irritation as the Steadholder's words bit home. His reaction surprised him. For a moment, he considered the possibility that the woman might be speaking more accurately than he was prepared to admit. It had been quite some time since he'd had occasion to behave according to motives other than necessity and self-preservation.

Since the day he had betrayed Amara, in fact.

Fidelias frowned. He hadn't thought of her in some time. In fact, it seemed a bit odd that he had not done so. Perhaps he had been pushing her out of his mind, deliberately forgetting to consider her. But for what reason?

He closed his eyes for a step or two, thinking of the shock on Amara's face when she had been buried to her chin in rough earth, captured by Aquitaine's most capable henchmen. She had deduced his change in loyalties like a true Cursor, but her logic had not prepared her for her emotional reaction. When she accused him, when he admitted that her accusation was true, there had been a flash of expression in her eyes he could not seem to forget. Her eyes had been filled with pain, shocked anger, and sadness.

Something in his chest twisted in a sympathetic reaction, but he ruthlessly forced it away.

He wasn't sure he regretted that he had pushed his emotions so completely aside, and it was that lack of regret that caused him concern. Perhaps the Steadholder was correct. Perhaps he had lost something vital, some spark of life and warmth and empathy that had been extinguished by his betrayal of the Crown and his subsequent actions in the Calderon Valley. Could a man's heart, his soul, perish and yet leave him walking and talking as if alive?

Again, he pushed the thoughts aside. He had no time for that kind of maudlin introspection now. The bounty hunters had begun to close the distance on Fidelias and Isana.

Fidelias drew his short, heavy bow clear of his cloak and slipped a thick and ugly arrow onto the string. With the practiced speed of a lifetime of experience as an archer and woodcrafter, he turned, drew, and sent his shaft home into the throat of the rearmost bounty hunter.

The bounty hunter's partner let out a shout and charged, evidently unaware that the first man was already dead, Fidelias noted. Amateurs, then. It was an old archer's trick, shooting the rearmost foe so that his companions would continue advancing in the open unaware of the danger instead of scattering for cover. Before the would-be bounty hunter had closed the distance, Fidelias nocked another arrow, drew, and sent the heavy shaft through the charging man's left eye at a range of about five feet.

The man dropped, already dead. He lay on the ground, one leg twitching steadily. The first bounty hunter thrashed around for a few more seconds, his spraying blood spattering on the cobblestones. Then he went still.

Fidelias watched them for a full minute more, then set down his bow, drew his knife, and checked the pulse in their throats to be sure they were dead. He had few doubts that they were, but the professional in him hated sloppy work, and only after he was sure both men were dead, did he take up his bow again.

Perhaps Isana was more right than she knew.

Perhaps he had lost the capacity to feel.

Not that it mattered.

"Steadholder," he said, turning to face her. "We should keep moving."

Isana stared at him in total silence, her face pale. Her schooled mask of confidence was gone, replaced with an expression of sickened horror.

"Steadholder," Fidelias said. "We must leave the streets."

She seemed to shake herself a little. She looked away from him, narrowed her eyes, and assumed her mask again. "Of course," she said. Her voice shook a little. "Lead on."

"Come on," Tavi said. "We've got to go."

"Not yet," Kitai said. She turned to the entry of the tunnel and slipped down into it.

"Crows," Tavi muttered. He set the bottle aside and followed her, hissing, "It drops off on the right. Stay to your left."

He followed Kitai back onto the ledge above the alien chamber, and crouched beside her as she stared down at the *croach*, the slow-moving wax spiders, the motionless Canim.

"By The One," she whispered, her eyes wide. "Aleran, we must go."

Tavi nodded and turned to go.

A wax spider appeared over the rim of the ledge, between them and the way back, and moved with lazy grace down the stone ledge toward Tavi.

Tavi froze. The wax spiders were venomous, but, more to the point, they worked with others of their kind. If this one signaled its companions, they would all come after him together—and while he might escape the slow-moving spiders, he would never outrun the bewitched Canim. He might be able to kill the spider, but not without its alerting the rest of its kind.

He glanced back over his shoulder at Kitai. She could only stare back at him, her eyes wide.

And then the spider's front leg touched lightly down on Tavi's hand, and he had to clench his teeth over a scream.

The spider stopped, luminous eyes whirling. It touched his hand with one forelimb for a moment, then used two of its front legs to gently run over his arm and shoulders. He remained rigidly still. The spider's limbs traced lightly over him, darting from his skin to the underside of his head and back several times, before it simply moved forward, stepping on his hand, elbow, then shoulder and crawled over him without attacking, without raising its whistling alarm cry, and without seeming otherwise to notice him.

Tavi turned his head slowly, only to watch the spider repeat its performance upon Kitai, then glide over her and down to the end of the ledge where it crouched and vomited out a patch of pale green *croach*, which it then began spreading over the ledge.

Tavi traded a long stare with Kitai, perplexed, and wasted no more time in heading back into the tunnel and away from the *croach*-filled cavern.

"Why did it do that?" Tavi blurted as soon as he had left the tunnel. "Kitai, it should have raised a warning and attacked. Why didn't it?"

Kitai emerged from the tunnel a second later, and even in the sullen light of the Canim lamp, he could see that she was pale and trembling violently.

Tavi stood absolutely motionless for a second. "Kitai?" he asked.

She rose, her arms wrapping around herself as if cold, and her eyes did not focus upon anything. "It must not be," she whispered. "It must not be."

Tavi reached out to her, laying his hand upon her arm. "What must not be?"

She looked up at him, her expression fragile. "Aleran. If . . . the old tales. If my people's tales are correct. Then these are the vord."

"Um," Tavi said. "The what?"

"The vord," Kitai whispered, and shuddered as she did. "The devourers. The eaters of worlds, Aleran."

"I haven't ever heard of them."

"No," Kitai said. "If you had, your cities would lie in ashes and ruin. Your people would be running. Hunted. As ours were."

"What are you talking about?"

"Not here, Aleran. We must go back." Her voice rose in panic. "We cannot stay here."

"All right," Tavi said, trying to sound soothing. "All right. Come on." He took up Varg's lamp and headed back up out of the Deeps, looking for the markings he'd left on the walls at intersections as they walked.

It took Kitai several moments to slow her breathing again. Then she said, "Long ago, our people lived elsewhere. Not in the lands we have today. Once we lived in a manner like your own people. In settlements. In cities."

Tavi arched an eyebrow. "I've never heard that. I didn't think your folk had any cities."

"No," Kitai said. "Not anymore."

"What happened to them?"

"The vord came," Kitai said. "They took many of our people. Took them as you saw those wolf-creatures in that cavern. They, too, had been taken."

"Taken," Tavi said. "You mean controlled? Enslaved, somehow?"

"More than that," she said. "The wolf-creatures you saw have been devoured. Everything within them that made them who they were is gone. Their spirit has been consumed, Aleran. Only the spirit of the vord remains—and the taken are without pain, or fear, or weakness. The vord spirit gives them great strength."

Tavi frowned. "But why would the vord do such a thing?"

"Because that is what they do. They spawn. Make more of themselves. They take, devour or destroy all life, until there is nothing else under the sky. They create themselves into new lives, new forms." She shuddered. "Our people have kept the tales of them. Dozens of horrible stories, Aleran, preserved over lifetimes beyond knowing. The kind that make even Marat stay close to their fires and huddle shivering in their blankets at night."

"Why keep those stories, then?" he asked.

"To help us remember them," Kitai said. "Twice, the vord all but destroyed our people, leaving only small bands running for their lives. Though it was long ago, we keep the stories to warn us should they come again." She bit her lip. "And now they have."

"How do you know? I mean, Kitai. If the Marat have worked so hard to remember them, why didn't you just point at them two years ago, and say, 'Oh look, it's the vord'?"

She let out an impatient hiss. "Am I speaking only to myself?" she demanded. "I told you, Aleran. They renew and reshape their forms. They are shapechangers. Each time the vord destroyed my people, they appeared as something different."

"Then how do you know it's them?"

"By the signs," she said. "Folk going missing. Being taken. The vord begin their work in secret, so that they are not discovered before they have a chance to multiply and spread. They strive to divide those who oppose them so that their enemies may be weakened." She shuddered. "And they are led by their queens, Aleran. I understand it only now: That creature, the one from within the heart of the Valley of Silence, the one you burned—it was the vord queen."

Tavi paused to look for the next marking. "I think I saw it. Here."

"In the cavern?"

"Yes. It was covered in a cloak, and issuing orders to a Cane who had not been . . . been . . ." He made a vague gesture.

"Taken," Kitai said.

"Taken." Tavi told her about the conversation between the cloaked figure and Sarl.

Kitai nodded. "You saw it. The vord plans to kill your headman. It wishes to create enough chaos to increase their numbers without being noticed. Until it is too late."

Tavi found his paces quickening. "Crows. Could they do such a thing?"

"The second time they ravaged my people, we were not able to stop them—and we had faced them before. Your people know nothing of them. So they seek to weaken you, divide you."

"The vord queen is using Sarl," Tavi murmured. "Divide and conquer. He provided her with soldiers to begin her work, and his caste has been hurling storms at Gaius in order to weaken him and force him to spend most nights in his meditation chamber, so that they have an idea of where he will be when they try to kill him. And the queen knows that if Alera is weakened, the Canim will attack us. She wants the Canim to attack and weaken us further—and in the process they will take losses as well. They'll leave themselves more vulnerable to the vord."

Kitai nodded. "In our tales they turned our peoples upon one another in much the same way."

"Crows," he swore quietly. Tavi thought of the long stair

down to the First Lord's meditation chamber. After the first guard station, there were no other entrances or exits from the stairwell or the chambers below.

It was a death trap.

Tavi walked even faster. "They know where Gaius is. Twenty Canim might be able to fight their way to him. We have to stop them."

Kitai kept pace. "We will warn your warriors, lead them here, and destroy the vord."

"Sir Miles," Tavi said.

Kitai looked at him blankly.

"He's a war leader," Tavi clarified. "But I'm not sure he'll attack."

"Why would he not?"

Tavi clenched his jaw and pressed ahead, in a hurry but not stupid enough to go sprinting through the tunnels until he was hopelessly lost. "Because he doesn't like me very much. He might not believe me. And if I tell him I got the information from a Marat, I'll be lucky if he only storms out of the room."

"He hates us," Kitai said.

"Yes."

"Madness," Kitai said. "The vord are a threat to one and all."

"Sir Miles will understand that, too," Tavi said. "Eventually. I'm just not sure there's enough time for him to be stubborn." Tavi shook his head. "Maestro Killian is the one to convince. If I do that, he'll order Miles to do it."

They reached the last marking Tavi had left on the wall and entered familiar tunnels again. Tavi picked up his pace to an easy run, mind racing over what he had to do, how best to get it done.

He registered a sudden motion in front of him, and he flinched to one side just as a hooded attacker with a heavy truncheon appeared from behind a veil of furycrafting and swung it at him. The club glanced off his left arm, and Tavi felt it go suddenly numb. Kitai snarled somewhere behind him. Tavi hit the wall, stumbled, and barely managed to keep from falling. He drew his knife and turned to confront the attacker, just in time to see the truncheon in motion only inches from his face.

There was a flashing burst of bright lights, then everything went black.

Dawn had not yet come when Amara and Bernard woke together. They shared a slow, soft kiss, then without a word they both rose and began to don their arms and armor. Just as they finished, there was a step outside the makeshift room, and Doroga pushed the curtain of cloaks aside. The Marat's broad, ugly face was grim.

"Bernard," he rumbled. "It is dawn. They come."

CHAPTER 41

Isana accompanied the assassin to a wine club on a quiet, dimly lit section of Mastercraft Lane, where the finest craftsmen in all of Alera plied their trades to the wealthy clientele of the city. The wine club itself was located between a small complex of buildings specializing in statuary and a furylampmaker's workshop. There was no sign over its door, no indication that it was anything but a service entrance or possibly the entrance to a countinghouse or some other business that did not require walk-in customers.

Despite the late hour, the door opened promptly when the assassin knocked, and a liveried servant conducted them down a hall and into a private room without speaking to them.

The room was cozy and lavishly appointed—a circle of small divans meant to be lounged upon on one's side while chatting and sipping wine. One of the divans was occupied.

Invidia Aquitaine lay upon her side, beautiful in the same silk gown she had worn at Kalare's fete. A crystal goblet in her hand was half-filled with a pale wine. Additionally, she wore a translucent drape of fabric over her features—a veil, Isana judged, meant to provide the legal pretense of anonymity should the evening's discussion somehow come under the scrutiny of the law.

Lady Aquitaine looked up as they entered and inclined her head pleasantly. "Welcome, Steadholder. I presume that my associate talked you into the meeting."

"He was persuasive—under the circumstances," Isana replied.

Lady Aquitaine gestured toward the divan across from her. "Please, relax. Would you care for a taste of wine? This is an excellent vintage."

Isana stepped over to the indicated divan but did not recline upon it. Instead, she sat upon its very edge, her back rigidly straight, and frowned at Lady Aquitaine. "I've no stomach for most wine," she replied. "Thank you."

Lady Aquitaine's pleasant smile faded into a neutral mask. "This might be easier for you if you indulged somewhat in the pleasantries, Steadholder. They do no harm."

"Nor serve any purpose, except to waste time," Isana replied. "And time is of importance to me at the moment. I came here to discuss business."

"As you wish," Lady Aquitaine replied. "Where would you like to begin?"

"Tell me what you want," Isana said. "What would you have of me?"

She took a slow sip of wine. "First, your public support of Aquitaine and my lord husband," she said, "who would become your political patron. It means that you would appear in public wearing the colors of Aquitaine—particularly at the presentation at the conclusion of Festival. You may be asked to attend dinners, social functions, that sort of thing, with my husband providing transport and covering any of your expenses."

"I work for a living," Isana said. "And I am responsible for a steadholt with more than thirty families in it. I'd do poor service to them constantly running off to social occasions."

"True. Shall we negotiate upon a reasonable number of days each year, then?"

Isana pressed her lips together and nodded, forcing herself to contain her emotions carefully.

"Fine. We'll work that out. Secondly, I would require your support as a member of the Dianic League, which would require you to attend a convocation of the League once each year and engage in written discourse over the course of the rest of the year."

"And within the League, you wish me to support you."

"Naturally," Lady Aquitaine said. "And finally, we may ask you to support certain candidates for the Senatorial elections in Riva. As your home city, you will be able to vote in the elections, and your opinion will inevitably carry some weight with your fellow Citizens."

"I want something understood, Your Grace," Isana said quietly.

"What might that be?"

"That I know full well the extent of you and your husband's ambitions, and have no intention of breaking the laws of the Realm to help you. My support and participation will extend as far as the letter of the law—and not an inch farther."

Lady Aquitaine raised both eyebrows. "Of course. I wouldn't dream of asking you for that."

"I'm sure," Isana said. "I simply want us to understand one another."

"I think we do," Lady Aquitaine replied. "And what would you ask in return for your support?"

Isana drew in a deep breath. "My family is in danger, Your Grace. I came here to contact the First Lord and get help sent back to Calderon, and to warn my nephew of a potential threat to his life. I have been unable to contact either of them on my own. If you would have my support, then you must help me protect my kin. That is my price."

Lady Aquitaine took another slow sip of wine. "I shall need to know more about what you require, Steadholder, before I can make any promises. Please explain the circumstances in greater detail."

Isana nodded, then began to recount everything Doroga had told them about the vord, the way they spread, where they had gone, and the danger they represented to the whole of the Realm. When she finished, she folded her hands in her lap and regarded the High Lady.

"That's . . . quite a tale," she murmured. "How certain are you of its truth?"

"Completely," Isana said.

"Even though what you know of it came from, if I understand you correctly, a barbarian chieftain."

"His name is Doroga," Isana said quietly. "He is a man of integrity and intelligence. And his wounds were real enough."

Lady Aquitaine murmured, "Fidelias, what assets have we near Calderon?"

The assassin spoke up from where he had taken an unobtrusive position against the wall beside the door. "The Windwolves are on training maneuvers in the Red Hills, Your Grace."

"That's . . . twenty Knights?"

"Sixty, Your Grace," he corrected her.

"Oh, that's right," she said, her tone careless, though Isana did not believe for a moment that she hadn't remembered precisely what resources she had, and where. "They've been recruiting. How long would it take them to reach Calderon?"

"As little as three hours, Your Grace, or as long as seven, depending upon wind currents."

Lady Aquitaine nodded. "Then please inform His Grace, when you report to him, that I am dispatching them to the relief and reinforcement of Calderon's garrison on behalf of our new client."

Fidelias regarded her for a moment, then said, "Lord Riva might not appreciate our sending troops into action in his own holdings."

"If Riva was doing his job, his own troops would already be there to reinforce the garrison," Lady Aquitaine said. "I am quite certain he would much rather snub the new Count Calderon than respond with a swift and expensive mobilization, and I should dearly love to openly humiliate Riva in front of all the Realm. But assure my husband that I will order the men to keep the lowest profile possible, and thereby only humiliate him in front of all the peerage.

The assassin smirked. "Very good, Your Grace."

She nodded. "The next order of business will be to find the Steadholder's nephew and make sure that he is safe from both this vord creature and from Kalare's bloodcrows."

"Alleged bloodcrows, Your Grace," Fidelias corrected her. "After all, we don't know for a fact that they belong to Lord Kalare."

Lady Aquitaine gave Fidelias an arch look. "Oh yes. How thoughtless of me. I presume you have Kalare's holdings in the capital under surveillance?"

Fidelias gave her a mildly reproachful look.

"Of course you do. Find out what your watchers have seen most recently and put absolutely anyone you can spare on this matter at once. Secure the boy and ensure his safety."

He ducked his head into a polite bow. "Yes, Your Grace. Though if I may offer a thought before I leave?"

Lady Aquitaine waved her hand in an acquiescing gesture.

The assassin nodded. "My investigation since arriving here revealed a pattern of unusual activity in the Deeps. A significant number of people have gone missing over the winter, and in my judgment it wasn't as a result of infighting between the local criminal interests. These creatures the Marat warned about could be involved."

Lady Aquitaine arched an eyebrow. "Do you really think so?"

Fidelias shrugged. "It certainly seems possible. But the Deeps are extensive, and given our limitations in manpower, it would require a considerable amount of time to search them."

Lady Aquitaine flicked her finger in a gesture of negation. "No, that will not be for us to accomplish. The security of the Deeps will certainly be of concern to the Royal Guard and Crown Legion. We will advise them of the potential danger at the first opportunity. For now, focus on the boy. He is our interest here."

"Yes, my lady." The assassin inclined his head to her, nodded to Isana, and departed the room.

Isana sat in silence for a moment and found her heart pounding too swiftly. She felt her hands shaking and clasped them together, only to feel a clammy sweat prickling over her brow, her cheeks.

Lady Aquitaine sat up, frowning as she stared at Isana. "Steadholder? Are you unwell?"

"I am fine," she murmured, then swallowed a bitter taste from her mouth, and added, "my lady."

Lady Aquitaine frowned, but nodded to her. "I'll need to go shortly in order to contact our field commander via water."

Isana paused in startled shock. She herself had been able to send Rill out through the streams of most of the Calderon Valley—but that was largely because she had lived there for so long and knew the local furies so well. With effort, Isana could perhaps have communicated through Rill as far as Garrison, but Lady Aquitaine was casually speaking about sending her furies five hundred times as far as the extreme limits of Isana's talents.

Lady Aquitaine regarded Isana for a moment more, before saying, "You really do believe that they are in mortal danger. Your family."

"They are," Isana said simply.

Lady Aquitaine nodded slowly. "You would never have come to me, otherwise."

"No," Isana said. "No, I would not."

"Do you hate me?" she asked.

Isana took a slow breath before answering, "I hate what you represent."

"And what is that?"

"Power without conviction," Isana replied, her tone lifeless, matter-of-fact. "Ambition without conscience. Decent folk suffer at the hands of those like you."

"And Gaius?" Lady Aquitaine asked. "Do you hate the First Lord?"

"With every beat of my heart," Isana replied. "But that is for a different reason entirely."

Lady Aquitaine made a noise in her throat to indicate that she was listening and nodded, but Isana did not continue. After a moment of silence, the High Lady nodded again, and said, "You seem to be one who appreciates forthright honesty. So I will offer you that. I regret what happened in Calderon two years ago," she said. "It was a senseless waste of life. I opposed it to my husband, but I do not rule his decisions."

"You opposed it out of the goodness of your heart?" Isana asked. She tasted the faint sarcasm on her words.

"I opposed it because it was inefficient and could too easily fail and recoil upon us," she said. "I would much prefer to gain power through the building of solid alliances and loyalties, without resorting to violence."

Isana frowned at her. "Why should I believe you?"

"Because I'm telling you the truth," Lady Aquitaine said. "Gaius is old, Steadholder. There is no need for violence to remove him from the throne. Time will eventually play the assassin for us, and he has no heir. Those in the strongest position to rule when Gaius passes may be able to assume the throne without allowing matters to devolve into an armed struggle for power." She offered Isana her hand. "Which is why I am quite serious when I tell you that your loyalty places upon me an obligation to protect your family as if it was my own. And I will do so by every means at my disposal." She nodded to her hand. "Take it and see. I'll not hide myself from you."

Isana stared at the High Lady for a moment. Then she reached out and took her hand. She felt nothing for a second, then there was a sudden gentle pressure of emotion from Lady Aquitaine.

"Are you telling me the truth?" Isana asked her quietly. "Do you intend to help me and my kin?"

"I am," Lady Aquitaine said. "I do."

Through their clasped hands, Isana felt Lady Aquitaine's presence as a subtle vibration on the air, and her words rang with the clarity of truth and confidence. It was not an affectation of furycrafting. That tone of truth was not something that could be falsified, not to someone of Isana's skill. Lady Aquitaine might have been able to conceal falsehoods behind vague clouds of disinterest and detached calm, but there was the quivering power of sincerity in her statements, and nothing cloudy about it.

She might be ambitious, calculating, relentless, and merciless—but Invidia Aquitaine meant what she said. She fully intended to do everything in her power to help Bernard, to protect Tavi.

Isana shuddered and could not stop a slow sob of relief from surging through her. The past days had been a nightmare of blood and fear and helpless frustration, a struggle to reach the man with the power to protect her family. She had reached Lady Aquitaine instead.

But, Isana realized, if Invidia could do as she claimed, if she could make certain that Bernard and Tavi were safe, then Isana would have no choice but to return that loyalty in good faith. She would become a part of something meant to tear down the First Lord, and willingly, if that was the price for protecting her own. She had committed herself.

But that didn't matter. As long as Tavi and her brother were safe, it was worth the price.

Lady Aquitaine said nothing, and did not withdraw her hand, until Isana finally looked up again. The High Lady then rose, glanced down at her gown, and frowned at it until its color darkened from scarlet to a red so deep it was almost black and better suited to avoiding notice in the night. Then she regarded Isana with cool eyes not entirely devoid of compassion, and said, "I must see to our communications, Steadholder. I've arranged for you to be taken under guard to my manor, where quarters await you. I will bring you word of your brother and your nephew the moment I have it."

Isana rose. Her head's pounding had eased significantly, and the lack of pain was a powerful soporific. She wanted little more than to get some rest. "Of course, my lady," she said quietly.

"Come with me, then," she said. "I'll walk you to the coach."

Isana followed Lady Aquitaine out of the building and found a coach waiting outside. It featured positions for half a dozen footmen, and each was occupied by an armed man with a hard expression and confident hands. Lady Aquitaine steadied Isana with one hand as she mounted the steps into the coach, and the footman closed the door behind her.

"Rest if you are able," Lady Aquitaine said, making a curt gesture to the night with one hand. A tall grey steed walked amicably out of the darkness, stopping to nuzzle Lady Aquitaine's shoulder. She pushed the beast's head away from her dress with an expression of annoyed fondness. "I will do all in my power to act immediately, and I will do everything I am able to get immediate word to the First Lord regarding the dangers here and in Calderon. You have my promise."

"Thank you," Isana said.

"Do not thank me, Steadholder," Lady Aquitaine said. "I do not offer this to you as a gift of patron to client. We have entered into a contract as peers—and one that I hope will benefit us both for years to come."

"As you wish, my lady."

Lady Aquitaine mounted gracefully, inclined her head to Isana, and said to the driver, "Martus, be cautious. Hired cutters have already sought her life once this night."

"Yes, Your Grace," the driver answered. "We'll see her there safe."

"Excellent." Lady Aquitaine turned her horse and set off at a brisk trot down the street, veil and gown flowing around her. One of the footmen drew down heavy leather curtains over the side of the coach, plunging it into darkness and preventing anyone from getting a look at its passenger. The driver clucked to his team, and the coach jolted into motion down the streets.

Isana leaned her head back against a cushion and lay limp, too exhausted to do more. She'd done it. She had paid a price that she knew would haunt her, but it was done. Help was on its way to Tavi and Bernard. Everything else was immaterial.

She was asleep before the coach was out of sight of the wine club.

CHAPTER 42

Tavi woke up with his head pounding, but his instincts screamed warnings, and he most carefully did not move or alter the patterns of his breathing. If he was still alive, it meant that his captors intended him to be that way. Announcing that he was alert would profit him nothing. Instead, he kept himself limp and passive and sought to learn whatever he could about his surroundings and his captors.

He was sitting in a chair. He could feel the hard wood under him, and his legs were bound, one to each leg of the chair. His elbows rested at the right height for the arms of a chair, though he could not feel his hands. He surmised that his wrists were bound, and that his bonds had cut off the circulation to his hands.

He could hear the creaking of wood around him. Most of the buildings in the city were constructed of stone. The only wooden structures were outside the walls of the capital itself, or else were the storage houses and shipwrights down at Riverside. He took part of a breath through his nose and caught the faint smell of water and fish. The river, then, and not outside the capital's walls. He was in a warehouse or a shipwright's—or, he amended, upon a ship. The Gaul was a wide, deep river, the largest in all Alera, and even deepwater vessels could sail up it to the capital.

"Were you able to fix him?" growled a male voice. From the sound of it, it was coming to him from an adjacent room, or possibly from the other side of a thin door or heavy screen. The voice itself had the quality of one shut indoors. His captors, then, most likely.

"I stopped the bleeding," said a voice, a woman's. It had an odd accent, from somewhere in the south of the Realm, Tavi thought, perhaps Forcian. "He'll have to see a professional about getting his nose back, though."

The man let out a laugh that had nothing to do with merriment. "That's rich. Serves him right for letting a little girl get to him."

There was an oppressive silence.

"You aren't little, Rook," the man said, his tone defensive.

"Bear in mind," Rook said, "that the girl is a Marat. They are physically stronger than most Alerans."

"Must be good exercise, bedding all those animals," he said.

"Thank you, Turk, for reminding me why some of us attend to the jobs that require intelligence, while others are restricted to the use of knives and clubs."

Turk snorted. "I get the job done."

"Then why is the Steadholder not dead?"

"Someone interfered," Turk said. "And no one told us that the old man was that good with a blade."

"Very true," Rook said. "The armsman protecting the coach was, goodness, skilled at arms. I can see why you were taken off guard."

Turk growled out a vitriolic curse. "I got the boy, didn't I?"

"Yes. The old crow might even decide not to make you sorry you weren't with the men at Nedus's manor."

"Don't worry," Turk said, sullen. "I'll get her."

"For your sake, I hope you are correct," Rook said. "If you will excuse me."

"You're not staying? I thought you were done."

"Try not to think too much," she said. "It doesn't do anyone any favors. I have a few loose ends to trim before I go."

"What do you want us to do with these two?"

"Keep them until the old crow arrives to question them. And before you ask, the answer is no. You aren't to touch either one of them meanwhile. He'll tell you how he wants you to handle it afterward."

"One of these days," Turk said in an ugly tone, "someone is going to shut your mouth for you."

"Possibly. But not today. And never you."

A door opened and closed, and Tavi chanced a quick peek up through the veil of his hair. He was in a storage house, surrounded by wooden shipping crates. A muscular, ill-favored man, dressed in a sleeveless river rat's tunic, stood glaring at the door as it closed. To Tavi's right, there was another chair, and Kitai was tied into hers just as he was into his—except that she'd had a leather satchel drawn over her head and tied loosely shut around her neck.

Tavi lowered his head again, and a second later Turk, the ugly man, turned and walked across the floor toward him. Tavi remained still as the man pressed fingers against his throat, grunted, and stepped over to Kitai. Tavi opened an eye enough to see him touch her wrist, then turn and stalk out of the warehouse. He slammed the door shut behind him, and Tavi heard a heavy bolt sliding into place.

Tavi agonized for a moment over what to do. The place may have had some sort of furycrafted guardian set to watch him—but on the other hand, the presence of any kind of formidable guardian would have drawn the attention of the Civic Legion's furycrafters, who regularly inspected the warehouses in Riverside. That meant that if there were any furies set to watch him, they would probably only raise the alarm, rather than attacking.

Tavi tested his bonds, but there was not an inch of the ropes that were not inescapably tight. If he'd been conscious when tied, he could have attempted to keep his muscles tight so that when he relaxed them there would have been some margin of slack in the ropes to allow him to wriggle out of them. But it hadn't happened that way, and there seemed little he could do now.

Even if he had been free, it might not have done him any good. There was only one door to the storage house—the one Turk had just walked out. Tavi tested his chair. It wasn't fastened down, and the legs thumped quietly on the floorboards as he wiggled back and forth.

Kitai's head jerked up, lifting the leather satchel. Her voice was muffled. "Aleran?"

"I'm here," he said.

"You are all right?"

"Got a headache I'm going to remember for a while," he responded. "You?"

She made a spitting sound from inside the hood. "A bad taste in my mouth. Who were those men?"

"They were talking about trying to kill my aunt Isana," Tavi said. "They probably work for Lord Kalare."

"Why did they take us?"

"I'm not sure," he said. "Maybe because getting rid of me will make Gaius look weak. Maybe to use me to try to lure Aunt Isana into a trap. Either way, they aren't going to let us go after this is over."

"They will kill us," she said.

"Yes."

"Then we must escape."

"That would follow, yes," Tavi said. He tensed up, testing his bonds again, but they were secure. "It's going to take me hours to get out of these. Can you get loose?"

She shifted her weight back and forth, and Tavi heard the wood of her chair creaking under the strain. "Perhaps," she said, after a moment. "But it will be loud. Are we guarded?"

"The guard left the building, but there might be furies watching us. And the men who took us won't be far away."

The satchel tilted suddenly, and Kitai said, "Aleran, someone comes."

Tavi dropped his head forward again, as it had been when he awoke, and a second later the bolt rattled and the door opened. Tavi caught a quick glimpse of Turk and another, taller man entering the warehouse.

". . . sure you can see that we'll have her before sunrise, my lord," Turk was saying in an unctuous tone. "You can't listen to everything Rook has to say."

The other man spoke, and Tavi had to force himself not to move. "No?" asked Lord Kalare. "Turk, Turk, Turk. If Rook had not asked me to give you a second chance, I'd have killed you when we came through the door."

"Oh," Turk mumbled. "Yes, my lord."

"Where is he?" Kalare asked. Turk must have answered with a gesture, because a moment later, footsteps approached. From a few feet in front of him, Tavi heard Kalare say, "He's unconscious."

"Rook rang his bells pretty good," Turk replied. "But there shouldn't be any lasting damage, my lord. He'll be awake in the morning."

"And this?" Kalare asked.

"Barbarian," said Turk. "She was with the other one."

Kalare grunted. "Why is she hooded?"

"She put up a fight before we got her bound. She bit Cardis's nose off."

"Off?" asked Kalare.

"Yes, my lord."

Kalare chuckled. "Amusing. The spirited ones always are."

"Rook said to ask you what you wanted done with them, my lord. Shall I detach them?"

"Turk," Kalare said, his tone pleased. "You've employed a euphemism. Next thing you know, you'll be showing signs of sagacity."

Turk was silent for a blank second, then said, "Thank you?"

Kalare sighed. "Do nothing yet," he said. "Live bait will do us more good than a corpse."

"And the barbarian?"

"Her, too. There's a chance she's the result of some kind of fosterage agreement between the barbarians and Count Calderon, and until there is leisure to extract the information from them, there's little point in making myself a blood enemy of the Marat. Not until it will profit me."

Suddenly fingers tangled in Tavi's hair, painfully strong, and jerked his face up. Tavi managed to keep himself totally limp.

"This little beast," Kalare said. "If the woman wasn't a greater threat, I think I would enjoy seeing him flayed and thrown into a pit of slives. That such a waste of a life could have dared to lay a finger on *my* heir." His voice shook with anger and disdain, and he released Tavi's hair with a flick of his wrist that made the muscles in Tavi's neck scream.

"Shall I arrange for his transport, my lord?"

Kalare exhaled. "No," he decided. "No. There's no point in giving him a chance to survive, given what I have planned for his family. Even something like this could grow into a threat, given time. We'll throw them all into the same hole."

His boots thudded on the floor as he walked back to the door. Turk's heavier, clumsier steps followed, and the door opened and closed again, the bolt fastening.

Tavi checked to make sure that they were alone, then said to Kitai, "You bit off his *nose*?"

Her voice was muffled by the satchel as she replied. "I couldn't reach his eyes."

"Thank you for the warning."

"No," she said. "I said someone was coming. I didn't mean through the door."

"What?"

"The floor," she said. "I felt a vibration. There, again," she murmured.

Tavi could hardly feel his feet, but he heard a faint, scraping noise from somewhere behind him. He twisted his head enough to see a floorboard a few feet away quiver and then suddenly bow upward, as if made from supple, living willow rather than dried oak. He saw someone beneath the floor work the floorboard free and draw it down out of sight. Two more floorboards followed it, and then a head covered with a shock of tousled and dusty hair emerged from the hole in the floorboards and blinked owlishly around.

"Ehren," Tavi said, and he had to labor to control his excitement and keep his voice down. "What are you doing?"

"I think I'm rescuing you," Ehren replied.

"There are guards here," Tavi told his friend. "They'll sense what you've done to get in here."

"I don't think so," Ehren said. He gave Tavi a shaky smile. "For once it's a good thing my furies are so weak, huh? They don't make much noise." He winced and began to wriggle up through the hole in the floor.

"How did you find us?" Tavi asked.

Ehren looked wounded. "Tavi. I've been training to be a Cursor as long as you have, after all."

Tavi flashed him a fierce grin, which Ehren struggled to return as he gave up on crawling up through the hole, and lowered himself to start passing a hand steadily over another of the boards, which quivered and slowly began to bend. "I was out asking questions, and I noticed that a man was following me. It stood to reason that whoever took your aunt might have an interest in following me around. So I went back up to the Citadel, turned around once I was out of his sight—"

"And tailed him back here," Tavi said.

Ehren coaxed the board into bending still more. "I swam out under the pier and listened to a couple of men talking about the prisoners. I thought maybe it could have been your aunt, so I decided to take a look."

"Well done, Ehren," Tavi said.

Ehren smiled. "Well. It was sort of a happy accident, wasn't it? Here, almost got it."

The board creaked and began to move, when Kitai hissed, "The door."

The bolt on the warehouse door rattled, and the door opened.

Ehren hissed and dropped down into the hole and out of sight, except for the white-knuckled fingers of one hand, holding the warped board flat against the floor with his weight.

Tavi licked his lips, thinking furiously. If he remained inert, the guards would have nothing better to do than notice the missing boards.

He lifted his head to face Turk. The broad-chested man wore a curved Kalaran gutting knife on his belt, and his eyes were stormy. Behind him walked a lean, skinny man in the same river sailor's clothing, and another curved knife rode on his belt. He was bald and looked as though he had been made from lengths of knotted rawhide—and his nose was missing. Watercrafting had left what remained a shade of fresh pink, but it gave him a skeletal look, his naval cavities reduced to a pair of oblong slits in his face. Cardis, then.

"Well," Turk said. "Look at that. Kid's awake."

"So what?" Cardis snarled, stalking over to the bound and hooded Kitai. He tore off the leather hood, took a fistful of the girl's hair, and savagely tore it out of her scalp. "I don't give a bloody crow about the boy."

Kitai's eyes blazed with emerald fire, something wild and furious rising up behind them. Her face bore bruises on one cheek, and dried blood clung in brown-black clots to the lower half of her face.

"Don't touch her!" Tavi snarled.

Cardis almost idly dealt Tavi's face a sharp, stinging blow with his open hand, then turned back to Kitai.

The Marat girl stared at Cardis without flinching or making a sound, then deliberately slipped her tongue between her lips and licked at the blood on her upper lip, a slow and defiant smile crossing her face.

Cardis's eyes went flat and dangerous.

"Cardis," Turk snapped. "We're not to harm either of them."

The other man stared down at Kitai and tore out another heavy lock of hair. "So we don't mark them up. Who's to know?"

Turk growled, "My orders are from the old crow himself. If I let you cross him, he'll kill you. And then he'll kill me for not stopping you."

Cardis's voice rose to a furious scream as he gestured at his face. "Do you *see* what that little bitch did to me? Do you expect me to just stand here and *take* that?"

"I expect you to follow orders," Turk spat.

"Or what?"

"You know what."

Cardis bared his teeth and drew his knife. "I've had about as much of this dung as I'm going to take for one day."

Turk drew his knife as well, eyes narrowed. He flicked a glance aside at Tavi, then his eyes paused on the floor behind them. "Bloody crows," he muttered. "Look at this." He took a couple of steps to stand over the hole in the floor.

"What?" Cardis asked, though his voice was less angry.

"Looks like someone is trying to—"

Ehren's head and shoulders popped up out of the hole, and the little scribe drove his knife straight down through Turk's heavy leather boot and the foot inside it to bury its tip in the floor. Turk let out a startled cry and tried to dodge, but his pinned foot could not move with him, and he fell to the ground.

Kitai let out a sudden and bloodcurdling howl of primal wrath. Her body jerked once, twice, and the chair she was tied to shattered into pieces still attached to her limbs. She swung one arm in a broad arc, and smashed the heavy wooden arm of the chair still tied to her wrist into Cardis's knife arm. The knife tumbled free and rang as it hit the floor.

Ehren shouted and the fourth board popped free. Then he swarmed up out of the hole in the floor and started kicking Turk in the head. Turk managed to slash clumsily at Ehren's leg with his curved knife, and scored. Ehren staggered back, his leg unable to support his weight. He fell to the ground just behind Tavi, scrambled to seize Cardis's dropped knife, and hacked desperately at Tavi's bonds.

Tavi saw Turk jerk the dagger impaling his foot clear of his flesh, toss the knife into a half flip, seize the blade, and fling it at Ehren's back.

"Down!" Tavi snarled. Ehren might not have been physically imposing, but the young scribe was quick. He dropped to the floor and the flung knife struck flat against the back of Tavi's chair and clattered down.

The ropes came free from his arms as Turk charged toward them. Tavi hopped in the chair to twist it around, then overbalanced himself to land hard on his side. He'd been too slow. Turk darted in with his curved Kalaran knife.

Kitai let out a shriek and swung at Turk. She missed, but it forced the man to dodge and bought Tavi a precious second. He seized Ehren's knife from the floor and turned just as Turk seized his hair. The knife flashed down. Tavi blocked the slash by interposing his forearm with Turk's wrist, simultaneously slashing up with his knife.

The blow whipped across Turk's inside upper thigh and bit deep. Blood sprayed.

Kitai seized Turk from behind, her encumbered hands gripping the back of his skull and the point of his chin. She howled and twisted her body in a sudden, savage motion, and broke the man's neck. He fell in a jellylike heap to the floorboards. Kitai promptly seized Turk's knife in one hand and ripped his shirt clear of his chest with the other, her eyes wild, focused on his heart as she drove the knife down and started cutting.

"Kitai," Tavi panted, cutting the bonds on his legs free. "Kitai!"

Her face snapped up toward him, a terrifying mask of rage and blood. Blood dripped from the curved knife, and the fingers of her other hand were already set inside the opening she had cut, ready to tear the body open and take the heart.

"Kitai," Tavi said again, more quietly. "Listen to me. Please. You can't do this. There's no time."

She stared, frozen, the wild light in her eyes fluttering uncertainly.

"My legs," he said. "I can't feel them. I need you to help me get out of here before more of them come."

Her eyes narrowed with an anticipation that was almost lustful. "More. Let them come."

"No," Tavi said. "We have to leave. Kitai, I need to cut you loose. Give me the knife." He offered her his hand.

She stared at him, and the wild energy seemed to recede, leaving her panting, bruised, and covered in welts, small cuts, and rope burns. After a second of hesitation, she reversed her grip on the knife and passed him its hilt before kneeling beside him.

"Great furies," Ehren breathed quietly. "Is . . . is that a Marat?"

"Her name is Kitai," Tavi said. "She's my friend." He started cutting the ropes from her as gently as he could. She simply sat, waiting passively, her eyelids drooping lower and lower as the wild and furious energy that had filled her ebbed away.

"Ehren," Tavi said. "Can you walk?"

The other boy blinked, nodded once, and cut cloth from the hem of his tunic. He wound it several times around his calf and tied it off. "Thank goodness they didn't have any furies."

"Maybe they did," Tavi said. "Thugs like that tend to be earthcrafters, and this warehouse is on the pier. They aren't touching the ground. But we've got to get out of here before someone else shows up." He rose and tugged on Kitai's hand. "Come on. Let's go."

She rose, and hardly seemed conscious of her surroundings.

"There's a knotted rope on your left," Ehren said. "Take it down to the water. Go in as quietly as you can and head for shore. I'll be along in a moment."

"What are you going to do?" Tavi asked.

Ehren gave him a tight smile. "Put those boards back and let them wonder what the crows happened in here."

"Good thinking," Tavi said. "Well done." He climbed down to the rope, got his feet steadily on one of the knots, and paused. "Ehren?"

"Yes?"

"What time is it?"

"Not sure," Ehren replied. "The moon's going down, though."

Tavi's flesh went cold and crawled with goose bumps. He started down the rope, encouraging Kitai to follow him, desperate to hurry but forced to move deliberately, quietly, until he was safely away from Lord Kalare's killers.

The moon was going down.

The Canim were coming for the First Lord.

CHAPTER 43

Amara stared out of the mouth of the cave at the taken as the morning light grew. "Why aren't they moving faster? It's as though they want us to come out and slaughter them before they're in position."

"We should already be doing it," grumbled a new voice from behind Amara.

"Giraldi," Bernard growled. "You shouldn't be standing on that leg. Get back with the rest of the wounded."

Amara glanced aside as the centurion limped heavily to the front of the cave to stand beside Bernard, herself, and Doroga. "Yes, sir. Right away, sir." But he found a place on the wall and leaned on it with no evident intention of moving anywhere, and regarded the enemy line of battle—such as it was.

"Giraldi," Bernard said, his voice a warning.

"If we get through this, Count, you can demote me for insubordination if it makes you feel better."

"Fine." Bernard grimaced and nodded reluctantly to Giraldi, then turned to watch the enemy.

The taken had been forming into a column of a width approximately equal to that of the cave's mouth for several minutes. The formation was not complete yet, and the front ranks, well out of bow range even for Bernard and his Knights Flora, consisted of the largest of the taken holders and *legionares*, the youngest and strongest of the men the vord had captured. The queen simply crouched at the head of the column, never moving, unsettling and shapeless in her dark cloak.

"Looks like they're going for quick and dirty," Giraldi growled. "Form up a column and push it right down our throats."

"The taken are very strong," Doroga rumbled. "Even Aleran taken. And we are outnumbered."

"We'll take a stand ten feet down the tunnel," Bernard said. "That will keep our fronts matched, reduce the advantage of numbers." He drew his heel across the dirt floor. "We form the shieldwall here, on this side of the tunnel, and leave the other to Walker and Doroga."

Giraldi grunted. "Three shields across, it looks, sir."

Bernard nodded. "Swords on the front rank. Spears in the next two." He nodded to a slightly raised shelf along one wall that had been used as a place for sleeping mats. "I'll be there with the archers and take what shots we can. We're low on shafts, though, so we'll have to be cautious. And you'll have our Knights Terra on the ground level in front of us, ready to assist either Doroga or the *legionares* if they need the pressure taken off them."

Giraldi nodded. "Nine men fighting at a time. I suggest six squads, Count. Each of them can take ten minutes of every hour. That will keep them as rested as we can get them and let us hold out the longest."

"Doroga," Bernard asked. "Are you sure you and Walker won't need resting time?"

"Walker can't back much farther down this tunnel," Doroga said. "Get us a couple minutes to breathe now and then. That will be as much as we can ask for."

Bernard nodded. "We'll need to give some thought to what craftings we'll want to use, Giraldi," Bernard began. "Brutus is still hiding us from Garados. What have your men got that isn't on the official list?"

"All of them have some metalcraft, sir," Giraldi said. "I've got one man who's a fair hand at firecrafting. He was a potter's apprentice for a while, and managed the fires there. I'm not saying he could call up a firestorm, but if we set up a trench with fuel and a low flame, he could maybe turn it into a barrier for a little while. Two men with enough windcraft to blow up a lot of smoke and dust. I daresay that they could probably help the Countess, if she's of a mind to try another windstorm. We've got a man who knows enough water to be damned good at poker, and he says that there's a stream at the back of the cave he might be able to call out when we run short on water. And I've got one more man who had a smart mouth when he first signed on, and he wound up digging most of the latrine trenches for about three years."

Bernard snorted. "He get his mouth under control?"

"No," Giraldi said. "He built up enough earthcraft that it wasn't a challenge for him anymore. With your permission, I thought I would have him help me prepare a fallback position deeper in the cave. Trench, earthwork, nothing fancy. If we need it, it won't save anyone, but it might make them pay more to get to us."

"Fine," Bernard said. "Go ahead and—"

"No," Amara said. Everyone stopped to blink at her, and she found herself fumbling for a way to put her thoughts into words. "No overt crafting," she said, then. "We don't dare use it."

"Why not?"

"Because I think it's what they are waiting for," she said. "Remember that the taken could indeed employ crafting, but that they only did so after we had called up craftings of our own. After we had set forces in motion."

"Yes," Bernard said. "So?"

"So what if they waited because they *couldn't* initiate a crafting?" Amara said. "We all know how critical confidence and personality is to initiating a furycrafting. These taken may have Aleran bodies, but they aren't Alerans. What if they can only use their talent at furycraft once someone else gathers enough furies into motion?"

Bernard frowned. "Giraldi?"

"Sounds pretty thin to me," the centurion said. "No offense, Countess. I'd like to believe you, but there's nothing to suggest that your guess is anything more than that."

"Of course there is," Amara said. "If they could use crafting, why haven't they? Wind or firecraft could have taken or burned the air from this cave and left us all unconscious. A woodcrafter could have grown the roots of the trees over this cave down and choked us on dust, and an earthcrafter could manage the same and worse. A watercrafter could have flooded the cave from that stream your *legionare* sensed, Giraldi. We know that the vord are under time pressure to finish us and vanish before the Legions arrive. So why haven't they used crafting to bring things to a swift conclusion?"

"Because for some reason they can't," Bernard said, nodding. "It explains why they didn't attack last night. They wanted to draw us out so that we would call up our battle-craftings and assault them. Especially since the vord believe that we still have a strong firecrafter with us. That many taken holders—maybe even a Knight or two, now—could turn all that energy against us and finish us in minutes."

Giraldi grunted. "It would also explain why they are forming up so slow now, and right where we can see them. Crows, if it was my command and we *did* have a firecrafter, I'd hit them right now, before they got themselves into order. Hope to knock them all out at once."

"Exactly," Amara said. "They're an intelligent foe, gentlemen. If we continue to react as predictably as we have been, they'll kill us for it."

Outside, the sky flickered with silver light, and thunder rumbled down from the looming peak behind the cave. Everyone paused to look up, and Amara took a few steps outside the mouth of the cave to send Cirrus questing through the air and the winds.

"It's a furystorm," she reported a moment later. "Something is building it up awfully quickly."

"Garados and Thana," Bernard said. 'They're never happy when the holders are moving around their valley."

"The cave should offer us some shelter from the windmanes," Amara said. "Yes?"

"Yes," Bernard said. "If we last that long. Even Thana can only build up a storm so fast."

"Will the windmanes attack the vord?"

"Never bothered my people," Doroga said. "But maybe they got good taste."

"Giraldi," Bernard said. "Organize the fighting squads and get the first two teams up into position. Get that stream brought up for water and that trench dug now."

"But—" Amara began.

"No, Countess. The men will need water if they're fighting. So we do it now, before the taken come any closer, and while we're at it, we dig those last ditch fortifications. Move, centurion."

"Yes, my lord," Giraldi said, and limped heavily back into the cave.

"Amara," Bernard said. "Get our Knights into position by

that shelf, and get whatever water containers we have available up here for the fighting men."

"Yes, Your Excel—" Amara paused, tilted her head, and smiled at Bernard. "Yes, my lord husband."

Bernard's face brightened into a fierce smile, his eyes flashing. "Doroga," he said.

The Marat headman settled onto the ground between Walker's front claws. "I will sit here and wait for you people to stand in lines so that we can fight."

"Keep an eye on the queen," Bernard said. "Make sure she doesn't pass a cloak off to one of her taken and use them as a false target. Call me if she gets to within arrow range."

"Maybe I will," Doroga agreed laconically. "Bernard. For the only man here who had a woman last night, you are strung pretty tight."

Amara let out a nervous little laugh, and her cheeks flushed hot. She took two steps to Bernard and leaned up to kiss him again. He returned it, one hand touching her waist, a possessive gesture.

She withdrew from the kiss slowly, and searched his eyes. "Do you think we can hold out?"

Bernard began to speak, then stopped himself. He lowered his voice to a bare whisper. "For a little while," he said quietly. "But we're outnumbered, and the enemy has no fear of death. The men will get injured. Tired. Spears and swords will break. We'll soon run out of arrows. And I'm not so confident that Giraldi's man can bring up any water. With furycrafting, we might hold out for several hours. Without it . . ." He shrugged.

Amara bit her lip. "You think that we should use it after all?"

"No," Bernard said. "You've made your case, Amara. I think you've seen what we haven't. You're one damned sharp woman—which is one of the reasons I love you." He smiled at her, and said, "I want you to have something."

"What?" she asked.

"It's an old Legion custom," he said quietly, and took the thick silver band set with a green stone from his right hand. "You know that *legionares* aren't allowed to marry."

"And that most of them have wives," Amara said.

Bernard smiled and nodded. "This is my service ring.

Marks my time with the Rivan Fourth Legion. When a *legionare* has a wife he isn't supposed to have, he gives her his ring to hold for him."

"I could never wear that," Amara said, smiling. "It's not quite big enough for my wrist."

Bernard nodded and drew a slender silver chain from his pocket. He slipped the ring through it, and placed the necklace gently about her throat, clasping it with a dexterity surprising for a man so large. "So a soldier will put his ring on a chain like this," he said. "It isn't a marriage band. But he knows what it means. And so does she."

Amara swallowed and blinked back sudden tears. "I'll be proud to wear it."

"I'm proud to see it on you," he said quietly. He squeezed her hands and glanced past her as a light drizzle began to come down. "Maybe it will make them miserable."

She half smiled. "It's a shame we don't have another, oh, thirty or so Knights Aeris. With that many, I might be able to do something with that storm."

"I wouldn't mind another thirty or forty earth and metal-crafters," Bernard said. "Oh, and perhaps half a Legion to support them." His smile faded, eyes sharpening as he watched the vord. "Better get moving. They'll be here in a moment."

She squeezed back hard, once, then hurried into the cave to round up their Knights, as grim-faced veteran *legionares* began to arise, weapons and armor prepared, and fell into ranks with quiet, confident purpose. Giraldi hobbled by, using a shield as a kind of improvised crutch, giving quiet orders, tightening a buckle here, straightening a twisted belt there. He broke the century into its "spears," its individual files, ordering each file into its own squad. The men of the first squad marched in good order to the front of the cave, while the others formed up behind them, ready to move forward if needed.

Amara rounded up the Knights, placing the archers on the elevated shelf and setting their remaining four Knights Terra on the ground before them. Each of the large men had strapped on their heavy armor and bore the monstrously heavy weaponry that only fury-born strength could wield. When those men cut into the unarmored ranks of the taken, it would be pure carnage.

Thunder rolled again, loud enough to shake the cave, and on the heels of the thunder, an eerie howl rose up through the morning air and sent rivulets of cold fear rippling over Amara's spine. Her mouth went dry, and she took a step up onto the elevated shelf to be able to see.

Outside, the file of taken was on the march, moving swiftly toward the cave. It was an eerie sight. Men, women, even children, dressed in Aleran clothing and Legion uniforms, all the clothing stained, twisted, rumpled, dirty, with no effort made to correct it. Faces stared slackly through the rain, eyes focused on nothing, but they moved in inhumanly perfect unison, step for step, and each of them bore weapons in their hands, even if they gripped only a heavy length of wood.

"Furies," breathed one of the *legionares*. "Look at that."

"Women," said another man. "Children."

"Look at their eyes," Amara said, loudly enough to be heard by everyone around her. "They aren't human anymore. And they all will kill you if you give them the chance. This is the fight of your lives, gentlemen, make no mistake."

The queen prowled along aside the lead rank until they reached bow range, at which time she fell back along the far side of the column, shielded from view by the file of taken. From behind the file, that eerie call rose up again, and Walker shook himself as he rose from his crouch, enormous claws flexing, and answered the call with a rumbling, trumpeting battle call of his own.

Bernard came up from the back of the cave and leapt up onto the shelf, his great bow in hand. "Men, you'll be happy to know that we'll have plenty of water to drink, compliments of Rufus Marcus. And it only tastes a little bit funny."

There was a rumble of low laughter from the readied *legionares*, and a couple of calls of, "Well done, Rufus!"

Outside, the column of empty-eyed taken grew closer, marching with steady speed through the rain.

"Careful now," Bernard said. "Front rank, keep your shields steady, mind your bladework, and don't get greedy with the spears. Second rank, if a man goes down, do not pull him back. That's for third rank to do. Get your shield into place."

The steady tramp of hundreds of feet striking in unison grew louder, and Amara felt her heart begin to race again.

"Keep them from closing if you can!" Bernard called over the noise. "They're all going to be stronger than they look! And by the great furies, don't let any of your swings hit the allied auxiliaries."

"Just me and you," Doroga rumbled to Walker. "But they are calling us allied auxiliaries."

The gargant snorted. Another low round of chuckles rustled among the *legionares*.

The tramp of feet grew louder.

And hundreds, if not thousands, of crows came flashing over the crown of the hill outside the cave in a sudden, enormous, raucous cloud.

"Crows," breathed a number of voices in a whisper, including Amara's. The dark fliers always knew when there was a slaughter in the making.

Crows screamed.

Thunder rumbled.

The tread of feet shook the earth.

Doroga and Walker bellowed together.

The Alerans joined them.

And then the first rank of the taken raised their weapons, crossed into the cave, and slammed into a wall of Legion shields and cold blades.

Tavi had already done so many foolish things for one evening that he decided that stealing three horses wasn't going to significantly change the amount of grief he would receive whenever official attention finally settled on him. There was an ostler's filled with riding horses brought in from all over the countryside around the capital, some from as far as Placida and Aquitaine.

One step upon the property revealed the presence of an unfriendly earth fury, and Ehren warned them that there was a watchful wind fury around the barn. Tavi and Kitai, not without a certain amount of smug satisfaction, used the methods Kitai had shown him and broke into the barn as they had the prison. Within moments, furies circumvented, locks picked, horses and gear liberated from the dark quiet of the stables, Tavi and Kitai rode out, leading a third horse for Ehren, who swung up into the saddle as they came out of the ostler's. They were half a block away before the furylamps around the burgled stable started flashing on, and though the proprietor attempted to raise a proper hue and cry, the attempts were lost amidst the general merry confusion of Wintersend.

"Do you understand me, Ehren?" Tavi demanded. He held the horses to a canter or a high trot at the very slowest, as they cut through the streets of the city, finding the swiftest way back up to the Citadel. "It's important that you tell her exactly what I said."

"I've got it, I've got it," Ehren said. "But why? Why go to *her* of all people?"

"Because the enemy of my enemy is my friend," Tavi said.

"I hope so," Ehren said. The scribe managed to stay mounted, which given the pain of the wound in his leg was no small feat. A canter seemed easier for him, but the bouncing trot they kept to most of the time had to have been sheer torture. "I'll manage," he said. "I'm slowing you down. Go on without me."

Tavi tilted his head. "You don't want to know what we're doing?"

"You're on the First Lord's business, obviously. I'm studious, Tavi, not blind. It's obvious that he's been keeping you close since Festival started." Ehren's face whitened, and he clutched at his saddle. "Look, just go. Tell me later." He half smiled. "If they'll let you."

Tavi stopped long enough to lean across his saddle and offer Ehren his hand. They traded a hard grip, and Tavi realized that Ehren's grip, while lacking the crushing power of Max's paws, was easily Tavi's equal. He hadn't been the only one who had been holding back around other Cursors.

Ehren turned off on Garden Lane, while Tavi and Kitai kicked their horses to a headlong run. Tavi gritted his teeth at the reckless pace, and had to hope that no one was too full of holiday spirit (or spirits) to get out of their way.

Kitai communicated in short sounds and curt gestures, as she had since leaving the warehouse. She seemed alert enough, but followed Tavi's lead without comment, and once he caught her staring down at her hands with exhausted eyes.

They drew up to the final approach to the gates of the Citadel, a long walkway flanked on either side by high walls of stone from which terrors of every sort could be rained down upon an invading army—as though any force would ever draw *near* the capital of all the Realm. Every few paces were heavy statues of bleak stone on either side of the walkway. They were of odd, part-human creatures that the oldest writings had called a "sphinx," though nothing like it had ever been seen in Alera, and historians considered them an extinct species if not an outright hoax. But each statue posed a very real danger to enemies of the Realm, as a few of a legion of earth furies bound into stone statues all over the Citadel and under the direct command of the First Lord himself. A single gargoyle, it was said, could destroy a century of Aleran infantry before it was brought down—and the Citadel had hundreds of them.

Of course, they would not be bringing down anything without a First Lord to loose them from their immobility. Tavi clenched his teeth and reined his horse in, slowing the beast to a jog, and Kitai followed suit.

"Why do we slow?" she murmured.

"This is the approach to the gate," he told her. "If we come in at a full gallop in the dark, the guards and furies here might try to stop us. Better put your hood up. I have the passwords to get us into the Citadel, but not if they see you."

"Why do we not use the tunnels?" she asked.

"Because the vord are running around down there," Tavi said. "And for all we know, Kalare's men might still be watching the tunnels like they were before. They'd be watching some of the key intersections, and if we had to go around them, it would take us hours out of our way."

Kitai pulled up her hood. "Can you not simply tell the guards what is happening?"

"I don't dare," Tavi said. "We have to assume that the enemy is watching the palace. If I try to raise the alarm here, it might take me time we don't have to convince them, and they sure as crows won't let me leave to go to the First Lord until everything is sorted out. Once the alarm goes out, the enemy will hurry to strike, and the First Lord still won't be warned."

"They might not believe you," Kitai said, disapproval in her tone. "This entire falsehood concept among your people makes everything a great deal more complicated than it needs to be."

"Yes, it does," Tavi said. The horses' breath steamed in the night air, and their steel-shod hooves clicked on the stones of the entryway, until they drew up even with the Citadel gates.

A centurion on guard duty challenged them from over the gate. "Who goes there?"

"Tavi Patronus Gaius of Calderon, and companion," Tavi called back. "We must enter immediately."

"I'm sorry, lad, but you'll just have to wait for morning like everyone else," the centurion said. "The gate is closed."

"Winter is over," Tavi called to the man. "Respond."

There was a second of blank, startled silence.

"Winter is over," Tavi called again, more sharply. "Respond."

"Even summer dies," the centurion called back. "Bloody crows, lad." His voice rose to an orderly bellow. "Open the gate! Move, move, move! Osus, get your lazy tail out of that chair and craft word to the stations ahead of the messenger!"

The great iron gates swung open with a low, quiet groan of metal, and Tavi kicked his horse forward into a run, passing through the gates and into the city-within-a-city of the Citadel. Two more tiers upon the Citadel consisted of housing for the Royal Guard and Crown Legion, the enormous support staff needed to keep the palace, the Hall of the Senate, and the Hall of Lords running smoothly. The road ran in a straight line until it reached the base of another tier, sloped into a zigzagging ramp up to the new level, then straightened out again, into the upper level where the Senate, Lords, and Academy lay.

Tavi passed them all, to reach the final, fortified ramp. Guards at the base and head of the ramp alike waved them through without stopping them, and Tavi reined his horse in sharply at the palace gates, which were opening even as he dismounted. Kitai followed suit.

Several guardsmen came forth, two of them taking the horses, while the centurion on duty nodded briskly to Tavi — but his eyes were more than a little suspicious. "Good evening. I just got word from the Citadel gates that a Cursor was coming through with tidings of a threat to the Realm."

"Winter is over," Tavi replied. "Respond."

The centurion scowled. "Yes, I know. You're using the First Lord's personal passwords. But I can't help wondering what the crows you think you're doing, Tavi. And who is this?" He looked at Kitai and flipped his wrist lightly. A little breath of wind blew the hood back from Kitai's face, her canted eyes, her pale hair.

"Crows," spat one of the guardsmen, and steel grated on steel as half a dozen swords hissed from their scabbards. In an eyeblink, Tavi found himself facing a ring of bright swords and soldiers on guard and about to use them. He felt Kitai tense beside him, her hand dropping to the knife on her belt.

"Drop the blade!" barked the centurion.

Guardsmen quivered on the edge of battle, and Tavi knew that he had only seconds to find a way to stop them before they attacked.

"Stop this at once," Tavi trumpeted. "Unless you would prefer to explain to the First Lord why his guardsmen murdered the Marat Ambassador."

Stillness settled on the scene. The centurion lifted his left hand, slowly, fingers spread, and the guardsmen eased out of their fighting stances—but they did not sheathe their blades.

"What is this?" he asked.

Tavi took a deep breath to keep his voice steady. "Gentlemen, this is Ambassador Kitai Patronus Calderon, daughter to Doroga, Headman of the *Sabot-ha*, Chieftain of the Marat. She has only now arrived in the capital, and my orders are to escort her inside at once."

"I haven't heard anything of this," the centurion said. "A female ambassador?"

"Centurion, I've given you my password, and I've explained more than I should have. Let us pass."

"Why are you in such a hurry?" he said.

"Listen to me," Tavi said, lowering his voice. "Ambassador Varg's chancellor has spent the last six months smuggling Canim warriors into the Deeps. As we speak, at least a score of them are on their way to the First Lord's meditation chamber to kill him."

The centurion's mouth dropped open. "What?"

"There may be a spy within the palace, so I want you to get every fighting man you have as quietly as you possibly can and head for the stairs to the meditation chamber."

The centurion shook his head. "Tavi, you're only a page. I don't think—"

"*Don't* think," Tavi snapped. "Don't ask questions. There is no time for either. If you want the First Lord to live, just *do* it."

The man stared at him, evidently shocked at the authority in his tone. Tavi had no more time to waste on the centurion. The guards in the stations on the stairs had to be alerted at once, and they were too deep in the mountain for a wind-crafting to carry word to them. He turned and sprinted into the palace, calling over his shoulder, "Do it! Hurry!"

He went up the long, smooth slope of broad marble stairs leading into the palace, into a reception hall topped with a rotunda the size of a small mountaintop, turned right, and went flying through the dimly lit halls. It seemed that it took him forever to reach the stairs, and he was terrified that he might already be too late. He slammed open the door to the first guard station, his heart in his teeth.

Four guardsmen lurched up from their card table, coins and placards scattering as the table overturned and they drew their weapons. Two more men, one sharpening a blade and another mending a torn tunic, also came to their feet, weapons in their hands.

Centurion Bartos opened a door and emerged from the jakes, his sword in one hand while the other held up his trousers. He blinked for a moment at Tavi, then his face darkened into the beginnings of a thunderous rage. "*Tavi*," he snarled. "What is the meaning of this?" He stared from Tavi to Kitai. "A *Marat*? *Here*? Are you *insane*?"

"Winter is over," Tavi said. "Respond. No, wait, don't bother, there's no time. Centurion, there are more than twenty Canim on their way here as we speak. They're coming to kill Gaius."

No sooner had Tavi spoken the words than a wailing scream of pain and terror echoed down the hall behind him. His heart leapt into his throat and he whirled, eyes wide, his knife in his hand though he hadn't realized he'd drawn it.

"Was that Joris?" muttered one of the guardsmen. "It sounded like Joris."

Another scream, this one closer, louder, came echoing through the halls. It was followed by shrieking, pleading babbles of sound that abruptly ended. Then, from the direction of the Black Hall, an enormous, lean form stepped around the corner at the end of the hall with lupine grace. It dropped into a crouch, the Cane's muzzle all but hidden in the deep cowl of its cloak. Blood dripped from its nose, muzzle, and fangs. The Cane was spattered in scarlet, and its blade of crimson steel shone wetly. It stood motionless for a moment, then a second Cane came around the corner. And another. And another. They prowled forward, their lazy-seeming steps deceptively swift, and the hall filled with silent Canim warriors.

The Royal Guard's alarm bells began belatedly ringing throughout the Citadel.

Bartos stood at Tavi's shoulder for a second, staring at them in wide-eyed shock. "Great furies be merciful," he whispered. Then he whipped his head around, and shouted, "Shields! Prepare for battle!"

Tavi grabbed the iron door and swung it shut, then shoved

the three heavy bolts into position, locking it. Guardsmen slapped on their helmets, strapped on their shields, and kicked an open area around the doorway, clearing it so they had a place to fight. Tavi and Kitai backed away to the far side of the room, where the stairs down began.

"Tavi," Bartos snarled, "get down to the next station and send them up here. Then get down to the First Lord. This door should hold until he's here, then we'll get him out of—"

There was a sound like a shock of thunder, a screaming of metal as the heavy bolts and hinges tore, and the heavy iron door was smashed nearly flat to the stone floor.

It crushed Centurion Bartos beneath it.

Blood splattered over the entire room, slapping against Tavi like a burst of hot rain. The torn metal of the bolts and hinges glowed orange-red with heat where they had torn.

The bloody-mouthed lead Cane, one of its pawlike hands now crushed to swollen pulp, stepped onto the door with lethal grace and slashed at the nearest guardsman. The guardsmen hesitated for no longer than a panicked heartbeat, but in that time a second Cane came through the door. The guardsmen formed a line in front of the Canim, their shields smaller than standard Legion issue, their swords glinting wickedly.

One guardsman struck at the nearest Cane, his sword blurring with fury-born speed. The thrust sank home in the Cane's belly; but the taken Cane did not seem to notice, and its return stroke nearly took the guardsman's head from his shoulders before the man could draw his sword back and raise his shield. A second guardsmen caught a downstroke on his upraised shield, only his fury-born strength allowing him to hold the blow from his body, then swept his *gladius* in a scything upward arch, striking the Cane's weapon arm several inches from the wrist and sending its hand and weapon spinning through the air.

The Cane never so much as blinked. It simply slammed the stump of its arm into the guardsman's shield, the force of it driving his boots across the floor, and leapt at him, jaws snapping. The guardsman went down, desperately trying to interpose his shield between his throat and the Cane's teeth. Kitai's hand blurred as she drew her knife and threw it all in the same motion. The blade tumbled end over end and sank into the

Cane's left eye. The Cane convulsed with a spasm of reaction, perhaps even with pain, and in that moment the man beside the downed guardsman struck cleanly through the Cane's neck, taking its head clear off its shoulders.

But more Canim pressed through the doorway, driving the guardsmen back step by step. Each step made more room for an attacking Cane to fight, and now three of them were battling the guardsmen instead of two. Tavi realized that the disparity of numbers and raw power meant that there was no way the guardsmen would be able to hold the room for long.

"Go!" screamed another of the guardsmen. "Warn the First Lord!"

Tavi nodded at him, his heart pounding with fear, and turned to bound down the long staircase as swiftly as he had ever done it in his life. Kitai followed close behind.

CHAPTER 45

Screams followed them down the stairs. Defiant, angry shouts blended in with shrieks of agony, and steel rang on steel. Just before they reached the second guard station, Tavi nearly ran headlong into a guardsman coming up the stairs, his expression concerned.

"Tavi," the guardsman said. "What's going on up there?"

"Canim," Tavi panted. "They're trying to get to the First Lord."

"Crows," the guardsman said. "Bartos is holding them?"

"He's dead," Tavi said, his voice flat and bitter. "They're in bad shape up there, but the alarm has been raised. If they hold, they can keep the Canim in the hallway until reinforcements arrive, but if the Canim can get onto the stairs . . ."

The guardsman nodded, and his eyes flicked to Kitai.

"She's with me," Tavi said hurriedly.

The guardsman hesitated, then gave him a sharp nod, ducked back into the second guardroom, and started snapping orders, getting the men on their feet and heading on up the stairs. Tavi stayed out of their way and continued down, the faint sounds of battle and alarm fading to silence by the time he reached the bottom. Tavi flew through the antechamber into Gaius's meditation room.

Gaius lay as he had before, unmoving, with Fade crouching close by. Max was stretched out on the cot in the same position Tavi had left him in, more unconscious than asleep. As Tavi came through the door, Maestro Killian came to his feet in a single smooth motion, his cane gripped tight. Sir Miles stood up at the desk, sword in hand.

"Marat!" Miles snarled, and bounded forward, sword extended.

"No!" Tavi cried.

Kitai dodged the thrust, whipped her cloak from her shoulders and flung it wide, like a net, at Sir Miles. He cut it out of the air, but in the time it took him to do it, Kitai had darted out of the room, back to the stairway, and crouched there, her pose feline, her eyes bright and unafraid.

Tavi got between Miles and the door. "She's unarmed!" he shouted. "Sir Miles, she is not our enemy here."

"Miles." Killian's voice cracked like a whip. "Stay your hand."

Sir Miles, his eyes flat with hatred, halted in place, but his eyes never left Kitai.

"Tavi," Killian said. "I presume this is your partner in Maximus's jailbreak."

"Yes, Maestro," Tavi said. "This is Kitai, the daughter of the Marat Chieftain, Doroga. And my friend. Without her help tonight, Max would still be in jail, and I would be dead, and there is no time to discuss this."

Killian's face clouded with anger, but Tavi could almost see him force himself to remain calm, and ask, "And why is that?"

"Because twenty Canim are coming down the stairs to kill the First Lord," Tavi said, trying not to let the mild vindictive satisfaction he felt show in his voice. "The alarm has been raised, but they were already at the first guard station when I came down. Centurion Bartos is dead, and I don't think that they can hold them in the stairway for long."

Miles spat out a sulfurous curse and started for the doorway.

"No, Miles," Killian said.

"The men are in danger," the captain growled.

"As is the First Lord," Killian said. "We leave together. Miles, you'll lead. Tavi, get Max up. He'll be next. You and Fade put Gaius on Max's cot and carry it up."

Tavi crossed the room to his friend before Killian had finished talking, and simply picked up one edge of the cot and dumped Max onto the floor. The large young man landed on the ground with a grunt and thrashed his way to wakefulness. "Oh," he said. "It's you."

"Max, get up," Tavi said quietly. "Get a sword. There are Canim warriors coming down the stairs." He grabbed the cot and dragged it over to the bed, where Fade rose up and lifted Gaius without evident effort. The slave settled him on the cot and wound blankets around the old man. Tavi glanced up and saw that Fade wore his sword on his belt, though it was largely hidden by the fall of his long, ragged overtunic.

Max pushed himself to his feet, tugged his shirt back on, and muttered, "Where's a sword?"

"Antechamber," Killian provided. "Lower drawer of the liquor cabinet. It's Gaius's."

Max paused, and said, "If you give me a minute, I can get into costume. It might . . . I mean, if they're here for Gaius, and they think they get him . . ." He let his voice trail off.

Killian's expression was nothing but stone. He nodded, and said, "Do it."

"Right," Max said. He exchanged a look with Tavi that couldn't hide his fright, then stalked out into the antechamber.

Tavi took a moment to take a sheet from the bed and loop it around the unconscious First Lord, then tied it as tightly and securely as he could, to help hold the old man on the cot, should it tilt. "We're ready to move him," Tavi said quietly.

"Very well," Killian said. "Maximus?"

Tavi and Fade picked up the cot and carried it from the meditation chamber. There was a pause, a quiet groan, then Max, wearing Gaius's form, appeared in the doorway. He bore the First Lord's long, heavy blade naked in his hand. "Ready," he said, though his voice was still Maximus's. He frowned, coughed a couple of times, one hand touching his throat, and said, this time speaking as Gaius, "Ready. Not sure how much crafting I can do, Maestro."

"Do your best," Killian said quietly.

Kitai made a hissing sound from the stairway, her eyes focusing up the steps. Without really thinking about it, Tavi drew his knife from his belt and flipped it through the air to her. She glanced aside, caught it by the handle as it came to her, and dropped it into a low fighting grip, her eyes searching up the stairway.

Killian tilted his head to one side a second later, blind eyes narrowing. "Good ears, girl," he murmured. "Miles."

The captain slipped up to stand a few steps above Kitai and crouched down low, sword ready. Then something came around the corner, and Miles rose, blade in hand. There was a flash of steel, a ringing sound, and a panicked cry. Then Miles grunted, and said, "Prios, man, it's me. Easy, easy."

Miles came back down, half-supporting a wounded guards-man. Prios was a man of medium height and build who was bet-ter known for his sharp eyes than his sword arm. His right arm was dangling limply and covered in blood, and he had lost his helmet. A scalp wound matted his hair to his skull on the left side. He bore his sword in his left hand, and was pale.

Tavi surreptitiously drew a blanket up to conceal most of Gaius's face. There was a moment of silence, then Killian nudged Max with his elbow.

Max coughed again, and said, "Report, guardsman. What is happening?"

"They're mad," the guardsman panted. "Mad, sir. They don't bother to defend themselves. They ignore wounds that should put them on the ground. It's as if they don't care about living."

Max put a hand on the man's shoulder and said, "Prios. I need you to tell me the tactical situation."

"Y-yes, my lord," the guardsman panted. "The Canim pushed us out of the first room, and some of them are holding it against the reinforcements. There are at least a dozen more coming down. My sword arm was out, and Red Karl was the senior spear. He ordered me to head to the second position, bolt all the doors behind me, then report to you, my lord."

Which meant, Tavi thought, that the guardsmen on the stairs above had just trapped themselves with the Canim and thrown their lives away in an effort to buy the First Lord more time. Max inhaled sharply and shot a glance at Killian. "They've lost, then. And they knew it."

"My lord," Miles said. "If we can beat them to the second room, it will give us the best chance to hold them. They'll have to come through the doorway, and we'll be facing them on even ground instead of on the stairs."

"Agreed," Max said. "Move out."

Miles nodded sharply and started up the stairs. Prios and then Max followed him, then Killian. As the Maestro took the stairs, he paused, and said, "The Marat girl goes last."

Fade glanced at Tavi, then took the stairs behind Killian, carrying the cot without apparent effort. Tavi had to grunt and strain for a moment as more of the weight settled on him, but he held his end up and kept pace with Fade.

Kitai pressed closely behind him, and hissed, "Will your warriors' sorceries not simply burn them?"

Tavi grunted and panted, answering as they climbed. "They don't dare in quarters this close. A firecrafting would suck out most of the air and heat the rest until it scorched our lungs. And we're so deep that an earthcrafting could bring the roof down on us, and an aircrafting would be so weak it's useless. We have to fight."

"Quiet," Miles snarled.

Tavi gritted his teeth and set his mind to keeping his end of the cot lifted and moving steadily. A hundred stairs later, his arms and shoulders began to quiver and ache. Kitai promptly stepped up beside Tavi on the stairway, and said, "Let me take this corner."

Too out of breath to argue, Tavi shifted his grip to allow Kitai to take half of his load, and they continued on up.

"Halt," came a low order from up the stairs. "We're close. Wait here."

Tavi heard Miles's boots on the stairs once, then silence. A moment later, Miles called, "We're clear to the second station. Both doors are still up. Hurry."

They resumed their pace and spilled into the guardroom. "Stay clear of the door," Tavi warned Miles. "They smashed the other one straight down to the floor. That's how they killed Centurion Bartos."

Miles eyed Tavi, then stayed to one side of the iron door, placed his left hand on it, and closed his eyes. There was a low, deep hum. Miles frowned, eyes still closed, and said, "Sire, I recommend we do everything we can to strengthen this steel before the Canim get here."

"Of course," Max replied. He went to the other side of the door and leaned his own hand against it in a mirror image of Miles. The humming sound grew louder.

"Fade, this corner," Tavi said. He, Fade, and Kitai carried the First Lord into the back corner of the room and set the cot down carefully. Tavi then dragged the heavy table over to the corner and dumped it onto its side to set up a makeshift barrier. Fade hurried around to crouch behind the barrier, dull eyes unfocused, his mouth open in a witless expression.

"Good," Killian approved, then swept the tip of his cane

up to point at the weapons rack on the wall. "Arm yourselves."

Kitai went to the rack and seized a pair of short, heavy blades and a short-hafted spear. She tossed the latter to Tavi, who caught it and tested its balance. Killian took a sword as well, keeping his cane in his left hand.

There was no warning. Just a thundering roar of impact and a shriek of warping metal, as a section of the door the size of a Wintersend ham bulged out under the force of a blow. It happened twice more, enormous dents driven into the bolted door, but the bolts held.

"Won't be able to hold this for long. Bending the metal is heating it up," Miles grunted.

Dents continued to erupt from the door, one every four or five seconds. Tavi set his spear aside, fetched a ewer, and dipped it into the water barrel against the wall, then splashed cold liquid over the door without ceremony. Steam rose in a hissing cloud.

"Well done, boy," Miles said. "It might buy us time."

Tavi rushed back to the barrel and returned with more water, slopped it over the door, and repeated the exercise. More dents bloomed up from the steel, and others grew under repeated blows, until the frame of the door itself groaned, and the steel bent and warped until it no longer matched the doorway. Tavi glimpsed a cloaked Cane on the other side as he threw more water onto the heated metal.

There was a sudden acrid, burnt odor in the air, and Miles ground his teeth. "Can't hold it. Have to pull off the door in half a minute, then they'll be in here. Everyone stand ready."

Tavi's heart pounded in his chest, and he exchanged the ewer for the spear. Fade crouched behind the table. Prios stood several feet back from the door. He had bound his mangled right arm into a sling and held his *gladius* in an awkward left-handed ready position. Kitai, her expression unconcerned, twirled the sword in her right hand, then the one in her left, and stood beside Tavi, just in front of the overturned table.

"You know how to use one of those?" Tavi murmured to her.

"How difficult could it be?" Kitai replied.

Tavi arched an eyebrow.

"Hashat showed me how once," Kitai explained.

"Oh," he said. "Well. When it starts, try to stay close to me. I'll look after you."

Kitai threw back her head and burst into a silvery belly laugh. It belled through the room in a wave of utterly incongruous amusement, and everyone but Miles and Max paused to look back at her.

"You will protect me. That is funny," Kitai said, shaking her head, laughter bubbling under her words. "That is very amusing, Aleran."

Tavi's cheeks heated up.

"All right," Miles said to Max, his voice strained. "After the next hit, we back off, let the door fall, hit the first one as he comes in."

"I have a better idea," Max panted.

The door shuddered under another impact, and Miles shouted, "Now!" and whipped his hand away from the door.

But Max didn't do that. Instead, he drew back his right hand, teeth clenched, and as he did the stone around him quivered with sudden tension. Max let out a roaring shout and drove his fist forward.

The door, no longer made stronger and more flexible by Max's and Miles's furycrafting, tore from its hinges in a shriek of shearing metal. The door slammed straight down, just as it had before the fists of the Canim in the first guardroom, and the Cane standing before it was crushed flat. There was a single beat of stunned silence, then Miles bounded out over the fallen door, his sword whirling in an all-out attack.

There was as much difference between Sir Miles's swordplay and that of the average guardsman as there was between a burrowbadger and its enormous cousin, the gargant. His sword sheared through mail, flesh, and bone with contemptuous ease, shattered the scarlet steel swords of two Canim, and spattered the stairs and walls with blood. Before any of the Canim could regain their balance, Miles had already danced back over the fallen door and back into the guardroom. One Cane followed on Miles's heels, but Max was ready, and the First Lord's sword swept straight down from an overhand grip, and all but split the Cane's torso in two.

Gouting blood and dying, the silent Cane's head snapped around to view its slayer. Then the Cane's eyes widened and a weak, bubbling snarl rippled from its muzzle. The Cane threw itself at Max, slammed hard against the young man wearing Gaius's features, and crushed him against the stone wall. It started ripping and tearing at Max with its fangs.

Miles shot a glance at Max and began to step his way, but a second Cane came through the doorway, and Miles was forced to engage it before it could escape the hampering confines of the doorway and fully enter the room.

Prios leapt forward, sword cutting hard at the horribly wounded Cane. The swing was clumsy but powerful, and it bit deep into the Cane's near thigh, drawing even more blood.

The Cane didn't seem to notice. The mangled warrior should already have died, but the horrible will of the vord refused to surrender to mere death and imbued the Cane with increasing ferocity as more savage blows struck home. Max screamed.

"Max!" Tavi shouted, and ran forward. He darted to the left flank of the Cane and charged, driving his spear home between the Cane's ribs. The spear's crosspiece struck hard, and the weight of Tavi's charge shoved the Cane away from Max. It twisted and fell, snapping at the spear in its flank, but the gesture was a futile one. The Cane collapsed abruptly to the ground, jaws still clashing.

Tavi jerked the spear out of the fallen Cane and whipped his head around to look at Max. In Gaius's form still, he was covered in blood. There was a savage wound on his left forearm, bleeding profusely, and there was blood running from his head. One of his legs was twisted so that his foot faced opposite the way it should have. Tavi seized the collar of Max's shirt and hauled him back toward the makeshift barrier. Max was limp and heavy, and Tavi had all that he could do to move him a couple of feet at a time, until Fade showed up at Tavi's side and seized Max beneath the arms and drew him back behind the barricade.

Maestro Killian followed them behind the barricade, grimacing as he stared down with blind eyes and let his fingers run over Max's form. He drew a knife, slashed Max's sleeve away, then used it to bind the wound on his forearm tightly closed to stop the bleeding. "Tavi, help Miles and Prios. That door must be held at any cost."

Tavi nodded and dashed back to the doorway, already gasping for breath and growing no less terrified. Miles had already opened a dozen wounds on the Cane trying to batter its way into the room. The bloody-eyed wolf-warrior showed no signs of pain, nor of fear, and fought in silent, steady ferocity. The Cane's sword was no match for Miles's speed and skill, and Miles was untouched, but the heavy blows raining down on him were forcing him back, inch by inch.

As Tavi got close, Miles snarled, "Tavi, bind him high."

Tavi reacted with instinctive, thoughtless speed. The Cane's sword swept down, and Tavi reached over Miles's shoulder to catch the blade on the cross brace of the spear and sweep it to one side, pinning the sword against the doorway.

"Good!" Miles barked, already moving. He closed in and slashed in an upward arch that opened the Cane from groin to throat, spilling blood and worse into the doorway as the Cane thrashed uselessly and collapsed to the floor dead. The next Cane on the stairs leapt forward with reckless speed, only to be met by the glinting silver arcs of Miles's deadly slashes. Tavi had to duck to one side to be out of the path of the Cane's leap, and it fell writhing wildly to the floor—in three separate pieces.

And then there was a flash of motion on the stairs and a blur of grey cloak. Tavi only had time enough to be astounded that *anything* could move that fast, then the figure leapt to one side, bounded off the wall, and vaulted up, over Miles's head. The captain whipped his sword through another attack, but was a hair too slow, and the figure went right by him. It turned in midair to meet the ceiling with all fours and propelled itself down upon the wounded Prios.

The guardsman never had time to shriek before a slender hand, skin a shining and reflective green-black, fingers tipped with gleaming claws, tore his throat open to the spine.

Tavi drove his spear at the figure, but it was simply too swift, and the spearhead struck sparks against the stone floor as the figure leapt again, floor to wall, kicking off the wall to drive at Sir Miles. Miles's sword lashed out and struck the figure with a sudden shower of sparks. The figure screamed, a horrible, metallic scream that had haunted Tavi's nightmares, off and on, for two years.

"Aleran!" Kitai snapped. "Ware! The vord queen!"

Claws lashed at Miles, literally too quickly to see, but the Captain of the Crown Legion had a lifetime of experience, and his sword was there to counter the vord queen, his feet shuffling to keep the deadly balance of distance from falling to the queen's favor, circling to one side—and Tavi suddenly realized that Miles was forcing the vord queen to turn her flank and back to Tavi.

Miles danced another two steps to one side and Tavi drove the tip of his spear at the vord queen's back—only to be astounded again at the creature's speed as she spun, seized the haft of the spear, and in a surge of motion hurled Tavi away.

Tavi's vision blurred as he flew through the air. He had a flickering glimpse of Prios's sightless, terrified eyes, then he bounced off something hard, fell, and landed on stone.

His head spinning, Tavi fought to lift it, looking around wildly. He was sprawled upon the steel door Max had crushed to the floor, and it was painfully hot.

He was also surrounded by Canim.

Two had already entered the guardroom. Another had one foot on the fallen door, and its empty scarlet eyes stared directly down at Tavi. Even as he watched, another taken Canim appeared behind that one, scarlet eyes flat. And another beyond that one.

Every single one of them bared bloody fangs and gripped bloodier weapons.

Every single one of them could tear him to literal pieces in a heartbeat.

And every single one of them turned to Tavi.

CHAPTER 46

Amara clenched her sword until her knuckles ached as the taken holders assaulted the cave. The fighting was elemental, brutal. Empty-eyed holders attacked the Legion shield front with spades and farm implements and their naked fists, with axes and old swords and hammers from the smithy. The heavier weapons struck with unbelievable force, deforming shields, denting helmets, crushing bones even through the *legionares'* heavy armor.

Two men in the first squad were killed when the first taken holders with hammers attacked, and after that Bernard began allowing his archers to expend arrows on the taken armed with heavy weaponry. Only a hit in the eyes or mouth would put one of them down reliably, but Bernard himself was an archer of nearly unbelievable skill, and he demanded that the woodcrafters in his command keep pace. When one of Bernard's archers shot, their arrows struck home and one of the taken went down.

Though she hadn't yet lifted her blade, Amara found herself panting in sympathy with the struggling *legionares*, and she started shooting looks at Bernard when the men began to tire. After what seemed like a small eternity, Bernard called, "Countess, drive them back."

Amara nodded sharply to the Knights Terra with her, and the *legionares* parted as they came through. Amara's arm flashed up, her blade intercepting a descending club and sliding it away from her before it struck her helm. Then her Knights Terra waded into the fray with fury-born strength, heavy swords ripping through the taken with hideous efficiency while Amara watched their flanks and backs. Within a minute, they had driven the taken back to the cave's mouth, and Amara called them to a halt before her Knights advanced outside the cave, where the taken could have enfolded them and swamped them under sheer numbers.

Getting back took longer. They did not dare simply retreat, allowing the enemy to follow them closely, building up deadly momentum and risking confusion in their own ranks during frantic movement. It had to be slow, controlled, to enable them to hold their lines, so Amara and the Knights Terra fought a steady, deliberate retreat back to their original position. The second squad had taken up the defensive line while the first squad retreated to breathe, drink, and rest.

She was panting and badly winded even from the brief engagement. It was one of the fundamental truths of battle that there was nothing, absolutely *nothing* more wearying than the exertion, exhilaration, and terror of combat. Amara made sure the fighting men had water before taking a tankard of it herself, and watched the battle. Second squad lost a man when a stray blow from an axe split his foot like a stick of cordwood and he had to be hauled back to what passed for their hospital. A second man hesitated when a taken holder who looked like a middle-aged woman came at him, and it cost him his life when she threw him out of the shieldwall and into the midst of the taken attackers. Moments later, another man was struck senseless by a blow to his helmet, but before his companions could haul him back, the taken holders seized his wrist, and in the ensuing tug-of-war ripped his arm from the socket.

The plan called for second squad to last at least another four or five minutes. Amara didn't see how they could possibly do it without losing more men. The taken holders had no interest in self-preservation, and they were willing to die to cripple or kill a *legionare*—and there were three or four times as many of them as there were Alerans. They could absorb the losses, and there was very little that the Alerans could do about it.

The sun had fully risen by then, and no Aleran relief force had come roaring down from the skies or across the fields. Nor, she thought, was it likely that any was coming. The rain began to fall more heavily, the wind to gust and howl, and crows haunted every tree in sight, settling down in the frigid wind to wait for corpses to fall.

Their fight was a hopeless one. If the rate of casualties remained steady—and it wouldn't, as the *legionares* grew more winded and wounded, and as Bernard's archers ran entirely out of arrows—then half of the combat-capable *legionares* would be out of action by late morning. And when the decline came, it would come swiftly, a sudden collapse of discipline and will under the relentless violence of the taken holders' assault.

They were unlikely to live until midday.

Amara forced that cold judgment from her thoughts and attempted to focus on something more hopeful. The most stable factor in the engagement was, surprisingly, Doroga and his companion. Walker proved a dominating, even overwhelming presence in the battle, his immense power in the confines of the tunnel unmatched by anything the vord had to throw at them. The Gargant seemed to operate under a very simple set of ground rules: He crouched more or less at his ease on his side of the cavern. Anything that walked within reach of his vast sledgehammer paws and stone-gouging claws got crushed or torn apart in swift order. Doroga, meanwhile, crouched between Walker's front paws with his war cudgel, knocking weapons from the hands of the taken and dispatching foes crippled to immobility by Walker's claws. The taken never slacked in their assault, but they began to show more caution about approaching Walker, attempting to draw the gargant out with short, false rushes that did not manage to lure him into the open.

Amara watched in awe as the gargant's paw batted a taken *legionare* through the air to land thirty feet from the mouth of the cave, and thought that even though they could not furycraft the cave's entrance into a narrower, more defensible position, Doroga and Walker, savagely defending half the cave's mouth on their own, were in fact more effective than a wall of stone. A stone wall would only have stopped the taken holders. Doroga and Walker were doing that and additionally dispatching enemies very nearly as swiftly as the Alerans. It had never occurred to Amara how the confined space of the cave would magnify the gargant's combat ability. Gargants in an open field of combat were largely unstoppable, but not generally difficult to avoid or to flank. But in the cave's confines, that changed. There was simply nowhere to run to get out of the beast's way, no way to encircle it, and the gargant's raw, crushing power made Walker much more dangerous than Amara had assumed he would be.

Amara had barely finished her water when Bernard ordered her into the fray again, moments short of the time that had been allotted the second squad to hold. She and the Knights Terra once again bought the *legionares* time to switch fresh bodies for winded ones.

Third squad did better than either second or first, but the fourth simply ran into a patch of horribly bad luck and lost their entire front rank in the space of a few seconds, necessitating an early advance from the fifth squad, and Amara and her Knights had to enter the battle again before they'd had a chance to breathe properly. Doroga took note of the situation and guided Walker into a short rush forward in time with Amara's Knights, and the gargant's bellowing challenges shook dust from the cave's roof.

It was only with Walker's help that they managed to successfully press the enemy back to the cave mouth again, giving the *legionares* behind them a chance to change out with fresh fighters. There was a quivering quality to the fight now, an uncertainty in the movements of her Knights. They were tiring, their movement hampered by the remains of fallen foes and *legionares* alike, making it more difficult to move and fight together. Worse, each drive forward only showed them how many of the enemy yet remained outside. For all their efforts, there were still too many of the taken to count easily, and no sign at all of the queen.

They reached the mouth of the cave, and Amara called a halt. They began their steady, ordered withdrawal back to their original positions.

An abrupt blur of grey cloak streaked into the cave along the ceiling, crawling like some unthinkably huge and swift spider.

The vord queen.

Amara had seen it the instant it appeared, but before she could draw a breath to shout a warning, the shape flung itself from the ceiling of the cave and hammered into the Knight on the left end of their line, a large and good-natured young man with red hair bleached to straw by hours in the sun. He was in the middle of a backswing, warding off a taken *legionare* with his blade, and never saw the queen coming. The vord hit him in a tangle of whipping limbs. There was a sound like a small cloud of whip cracks, and the queen flung itself to the opposite wall, behind Walker, only to bound off it like a coiled spring and pounce upon the rightmost Knight in the same fashion, while blood blossomed up in a sudden shower from the redheaded Knight.

The second Knight was an older man, a career soldier, and he had enough experience to dodge away from the queen and whip the crown of his heavy mace in an overhand, shattering blow.

The vord caught the mace in one hand, and stopped it cold. The queen's skin was a shade of deep green-black, shining and rigid-looking, and with a twist of its body it threw the Knight off-balance and sent him staggering into the waiting taken. Before the Knight could regain his balance, they seized him and mobbed him as slives did a wounded deer, while the queen bounced to the left-hand wall again, barely avoiding a crushing kick from Walker's left hind leg. More taken, this time moving with some kind of horrible excitement, began to press recklessly into the cave.

The creature was so *fast*, Amara thought in a panic, and called upon Cirrus, borrowing of the fury's fluid speed.

Time did not slow—not precisely. But she suddenly became aware of every detail of her surroundings. She could see the gleam of light and the stains of blood upon the vord queen's claws. She could see and smell the pulsing fountain of blood pouring from the first Knight's throat, slashed open to the bone. She saw individual raindrops as they fell outside, and the sway of the vord queen's rain-soaked cloak.

Amara's head turned to follow the queen, as she shouted, "Bernard!" The queen bounded off the wall and flew at Amara, an alien nightmare of grace and ferocity and power.

Amara slipped to one side, as legs of the same green-black chitin extended, their claws poised to rake in tandem with the claws upon the queen's hands. Amara's sword swept up to strike at the nearest leg, sweeping it away from her and biting into green-black chitin, and the queen went into a tumble as the blow robbed her of balance. One claw flailed at Amara as it went by, missing her eye by inches, but she felt a sudden fire high on her cheek.

The queen landed on all fours, recovering its balance in an instant, and even with Cirrus's help, Amara was too slow to change her stance to defend against an attack from the opposite side of the first. She turned desperately, sword raised, but the vord queen was already coming, deadly talons set to rend and rip.

Until the last of the Knights Terra, Sir Frederic, whipped his spade straight down across the queen's back, a sledgehammer blow that drove her into the cave floor. The queen twisted like a snake, claws raking at Frederic's near leg, and the young Knight screamed in agony and fell to his knees. The queen tried to roll closer, claws poised to strike at the arteries in Frederic's thigh, but Frederic had bought Amara enough time to complete her turn and thrust her sword into the queen's back.

The blow struck savagely, enhanced with fury-born speed, and would have spit a man in mail clean through. The vord queen, however, was another matter. The tip of Amara's blade barely sank in, not even to the full width of the sword. The queen changed directions, horribly swift, one leg sweeping a cloud of dirt on the cave floor into Frederic's eyes while the other three flung her at Amara.

"Down!" Bernard roared, and Amara dropped to the cave floor like a stone. An arrow swept by her, so close that she felt the wind of its passing, and the broad, heavy head bit into the vord queen's throat.

She let out a deafening shriek and fell into a roll. Amara struck again, inflicting no greater injury than the last; then the queen, Bernard's arrow protruding from both sides of her neck, shot between the ranks of the taken and out of the cave. The queen shrieked again as she went, and the taken let out wailing howls in unison and charged forward with a sudden, vicious ferocity.

Amara heard Bernard order an advance, and the *legionares* screamed their defiance as they came on. Frederic, blood streaming from his wounded leg, could not rise. He swept the edge of his spade along at ground level, the steel cutting hard into the knee of the nearest Taken, sending it crashing to the floor. Another taken dived and hit Amara at the thighs, knocking her down, and she saw three more already leaping toward her. Beside her, more taken flung themselves upon Frederic.

The *legionares* were still a dozen strides away. She tried to cut the nearest, but the taken were simply too strong. They smashed her sword arm to the floor, and something slammed into the side of her head with a flash of nauseating pain. Amara could only scream and struggle uselessly as the taken Aric, former Steadholder of Aricholt, bared his teeth and went for her throat with them.

And then Aric went flying away from her, hitting the wall with a bone-crushing impact. There was an enormous roar of sound, and Walker's foot slammed another of the taken holders to the cave floor. Amara saw a heavy war club descend and crush the back of the last Taken attacking her, then Doroga kicked the creature off her, lifted his war cudgel, and finished it with a blow to the skull.

Doroga whirled to strike at another taken before it could crush Frederic's throat, while Walker turned his enormous body about to the front of the cave again, more lithe than Amara would have thought possible. The gargant rumbled its battle cry and slammed into the incoming taken with rage and abandon, ripping and tearing and crushing in a frenzy. The taken attacked with mindless determination, swinging blades, clubs, stones, or simply ripping out scoops of flesh from the gargant with their naked hands.

The *legionares* thundered forward to support the gargant, but the corpses and spilled blood made it impossible for them to maintain ranks, and the taken that got around Walker tore into them with insane fury.

A strong hand closed on the back of Amara's hauberk, and Giraldi hauled her along the floor, seized Frederic's hauberk in the same way, and pulled them both toward the back of the cave, wounded leg and all.

"They're breaking through!" someone shouted from directly behind her, and Amara looked up to see a *legionare* fall and half a dozen taken spill past the lines, while outside the cave, even more of them pressed in with inevitable determination, pushing their way through with sheer mass.

"Loose at will!" Bernard called, and suddenly the air of the cave hummed with the passing of the woodcrafters' deadly shafts. The half dozen taken who had broken through fell in their tracks. Then the woodcrafters started threading shots through the battle lines, passing in the space under a *legionare*'s arm when he lifted his sword to strike, sailing over one's head when he ducked a swing from a clumsy club, flitting between another's shield and his ear when he lunged forward, changing his center of balance.

It was, barely, enough. Though the Knights Flora's few arrows had been quickly spent, they had checked the taken's assault long enough for more *legionares* to advance from the rear of the cave, and they filled the weakness in the line, fighting with desperate strength.

The vord queen shrieked again from somewhere outside the cave, the sound loud enough to drown out the noise of battle and put painful pressure on Amara's ears. Instantly, the taken who had been fighting turned to retreat from the cave at a dead run, and the *legionares* pressed forward with a roar, cutting down the enemy as they fled.

"Halt!" Bernard bellowed. "Stay in the cave! Fall back, Doroga, fall back!"

Doroga flung himself in front of the furious gargant, shoving against Walker's chest while he tried to pursue the enemy. Walker bellowed his anger, but a few feet outside the cave he came to a halt, and at Doroga's urging retreated back to their original position.

The cave was suddenly silent, except for the moans of wounded men and the heavy breathing of winded soldiers. Amara stared around the cave. They'd lost another dozen fighting men, and most of the rest who had engaged the taken were wounded.

"Water," Bernard growled, then. "First spear, collect flasks and fill them up. Second spear, get these wounded to the rear. Third and fourth spears, I want you to clear the floor of these bodies." He turned to the Knights Flora with him, and said, "Help them, and recover every arrow you can while you're at it. Move."

Legionares set about the tasks given them, and Amara was appalled at how few of them were in condition to be up and moving. The wounded at the rear of the cave now outnumbered those still in fighting condition. She simply sat and closed her eyes for a moment.

"How is she?" she heard Bernard rumble.

Her head hurt.

"Lump on her head, there," Giraldi drawled. "See it? Took a pretty good hit. She hasn't been responding to my questions."

"Her face," Bernard said quietly. There was a note of pain in his voice.

Fire chewed steadily, ceaselessly at her cheek.

"Looks worse than it is. Nice clean cut," Giraldi replied. "That thing's claws are sharper than our swords. She was lucky not to lose an eye."

Someone took her hand, and Amara looked up at Bernard. "Can you hear me?" he asked quietly.

"Yes," she said. Her own voice sounded too quiet and weak to be her. "I'm . . . starting to come back together now. Help me up."

"You've got a head wound," Giraldi said. "It will be safer if you didn't."

"Giraldi," she said quietly, "there are too many wounded already. Bernard, help me up."

Bernard did so without comment. "Giraldi," he said. "Find out who is fit to fight and re-form the squads as necessary to fight in rotation. And get everyone some food."

The grizzled centurion nodded, rose to his feet, and withdrew to the back of the cave again. Moments later, the *legionares* at the front finished their gruesome task and retreated to the back of the cave, leaving Amara, Bernard, and Doroga the only people near the cave mouth.

Amara walked over to Doroga, and Bernard kept pace.

Walker was lying down again, and breathing heavily. Patches of his thick black fur were plastered down to his body, wet with blood. His breaths sounded odd, raspy. Blood made mud of the dirt floor beneath his chest and chin. Doroga crouched in front of the gargant with a stone jar of something that smelled unpleasantly medicinal, examining Walker's injuries and smearing them with some kind of grease from the jar.

"How is he?" Amara asked.

"Tired," Doroga replied. "Hungry. Hurting."

"Are his injuries serious?"

Doroga pressed his lips together and nodded. "He's had worse. Once." Walker moaned, a low, rumbling, and unhappy sound. Doroga's broad, ugly face contorted with pain, and Amara noticed that Doroga himself had several minor injuries he had not yet seen to.

"Thank you," Amara said quietly. "For being here. You didn't have to come with us. We'd all be dead right now but for you."

Doroga smiled faintly at her and bowed his head a little. Then he went back to his work.

Amara walked to the mouth of the cave and stared out. Bernard joined her a moment later. They watched taken moving purposefully around in a stand of trees on one of the nearby hills.

"What are they doing?" Bernard asked.

Amara wearily called Cirrus to bend light, and she watched the taken for a moment. "They're cutting trees," she reported quietly. "Working with the wood somehow. It's difficult to tell through the rain. I'm not sure what their aim is."

"They're making long spears," Bernard said quietly.

"Why would they do that?"

"The gargant is too much of a threat to them," he said. "They're making the spears so that they can kill him without paying as dearly to do it."

Amara lowered her hands and glanced back at Doroga and Walker. "But . . . they're not even proper spears. Surely they won't be effective."

Bernard shook his head. "All they need to do is carve sharp points. The taken are strong enough to drive them home if Walker doesn't close with them. If he does, they'll set the spears and let him do the work."

They stood watching the rain for a time. Then Bernard said quietly, "No one is coming to help us."

Amara said quietly, "Probably not."

"*Why?*" Bernard said, one fist clenched, his voice frustrated. "Surely the First Lord sees how dangerous this could be."

"There are any number of reasons," Amara said. "Emergencies elsewhere, for one. Logistics issues delaying the departure of any of the Legions." She grimaced. "Or it could be a problem in communications."

"Yes. No help has come," Bernard said. "Which means that Gaius never got the word. Which means that my sister is dead. Nothing else would stop her."

"That is only one possibility, Bernard," Amara said. "Isana is capable. Serai is extremely resourceful. We can't know for certain."

Doroga stepped up to stand beside them. He squinted at the taken, and said, quietly, "They are making spears."

Bernard nodded grimly.

Doroga's eyes flashed with anger. "Then this is almost over. Walker will not hide in the cave and let them stab him to death, and I will not leave him alone."

"They'll kill you," Amara said quietly.

Doroga shrugged. "That is what enemies do. We will go out to them. See how many of them we can take with us." He looked up at the clouds. "Wish it wasn't raining."

"Why not?" Amara asked.

"When I fall, I would like The One to look on." He shook his head. "Bernard, I need a shield so I can bring Walker some water."

"Certainly," Bernard said. "Ask Giraldi."

"My thanks." Doroga left them at the mouth of the cave.

Thunder rolled. Rain whispered.

Amara said, "We'll be lucky to have three squads, now."

"I know."

"The men will tire faster. Less time to rest and recover."

"Yes," he said.

"How many arrows did your Knights Flora recover?"

"Two each," he said.

Amara nodded. "Without Walker and Doroga, we can't hold them."

"I know," Bernard said. "That's why I've decided that I have to do it."

Amara shook her head. "Do what?"

"I led these men here, Amara. They're my responsibility." He squinted outside. "If we are to die . . . I don't want it to be for nothing. I owe them that. And I owe Doroga too much to let him go out there alone."

Amara stopped and looked at him. "You mean . . ."

"The queen," Bernard said quietly. "If the queen survives, it won't matter how many taken we've killed. She'll be able to start another nest. We must prevent that. At any cost."

Amara closed her eyes. "You mean to go out to them."

"Yes," Bernard said. "Doroga and Walker are going anyway. I'm going with them, along with any man who can walk and hold a weapon and is willing. We'll head for the queen and kill her."

"Outside the cave, we won't last long."

Bernard gave her a bleak smile. "I'm not so sure that's a bad thing."

She frowned and looked away from him. "It will be difficult to force our way through them without any Knights Terra left to us."

"Walker can do it," Bernard said.

"Can we reach her before they kill us?"

"Probably not," Bernard confessed. "I put an arrow right through that thing's neck, and all it did was startle her away. I saw how hard you hit it." He shook his head. "It's so fast. And with all those taken around it, it's unlikely that we'll have the time to land a killing blow. But we have no choice. If we don't kill the queen, everyone who gave his life has died for nothing."

Amara swallowed and nodded. "I . . . I think you're right. When?"

"I'll give the men a few moments more to breathe," Bernard said. "Then call for volunteers." He reached out to her and squeezed her hand. "You don't have to go with me."

She squeezed back as tightly as she could and felt tears blur her eyes. "Of course I do," she said quietly. "I'll not leave your side, my lord husband."

"I could order you to," he said quietly.

"I'll not leave your side. No matter how idiotic you are."

He smiled at her and drew her against him. She stood there in the circle of his arms for a moment, her eyes closed, breathing in his scent. Moments went by. Then Bernard said, "It's time. I'll be right back."

Thunder and rain filled the world outside, and Amara's head and her face hurt horribly. She was afraid, though so tired that it hardly seemed to matter. Bernard spoke quietly to the *legionares*.

Amara stood staring up the hill at the implacable enemy intent on tearing them all to pieces, and prepared to go out to meet them.

The nearest Cane reached down, seized the front of Tavi's tunic, and hauled him up close to its muzzle. It sniffed at him once, twice, drool and blood dripping from its fangs.

And then the Cane simply dropped him.

It ignored him and continued on into the guardroom.

Its companions followed suit.

Tavi stared in utter confusion as the Canim simply ignored his presence, but gritted his teeth and kicked himself into motion, darting between a pair of the enormous wolf-warriors and back into the guardroom, where Miles still fought against the cloaked creature, the vord queen. There was blood dripping from his left elbow, but his face was smooth and utterly expressionless as he fought, his battle with the queen one of constant, flowing grace and technique pitted against raw power and speed.

Nearer him stood another Cane, facing Kitai, while Fade hovered nervously in the background. Evidently, the two of them had immediately run to try to reach Tavi when the queen had thrown him out of the room, but the Cane had blocked their path. Even as Tavi watched, the Cane swept its sword in an overhand arch intended to split Kitai in half down the middle. The Marat girl crossed the blades of her swords and caught the blow upon them, sliding it to one side with a dancer's grace and struck out with one of her blades, drawing a flash of blood from the Cane's abdomen. The Cane didn't fall, but Tavi could see several other similar wounds upon it—painful but not debilitating.

Fade let out a hooting sound when he saw Tavi. The slave held up a second spear and flung it at Tavi. Tavi sidestepped and caught the spear in flight, set his grip, and spun to drive the weapon hard at the back of the vord queen.

The steel head of the spear penetrated the queen's green-black hide only modestly—that had not been Tavi's intent.

The strike inflicted little injury upon the vord queen, but the force of the blow drove her forward and off-balance, if only for an instant.

It was all the time Sir Miles needed.

The captain snarled in sudden exultation, and his fluid retreat reversed itself in a heartbeat. His blade whipped in two savage slashes, each one scattering droplets of strange, dark blood, and the vord queen shrieked, the sound metallic, high-pitched, and deafening, filled with pain. Miles followed up, sword flashing through a whirling web of cold steel, striking the queen twice more, driving the creature into a corner.

Then the queen let out a strange, eerie hiss of sound, her head snapping toward Miles, eyes a glow of furious scarlet within the hood of her cloak.

Miles's eyes widened and he faltered, head snapping left and right, sword darting in uncertain parries of no visible attacks. One of the Canim turned and lunged at his back, but Miles gave no sign of noticing.

"Sir Miles!" Tavi shouted.

The captain spun in time to deflect the Cane's sword, but before he could whirl back to the queen, she had recovered her balance and attacked him. Dark claws struck simultaneously with the captain's sword.

With another eerie hiss, the queen leapt away from Miles and clung up high on the wall over the door. Her head whirled around to Tavi, who saw two scarlet eyes blazing within the cloak's hood, and abruptly the two Canim nearest him turned toward Tavi, blades slashing toward him. The queen howled again, and the remaining Canim surged through the doorway toward the makeshift barrier in the back corner.

"The stairs!" Maestro Killian called. "Take the wounded down the stairs!"

Tavi ducked under a curved blade and thrust his spear against the guard of the other Cane's sword, fouling the stroke before it could properly land, and retreated to stand shoulder to shoulder with Miles. More Canim stalked into the room and advanced on Tavi and Miles, half a dozen of the enormous warriors now in the room. The vord queen dropped down to the floor behind the screen of Canim warriors, out of sight.

"Captain?" Tavi asked. "Are you all right?"

"I can fight." Miles looked up defiantly at the oncoming Canim. The near side of his face was a mask of blood and torn flesh, and all that remained of his eye was a sunken socket. There was no expression of pain on his face, the discipline of metalcrafting allowing him to ignore distractions such as agony and weariness.

One of the Canim swung its blade, and Miles blocked the blow almost contemptuously. Tavi lashed out with the spear as he did, and the blade struck the Cane's weapon arm, drawing blood. The queen shrieked again, from somewhere beyond the room, and the Canim snarled, weapons sweeping and cutting. The cramped space—for things so large as the Canim, at least—gave them only a few angles on which they could attack, and Tavi managed to dance and weave in place, dodging or fending off most strikes with the spear. Miles's blade never slowed, intercepting every strike, lashing out to bite deep into the foe. Tavi's heart pounded in terror, but he did not leave Miles's blind side.

"Kitai, Fade," Tavi shouted. "Help Killian! Get them down the stairs!"

Miles struck down another of the foe, but a second Cane drove the tip of its sword hard into Miles's chest. The captain turned, catching the blow on the keel of his breastplate, but the impact staggered him. Tavi let out a scream and assaulted the Canim with wild, repeated thrusts of his spear, trying to buy enough time for Miles to recover. The Canim did not retreat. A sword swept by, so close that it cut locks of hair from the top of Tavi's head. Another blow came at him, and Tavi had to block with the spear's shaft. It held, but only barely, the scarlet steel of the Canim's sword biting almost entirely through the length of oak. The Cane jerked its weapon clear to swing again, and the haft of the spear buckled.

Killian entered the fight in total silence. His cane struck the Cane's weapon arm, driving it up enough that the next blow missed Tavi altogether. The Maestro's sword slashed down, cutting through the tendon low on the Cane's leg, and the wolf-warrior faltered and staggered to one side. "They're through!" Killian called, shoving the hilt of his sword at Tavi. "Fall back!"

Tavi took the sword and obeyed, helping the staggering Sir Miles back to the door. Killian dodged another attack, brought his cane down sharply on the very tip of one wolf-warrior's sensitive nose, and drew a pouch from his pocket and whipped it out, scattering sand and iron filings into the air. He clenched his hand into a fist, a grunt of effort sliding from him as he did, and a sudden, tiny tempest arose, whirling the grains of sand and metal into the sensitive eyes and noses of the Canim. It neither lasted long nor inflicted any real harm, but it bought them time enough to hurry to the stairs. Once everyone was through the doorway, Fade slammed the door shut and threw the bolts, before jumping back away from it.

"That won't hold them for long," Tavi panted. He looked back down the stairs to see Kitai gently settling Max down on them. Gaius was still tied to his cot, and it lay across several stairs. Neither of them moved.

"Doesn't matter," Miles replied, also breathing heavily. "Stairs are our best chance now. They'll have to come single file. That's how we'll hold them back longest."

"We'll fight in order," Killian said. "Miles, then me, then you, Tavi. But first I want you to get Gaius back down to the meditation chamber."

"Max, too?" Tavi asked.

"No," Killian said. His voice sounded rough. "Leave him there."

Tavi stared at the blind Maestro. "What?"

"If these things think they've killed Gaius, it's possible that they won't continue to the bottom of the stairs," Killian said.

"You'll . . . sir, but Max. He's unconscious. He can't fight them."

"He knew what he was doing when he crafted himself into that form," Killian said quietly.

"At least let me move him to the bottom of the stairs," Tavi said. "If the trick works, it will work there as well as up here."

Killian hesitated, but then gave him a sharp nod. "Take the Marat and the slave to help you, and get back here as quickly as you can. Will your slave fight?"

Tavi swallowed. "I don't think he likes to, sir. But if you

need him to, tell him." He glanced back over his shoulder at Fade and met the man's eyes. "He's loyal, sir."

"Very well. Miles," Killian said. "What happened to you when you fought that creature? I thought you had it."

"So did I," Miles replied. "It must have done some kind of crafting on me. For a second, I saw two more of them, there with it, and I lost focus."

"Your injuries?" Killian asked.

"It took one of my eyes," Miles said, his voice calm. "It's going to limit how aggressively I can attack."

"Did you slay the thing?"

Miles shook his head, then said, "Doubtful. I struck its throat, but it didn't bleed the way it should have. Between the two of us, the queen may have gotten the better of the trade."

Above them, the steel door shook under a heavy impact.

"Tavi," Killian said, his voice urgent, "go on down. Miles, don't focus on cutting them down. Fight defensively and retreat as you need to. Buy us time for the Guard to break through."

"Understood," Miles said, his tone grim. "Tavi, give me that sword, please."

Tavi passed the sword he held to the captain, and Miles stood with one blade in either hand. He twirled each once, then nodded sharply and turned to face the door.

"Go, Tavi," Killian said, quietly. "There's no more time."

Fidelias knocked twice on the doors to Lady Aquitaine's private chambers in the Aquitaine manor, paused for a beat, then opened them. "My lady," he began.

Lady Aquitaine stood in profile before the room's great hearth, naked except for the fine silk gown she pressed to the front of her body with both hands. Her dark hair had been let out of its pins and dressing and spilled to her hips. Her long limbs were fit and lovely, her pale skin flawless, and a small and wicked smile curled one corner of her mouth.

Standing behind her, his hands on her hips, was Lord Aquitaine, naked to the waist. A leonine man, built with as much grace as power, his dark golden hair fell to his shoulders, and his black eyes glittered with intelligence—and annoyance.

"One wonders," he said, his voice mellow and smooth, "why my spymaster feels comfortable with a single knock upon my wife's private chamber door, followed by an immediate entrance."

Fidelias paused and bowed his head, keeping his eyes down. "In point of fact, my lord," he replied, "I knocked twice."

"Well. That changes everything then, doesn't it?" Aquitaine murmured, his tone dry. "I assume that there is a very good reason for this intrusion that will convince me not to kill you in your tracks."

Aquitaine's voice was mild, but there was a current of amusement in it which Fidelias knew removed most of the danger from the threat.

Most of it.

"Attis," Lady Aquitaine chided gently. Fidelias heard silk sliding on naked skin as she slipped her robe back on. "I'm quite certain only an urgent matter would bring him here like this. Very well, Fidelias, I am decent."

Fidelias looked up again and bowed his head to Lady Aquitaine. "Yes, my lady. Some information has come to my attention that I feel merits your immediate attention."

"What information?"

"If you would accompany me to the library, my lady, the people in question can give it to you directly and respond to your questions."

Lady Aquitaine arched an eyebrow. "Who?"

"A young man I am not acquainted with and Lady Placida Aria."

"Placida?" Lord Aquitaine murmured. "I never expected Placida or his wife to involve themselves in politics. Why would she be here?"

"Shall we ask her?" Lady Aquitaine said.

Lord Aquitaine idly pulled his loose white shirt over his head. Lady Aquitaine reached up to untuck a few errant locks that hadn't come all the way through, and the two of them left the room. Fidelias held the door, then followed them to the library.

The room wasn't large by the standards of the rest of the house, and it had seen more use than most of the rest. The furniture there was of excellent quality, of course, but it was warm and comfortable as well. A fire blazed in the hearth, and two people rose to their feet as the Aquitaines entered.

The first was a tall woman with vibrant red hair and a rich dress of emerald green. "Invidia, Attis," she murmured as they entered. She arched an eyebrow at them, and said, "Oh, dear. I must apologize for the awkward timing."

She exchanged a polite embrace with Lady Aquitaine and offered her hand to Lord Aquitaine, who kissed it with a small smirk on his mouth. "It will be the sweeter for the anticipation," he replied, then gestured for her to sit and waited for his wife to do the same before seating himself. "What brings you here?"

Fidelias remained standing in the background, against the wall.

"He does," Lady Placida replied, and gestured at the boy, still standing awkwardly, fidgeting. He wore plain but well-made clothing, and an academ's lanyard hung around his neck with but three small beads to vouch for his crafting ability.

"This is Ehren Patronus Vilius, a student at the Academy, who came to me with an unusual message." She smiled at Ehren, and said, "Please tell them what you told me, young man."

"Yes, Your Grace," Ehren replied. He licked his lips nervously, and said, "I was bid tell Lady Placida by Tavi Patronus Gaius ex Calderon that he sends his most respectful greetings and sincere apologies for the ruse he used to speak to you at Lord Kalare's garden party. He further bids me say that one hour ago, he and a companion were taken by force to a warehouse on Pier Seven, Riverside, and held there by agents calling themselves bloodcrows, whom he believed to be in the employ of Lord Kalare or someone in his household."

Lord Aquitaine's expression darkened. "Tavi Patronus Gaius. The same boy from Second Calderon?"

"Yes, dear," Lady Aquitaine told him, patting his arm. She tilted her head. "How is it that he was able to send this message, if he was held prisoner?"

"He effected an escape, Your Grace," Ehren said.

Aquitaine shot a look at his wife. "He escaped the blood-crows?"

"I told you he was resourceful," Lady Aquitaine murmured. She regarded Lady Placida, and asked, "Aria, this is fascinating, but I cannot help but wonder why you brought this news to us."

"I assume you know of the attack upon Steadholder Isana and her retinue here in the city," Lady Placida said. "And I thought it quite intriguing that she and her kin were both attacked in the same evening. Clearly, someone is attempting to embarrass Gaius before the Lords Council and Senate by killing them here, virtually under his nose."

"Clearly," Lady Aquitaine said, her expression serene.

"I know how loyal you and your husband are to the First Lord, and how highly you value the welfare of the Realm," Lady Placida went on, and there was not a trace of either sarcasm or humor in her voice. "And I thought it might be a matter of concern to you, as steadfast supporters of the Realm, that one of our own might be raising their hand against Gaius."

There was an utter silence in the room for several long seconds, then Lady Placida rose, all grace and polite reserve.

"Ehren, I believe we have imposed upon our hosts long enough. I must thank you for taking the time to come here."

"Of course, Your Grace," the young man answered, rising.

"Come along. I will have my driver take you up to the Academy."

The Aquitaines rose and exchanged polite farewells with Lady Placida, and she and the young man left the room.

"Earlier today," Fidelias said, "one of my sources discovered that the Canim were mysteriously absent from the Black Hall. Fifteen minutes before Lady Placida's arrival, word reached me of unusual activity in the Deeps. One of my sources saw a pair of Canim warriors battling in the alley behind the Black Hart on Riverside, leaving one of them dead. The Cane who won the battle was almost certainly Ambassador Varg. According to my source, the dead Cane had fought in total silence, without any sort of emotional reaction—not even to his own death. He said it was like the fighting spirit had simply been taken from the Cane."

"Taken," Lady Aquitaine breathed. "These vord the Steadholder spoke of?"

Fidelias nodded grimly. "A possibility. Five minutes ago, word reached me of fighting in the highest tunnels of the Deep, near the Citadel, and that the alarm bells have been ringing within the palace."

Aquitaine let out a hiss. "That fool, Kalare. He strikes at the First Lord *now*?"

"Too bold," Lady Aquitaine replied. "He would never try something so overt. This is a move that begins with the Canim, I think."

"Then why would their leader be killing his own guards in fights in dark alleys?" Aquitaine asked.

She shook her head. "It is possible that their loyalty has been taken." She frowned in thought. "But if there is alarm enough and confusion enough, Kalare will take the opportunity to strike. The man is a slive."

Lord Aquitaine nodded, continuing the thought to its conclusion. "He would never pass up the opportunity to strike at a weakened foe. We must therefore ensure that he does not profit from this situation." He frowned. "By preserving Gaius's rule. Crows, but that doesn't sit well with me."

"Politics make strange bedfellows," Lady Aquitaine murmured. "If Gaius is slain now, before we've dealt with Kalare, you know what will happen. In fact, it would not surprise me if the Canim are attempting to kill Gaius in order to foment an open civil war between Kalare and Aquitaine—"

"—in order to weaken the Realm as a whole." Aquitaine nodded once. "It is time we relieved Kalare of his blood-crows. Pier Seven, I believe the boy said, Fidelias?"

"Yes, my lord," Fidelias replied. "I dispatched observers who reported increasing activity. In my estimation, Kalare has sent out word to his agents, and they are gathering there to move in concentrated force."

Aquitaine exchanged a glance with his wife, then gave her a bleak smile. "Tunnels or river?"

She wrinkled her nose. "You know I hate the smell of dead fish."

"Then I'll handle the warehouse," Aquitaine said.

"Take one of them alive if you can, Attis," Lady Aquitaine said.

Lord Aquitaine gave her a flat look.

"If I don't tell you," she said calmly, "and you don't think to save one, afterward you'll complain that I didn't remind you, darling. I'm only looking after your best interests."

"Enough," he said. He leaned over to kiss Lady Aquitaine on the cheek, and said, "Be careful in the tunnels. Take no chances."

"I'll be good," she promised, rising. "Fidelias knows his way around them."

Aquitaine arched an eyebrow at Fidelias, and said, "Yes. I'm sure he does." He kissed her mouth and growled, "I'll expect to resume our conversation later."

She returned the kiss and gave him a demure smile. "I'll meet you in the bath."

Aquitaine's teeth flashed in a flicker of a smile, and he stalked from the room, intensity blazing from him like an unseen fire.

Lady Aquitaine rose, her own eyes bright, and crossed to an armoire beside the liquor cabinet. She opened it and calmly drew out a scabbarded sword on a finely tooled leather belt. She drew the sword, a long and elegantly curved saber, slipped it back into its sheath, and buckled it on. "Very well, dear spy," she murmured. "It would seem we must enter the Deeps."

"To save Gaius," Fidelias said. He let the irony color his tone.

"It wouldn't do to let Kalare poach him, now would it?" She drew a cloak of dark leather from the armoire and donned it, then slipped a pair of fencing gauntlets through the sword belt.

"I'm not an expert in fashion," Fidelias said, "but I believe steel is generally considered more tasteful than silk for any event that involves a sword."

"We're going to be near the palace, dear spy, with hundreds of angry, paranoid members of the Royal Guard. Better to appear as a conscientious Citizen happening by to help in a moment of crisis than as an armed and armored soldier creeping through the dark toward the palace." She swiftly bound her hair back into a tail with a dark scarlet ribbon. "How quickly can you get us to the palace?"

"It's a twenty-minute walk," Fidelias said. "But there's a long shaft that drives almost all the way up to the palace. It can't be climbed, but if you can lift us up it, I can have you there in five minutes."

"Excellent," she said. "Lead on. We have work to do."

CHAPTER 49

Tavi gritted his teeth as the door shook again under another blow from the taken Canim. He turned to Fade and Kitai. "Carry the cot," he said. "I'll get Max, go down ahead of you so if I lose him, he doesn't fall onto Gaius."

Kitai frowned. "Are you strong enough?"

"Yeah," Tavi sighed. "I haul him home like this all the time." He went to his senseless friend and got his weight underneath one of Max's shoulders. "Come on, Max. Move it. Got to walk you back to bed."

One of Max's eyes opened part of the way and rolled around blearily. The other had been sealed shut with crusted blood. Blood dripped from his badly wounded arm, but the bandages had held the loss to a trickle rather than a stream. His legs moved as Tavi started down the stairs. It could not by any means have been confused with actually walking, but Max managed to support enough of his own weight that Tavi's strained body could manage the rest. They went down steadily, if not swiftly.

Somewhere above them, iron screamed protest again, and a hollow, thumping boom swept down the staircase. A few seconds later there was the clash of steel on steel, which faded as they went on down away from where the wounded captain fought to hold the Canim at bay.

For the first time since he had escaped the warehouse, Tavi had a spare moment for thought. Dragging Max around was a familiar task, and while not exactly easy, it did not require his attention, either. He started piecing together the things he had seen, trying to get an idea of what might happen next.

And suddenly he couldn't breathe. It wasn't an issue of labor or lack of air. He simply could not seem to get enough air into his lungs, and his heart was pounding with such terror that he could not distinguish individual beats.

They were trapped.

Though the Royal Guard was no doubt trying to fight their way down to the First Lord, some of the Canim had to have been holding them off. The wolf-warriors were deadly in such closed spaces, where there was less room to avoid them or circle to their flanks, and where their superior reach and height made them more than a match for all but the most seasoned *legionare*. Without a doubt, the Knights of the Royal Guard would use furycrafting against them, but they would be sharply limited in what they could do for the same reasons Tavi had explained to Kitai. Not only that, but it was entirely possible that most of the Knights had not yet arrived at the top of the stairway. The attack had come in the darkest hours of the night, when most were abed, and it would take long moments for them to awaken, arm, and rush to the fight.

They were moments the First Lord simply did not have. Eventually, the Guard would overcome the Canim, of course. But the Canim only needed to hold them off for a few moments more, and in a mortal struggle those moments seemed like hours. They would simply throw themselves at Miles, exchanging themselves for blows that would merely cripple the captain. They had numbers enough to do it and still leave more to finish Miles off and tear apart those behind him.

There was no way out of the deep chamber but for the stairs. There was nowhere to run. The Canim were still coming, and Sir Miles had not managed to kill the queen. Miles, the only one of them who could hope to stand up to the Canim for long, was already wounded, bleeding, and half-blind. The smallest of mistakes or misjudgments could cost him his life, and while Tavi was confident Miles could have handled it at any other time, with his injuries it would only be a matter of minutes before he was too slow or too hampered by his damaged vision to fight perfectly.

When Miles fell, the Canim would kill the Maestro. They would kill Tavi and Kitai. They would kill Max, of course. And, unless they were extremely stupid, they would kill Gaius, as well, despite Max's willing sacrifice as the First Lord's decoy.

Gaius was still unconscious. Max was incoherent. The Maestro was an excellent teacher of the fighting arts, but he was an old man, and no soldier. Kitai had seemed to handle herself in a fight at least as well as Tavi, but she was simply not a match for one of the Canim, much less a dozen of them. Tavi himself, while a trained fighter, could hardly hope to face one of the Canim with any significant chance of victory. The disparity in size, reach, experience, power, and training was simply too great.

If the First Lord died, it would provoke a civil war—a civil war the Canim would gleefully use to their advantage. Gaius's death could quite possibly prove to be the event that signaled the end of the Aleran people.

More thoughts bounced and spun through his head, and he gritted his teeth, trying to clear his mind and focus. The best he could do was to isolate two concrete thoughts.

Gaius had to be saved regardless of the cost.

Tavi did not want to die, nor see his friends and allies harmed.

There was only one person trapped in the First Lord's defense who could make a difference.

They reached the bottom of the stairs, and Tavi settled Max down as gently as he could beside the cabinet. The larger boy, though he looked identical to the First Lord, slumped down at once, sinking into immobility and unconsciousness again. A heavy snore rattled from between his lips. Tavi laid his hand on his friend's shoulder for a moment, then rose as Kitai and Fade emerged from the meditation chamber and shut the door behind them. They started for the base of the stairs, but Tavi stepped into Fade's way, his teeth clenched, and glared at him from a handbreadth away.

"Fade," Tavi said, his voice hard. "Why didn't you fight?"

The slave eyed him, then looked away, shaking his head. "Couldn't."

"Why *not*?" Tavi demanded. "We needed you. Max could have been killed."

"I *couldn't*," Fade said. His eyes shifted warily, and Tavi saw real fear in them. "Miles was fighting that thing, that vord. It was too fast. If I'd drawn steel, he would have recognized me immediately." Fade took a slow breath. "The distraction would have killed him. It still might."

"He's hurt," Tavi said. "And we have no idea how long he can fend them off."

Fade nodded, his expression bleak, full of old pain. "I . . . Tavi, I don't know if I can. I don't know if I could bear it if . . ." He shook his head and said, "I thought I could, but being back here . . . So *much* will change, and I don't want that."

"Dying is a change," Kitai put in. "You don't want that, either."

Fade shrank a little.

Tavi made a gesture to Kitai to let him do the talking. "Fade, the First Lord needs you."

"That arrogant, pompous, egotistical old *bastard*," Fade spat, his voice suddenly filled with an alien, entirely vicious hatred, "can go to the bloody crows."

Tavi's fist caught the ragged slave on the tip of his chin and knocked Fade onto his rear on the smooth stone floor. Fade lifted his hand to his face, his expression one of pure shock and surprise.

"Since you don't seem to be thinking well," Tavi said, his voice cold, "let me help you. Your feelings toward Gaius are irrelevant. He is the rightful First Lord of Alera. If he dies here tonight, it will cast our entire people into a civil war that will be a signal to our enemies to attack us. The vord pose a threat that could be worse than the Canim, Marat, and Icemen combined if it is left to fester, and we need a strong and uni-fied central command to make sure it doesn't happen."

Fade stared up at Tavi, his expression still stunned.

"Do you understand what is happening here? Millions of lives depend on the outcome of this hour, and there is no time to be distracted by personal grudges. To save the Realm, we must save Gaius." Tavi leaned down, seized the hilt of Fade's worn old sword, and drew it from its scabbard. Then he knelt on one knee and stared into Fade's eyes while he reversed his grip on the blade and offered the hilt to the slave over one arm.

"Which means," Tavi said quietly, "that the Realm needs Araris Valerian."

Fade's eyes brimmed with tears, and Tavi could almost feel the terrible old pain that brought them, the fear that filled the scarred slave's haunted eyes. He lifted his hand and touched his fingers to the coward's brand on his maimed cheek. "I . . . I don't know if I can be him again."

"You were him at Calderon," Tavi said. "You saved my life. We'll work something out with your brother, Fade. I promise that I'll do everything I possibly can to help you both. I don't know the details of what came between the two of you. But you're his brother. His blood."

"He'll be angry," Fade whispered. "He might . . . I couldn't hurt him, Tavi. Not even if he killed me."

Tavi shook his head. "I won't allow that to happen. No matter how angry he might be, underneath it he loves you. Anger subsides. Love doesn't."

Fade folded his arms over his chest, shaking his head. "You don't understand. I c-can't. I can't. It's been too long."

"You must," Tavi said. "You *will*. You gave me your sword. And you didn't mean it as a present for me to hang on my wall. You meant it as something more. Didn't you? That's why Gaius was so disapproving when he saw it."

Fade's face twisted with some new agony, but he nodded.

Tavi did, too. "With or without you, I'm going back up those stairs," he said, "and I'm going to fight those animals until I'm dead or until the First Lord is safe. Take up your sword, Fade. Come with me. I need your help."

Fade exhaled sharply and bowed his head. Then he took a deep breath, lifted his right hand, and took the sword Tavi offered him. He met Tavi's eyes, and said, quietly, "Because you ask it of me."

Tavi nodded, clasped Fade's shoulder with one hand again, and they rose together.

CHAPTER 50

"They're forming up again," Amara reported, staring out at the taken holders. A score of them held long, rough spears of raw wood, crude points hacked into them with knives and sickles and swords. "Looks like they're using the *legionares'* shields, too."

Bernard grunted and came up to the front of the cave to stand beside her. "They'll use the shields to cover the spears from our archers. That volley must have been worse than they expected." The rain came down in steady, heavy drops outside the cave. Flashes of green-tinged lightning continued to dance through the clouds veiling the summit of Garados, and the air had grown steadily thicker and more oppressive, a sense of old, slow malice permeating every sight and sound. "And the furystorm is about to break, if I'm any judge. We'll have windmanes coming down on us in half an hour."

"Half an hour," Amara mused. "Do you think it will matter to us by then?"

"Maybe not," Bernard said. "Maybe so. Nothing is written in stone."

A wry smile twisted Amara's mouth. "We might survive the vord to be killed by windmanes. That's your encouragement? Your reassurance?"

Bernard grinned, staring out at the enemy, defiance in his eyes. "With any luck, even if we don't take them, the furystorm will finish what we started."

"That really isn't any better," Amara said. She laid a hand on his shoulder. "Could we wait here? Let the furystorm take them?"

Bernard shook his head. "Looks to me like they know it's coming, too. They've got to take the cave before the storm breaks."

Amara nodded. "Then it's time."

Bernard looked over his shoulder, and said, "Prepare to charge."

Behind him, waiting in ranks, was every *legionare* still able to stand and wield a blade. Twoscore swords hissed from their sheaths with steely whispers that promised blood.

"Doroga," Bernard called. "Give us twenty strides before you move."

The Marat chieftain lay astride Walker's broad back, the cave's ceiling forcing his chest to the gargant's fur. He nodded at Bernard, and said something in a low voice to Walker. The gargant's great claws gouged the floor of the cave, and his chest rumbled an angry threat for the enemy outside.

Bernard nodded sharply and glanced at the archers. The Knights Flora each held an arrow to the bowstring. "Wait until the last moment to shoot," he told them quietly. "Clear as many of those spears from Walker's path as you can." He fit a string to his own bow and glanced at Amara. "Ready, love?"

She felt frightened, but not so much as she had thought she would be. Perhaps there had simply been too much fear over the past hours for it to overwhelm her now. Her hand felt steady as she drew her sword from its scabbard. Really, she felt more sad than afraid. Sad that so many good men and women had lost their lives. Sad that she could do nothing better for Bernard or his men. Sad that she would have no more nights with her new husband, no more silent moments of warmth or desire.

That was behind her now. Her sword was cold and heavy and bright in her hand.

"I'm ready," she said.

Bernard nodded, closed his eyes, and took a long breath, then opened them. In his left hand, he held his great bow, arrow to the string. With his right, he drew his sword, lifted it, and roared, "*Legionares!* At the double, forward march!"

Bernard stepped forward into a slow jog, and every *legionare* behind him started out in that same step, so that their boots struck the ground in unison. Amara followed apace, struggling to keep her steps even with Bernard's. Once the *legionares* were all clear of the cave mouth, Bernard lifted a hand and slashed it to his left.

Amara and the Knights Flora immediately peeled away, to the left of the column's advance, making their way up a low slope that would allow them to shoot over the heads of the column almost until they engaged the taken.

Once they were clear of the column's path, Bernard lifted his hand and roared, "*Legionares!* Charge!"

Every Aleran throat opened in a roar of, "Calderon for Alera!" The *legionares* surged forward in a wave of steel, and their boots were a muffled thunder upon the rain-soaked earth as they followed the Count of Calderon into battle. At the same time, Walker emerged from the cave mouth, the bloodied gargant's battle roar joining that of the *legionares* as it accelerated into a lumbering run, deceptively swift for all its apparent clumsiness, his claws biting into the earth. Walker began to gain on the *legionares* at once, gathering momentum while Doroga whirled his long-handled cudgel over his head, howling.

An unearthly yowl rolled out from the stand of trees, and the taken moved in abrupt, silent, and perfect concert. They formed into a loose half circle, shields in the front rank, while those holding spears set them to receive the charge, making the taken shieldwall bristle with the crude weapons.

Amara beckoned Cirrus as she ran, struggling to exert the bare minimum of effort necessary for the fury to bend light and let her see the enemy. She had only one duty in this battle—to find the vord queen and point her out to Bernard.

Beside her, the Knights Flora raised their bows. Arrows flashed out through the rain, striking eyes and throats with unerring precision, and over the next ten seconds half a dozen of the spearmen fell despite the use of the Legion shields. The taken moved at once, others picking up the spears and moving into the place of the fallen—but the disruption was enough to create an opening in the fence of rude spears, allowing the *legionares* to drive their charge home.

Shield met shield with a deafening metallic thunder, and the *legionares* hewed at the crude spears with their vicious, heavy blades, further widening the opening and disrupting the formation of the taken.

"Shift left!" Bernard cried. "Shift left, left, left!"

The *legionares* immediately moved together, a sudden lateral dash of no more than twenty feet.

And a heartbeat later, Doroga and Walker crashed onto the breach in the thicket of spears.

Amara stared in utter shock for a moment at the gargant's impact. She had never heard a beast so loud, never seen anything so unthinkably strong. Walker's chest slammed into the shieldwall, crushing several of the taken who bore them. His great head swung left and right, slamming more of the taken around like an angry child with his toys, and Doroga leaned far over the saddle-mat with his cudgel, striking down upon the skulls of the taken. The gargant plowed through the ranks of the taken without slowing, leaving a corridor of destruction behind him, halted, whirled, and immediately laid into the ranks of the taken with savage claws.

Before the charge was complete, the *legionares* roared together and slammed forward in a frenzied, all-out attack, catching the taken between them and the blood-maddened gargant.

Amara bit her lip, sweeping her gaze around the battle, desperate to find the queen, to do *something* to help Bernard and his men. She could only watch the battle, seeing flashes of it in horrible clarity as she searched for the queen.

After the initial shock of the gargant's charge, the taken moved together into a counterattack. Within a minute, several with spears had spread out to either side of Walker, and thrust the weapons at the gargant while Doroga attempted to parry them away with his great club. The others focused on the *legionares*, and though the men fought with undeniable skill and courage, the numbers against them were simply too great, and their momentum began to falter.

She watched as Bernard ducked the swing of an axe wielded by an old grey-haired man, and the *legionare* beside him struck a killing blow upon his attacker with a downsweep of his sword. Seconds later, a child, a girl of no more than ten or twelve summers, hauled a *legionare*'s leg out from beneath him and twisted with savage power, breaking it. The *legionare* screamed as other taken hauled him away and fell upon him with mindless savagery. An ancient crone thrust a wooden spear into Walker's shoulder and the gargant whirled with a scream of pain, swatting at the spear and shattering its shaft.

And then Amara saw a flicker of motion, behind Doroga and Walker, something darting out of the shadow of the trees, covered by the folds of a dark cloak and hood.

"There!" she cried to the archers, pointing. "There!"

Moving swiftly, two Knights touched their last arrows, bound with oiled cloths just beneath the heads, so the embers in the small firepots on their belts set the arrows aflame. They drew and loosed, sending twin streaks of fire hissing through the rain. One arrow struck the shape directly, shattering as if it had impacted upon a heavy breastplate. The other arrow missed striking anything solid, but lodged in the folds of the vord queen's cloak.

That was the signal. Bernard's head whipped around to trace the flight of the fire arrows, and he roared commands to his *legionares*, who wheeled and surged toward the vord queen with desperate power. Doroga whipped his head around as the vord queen leapt at him. He threw himself to one side, rolled off the gargant's back, and landed in a heavy crouch. The vord queen whirled and rushed him, only to alter her course when Walker threw himself into the queen's path.

"Swords!" Amara snapped to the Knights with her. "With me!" They drew steel and sprinted forward, circling the chaos of the melee to head for the queen. Amara sprinted ahead of the Knights, swifter than they on foot, sidestepping a clumsy grab from one of the taken and striking it down as she flew past it. She saw the queen leap again, claws flashing in an effort to put out one of the gargant's eyes. Walker turned his head into the leap, gashing the queen with his tusks, and sending her bouncing across the earth not ten yards from Amara.

The Cursor shouted a wordless battle cry, sword raised, and called to Cirrus for swiftness enough to challenge the queen. The queen whirled to face Amara, claws spread, and let out another shriek. Half a dozen taken peeled away from the fight to charge Amara, but the Knights with her intercepted them, swords raised, and kept them from moving forward.

Amara swept her sword in a feinting cut, then reversed direction and drove her blade in a thrust aimed for the queen's eyes. The queen swatted the blade away, but not before it bit into the creature's face, tearing the hood away and giving Amara a full look at the vord queen's features for the first time.

It looked human.

It almost looked familiar.

Though its skin was green-black, shining and hard, the creature's face looked almost Aleran, but for slightly canted eyes like the Marat. Curly black hair writhed in a mussed wreath around the vord queen's head. Fangs dimpled full feminine lips. But for the fangs, the shade of its skin, and its luminous eyes, the vord queen could have been a young and lovely Aleran girl.

The queen recoiled, and a trickle of a thick, greenish fluid oozed from the cut across her cheekbone. The queen touched her cheek and stared at the blood on her fingers, raw and somehow childlike amazement on her face. "You harmed me."

"That makes us even," Amara said, her voice grim. She shouted and closed again, her sword whipping fast and hard at the queen.

The vord queen darted away from the blow and came back toward Amara with a counterattack of blinding speed that the Cursor barely avoided. The queen shrieked as they fought, and Amara heard and felt the sudden presence of more taken at her back, breaking off from the melee to assist the queen. She ruthlessly suppressed a sudden urge to call Cirrus and sail above the battle to engage the queen in classic flying passes, and stayed focused on her enemy. She exchanged another rapid series of attack and counter with the vord queen, all too aware that the taken were closing on her with every second that passed.

"Countess!" called one of the Knights, and she turned in time to see one of them struck down by a swing of a worn woodsman's axe. Not a heartbeat later, a taken fist slammed against the neck of a second Knight, and he dropped into a limp heap.

The third Knight panicked. Half a dozen taken closed on him, and in obvious desperation he looked back at the outstretched branches of a nearby oak. He made a sharp gesture and one of those branches bent and stretched down enough for him to seize it in one hand. The branch sprang back, hauling him out and away from the hands and weapons of the taken.

But the instant he gestured, at least a dozen taken faces whirled toward the desperate Knight. Amara could almost *feel* a sudden, alien pressure against her eyelashes as the taken holders focused on the Knight.

Every branch of that tree, and every branch of every tree within twenty yards began to whip and thrash madly, bending and smashing and wrenching.

Seconds later, what was left of the doomed man pattered down from branch and bough in a grisly rain. None of the remains could ever have been identified as belonging to a human being.

The vord queen smiled at Amara then, as two dozen taken flung themselves toward her back.

And Amara smiled at the queen as Doroga spun in a running circle to gather terrible momentum into his war cudgel and struck.

The queen turned at the last second, and while unable to avoid the blow entirely, she slipped enough of it to survive the terrible impact of the war club, though it threw her across twenty feet of muddy ground. She rolled and came to rest crouched oddly, her weight upon her toes and her left hand. The other hung uselessly. The queen hissed and whirled to retreat—only to see Walker crash into the ranks of the taken. To one hand, Doroga closed in, his cudgel held ready, cold fury in the barbarian's eyes. To the other Amara waited, cold and bitter blade in hand, already stained with the queen's blood. And as the queen turned toward the last quarter, Bernard's *legionares* cut the last taken from their lord's path, and the Count of Calderon, his men holding back the taken behind him, drove his sword into the soft earth and raised the great black bow.

The queen turned to the nearest of her foes, Amara, wild eyes staring—and Amara suddenly felt an alien presence against her thoughts, like a blind hand reaching out to touch her face. Time slowed and Amara understood what was happening—earlier, the queen had listened to her thoughts. Now she was attempting to rake through them, though in doing so, she revealed her own to Amara.

Amara could all but see the queen's mind. The queen was simply stunned at what was happening. Though the Alerans had managed to entrap the queen, they had doomed themselves to do so. There was no way they would be able to escape the wrath of the taken around them, no chance that they would survive—and it had never occurred to the queen that her foe's tactics would simply decline to take survival into account.

Sacrifice.

The vord queen's thoughts locked upon the word, found there in Amara's mind.

Sacrifice.

She did not understand. Though the vord queen could comprehend that those facing it were willing to give up their own continuation to destroy hers, she did not understand the thought behind it, beneath it, motivating it. How could they regard their own deaths as a victory, regardless of what happened to their foe? It was not reasonable. It was not a manner of thought that promoted survival. Such deaths could serve no Purpose whatsoever.

It was madness.

And as she gazed upon the vord queen, Amara suddenly found herself entangled in the racing thoughts of the creature. She saw the vord queen tense, saw her leap forward, saw fangs and claws gleaming as the queen came—and Amara *felt* the queen decide upon her as the weakest target, the most likely path of escape. She felt the queen's detached certainty, the gathering tension as claws swept toward Amara's throat.

There was a heavy thrumming sound, a thud of impact, then Bernard's first arrow struck the vord queen beneath the arm and sank to the fletchings in her flesh. The power of the impact threw her to one side and cast her to the ground, and Amara was abruptly freed from the horrible entanglement of her thoughts with the queen's.

She watched as the queen rose again, and Bernard's last arrow hammered into her throat, bloodied head erupting from her armored flesh. Again, the queen was thrown down. Again, she staggered erect, blood pouring from her wounds. She wavered, then those luminous eyes focused on Amara, and the queen flung herself into one last, desperate leap toward the Cursor.

"Amara!" Bernard cried.

Amara lifted her sword, and as the queen leapt upon her, she stood her ground, legs wide and steady. She ignored the deadly talons and claws, though she knew the queen intended to kill until no life remained in her body, and focused instead on the distance between them, on the glimmer of fangs in the queen's shrieking mouth.

And then Amara moved, all at once, a concentrated explosion of every nerve and muscle fiber that moved her sword arm alone. She drove the sturdy *legionare*'s blade forward, and its tip dived into the queen's mouth, into her throat, and on through, parting bone and tissue. There was a horrible sensation of impact, hot pain in her arm, her leg, and a shattering collision with the ground.

Amara lay stunned for a confused moment, unable to understand why she suddenly could not see, and why someone was pouring water into her face. Then a weight was lifted from her, and she remembered the cold rain falling from the sky. Bernard lifted her, helped her sit up, and Amara stared for a moment at the unmoving corpse of the queen beside her, a *legionare*'s blade driven to the hilt into her mouth.

"You did it, love," Bernard said. "You did it."

She leaned wearily against him. Around them, she could see perhaps twenty *legionares* fighting shield to shield. Doroga, wounded with a dozen small cuts, stood beside Walker. Though the beast shook its tusks defiantly, it hardly seemed able to remain standing, much less to fight, and when it lunged at one of the taken, the thing easily evaded the clumsy, limping motion.

Amara blinked the rain out of her eyes and watched as scores of taken fought to overwhelm the exhausted, outnumbered Alerans.

"We did it," she said, and just speaking the words was exhausting. "We did it."

Thunder rolled again, amidst angry lightning, and the firelit clouds of the furystorm rolled down the mountainside toward the embattled scene.

"Hold me?" Amara asked quietly.

"All right," Bernard said.

And then a storm of fire and deafening sound roared down from the low clouds and charred two dozen of the taken holders to ash and blackened bones.

Amara gasped, leaning weakly against Bernard.

"Close in!" Bernard bellowed. "Close in, stay together, stay low!" Amara was aware of the *legionares*, struggling to obey Bernard's orders, of Doroga urging Walker in one of the Marat tongues. But mostly she was conscious of another flicker of light in the clouds, an eight-pointed star formed of lightning that danced from point to point so swiftly to make it seem a wheel of sudden fire—a fire that coalesced, flashed down, and charred another, even broader swath of the taken to corpses.

She had to have been imagining it. From the furious sky appeared dozens of forms—Knights Aeris, both flying formation and serving as bearers for open aerial litters. Twice more, lightning tore from the heavens, rending the ranks of the taken, and then another eight Knights Aeris descended low enough to be seen, gathering a final burst of lightning into an eight-pointed star between them, and hurling it down at the taken.

Men in armor, mercenaries she thought, dismounted from the litters and engaged the remaining taken. There was a stunned moment of shock. And then came a roar from the surviving *legionares* as impossible hope washed over them.

Amara struggled to rise, and Bernard supported her, his sword held still in one hand, as the mercenaries and the *legionares*, between them, shattered the rest of the taken and put them down. Most of the fighting mercenaries wielded blades with the devastating grace and skill of master metalcrafters.

"Knights," Amara whispered. "They're all Knights. Every one of them."

A man cut down three of the taken in as many strokes, then casually turned and began walking toward Bernard before the last one had fully fallen to the ground. He was a giant of a man, heavily armored, and as he approached he took off his helmet and bore it under one arm. He had dark hair, a beard, an angry scar, not too old on one cheek, and his eyes were calm, detached, passionless.

"You," Bernard said to the man.

"Aldrick ex Gladius," Amara said. "Of the Windwolves. In service to the High Lord Aquitaine. I thought you were dead."

The captain of the mercenaries nodded his head. "That was the idea," he said. He gestured around at the mercenaries now engaged in mopping up the last of the enemy and looking for wounded in need of assistance. "Compliments of Steadholder Isana, Lord Count, Countess Amara."

Bernard pursed his lips. "Really? Then she did find help at the capital."

Aldrick nodded once. "We were dispatched here to aid the garrison by whatever means we could. I apologize we were not here sooner, but bad weather slowed us. Though I suppose it meant we had a nice, ripe storm to play with when we did arrive." He glanced up at the skies and mused, "It takes the fun out of things, but it isn't professional to let that kind of resource go to waste."

"I cannot say that I am sorry to have your help, Aldrick," Bernard said. "But neither can I say that I am glad to see you. The last time we met, you all but gutted me on the walls of Garrison."

Aldrick tilted his head to one side, and said, "You've been a soldier. That wasn't personal, Your Excellency. I neither offer you any apology nor take any particular pleasure in what I did. But I need you to tell me if you can live with that, right now. One way or another, it's got to be settled immediately."

Bernard frowned at the man and nodded once. "I can. I would have word of Steadholder Isana."

Aldrick nodded. "Of course, though I have little enough to give you. But first, Your Excellency—"

Bernard slashed a hand at the air. "Bernard. You've saved my men's lives. You don't need to use the title."

Aldrick tilted his head to one side, and his expression changed by some subtle degree. He inclined his head, a minor but significant gesture of respect, and continued, "I suggest that we take shelter in that cave, then. My Knights Aeris stole a great deal of a powerful wind fury's thunder, and it will send windmanes to seek vengeance. With your permission, Count, we'll move into the caves to shelter until the storm is past. My watercrafters can see to your wounded while we are there."

Amara frowned steadily at Aldrick, but when Bernard glanced at her she nodded weakly. "We can sort out our past differences after we've all survived the storm."

"Excellent," Aldrick said, turning away with professional preoccupation. He flipped his hand in a short series of gestures at one of his fellow mercenaries, who spread word to the rest of them. Bernard passed on orders to gather up the Aleran wounded and make for the cave in order to find shelter from the still-coming storm.

"I can walk," Amara told Bernard. She took a step to prove it and almost fell down.

He caught her, and said, "Gently, love. Let me take you. You've hit your head."

"Mmmm," Amara murmured with a sigh. Then she blinked her eyes slowly open and said, "Oh, dear."

"Oh dear?" Bernard asked.

She reached up and touched her throat, where Bernard's ring still hung by its chain. "Oh, dear. We've survived. We're alive. And . . . and we're wed."

Bernard blinked a few times, then mused, "Why, yes. I suppose that's true. We've lived. And we've married. I suppose now we'll have to stay together. Perhaps even be in love."

"Exactly," Amara repeated, closing her weary eyes with a sigh and leaning against the broad strength of his chest. "This ruins everything."

He walked several steps, carrying her without apparent effort, before he said, "Will you still have me, then?"

She lifted her face to press a kiss against his throat, and murmured, "Forever, my lord, if you will have me."

He answered her with his voice thick with emotion. "Aye, my lady. And honored to."

Tavi went first, rushing back up the winding stairway. The clash of steel on steel warned them that they were drawing near, and several steps later, the steps went dark and slick with spilled blood. Tavi looked up to see Captain Miles holding the stairs against the Canim. One Cane was down, crumpled life-lessly to the stone stairs, and its blood had formed the stream that stained them. The dead Cane's companions had simply walked over the corpse, digging clawed toes into it to secure their footing on the treacherous, slick stairway.

Miles had been driven slowly down the stairs by the sheer power of his foes, and he had been wounded again; his left leg was soaked in blood from the knee down. As a result, his bal-ance was awkward and precarious on the curl of the stairway, and he had to shuffle his balance clumsily to retreat down an-other step, while his opponent showered blow after blow down at the wounded captain.

Behind Miles, leaning heavily against a wall, was Maestro Killian. His sword lay several steps below where he stood, and he clutched his cane tightly to his chest. His chest and shoulder were soaked with blood: He'd been wounded as well.

"Tavi?" Killian gasped. "Hurry. Hurry, boy!"

"Fade," Tavi snapped, and pressed his back to the wall to give the scarred slave room to pass.

Fade lifted his eyes to Tavi, then past him, to Miles, widen-ing as they saw the man's injuries, and how obviously he'd been slowed and weakened by them. Fade's eyes narrowed, then he was in motion, darting past Tavi to rush forward to Sir Miles.

"Miles!" Fade barked. "Step out low!"

Captain Miles moved with the kind of instant response that can only come from training and long practice. He feinted high with his blade, then just as Fade reached him, he dropped into a crouch and rolled to his left, bumping awkwardly down several stairs.

Fade did not draw his sword until Miles first dropped, then it sprang from its sheath in a strike that cut the air with a vicious hiss. It struck the Cane's weapon at its weakest point, just above the hilt, and shattered it into shards of scarlet steel that struck sparks from the stone wherever they hit. A second strike removed the Cane's leg at the knee, and as it fell a third blow struck the creature's head from its neck. Fade delivered a kick to the falling body's belly, and it tottered backward, blood spraying in a fountain into the noses and eyes of the next Cane in the line.

Fade advanced, stepping on the fallen Cane to keep his footing, and his blade slithered through the guard of the blinded Cane, opening its belly in an S-shaped cut that spilled blood and worse onto the stairs. The Cane fell, snapping with its jaws and slashing with its blade as it died, but Fade blocked both with almost contemptuous skill, and finished the Cane with a flickering cut to the throat that flowed directly into another step forward and up, coupled with a sweeping stroke aimed at the next Cane in the line.

Tavi ran up to the Maestro, checking Killian's injuries. He'd taken a nasty blow to the slope of muscle between neck and shoulder, and had been fortunate that the blow had cut no deeper than it had. Tavi drew his knife and cut off a section of his cloak, folded it into a pad, and pressed it to the injury. "There," he said. "Hold this there."

Killian did so, though his face was pale with pain. "Tavi. I can't see them," he said, voice tight. "I can't . . . tell me what is happening."

"Fade is fighting," Tavi said. "Miles is hurt, but he's alive. Three Canim are down now."

Killian let out a soft groan. "There are ten more beyond them," he said. "Felt them earlier. One of them tore up Miles's leg when he struck it down. Got his teeth into him before he died, and Miles fell. I had to step in until he could rise. Stupid. Too old to be thinking I can do this nonsense."

"Ten," Tavi breathed. The shock of Fade's arrival to the fight had worn off, and now he fought without any sort of forward movement, his blade clashing with that of the snarling Cane, each striking and parrying with deadly speed.

There was a sudden rush of air sweeping up from the

stairway beneath them, then a hollow, deafening boom that shook the stone beneath them.

"Bloody crows," Tavi swore, bracing himself against the wall. "What was that?"

Killian tilted his head, blind eyes focused on nothing. "Firecrafting," he said. "A big one. Maybe in the hall at the top of the stairs."

"The Guard," Tavi said, sudden hope a surge in his chest. "They're coming."

"H-have to hold—" Killian said. "Must—" Then the Maestro sagged and almost fell.

Tavi caught his slight weight with a curse. "Kitai!" he called.

She came up to him immediately, sword in hand, her eyes on the fight a few steps above them. "Is he dead?"

"Not yet," Tavi said. "Take him. Get him back down the stairs, by Max."

Kitai nodded once and slipped the sword through her belt, before picking up Killian at least as easily as Tavi had. "Wait," he told her, and hurriedly cut another strip from his cloak, using it to bind the blood-soaked pad he'd fashioned over the Maestro's injuries. "There," he said. "Go, go."

Kitai nodded, and met his eyes. Her own were worried. "Be cautious, Aleran."

"Don't be gone long," Tavi replied, and she nodded shortly before turning to descend the stairs.

Tavi went to Miles next. The captain had hauled himself up to a sitting position, back against the wall, and lay there panting, his eyes closed. He looked almost violently weary, chest heaving, his face bloodied and horrible with its empty eye socket, and creased with pain despite his crafting. Tavi knelt near him, and Miles's sword arm twitched seemingly of its own volition, blade darting out to touch its tip to Tavi's throat.

Tavi froze, eyes wide, and said, "Sir Miles, it's Tavi."

The wounded captain opened his eye and blinked blearily at Tavi. The sword wavered and dropped. Tavi knelt immediately, examining Miles's injuries. The wounds on his face looked hideous, but they weren't deadly. Some of them had already clotted with blood. His wounded leg was much worse. The Cane's teeth had sunk into the meat of his thigh, just above his knee, and then ripped savagely through his flesh, until it looked like so much raw meat. Tavi jerked his cloak off and used the remaining material to fashion another thick pad and tie it tight.

"Guard?" Miles muttered. His voice was thready and weak. "The Guard got here?"

"Not yet," Tavi said.

"Wh-who, then? That's . . . that's old battlespeak. Step out low. Haven't heard it in years." He blinked his eye at Tavi, then turned his head almost drunkenly to the battle raging only a few stairs away.

Miles froze. His eye opened wider, and then his lips parted to let out a soft, weak little sound. He started trembling, so violently that Tavi could feel it in his hands as he finished with the bandage on the captain's thigh. "This isn't . . ." His face twisted into a grotesque grimace. "No, this isn't possible. He's dead. He died with Septimus. They all died with Septimus."

Fade dodged a sweeping blow of the Cane's sword by the width of a blade of grass, then struck out in a pair of blows that maimed the Cane's weapon arm, then struck its muzzle from its skull. The Cane fell toward him in a sudden frenzy of motion, trying to seize him with its remaining paw-hand, but Fade ducked away, retreating down three steps as the Cane fell, and struck a blow that sheared off a portion of its skull and killed it at once. He barely got his blade up fast enough to block the next Cane's sword, and the creature's vicious attack put him on the defensive, driving him down another step.

"Now draw him out," Miles said in a dull voice. "Make him overextend, and take the weapon arm and leg."

The Cane missed a throat slash by a hair, nearly struck Fade with the scything return stroke, and had Fade wobbling on the edge of the next step as the Cane surged forward. In the instant before it struck, Fade recovered his balance, so quickly that Tavi knew it had been a ruse from the outset, ducked under the Cane's blade, then surged inside its guard, struck a crippling blow to its weapon arm, then down to its forward leg in one single circular motion. The Cane fell, but not before Fade's sword had circled around again, using the Cane's own weight to add power to its upswing and all but severing the wolf-warrior's head as it fell.

"Perfect," Miles said quietly. "Perfect. He was always perfect." He blinked his eye several times, and Tavi saw a tear slice down through the blood on Miles's face. "Furies. He's gotten better since that day. But it can't be. It can't be."

"Miles," Tavi said quietly. "You aren't seeing things. It's your brother."

"Araris is *dead*," Miles snarled.

"He looks fairly lively to me," Tavi said.

Miles shook his head again, weeping, as Fade's sword wove an impenetrable sheet of steel between himself and the next Cane warrior. "See, there," he mumbled, his tone suddenly distant again. "That was Septimus's favorite defense. He learned it from pirates, for fighting on slick decks in rough seas. The Princeps taught it to all of us. Or tried to. Only Aldrick and Araris really understood it. How could I not have seen him?" He turned his eye from Fade to Tavi, his expression bewildered. "How could this be? How can he be here?"

"He came with me," Tavi said quietly. "From Calderon. He'd been a slave in my uncle's steadholt since I was a child. Gaius brought him here when I came."

"Gaius. Why would Gaius . . ." His voice suddenly trailed off, and his eye widened again. Beneath the blood on his face, Miles's skin went white, and he stared at Tavi. "Great furies," he whispered. "Great bloody furies."

Tavi frowned at Miles. "What is it?"

Miles opened his mouth, then hesitated, his expression an anguish of pain, exhaustion, and shock.

"Tavi!" Fade shouted suddenly, and Tavi whipped his eyes upward.

Fade still fought furiously, his plain old blade striking sparks from the bloodsteel of the Canim weapons, but motion on the ceiling drew Tavi's eyes as spindly, many-legged forms glided swiftly and gracefully along the stone.

Wax spiders. Keepers.

Miles gripped his sword, but the wax spiders did not attack them. They simply flowed overhead, moving in an undulating line of a dozen or more, and vanished around the curve of the stairs below them.

The First Lord. Max. The Maestro. They all lay helpless down there. The deadly venom of the wax spiders would finish them. Only Kitai was capable of defending herself, and she did not know that the spiders were coming. She would never be able to defend all the wounded if they caught her unawares. She would be lucky to survive it herself.

"Gaius," Miles hissed. "They're going down for Gaius." He tried to get his leg underneath him and rise—but Tavi suddenly realized that the Cane had savaged Miles's good leg. His other, the one that had never fully healed, that had given him a permanent limp, could not support him entirely on its own. Even had his injuries left his leg functional, Tavi was unsure Miles could have risen on his own. Exhaustion and loss of blood had taken a horrible toll, and Tavi realized that it was everything Miles could do simply to remain conscious.

Tavi pushed Miles back against the wall, and said, "Stay here. I'll go."

"No," Miles growled. "I'm coming with you."

He tried to rise again, but Tavi slammed him back against the wall with ease. "Captain!" He met Miles's eyes, and said, without rancor, "You're no good to anyone in this condition. You'll slow me down."

Miles closed his eyes for a moment, mouth pressed into a bitter line. Then he nodded once, took his sword, and offered its bloody hilt to Tavi.

Tavi took the captain's sword and met his eyes. Miles tried to smile at him, then grasped Tavi's shoulder with one hand, and said, "Go, lad."

Tavi's heart pounded with terror more pure and awful than anything he had felt in all of his life—not fear for himself, though he certainly was afraid. He was terrified not so much by the prospect of his death as by the possibility that he was insufficient to the task. He was the only one who might warn Kitai and defend the wounded from the wax spiders.

The consequences of failure were too horrible to contemplate, and every second that passed counted against him.

Even as those thoughts played through his mind, Tavi laid the sword back along his forearm in case he should slip on the stairs, then flung himself down them with wild abandon.

CHAPTER 52

Fidelias hated flying.

Granted, shooting up the long shaft in the Deeps had little in common with soaring above the countryside, at least superficially, but cut each of the experiences to the bone and the only real difference was that outdoor flight had a better view. He was still traveling at a terrifying rate of speed, and he had no control whatsoever over either his speed or his course— and, most importantly, his life was utterly dependent upon someone else.

Lady Aquitaine could kill him at any moment, simply by doing nothing at all. Gravity would hammer him to the floor far below, and it was unlikely anyone who found his corpse would be able to identify it, much less trace it to her. He would be helpless to stop her, and he knew perfectly well that she was capable of a calculated murder. If ever he became a liability to her ambitions, she might well decide to remove him.

Of course, he mused, Lady Aquitaine could arguably murder him at any moment, for any reason or none at all, and there would be as little he could do to stop her. He had turned against the Crown and committed himself to the cause of her husband's house, and only their continued satisfaction with his service prevented them from turning him over to the Crown or, more likely, quietly doing away with him. There it was. His reaction to the flight up the long shaft was irrational. He was in no more danger now than at any other given moment.

But he still hated flying.

He glanced aside at Lady Aquitaine as they rose on a column of wind. The dark banner of her hair whipped back and forth like a pennon in the gale, and her silk dress did the same, offering the occasional flash of her pale and shapely legs. Fidelias had long since dispensed with the natural hesitation of most people to treat watercrafters as contemporaries despite the apparent youth of their features. He had dealt with far too many outwardly youthful men and women who possessed the experience and judgment far exceeding what their appearance suggested. Lady Aquitaine was little younger than Fidelias, but her face, form, and figure was that of a young woman in her prime.

Not that Fidelias hadn't seen her legs and a great deal more before now.

She saw him looking and quirked a small smile at him, her eyes sparkling. Then she nodded above them, to where the distant pinpoint of light that marked the end of the shaft had grown steadily nearer, until Fidelias could see the iron bars placed over the opening of the shaft.

They slowed to a halt, just below the bars, and Fidelias counted out to the third from the right, then gave it a twist and a sharp tug. The bar slid from its mounting, and Fidelias pulled himself up through the gap, then leaned down to offer Lady Aquitaine his hand to help guide her through as well.

They emerged into a hallway inside the palace itself, a service corridor that ran from the kitchens to the banquet halls and the royal apartments. Alarm bells rang, and Fidelias knew the sound would be carrying through virtually every hallway in the palace. At this time of night, the service corridor would probably be deserted, but there was always the chance that a guard, responding to the alarm, might use it as a shortcut. Not only that, but within the hour the first few servants would head for the kitchens to begin readying the morning meals. The more quickly they left, the better.

"I still regard this as unwise," Fidelias murmured. He strung his short, heavy bow, laid an arrow to its string, and checked to make sure the rest were at hand. "It's foolish for you to risk being seen with me."

Lady Aquitaine made a clucking sound and waved a hand in airy dismissal. "All you need do is guide me to the disturbance, then depart," she said. She winced, and touched a hand to her forehead.

"Are you well?" Fidelias asked.

"Windcrafting sometimes gives me headaches," she replied. "I had to draw that air all the way from the river and up through the Deeps to lift us. It was extremely heavy."

"Air?" Fidelias asked. "Heavy?"

"When you're trying to move enough it is, dear spy, believe me." She lowered her hand and looked around, frowning. "A service corridor?"

"Aye," Fidelias said, and started down it. "We're close to the royal suites and the stairway down to the meditation chamber. There are several ways down to the Deeps throughout that portion of the palace."

Lady Aquitaine nodded and kept pace, following slightly behind Fidelias. He led her down the hall a short distance, to an intersection that would allow them to bypass a sentry post—though he suspected that the entire Royal Guard was responding to the alarm bells, there was no point in taking chances. Fidelias took the servant's entrance into a richly appointed sitting room, dim and quiet since Gaius's first wife had died some twenty years before, now opened only for dusting and tidying. Inside the sitting room, a section of the oak paneling over the stone walls swung out to reveal a small passageway.

"I love these," Lady Aquitaine murmured. "Where does this one lead?"

"To Lady Annalisa's old chambers," Fidelias murmured. "This room here used to be Gaius Pentius's study."

"With a direct passage to his mistress's chambers, hmm?" Lady Aquitaine shook her head, smiling. "Palace or not, it's all so petty once you've scratched the surface."

"True enough." They shut the hidden panel behind them and emerged into a large bedroom suite centered around an enormous bed on a slightly elevated section of floor. This room, too, had the look of something that had been largely discarded, and Fidelias crossed to the door, cracked it open very slightly, and peered out into the hallway.

The crash and cry of combat rang out as soon as he had opened the door. Not thirty feet away, the Royal Guard crowded against the doorway leading down to the First Lord's meditation chamber. Fidelias sucked in a quick breath. The metal door had been smashed flat to the floor inside the room by some unthinkably powerful impact. Even as he watched, a guardsman went through the door, weapon at the ready, and stumbled back a breath later, clutching his hands to a long wound across his abdomen. He was hauled to one side, where other wounded were being seen to by a harried-looking healer, who kept trying to craft the worst injuries closed enough to keep the wounded alive until more could be done for them. The other members of the Guard struggled to fight their way through the door, but it was clear that the alarm had found them unprepared, and there didn't seem to be any organization to their efforts.

"Wait here," Lady Aquitaine said, and strode out into the hallway. She walked purposefully over to the nearest guardsman, and said, tone steady and crackling with authority, "Guardsman, who is in charge of this riot?"

The man whipped his head around and blinked at the High Lady. His mouth worked a couple of times, and he said, "This way, Your Grace." He led her over to the healer, and said, "Jens! Jens! Lady Aquitaine!"

The healer looked up sharply, studying Lady Aquitaine for a brief second, before nodding to her and returning to his work. "Your Grace."

"You are the commanding officer here?" she asked.

A spear flew out of the guardroom as though cast by some enormous bow, spitting another one of the guardsmen. The man started screaming.

"Get him over here!" the healer shouted. He glanced up at the High Lady again, and said, "The captain is nowhere to be found. Every regular centurion on duty has been killed, but technically I carry the rank of centurion." The guardsmen brought the impaled man to him, and the healer seized his kit and whipped out a bone saw. He started hacking through the spear's shaft with it. "Crows take it," he snarled, "hold him still!" He grimaced as he cut the spear shaft and slid the weapon out of the wounded guardsman. "If you will excuse me, Your Grace. If I don't give these men all my attention, they'll die."

"If someone doesn't lead them, you're going to have a great deal more of them to tend to," Lady Aquitaine said. She frowned down at the healer, then said, "I'm assuming command until one of your centurions or the captain arrives, healer."

"Yes, fine," the healer said. He looked up at the guardsmen, and said, "Let Lady Aquitaine get things organized, Victus."

"Yes, sir," the guardsman said. "Uh, Your Grace. What are your orders?"

"Report," she said sharply. "Exactly what is happening here?"

"There are four or five Canim holding the first guard station against us, the guardsman said. "They've killed the guards in the room, and about a dozen who have tried to get in, including Centurion Hirus. More of the men are on the way, but our Knights were off duty tonight, and we're still trying to find them."

"Who is down there?"

"We can't be sure," the guardsman replied. "But the First Lord's page came through and warned us of an attack, and Gaius is usually in his meditation chamber at this time of night. The men in the first room went down fighting, so he must have warned them."

"The Canim left some to hold the door against you while the others go after the First Lord," Lady Aquitaine said. "How long have the alarms been sounding?"

"Ten minutes, perhaps, Your Grace. Give us another ten, and our Knights will be here."

"The First Lord doesn't have that long," she said, and spun toward the doorway. She spoke in what seemed a normal tone of voice, but it rang clearly over the sounds of battle and carried the tone of absolute authority. "Guardsmen, clear the doorway at once."

Lady Aquitaine strode to stand in front of the doorway, the guardsmen falling back as she did so. She faced the room, frowned, and raised her left hand, palm up. There was a sullen flash of red light, then a sphere of fire the size of a large grape swelled into life there.

"Your Grace!" the guardsman protested. "A firecrafting could be dangerous for those below."

"A large fire would," Lady Aquitaine replied, and then she hurled the sphere of fire through the doorway.

From where he was standing, Fidelias couldn't see precisely what happened next, but there was a thunderous sound, and wildly dancing light spilled from the room. He saw the sphere flash past the doorway several times, moving in a swift blur and rebounding off every surface within. Lady Aquitaine stood staring at the room for perhaps a minute, then nodded once, decisively. "The room is clear. Gentlemen, to the First Lord at once!"

Something set Fidelias's instincts screaming, and he opened the door enough to look the other way down the hall as the Royal Guard poured forward into the room.

It was the first time he had seen the vord.

A pair of hunchbacked, black shapes were coming down the hall, each one the size of a small horse and covered in chitinous black plates. They had legs like those of an insect, and moved with an awkward, scuttling gait that nonetheless covered ground very swiftly. On the floor beside them, on the walls around them, even on the ceiling above they were accompanied by dozens and dozens of pale forms the size of a wild dog, also covered in chitinous plating, gliding along on eight graceful, insect limbs.

He stared at them for half a second, and began to shout a warning. He clamped down on the urge. There were thirty or forty guardsmen in the hallway and more arriving at every moment. If one of them saw him, odds were good that he would never leave the palace alive. The only rational thing to do was remain silent.

The creatures drew closer, and Fidelias saw the heavy mandibles on the larger beasts, the twitching fangs on the smaller ones. Though it seemed impossible, no one in the hall had seen them yet. Everyone was focused on getting forward through the doorway to aid the First Lord. Lady Aquitaine had her back to the oncoming vord, listening to an appeal from the frantic healer.

The vord drew closer.

Fidelias stared at them, then realized something. He was afraid for the men in the hall. He was afraid for those wounded lying helplessly on the marble floor, for the desperate healer trying to care for them, and afraid for Lady Aquitaine, who had acted with such decisive precision to control the chaos she had found there when she arrived.

One of the pale spiders made a gliding, twenty-foot jump, landing ahead of its fellows on the marble, and only twenty feet from Lady Aquitaine's back. Without pause, it flung itself through the air at her.

To expose himself would be the height of irrationality. Suicide.

Fidelias raised his bow, drew the string tight, and shot the leaping spider out of the air three feet before it touched Lady Aquitaine. The arrow impaled the spider and sank into the wooden paneling of the wall, where the creature writhed in helpless agony.

"Your Grace!" Fidelias thundered. "Behind you!"

Lady Aquitaine turned, her eyes flashing in time with the blade of her sword as she drew and saw the oncoming threat. The guardsmen, once warned, reacted with trained speed, weapons appearing as if by magic, and a cloud of pale spiders flung themselves forward through the air in an alien flood.

Men started screaming, their voices joining with a chorus of shrill, whistling shrieks. Steel tore into the pale spiders. Fangs found naked flesh of throats and calves and anywhere else not protected by armor.

Fidelias had seen many battles. He had seen battlecrafting on both large and minor scales. He had worked closely with units of Knights, pitted himself against other furycrafters of various levels of strength, and he had seen the deadly potency of such crafting.

But he had never seen one of the High Blood of Alera enter into open battle.

Within seconds, he understood the vast chasm of power that yawned between a Knight's power, or his own, and that of someone of the blood and skill of Lady Aquitaine.

As the spiders hurled themselves forward, the hallway dissolved into chaos, but for the area near Lady Aquitaine. Her sword moved like a shaft of light, intercepting one spider after another and striking with lethal precision. Her expression never altered from the serene mask she habitually wore, as she weathered the initial wave of leaping creatures, and the instant she had bought herself a few seconds free of attack, she lifted a hand and cried out, her eyes flashing.

Half the hallway beyond exploded into flame, consuming the vord in blinding heat. A furnace-hot gale exploded through the halls in another rattling detonation, but the crafting had stopped the tide of spiders only briefly. Those that survived the fires flung themselves onward over the smoldering remains of their kin.

And then their larger kin arrived.

One of the warrior vord seized a guardsman, its armor

turning aside several blows from the man's heavy sword, and shook him back and forth like a dog with a rat. Fidelias heard the man's neck break, and the vord threw him aside and lunged for the next in line—Lady Aquitaine.

The High Lady dropped the sword as the vord warrior closed, and caught the creature's mandibles in her gloved hands as it tried to close them on her neck.

Lady Aquitaine's mouth quirked into an amused little smile, and the earth shook as she called forth power from it and slowly shoved the creature's jaws back open. It began to struggle frantically, but the High Lady of Aquitaine did not release it, pushing its jaws wider until there was a sickly cracking sound, and the vord began flailing its limbs wildly. Once that happened, she seized one of the mandibles in both hands, spun, and hurled the warrior fifty feet down the hall, into a tall marble pillar, where its armor shattered and it fell like a broken toy, gushing alien fluid, twitching, and dying.

The second warrior flung itself directly at her. Lady Aquitaine saw it coming, and with that same amused little smile, she leapt back and up into the air into graceful flight, a sudden wind rising to support her, just out of reach of the vord warrior.

But for all her power, she did not have eyes in the back of her head. Spiders she had not seen dropped down toward her from the ceiling. Fidelias did not waste his time in thinking. He focused on his task, sending a pair of heavy arrows flashing over the distance between them, tacking one of the spiders to the ceiling before it had fallen six inches, and hammering the other away from Lady Aquitaine a bare foot above her head.

She snapped her head around and saw the results of Fidelias's shooting, then flashed him a fierce, heated smile. Below her, the guardsmen were fighting together now, after the initial shock of the vord attack, and reinforcements were arriving, including two Knights Flora and half a dozen Knights Ferrous, whose archery and swordplay brought the second vord warrior down in short order.

Lady Aquitaine darted over to hover above the wounded guardsmen on the ground, almost casually striking down spiders that approached them with fists of wind and flame. Once more guardsmen arrived, she alighted to the marble floor outside the doorway of the room Fidelias remained within.

"Well done, Fidelias," she said quietly. "Your archery was superb. And thank you."

"Did you think I would not support you when the action began, my lady?"

She tilted her head. Then she said, "You exposed yourself to warn me, Fidelias. And to warn the guard. These men, if they didn't have larger worries at hand, would hunt you down and kill you."

Fidelias nodded. "Yes."

"Then why did you risk yourself for them?"

"Because, my lady," he said quietly, "I turned against Gaius. Not Alera."

She narrowed her eyes and nodded thoughtfully. "I see. It wasn't something I had expected of you, Fidelias."

He inclined his head to her. "Some of those spider creatures got through, my lady. They went on down the stairway."

"There's little to be done for that," she replied. "Best you take your leave now, before the fighting is finished and someone remembers seeing you. Guardsmen are already on the way down to the stairs. We are fortunate to have had your warning. Without it, their attack might have succeeded."

"I don't believe it was meant to succeed," Fidelias said, frowning. "It was meant to delay us."

"If so, it only did so for a few minutes," Lady Aquitaine said.

Fidelias nodded and withdrew from the doorway toward the hidden passage. "But critical minutes, my lady, in a desperate hour," he said. "Great furies grant that we are not now too late."

As he ran full tilt down the stairs, Tavi thought to himself that it was probably just as well Gaius had him running up and down the crows-eaten things over and over for the past two years. Because if he had to run down them one more time, he was going to start screaming.

He reached the last several dozen yards of them and caught up to the wax spiders. "Kitai!" he screamed. "Kitai, more Keepers! Look out!"

He heard the sudden clash of breaking glass, then he came down the last of the stairs and into the antechamber.

Kitai had evidently heard Tavi's warning in time, and her response had been to fling herself at the First Lord's liquor cabinet, where she seized bottles of hundred-year-old wine and started flinging them with deadly accuracy at the oncoming wax spiders. By the time Tavi's feet hit the floor, three of them were already lying on their backs, partially crushed by Kitai's missiles. Even as Tavi ran forward, a pair of spiders dropped down onto Max's recumbent form, and three more headed for Maestro Killian.

Kitai leapt to protect Killian, whipped her swords out of her belt, and shouted a challenge at the wax spiders. Tavi rushed over to Max and seized the sword nearby him—Gaius's blade, which Max had been using earlier. One of the spiders ducked down to bite at Max. Tavi swung the sword before he'd really gotten a good grip on it, and he struck mostly with the flat of the blade. The blow at least knocked the spider off Max, and Tavi followed it with a hard kick aimed at the second beast.

"What's happening?" Killian demanded, his voice thready and thin. "Tavi?"

"Wax spiders!" Tavi shouted. "Get into the meditation chamber!"

Kitai drove one of her blades into a spider. The creature

convulsed, tearing the blade from her hand as it dashed drunkenly across the room. She swung a kick at another, which bounded backward in a dodge, but the third leapt upon Killian and sank its fangs into the old Maestro's bloodied shoulder.

Killian screamed.

Kitai seized the spider and tried to pull it off the old man. It hung on stubbornly, and every time she tugged on the beast it drew another cry of pain from the Maestro.

Tavi took two steps over to Killian and snapped a swift warning. Before he'd gotten the words fully out, Kitai had dropped the spider and rolled to one side. Tavi swept the First Lord's blade at the spider, and the razor-edged steel cut cleanly through the body of the spider, severing it at what passed for the creature's neck. "More bottles!" Tavi snapped aloud, and knelt to help the old man.

Killian thrashed and shoved the Keeper's body aside, and Tavi reached down to jerk the head—still biting—from the old man's shoulder. He had deep puncture wounds, and they were already swollen. Some kind of yellow-green slime oozed out of the punctures. Poison.

Tavi bit his lip, seized the handle of the door to the inner chamber, and shoved it open. Then he grabbed the old Maestro by the collar and hauled him across the floor and into the room. The old man cried out with pain when Tavi moved him, the sound pitiable, undignified, and Tavi had to steel himself against it. He got the Maestro inside the room as more glass began breaking in the antechamber, then dashed back out.

Kitai, back at the liquor cabinet, flung a heavy bottle at one of the spiders near Max, striking it and sending it flying. Another leapt at her, and she seized another bottle and swung it like a club, shattering it and crushing the spider.

"Here!" Tavi barked. "Break them right here, in front of the door!" He grabbed Max's collar and started pulling. His friend weighed twice what Killian did, but Tavi found that he could move him. It was an enormous strain, but Tavi's additional training and conditioning with the Maestro was paying off, and the fear and heat of battle made him stronger yet.

A spider leapt at Max, and Tavi took a clumsy swing at it with the First Lord's blade. To his shock, the spider simply caught the blade in its jaws, then swarmed up it in a blur of spindly legs to Tavi's arm.

It didn't bite him. It only swarmed up over his shoulders and down the other arm, toward Max. Tavi released his friend and flapped his arm around wildly, tossing the spider upward and away from him, precisely in time to see a deep green bottle crash into the beast, taking it down.

"Hurry!" Kitai cried. "I am running out of bottles!"

Tavi seized Max, dragged him through, and screamed, "In front of the door, hurry!"

Glass shattered upon the floor, splattering wine and harder liquors everywhere, as Tavi pulled Max into the inner chamber.

"Aleran!" Kitai shouted.

"Come on, get in here!" Tavi yelled. He ran back to the door.

Kitai flung herself across the antechamber, scooping up her dropped blade on the way. Two more spiders came down the stairs, joining the half dozen or so remaining, and flung themselves through the air toward Kitai.

"Look out!" Tavi screamed.

Again, before he'd completed the first word, Kitai was in motion, ducking to one side—but she slipped on the spilled liquids and fell to one knee.

Both spiders landed upon her and started biting viciously. She let out a wail of terror and rage, tearing at them, but she had no more luck peeling them off her than she had with Killian. She struggled to rise and slipped again.

A third spider hit her.

And a fourth.

They were killing her.

A rage like nothing he had ever felt engulfed Tavi in a sudden cloud. His vision misted over with scarlet, and he felt the fury run like lightning through his limbs. Tavi launched himself forward, and the First Lord's sword was suddenly not too heavy for him to wield effectively. His first strike split one of the spiders in half and knocked another one clear.

He thrust the blade through one of the remaining spiders, then had to kick it off the end of the sword. He killed the other in the same way, grabbed the girl by the wrist, and hauled her into the inner chamber.

The remaining spiders were right behind them, chirruping in those eerie whistles. Tavi whipped around to the doorway, seized a furylamp off the wall, and hurled it down onto the liquor-covered floor in front of the door.

Flame exploded in a rush, engulfing the remaining spiders. They let out shrieking whistles and dashed mindlessly around the room. One of them bounded through the doorway, evidently by blind chance. Tavi knocked it to the floor with his first slash, crippling it, then finished it with a swift thrust, impaling it on Gaius's sword. Then he spun and hurled the dying spider from the blade, at the partly open door to the outer chamber. The spider hit it in a burst of greenish gore, and its weight slammed the door shut.

Tavi dashed to the door, threw the bolt, then ran to Kitai.

She lay there shivering, bleeding from a dozen small wounds. Most of them were swollen and stained with poison, as Killian's was, but others were more conventional injuries, cuts from the broken glass littering the floor.

"Kitai," Tavi said. "Can you hear me?"

She blinked green eyes up at him and nodded, a bare motion. "P-poison," she said.

Tavi nodded, and sudden tears blinded him for a moment. "Yes. I don't know what to do."

"Fight," she said, her voice a bare whisper. "Live." She looked like she might have said something else, but her eyes rolled back, and she went limp except for tiny, random twitches.

A few feet away, Killian had managed to partially sit up, leaning on one elbow. "Tavi?"

"We're all in the meditation chamber, Maestro," Tavi said, biting his lip. "You've been poisoned. So has Kitai." Tavi bit his lip, looking around desperately for something, anything that could help them. "I don't know what to do now."

"The First Lord?" Killian asked.

Tavi checked the cot. "Fine. Breathing. The spiders never got close to him."

Killian shuddered and nodded. "I'm very thirsty. Perhaps the venom. Is there any water?"

Tavi grimaced. "No, Maestro. You really should lie down. Relax. Try to conserve your strength. The guard is sure to be here soon."

The old man shook his head. The pulse in his throat fluttered wildly, and there were veins on his forehead and temple swelling into twitching visibility. "Too late for that, lad. Just too old."

"Don't say that," Tavi said. "You're going to be all right."

"No," he said. "Come closer. Hurts to talk." He moved his hand and beckoned Tavi.

Tavi leaned close to him to listen.

"You must know," he said, "that I have been involved with Kalare. Working with his agents."

Tavi blinked down at Killian. "What?"

"It was meant as a ploy. Wanted them close, where I could see them moving. Feed them false information." He shuddered again, and tears ran from his blind eyes. "There was a price. A terrible price. To prove myself to them." A sob escaped his throat. "I was wrong. I was wrong to do it, Tavi."

"I don't understand," Tavi said.

"You must," Killian hissed. "Spy. Kalare's . . ." He suddenly fell back to the floor, and his breath started coming faster, as though he'd been running. "H-here," he gasped. "Kalare. His chief assassin. You m—"

Suddenly Killian's blind eyes widened and his body arched up into a bow. His mouth opened, as if he was trying to scream, but no sound came out—nor any breath, either. His face purpled, and his arms worked frantically, clawing at the floor.

"Maestro," Tavi said quietly. His voice broke in the middle of the word. He caught one of Killian's wrinkled hands, and the old man clutched Tavi's fingers with terrified strength. Not long after, his contorted body began to relax, deflating like a leaking leather flask. Tavi held his hand and laid his own hand on the Maestro's chest, feeling his frantically beating heart.

It slowed.

And stopped a moment later.

Tavi gently put Killian's hand back down, frustration and pain a storm in his chest. Helpless. He had watched as the old man died, and there was not a bloody thing he could have done to help him.

He turned away and went to Kitai. She lay on her side,

half-curled upon herself. Her eyes were closed now, her breath coming in swift rasps. He touched her back, and could feel the frenzied pounding of her heartbeat. Tavi bit his lip. She'd been bitten many more times than the Maestro. She was younger than Killian, and unwounded, but Tavi did not know if it would make any difference in the end.

He took Kitai's hand, and now he did weep. His tears fell to the tiled mosaic floor. Pain stabbed at his heart with every beat. Rage followed close behind it. If only he could perform watercrafting like Aunt Isana. He might be able to help Kitai. Even if he wasn't as powerful as his aunt, he might be able to help her remain alive until help came. If he had even a laughable talent with watercrafting, he could have at least given Killian some water.

But he had none of that.

Tavi had never felt more useless. He'd never felt more powerless. He held her hand and stayed with her. He had promised her that she would not be alone. He would stay with her to the end, regardless of how painful it would be to watch her die. He could, at least, do that.

And then the door to the meditation chamber exploded from its hinges and slammed flat to the stone floor.

Tavi jerked his head up. Had the Guard arrived at last?

The taken Cane stepped onto the fallen door and swept its bloodred gaze around the chamber. The Cane was wounded, blood wetting the fur of its chest and one thigh. It was missing one ear completely, and a slash to its face had opened one side of its muzzle to the bone and claimed one of its eyes.

For all of that, it moved as if it felt no pain at all. Its eye settled on Max. Then on Gaius. It looked back and forth between them for a moment, then turned and stalked forward, toward Max.

Tavi's heart erupted with pure terror, and for a moment he thought he might swoon. The Canim had gotten by Fade and Miles. Which meant that they were probably dead. And it meant that the guard was not closing in to save them.

Tavi was on his own.

CHAPTER 54

Tavi looked down at Kitai. At Max. At Gaius.

The Cane stalked forward with a predator's deadly beautiful grace. It was so much larger than he, stronger, faster. He had little chance of surviving a battle with the Cane, and he knew it.

But if it was not stopped, the Cane would kill the helpless souls behind him. Tavi's imagination provided him a vivid image of the carnage. Max's throat torn out, his corpse grey-skinned from blood loss. Gaius's entrails spilling forth from his ravaged body. Kitai's head lying a few feet away from her body, cut away by the Cane's curved blade.

Tavi's fear vanished utterly.

All that remained was the red-misted haze of rage.

He released Kitai's hand. His fingers closed hard around the hilt of the First Lord's blade as he rose, and he felt his mouth stretch into a fighting grin. He raised the sword to a high guard, both hands on the hilt. A healthy Canim warrior would have torn him limb from limb, literally. But this one was not healthy. It was injured. And while he could never hope to overpower the Cane, his sword was sharp, his limbs were quick, and his mind quicker. He could outthink the creature, fight it with not only strength but with guile. His eyes flicked around the room, and his grin became fiercer.

And then he gave his rage a voice, howling at the top of his lungs, and attacked.

The Cane bared its teeth and swept its curved blade at Tavi as he came in, its height giving it a deadly advantage in reach. Tavi met the slash with his sword, both hands gripping it as tightly as he could. The Cane's scarlet blade rang against Aleran steel. Tavi felt the bone-deep shock of the impact all the way up to both shoulders, but he stopped the Cane's heavy blade cold, beat it aside, and reversed the sword into a horizontal slash. The blow struck sparks from the Cane's mail, severing a dozen links that sprang away from the armor and rang tinnily as they struck the stone floor.

Tavi dared not close to more exchanges of main force. His fingers were already tingling. Another blow or two like that from the Cane and he wouldn't be able to hold a sword—but the first such attack had been necessary.

Tavi had proven himself a threat, and the Cane turned to engage him.

The Cane's counterattack was quick, but Tavi continued his movement past the wolf-warrior, circling to the side of the Cane's wounded leg to force it to turn on the injured limb. It slowed the Cane, and Tavi ducked under the scything blade and struck again, a heavy slash that landed hard on the foot of the Cane's unwounded leg. Tavi rose from that strike in a two-handed upward slash that might have opened his foe from groin to chest—but the Cane blocked Tavi's attack, flicked his sword to one side, and surged toward him in a primal assault, teeth snapping.

The Cane was far too swift for its size; but with both legs injured, its balance was precarious, and Tavi managed to jerk his face back and away from the Cane's jaws before they snapped shut. He felt a flash of heat over one eye, then fell into a backward roll, toward Killian's body, tucking himself into a ball until he came back up to his feet. Tavi brought his sword up to guard almost before he was finished with the roll, and he managed to deflect the Cane's sword as it swept straight down at his skull.

The Cane snapped at his face once more. Tavi ducked under the Cane's foaming jaws to come up on the creature's opposite side—its blind side. The Cane slashed wildly toward him, but the blow came nowhere close, and it whirled to snap at him with its teeth once more, swift and monstrously strong—and blind. Tavi shifted his grip on the First Lord's blade and drove its pommel forward with another battle cry. The weighted metal hammered into the Cane's snapping jaws, and fragments of broken teeth flew up from the blow.

The taken Cane whipped its head back and forth with a high-pitched snarl of pain, evidently more than even the vord taken could totally suppress. Tavi took the opportunity to drive a short, hard slash into the Cane's muzzle. The blow was not a forceful one, but it sliced into the Cane's blunt nose, and drew another howl of agony from the creature. It staggered back, as Tavi had intended, slipping on the blood beside Killian's corpse. Its feet slipped and twisted treacherously as it snarled in maddened rage and raised the curved sword again.

In the time that took, Tavi danced once more to its blind side, out onto the tiles of the map-mosaic of Alera itself. He struck across the Cane's throat, splitting its leather war collar with the First Lord's blade. The flesh beneath opened in a fountain of gore. The taken Cane swept its blade in a wide slash, but slowed by its injuries and its uncertain footing, Tavi ducked it easily enough—and then he screamed out his defiance as he drove the tip of the sword into the Cane's chest.

Mail rings shattered and scattered over the tiles as the First Lord's sword bit deep. The Cane hacked down at him, but Tavi pressed in close, inside the effective arc of the blade. He felt a fiery flash on the calf of one leg, and heard himself screaming and howling as he forced himself hard against the Cane, driving his sword deeper, shoving the much larger creature into a backward stumble.

The Cane, lamed in both legs, slipping on bloody tiles, went down with a crash of mail. Tavi, holding on to the hilt of the sword, came down on top of his opponent. The Cane tried once more to tear at Tavi with its teeth, but the vicious power of the thing was fading by the heartbeat, as blood spilled from its throat.

Still screaming, Tavi slammed himself against the sword, trying to drive it deeper, to pin the Cane down to the stone of the floor if need be. If he let it rise, the Cane could still murder Gaius or Max or Kitai, and he was determined that it would not happen.

He wasn't sure how long he struggled to keep the thing down, but at some point he found himself lying still atop an unmoving foe, his breathing labored. The Cane's lips were peeled back from its fangs in death, and its remaining eye was glassy. Tavi rose slowly, aching in every limb. The wild energy of the battle fever he'd felt was gone, and he was cut both on his forehead and on his leg. He wasn't bleeding badly from either injury, but he felt himself shaking in sheer exhaustion.

He'd done it. Alone. Had the Cane not been already injured, or had he not exploited its injuries, he might not have
survived the battle. But he, Tavi, alone, without furies of his
own, without allies, had overcome one of the monstrous warriors in open battle.

He heard footsteps outside, coming down the stairway.

Tavi took a deep breath. He reached down to the sword,
and with an enormous effort he hauled it from the Cane's
corpse. His wounded leg buckled, but he brought the sword
upright into his hands, most of the weight on his back leg, the
other planted on the fallen Cane's chest as he waited for whatever else might come.

The footsteps grew louder, and Fade, his slave's rough
clothing covered in blood, leapt down the last several steps,
blade in hand. He let out a cry and threw himself toward the
doorway, but came to a sharp halt as he saw the room beyond.
Behind him, several of the Royal Guard, one of them assisting Sir Miles, came running down the stairs as well. Miles
hobbled over to the door at once, ordering guards out of his
way—and then he, too, stopped, staring at Tavi with his
mouth open.

Tavi faced them all for a second, sword in hand, and it registered slowly on him that it was over. The battle was over,
and he had survived it. He let out a slow breath, and the sword
fell from his suddenly nerveless hands. His balance wobbled,
and he abruptly forgot how to stand upright.

Fade's sword clanged as it hit the floor, and he was underneath Tavi before the boy could fall.

"I've got you," Fade said quietly. He lowered Tavi gently
to the floor. "You're wounded."

"Kitai," Tavi panted. "Poisoned. She'll need help. Max
still wounded. Killian . . ." Tavi closed his eyes, to avoid
looking at the Maestro's still form. "The Maestro is dead,
Fade. Poisoned. The spiders outside. Nothing got to Gaius."

"It's all right," Fade said. He murmured something, then
pressed the mouth of a flask to his lips. Tavi drank the luke-
warm water thirstily. "Not too fast. Thank the great furies,
Tavi," Fade said as he drank. "I'm sorry. One of the Canim
threw himself on my sword to let another go past me. I got
here as swiftly as I could."

"Don't worry about it," Tavi told him. "I got him."

Tavi could hear the sudden, fierce smile on Fade's mouth as he spoke. "Yes. You did. There are watercrafters and healers on the way, Tavi. You'll be all right."

Tavi nodded wearily. "If it's all the same to you, I'm just going to sit here for a minute. Rest my eyes until they get here." He leaned his head back against the wall, exhausted.

Tavi didn't hear if Fade made any reply before he gave himself to sleep.

". . . absolute mystery to me how the girl survived it," Tavi heard a sonorous male voice saying. "Those creatures poisoned two dozen guardsmen, and even with watercrafters at hand, only nine of them survived."

"She is a barbarian," replied a voice Tavi recognized. "Perhaps her folk aren't as susceptible."

"She seemed more like one who has endured it before," the first voice said. "Gained a resistance to it through exposure. She was already conscious again by the time we began to treat her, and she needed almost no assistance. I'm certain she would have been all right without our help."

The first voice grunted, and Tavi opened his eyes to see Sir Miles speaking quietly with a man in an expensive silk robe worn over rather plain, sturdy trousers and shirt. The man glanced at him and smiled. "Ah, there you are, lad. Good morning. And welcome to the palace infirmary."

Tavi blinked his eyes a few times and looked around him. He was in a long room lined with beds, curtains hung between each. Most of the beds were occupied. The windows were open, a pleasant wind stirring them gently, and the scent of recent rain and flowering plants, the scent of spring filled the room. "G-good morning. How long have I been asleep?"

"Nearly a full day," the healer replied. "Your particular injuries were not threatening, but you had so many of them that they amounted to quite a strain. You'd gotten some of that spider venom into some of your wounds as well, though I don't think you'd been bitten. Sir Miles ordered me to let you sleep."

Tavi rubbed his face and sat up. "Sir Miles," he said, inclining his head. "Is Kitai . . . the First Lord . . . Sir, is everyone all right?"

Miles nodded to the healer, who took it as a hint to depart. The man nodded and clapped Tavi's shoulder gently before making his way down the row of beds, attending to other patients.

"Tavi," Miles asked quietly, "did you slay that Cane we found you on top of?"

"Yes, sir," Tavi said. "I used the First Lord's blade."

Miles nodded, and smiled at him. "That was boldly done, young man. I expected to find nothing but corpses at the bottom of the stairs. I underestimated you."

"It had already been wounded, Sir Miles. I don't think that . . . well. It was half-dead when it got there. I just had to nudge it along a little."

Miles tilted his head back and laughed. "Yes. Yes, well. Regardless, you'll be glad to know that your friends and the First Lord are all well."

Tavi's back straightened. "Gaius . . . He's . . . ?"

"Awake, irritable, and his tongue could flay the hide from a gargant," Miles said, his expression pleased. "He wants to speak with you as soon as you're strong enough."

Tavi promptly swung his legs off the side of the bed and began to rise. Then froze, looking down at himself. "Perhaps I should put some clothes on, if I'm to see the First Lord."

"Why don't you?" Miles said, and nodded to a trunk beside the bed. Tavi found his own clothes there, freshly cleaned, and started slipping into them. He glanced up at Sir Miles as he did, and said, "Sir Miles. If . . . if I may ask. Your brother—"

Miles interrupted him with an upraised hand. "My brother," he said, with gentle emphasis, "died nearly twenty years ago." He shook his head. "On an unrelated note, Tavi, your friend Fade, the slave, is well. He distinguished himself for his valor on the stairway, assisting me."

"Assisting you?"

Miles nodded, his expression carefully neutral. "Yes. Some idiot has already composed a song about it. Sir Miles and his famous stand on the Spiral Stair. They're singing it in all the wine clubs and alehouses. It's humiliating."

Tavi frowned.

"It makes a much better song than one about a maimed slave," he said quietly.

Tavi lowered his voice to almost a whisper. "But he's your brother."

Miles pursed his lips, looked at Tavi for a moment, then said, "He knows what he's doing. And he can't do it as well if every loose tongue in the Realm can wag on about how he has returned from the grave." He nudged Tavi's boots over to him from where they sat near the foot of the bed, and added, so quietly that Tavi could barely hear him, "Or why."

"He cares for you," Tavi said quietly. "He was terrified that . . . that you would think ill of him, when you saw him."

"He was right," Miles said. "If it had happened any other way . . ." He shook his head. "I don't know what I might have done." His eyes went a bit distant. "I spent a very long time hating him, boy. For dying beside Septimus, off in the middle of nowhere, when my leg was too badly injured to allow me to be there beside him. All of them. I couldn't forgive him for dying and leaving me behind. When I should have been with them."

"And now?" Tavi asked.

"Now . . ." Miles said. He sighed. "I don't know, lad. But I have a place of my own. I have my duty. There seems to be little sense in hating him now." His eyes glittered. "But by the great furies. Did you *see* him? The greatest swordsman I've ever known, save perhaps Septimus himself. And even then, I always suspected that Rari held back so as not to embarrass the Princeps." Miles's eyes focused elsewhere, then he blinked them and smiled at Tavi.

"Duty?" Tavi suggested.

"Precisely. As I was saying. Duty. Such as yours to the First Lord. On your feet, Acad—" Then Miles paused, head tilted to one side as he regarded Tavi. "On your feet, man."

Tavi pulled his boots on and rose, smiling a little. "Sir Miles," he asked, "do you know if there's been any word of my aunt?"

Miles's expression became remote as he started walking, his limp now more pronounced. "I've been told that she is safe and well. She is not in the palace. I don't know more than that."

Tavi frowned. "What? Nothing?"

Miles shrugged.

"What about Max? Kitai?"

"I'm sure Gaius will answer any questions you have,

Tavi." Miles gave him a faint smile. "Sorry to be that way with you. Orders."

Tavi nodded and frowned even more deeply. He walked with Miles to the First Lord's personal chambers, passing, Tavi noted, three times as many guardsmen as normal. They reached the doors to Gaius's sitting room, where he received guests, and a guard let them in, then vanished behind curtains at the end of the room to speak quietly to someone there.

The guard reemerged, and left the room. Tavi looked around at the furniture, really rather spartan for the First Lord, he thought, everything made of the fine, dark hardwoods of the Forcian forests on the west coast. Paintings hung on one wall—one of them only half-finished. Tavi frowned at them. They were of simple, idyllic scenes. A family eating a meal on a blanket in a field on a sunny day. A boat raising sails to meet the first ocean swells, a dim city somewhere in the fog behind it. And the last, the unfinished one, was a portrait of a young man. His features had been painted, but only about a third of his upper body and shoulders were finished. The portrait's colors stood out starkly against the blank canvas beneath.

Tavi looked closer. The young man in the portrait looked familiar. Gaius, perhaps? Take away the weathering of time in his features, and the young man could perhaps be the First Lord.

"Septimus," murmured Gaius's deep voice from somewhere behind Tavi. Tavi looked back to see the First Lord step out from behind the curtain. He was dressed in a loose white shirt and close-fitting black breeks. His color was right again, his blue-grey eyes bright and clear.

But his hair had turned stark white.

Tavi bowed his head at once. "Beg pardon, sire?"

"The portrait," Gaius said. "It's my son."

"I see," Tavi said, carefully. He had no idea what the proper thing to say in this sort of situation might be. "It's . . . it's not finished."

Gaius shook his head. "No. Do you see that mark on the neck of the man in the portrait? Where the black has cut over onto his skin?"

"Yes. I thought perhaps it represented a mole."

"It represents where his mother was working when we got word of his death," Gaius said. He gestured at the room. "She painted all of these. But when she heard of Septimus, she dropped her brushes. She never picked them up again." He regarded the painting steadily. "She took sick not long after. Had me hang it in the room near her, where she could see it. She made me promise, on that last night, not to get rid of it."

"I'm sorry for your loss, sire."

"Many are. For many reasons." He glanced over his shoulder. "Miles?"

Miles bowed his head to Gaius and backed for the door. "Of course. Shall I have someone bring you food?"

Tavi started to agree very strongly but held off, glancing at Gaius. The First Lord laughed, and said, "Have you ever known a young man who wasn't hungry—or about to be so? And I should be eating more, too. Oh, and please send for those others I mentioned to you?"

Miles nodded, smiling, and retreated quietly from the room.

"I don't think I've seen Sir Miles smile so much in the past two years as I have today," Tavi commented.

The First Lord nodded. "Eerie, isn't it?" He settled in one of the two chairs in the room and gestured for Tavi to take the other. "You want me to tell you about your aunt," Gaius said.

Tavi smiled a little. "Am I that predictable, sire?"

"Your family is very important to you," he replied, his tone serious. "She is unharmed, and spent the entire night sitting beside your sickbed. I've sent word to her that you've woken. She'll come up to the Citadel to visit you shortly, I should imagine."

"To the Citadel?" Tavi asked. "Sire? I had thought she'd be staying in guest quarters here."

Gaius nodded. "She accepted the invitation of Lord and Lady Aquitaine to reside in the Aquitaine manor for the duration of Wintersend."

Tavi stared at the First Lord in shock. "She *what*?" He shook his head. "Aquitaine's scheme nearly destroyed every steadholt in the Calderon Valley. She despises him."

"I can well imagine," Gaius said.

"Then in the name of all the furies, *why?*"

Gaius twitched one shoulder in a faint shrug. "She did not speak to me of her motivation for such a thing, so I can only conjecture. I invited her to stay here, near you, but she politely declined."

Tavi chewed on his lower lip in thought. "Crows. It means more, doesn't it?" His belly suddenly felt cold. "It means she's allied herself with them."

"Yes," Gaius said, his tone neutral and relaxed.

"Surely she . . . Sire, is it possible that she has been coerced in some way? Furycrafted into it?"

Gaius shook his head. "No such thing was affecting her. I examined her myself. And that kind of control is impossible to hide."

Tavi racked his mind frantically to find an explanation. "But if she was threatened or intimidated into it, then couldn't something be done to help her?"

"That is not what has happened," Gaius said. "Can you imagine fear moving your aunt to do anything? She showed no signs of that kind of fear. In fact, in my judgment she traded her loyalty as part of a bargain."

"What kind of bargain?"

There was a polite knock at the chamber door, and a porter entered pushing a wheeled cart. He placed it near the chairs, opened its sides into the wings of a table, and began placing silver-covered dishes and bowls on the table, until he had laid out a large breakfast, complete with a ewer of milk and another of watery wine. Gaius remained silent until the porter took his leave and shut the door again.

"Tavi," Gaius said, "before I tell you more, I would like you to go through everything that happened in as much detail as you can recall. I don't want my explanations to muddy your own memories before you've had the chance to tell them to me."

Tavi nodded, though it was frustrating to be forced to wait for answers. "Very well, sire."

Gaius rose, and Tavi did as well. "I imagine you're even hungrier than I am," he said with a small smile. "Shall we eat?"

They piled plates with food and settled back down into the chairs. After the first plateful, Tavi went back for more, then started recounting events to the First Lord, beginning with his confrontation with Kalarus Brencis Minoris and his thugs. It took him most of an hour. Gaius interrupted him a few times to ask for more details, and in the end he leaned back in his chair, a cup of mild wine in his hand.

"Well," he said. "That explains Caria this morning, at any rate."

Tavi's cheeks flushed so hot that he thought they must surely blister at any moment. "Sire, Max was only—"

Gaius gave Tavi a cool look, but he could see the smile at the corners of the First Lord's eyes. "In most of my life, I would not have minded a lovely wife inviting herself to join me in my bath. But this morning was . . . I was taxed enough. I'm nearly fourscore years, for goodness' sake." He shook his head gravely. "I adjusted to the demands of my station, of course, but when you speak to Maximus, you might mention to him that in the future, should this situation arise again, he should seek some course *other* than to fondle my wife."

"I'll let him know, sir," Tavi said, his own voice solemn.

Gaius chuckled. "Remarkable," he murmured. "You acquitted yourself rather well. Not perfectly, but you might have done a great deal worse, too."

Tavi grimaced and looked down.

Gaius sighed. "Tavi. Killian's death was not of your making. You needn't punish yourself for it."

"Someone should," Tavi said quietly.

"There was nothing you could do that you had not already done," the First Lord said.

"I know," Tavi answered, and was surprised by the bitter anger in his own voice. "If I wasn't a freak, if I'd had even a little skill at furycraft—"

"Then, in all likelihood, you would have relied upon your crafting rather than upon your wits, and died because of it." Gaius shook his head. "Men, good soldiers and good crafters alike, died in fighting these foes. Furycraft is a tool, Tavi. Without a practiced hand and an able mind behind it, it's no more useful than a hammer left on the ground."

Tavi looked away from the First Lord, staring at the floor to one side of the fireplace.

"Tavi," he said, deep voice quiet, "I owe you my life, as do the friends you protected. And because of your actions, countless others have been saved as well. Killian died because he chose a life of such service, to put himself between the Realm and danger. He knew what he was doing when he entered that fight, and the risk he was taking." Gaius's voice became more gentle. "It is childishly arrogant of you to belittle his choice, his sacrifice, by attempting to take responsibility for his demise upon your own shoulders."

Tavi frowned. "I . . . hadn't thought of it in those terms."

"There's no reason you should have," Gaius said.

"I still feel as if I failed him somehow," Tavi said. "His last words to me were important, I think. He was trying so hard to get them to me, but . . ." Tavi remembered the last seconds of Killian's life and fell silent.

"Yes," Gaius said. "It is unfortunate that he did not manage to reveal the identity of the assassin—though I suspect that with Killian dead, Kalare's agent will depart."

"Isn't there any way for us to tell who it is before he—or she—leaves?"

The First Lord shook his head. "There is a great deal for me to do to repair some of the damages done. To exploit an advantage or two. So, young man, I'll pass the search to you. Can you apply your mind as ably to finding this assassin as you did to stopping the attack? I should think Killian would like that."

"I'll try," Tavi said. "If I'd only been a few seconds faster it might have helped him."

"Perhaps. But one might as easily say that if you had been a few seconds slower, all of us would be dead." Gaius waved a hand. "Enough, boy. It's done. Remember your *patriserus* for his life. Not his death. He was quite proud of you."

Tavi blinked his eyes a couple of times, fought back tears, and nodded. "Very well."

"Upon the subject of your aunt," Gaius said. "You should know two things. First, that there was an attack of these creatures within the Calderon Valley. Your uncle and Countess Amara led a force against it, while your aunt carried word to me to ask for reinforcements."

"An attack?" Tavi said. "But . . . what happened? Is my uncle all right?"

"I dispatched two cohorts of Knights Aeris and Ignus to their aid about twelve hours ago, as well as informing Lord

Riva of the issue and strongly suggesting that he take steps to investigate, but there hasn't yet been time enough for word to reach us of what they found."

"Great furies," Tavi murmured, shaking his head. "When will you know?"

"Perhaps by tomorrow morning," Gaius said. "Certainly before tomorrow sunset. But I suspect that they have already received aid."

Tavi frowned. "But how?"

"The Aquitaines," Gaius said. "They control a formidable number of Knights Aeris and other Knight-quality mercenaries. I believe that was one of the things your aunt secured in exchange for her political support."

"One of them?"

"Indeed," Gaius said. "When the vord and the taken Canim attempted to storm the stairway, time had become a critical issue. The Royal Guard would have ultimately prevailed, but in the confusion it was unlikely that they could have done so in time. Until Invidia Aquitaine arrived, took command of the counterattack, destroyed most of attacking vord creatures, then broke the Canim rear guard so that the guards could descend the stairs."

Tavi blinked. "*She* was protecting *you*?"

Gaius's mouth quirked. "I suspect she was preserving me from death in order to prevent Kalare from attempting a coup of his own until she and her husband were ready for theirs. It's remotely possible that she was concerned that a succession war could have erupted and left the Realm vulnerable to its foes." He smiled. "Or perhaps she was simply protecting you, as part of her bargain with your aunt. In either case it's a winning tactic for her. By the crows, I'm going to have to give her a medal for it, right in front of everyone—the First Lord saved by a woman. The Dianic League may collapse in a fit of collective ecstasy at the opportunity."

"And she'll use Aunt Isana to help rally the League around her, too." Tavi shook his head. "I just can't believe it. Aunt Isana . . ."

"It isn't hard to understand her, boy. She came to me to ask my help and protection. I did not give them to her."

"But you were unconscious," Tavi said.

"And why should that matter?" Gaius asked. "Her home was in danger. Her family was in danger. She was not able to reach me for help, so she took it where she could find it." He frowned down at his glass, his brow troubled. "And it was given to her."

"Sire," Tavi asked, "do you know who slew the vord queen? After the initial attack, I did not see her again."

Gaius shook his head gravely. "No. So far as we know, the creature escaped—as did the Canim chancellor. Miles already has the Crown Legion sweeping the Deeps, which I should think will put a large dent in the smuggling business for the year, but, I suspect, little else. All the shipping that has left in the past two days has been hunted down and searched, but to no avail."

"I think Sarl was using the courier ships and working with the vord."

Gaius tilted his head. "Oh?"

"Yes, sire," Tavi said. "Canim guards changed out every month. There were always a couple of them coming or going at least, and all of them in those big, heavy capes and hoods. My guess is that Sarl and the vord would take the largest and tallest men they could find, dress them up in a Cane's armor, drape the hood over them, then take them to the ship, while the two Canim who were supposed to be going back home were taken instead, and stored at the vord nest in the Deeps. That's how they built up that many Canim."

Gaius nodded slowly. "It makes sense. This information about factional struggles within the Canim nation is rather encouraging. It's nice to know that our enemies can be as fractious as we are."

"Sire?" Tavi asked. "What of Ambassador Varg?"

"He returned to the palace last night and surrendered his sword, accepting full responsibility for the actions of his chancellor. He's under house arrest."

"But he helped us, sire, when he need not have done so. We owe him our thanks."

Gaius nodded. "I know that. But he's also a war leader of a nation whose warriors just tried to openly murder the First Lord of Alera. I believe I can ensure that his life is spared, for the time being at any rate. But I can promise him little more."

Tavi frowned but nodded. "I see."

"Oh," Gaius said. He picked up an envelope and passed it to Tavi. "I think you've very nearly outgrown your position as my page, Tavi, but this is a last message to deliver to the new Ambassador, in the northern hall."

"Of course, sire."

"Thank you," he said. "I've arranged to take dinner with your aunt and your fellow trainees this evening, as well as with the Ambassador. I'd like you to be there as well."

"Of course, sire."

Gaius nodded, the gesture one of dismissal.

Tavi turned to go to the door—but once there, he paused and turned. "Sire, if I may ask about Fade?"

Gaius frowned and lifted a hand to pinch the bridge of his nose between thumb and forefinger. "Tavi," he said tiredly, "there are some questions in life only you can answer for yourself. You have a mind. Use it." He waved a hand vaguely. "And use it elsewhere, hmm? I'm growing fatigued quite easily, and my healers tell me that if I am not cautious, I might have another episode."

Tavi frowned. Gaius hadn't seemed to be getting more weary as they talked, and he suspected it was merely an excuse to avoid the subject. But what could he do? One didn't try to pin the First Lord of Alera down in a conversation. "Of course, sire," Tavi said, bowing at the waist and departing.

He left the First Lord's suites and walked slowly into the north hall. He paused to ask a passing maid where the new Ambassador's quarters were located, and she directed him to a large set of double doors at the far end of the hall. Tavi walked down to them and knocked quietly.

The door opened, and Tavi found himself facing Kitai as he had never seen her before. She was dressed in a robe of dark emerald silk that fell to her knees and belted loosely at the waist. Her hair was down, brushed out into long and shining waves of white that fell to her hips. Her feet were bare, and fine, glittering chains of silver wrapped one ankle, both wrists, and her throat, where the necklace was set with another green stone. The colors were a perfectly lovely complement to her large, exotic eyes.

Tavi's heart suddenly beat very quickly.

Kitai studied Tavi's expression, her own face somewhat smug, and she smiled slowly. "Hello, Aleran."

"Um," Tavi said. "I have a message for the Ambassador."

"Then you have a message for me," she said, and held out her hand. Tavi passed the envelope to her. She opened it and frowned at the letter within, then said, "I cannot read."

Tavi took the letter and read it. "Ambassador Kitai. I was pleased to hear from the crown guardsman you passed on the way into the palace yesterday morning that Doroga had dispatched an envoy to Alera to serve as an ambassador and emissary between our peoples. While I did not expect your arrival, you are most welcome here. I trust your quarters are satisfactory, and that your needs have been adequately attended to. You have only to inquire of any of the serving staff if you have need of anything else."

Kitai smiled, and said, "I have my own pool, in the floor. You can fill it with hot water or cold, Aleran, and there are scents and soaps and oils of every kind. They brought me meals, and I have a bed that could fit a mother gargant giving birth." She lifted her chin and pointed at the necklace. "You see?"

Tavi saw very soft, very fair skin, more than anything—but the necklace was lovely, too.

"Had I known of this," Kitai continued, "I might have asked to be an Ambassador before now."

Tavi coughed. "Well. I, uh. I mean, I suppose you *are* an Ambassador, if the First Lord says so, but for goodness' sake, Kitai."

"Keep your opinions to yourself, message boy," she said disdainfully. "Continue to read."

Tavi gave her an even look, then read the rest of the note. "In order to help you better understand your duties here, I suggest that you take the time and effort to learn to understand the written word. Such a skill will be an immense advantage to you in the long run, and enable you more accurately to record your experiences and knowledge so that you may pass it on to your people. To that end, I am placing at your disposal the bearer of this message, whose sole duty for the next several weeks at least will be to teach you such skills with words as he may possess. Welcome to Alera Imperia, Ambassador, and I look forward to speaking with you in the future. Signed, Gaius Sextus, First Lord of Alera."

"My disposal," she said. "Hah. I think I like that. I can have you do anything, now. Your chieftain said so."

"I don't think that's what he meant when—"

"Silence, errand boy!" she said, green eyes sparkling with mischief. "There are horses here, yes?"

"Well. Yes. But . . ."

"Then you will take me to them, and we will go for a ride," she said, still smiling.

Tavi sighed. "Kitai . . . perhaps tomorrow? I need to make sure Max is all right. And my aunt. We're having dinner this evening."

"Of course," she said at once. "Important things first."

"Thank you," he said.

She bowed her head to him a little. "And you, Aleran. I saw you against the Cane. You fought well. It was cleverly done."

And then she stepped up to him, stood on tiptoe, and kissed him on the mouth.

Tavi blinked in surprise, and for a second he couldn't move. Then she lifted her arms and twined them around his neck, drawing him closer, and everything in the world but her mouth and her arms and the scent and fever-hot warmth of her vanished. It was sometime later that the kiss ended, and Tavi felt a little wobbly. Kitai looked up at him with languid, pleased eyes, and said, "Cleverly done. For an Aleran."

"Th-thank you," Tavi stammered.

"My disposal," she said, satisfaction in her tone. "This promises to be a pleasant spring."

"Uh," Tavi said. "Wh-what?"

She made a little sound, half of impatience, half of disgust. "When will you stop talking, Aleran?" she said in a low, throaty growl and kissed him again, drawing him back into the room, until Tavi could kick the door closed behind them.

Amara stood beside Bernard as the *legionares* who had survived the battle fell into neat ranks facing the mound they'd raised over the battlefield.

The mercenaries and their commander had departed as soon as their healers had done their work. Before the day was out, two hundred Knights had arrived at the direct command of the First Lord, and a relief force on a swift march from Riva's Second Legion arrived the next morning, to ensure the security of Garrison and the valley. They had brought with them word of a minor miracle. Healer Harger had kept his head in the face of the vord's surprise attack on the wounded at Aricholt, and though wounded, had managed to lead the children who had survived the first attack from the doomed steadholt. It was a small ray of light in the gloom of death and loss, but Amara was grateful for it.

Bernard had never given any such order, but those men who had survived did not mention the presence of the Windwolves or their outlaw commander. They owed their lives to the mercenaries, and they knew it.

There were far more dead to bury than living capable of digging graves, and so they had decided to use the cave as a resting place for the fallen. *Legionares* and taken holders alike were carried into the cave and composed with as much dignity as possible, which generally meant little. Those fallen on the battlefield seldom met death in positions like those of gentle sleep, but whatever could be done for them was done.

Once the bodies had been taken into the cave, the survivors of the battle gathered to say their farewells to fallen acquaintances, sword-brethren, and friends. After a silent vigil of an hour's passing, Bernard walked to the front of the formation and addressed the men.

"We are here," he said, "to lay to rest those who have fallen in defense of this valley and this Realm. Not only those *legionares* who fought beside us, but also those holders and soldiers alike who fell to our enemy and whose bodies were used as weapons against us." He was silent for a long moment. "They all of them deserved better than this. But they gave their lives to stop this threat from spreading and growing into a plague that could have ravaged all the Realm, and it is only by the whims of chance that we stand over their graves rather than them standing over ours."

Another long silence fell.

"Thank you," Bernard said quietly. "All of you. You fought with courage and honor, even when wounded, and when the fight seemed hopeless. You are the heart and soul of Aleran *legionares*, and I am proud, honored, and privileged to have commanded you." He turned to the empty mouth of the cave. "To you," he said, "I can offer only my apologies, that I could not protect you from this fate, and my promise that your deaths will make me more vigilant and dedicated in the future. And I ask that whatever power governs the world after this one to look upon our fallen with compassion, mercy, and gentleness that was not given them by their slayers."

Then Bernard, Sir Frederic, and half a dozen Knights Terra who had arrived with the relief force knelt upon the ground, calling to their furies. Some kind of rippling wave ran through the earth, toward the cave, and with a low rumble, the shape of the hillside the cave was in began to change. It was a slow, even gentle motion, but the sheer scale of it made the ground tremble under Amara's feet. The mouth of the cave sank and began to close, the motion slow, ponderous, inevitable, until the opening in the rock was gone, and only the hillside remained.

Silence settled over the valley, and the earthcrafters rose to their feet together. Bernard turned to face the fifty-odd surviving veterans of Giraldi's century. "*Legionares*, fall out. Pack up your gear and make ready to march back to Garrison."

Giraldi gave a few subdued orders, and the weary men began the walk back to Aricholt. Bernard stood watching them go. Amara remained beside him until they were out of sight.

Walker came pacing slowly out of the sheltering trees, Doroga padding along beside him, his cudgel over one shoulder. They walked over to Bernard and Amara, and Doroga nodded to them. "You fight well, Calderon. The men who serve you are no cowards."

Bernard smiled a bit, and said, "Thank you for your help, Doroga. Again." Then he faced Walker, and said, "And thank you as well, Walker."

Doroga's broad, ugly face spread into an honest grin. "Maybe your people can learn something," he said. Walker let out a rumbling snort. Doroga laughed.

"What did he say?" Bernard asked.

"Not say, so much as . . . mmph. It is something like, spoiled fruits all taste the same. He means your people and mine shared a common enemy. He allows that you are passably good substitutes for the *Sabot-ha*, my clan, if there is fighting to be done."

"He's the reason we survived that rush in the cave," Bernard said. "I won't forget it."

The big Marat rolled his massive shoulders in a shrug, smiling. "Send him some apples. Maybe not spoiled."

"My word on it." He offered Doroga his hand. Doroga traded grips with him without hesitation.

"And you, Windrider," he said, turning to Amara. "You will not make a good Aleran wife, I think."

She smiled at him. "No?"

He shook his head gravely. "I will wager that you will not clean much. Or cook much. Or make blankets and things. I suspect you will find yourself in trouble, all the time."

"It's possible," she agreed, smiling.

"Good in bed, though, from the sound of it."

Amara's face heated until she thought steam must surely rise from it. "Doroga!"

"Woman of trouble," Doroga said. "But good to hold. My mate was one such. We were happy." He struck his fist lightly to his heart, Aleran style, and bowed his head to them. "May you be. And may your fallen people be at peace."

"Thank you," Amara stammered.

Bernard inclined his head as well. Without further words, Doroga and Walker departed, walking slowly and steadily without looking back.

Amara watched him, standing close beside Bernard. She

didn't remember when she'd twined her fingers with his, but it felt natural and right. Bernard sighed. She could feel the pain in him, even without looking at him, without speaking to him.

"You did all that you could," she said quietly.

"I know," he answered.

"You should not blame yourself for their deaths."

"I know that, too," he said.

"Any decent commander would feel what you do now," Amara said. "They'd be just as wrong as you are to feel it. But all the best ones do."

"I lost the folk of an entire steadholt under my protection," he said quietly, "and almost three quarters of my *legionares*. I'm hardly one of the best."

"Give it time," she said quietly. "It will hurt less."

His fingers squeezed back, very gently, and he made no other answer. He stood looking at the hillside where the cave had been for a time, then turned and walked away. Amara kept pace with him. They were halfway back to Aricholt before she said, "We need to talk."

He exhaled through his nose and nodded. "Go on."

"Bernard," she said. She sought for the right words. None that she found seemed equal to the task of conveying what she felt. "I love you," she said finally.

"And I, you," he rumbled.

"But . . . my oath to the Crown, and yours . . . they both have prior claim on us. Our vows . . ."

"You wish to pretend that they did not happen?" he asked quietly.

"No," she said at once. "No, not that. But . . . have we not foresworn ourselves?"

"Perhaps," he said. "Perhaps not. If you could bear children—"

"I can't," she said, and she hadn't meant it to fly out from her mouth so harshly, so bitterly.

"How do you know?" Bernard asked quietly.

Her face flushed. "Because . . . you and I have . . . bloody crows, Bernard. If I could have I'm sure I would have by now, with you."

"Perhaps," he said. "Perhaps not. We see each other perhaps one night or two in every moon. At the most. It isn't the best way to assure children."

"But I was blighted," she said quietly. "Even if you can hardly see the scars."

"Yes," Bernard said. "But there are women who have contracted the blight and yet borne children. Not many, perhaps, but it has happened."

She let out an exasperated breath. "But I am not one of them."

"How do you know?" Bernard asked. "How do you know for certain?"

She looked at him for a moment and shook her head. "What are you driving at?"

"That it is at least possible that you might yet be able to bear children. And that until we know that it is not so, there is no reason for us not to be together."

She looked at him uncertainly. "You know what the laws say. You have an obligation to the Realm, Bernard, to produce heirs of your blood and to pass on the strength of your furycraft."

"And I intend to fulfill that obligation," he said. "With you."

They walked in silence for a while, before she said, "Do you really think it might be possible?"

He nodded. "I think it is possible. I want it to happen. The only way for it to happen is to make the effort and see."

Amara was quiet for a time, then said, "Very well." She swallowed. "But . . . I do not want Gaius to know of it. Not unless—" She cut herself off and began the sentence again. "Not *until* we bring forth a child. Before that, he could command us to part. But if there is a child, he will have no legal or ethical grounds to object."

Bernard studied her for several steps. Then he stopped, lifted her chin with one broad hand, and kissed her, very slowly and very gently, on the mouth.

"Agreed," he murmured, after that. "For now. But the day may come when we can no longer hide our marriage vows from others. On that day, I want to know that you will stand beside me. That if it comes to that, we will defy the will of the First Lord and the law together."

"Together," she said, the word a promise, and kissed him again.

He half smiled. "What's the worst that could happen? To be dismissed from service. To have our Citizenships revoked. At which point, well, we'd not have to worry about the legal obligations of the Citizenry, would we?"

"We'd be ruined, but together," Amara said, a dry smile on her lips. "Is that it?"

"So long as I had you, I wouldn't be ruined," he said.

Amara wrapped her arms around her husband's neck and held on very tightly. She felt his arms around her, strong and caring.

Perhaps Bernard was correct. Perhaps everything would be all right.

Fidelias finished brushing out the leather of his boots and sat them beside the bed. His pack, already filled and buckled shut, sat beside them. He looked around the room for a moment, musing. The servant's quarters he occupied in the basement of the Aquitaine manor were, he realized, almost precisely the same dimensions as those he had formerly occupied in the Citadel. The bed was softer, perhaps, the sheets and blankets finer, the lamps of slightly better quality. But otherwise, almost the same.

He shook his head and stretched out on the bed, for the moment too tired to make the effort to get undressed and under the blankets. He stared up at the ceiling instead, listening to the dim sounds of movement and conversation in adjacent rooms and in the halls above.

The door opened without a knock, and Fidelias did not need to look to see who was there.

Lady Aquitaine was quiet for a moment, before she said, "Already packed, I see."

"Yes," he said. "I'll leave before first light."

"Not staying for the presentation ceremony?"

"You don't need me for that," Fidelias said. "I saw the gown you bought the Steadholder. I'm sure it will make the impression you wanted. I have other business to occupy my attention."

"Oh?" she asked. "I have not even given you your next assignment."

"You'll be sending me to Kalare," Fidelias said. "To get into touch with my contacts there. You'll want to know what links Kalare has to the southern High Lords and get an idea of how to disrupt or sever them."

She let out a low laugh. "Should I feel this smug about going to the effort to recruit you, my spy?"

"Don't bother," he said. "I chose you and your husband. It wasn't the other way around."

"How cynical," she murmured. "A gentleman would have danced around the point."

"You didn't hire me to dance," Fidelias said quietly.

"No. I didn't." She was quiet for a moment, before she said, "You'll take water from the font here?"

"Yes. As long as I don't get too thirsty. Southern summers are hot."

"Have a care, Fidelias," Lady Aquitaine said. "You are a valuable asset. But my tolerance for your occasional insubordination will only last so long."

"If I were you, Your Grace," Fidelias said, "I would give a thought to conserving your intelligence resources."

"Meaning you?" she asked.

"Meaning me."

"And why is that?" There was a dangerous edge to her voice.

Fidelias lowered his eyes from the ceiling for the first time. She stood in his doorway, tall and elegant and lovely, covered in a voluminous grey cape, light slippers on her feet. Her dark hair was pinned up with a number of ivory combs. He regarded her beauty for a moment, and felt a stir of both desire and anger. No man could see a woman of such beauty and feel nothing, of course. But his anger was a mystery to him. He kept it carefully contained, hidden from her.

Instead of answering her, he nodded to the dresser beside the door.

She frowned and looked. She tilted her head for a moment and reached out to take a worn traveling cloak from the top of the dresser. "It is a cloak," she said, slightly exaggerated patience in her tone. "And what possible threat does this represent?"

"It isn't a cloak," Fidelias said quietly. "It's a seacloak. They're made in Kalare, Forcia, and Parcia. The hides are taken from a breed of large lizard that feeds on bulbs and roots in the swamps and rivers. Get them a little wet and they swell, become waterproof. Anyone traveling there needs one of these cloaks, either for wear on board ships or for protection during the rainy season. Without a seacloak, it's very easy to be taken sick."

Lady Aquitaine nodded patiently. "I still do not perceive how it might be a danger to us, dear spy."

"This cloak is my cloak," Fidelias said.

She regarded him, expression remote.

"I left it in my quarters in the Citadel, the day I left for the south with Amara, for her graduation exercise. The day I abandoned Gaius." He shook his head. "I found it here this evening."

A line appeared between her brows. "But . . . that would mean . . ."

"It would mean that Gaius himself was here, in your own manor, and you never had an inkling of it. It means that he knows where I am. It means he knows whom I serve. It means that he is perfectly aware that you are sending me to the south to stir up trouble for Kalare—and that I have his blessing to do so." He crossed his arms behind his head and went back to staring at the ceiling. "Beware, my lady. The lion you hunt may be old—but he is neither dotard nor weak. Miss a step, and the huntress may become the prey."

Lady Aquitaine stared at him in silence for a moment, then left without a word, shutting the door behind her. Her steps as she walked away were a very little bit quicker than usual. She was frightened.

For some reason, that pleased Fidelias, just as it had pleased him to shout a warning to Aleran guardsmen when the vord had been stealing up upon them. There were thoughts tied up in it, dangerous thoughts, dangerous feelings he did not wish to examine too closely lest they cripple him. So he accepted the feelings for what was upon their surface alone.

It had pleased him.

As feelings went, it was not an intense one—but it was far, far better than nothing.

That night, he fell asleep easily for the first time in nearly three years.

CHAPTER 58

Isana folded her hands in her lap and tried not to let them shake too much. She was alone in the carriage, but it would not do to allow herself to be seen in such a state when she arrived at the palace.

Even if, at least in spirit, she was now a traitor to the Crown.

She closed her eyes and breathed slowly in and out. It was only a dinner, and doubtless the First Lord would not linger after the meal. And she would get to see Tavi again, whole and well. She had thought she might have strained her chest to sickness, so hard had she wept when she came to the infirmary and found him there, wounded, exhausted, unconscious, but whole. She had brushed away the Citadel's healers in irritation and healed his wounds herself, the hard way, through wet cloths and slow, grueling effort.

She had stayed beside Tavi until she began to drift off to sleep herself, then Gaius had arrived. The First Lord moved very slowly and very carefully, like a weary old man—though he did not look older than a man in his late prime, but for his hair, which had gone entirely grey and white since the last time she had seen him. He had offered her a room, but she had declined, telling him of Lady Aquitaine's offer of hospitality.

He had stared at her then, his eyes steady, piercing, and she knew that he had understood far more than the simple statements she had made. He made no objection to her leaving— and in fact, had gone out of his way to invite her to the palace for a meal with himself and her nephew.

He'd known she would come, of course, if it was to see Tavi. Lady Aquitaine was not to be trusted, but there was some truth in her accusation that Gaius was holding Tavi as a prisoner to her good behavior. In this instance, at least, he was using the boy to make sure she would come to the palace.

But at least she had gotten what she wanted. Word had

come back from Aquitaine's mercenaries that her brother was whole, though the people of an entire steadholt had been slain along with many of her brother's soldiers. They had destroyed the vord nest.

The coach drew to a halt, and the footman folded down the stepladder and opened the door. Isana closed her eyes and took a deep breath, willing herself into at least a semblance of calm. Then she descended from the coach, under the watchful eyes of the hard-faced armsmen of Aquitaine, and was escorted by a centurion of the Royal Guard—very young, for his rank, she thought—into the palace and to what was, by the standards of the highborn of Alera, a cozy, intimate dining room.

It was larger than the great hall back at Isanaholt, and may have been almost the size of the steadholt's stone barn. An enormous table had been laid out, with places evenly spaced every bowshot or so along it, but someone had evidently decided that the arrangement wouldn't do. The chairs had all been dragged down to an uneven clump at one end of the table, the plate settings similarly rearranged, and several voices were raised in laughter.

Isana paused for a moment at the door, studying the scene. The large young man in the midst of a tale had to be Antillar Maximus, about whom Tavi had written much in his letters home. He had the kind of rugged good looks that made him look something of the rogue now, but which would in time, weather into something stronger, more solemn, if no less appealing, and he was telling a story of some kind with the panache of a practiced raconteur. Beside him sat a slight young man with intelligent eyes and a wide smile, though there was something of a mouselike quality to the way he sat, and listened, as if he expected to be overlooked and liked it that way. Ehren, by Tavi's letters. A girl, plain but pleasant-looking, sat across from Max and Ehren, beside Tavi, her cheeks pink with laughter.

On Tavi's other side sat an exotic beauty, and it took Isana a moment to recognize her as Kitai, the daughter of the Marat chieftain. She was dressed in a fine silken shirt and closely fitting pants, and her pale feet were bare. Her long, white hair had been plaited into a braid that fell straight down her spine, and silver gleamed on her throat and her wrists. There was mischief in her eyes—eyes precisely the shade of Tavi's, Isana noted.

And Tavi sat listening to Max. He had grown, she saw at once, and in more than just height. There was a quality to his quiet that had nothing to do with insecurity. He sat listening to Max with a silent smile that rested partly upon his mouth but mostly in his eyes, and he held himself with an easy confidence she had not seen before. He interjected some comment when Max paused to take a breath, and the table exploded in laughter again.

Isana felt a sudden presence beside her, and Gaius Sextus murmured, "It's a good sound. Laughter like that, from the young. It's been far too long since it has been heard in these halls."

Isana felt her back stiffen as she turned to face the First Lord. "Your Majesty," she said, making the little curtsey Serai had taught her. *On the day she died*, Isana thought.

"Steadholder," he said. He looked down her and back up and said, in a neutral, pleasant tone, "That's a lovely gown."

The dress Lady Aquitaine had provided her was of the same exotic and expensive silk she'd shown off at the garden party, though in a much more modest cut. The deep scarlet of the silk darkened by degrees to black at the ends of the sleeves and the hem of the skirt. Scarlet and sable, the colors of Aquitaine.

Gaius's own tunic was of red and blue, of course—the colors of the royal house of the First Lord.

"Thank you," she replied, keeping her voice steady. "It was provided me by my host. It would have been impolite not to wear it."

"I can see how that would be," Gaius said. There was both reserve and compassion in his tone. Again, she was struck with the impression that he understood much more than she said—and that she, in turn, understood much more than the overt meaning of his words. "You may be interested to know that I had Maximus pardoned and cleared of the charges against him. I offered Kalare an in-depth investigation of the happenings that night, and he shied away from it quite swiftly. So, in the absence of a willing accuser, I had the charges dismissed."

"Does this matter to me?" Isana asked.

"Perhaps not to you," Gaius said. "Perhaps someone you know would find it interesting."

By which he meant the Aquitaines, of course. "Shall we join them?" she asked.

Gaius looked up at the group of young people, still laughing. He watched them, his face unreadable, and though her own skill at watercrafting was insufficient to sense truly what he felt, Isana was struck with the sudden impression that his life, as the First Lord, had to have been, more than anything else, a horribly lonely one. "Let's wait a moment more," he said. "Their laughter would never survive our arrival."

She regarded him for a moment, then nodded. The unspoken tension between them did not vanish, but it dwindled for a time.

When they finally did enter the hall, she spent a very long time holding Tavi to her. He had grown unbelievably, and when before she had been a half hand taller than he, he was now at least half a foot taller than she was. His shoulders had widened by a similarly preposterous measure, and his voice was no longer the warbling tenor he'd had when he left home, but a steady baritone.

But for all of that, Amara had been right. He was still Tavi. She could feel it in his warmth and smile, in the love for her as he hugged her in turn. The sparkle in his eyes, his sense of humor, his smile—though more serious, more thoughtful, it was all still his own. His time at the Academy had not taken anything from him. It had, perhaps, made him even more of what he had been: a young man with a swift mind, occasionally questionable judgment, and a good heart.

The meal was excellent, and the conversation pleasant until the First Lord asked Tavi to share his story of the events of the past few days. Isana suddenly understood why the gathering had been as small as it was. Not even servants were allowed in the hall, as Tavi spoke.

She could hardly believe what she heard, and yet it was all true. She could feel that much from him. Isana sat stunned that Tavi should have held so very, very much power in his hands. He had been only a young student, but the fate of the Realm itself had hung upon the choices he had made. Not solely upon him, to be sure, but by the great furies, he had once more acted as a hero.

She sat bemused by the tale, hardly surprised that Tavi had been training as a Cursor. It was very much in line with what she had supposed would happen when he came to the capital. She listened to Tavi, but spent much of the time judging the expressions and emotions of the others at the table. She suspected, as well, that Tavi was leaving things out, here and there, though she was not sure why he would conceal portions of Max's masquerade as the First Lord or the death of the Maestro, Killian.

The hour was very late when the First Lord suggested that the evening had gone on long enough. Isana loitered until everyone had departed but Tavi and the First Lord.

"I had hoped," she said quietly to Gaius, "to speak to Tavi alone for a while."

Gaius arched an eyebrow and regarded her gown for a time. Isana had to have Rill's help to keep her face from flushing, but met Gaius's gaze without moving.

"Steadholder," he said gently, "this is my house. I would hear what you have to say to one of the Cursors."

Isana pressed her lips together, but inclined her head. She had no wish to speak of this in front of Gaius—but that was part of the price she would now have to pay to have secured the aid of the Aquitaines. So be it.

"Tavi," she said quietly, "I have concerns about your friend. Gaelle, I believe. I can't pinpoint it, but there is something . . . not right about her."

Tavi glanced at Gaius, to Isana's annoyance. The First Lord nodded to him. "I know, Aunt Isana," he said, his voice quiet and very serious. "She isn't Gaelle. Or at least she isn't the real Gaelle."

Isana frowned. "How do you know?"

"Because the men who took me and Kitai in the tunnels were Kalare's," he said, "and they were waiting for us. Maestro Killian told me, as he died, that Kalare's chief assassin was still close, and that he had paid a terrible price to establish the assassin within the Citadel. He was playing the traitor to Kalare, hoping to learn more about the enemy through his contact with the chief assassin—a woman named Rook.

Whoever Rook was, it had to be a woman, someone often in contact with the Maestro to avoid arousing suspicion, and someone who had seen me enter the tunnels that night, and who knew where I would have to start marking the walls to find my way. In short, it almost had to have been one of the trainees."

"That was the price Killian mentioned," Gaius murmured. "The actual girl selected for the training was replaced by Rook, by means of watercrafting herself into a double. She was probably killed a few days after her selection as a trainee."

Isana shook her head. "That's . . . Your Majesty, you know as well as I that anyone with that much watercraft would have a strong contact with the emotions of those around them."

"It would be an enormous advantage in convincing those around you that you are merely a harmless girl," Gaius murmured.

"Yes. And if one killed often enough, it would almost certainly drive one mad."

"More than likely," Gaius said, nodding.

"You allowed that poor girl to be killed," Isana said, "so that you could gain some kind of advantage?"

"Killian never spoke to me of it," Gaius said. "He did it on his own."

Isana shook her head, disgusted. "All the same. It's monstrous."

"Yes," Gaius said, without a trace of shame. "It is. But Killian felt it necessary."

Isana shook her head. "This killer. Rook. When will you arrest her?"

"We won't," Tavi said quietly. "Not at once, in any case. Right now, Rook does not know we are aware of her identity. We can use that against her, and against Kalare."

"She's an assassin," Isana said quietly. "Quite likely a madwoman. And you would have her roaming loose?"

"If the First Lord removes her," Tavi said, "has her arrested or exiled, Kalare will only recruit someone else and try it again—and this time we might not be lucky enough to discover them. There is less danger in leaving her than not. At least for the moment."

"Monstrous," Isana said. She felt tears in her eyes and did not bother to hide them.

Tavi saw her expression and flushed, looking down. Then he looked up, and said, "I hope you are not too much disappointed in me, Aunt Isana."

She smiled slightly. "I hope you are not too much disappointed in me, Tavi."

"Never," he said quietly. "I understand why you . . ." He waved a vague hand. "You did what was necessary to protect the people you loved."

"Yes," Isana said quietly. "I suppose I should not be the first to cast stones." She stepped up close to him, cupped his face in her hands, kissed his forehead, and said, "Promise me that you will be careful."

"I promise," he said quietly.

She held him again, and he hugged her back. Gaius made an unobtrusive exit, while Tavi escorted her down to the entrance, where the Aquitaines' coach was waiting once more. She walked with her hand on Tavi's politely extended arm, and he provided a supporting hand when she stepped up to the carriage.

"Tavi," she said, before the door closed.

"Yes, Aunt Isana?"

"I love you very much."

He smiled. "I love you, too."

She nodded. "And I am proud of you. Never think that I am not. I worry for you. That's all. But you're growing up so tall."

He grinned. "Cost the First Lord a fortune keeping me in pants," he said.

Isana laughed, and he leaned up to kiss her cheek again. She ruffled his hair and said, "Write often. Regardless of where we find ourselves, it will never change what you mean to me."

"I feel that, too," he assured her. He stepped back and nodded with a quite natural authority to the coachmen, who began closing it up. "Write me as often as you can. Be safe."

She nodded and smiled at him, then the coachmen had closed things up, and the carriage was rolling away from the palace. She leaned slowly back in her seat, her eyes closed. She felt very, very alone in the Aquitaines' carriage.

She *was* alone there.

"Be safe," she whispered, her eyes closing, holding the image of his smile in her mind. Her hand drifted to the shape of the ring, still on its chain around her neck, still hidden. "Oh, be safe, my son."

Miles came down the last few steps and crossed the antechamber to the First Lord's meditation chamber. There were still scorch marks on the floor from the fires Tavi and Kitai had started, but the various kinds and colors of blood had been cleaned away. The door to the meditation chamber was half-open, but Miles paused outside it and knocked quietly.

"Come in, Miles," came Gaius's voice.

Miles pushed the door open and went in. Gaius sat in a chair by the little desk, lips pursed thoughtfully as he wrote something on a page. He finished it, signed it, and calmly folded the page and sealed it shut with wax and the hilt of his signet dagger. "What brings you here, Miles?"

"The usual," Miles said. "We have found nothing in the Deeps, beyond that odd cavern the vord had taken as a nest. There has been no sign of them elsewhere, but I have dispatched word to the Legions of every city to exercise extreme caution should anything happen that might indicate a vord presence."

"Fine," Gaius said. After a moment, he mused, "Did you know that the vord, in one form or another, utterly ignored Tavi's presence in at least three instances?"

Miles frowned. "I saw him scamper out of a crowd of them. At the time, I just assumed he'd been quick enough to get away. And they did attack him immediately after."

"But not until he struck at the queen with a spear," Gaius mused.

"You aren't suggesting that the boy is in league with them, are you?" Miles said.

Gaius arched an eyebrow. "Naturally not. But it is an anomaly which I do not yet understand. Perhaps it was nothing—mere luck. But what if it wasn't? It might tell us something important about them."

"Do you think they are yet here?"

"I am not entirely certain. It's odd," Gaius said, thought-fully. "I've looked for their presence. I haven't sensed it."

"According to Count Calderon, they were very difficult to detect with crafting, sire."

Gaius nodded and waved a hand. "Well. We are aware of them. We are on the watch for them. It is all we can do for the time being."

"Yes, sire." He looked around the room. "It cleaned up nicely."

Gaius sighed. "I can't believe those two employed my en-tire liquor cabinet as a weapon against the enemy."

Miles pursed his lips and frowned. "Sire, may I—"

"Speak candidly, yes, yes." He waved an irritated hand. "How many times must I tell you that you do not need to ask?"

"Once more at least, Sextus," Miles said. "I don't mourn your liquor cabinet. Blessing in disguise. You were drinking too much."

The First Lord frowned pensively, but did not dispute the captain.

"You did it on purpose, didn't you?" Miles said.

"Did what?"

"You brought Fade here. You arranged for Tavi to share a room with Antillar Maximus. You wanted them to become friends."

Gaius smiled faintly, but he said nothing.

"Is he what I think he is?" Miles asked.

"He's a Cursor, Miles. He's a former apprentice shepherd."

"Crows, Sextus," Miles said, irritated. He scowled at the First Lord. "You know what I mean."

The First Lord gave Miles a very direct look. "He has no crafting, Miles. So long as that is true, he will never be any-thing more than what he is."

Miles frowned and looked away.

"Miles," Gaius chided, "is it such a bad thing, what he is now?"

"Of course not," Miles said, and sighed. "It's just that . . ."

"Patience, Miles. Patience." Gaius took the letter he'd written in hand and rose. Miles fell in beside him as the First Lord walked to the door. "Oh," Gaius said. "Which reminds me. Don't restock that liquor cabinet. Have it removed."

Miles stopped in his tracks and blinked. "You aren't . . ." He gestured vaguely at the mosaic.

Gaius shook his head. "I need my rest."

Miles frowned faintly at the First Lord. "I don't understand."

"I must bear up a little longer, Miles. To do that, I need my health." He looked back at the mosaic, and there was sudden grief in his expression. "It was arrogant of me, to behave as if I had no limits. If I don't respect them now . . ." He shrugged. "The next time I might not wake up."

"Bear up a little longer?" Miles asked.

Gaius nodded. "Hold on. Prevent Aquitaine and Kalare from sinking us into a war of succession—and there *will* be one, Miles, once I am gone. But I can buy time."

"For what?"

"For a change in the boy."

Miles frowned. "If he doesn't change?"

Gaius shook his head. "Then he doesn't. Unless matters change, no one hears of this, Miles. Even rumor and suspicion would make him a marked man. We must protect him, inasmuch as we can."

"Aye, sire," Miles replied.

Gaius nodded and started walking steadily up the stairway.

Miles followed the First Lord back up the steps to the palace, silently afraid of the future.

The power-hungry High Lord of Kalare has launched a mer-
ciless rebellion against the aging First Lord, Gaius Sextus.
Caught off guard by the sheer power of Kalare's attack, Gaius
and the loyal forces of Alera must fight for the survival of the
Realm beside the unlikeliest of allies—the equally contentious
High Lord of Aquitaine.

Countess Amara, Cursor to the First Lord, is tasked with the
desperate rescue of valuable noble hostages taken by Kalare.
The survival of the Realm may hinge on the success of her
mission. But is her ally, Lady Aquitaine, sincere in her efforts
to assist—or will she betray the young Cursor and the First
Lord she serves?

Sent away from the fires of war by the protective First Lord,
young Tavi of Calderon joins a newly formed Legion under
an assumed name. Then the ruthless Kalare does the unthink-
able: He unites with the Canim, bestial enemies of the Realm
whose vast numbers spell certain doom for Alera. When
treachery from within destroys the army's command structure, the young Cursor finds himself leading an inexperienced, poorly equipped Legion—the only force standing
between the Canim horde and the war-torn Realm . . .

Now available from Ace Books